Embrace the Fire

Stephen England

Also by Stephen England

Sword of Neamha

Shadow Warriors Series

LODESTONE
NIGHTSHADE
Pandora's Grave
Day of Reckoning
TALISMAN
Embrace the Fire

Lion of God Trilogy

Lion of God: Episode I

Copyright © 2016 by Stephen England
Cover design by Louis Vaney
Author photo by Jonathan Williams
Formatting by Polgarus Studio

All rights reserved. No part of this publication may be reproduced, stored in a retrieval system, or transmitted in any form or by any means—electronic, mechanical, photocopy, recording, or any other—without the prior written permission of the author.

This is a work of fiction. Names, characters, places, and incidents either are the product of the author's imagination or are used fictitiously, and any resemblance to actual persons, living or dead, business establishments, events, or locales is entirely coincidental. Views expressed by the characters in this novel are their own, and do not necessarily reflect the views of the author.

In memoriam of the late Tom Clancy and Vince Flynn, both of whom passed away during the writing of *Embrace the Fire*.
Two legends whose influence upon the thriller genre can hardly be overstated, and whom I have to thank for a great deal of inspiration over the years.
It is to their memory that this novel, and the character of John Patrick Flynn, is respectfully dedicated.

"Vengeance is mine, I will repay, saith the Lord." – Romans 12:19

"Revenge. . .it is like a rolling stone, which, when a man hath forced up a hill, will return upon him with a greater violence, and break those bones whose sinews gave it motion." – Jeremy Taylor, *Apples of Sodom*

Glossary

BND—Federal Intelligence Service of Germany
CCTV—Closed Circuit Television
CO-19—Specialist Firearms Command
CONUS—Continental United States
CS—tear gas
DCIA—Director, Central Intelligence Agency
DCS—Director, Clandestine Service
DG—Director-General
DGSE—Directorate-General for External Security
GCHQ—Government Communications Headquarters
HAHO—High Altitude, High Opening
HUMINT—Human Intelligence
IED—Improvised Explosive Device
IRA—Irish Republican Army
JSOC—Joint Special Operations Command
MI-5—The Security Service
MI-6—Secret Intelligence Service
MoD—Ministry of Defence
MP—Member of Parliament
MRE—Meals Ready to Eat
NCA—National Crime Agency
NCO—Non-comissioned officer
NCS—National Clandestine Service
NODs—Night Optical Device
NSA—National Security Agency
PIRA—Provisional Irish Republican Army
PM—Prime Minister
PMC—Private Military Contractor
RAF—Royal Air Force
RUMINT—Rumor Intelligence
RUC—Royal Ulster Constabulary
SAD—Special Activities Division
SAS—Special Air Service
SCIF—Sensitive Compartmented Information Facility
SDR—Surveillance Detection Run

SIGINT—Signals Intelligence
SO-13—Metropolitan Police Anti-Terrorist Branch
SO-14—Metropolitan Police Royalty Protection Branch
SO-15—Metropolitan Police Counterterrorism Command
UAV—Unmanned Aerial Vehicle
VBIED—Vehicle-Borne Improved Explosive Device

Prologue

8:03 P.M. Greenwich Mean Time, March 22nd
London, England

They were watching. He knew that—they were always watching, a hundred lidless eyes gazing down through the night.

Never blinking. Never resting. Just always *there*.

And they knew his face.

The rain came tumbling down out of the sky above him—nothing heavy, just a steady drizzle—ice-cold water running down his cheeks, collecting in the rough stubble that masked the lower half of his face.

A dead zone lay ahead, between him and the bus stop, or at least there had once been—a twenty-foot gap in London's legendary CCTV coverage. Enough space for a man to disappear.

Disappear. There'd been times he'd wanted nothing more than to do just that. To disappear, to *run*—into the night.

Not yet.

There was only one camera across the street from the stop and he ducked his head as if against the rain as he approached the far side of the double-decker bus. Shielding his face.

Public transportation was a risk, but one he had to take. A thirty-minute ride would put him at his destination. After that. . .

He could only keep this up for so long, that much he knew. Had known it ever since he'd set out, he thought, ascending into the bus just behind a young Muslim woman in a hijab and jeans—her small son clutching her hand.

But it would have to be enough.

So many memories. He paused for a long moment on the curb, alone once more—the bustle of the bus ride left far behind. Looking up at the flat before him, rain soaking him to the skin as he stood there. Sadness glinting in his gunmetal blue eyes.

So many years, passed and gone.

It was the kind of place he would have expected her to have sought out, he realized—the low gate giving beneath his hand as he moved like a ghost toward the door, the black windbreaker hanging loose and wet from his tall, powerful frame.

Quiet, nondescript. Just another in a long row of terraced houses. *Anonymous.* There was nothing more valuable. . .not in their business.

He glanced at the plate mounted to the right of the door, verifying the address once more before he lifted his hand to press the bell.

Hearing the vague, distant sound of it ringing through the flat as he waited, his eyes flickering back to the deserted street. *Ever alert.*

Footsteps within, the sound of someone cautiously approaching the door. "Who's there?"

He turned so that his face was visible through the peephole. "It's me, Mehreen."

"*Ya, Allah.*" He could hear her gasp of surprise through the door. The Arabic so familiar to his ears. Oh, God.

Another moment, and he heard the rattle of a chain, a bolt being slid back as the door swung open.

The woman who stood in the doorway was in her mid-forties, nearly eight years his senior—her shoulder-length black hair now shot with tell-tale streaks of silver. Framing the dark features of her native Pakistan. "It's been a long time, Mehr."

It was a long moment before she replied, a mixture of emotions playing out across her face—and for a moment he thought she might shut the door in his face. Turn him away.

"Yes. . .yes it has." She turned back from the door, seeming to choose her words with reluctance. "Come in, if you want—I'll make a pot of tea."

He followed her into the small living room of the apartment, removing his hat and running long fingers through his rain-slick black hair as she disappeared into the kitchen.

There was a framed picture on the small table, a picture of a bride in shining white on the arm of a sandy-haired man in full dress uniform—passing underneath the arched sabers of the Regiment. Something about the way they were looking at each other, eyes full of laughter. Of hope. Of love.

A wistful smile touched his lips as he picked up the frame, the memories flooding back. He'd been there that day. Experienced the majesty of that wedding.

There were other memories, and. . .well, majestic was hardly the word.

"Nick was a good man," he announced, feeling almost shame-faced as she reentered the room to find him holding the picture.

She nodded, passing him the hot cup and saucer and taking the frame from his hands. His own sadness reflected in her eyes. "Yes—he was."

"I'm sorry I couldn't be there for you. . .at the funeral." He'd been in Darfur at the time. No way to get back—a job to do. "They told me it was another splinter group of the Provos. A bomb."

Another nod, as she eyed him guardedly.

"I thought that had all died away," he said, raising the cup of Darjeeling to his lips. Steam drifted off the pale golden liquid, warming him against the rain that had chilled his body. "That the Troubles were behind us."

A bitter smile crossed her lips. "We always think that, don't we? But hate. . .hate never dies. Old men pass it on to the young in the blood. Playing at war—their 'patriot game.' And good men die."

Good men die. The refrain of his life.

If he closed his eyes, he could still remember it. The HAHO jump over Lebanon, standing there on the ramp of the C-130 with Nick Crawford and another SAS sergeant at his side. Preparing to jump out into the pitch black of the night.

He could feel the shock of the parachute opening, hear the crackle of automatic weapons fire, smell the gunfire—the blood. He'd saved Nick's life that night. Brought him home safe to her.

But good men die.

He looked up to find her regarding him intently. Her tea untouched by the side of her chair. "You're here to kill a man. . .aren't you, Harry?"

Harry Nichols leaned back in the armchair, watching her—

measuring his words carefully. "I don't work for the Agency any longer, Mehr."

Her fingers trembled slightly as she picked up her teacup, something akin to fear in her dark eyes.

"That's not what I asked."

Chapter 1

6:09 A.M., March 23rd
A flat
London, England

The light of early dawn through the low window struck him in the face as he lifted his face from the prayer rug, gazing east toward Mecca. "*Assalaamu 'alaykum wa rahmatu-Allah.*"

The blessings and peace of God be upon you. Hands flattened out upon his knees, he finished performing the *taslim*, rising as the last of the sacred words passed across his lips.

He rose to his feet, folding the rug reverently and placing it in the small closet beside his bed. Right beside the shoebox containing a pair of mobile phones—and his double-action Browning High Power.

The gun was illegal in the UK, but so were many other things. And with what was coming, it was not a time for followers of the Apostle to be unarmed.

He left his room, pulling the door shut quietly behind him as he walked down the narrow hallway of the flat toward the kitchen.

"*Salaam alaikum, shaikh,*" a voice greeted him. Tarik Abdul Muhammad smiled, reaching out to embrace his host.

"And blessings and peace be upon your house, my brother."

A basket of garlic bread was placed before him as he took his seat at the breakfast table and he glanced briefly upward into the face of his host's wife. "*Jazak'allah khair.*"

May God reward you with goodness. She didn't respond, modest woman that she was, merely smiled as she moved away from the table, her hair covered in a flowing *hijab*.

Which was as it should be.

For weeks he had lived this way, Tarik thought, tearing off a piece of the bread and placing it in his mouth. Moving from place to place among the faithful, never staying with one family for more than a few days.

Evading the watchers.

He reached out to tousle the jet-black hair of their five-year-old daughter as she moved past his chair, smiling at her laugh. Children were a gift from God.

A gift he had himself forfeited, for a greater cause.

Without warning, a knock came on the door of the flat—hard and urgent. His hosts exchanging glances, fear all too visible in their eyes.

Fear that the door would come crashing in the next moment, battered in by a ram in the hands of the thugs they knew as the Special Branch. Fear that their children would be caught in the cross-fire.

Tarik replaced the uneaten portion of the garlic bread in the basket, eyeing the distance down the hallway back to the small room where he'd been sleeping. *Was there time?*

The knock came again, and his host rose from the table. "I'll get it," he whispered, motioning with his hand for his family to leave the room.

Tarik nodded, speaking softly in his native Pashto as he shepherded them down the hall and back into the room he had come to call home. "Stay here," he instructed the wife, grabbing the box out of the closet, the little girl's eyes opening wide at the sight of the gun in his hand.

Voices. He moved down the hallway toward the sound, the muzzle of the Browning leading the way—the weapon cold in his hands.

"Brother Tarik," his host called out just as he rounded the corner. There was a young man standing just within the flat's door, speaking rapidly. Light-skinned, his face covered in dark stubble, his hands were moving quickly as he talked.

And then he saw the gun. "Please, please, *no*. I am not your enemy."

"Then who are you?"

His host stepped between them, holding up his hand. "*Salaam*, Tarik. Abdul comes to us as a courier from the Brothers."

The *Ikhwan*.

Tarik smiled, de-cocking the Browning as he waved the courier forward, gesturing for him to take a seat at the table. "*Salaam alaikum*, my brother."

"*Wa' alaikum salaam*." And unto you peace.

"What word do you bring me, Abdul?" Tarik asked, taking a seat opposite the young Arab, the Browning laying there on the table between them. With the Western intelligence agencies monitoring every call placed, every e-mail sent. . .the faithful had been reduced to this for messages too important, too specific to trust otherwise. Meeting face-to-face.

A man, carrying a message.

Reduced? For as it had been in the days of the Prophet, so it was now.

The Arab licked his lips nervously, his dark eyes darting from one to another as if uncertain whether he should speak. "I bring evil news, *shaikh*. The prince is dead."

For a long moment, Tarik thought he must have misunderstood his words. His once-tranquil blue eyes blazed as he leaned across the table, his voice lowering to a hiss. "Prince *Yusuf?*"

"The same."

"How did this happen? When?"

Once again, the man's tongue darted out nervously, moistening his lips.

"He was shot dead aboard his yacht *Khaybar*, four days ago. This," he said, his fingers trembling as he laid a small, coin-shaped object on the table between them, "was found in his mouth."

Hesitating for only a moment, Tarik reached forward, picking up the object. It wasn't a coin, but rather a poker chip.

A poker chip with the word *Bellagio* emblazoned in the center.

It was as if the shadow of Death itself had fallen over the room, a chill pervading his body.

He reached forward, grasping the messenger by the wrist. "Why have you brought this to *me?*"

6:21 A.M.
The United States Embassy
Grosvenor Square, London

". . .only following the instructions I was given. Forgive me, *shaikh*."

"*Got* you," Carlos Jimenez whispered, a grin of triumph crossing his face. Their gambit had paid off, succeeding where nearly a month of joint surveillance had failed. *Locating their target.* He leaned back in his chair, running a hand over his chin as the audio stream continued. "How long do you think it will take him to figure out that poker chip was embedded with a tracker?"

The tall man sitting on the edge of his desk smiled ever so faintly. "Hard to say, but I wouldn't want to be 'Abdul' when he does."

That was God's honest truth, Jimenez thought, glancing around at his windowless office. The furnishings were Spartan enough, considering the former Marine's position at the Court of St. James.

He'd been a Marine for ten of his forty-five years, had served with the Agency another nine.

Station Chief London—that was his title, one that he had held for the last two years. Not that anyone aside from his own team and his colleagues at Thames House—the headquarters of the UK's Security Service—used it.

Anonymity. . .it was more to be desired than anything else in this business.

"You were there, weren't you, Parker?" he asked, looking up into his colleague's eyes. "In Vegas."

Vegas. Thomas Parker glanced across the room at the empty wall, a thousand images passing before his eyes in the long moment before he responded. Remembering that night, the Nevada sky filled with fire, the stench of blood and gunpowder filling the Bellagio's theatre.

The scent of camphor in his nostrils. Soman nerve gas.

"Yes," the paramilitary operations officer replied. "I was there."

And wasn't able to stop it, his mind finished for him, unspoken words of self-condemnation. For terror had come to America that night—on the very eve of Christmas itself.

When he looked back, it was to find the station chief staring at him. The man might not have quite looked the image of a Marine, nine years after leaving the Corps for the intelligence community, but there were traces still present—the prematurely greying hair cropped up high and tight, the voice of command that every recruit knew so well.

"Is that going to be a problem?" he asked, the meaning clear in his voice.

Thomas chose to ignore it. "What do you mean?"

With a heavy sigh, Jimenez opened the bottom drawer of his desk, pulling out a bottle of Jim Beam and a pair of shot glasses with the USMC logo etched into the crystal. "Don't give me that, Parker. You know exactly what I mean—you know our orders, yours and mine. You're here to surveil Tarik Abdul Muhammad, not take him down. Now we've found him, so I'm asking: can you handle that?"

He watched him tilt the bottle of bourbon, amber liquid splashing into the glasses. Temptation gnawing at his heart.

"Do you think Kranemeyer would have sent me if I couldn't?" he asked, referencing the Director of the Clandestine Service.

The CIA station chief shook his head, replacing the cap on the bottle. "No, I don't. . .but Kranemeyer is three thousand miles away. And you're operating in my bailiwick now. So how about it?"

"I've been down this road a time or two before as you well know, Carlos," Thomas replied, drawing himself up. Looking the Marine in the eye. "It's not going to be a problem."

Jimenez searched his eyes for another long moment, then reached for both of the shot glasses.

"I can drink to that," he said, handing one of them to Thomas. "Devil's Cut—just got the bottle in from the States."

He smiled easily. "You wouldn't believe what can fit in a diplomatic pouch."

Thomas almost didn't hear him, looking down at the drink in his hand. *Torn.* He knew what he should do, what he *had* to do. Knowing and doing were two different things.

"There a problem?" Jimenez asked, pausing even as his own shot glass touched his lips. "You take your bourbon neat, as I recall."

He laughed. "I remember that time in Kabul back in '09—the two of us, that brunette lieutenant, and the only bottle of liquor in the whole godforsaken country. What a party."

Yeah. He remembered that night, a few hours' respite in a war without end. A faint smile touched his lips at the memory.

He could feel the station chief's eyes on him, knew the questions which would come. Questions with no answers. . .or none that he wanted to give. Knowing the alternative to those questions was defeat itself.

And he raised the glass to his lips with a rough motion, feeling the whisky slide down his throat, the fire mellowed by notes of cinnamon.

Surrender. . .

7:03 A.M.
The flat
Ealing, London

The couch on which he'd slept was empty when Mehreen came out of the bedroom, its cushions cool to the touch. He'd been gone for hours.

Where. . .she had no idea.

She pulled her mobile from the pocket of her jeans as she moved into the kitchen, gazing down at the luminous screen in the semi-darkness.

Knowing what her job required her to do, knowing that she should place the call. Any contact with a foreign—even friendly—intelligence officer was to be reported. No exceptions.

And yet something held her back. There'd been something different about Nichols, something she'd sensed since the moment he had entered her flat.

He had changed.

She knew his history almost as well as she knew her own. The Security Services were very particular about that sort of thing. Nichols had entered the employment of the American Central Intelligence Agency in the years before 9/11, back in the old days of the Directorate of Operations.

A paramilitary operations officer, that's what he was. Or had been, assuming his story of leaving the Agency was true. One of the men out at the sharp end—fighting in the shadows of a war most people didn't even know was being waged. *Like Nick.*

She'd always known the work that he did—that *they* did. They were hunters. Hunters of men. No sense in evading that reality.

But last night had been different, and for the first time she had felt it, seen its dark presence in his eyes. *Death.* A fatalism she had never seen him exhibit before.

He hadn't asked her *not* to make the call. Hadn't even mentioned it, though he knew full well the protocols that were in place. Just left the decision to her, without judgment. Without reproach.

It was trust, alien though that was to a man like him.

Mehreen paused by the refrigerator, looking at the photo of her and Nick hanging there. A casual shot, his shirt off, a sinewy arm wrapped tightly around her shoulders—the white sands of Sanna Bay stretching out behind them.

Nichols had taken the picture.

She closed her eyes, remembering the moment as if it were yesterday. The men had just come back from a run on the beach, a hell-for-leather footrace. Come back laughing like boys, slapping each other on the shoulder and flinging insults like the friends they were. Brothers in all but blood.

Nick had knelt down beside her as she lay there on the beach blanket, raising her hand to his lips. Laughed and told her she was beautiful, brushing her dark hair back from her eyes. The war forgotten for that moment in time.

Eleven months later, he was dead.

Brothers, she thought, their laughter echoing through her mind as she put the mobile back in her pocket. They'd have laid down their lives for each other, without a moment's hesitation.

And she knew, in that moment. There were trusts which could never be betrayed.

7:07 A.M.
Mortlake Cemetery
Southwest London

Robert Montfort. That was the name on the headstone, along with the dates *1898-1975*. A granite angel keeping watch, head bowed in prayer.

Two feet down. And a foot from the head of the coffin. Harry bent down on one knee in the crisp, powdery snow, using an entrenching tool to scoop out earth from the old grave.

He'd taken the R68 bus to the cemetery, using the hat to shield his face as he climbed aboard. An hour's ride, sitting two seats behind an elderly Sikh clad in the traditional clothing and turban of his faith, his face shrouded in a snow-white beard.

Two young men had gotten on at the second stop, he remembered, a flashlight clenched between his teeth as he checked his measurements one more time.

Street toughs, by the look of them.

The older of the duo had sidled up to the Sikh, his breath reeking of liquor—opening his faded leather jacket to reveal a white t-shirt emblazoned with the blood-red cross of St. George.

"Look, we've got us a bleedin' Paki," he'd heard him announce—laughing drunkenly with his mate as obscenities slurred from his lips.

Leaning in close, a bony finger extending from his hand, only inches away from the Sikh's face. "Done any little girls lately?" the thug had asked, his face twisted in intoxicated disgust. "You muzzies are all the same—paedos the lot of you. Don't belong in *our* country."

He'd looked away as the verbal abuse continued. Looked away, when he could have stood up for the old man. Could have. Maybe *should* have—but he'd learned a long time ago that you couldn't save the world.

Then, as now, remaining the gray man was paramount. Staying in the shadows, unremarked.

Unremembered.

It meant turning a blind eye to a thousand wrongs. Dismissing them as. . .irrelevant. All so that the mission might succeed.

The mission. He heard the entrenching tool strike metal, leaned forward to aim the flashlight down in the hole.

He only had one mission now.

The cold metal edge of a box touched his probing fingertips and he began brushing away dirt with a gloved hand, his motions hurried. Dawn was coming, and it was time for him to be gone.

The box was twelve inches long—five wide, he realized as he lifted it from the hole. Smaller than he had hoped, much smaller. Secured with a rusty lock.

He could only hope its contents, first buried for use in last resort by Agency officers back during the Cold War, were in better condition. He laid the edge of the entrenching tool against the lock, striking it a vicious blow with the palm of his hand. One blow, then a second—and the lock snapped open with a sound like a pistol shot, echoing off the brick cloisters of the nearby crematorium.

The lid came up, revealing the old insulation that had sealed the box from the inside, keeping out the moisture in the nearly four decades since it had been placed in the ground.

And there it was—a box of ammunition tucked into one corner of the box. Twenty rounds of .380 ACP hardball. Full metal jacket.

Reaching in, he lifted an object wrapped in oilcloth from its resting place.

The familiar shape of a pistol beneath his fingers.

And the cloth fell away, the distinctive outline of a Walther PPK revealed in the beam of his flashlight.

He leaned back into the cold headstone, his shoulder pressed against the graven angel as he stared down at the pistol in his hand, his fingers trembling ever so slightly.

It wasn't fear, he knew that. Fear was the province of men who had something to lose—and he had already lost more than he cared to remember. Everything he had once held dear.

It wasn't nerves, those hesitations that came with the thought of killing a man. He knew those feelings. . .and he had killed many times before. The thought no longer gave him pause, a piece of his soul that had disappeared a long time before. Seared away in the fires of war.

But this time was different. This time was personal. And he knew what it was he felt. Knew how dangerous it could become.

Hate.

Chapter 2

8:28 A.M.
Central London

Returning to the city was always somewhat of a shock, and the longer he had been gone, the more alien it seemed. Was this home—or was home the desert he had left behind?

Three months in Somalia, Darren Roth thought, glancing impatiently at the crosswalk sign, waiting for the symbol to flash. If he closed his eyes he could still hear it all, the bleating of goats in the villages, the rumble of a lorry's engine. The crackle of small-arms fire in the night.

Three months hunting an elusive enemy, militants loyal to Al-Shabab.

A chill ran through the black man's body as he pulled his jacket more tightly about his shoulders. It wasn't cold, not really—but less than thirty hours had elapsed since he'd left behind the hundred-degree temperatures of the Somalian desert, and the air seemed to bite at his ears, at his shaved scalp.

His eyes searched through the crowd surrounding him as he waited for the light to change, a mass of humanity halted for a moment there on that London street. Most of them were on their mobiles, head lowered like the slightly built girl beside him, her thumbs dancing over the phone's small keyboard. Texting a friend, a lover.

None of them would have lasted three days in Somalia.

The symbol flashed and the crowd began to move, people jostling against him as he made his way toward the crosswalk. Ahead of him he could see the security guards, the massive archway of Thames House.

The headquarters of the Security Service. MI-5. . .

"Marsh is waiting for you in his office," were almost the first words Roth heard as he walked into Five's Operations Centre, stripping off his jacket and draping it over the empty chair at his desk.

Or what had been his desk before he left.

He raised an eyebrow, glancing over at the woman. "No rest for the wicked?"

She smiled. "His orders were to send you in the moment you arrived."

Marsh. A legend in the intelligence community, Julian Marsh had been part of the Service for decades, ever since the twilight years of the Cold War.

Roth looked back from the operations center toward the glass-enclosed room that served as the director-general's office and nodded grimly. "Right you are."

"Come in," Marsh announced at his knock. The director had his back to him, hands shoved deep into the pockets of his dress pants as he gazed out on the floor, but he could see the man's reflection in the glass. A stern face surmounted by thinning grey hair staring back at him.

Tailored grey pants, a matching vest, and a pale blue tie against a starched white shirt—that was the uniform of the day for Marsh. Always had been. His suit jacket was discarded over the back of a chair in the sparsely appointed office.

"Moral of the story," he began, still not facing him, "never loan one of your best field officers to Six. You may never get him back."

He turned, favoring Roth with an expression that was as close Marsh ever came to a smile. "Have a seat," he continued with a small gesture of his hand. "How was Somalia?"

"It went well, sir," he replied guardedly. "Need to know" was ever applicable, even with someone of Marsh's clearance. "I'm sure the notes from my debriefing with Six will be arriving on your desk presently."

"When Babylon-on-Thames gets around to it," the older man snorted, referencing the nickname for MI-6's ziggurat-style headquarters. He picked up a folder lying on top of his desk. "No matter. . .we have more pressing issues. Namely, Operation PERSEPHONE. Read this."

Roth took the folder from his hand, opening it in his lap and scanning through page after page of computer print-outs and surveillance photos. It seemed impossible, but there it was. All spelled out before him in black and white. "We're running a joint surveillance operation with the CIA—here in London?"

"We are," Marsh responded. "And now *you* are. With the target finally located as of earlier this morning, I'm placing you in charge of liaising with our American cousins as we prepare to go fully operational."

"Why do you need me?" he asked, picking up the photo of their target, reading the name printed below. *Tarik Abdul Muhammad.*

"For the same reason I petitioned the Home Office to have their request denied," came Marsh's acid reply. "But you know how that goes. Petitioning the Home Office is like mating with an elephant. There's precious little pleasure to be derived from it, you're liable to be squashed—and nothing will come of it for years."

If that had been meant as a joke, Marsh showed no signs of laughing as he continued, "The new American president made the request personally, and the PM was in an accommodating mood. Everything signed, sealed, and delivered, with the Security Service read in as a polite afterthought. And that's why I'm bringing you in—the Americans are up to something, and I need you to find out what it is."

There was something there in the director's voice, something veiled.

"What are you telling me?"

Marsh took a second, noticeably thinner folder and tossed it into his lap. "That's the man the CIA sent over to take operational command of their half of the operation. Thomas Parker. In the years before 9/11, he was the highly successful manager of a Fortune 500 tech company—a company which went down with the World Trade Center Towers. Most of what we have on him is from those years—the final single-sided sheet is everything we've been able to gather through 'channels' since he joined the Agency. Draw your own conclusions."

Roth's eyes scanned quickly down the sheet, connecting the dots. He was weary, the stress of the flight back from Somalia taking its toll.

But not so weary as to miss the obvious.

"He's a paramilitary operations officer," he announced, looking up from the dossier.

"Exactly," Marsh responded, extending a hand for the folder. "Ostensibly, the Americans are here for surveillance purposes and surveillance purposes alone. . .and yet they place a member of the Special Activities Division in charge."

"You're thinking extraordinary rendition?" It would have been their best play, if an almost unbelievably audacious one. Grab the Pakistani and fly him out of the UK under the cover of night. Take him to Jordan, one of the last countries in the Middle East still cooperating with the CIA's rendition program in the wake of the Arab Spring. Throw him in a cell in Amman, let King Abdullah's *Mukhabarat* have a few turns at him. It could work.

It *had* worked, many times before.

Marsh just looked at him, unanswering, and it was in that moment that Roth realized the older man was contemplating the unthinkable.

Assassination. . .

8:53 A.M.
The May Fair Hotel
Central London

The Agency did nothing by half measures, Thomas thought, closing the door behind him. They had secured the entire floor of the May Fair Hotel for their personnel, with armed officers of the UK Counter Terrorism Command standing guard at the elevators.

A month in, and he still wasn't sure whether that was for their protection. . .or just to keep an eye on them. Knowing the tenuous state of the "special relationship" these days, it was probably more than a bit of both.

And it certainly did nothing to lower their profile.

He tossed his overcoat onto the bed, rubbing his face with a weary hand. Surveillance work wasn't nearly as glamorous as the movies made it out to be—long nights huddled in the back of a van with bad heat, trying to take decent photographs from half a kilometer away.

Only the very best could maintain their edge over the course of a long surveillance op. Only the voyeurs enjoyed it.

He'd once been one of the best. Wasn't sure about that—not anymore. Wasn't sure about much of anything, these days.

There was a sticky note pressed against the mirror in the suite's bathroom, where he'd left it the preceding night, before heading out. It bore the words "nine days", with a crudely drawn smiley face beneath it.

It seemed to be mocking him now. *Nine days dry.* It was probably the longest he'd gone without a drink since he'd started drinking at the age of sixteen—a party after the junior prom at his upstate New York high school, if memory served.

Nine days, and now the count started all over again. So damnably *weak*.

The first step is admitting you have a problem. He could still hear his sponsor's voice, half a world away now. The trouble with that when you were part of the intelligence community was not letting anyone else know that you had the problem.

He'd always been known as a hard drinker—that was more common than not in the community, he thought, staring at his reflection in the mirror. But it had never affected his work. *Ever.* He was too much the professional for that.

Or so he'd thought.

He unbuttoned his shirt to reveal the ballistic vest underneath. The Brits were dead set against them carrying weapons, but body armor they were okay with. Couldn't shoot, but maybe they'd survive *being* shot.

Yeah, he mused sourly—that made perfect sense.

Time to get some sleep. Four hours of it. . .and then it all started again.

9:08 A.M.
Thames House

"Running late this morning, Mehr?" were almost the first words she heard as she slipped into her workstation, tucking her lunch down by her feet. Another day at the office.

"Yes," she responded, forcing a smile to her face as she glanced up into the grey eyes of her supervisor, Alec MacCallum. "A lot of people on the Tube this morning."

Which was true, if not the reason for her delay. She'd delayed leaving her flat until the last moment, second-guessing her decision regarding Nichols. Wondering if he had any plans to return.

Her boss nodded, seeming to accept her response. "The weekly threat assessments are on your desk, fresh in from GCHQ. Get them worked up as soon as possible."

She watched as he moved on, winding his way through the maze of workstations in the Centre, pausing to speak to several of the other officers. Having spent twenty-one of his fifty-six years with SO-13, the Anti-Terrorist Branch of the London Metropolitan Police Department, MacCallum had been a natural choice to take charge of Five's Section G, one of Marsh's first appointments upon arrival.

Aside from the Director-General, she and Alec anchored the old guard among the Security Service's predominantly youthful workforce, a fact that had resulted in the two of them working closely together since his arrival at Five.

Her fingers flickered across the keyboard, entering her system passcode. There'd even been a time when she had thought he fancied her, in the years since Nick's death. There was comfort to be found in the friendship—a lonely divorcee, a grieving widow—but the professional reserve had proven impossible to strip away. The walls each of them had built far too high.

She let a heavy sigh escape from her lips as she turned to the thick stack of threat assessments. *New* threats. . .and they never stopped coming. Assessing their credibility—that was her job.

There was no time to reflect on the past, and as she opened the first folder, her eyes scanning down the cover sheet—she found herself wondering why she had done so this morning.

Nichols.

11:04 A.M.
Northwest London

"He's moving," the man in the chase car announced, raising a camera surreptitiously to his eye and snapping a quick picture as their target emerged from the door of the flat, looking first left, then right. "I repeat, I have eyes on CERBERUS. On foot, and moving east. Sierra Two, do you copy?"

A moment passed before his earpiece crackled, a voice announcing, "Aye, Sierra One—taking up a following position."

Tarik Abdul Muhammad shoved both hands deep into the pockets of his jacket as he moved down the sidewalk, lost in his own thoughts.

His friend was *dead*. It seemed impossible to comprehend, to process the reality of what had happened. He could still remember the first meeting with Prince Yusuf in Lahore all those years ago, scant weeks after his release from Guantanamo Bay.

It had been a meeting ordained of God, a communion between a man with vision and a man with the money to bring that vision to pass.

A vision which had come to fruition only a few months before as the skies over Las Vegas erupted in fire, bits and pieces of Delta Airlines Flight 94 raining down over the city. As his *mujahideen* stormed through the doors of the Bellagio, seeking death and meeting their own.

Bellagio. His fingers met the ridged edge of the poker chip, turning it over and over as he walked. The Americans had killed his friend, and now they were sending him a message.

The message that no matter where he ran, no matter where he sought refuge, they could find him. They could kill him.

As though they thought themselves God, he mused, staring up into the eye of a surveillance camera as he stood at the edge of a crosswalk, waiting for the traffic to pass.

The arrogance of it was unbelievable, the hubris of the West. Vulnerable as they had been proven to be, and still they exalted themselves.

His eyes flickered over the busy street, serene calm radiating from their blue depths as pedestrians jostled around him. Yusuf's death was no doubt a test, all just another part of God's plan for him.

And if he knew nothing else, he knew this. No matter what the Americans schemed in their pride, the time and the place of his death would be of Allah's choosing.

Not until.

12:24 P.M.
Thames House
Central London

It felt like he was back in Somalia again, Darren thought, spreading out the PERSEPHONE briefing folders on the desk of his workstation as he reflected on Marsh's words.

Working with allies you couldn't trust, having to keep as close an eye on your "friends" as your enemies. That was reality.

As was the enormity of a twenty-four-hour surveillance operation. You couldn't run one with just a few officers, the way they showed it on the telly. From what he could see of the roster, there were nearly forty people read in on the mission already. More people than had even known he was in Somalia—nearly half of them brought on after Five had "lost" Tarik Abdul Muhammad in Leicester over a month previous.

A trail that had run cold, until this morning.

He glanced down at the hard polymer case at his feet, a "gift" from Marsh. If you wanted to call it that.

"You'll be liaising with SO-15," Marsh had said, referencing the official designation for the Counter Terrorism Command, *"but I want you to be prepared for any eventuality. . .no matter how suddenly it may arise."*

Be prepared, indeed. The polymer case housed a Sig-Sauer P229 semiautomatic pistol chambered in 9mm Luger, along with a pair of thirteen-round magazines. And a suppressor designed to be screwed into the threaded barrel.

MI-5 officers weren't supposed to be armed. Not on British soil, at least. Something he had voiced to the DG.

Marsh had shrugged, as if that were nothing of concern. *"I secured a special dispensation for you in this case, despite much reluctance on the part of the Home Secretary. Just keep an eye on the cousins for me. Make sure they don't do anything. . .untoward."*

Darren glanced at his watch. Just under five hours until he was due at Grosvenor Square to meet with his opposite numbers with the Agency.

He picked up Parker's thin folder again, flipping it open to reveal the American's picture. Did the man match the file? He'd know, soon enough. . .

2:39 P.M.
Hendon Cemetery
Northern Greater London

Cemeteries. They had always been a familiar part of his life, Harry thought, walking slowly amongst the tombstones. An all too familiar part.

He'd been burying people for years. Watching as a flag-draped casket was lowered into the ground—holding a sobbing widow tight against his chest as shots rang out in final salute to her love. Row on row of white crosses standing in mute testimony to the lives departed.

And yet he had lived, where others died. The unbearable grief of being left behind—the inescapable guilt of the survivor.

Wishing more than words that you could have taken their place, stood in their shoes when the bullet came for them.

A granite stone stood upright near the end of the row, his boots crunching in the light snow as he came abreast of it. It was an old stone, the name nearly worn away by the years, but the inscription remained. *For she walked with God. . .and she was not, for God took her.*

The words hit him with the force of a physical blow, and for a moment he felt as if he might become sick, the foul taste of bile pervading his throat. *For God took her.*

Carol. He could scarce bear to speak her name, but in that moment, he found himself transported back to that night in Vegas, those stolen moments just before their world fell apart.

The taste of her lips on his, salty with tears, her back pressed against the door as he pressed her body close to his.

"You have to promise me. . .this won't be the end."

And yet end it had, he thought, running an angry hand across his face. *For God took her.*

He gazed up into the slate-gray heavens, clouds drifting slowly across the face of the earth—blocking out the sun. He'd asked *why*, but found no better answer to that question than he ever had through the years. *The one shall be taken and the other left.*

Far better to be the mourned than the mourner.

Another twenty minutes of searching led him to that which had brought him here, a stone in a corner near the chapel—small, nondescript, the inscription reading *Company Sergeant Major Nicholas Crawford, British Army.* And then the line below, *Who Dares Wins*—the motto of the Special Air Service since its inception. The Regiment. The creed by which Nick had lived his life.

Harry had half-expected the stone to have born the escutcheon of the SAS, the downward-slashing Excalibur wreathed in flames—but the granite was bare. Perhaps Mehreen had been unable to afford the engraving. That wouldn't have surprised him, the salary of a civil servant was nothing to boast of.

Kneeling down in front of the stone, he removed his glove, tracing a hand over the inscription.

Good men die. Mehreen's words from the previous night—and there had been none better than Nick. None braver.

He'd been at home that weekend. *For once.* A rare moment of peace, of tranquility, in lives marred by war.

So soon shattered. Nick had kissed his wife good-bye that bright spring morning, headed out the door. *Off to work.* Taking her car, for once—his own down with engine trouble.

He'd tossed his kit in the back seat, opened the driver's door and slid inside. Turned the key in the ignition. . .and it was all over, in the space of a moment. *A blinding flash.*

There had been a bomb in the car, Special Branch confirmed later. Planted there by a previously-unknown splinter group of the Real IRA.

It had killed him instantly, that much was sure—the shockwave rippling outward from the epicenter of the blast, shattering every window in the small Bromley flat he and Mehreen had called home.

Dead. Long before she had pulled his broken body from the burning wreckage, her feet cut and bleeding. Tears streaming down her cheeks as she felt frantically for a pulse that wasn't there.

No goodbyes.

"I'm sorry," he breathed, unsure whether his apology was for past regrets. . .or what he was about to do, the steel of the Walther cold against his side, beneath his shirt.

The faiths he was about to betray.

5:04 P.M.
The US Embassy
Grosvenor Square, London

"Always good to have you visit us, Jules." Carlos Jimenez smiled, ushering Julian Marsh and his subordinate around the security checkpoints that guarded the Grosvenor Square building from unauthorized access. "Welcome to the United States of America."

It was true, strange as it sounded. An embassy was the sovereign soil of its respective nation, an inviolable refuge. *Home court advantage.*

"A pleasure to meet you, Mr. Roth," Thomas greeted, reaching out to shake the black man's hand. Knowing a man's name without being introduced, that was one of the benefits of being an intelligence officer.

Knowing everything about him. . .was another. Darren Roth was a former Royal Marine warrant officer, part of the elite Special Boat Service and a veteran of both Iraq and Afghanistan, where he had been awarded the Conspicuous Gallantry Cross for his actions in the middle of a Taliban ambush in 2008. He'd left the military for the Security Service three years before, and word had it he was Marsh's right-hand man.

Word had it. For the moment, Thomas would content himself with the hard intel at his disposal. All the RUMINT aside, Darren Roth was a very dangerous man. Good thing he was on their side.

Or something like that.

"Likewise," the MI-5 officer replied, a disarming smile crossing his face.

That wasn't going to work, Thomas thought, forcing a smile of his own as the CIA station chief turned, leading the way down the corridor toward the elevators.

They were both old hands at this game.

6:30 P.M.
The flat
Ealing, London

The door of her flat had been locked when she left. She was always very particular about that. . .had been even when Nick was still alive.

It wasn't something she forgot.

And yet, as she hung her coat in the small entry hall, she could smell chicken cooking, the aroma of ginger and curry filling her nostrils.

Nichols was standing by the stove when she came in from the hall, his back to her. Black t-shirt and dark jeans, a not uncommon uniform for him over the years. But he looked thinner now, more fragile, somehow.

"Didn't know what to think when I found you gone this morning," she said, running a hand through her damp hair.

"I'm sorry," he said, still not turning to face her—and the apology sounded sincere to her ears. Then again, it would.

That was Nichols, and he was nothing if not good at dealing with people. It had been his job. "Dinner is almost ready, I picked a few things up at the market."

"You didn't need to do that."

He looked back at her for the first time, a tinge of sadness in those blue eyes. "I did."

She shrugged. "It smells good, whatever it is. Smells like home."

"Murgh handi," he responded, reaching a finger into the pot to taste his cooking. It was a traditional dish of chicken and spices, mixed together in a *handi*, a narrow-mouthed cooking vessel used commonly in Pakistani cooking.

She smiled, pain clouding her eyes as she sat down at the table. Tasting the food with his fingers—it reminded her of Nick.

The legacy of too many years spent out in the field. Squatting around a goatherd's fire, nestling deep in a "hide" eating cold MREs with one's bare hands. Only a rifle for company. The two of them had been so much the same.

"You spent a lot of time in Pakistan over the years, didn't you?"

A nod. "Most of my career was spent in the 'Stans," he responded. "The best part was the food. Grew to love it."

Past tense. The 'Stans. . .Afghanistan, Pakistan, the handful of countries between Russia and the sea, most of them former client states of the Soviet bloc and whose names ended in the Farsi suffix which mean "the place of." But for her people—there was no place. Not anymore.

"I went for a walk in the city today," he said, setting the steaming bowl of meat between them as he took a seat opposite. It was a lie, she was certain of that—almost imperceptible, but she knew him. A lie. . .or a half-truth? Either way, he was hiding something from her. "Been longer than I thought. It's changed."

"It has. More by the year," she acknowledged, her lips closing around a piece of the spice soaked chicken. Chewing it slowly as she watched him. "None of it good."

He forced a grim smile. "Change rarely is, these days."

"They're here now," came her observation, a distant anger entering her eyes. "But you know that, don't you?"

"The Islamists?"

She nodded. "Like parasites, moving on to a new host after the pillaged body of the old has collapsed underneath their weight. At any given time, we're monitoring up to thirty jihadi operations here in this country. Five of them in London alone, one not eight miles from where we're sitting."

"Are you sure that's something you should have told me?" he asked quietly.

There was something in his eyes that nettled her. "No more sure than I was when I chose not to fill out a contact report when I arrived at Thames House this morning."

6:41 P.M.
The US Embassy
Grosvenor Square, London

"We're going to need an officer in the Centre," Carlos Jimenez said, glancing up from his notes to look down the conference table at the director-general. "A round-the-clock presence, access to the complete operational details of PERSEPHONE as this continues to unfold."

"No." Thomas saw Marsh's eyes flash, drawing himself up in his seat as he transfixed Jimenez with a patrician glare. "Absolutely not. That's out of the question."

"Now, Jules. . ." The CIA station chief shook his head, smiling the smile of a man certain he held all the cards. "I happen to know the orders you received from the Home Office are to offer the Agency your full cooperation. We both know the authorizations on this op go way above my pay grade. *And* yours."

"And I will comply with my orders from the Home Secretary," came the icy reply. "But cooperation is one thing, giving your people *carte blanche* to go freewheeling around Thames House is quite another—no. Request denied."

Jimenez let out a sigh of exasperation, catching Thomas's eye as he replied, "I can't stress enough how seriously you need to take the presence of Tarik Abdul Muhammad in this country, Jules, given his involvement in the planning and execution of the Vegas attacks. If you're not going to take him down, you need to keep him under constant surveillance—monitor anyone he talks to, anyone he so much as passes on the street. Whether you choose to believe it or not, he poses a clear and present danger to the national security of the UK."

"As do many others," Marsh returned evenly. "The Security Service faces threats on a daily basis, everyone from al-Qaeda to the Islamic State. Which is not to mention the stray Irish dissident and fruitcakes covering the political spectrum from Left to Right."

"But this is—"

"And if the US government," the director-general went on, raising his voice to cut his CIA counterpart off, "hadn't decided to play catch-and-release with its Guantanamo detainees, Tarik Abdul Muhammad wouldn't be one of them. So, no, Mr. Jimenez. . .laudable as your motivations may be—you don't get to sit there and lecture me on not taking this seriously."

6:43 P.M.
The flat
Ealing, London

"Why didn't you, Mehr?" Still the same calm, as if the answer was of no consequence, instead of something that would decide his very fate.

Why? Why hadn't she? An impossible question to answer. As impossible as the decision between two rights. *Two wrongs.*

For turning him in would have been both.

Her hands balled into fists underneath the table, knuckles whitening as she struggled to maintain control. Or the illusion of it.

With a rough motion, she pushed away the half-eaten bowl of chicken, suddenly no longer hungry. His very presence bringing back all the memories.

"I'm going to take a shower, then go to bed," she announced, her voice brittle. On the verge of breaking.

Mehreen didn't look at him, nor did he say anything to stop her as she left the kitchen, moving down the flat's narrow hallway toward her bedroom.

Her hand reached out, closing the door behind her. She didn't lock it, didn't need to. Nichols would respect that. Always had.

Always had. Her face tightened with emotion, refusing to give way to tears. Her legs slowly giving out from under her as she sagged to the floor. Remembering. Whatever his faults—and she had no doubt they were many. . .he had been there for her when there'd been no one else.

She and Nick had tried for years to have a child. *Years.* He had wanted nothing more in the world than a son, but he would have been happy with whatever she had born, she knew that.

Fertility treatments were rare in the UK, the wait times long. Running out of time, her clock ticking down. But they had tried that as well, and succeeded at long last.

They'd named him Adrian, after Nick's father. Set up one room of that flat in Bromley as a nursery, painting it pale blue—the color of a robin's egg. She could still remember standing in the room, watching him paint. Painting had never been his strong suit, and his clothes had been speckled with blue.

She'd laughed at him and he had reached over, his hand darting out to dot her nose with paint, his eyes dancing with delight—the baby kicking within her. The three of them becoming one in that moment.

Then Nick had been called back to the war—without warning—the duty of the soldier taking precedence over that of the husband. As ever. And she was left alone, barely six months along.

The end of the fourth week since Nick's departure came around, and with it a knock on the door. Telling her that his patrol had been ambushed in the Iraqi desert outside Basra, leaving two SAS soldiers dead and Nick. . .missing in action.

She'd thought she was strong—seen everything during her years at Five. But nothing had prepared her for that moment.

And she'd gone into labor. Far too soon, alone in the city. She'd been estranged from her family years before. Moving to the UK had been one thing for all of them. Marrying a British soldier was another.

Harry had called her the day before from the American Embassy, checking in on his godson. Passing through the UK on his way back to the States.

When she called him from the back of the ambulance, he was still there, just getting ready to catch a flight.

He'd dropped everything to come to her side, to join her at the hospital. It was the brotherhood—Nick had been his mate, and you looked out for the wife and kid of your mate. No matter what it took.

He was there through the long hours, holding her hand as the birth pangs convulsed her body, as she cried out in pain. There at the end when Adrian was finally delivered. . .stillborn.

And he had stayed with her through the days of grief that followed, a pillar of strength—a shoulder to cry on. Taking care of all the arrangements for Adrian. Until the word came that they'd found Nick. That her husband was on his way home.

They had stood together on the tarmac at RAF Brize Norton, watching as the big C-130 Hercules taxied to a stop in front of them. As Nick came limping down the ramp.

So many years ago, and yet there were wounds that time didn't heal. They'd never tried again, hadn't had the heart for it. And then Nick had been taken from her as well.

Sorrow compounding sorrow, daggers stabbing at her heart. She brushed angrily at the tears now streaming down her cheeks, as if that could somehow check their flow.

The dictates of protocol. Of *duty*. And yet she owed him a debt.

The kitchen was ghostly quiet after her departure, leaving Harry sitting there, picking idly at his food. His own appetite had deserted him long before, but he was only too aware of how much he *needed* to eat.

Using people. You could rationalize it any way you pleased, but that's what it came down to in the end, the dirtiest part of this business. The most necessary part of the trade.

He knew what Mehreen would decide, *had* known before he had even lifted a hand to knock on her door the previous night. She wouldn't betray him. . .the only question remaining was what she would be willing to betray *for* him.

With a sigh, he reached for his bottle of spring water, draining what remained in a single swallow. Might as well start trying to get some sleep himself. Had a feeling it was going to come hard this night.

10:49 P.M.
London

Sleep. Whatever *that* actually was, he wasn't getting enough of it, Thomas thought, bringing the camera up to his eye and snapping off three shots. *Click-click-click.*

Almost as quick as a video camera, capturing Tarik Abdul Muhammad crossing the street less than a hundred meters east of their position.

"Any thoughts on where he might be going?" Darren asked from the driver's seat beside him.

Thomas shook his head. "A lot of his movement has seemed random—my best bet is that he's been running SDRs on us."

Surveillance detection routes. Standard protocol in the intelligence business, their best proof thus far that the Pakistani's business in the country was anything but on the level.

Click-click-click. "Two phone calls earlier today. Nothing actionable."

"You ran them?"

"Your man MacCallum did. Tarik placed a call to one Andy Gaveda in Dartford, asking about a used car in the classifieds."

"Legitimate?"

"Seems to be," Thomas replied, momentarily distracted by the chatter over his earpiece. "My latest report was that Special Branch was going to have a look in the morning."

"And the other?"

"He received a phone call from Hashim Rahman, the director of the Children of Al Quds Foundation in Leeds. They discussed meeting in person three days from now."

"Where?" the British officer asked, easing the car forward carefully. They were back-up, there to move into place if Tarik suddenly found transport. Till then, their foot teams would handle the job of shadowing the Pakistani, alternating places with dizzying precision.

"They were vague—deliberately so, in my opinion. Near as we can tell, the meeting place is the Masjid-e-Ali there in the city, the registered address of Rahman's foundation." Thomas laid the camera aside, sweeping the street with his binoculars. He picked up three of the MI-5 officers, but only because he knew them by sight.

Two men and one woman, their appearance was completely nondescript, utterly essential for an operation like this. Nothing to draw attention, just businesspeople headed home at the end of a long day.

A vagrant standing in the shadow of the building took a final drag of his cigarette before turning to follow Tarik. "Echo 2, I have CERBERUS."

A smile touched his lips. The "vagrant" was a fourth officer. Well played.

"Leeds," Darren mused. "Maybe that's why he's buying a car."

Likely. Thomas turned to face his companion in the darkness of the car. "Think we can get eyes and ears inside the mosque?"

The former Royal Marine pursed his lips. "You're talking a bureaucratic nightmare."

"Aren't they all?" Thomas asked with a laugh.

Caught off-guard, Darren hesitated for a moment, then started laughing. "Too right, mate. Too right…I'll see what I can do. No promises, you understand?"

"Of course." Radio chatter from the chase teams filled his ear and Thomas lifted the binoculars to his eyes once again, focusing on the figure of Tarik Abdul Muhammad standing on the steps of a run-down building.

Chatting amiably with a young woman who was, well…underdressed for the weather.

"You thinking what I'm thinking?"

Thomas nodded, chuckling. "He's a terrorist—not a eunuch."

10:54 P.M.

The inside of the building was dark, Tarik thought—darker than even he had expected—only a single flickering bulb illuminating the corridor as the prostitute led him along by the arm, a bored, disinterested look on her face.

No matter. She looked to be in her late twenties—almost his age, as nearly as he could tell. Older than he liked his women, but that wasn't the priority. Not tonight.

He could hear grunts and moans coming from the rooms surrounding them as they passed—and once, a woman's scream—as if in pain. The paint of the doors was faded and chipped, bearing an occasional room number, half-scratched off. Perhaps this had been a hotel once, in a by-gone age.

She led him past an elevator which didn't work anymore and up the stairs, ascending the steps ahead of him.

He found himself distracted by the sight, a smile pulling at the corners of his mouth. *Focus.* Everything depended on the next few moments.

The whore stopped outside a door at the top of the stairs, lifting a small hand to rap on the wood.

A moment passed, and he could hear footsteps from within, the bulge of the Browning Hi-Power feeling cold against his ribs.

She leaned against the door, speaking a few words in broken English—and it swung open to reveal a young negro standing behind it, a knife on his belt, a pistol shoved into the waistband of his jeans beneath a swinging gold chain, his eyes narrowing as they settled on Tarik.

The *kufi* nestling on top of his head was the only distinguishing sign of his faith. "And what is to be done of the Hell of which you were warned?"

Tarik smiled, recognizing the source of the codephrase. *Surah Ya-sin.* Knowing the reply which was expected of him. "Embrace the fire. . ."

The man's face finally relaxed into something that might pass for a smile and he stepped back, allowing Tarik to enter. He'd expected the woman to leave, but she entered the room behind him, his eyes adjusting to the semi-darkness within, picking out one man standing by the shuttered window.

"*Salaam alaikum,*" a voice greeted him from the bed, and he glanced over to see another man sitting there, half-dressed, a woman in his lap—one hand absently stroking her long hair, the curve of her back.

Clearly no one had any intention of getting rid of the women. He wondered if they had taken even the barest minimum of precaution.

"You are Sayyed Hassan?" he asked, not bothering to return the salutation. The manager of a used bookstore in Mayfair, the man had been entrusted with the leadership of a jihadist cell in London.

A nod.

Tarik turned back on the prostitute who had accompanied him up, favoring her with an indulgent smile.

"Take your knife," he began in Arabic, addressing the black man. "And slit her throat."

10:57 P.M.

"Any chance of getting eyes on the inside?" Thomas asked, glassing the building with a small pair of binoculars. He had a bad feeling, gnawing at him—the feeling that something was going wrong, even as they sat there. Perhaps it was just nerves, the knowledge of what this man had once done.

Not again. Not if he could stop it.

In the driver's seat beside him, Darren grimaced. "I can place a few calls. . .but, the authorization isn't going to be easy to obtain. Prostitution rings are the jurisdiction of the NCA, not Five."

The National Crime Agency, hailed in the UK media as "Britain's FBI."

"Then what's your plan?"

"We watch," the British officer responded coolly, pulling a mobile from his pocket. "And we wait."

10:58 P.M.

Nothing. He watched the faces of both the prostitutes as he spoke the words—there was no reaction to be seen in their eyes. They hadn't *understood* his words.

"Put up your weapon," he said calmly, motioning toward the black man, who was staring at him with a confused expression on his face, his knife half-drawn from its sheath. "We can talk freely now."

Sayyed Hassan laughed, slapping his woman lightly on the buttocks, motioning for her to slide down off his lap. "The brothers warned us you could be unpredictable, *shaikh*."

Tarik nodded, watching as the woman walked across the room toward the cheap wooden chest of drawers, pausing in front of the mirror. "It is why I am still alive, despite the best efforts of the *khafir*."

"*Insh'allah*," came the overly-pious rejoinder. As God wills.

"Do not tempt God," he replied, shooting Hassan a stern look, "by asking that He protect you against the consequences of your own stupidity."

He continued on before the man could muster the presence of mind to respond, taking command of the room. "Tell me you at least posted a lookout."

If Tarik had doubted the answer to his demand, he received undeniable confirmation in the confused look on Hassan's face. *They hadn't*.

"Go," he ordered, wheeling on the black man. "Go outside and keep a close watch. And remove your *kufi* first."

For a moment, the man hesitated, as though looking to his cell leader for confirmation of the order. Tarik's gaze brooking no disobedience.

A moment, and then he wilted under the stare, taking off the small Islamic skullcap as he ducked out the door, closing it behind him. *Fools*.

"Now tell me," he began, turning back to the leader of the London cell, "have you been able to obtain the weapons we spoke of?"

Hassan swallowed hard, seeming suddenly overawed, the confident self-assurance with which he had handled the whore now leaving him. "W-we are working on it, *shaikh*."

Chapter 3

12:03 A.M., March 24th
The flat
Ealing, London

Warm and wet. The sound of a bullet smashing into flesh, sickeningly familiar.

And she was swaying before him, her head striking his chest as she collapsed into his arms. A dull, lifeless thud.

A raw, inhuman cry escaping his lips as his hands came away from her back, sticky with her blood. "Carol!"

The shot of the sniper ringing in his ears, a haunting echo. Again and again.

Again and again and again.

Harry's eyes flickered open at the sound of the gunshot, his breathing fast and shallow, a sheen of perspiration covering his bare chest—his hand reaching under the pillow cushion for the holstered Walther.

His fingers closed around the butt of the small semiautomatic, flicking the safety off as he brought it out in one practiced motion, his eyes adjusting to the darkness.

Nothing. There was nothing there, absolutely nothing. Just the darkness of the flat, dim street noise from outside the window.

He sat there on the couch, pistol in hand, surveying the twisted mass of blankets at his feet, willing his breathing to return to normal. Wiping the sweat from his chest with a still-trembling hand. A *dream*. It had all been a dream.

Well. . .not all a dream, he thought, safing the Walther with an almost palpable reluctance. Carol was dead, that was real enough. *All too real.*

He let himself fall back against the cushions, struggling to shut the images from his mind. It wasn't the first time he'd had such dreams, not the first time he had awoke reliving that Vegas night. The night she had died, bleeding to death in his arms, a sniper's bullet in her back.

That was then, he thought. This was now—and he couldn't risk losing his focus. He reached into the pocket of his jeans, bringing out his prepaid cellphone and opening it till the glow of the screen illuminated his face in the darkness, playing across the rough stubble of his beard, the sunken hollows of his eyes.

There were two text messages in the inbox, both of them already opened, but he was only interested in the most recent one. *The meet is arranged*, it read, giving him an address. It was a bad part of the city, he remembered—but that was to be expected considering the man he was to meet.

"You get out there in the real world," he thought, smiling ever so slightly as the voice came back to him. The voice of his mentor when he had first joined the CIA's Directorate of Operations, in those years before 9/11. *"You get out in the real world and you realize that the saints won't be able to give you what you need. And if you're going to accomplish your objectives, you're going to have to get down there in that mud and fight shoulder to shoulder with the devil's own—people every bit as dirty, every bit as vile as the men you're trying to stop. Because that objective is the only thing that matters. And* that *is truth."*

John Patrick Flynn. He'd been gone for years now, but Harry could still remember meeting him for the first time there at Camp Peary, in his first days of training. A soft-spoken veteran of the CIA's first go-round in Afghanistan, arming the *mujahideen* against the Soviets, Flynn had brought the hard edge of reality to the training.

Life *and* death. No "or" about it.

He read the message again, a calloused thumb rolling down the screen. Noting the time of the meet: *1530 hours*. It wasn't a meeting he looked forward to, but it was necessary.

Because the objective was the only thing that mattered. . .

7:34 P.M. Eastern Time
An apartment
Washington, D.C.

It was an early evening for him, or would have been, the man thought, picking at his food, the low hum of a television in the background of the apartment.

He'd been up since the previous midnight, putting out fires. Figuratively speaking, of course—and none of them unexpected.

It came with the territory, the little sign on his desk that read *"Director of the National Clandestine Service."*

All of the current crises part of the fallout from the successful hit on TALISMAN.

His men had done their job and done it well, but the intelligence world placed heavy reliance on the time-honored question of *"Cui bono?"*, which translated roughly from the Latin as "To whom the good?"

And the list of suspects who would benefit from the death of a Saudi prince was not. . .overpopulated.

Which is why the Saudi intelligence chief would be flying into D.C. for a meeting before the week was out.

Prince Badr bin Abdul Aziz had been the head of the *Ri'āsat Al-Istikhbārāt Al-'Āmah* for most of the last year, tapped for the intelligence position as the aged King Salman shuffled more of his chess pieces around the board, solidifying power.

The meeting was as off-the-books as it got. Equal parts indignant denial and veiled threat. *Accidents happen. Don't want to lose your people? Keep them on the reservation.*

Something on the television attracted his attention, and he looked over to see the face of the man who had signed off on the assassination of Prince Yusuf ibn Talib al-Harbi.

The President of the United States.

The man wiped his hands on a napkin, reaching down to turn his wheelchair around until he faced the screen, phantom pain twitching through his right leg—a leg that wasn't there any more, the stump above the knee resting on the wheelchair's edge.

He'd left it in Fallujah years before, an Iraqi IED killing one of his team members and leaving his leg mangled below the knee, shrapnel peppering his thighs.

It had marked the end of one career. . .the beginning of another.

". . .promised transparency during my campaign for this office, and it is a promise I intend to keep."

The man reached for the remote, turning the volume all the way up as President Richard Norton continued to speak.

"The bureaucracy of the federal government has grown bloated, unresponsive, and increasingly opaque. And I intend to do what I was elected to do—turn on the lights, from the West Wing, to Capitol Hill. To the bastions of the intelligence community in Fort Meade, Maryland, and Langley, Virginia. It is long past time for the American people to know what is being done in their name. No more secrets. Long past time for those things which have been said in darkness to be heard in the light."

On-screen, the President continued, but the man in the wheelchair was no longer listening.

Much of what Norton had said was. . .true, so far as it went—but other forces were in motion behind the scenes.

Forces he didn't think the newly sworn-in President had even begun to come to terms with—or understand.

He pulled a phone from his pocket, glancing at the screen for a long moment as the President's address continued, punching in a number from memory.

Two rings and a voice answered.

He hesitated before speaking, just silence on the line. Remembering the last time he had called this number, the darkness that had unfolded from that call. What had been *necessary*.

"This is Kranemeyer. We need a face-to-face. As soon as you can make it happen."

12:49 A.M. Greenwich Mean Time
London

"He's been there a long time, hasn't he?" Thomas asked, raising his camera and snapping a couple pictures of a young black man lounging near the corner of the rundown hotel.

"Three cigarettes," Roth responded quietly, proof that he had been watching very closely indeed.

Further proof of his competence, Thomas thought. A valuable quality in an ally, but given the nature of the alliance. . .

They would cross that bridge when they came to it. Movement from the front steps of the hotel caught the corner of his eye and he looked over to see Tarik Abdul Muhammad emerging from the door.

"All teams," he said, touching his ear. "All teams, we have eyes on CERBERUS. I repeat, eyes on the subject—subject is on the move."

The Pakistani had taken maybe fifteen steps down the sidewalk toward them when the black man threw down his cigarette and started to walk back toward the hotel's door.

Lookout. He traded looks with Roth, saw the same question reflected in his counterpart's eyes.

"Victor One, Victor Two, take up following positions on CERBERUS," the British officer ordered, keying his mike. "Sierra elements, hang back and maintain surveillance on the brothel. I want pictures of every bleedin' punter that exits between now and daybreak."

Thomas glanced over at him. "Think we're looking at a meet?"

Roth grinned, the first genuine smile Thomas had seen from the man since meeting him earlier in the day. "He was in there for nearly two hours. . .what do *you* think?"

A chuckle as Thomas cycled back through the pictures, picking out a full frontal shot of the lookout, his face barely shadowed by a nearby streetlight. "I think we need to get a name for this guy."

5:30 A.M.
The flat
Ealing, London

Mehreen could hear the faint hum of voices when she woke, wrapping a housecoat about herself as she moved to the door of her bedroom.

Voices growing louder as she moved down the hall toward the main living area of her flat. Sleep had not come easy the night before, a fitful rest filled with memories.

Of times gone by. Of better days.

It was the telly, she realized, the glow of its screen illuminating the kitchen—a man's voice speaking.

". . .my opponents say that I am a radical, but I ask you, what is radical about the desire of a man to preserve his home? To ensure its future for his children? These. . .people—if you wish to dignify them in such a way—which we have welcomed into our country, they care nothing for what it means to be *British*, for the centuries of storied history and traditions which have made us what we are today. They despise our institutions, sneer at our culture, and revile our fallen heroes as though they were dung. What have we done? I'll tell you what we've done. . .we have taken a serpent into the bosom. And as I stand before you today, I tell you this. If we do not stand together as Englishmen now, to end this so-called 'multi-cultural' experiment—it will end *us*, and all we hold dear."

The voice faded away as she entered the kitchen, replaced by that of a Sky News reporter, ". . .MP Daniel Pearson in a speech given yesterday in Manchester at a rally for the British Defence Coalition. Pearson insists that the goals of the . . ."

Nichols was sitting there, his eyes fixed intently on the TV screen, a steaming mug of coffee warming his hands.

"How long do you suppose we have, Mehr?" he asked, without looking up. How he'd known she was standing there, she had no idea. He'd always had that ability.

"That's hard to say," she responded, tying the sash of her housecoat as she moved to the refrigerator. "The country is on the brink."

He snorted. "The whole world's on the brink."

True enough. "And it's being pushed closer to the edge every day," she said, looking back at him as he sat there in the semi-darkness, his unshaven face lit only by the glow of the now-muted television. "The clerics on the one side, the British far right on the other—each chanting for their own personal take on Armageddon. Drowning out everyone caught in the middle."

"And Pearson?"

She thought for a moment. "A decent enough man, I suppose. A patriot, certainly. But his alliances. . .the legitimacy he lends to the fascist thugs of the BDC. They'd split this country apart if they were given half a chance—all in the name of saving it."

"There's always someone," he replied, taking a long sip of his coffee. "I need you to do something for me, Mehr. Something no one else can."

She could feel her body tense at the words. "And what would that be?"

"The UK dead-ground map. London—all the rest of the major cities in Britain."

"You don't need me for that." She shook her head. "There are websites, blogs—any number of them official—giving a list of the positions of surveillance cameras in the city. You can work out the dead ground from there yourself."

He set the empty mug in front of him, his eyes never leaving her face. "There are lists, of course. And you and I both know they're incomplete. Project OSIRIS has never been disclosed to the public."

"OSIRIS?" The surprise showed in her face and she cursed herself for it. He had taken her off-guard, once again—and he could tell.

"Come on now, Mehr," he replied, and there was almost a sadness in his dark eyes. *Pain.* "We've known each other too long for these games. We both know that after 7/7, your government began exploring the potential of installing a network of facial-recognition cameras around London. It was code-named Project OSIRIS, an allusion to the all-seeing eye of Egyptian mythology—and completed in 2012. I haven't been in-country since, don't know where any of them are located. It's a risk I can't afford to take. Not now."

"Why?" she asked quietly.

He spread out his hands on the tabletop, appearing to weigh his words carefully. "To be honest. . .I'm not in the UK legally, Mehr."

"I know that," she replied, working to regain her composure. *Control the situation.* "I ran your name through the Customs database at Thames House yesterday—came back negative. Leads me to think that you're here on an Agency legend, working as a NOC. That you've been lying to me all along."

She'd been prepared to let this slide, to let him move on, in the hopes that this was nothing. That she was wrong.

Until this. . .

NOC stood for "non-official cover." An illegal CIA asset. She knew all too well the seriousness of the charge she was leveling, expected to see him flinch in the face of it.

Betray some tell.

"I wish." He shook his head, seeming strangely earnest in that moment. *Genuine.* Or was it an illusion? "I told you the truth, so far as it goes. I left the CIA two months ago."

"Then why are you here?"

He considered her question for a long moment, finding himself hesitant to speak. Reconsidering his decision to bring her into this. To *recruit* her.

But it was time. The moment when the time came to lay all your cards out on the table. Or, perhaps more precisely, to make the other person *believe* that you had done so.

Not an easy line to walk with someone of Mehreen's training.

"There's a man in the UK," Harry began, "Your government and mine know that he's here. And they won't take him down."

That the man of which he spoke was a terrorist went without saying. She knew the words to this song.

"Why?"

"They're afraid. Afraid of what might happen if they move, afraid of what might happen if they don't. Bureaucrats quivering in their armchairs on both sides the Atlantic, hoping that phone doesn't ring in the middle of the night."

"And who is this man?"

"His name is Tarik Abdul Muhammad." He expected to see recognition in her eyes, and there was. "The man they call 'The *Shaikh.*'"

"The man you suspect of engineering the Christmas Eve attacks on your country."

There was something in her tone, a skepticism. "Mehr, I 'suspect' nothing. I know. I was *there* that night," he whispered, his voice trembling with emotion. "I stormed that theater, saw the bodies of those he killed. Men, women—innocents who had just been enjoying a night in Vegas. And now he's here."

"I know that MacCallum has been running an op in coordination with Langley," she said thoughtfully, looking at him in the darkness of the kitchen. "A high-profile target, I can tell that much by the way it's being handled. . .but I've not been read in."

"That's him. And it's a surveillance op, nothing more."

"And how would you know that?" The sharpness of her question surprised him, a reminder not to underestimate her. Not to let his guard down, even for a moment.

"It was supposed to be my op." That was only half a lie, he thought, watching for her reaction. It *should* have been his. . .

"So why isn't it?" She moved a hand to brush dark hair back from her eyes. "Why are you in the UK as an illegal, instead of working out of Grosvenor Square? Liaising with Five?"

Harry shrugged. "The Agency moves in mysterious ways, their wonders to perform. One of my team members was tapped to lead the op instead."

She wasn't buying it. "If you're going to ask me to help, Harry, you're going to tell me the truth."

"The truth?" Most people thought of truth as something simple, something painless, but it wasn't. Not in their world. "The truth is that we're all expendable, in the end. Just weapons, not a one of us more important than the mission we're chosen to execute. And just like weapons. . .a gun breaks on you, you throw it away. That's what happened to me."

"You 'broke'?" Was it sympathy he saw in her eyes? It was hard to tell. "What does that even mean?"

"I told you I was there, but that wasn't all of it. I got bad intel on Vegas, intel I believed to be credible," he answered slowly, his hand clenching into a fist.

He had to remain calm, shove aside the other memories of that night. Fight one battle at a time. "And Americans died because of my intel. Three hundred and eighteen of them."

Three hundred and eighteen Americans dead, a number seared into his very soul. Scores more injured. The worst terrorist attack on American soil since 9/11.

It was a long time before she responded, silence falling over the darkened room. He had committed himself—there was no way back now.

It seemed like an eternity before she looked up, her eyes meeting his face once again. "I'm assuming you have a plan?"

7:31 A.M.
Barnet Hospital
North London

Internal hemorrhaging. Brain damage. Coma.

Words, that's all they were to Paul Gordon. . .or all they had once been. It wasn't real. *Not yet.* Not even after two days.

A tear fell from his eye as he looked down at the driver's license in his hand, her picture staring back at him. *Alice.*

She'd been smiling that day when he took her, nervous about the theory test, but smiling all the same at the idea of having her own license.

His kid sister, beautiful from the moment he'd first seen her. So *perfect*.

"Mr. Gordon," a voice announced flatly, and he looked up into the eyes of a policeman. Eyes that had seen too much of life, too much suffering. Broken beyond caring. "I need you to come with me for a moment."

"Of course," he responded, squeezing her hand once more as he rose from beside the hospital bed. There was no response, her hand falling back limply to her side, her once-beautiful face swathed in bandages, mercifully covering from view where the acid had burned into her flesh.

Her sight was gone forever, that was the prognosis of the doctors, themselves worn out and harried by more patients than they could begin to deal with. He swore under his breath, following the officer out of the hospital room and into the hallway.

The smell of urine filled his nostrils, but he barely noticed. He'd been a soldier, once upon a time. Spent years of life in Iraq—seen all the brutality life had on offer.

Or so he'd thought.

"Have you found them?" he asked, looking the policeman in the eye. "Have you found the men who. . .did *this* to my sister?"

He found himself unable to voice the words. That his sister had been raped, again and again. Used up and thrown out on the street, like a piece of garbage.

The officer shook his head. "We've not been able to positively identify any suspects as of yet. I'm sorry, sir. Bystanders identified your sister's assailants outside the club as a gang of Asian youths, one of whom threw acid into her face before shoving her into the back of their car."

And the bystanders had just *watched*, he thought, finding a helpless rage rise within him. *Sheep*. "Asians?" he asked skeptically, looking over at the officer. "You mean Pakis, don't you?"

Muslims. The officer just looked at him, that same emotionless expression plastered to his face like a mask. "I'm afraid I can't speculate, sir. I'm sorry."

Sorry. There was nothing in the voice, just *nothing*—the man might as well have been announcing the time of day. He felt his fists clench, longing to reach out, to strike.

And he really wasn't sure why he didn't, in the end. Just stood there feeling helpless as the London bobby mouthed a few more words, finally disappearing down the crowded hospital corridor.

Leaving Paul to curse his retreating form. *Helpless*. . .

10:47 A.M.
Thames House
London, England

"*There's a man in the UK. Your government and mine know that he's here. . .and they won't take him down.*"

Could it be possible that he was telling the truth? That bureaucratic indecision was leading them along the brink of disaster? It wasn't hard to believe.

The blind leading the blind, Nick had always said of politicians with a bitter laugh. *Till they all topple arse-over-teakettle into the ditch.*

No, Mehr thought, the words replaying themselves through her head as she gazed at her computer screen. There was no way they were going to let that happen. Not on their watch.

The truth was more complicated than that, of course. Truth always was.

She could remember sitting in this very chair as chaos unfolded on that dark day in 2005, four bombs ripping London apart across the space of the hour. *7/7*.

Taking fifty-two lives. Very nearly including her own.

She'd been running late that morning, train schedules hopelessly mucked up in the weeks preceding the attacks.

If she'd been ten minutes earlier. . .

They'd come so close to fingering Mohammed Siddique Khan during DOWNTEMPO. So very close, and yet the connections had eluded their best efforts.

Connections that seemed so obvious now. . .proving that hindsight truly was 20/20, even if that meant gazing back through a mist of blood and smoke.

Never again, she'd sworn that day. *Never.*

She lifted her head, the eyes of Tarik Abdul Muhammad staring back at her from the dossier photo displayed on her screen. A single question filling her mind.

What was it going to take to keep that vow?

6:03 A.M. Eastern Time
Foxstone Park
Vienna, Virginia

Running. It had saved his life, Bernard Kranemeyer thought, his head ducked down, the muscles of his good leg pumping as he pounded down the wooded trail at a punishing jog. The forest just beginning to wake around him, the first rays of sunshine not yet breaking over the horizon.

The desire to run again had been the only thing that had pulled him out of that hospital bed at Walter Reed, forcing him through the months of therapy until the prosthesis began to work as a part of his body.

The desire to run. The desire to get back to his men, back out in the field.

The first had happened—the second. . .well, Delta hadn't taken him back.

Oh, they'd given him the chance—and he'd given it his best shot, but he had failed the re-certification. Twice.

Couldn't say he blamed them, in the end. You couldn't take a chance that something might go wrong, out there on the edge of the knife.

And he could never have lived with himself if something had. The knowledge that one of his brothers had died because he had been a split-second too slow. The guilt that went with that knowledge.

He'd looked into enough widows' eyes as it was. Far too many.

His pace slowed as he came to the footbridge, a faint sheen of ice glazing one of the planks, water gurgling from the darkness below.

The last time he had come to this park. . .it was a night he didn't like to think about. He grimaced at the memory, chill morning air stabbing at his lungs. The memory of what had been *necessary*. Blood on his hands.

Ahead of him was the access road, a blacked-out Suburban parked behind his car, blocking his exit.

The figure of a man standing there in front of the vehicle, the glow of the cigar in his mouth visible in the early morning twilight.

Kranemeyer slowed instinctively, his hand slipping into his jacket, toward the butt of the Heckler & Koch USP .45 holstered on his hip in a cross-draw position.

"Nearly thought you wouldn't show," a familiar voice called out, and he felt himself relax. "Had in mind to finish my Cuban and head back out."

"I always keep my appointments, Roy," Kranemeyer replied, walking up to the older man.

Roy Coftey snorted, the lapels of his trench coat turned up against his neck against the cold, a silver-haired figure standing there in the semi-darkness.

A six-term senator from the state of Oklahoma, Coftey was the chairman of the powerful Senate Select Committee on Intelligence, a career politician who'd long since learned how to swim in the swamp that was the Beltway.

He'd also been in the Special Forces once upon a time, a nasty war its survivors remembered simply as "Nam." And a soldier was always a soldier, Kranemeyer had found. No matter the passage of time.

"You made sure you weren't followed?" Kranemeyer asked, glancing down the access road as if he expected to see lights, to hear the crunch of wheels against the gravel. His jacket was still unzipped, the pistol not far from his fingers.

"Of course," the senator replied with a wave of his hand. "Spent the last hour running one of those. . .SD—SDRs, I believe you called them?"

A nod. "A surveillance detection route."

"Yeah, exactly. Cloak and dagger." Coftey took another puff on the *Romeo y Julieta*, exhaling smoke into the dawn. "I thought I'd made it clear after all that happened with. . .Hancock, that we needed to put space between ourselves. Minimize the risk."

Roger Hancock, the predecessor to Richard Norton in the office of President of the United States. A man who had betrayed his oath and his country in order to gain re-election.

And my men, Kranemeyer thought, for Hancock's treason had led to the death of a CIA officer on the far side of the world. A young man, one of his country's finest. Davood Sarami.

A backroom deal for peace and oil, with Iran on the other side of the bargaining table. He'd never learned the details, had never cared to know. All that mattered was that his men had been betrayed.

An eye for an eye.

"And that's the reason for the cloak and dagger," Kranemeyer replied, looking the older man in the eye. "We don't need to be seen in public together. Now more than ever."

Hancock's re-election had been bogged down in a re-count of ballots alleged to have been cast by illegal immigrants in New Mexico, the case taken before the Supreme Court the previous December. And the administration had attempted to exert. . ."influence" on the high court, with Coftey carrying their water. Offering them deniability.

Until Kranemeyer had gotten to him.

"Then we're agreed," Coftey responded calmly. "So tell me, Barney, what's on your mind?"

"Walk with me."

They set off down the trail, back toward the wooden bridge, the smoldering cigar still clutched between Coftey's fingers. "Is this about the President?"

A nod from Kranemeyer. "Norton authorized the finding for TALISMAN, but it was touch-and-go all the way. And now with that last speech—he's going to come gunnin' for the intelligence community. All in the name of freedom."

"God save us all from the patrons of good intentions," Coftey intoned, flicking ash into the slushy snow. "His people on the Hill are organizing—have been ever since Snowden defected to Mother Russia. But Norton's election gave them the momentum they'd been looking for."

"What can you do to buy us time, Roy?"

There was a long silence before the senator replied. "Very little, I'm afraid."

Kranemeyer swore. "You're the chairman of the intel committee. If you can't slow them down, no one can."

A shrug. "A chairman can only do so much. I'd need allies. And I don't have any, not anymore. Cahill's been busy. Word has it that I'm to be primaried next election."

Coftey snorted, smoke curling from his nostrils. "Primaried, can you imagine that? And with our control of the Senate itself hanging in the balance. Fifty-one, forty-nine after last November."

A hundred men and women, Kranemeyer thought, listening disinterestedly as the senator went on. And scarce a one of them worth shooting. All of them consumed with their own petty agendas, obsessed with re-election. *With control.*

For most of them, "good of the country" was something which had fallen by the wayside long ago. If it had ever been reckoned among their priorities to begin with.

"A single seat flips to the Republicans two years from now, and Vice President Havern gets to break any tie votes Norton wants broken for the remainder of his term in office. But apparently that's less important than seeing me gone." Coftey shook his head, anger building in his voice. "Three decades of my life that I've given to the party, and this is how they repay me. All because I helped purge a traitor from our midst. Politics is a devil of a thing, Barney."

Which was why he hadn't voted since the early '90s. Why anyone who placed faith in their elected representatives to "save the country" was deluding themselves. "So there's nothing you can do?"

The senator held up a hand, gesturing with the stub of his cigar. "I didn't say that. Perhaps it's time to remind Norton who put him where he sits today."

There was just something about the way he said it that caused Kranemeyer to stop short, turning to face his friend. "What are you saying, Roy?"

For a moment, Coftey looked incredulous. "You didn't know?"

"Go on," Kranemeyer said, the night seeming to grow suddenly colder around him.

Coftey responded with a shake of his massive head. "I was brought in to make doubly sure that everything went smoothly with the high court. . .but Hancock won the election, Barney. As fair and square as any election like that ever is. You, me—the Chief Justice—we overthrew the duly elected President of the United States. . ."

3:18 P.M. Greenwich Mean Time
Deptford
South London, England

He had passed two pushers on the way in, hawking their wares from underneath the eaves of graffiti-anointed buildings, the sidewalk cracked and broken under his feet. A junkie fallen asleep on the stoop of a flat, his pockets turned inside out, his clothing torn.

The church that had been set as the rendezvous point for his contact was old, worn by the passage of time—a plaque embedded in the stone outside bearing the inscription, *Anno Domini 1897.*

In the year of our Lord.

Harry removed his hat as he stepped into the sanctuary, his eyes falling upon a single supplicant kneeling near the altar, an image of the crucified Christ staring down upon the scene.

He hadn't seen the inside of a church since. . .well, since Carol's funeral. Didn't know why.

Or didn't want to face the reason. That might have been closer to the truth of the matter.

He'd been outside for nearly two hours, maintaining surveillance on the site of the meet. Watching for activity, any sign of assets being pre-positioned.

It had been long enough to bring one of the pushers over his way, a thin black man who looked like he had been using too much of his own product. The hilt of a knife displayed prominently beneath his threadbare jacket.

He'd spoken, a hoarse "What you doin', bruv?" and Harry had just looked at him, a cold stare that had delivered his message more effectively than words. *Move on.*

And he had.

Eyes scanning the sanctuary for threats, Harry moved down the center aisle, toward the worshipper. The only man he'd seen enter since he had taken up watch.

"There were roses," he said quietly, coming up behind the man—staying just far enough back to avoid surprises. His jacket was open, the Walther in an inside pocket. Not ideal, but you made the best of what you had.

"That there were, mate," the man replied, rising from his knees. His rough clothes suited the neighborhood, his hands those of a worker, hard and callused. "What's it to you?"

It wasn't his contact, but the Belfast accent told Harry everything he needed to know.

"Flaharty sent you?" he asked, watching the man's eyes—his hand not far from the butt of the Walther.

"Aye, that he did," a second voice announced, Harry's head swiveling to see another man emerge from back near the confessional, a compact CZ 75 leveled in his right hand.

He looked back to see the "worshipper" standing before him, his Beretta drawn, only inches away from Harry's face.

Close enough to take.

He could have seized it, killed them both before they had time to react. Being held at gunpoint with a pistol wasn't the game-ender that Hollywood portrayed. Not if you had the training to deal with it.

But it wouldn't have gotten him a single step closer to his objective.

"Put this over your 'ead," the man with the CZ ordered, pulling a black hood from within his jacket and throwing it at Harry's feet. "We'll be goin' out the back."

6:17 P.M.
Thames House

"If you'll come right this way," Alec MacCallum said, looking back as Thomas hung the visitor ID around his neck, following Roth into Five's Operations Centre. "We have a conference room set up for the briefing."

He led them past bank after bank of screens, moving hurriedly, as if to minimize their exposure to the visitor. *So much for the special relationship*, Thomas thought. Maybe that really was a thing of the past.

"We've obtained a positive ID on the 'lookout', if that's indeed what he was," he announced, ushering them into a small soundproofed conference down a hallway off the "floor" of the op-center. He gestured toward a man already seated at the table. "Parker, I'd like you to meet Simon Norris, a fine analyst in his own right—and one of my best officers. Simon, this is Thomas Parker, the CIA liaison officer."

Thomas merely nodded by way of acknowledgment, taking a seat as MacCallum moved to the head of the table, throwing up the surveillance photo taken the previous night on the screen at the far wall.

"Keon Davison," he said, clicking his remote to put up another picture, this time a mug shot. "Twenty-two years of age, natural born citizen of the UK. No current address. Changed his name to Nadeem Abdul al-Qawi after converting to Islam while serving a stint up at Feltham for armed robbery."

Prison conversion. That was a familiar song and dance, Thomas thought, glancing over at Roth. Both sides of the Atlantic.

For some the conversion was genuine, for others it was just a way to stay alive. You needed to "belong" in prison if you wanted to survive. Either way, once you were in—getting out was more problematic.

"Does he have any family? Anyone we could lean on?"

MacCallum shook his head. "No father listed in our databases, his mother's been in and out of alky-clinics ever since he was a kid. Davison was first arrested when he was thirteen, sent up for shoplifting."

Alky-clinics, Thomas winced. Rehab for alcoholics. That struck a bit too close to home. "So we have no idea where to find him?"

"That's a different question," the British officer smiled. "He has a Twitter account. . .and we've been working to cross-reference his geo-location data over the past three weeks. Simon?"

The analyst nodded. "We have two possible addresses. I'm currently liaising with Special Branch to have them checked out, see if he shows up. In the meantime, we've pulled his phone logs and are combing through his contact history for any possible matches against our watchlists."

"And then what?" Thomas asked, glancing from Roth to MacCallum.

"Then we'll have to make the decision. Either maintain surveillance—or have Special Branch lift him so that the quizmasters can have a go."

"On what charges?"

Norris smiled. "He's not seen his probation officer in nine months."

7:03 P.M.
Somewhere in the UK

Darkness. A noise-filled, disorienting darkness, every bump in the road transmitting itself through Harry's body as he lay in the boot of the car, arms zip-tied behind his back, the hood over his head completely robbing him of sight.

Sensory deprivation. He'd never forget the first time the hood had been placed over his head, back during his training at Camp Peary, the inescapable feeling of panic, his breath quickening. It hadn't mattered that it was a controlled test—your mind didn't process that at first.

Just the panic.

But that was exactly what training was for, preparing you for the day when it would no longer be a test. *No control*. He rolled over on his back, feeling the bulge of a spare tire against his foot—trying to determine just how long he'd been in the car.

Hours. It had to have been close to four, maybe more, but it was impossible to say with any certainty. Trying to keep track of turns would have been pointless—he knew Flaharty, knew his men. They'd probably spent half their time running SDRs through southwest London, criss-crossing the city in an effort to determine if he had back-up.

It's what he would have done.

The car's pattern of movement had changed over the last couple hours, though—changing from the familiar stop-and-go of city traffic to the smoother acceleration of highway driving.

And then later on it had gotten rough, as if they had left the highway for more rural roads. Slowing down.

The vehicle swung suddenly into another turn and he felt himself roll, ending up with his cheek pressed against the wheel well as the car came to a stop, the sound of the motor fading away.

Footsteps crunching outside. *Gravel.* They were walking on gravel. Then the sound of the boot's lid being opened, hands seizing hold of his arms, lifting him out.

He felt the muzzle of the CZ jam into his ribs as he was shoved forward. "Keep it moving," a voice growled in his ear, so very close.

He heard a door open and shut behind him, the gun forcing him down a small set of stone steps—moving cautiously. Arms still bound, there was no way he was going to catch himself if he went down.

Voices murmuring around him, faint. Indistinct.

The hood was ripped from his head without warning, the zip-ties cut from his hands.

"It's been a long time since we last stood in the same room, Harry. A very long time."

He blinked against the sudden light, glancing about him, taking in the massive rough-hewn beams over his head, the walls of stone. *A farmhouse?* Over to where a short, balding man stood at the end of a table in the basement room, cleaning his glasses. *Flaharty.*

"That it has, Stephen," he replied, rubbing his wrists to restore circulation as he looked the former IRA bombmaker in the eye. "Do you have the weapons we spoke of?"

"All in good time," the man smiled, pushing his glasses back on the bridge of his nose. He picked up the small Walther from off the table, favoring it with a look of disdain. "Seriously, old son. . .a PPK?"

Harry shrugged. "You know what they say. Any port in a storm."

7:15 P.M.
The flat
Ealing, London

Treason. That's what it was, no getting around it—no matter how she might justify it. Every member of the Security Service knew the consequences for violating the Official Secrets Act. *No exceptions.*

Mehreen leaned back in her chair, the cup of tea warming her hands as she gazed at the small thumb drive on the table before her.

The drive containing London's dead-ground map...including OSIRIS. Smuggling the files out of the Registry without being detected had not been easy—she'd nearly reconsidered twice. Questioned what she was doing, risking all that she had worked so hard to achieve.

And now, as she sat in her home, the evidence of her crime before her, the questions had returned.

The flat had been empty when she'd arrived home, no sign of Nichols to be found. Vanished, like a ghost into the darkness.

What had she expected?

She'd known he was keeping something from her even yet—known and gone ahead to retrieve the files anyway. *"He's not going to live long enough to strike again, Mehr. I will see to that."*

And she was aiding an assassin.

7:22 P.M.
Somewhere in the UK

"I was surprised to hear from you, considering the circumstances of our last meeting," Flaharty said, gesturing for his men to give them the room as he placed a long gun case on the table between them, flicking back the catches.

Harry forced a smile, waiting until the door had closed behind the Irishman's enforcers before he spoke. "No more surprised than I was to be contacting you."

Once upon a time, Stephen Flaharty had been a legend—and for all the wrong reasons. One of the best bombmakers the Provisional Irish Republican Army had ever seen, back during the times of the Troubles.

The Provos.

But the world had changed, or so people liked to believe. And when the Provos had laid down their arms in 2005, rebels like Flaharty had been scattered to the wind, fanning out across the globe with Her Majesty's government still on their heels.

Flaharty had turned arms dealer, a career choice which had brought him across the path of the Agency. More than once.

"It was part of the bleedin' deal," Flaharty announced sharply, throwing back the lid of the gun case to reveal an Accuracy International L115A3, the thick barrel of the sniper rifle gleaming in the light. "I turned tout, and you sods stayed out of *my* business affairs."

Tout. An informant, in the British parlance. And that's exactly what Flaharty had been, in his last few years with the Provos—and since. An Agency asset.

Harry shrugged, lowering his voice. Only too aware of how risky this conversation was. For both of them. "In fairness, Stephen, we didn't know it was you."

And as odd as it sounded, he thought—it was the truth. Or at least *he* hadn't. God only knew what Langley had known.

His own first clue that Flaharty was involved had come when he'd found himself staring down the sights of his Barrett REC-7 at the Irishman, oily smoke billowing up into the Malian sky, small-arms fire crackling through the early morning dawn.

Harry's team had been in-country in covert support of the Touré government, tasked with destroying a convoy of weapons on their way to *Anṣār ad-Dīn*.

Flaharty's weapons, as it turned out. Unfortunate.

"But that's the past," Flaharty announced, smiling as he gestured toward the rifle. "And business is business. Everything, just as you requested. I have. . .'contacts' at Brecon."

The British Army sniper school. Harry lifted the rifle from the case, wondering for a moment how someone on active duty could have been persuaded to have dealings with a former Irish terrorist.

An irrelevant question in all likelihood—Flaharty might as easily be working through a cut-out. He hefted the big rifle in his hands, feeling the weight. Nearly fifteen pounds, unloaded.

"You were able to secure the ammunition I asked for?"

Flaharty nodded, reaching into a compartment of the case to extract a box labeled *8.59mm*. "Just a single box—twenty rounds. Pick your targets wisely, boyo."

"Always do," Harry replied, working the bolt, his hand sliding along the receiver. It was a good weapon, more than sufficient for his purpose. The hardest part would be working without a spotter, but he'd done so more than once before. No reason he couldn't do it again. "The scope is zeroed in?"

"It holds zero at five hundred yards, as you specified. And I'm telling you, finding a place to test it was a pain in the arse."

"I'm sure you managed. And as for the other two?"

"I have them," Flaharty acknowledged, motioning for one of his men to bring forward the final two weapons cases, setting them on the table between them. "And also the vehicle you asked me to procure. But first, I need to see my money in my accounts."

All business. That was the Irishman. Always had been. There were times when Harry wondered how he had become swept up with the Provos. Revolutions didn't tend to attract pragmatists.

"Of course," Harry nodded, moving his hands slowly to open his jacket, feeling Flaharty's eyes on him as he did so. *No sudden movements.*

It was to be the moment of truth, he thought, his fingers closing around the small USB thumb drive in the inner pocket of his jacket. Remembering where he had obtained it, remembering like it was yesterday that night out in the California oilfield. A night which had nearly borne witness to his death—looking down the muzzle of an assassin's pistol.

Sergei Ivanovich Korsakov.

He remembered pulling the drive off the corpse of a young man in Korsakov's employ—not knowing in that moment what it contained. Or how important it would become.

Routing information, access codes for over ten offshore bank accounts. Enough money to finance a small war.

He looked up to see the Irishman regarding him with a keen glance, the sharpness of the man's eyes hidden not at all by the glasses. As if he could read Harry's thoughts. *No matter.*

There was nothing but darkness to be read there. "All I need is a secure connection—you'll be able to verify the transfer within the hour."

10:25 P.M.
A pub
London, England

"I can't even look at her now," Paul Gordon whispered, raising the pint to his lips. It was the third time he'd said it, but the alcohol was finally numbing the pain, and he was losing track. "What sort of tosser am I? Alice needs me more than she's ever needed me, and I can't stand the sight of her. She was such a beautiful kid. . ."

His voice trailed off. "Those *animals.*"

He replaced the pint on the tabletop, his hand clenching into a fist as he looked across the booth into the eyes of his friend. Anger welling up within him. He shook his head. "This is the first time I've left the hospital since my mobile rang with the news. I rode the bus here—saw one of *them* get on. And I swear to you, Conor. . .I wanted nothing more than to rip that smirking Paki out of his seat and beat him till I saw the color of his brains."

His friend nodded, draining his own beer and setting it back down near Paul's. "You can't be goin' off and doing that, mate. You know that."

He smiled sadly back at the man across from him. *Conor Hale.* They'd served together in Iraq, both of them Paras in that time, before everything that followed. A year before they'd both taken a shot at selection for the Regiment. The Special Air Service.

"And why can't I?" he asked, more of himself than Hale. It had been hot out on the Beacons that summer, hot beyond reason. They'd made it through the first few days together—the cross-country marches growing in distance with each day. Farther, faster. Rifle in your hand and a full Bergen on your back.

"You don't understand, mate," Paul whispered, aware that the liquor was affecting him, his words slurring slightly. "Lost my job five months ago—been staying with her. And now. . .I don't have anything left to lose."

Lose. He'd made it, day after day.

Until they came to the Fan Dance—a brutal quick march up the Welsh mountain of Pen y Fan. He'd passed out half-way to the top from heat exhaustion.

To this very day, he could never remember breaking ranks. Just the sensation of lying there on his back, a medic leaning over him. The knowledge that he'd failed.

He'd been RTU'd two days later. Returned to unit. *A failure*.

And Hale had won where he had lost, going on to become an SAS sergeant. Decorated for bravery in Afghanistan. A sodding hero. Across the table from him, his old comrade shook his head. "Stuff and nonsense, mate. You have Alice, and she needs you now more than ever. Even if she doesn't realize it. She doesn't need you in prison. Besides, do you think beating up one wog is really going to accomplish anything?"

All he could see was her face, the way it had looked when they'd asked him to identify her—all eaten away with the acid, the wreckage of beauty. "Maybe not. . .maybe they'd go back to where they came from. Where their kind belongs. Maybe. I just don't know anymore, mate. You have any ruddy better ideas?"

There was no answer, just a long searching look across the table, the stare piercing his consciousness as he slowly realized Hale was nowhere near as drunk as he was.

It was nearly midnight, the clock in one corner of the pub striking the quarter hour—a sound barely audible over the sound of the soccer match on the telly over the bar. Arsenal was winning.

The former SAS sergeant leaned back in the booth, nursing the last of his beer. He was alone now, having called a cab for his friend an hour before.

Paul Gordon had been a good man, Hale thought, looking down at the mobile in his hand, the number displayed on his screen. One of the best.

The type of man they could use.

After a moment's further reflection, he leaned forward, bringing the phone to his ear as he pressed SEND.

"This is Hale," he said when a voice answered on the other end. "I think we have a new recruit. . ."

Chapter 4

2:03 A.M., March 25th
West Sussex
England

A23 North, the sign above the roadway read, the lights of the Vauxhall Cavalier striking it as the sedan sped underneath the overpass—the needle of the speedometer pegged just below the speed limit.

No sense in calling attention to oneself, Harry thought—checking his mirrors once again. Not with the weapons he had concealed under a tarpaulin in the boot of the car—the Sig-Sauer P228 in a holster inside his waistband, his jacket concealing the compact 9mm semi-automatic.

He'd been blindfolded again after his transaction with Flaharty was complete, driven around for a few more hours until they'd finally stopped by the side of the road—taken him out and handed him the keys to the old Vauxhall.

The former terrorist was obsessed with his security, and with good reason, considering what he had done for the CIA. Many of his old comrades had found themselves lying face-down in a ditch for less.

"You're no longer working for the Agency. . .are you?" Flaharty had asked as they sat there in the old stone farmhouse, waiting for the transactions to process.

"Why?"

"The way you're moving this money around—the multiple accounts, the small amounts with each transfer. Scrubbing it clean. It's not the way you'd do it if you were still on the inside."

The Irishman had laughed. *"Your bean-counters all but want a bloody receipt for their money. You can't fight a war like that, but that's something they'll never learn. No, Harry, you're out in the cold. Just like me. Working your own angles now."*

"No comment." But that was, in itself, a comment—and they both knew it.

The Accuracy International in the boot of the Vauxhall was a cousin of the rifle that Tarik Abdul Muhammad had used in Vegas. The weapon he had used to kill. . .

No. His fist slammed into the car's steering wheel, narrowly missing the horn as he pulled into the other lane, accelerating to pass the car in front. He couldn't allow himself to think about that. Not now. *Focus.*

The phone in his pocket rang in that instant, startling him from his thoughts. *Unknown number.*

"Yes?" he answered cautiously, cold air streaming in past his face as the Vauxhall's window lowered. A single moment, and he could throw the phone out into the traffic—lose whomever might be tracking him.

It was Mehreen's voice that replied.

Danger. "How did you get this number?" he asked, cradling the cellphone between his ear and shoulder as he continued to drive.

"There's always a way, Harry. You know that." There was a pause, as if she herself was uncertain what to say. Then, "We need to meet."

11:17 P.M. Eastern Time
National Clandestine Service Operations Center
Langley, Virginia

"Sir, we're just getting the feeds in from Bravo Team," a man announced, coming up to Daniel Lasker as he stood in the nerve center of the Clandestine Service. *Sir.*

The twenty-eight-year-old Lasker still wasn't used to being addressed that way, but he was the watch officer for the night, and the protocol applied. He turned as the man went on, "They just landed in Cairo and Nakamura is liaising with the *Mukhabarat.*"

The decision to turn Bravo Team right back around and dispatch them to Egypt scarcely hours after their return from Europe had been a difficult one. But snatching Umar ibn Hassan was an opportunity they couldn't afford to pass up—and Nakamura's people could be wheels-up faster than anyone else. "What's their ETA on the target, Ethan?"

"It's nearly dawn there," the intelligence officer replied. "Egyptian special forces are providing transport out into the Sinai and will be coordinating on the assault. The plan is to move into position after nightfall—spend a couple days surveilling the compound along with the Egyptians, then take it down if the intel on Umar ibn Hassan appears solid."

Good, the watch officer thought, acknowledging the information with a nod as he turned back toward his desk. *Past time they were putting him out of commission.* It was only a moment later that he realized the man was still standing there. "Was there something else?"

"Yes," came the reply as the man handed him a thin folder. "This is unconnected to the ongoing op, but we got this from the boys at Fort Meade. It hit their radar a couple hours ago and they thought it needed to be kicked up the stairs."

Lasker opened the folder, his eyes narrowing as he scanned down the sheet—his gaze falling upon a familiar name at the bottom. *So familiar.* "Is this credible?"

"That's the word."

He looked at the name again as if to assure himself that it was there. "Holy crap. . ."

6:24 A.M. Greenwich Mean Time
Regent's Park
London, England

The sun was just beginning to creep over the horizon by the time Harry walked out across the grass of the park past the deserted bandstand—his eyes searching the twilight for any sign of danger. For any indication that she had brought Five with her.

He'd stowed the car in long-term parking near Heathrow, leaving behind everything except the Sig-Sauer and two loaded magazines. One of them went into the butt of the gun, the other into the inner pocket of his jacket. Ready for use.

No overt signs of surveillance in the hour he had already spent in the park. . .just watching her.

Didn't mean there wasn't any. The Security Service had the manpower. His phone beeped, the message on the screen blinking *"Bluetooth Accessed."* He looked at it briefly and returned it to the pocket of his jacket.

Insurance.

Mehreen was standing near the boating lake, the hood of her jacket pushed back to reveal her long dark hair—her hands resting on the iron fencing that surrounded the lake as she looked out over the water. Water glistening in the light of the dawn.

Pigeons scattered along the footpath as he approached, taking flight, the drumming of their wings breaking the early morning stillness.

She glanced up at the sound, just looking at him. Not saying a word.

The early rays of sun warmed the back of his head as he took his place beside her at the fence. "Out beyond all concept of wrongdoing or rightdoing," he whispered, "there is a field. And there will I meet you."

The faintest of smiles touched her lips as he quoted the words of the Sufi mystic. "You know your Rumi."

"A wise man. Tell me, Mehr—what are we doing here this morning?"

"Nick loved this place," she said finally. "He brought me here when we were first going together—had a picnic and heard the Royal Green Jackets perform, just over there. Came back so many times."

That would have been Nick, Harry thought. He'd been a big-hearted, passionate man. Loved a good fight, a good soccer game. A good brass band.

In no particular order.

"Yeah," he said, smiling at the memory. "He had a bootleg CD of them in Afghanistan. Would play it over and over and over again, drove everyone in the FOB crazy."

"I still have it," she chuckled, a light shining briefly from her eyes. The smile faded from her face as she turned to him. "I secured the dead-ground map, Harry. Including the OSIRIS file."

But there was something in her voice. . .he looked down into her dark eyes, trying to read what was written in their depths. "What is it, Mehr?"

A pause. "Giving you this, it could be the end of everything I've worked for. It—"

"No one ever needs to know it came from you," he said, taking a step closer to her. "I've been discreet, you know that."

"Let me finish," she responded, putting up a hand. "None of that matters—but if I'm going to do this, I need something from you. I need you to tell me the truth. . .for *once* in your life."

"Of course." The assurance came quickly to his lips, automatically—even though he knew he had no intention of doing anything of the sort.

She reached forward, her hand covering his as it rested on the iron of the fence. "Tell me, Harry—who is Carol?"

6:30 A.M.
The May Fair Hotel
Central London

"He's on the move again," one of the female CIA officers announced as Thomas Parker stepped into the expansive hotel suite they had transformed into a makeshift communications center, still barefoot. A housecoat wrapped around his body.

There was only so much information they could access outside of a designated Sensitive Compartmented Information Facility—or SCIF, as it was called in community parlance—but it enabled them to stay abreast of PERSEPHONE on a minute-by-minute basis when necessary.

"Roth's people are on him?" he asked, pulling the belt of the housecoat tight as he crossed the room to stand behind the middle-aged woman, a veteran of the Agency's Intelligence Directorate.

She nodded, headphones covering her ears. "He's entering the Elephant & Castle tube station as we speak—they'll be going off comms in three."

The realities of working in the London Underground, Thomas thought, glancing toward the window—the curtains pulled, blocking out the early morning city lights. Go far enough down, and none of your communications equipment was going to work.

"Wait," she exclaimed suddenly, grabbing his attention as she held up a finger. "He's ditched the tracker. Dumped the poker chip into a litter bin just before descending the escalator into the station itself."

Thomas grimaced. *Two days*. Ah, well—they had known it couldn't last forever. But it had accomplished what they needed of it. "Good work, Jan," he said, turning away. "Let me know the moment Five makes contact again."

6:32 A.M.
Regent's Park

It was hard to know where to begin. . .how to sum up the focus of one's hopes and dreams in a few words. *Paradise lost.*

"How did you know?"

Mehreen paused, looking out over the water, smooth as a mirror in the dawn. "I heard you, last night. Calling out for her in your dream. And somehow I think that whoever she is—she's involved in this."

"*Was*," Harry replied flatly, forcing himself to speak the words. "She's dead, now."

The truth.

She didn't attempt to reply, to apologize—just stood there in silence, her dark hand covering his. Waiting for him to continue.

He closed his eyes, fighting against the pain of that night. "I didn't want to love her, Mehr. I knew better than that."

And so he had. The rules of personal protection were few, but they were simple, chief among them: *Never become emotionally involved with your principal. Stay detached.*

Carol Chambers had been his responsibility, her safety his only concern. But he had allowed it to become something more. So much more.

"I knew the price that comes from caring for someone. Anyone. But I wanted to dream. . .to hope for something beyond all of *this*. A normal life. A wife, kids. A home out in the country, just for us. *Peace*. The American dream." His face twisted in pain at the memory.

No one who hadn't lived the life could have truly understood, but Mehr knew. "She gave me a feeling I hadn't known for a long time—awoke dreams I'd thought long dead. And he took her from me."

She looked at him. "Tarik Abdul Muhammad?"

A nod. "How did it happen?" He could see the sorrow in her eyes at the question—the look of a woman who had known such grief.

How? Had he let his feelings for her cloud his judgment—even for a moment in time? Or had it been inevitable? *Fate*.

"She and I. . .we were in Vegas together," he responded slowly, every word stabbing into him like the blade of a knife, "trying to stop the attacks. We got the hostages out—evacuated the Bellagio just moments before the bombs blew. Had a congresswoman there with us, Laura Gilpin, one of the VIPs we'd been sent in to rescue. We came out of the building, out into a night filled with sirens and flashing lights. Chaos. And there was a sniper—on the roof of the resort across the street."

He could still remember that moment, still hear the first whip-lash *crack* of a bullet breaking the sound barrier, a crimson stain spreading across the congresswoman's blouse as she fell. Still feel Carol by his side as she lifted with him, helping him carry Gilpin to safety.

Too late.

"It was his second shot," Harry whispered, as much to himself as to her. Reliving those moments. "I should have gotten her to cover. I had the time."

Life and death. A binary choice, really. You turned right when you should have turned left—spent the rest of your life wondering how things might have been different if you'd just taken the other path.

He'd woken up nights in a cold sweat, reaching out for her, believing for a moment in that semi-lucid, subconscious state that he had made the *right* choice. That she was still alive. Still with him.

The eternal hell of *what if?*

"The bullet punched straight through the ballistic vest I'd had her wear," he continued, struggling to keep his voice level, "caromed around inside her like a wrecking ball. She bled out in my arms, Mehr, and there was nothing I could do. Nothing except hold her. . .and pray for a miracle that wasn't coming."

"I'm sorry," she whispered, her hand on his arm. The words would have sounded so trite coming from anyone else. *Meaningless.*

But she *knew.*

She reached out, her arms enfolding him, her face pressed against his chest as she pulled him close. If she felt the bulge of the Sig-Sauer beneath his jacket, she gave no sign.

"You'll need this," came the words and he felt her hand at the breast pocket of his jacket, the OSIRIS drive slipping beneath the leather. "Now go."

She didn't look up into his eyes, didn't say another word as she turned away. And he just stood there in the dawn, watching her go.

9:45 A.M. Eastern Time
The NCS Op-Center
Langley, Virginia

"We have a problem." Kranemeyer looked up from his desk to see his chief analyst standing in the doorway of his office. No greeting, no preamble. Just the announcement.

But that was Ron Carter. A short, thin black man, Carter had been running the Clandestine Service's Field Support & Analysis Group for the past three years. And while there was no one better at what he did, it wasn't a line of work that lent itself to pleasantries.

"What's going on, Ron?" The look on the analyst's face was cause for worry—there was *always* something going on in the world, much of it a problem in the eyes of the Agency. But this was different.

"This," he replied, handing a folder across the desk. "Part of it came from Fort Meade overnight—the rest of it is what I've had my team spend the morning working up."

It was financial data, the DCS realized, his eyes scanning down the first sheet. He looked up as Carter continued, "The NSA got pinged when money was transferred out of a flagged account in the Caymans. Not a large amount, not at all. If the account itself hadn't been red-flagged, it never would have attracted notice. So they let us know."

"Nice of them." A statement loaded with irony. Cooperation between the bureaucracies that comprised the American intelligence community had improved in the years since 9/11, that much was undeniable. But it was improvement measured with a micrometer. *Turf wars.*

"So I called in a few favors, had a friend at Meade run down every off-shore transfer of the same amount during the time window. There were over twenty of them, several from the same accounts, nearly forty minutes apart from the first round. Over a hundred thousand US dollars moved in the space of less than an hour."

"Who does the money belong to?" Kranemeyer asked, his finger tracing along the rows of figures. Each transaction precisely the same amount, down to the penny.

"You mean who *did* it belong to," Carter retorted. "The name on the flagged account was a known alias for Sergei Ivanovich Korsakov."

Kranemeyere just looked at him, swearing softly under his breath. "The *Spetsnaz* assassin?"

"The same."

"He's been dead for three months," the DCS retorted, still not entirely believing his ears. "His body was positively ID'd after Nichols killed him out in California. We even ran it by the FSB—Dmitri Andreyovich confirmed our findings."

"I know." The meaning was clear. . .someone else had accessed Korsakov's finances. Another player on the field.

"Where did the money go?"

Carter shook his head. "I have people working on that, nothing conclusive as of just yet. Europe definitely, perhaps the United Kingdom. Funds were being routed and re-routed all over the place—it's like trying to follow the hands of a blackjack dealer."

He seemed to pause, as if hesitant to go on. "What is it, Ron?"

"I think we have a bigger problem, sir." That was itself a sign of trouble. . .Carter knew better than to call him "sir." "It's the way the funds were transferred. There's a threshold at which the NSA begins tracking international financial transfers. It's been in place since 2009. Each of these transfers came within two dollars of that threshold. Nothing more, nothing less."

No. The face came to his mind unbidden, unwanted. Kranemeyer looked up to meet Carter's eyes. "You're saying it was someone who knew precisely how we operate. . ."

"Yes."

6:27 P.M. Greenwich Mean Time
Masjid-e-Ali
Leeds, England

"Imam Anwar al-Awlaki, blessed be his memory, once told the story of how Christian missionaries in Indonesia had tried so hard to sway believers from the true path. So hard, with no success, *insh'allah*," Hashim Rahman intoned, sitting cross-legged on the floor of the mosque as he looked out on the upturned faces on the young men before him. As God wills.

"Yet at long last they were able to convince one man, this very old man. . .by promising him that if he would accept Christ, they would grant his wish—a wish that he said he'd had all his life. So, when he had become a Christian, the missionaries came to him and asked, 'What is your wish?' And the old man looked at them, praise be to God, and replied, 'I wish to make *hajj.*'"

The imam smiled as the room erupted in laughter, along with a few more profane cries of approbation.

An unwelcome reminder that the crass culture of the *kaffir* had reached out to touch even these chosen.

"And so it is," he said, holding up a hand to once again still the room. "The devotion that we must have to Allah, *subhanahu wa ta'ala*, and His cause. You will see Muslims on your telly when one of your brothers is hauled away to prison, talking about how he was a 'terrorist,' telling you that you need to distance yourself, remain quiet, just go along, to 'assimilate.' Yet, I tell you this, as God is my witness, as soon as you allow one Muslim to be taken. . .Allah does not help you anymore. And why should He?"

6:35 P.M.

"How long before we can go in?" Thomas asked, glancing up at the screens in the back of the surveillance van. They had access to the CCTV feeds on a block radius surrounding the mosque, covering almost every approach. Getting the same type of coverage *inside* the mosque—that was their next objective.

"There's no "we" about this, mate," Darren Roth responded, stripping off his coat to reveal a work uniform beneath it, the emblem of Yorkshire Gas & Power emblazoned on the front. "You're staying right where you are."

A shrug. He'd figured as much. "This isn't my first séance, Darren. I've done this a time or two. The Agency isn't writing my checks so that I can sit on my hands."

The British officer shook his head. "That's something you and your conscience will have to get sorted with them—I'm not risking a 'visitor' on an op like this. Getting the warrant was hard enough."

He turned away, inserting his earpiece. "Testing. . .Sierra One, do you copy? Sierra Two?"

"Loud and clear, sir. Standing by."

"The lecture lets out in about twenty minutes, according to the mosque's website," Roth announced over the comm channel, looking around the interior of the van at Thomas and the female officer who was manning the surveillance equipment. "That's when we go in."

7:02 P.M.

So young, Rahman thought, bending down at the entrance of the mosque to recover his shoes. *And yet so devout.*

He had himself been young once, growing up in Egypt under the repressive Mubarak regime. The lapdog of the Americans. That had all been before he had himself turned to the path of truth, found purpose for his life in the struggle.

He laced his shoes, looking up then to see a boy of maybe sixteen years of age standing a few feet away—still barefoot. Hanging back.

"*Salaam alaikum,*" Hashim greeted, smiling at the young man. *Blessings and peace be unto you.*

"*Wa alaikum. . .as-salaam,*" came the stammering reply, the Arabic rough and unpracticed. *And unto you, peace.*

The imam rose from his knees, extending a hand. "You've been coming to my classes faithfully for some time now—what's your name?"

There was the broad, youthful smile at the thought that he had been noticed. *Remembered.* "Aydin."

Rahman nodded with a smile of his own, clasping the boy's hand in his. It was a question he had known the answer to before he asked it, but the time had come to see if this devotion could be developed into something. . .more.

"*The light of the moon.* It is a good name. Wear it proudly as a follower of the Prophet should do."

He sensed a hesitation there, glanced about them at the rest of the students filing out. "Was there something you wished to say to me, Aydin?"

The young man opened his mouth to speak, then closed it again as if he had thought better of his words. "Go on," Hashim urged him. "Please."

"Is it true what they say, imam—that you fought against the unbelievers in Afghanistan?"

He reached out, placing a gentle hand on the boy's elbow. "Where did you hear this, my son?"

Aydin shrugged. "Everyone says it," he replied, looking earnestly into the imam's face. "But is it true?"

He gestured toward the rack. "Go ahead and put your shoes on, Aydin. We'll walk together."

Cold air struck them in the face as they exited the mosque, the streetlights of Leeds glowing down upon them. "Why do you wish to know of this?"

The boy's eyes were shining, his words coming fast in the excitement. "I want to know how I can go overseas. To Syria. Or—or Afghanistan. I want to fight, to join in the struggle of God."

Rahman stopped on the sidewalk, turning to look his companion in the eye, searching his face. But there could be no doubting his sincerity. He smiled, squeezing the boy's shoulder affectionately. "May His name be praised. But you must understand, to join in God's struggle. . .it is not even necessary that you leave this country."

7:13 P.M.

"Sierra One, Echo One—you are cleared to proceed," Thomas announced, looking up at the screens as he keyed his headset mike. "The mosque's security system will go off-line in three. . .two. . .one. *Go!*"

He couldn't see the two MI-5 teams as they moved into position, one near the back of the mosque—another in the alley at the side, but he could feel them. Adrenaline pumping through his veins as he stared at the screens, a sympathetic reaction.

He'd been on enough of these ops in his time, knew exactly what was about to go down. Knew what they were feeling as they closed on their target.

You were never more alive than in these moments.

"We're in," Darren announced, replacing the lockpicks within the pocket of his shirt as he moved into the darkness of the mosque's interior. His shoes were still on, that act in itself a desecration. . .but only if they were discovered.

And that was the first commandment of espionage: thou shalt not get caught.

"Roger that, Sierra One," the American's voice responded coolly. "You have five minutes."

"Five minutes, aye." He raised a hand, motioning for the officer behind him to continue down the corridor toward the left while he proceeded straight ahead.

Within that time, the mosque would be wired for sound.

Thomas glanced over at the woman with whom he shared the van, her brown hair tucked back into a ponytail—beneath the headphones she wore. Monitoring the police bands was her job, making sure that no one had sounded the alarm.

Roth had been close-lipped, but from the best Thomas had been able to determine, Five wasn't coordinating with the North Yorkshire Special Branch.

Marsh was playing it close to the vest, Thomas thought. An admirable tactic, but it meant if they were discovered, they were going to have to clear out. Fast.

"Camera 3 in position, main hall," Darren announced. "Moving to the office. Do you copy?"

Thomas's fingers moved over the keyboard, bringing up the feed, watching as the video buffered and then came up. "Camera 3 is live, Sierra One. Eyes and ears. You have two minutes."

He saw the woman shake her head, her hand moving to toggle the mike. "No, you don't. Sierra One, you need to get your team out *now*."

It took Thomas only a moment to see what had prompted her reaction. The sight of an older man moving intently toward the mosque, his body cloaked against the cold in the traditional dress of an Albanian Muslim.

"One moment," Darren replied, the words escaping from around the flashlight clenched between his teeth, his eyes focused on the microphone he was implanting in the air vent. The vent itself was on the desk beneath him, a pair of small screws and a screwdriver beside it.

"That's not a moment you have, Sierra One. We've got company—get out of there."

Bugger.

There wasn't going to be time, Thomas thought, watching the man's approach through the CCTV cameras. Not nearly enough time. He ripped the headset from his ears, pulling on a jacket as he pushed open the back of the surveillance van.

"What—where are you going?" he heard the woman ask, but there was no time to stop and explain.

He shut the door of the van behind him, zipping the jacket up against the cold.

The man was coming toward his position, still out of sight beyond the Leeds storefront as Thomas set off down the sidewalk. On a collision course.

Screws were small, Darren thought, rolling one of them between his big fingers, feeling clumsy in that moment. Forcing himself to calm.

He fitted the vent up against the opening, holding it in place while he prepared to screw it tight. Everything back just the way they had found it. His earpiece crackled with static, the female officer's voice coming on. "Sierra One, we have another problem. The American just did a runner."

A curse escaped his lips and he nearly dropped the screw in his surprise. "*Why?*"

"He didn't say, sir. Was gone before I could stop him." She paused. "I still have him on CCTV...he's speaking to the subject. They're in conversation, looks like Parker is holding up a map."

Despite the tension of the moment, Darren found himself chuckling. He should have known better than to underestimate the CIA officer. He was as good as advertised. Maybe too good.

He reached down for the second screw, the glow of the flashlight playing around the dark office as he finished up. Time to get out of here. . .

"So I go down from here two blocks, turn right and walk to the bus station—another block and I'm there?"

The older man nodded, the skullcap nestled among his greying hair. "You are an American, yes?"

"How did you guess, man?" Thomas smiled affably, rattling on before his companion could respond. "I'm from New York—came here with my girlfriend on vacation. She's out shopping as usual, I'm supposed to meet her for dinner in, like, an hour."

He grinned, stalling for time. "And that's when I'm going to pop the question."

The cellphone in the pocket of his jeans buzzed quietly once, then twice. The recall code. Five's team was out of the mosque.

He glanced at his watch, as if just realizing the time. "Look, I gotta run. Thanks again for the directions."

A smile touched the man's lips. "May peace be upon you, my son."

7:39 P.M.
Brooks's
St. James, London

Conor Hale handed over his coat to the doorman, self-consciously brushing a speck of lint off the lapel of his jacket. It was strange for the former SAS sergeant to feel nerves, but he was feeling them now.

Perhaps it was the surroundings, he thought as the butler motioned for him to follow, feeling oddly out of place as they walked farther into the men's club. Or perhaps it had more to do with *why* he was here.

Brooks's was one of London's most exclusive social clubs, with a legacy dating back to the middle of the 18th-century. A membership that had counted kings among its ranks—walls that had once borne witness to the passionate oratory of Edmund Burke.

This was England, Hale thought, gazing up at the barrel-vaulted ceiling of the Great Subscription Room. England as she had once been.

England as she could be once more.

The drawing room was nearly deserted, a couple men conversing intently in armchairs over near the far wall.

The butler guided him past them, back toward where a towering bookcase rose toward the ceiling, a 19th-century globe of the world centered squarely on a heavy endtable carved from mahogany.

A man sat there, alone, the newspaper nearly obscuring his face, sipping at a tumbler of whisky.

"Ah, Sergeant Hale. I'm so glad you could join me," he smiled, setting aside the broadsheet as he gestured for Hale to have a seat in the leathern armchair across from him. "Please, Desmond. . .a whisky for my friend."

"It's a beautiful place, isn't it, Conor?" Arthur Colville mused, glancing up at the ceiling as the butler left them. At sixty-one years of age, the publisher of the *UK Daily Standard* was over two decades Hale's senior. "A reminder of just how great this country once was."

"That it is, sir," Hale responded, unsure what else to say. He'd had prior meetings with Colville, but none under these circumstances. In these surroundings—with their plan already underway.

"You knew the IRA bombed this building, didn't you? Back in the '70s. I was at Cambridge at the time, but Ted Heath gave me the details when we met in later years. What it *felt* like to be in the middle of that. The terror. It's coming again."

"I spoke with Flaharty," Hale interjected, conscious of the irony of his words. That was the way of the world. Enemies became allies. . .and allies, enemies. Having too rigid a morality only served to complicate affairs. "Everything is on schedule."

"Good," the publisher replied absently, seeming lost in thought.

Hale cleared his throat. "Does Pearson know what we're planning?"

The MP was their biggest backer in Parliament, the public champion of their cause. Their *face*. Yet he wondered if the man had the stomach for what was to come.

"No," came the reply. "Nor can he be allowed to know, at least not until the board has been set, the pieces already in motion. Daniel is a good man, but he is a politician and politicians are timid animals by nature."

Hale snorted his assent as his employer glanced around them once again, taking in the ornate furnishings.

"The bombings couldn't stop us, and yet what is Brooks's now? A shell," Colville added, answering his own question. "A shell of a memory, echoes of greatness. That's all clubs like this are, for all their history. Just a reminder of the England we are losing."

He gestured with his whisky toward the broadsheet. His own paper. "Have you seen the headlines from this morning?"

"No." Hale shook his head. "I don't subscribe, sorry. Get most of my news off the telly and the net."

"Like most people," the publisher responded. "If the *Standard* only had half the subscribers that we have in traffic on the website. . ."

He smiled, reaching forward and lifting up the paper. "It was another incident in Whitechapel overnight, they found a shopkeeper trussed up to the beams of his own shop, his clothing shredded—the skin flayed from his back with a whip. Forty lashes. . .the Islamic punishment for selling liquor. Here. In *our* country."

7:43 P.M.
A cafe
Leeds, England

"Have you spoken to your parents of your desires?" the imam asked, glancing keenly across the café table into the face of his young friend.

The shadow that entered the boy's eyes at the question gave him all the answer he needed. A simmering anger. "Once."

"I see." He leaned back in his chair, sipping at his tea. Giving the boy space.

"My father said that if he ever heard me speak of Syria again," Aydin continued after a long silence, "he would throw me out on the street. That the concerns of Iraq, of Palestine, were not ours here in England. 'Mind your business,' he says. 'Don't make waves.'"

Rahman nodded his understanding. "Your father is like so many who do not grasp the true nature of the *Ummah*. We are all one body, as was witnessed by Allah's Messenger, may peace be upon him. And wherever a faithful Muslim is being oppressed, you should *feel* that pain, as if it had happened to your own family."

"I do," the young man replied earnestly, the sandwich long since forgotten on his plate.

"And your father does not, and this troubles you. As well it should." Rahman paused, choosing his words carefully. "If you are only concerned with your own safety, with that of your immediate family and not that of the faithful. . .something is wrong. You have become detached, are no longer a part of the body."

"He wants me to go to college next year. To go into business. To be *normal*."

He spat the word as if it were a curse, his face twisting with the emotion.

Rahman inclined his head toward the front of the café, a young couple sitting there on the stools by the counter—a short skirt accentuating the woman's legs, her partner's right hand resting possessively on her bare knee. His left clutching a drink.

Their heads together, laughing. At each other, at everything—and nothing at all.

"You see them?" he asked, watching as the young man nodded. "'You only live once,' they say—but they do not truly *live* at all. They pretend to be happy, but their kind simply exist, moving like ghosts from one party to the next. Chasing their next fix. No purpose. Restless, hopeless. Empty."

The imam leaned forward in his seat, an edge of emotion entering his voice. "They promise you a dream if you only will be a 'good' Muslim—if only you will be like them—but it's a dream which turns to ashes in your mouth. A mirage. And you will *never* be like them."

Across from him, Aydin nodded, sadness clouding his features. "And what of my father?"

"It is truly as the Prophet has said. . .everyone will be with those whom he loves."

7:51 P.M.
Brooks's
St. James, London

"How did we get here?" Colville mused, staring across the drawing room at a massive oil painting of Trafalgar. "So far from those days of glory. . .wooden ships. Iron men. 'England confides that every man will do his duty.' That was Nelson's original message, you know, before they changed it for ease of transmission."

Hale nodded. He knew the story well, the day when the fate of all England had rested upon the men in those ships-of-the-line. Outgunned. Outnumbered. But not outmanned, for no one could outfight an Englishman.

Then.

"Our country has grown soft," the publisher continued, as if reading his thoughts. "There is nothing more sedentary than your average Briton, no one more loathe to be roused to action. Unless it's football or some other rot, of course. Then you can get them out in the bloody streets."

He shook his head disdainfully. "And all this in the face of the greatest threat Europe has known in centuries."

"Since Tours," Hale offered, a smile touching his lips as he took a sip of his whisky, the crystal tumbler poised awkwardly between rough, calloused fingers.

Colville laughed, a mirthless, bitter sound. "Nothing ever bloody changes. But we have no Charles Martel now. . .no Nelson. What we have is democracy—the weakest, most insipid form of government known to man. We could use a king."

"We'll have one, sooner or later," the former SAS sergeant said, shaking his head. "The Queen can't last forever."

"Charles?" Colville demanded, passing a hand over his face. "Don't jest. He wants no more to do with the throne—with the *leadership* of the country—than he did with his wife. He'll keep playing the gentleman farmer and leave it all to those same simpering fools in Whitehall. 'Uneasy lies the head that wears the crown,' as the saying goes. There are moments when I think that we're too late, that England is already lost."

Silence fell between the two men as they sat there in the drawing room. No answer which could be given to a truth which was all too plain.

Hale drained his glass and set it on the endtable between them, waiting for the other man to speak.

"But I tell you—one of the greatest evenings of my life was a few years ago when a friend invited me to the Special Forces Club. Less lavishly appointed than this, of course. . .but I was in the presence of *men*."

"My brothers," Hale observed quietly. He'd been to the club in Knightsbridge once, shortly after his return from Afghanistan. The black-framed photographs on the walls a grim reminder of the price Britain's special forces had paid in the decades since their formation during the Second World War. A legacy of blood.

"And that's why I'm counting on you to see this through to a finish, Conor." Colville tapped his fingers against the rim of his tumbler, staring keenly at him. "Your friend from the Paras—this Paul Gordon fellow. You trust him?"

"As I do all the rest. With my life."

9:14 P.M
The flat
Ealing, London

The flat seemed emptier since he had left, the emptiest it had felt since Nick's death.

Moving slowly to the window, Mehreen pushed back the shades, looking out at the light rain smacking against the pane—running in rivulets down the glass. The mercurial nature of London weather once again asserting itself.

She knew now what she had seen in his eyes when she had first opened the door on that rainy evening. *Grief.* Bitterness congealing within their depths. A familiar feeling.

Just a few days before, but it felt like forever. Maybe it was—it had been an eternity since Nick's death.

The death of the one you loved—it wasn't something you could move past. Get over. Forget. They took a part of your soul with them to the grave. Sometimes the only part that mattered. The part that made you. . .*better.*

He was out there, somewhere. A man with a mission. And a gun, she thought, remembering the hard bulge against his side—the feel of metal under her hand when she'd embraced him.

And where had he obtained that? Handguns weren't easy to come by in the UK, but Nichols had always had his sources.

Like her.

She had gone to the park with the intention of telling him no, of explaining why she couldn't help—why she couldn't lay that much on the line for him.

And she had done just the opposite. *Why?* Was it the repayment of a debt? Or did she just want justice? If not for her, for *someone* in this life. For Nichols, as he'd stood there by the fence—the pain so visible in his eyes. The loss.

There had been no justice for Nick. No one hauled into Old Bailey to answer for his murder. As far as the public was concerned, there hadn't even been a murder.

Just another dead soldier, in a war everyone was sick of hearing about on the telly.

Gone and forgotten.

No. Her fist clenched as she stared out into the rain, eyes shadowed by grief. Not forgotten. Never.

11:03 P.M.
Hadley Wood
London Borough of Enfield

It was a small house on the edge of the town, a five-block walk from the Route 399 bus stop.

Not far at all, Harry thought, looking up at the crumbling brick façade of the abandoned council house, jagged glass protruding from a broken window in one of the dormers. It looked as though it had been a beautiful home once—in better days—but it was little more than a ruin now.

It would keep out the rain, at the very least, he thought—pausing by the door. He'd brought a lockpick set, but it wasn't necessary. The lock was broken, the handle giving under his hand as he pushed down. Swinging open with a rusty groan from the hinges, a sound nearly masked by the falling rain outside.

He took a step back, into the open, raindrops splashing against his face as he slung the knapsack over his back, drawing the Sig-Sauer and bringing it up in both hands.

Darkness closed around him as he entered, his eyes adjusting as the glare of the streetlights faded away. Trash littered the floor at his feet, the detritus of past occupants. Or current? It was hard to say, but he had sought refuge in worse places in the weeks since arriving in the UK.

He couldn't have stayed with Mehreen much longer, he thought, suddenly aware of just how monumental the task he'd set for himself was.

The lone wolf archetype popularized by thriller novels was nothing more than the stuff of fantasy. To pull off an op—any op—you needed manpower, and that was something he didn't have.

Yet.

Beg. Borrow. Steal. . .

Chapter 5

7:03 A.M.
Thames House
London

"According to our teams, Tarik visited Gaveda yesterday but did not buy the car," Alec MacCallum summarized, looking up from his notes. "We're running down financial information and contact records for any matches on Gaveda. Nothing. There's been no further contact between him and Rahman, but we're assuming the meet is still on for today. The question remaining is how he's going to get there. As for Rahman himself—he spent time in Germany before immigrating, so we ran his name past the BND."

The *Bundesnachrichtendienst*, Julian Marsh thought, running a hand over his forehead—Germany's Federal Intelligence Service. The BND had been founded during the Adenauer chancellery, back in the days of a divided Germany. Dark days that Marsh remembered all too well.

The senior officer paused and Marsh shot him a look. "And?"

"And they believe he might have spent time in Afghanistan."

"What do they mean 'believe'?" the DG exclaimed. "Isn't Köhler minding his store over there?"

"I've seen their jacket on Rahman," Simon Norris interjected, tapping his pen on the conference table. "It's full of holes—empty spots, entire years where they have no idea where he was."

"Sounds like a player to me," Thomas Parker offered. He was in the conference as a professional courtesy, nothing more. *The Americans.*

MacCallum cleared his throat. "That might be good enough for your people at Guantanamo, Mr. Parker, but here in the UK we hold ourselves to somewhat more. . .rigorous evidential standards. We'll need more."

Problems—they came new every morning, particularly at briefing sessions like this one. Marsh lifted his eyes, glancing wearily down the table toward his field officer. "Tell me you have something uplifting for us, Darren?"

"Arsenal won last night's game?" the former Royal Marine offered helpfully, trading looks with his American counterpart.

"We no longer behead people in the Tower," Marsh observed, shooting his subordinate a baleful glance, "but I'm sure we can make an exception for 'extenuating circumstances.'"

"Sorry, sir," Darren Roth amended. "All the bugs we emplaced yesterday—the audio is coming through crystal clear. From the moment Tarik walks through the doors of that mosque, we'll have him. There's only one thing. I need more manpower."

Marsh waved his hand at the stack of folders sitting in front of him. "We're already trying to compartmentalize this as far as we possibly can. I have officers sifting through everything we can find on the eleven men we identified at the brothel. *Eleven* men. We're stretched thin."

It was the danger of any operation like this—you got overextended, started missing things. Started ignoring pieces. That was what had happened in DOWNTEMPO. Mohammed Siddique Khan had been on Five's radar early on, but the intelligence linking him to the main cell had been so weak. Like that linking these men at the brothel to Tarik.

They'd let him drop off their radar—only to have him show back up in the Edgeware Road Station on that July morning, a bomb strapped to his body.

He gave Parker a pointed look. "Perhaps Grosvenor Square would be inclined to lend a hand?"

Darren put his hand up before the American could respond, cutting him off. "In point of fact, sir, I had a specific officer in mind. I want Mehreen Crawford read in on PERSEPHONE. She's fluent in Arabic, Pashto, and Urdu—can give us a real-time translation of the audio."

"Crawford?" It was Norris again, MacCallum's analyst clearing his throat from the opposite end of the table. There was skepticism in his voice—along with something more.

The DG's eyes narrowed, trying to read the man. "Do you have an objection, Simon?"

There was a moment before the analyst responded, as he seemed to choose his words. "I just think we need to be very careful on this. If half of what our American cousins," he gestured toward Thomas Parker, "are telling us is true. . .we need to tread with caution. Mehreen Crawford still has family ties to the same part of the world from which this threat emanates."

He paused, just letting the suggestion hang there. Unspoken.

Marsh saw Darren straighten in his chair, his body stiffening. "Exactly what are you insinuating?"

Norris put up his hands, shaking his head. "I'm not insinuating anything, just advising caution. There's risk to be assessed when dealing with anyone of that background."

"That *background*?" The look on Darren's face was one of pure fury. "Nick Crawford was a good mate, one of the best I ever served with. Sod me if I'm going to bloody well sit here and listen to you disparage his—"

"Enough." Marsh leaned forward, his elbows on the table—fingers tented as he glared at the two men. "We shall, I trust, save some of these energies for dealing with the enemy, yes? The decision is mine to make, and I have made it. Alec, you will brief Mehreen on PERSEPHONE when she arrives. As for the rest of you, please make an *attempt* to focus on the mission before us. We still have a team on Tarik, correct?"

Darren nodded, his eyes still smoldering.

"Good," the DG continued, ignoring the glance. "Now I want CCTV coverage on every train station, every bus terminal out of London. If possible without spooking him, I want an officer with Tarik on his journey north. Let's make this happen, people."

2:00 A.M. Eastern Time
Vienna, Virginia

Somewhere in the old house, the clock struck the hour. Once, then twice, before quiet descended once again. Almost an unnatural quiet—the type of early morning stillness that comes with not having slept.

Roy Coftey leaned back against the headboard of the bed, staring up at the bedroom ceiling as he listened to the breathing of the young woman lying there beside him. Slow and measured.

He looked down at her sleeping form, bringing up a hand to caress her bare shoulder. She stirred but didn't awaken, her lips parting as if to speak.

Melody.

They'd been together for six months, longer than he typically kept any one woman around. Stay in D.C. for long enough and you picked up a reputation whether you liked it or not—and Coftey didn't mind being known as a womanizer. It helped him forget.

He'd only been in Congress for nine years when his wife passed from Lou Gehrig's, a long illness that had slowly stolen away the woman he had loved so much.

Moment by moment.

They had never had children—and he'd never fallen in love again. Until now.

Now. He smiled in the darkness, a war-weary smile. Now, when everything he had built was so close to collapse, with Cahill gunning for him.

Ian Cahill. It seemed ironic—given how closely the two of them had worked together over the decades. Friends? No, because neither of them had believed in such a thing, but firm allies.

An utterly ruthless strategist with all the morality of a street fighter, Cahill had risen to power in the Hancock administration, becoming the President's chief of staff. Roger Hancock's closest advisor.

He'd known from that moment at Camp David that Cahill would never forgive him his role in bringing down the administration. *Never.* And it didn't matter that the former President was dead now—Hancock stabbed to death by a woman in a California hotel room, a lover's quarrel gone wrong.

None of that mattered. For Cahill, it was war.

Coftey smiled, reaching over in the darkness for his reading glasses on the nightstand. He'd been in D.C. for as long as Cahill, maybe a bit longer. What was that old saying from the opening of the American Revolution?

If they wish to have a war. . .let it begin here.

10:27 A.M. Greenwich Mean Time
King's Cross Station

He was *chosen*. That much Tarik knew, glancing around at the Victorian architecture of the train station, looking for Nadeem. The young man had volunteered to accompany him to Leeds, offered to be his bodyguard.

That much he had known for many years. His faith had wavered in those early months in Cuba, staring out from behind the wire of Camp X-Ray, the blue water of Guantanamo Bay beckoning to him. Taunting him with its promise of freedom.

Wavered? No, his faith had done far more than waver. He had given up, on the cause, on the promises of Allah. Turned his back on his faith. He could still remember lying there, curled up into a ball on the concrete floor of his cell. Refusing to eat.

Day after day, a resistance born of despair. He'd wanted to die more than anything else, prayed that the darkness would swallow him up.

He looked over his shoulder again as he moved toward the machines to take his railway pass. Once or twice in recent days, he had thought that he was being followed, but it remained a feeling. Nothing more.

But his death had not been so ordained, there in that cell. And as he lay there, starving, his mind swirling in delirium, he had seen a vision—a supernatural light shining down upon him from above, a voice in the midst of the darkness.

The voice of an angel speaking to him, words of hope. Of purpose. Of truth.

And from that moment, he had *known*. There was a mission for him to perform, a purpose from on high. A part to be played in Allah's struggle.

An Englishwoman bumped into him as he moved to the turnstile, and felt her turn toward him, as if expecting an apology.

He turned but for a moment, his blue eyes drifting over her. Transfixing her with a gaze as serene as it was penetrating before he turned back, pushing through the turnstile on his way toward the train pulling into the station, an electric locomotive painted in the silver livery of the East Coast line.

The young man came hurrying up at the last moment, following him through the turnstile. Tarik ignored his apology, choosing to overlook the failure. For now.

So many years, and all through the darkness God had guided his steps in his jihad against the West. Surely He would not fail them now, in this hour of testing.

"Now boarding. . ."

10:31 A.M.

"He's here," Mehreen announced into her earpiece, moving out onto the platform toward the Mk 4 passenger carriage, about ten feet back from their target. "He's entering the third coach back from the engine. I say again, I have eyes on Tarik Abdul Muhammad. And he's not alone."

She didn't recognize his companion, a black man perhaps ten years younger than Tarik himself.

"That's a known associate. Nadeem Abdul al-Qawi, no doubt along as muscle. We have the three of you on CCTV. Get on the same coach with them, but stay back." It was MacCallum's voice, calm and measured. The voice of an old hand.

Mehreen resisted the urge to nod, keeping her focus. "I've done this once or twice, Alec."

"As have we all. A reminder never goes amiss."

"Of course." It was standard procedure, she knew that. Nothing unusual.

She stepped through the doors, glancing up the rows of upholstered seats, grey alternating with blue. *There.* A window seat, eight rows from the end of the coach—his face turned, looking out on the platform. It looked as if his companion was trying to start a conversation, that Tarik was having none of it.

There was an empty seat four back from him and she began working her way toward it. "What's our status in Leeds?"

"You'll turn over direct surveillance to our teams at the station. Darren is already in place, will be there to pick you up. Normal contact protocols apply."

Of course. The decision to place her in the field again for this op had been a tactical one. They'd had teams in place on Tarik for two weeks, but this was the closest they had ever shadowed him. Didn't want him recognizing a familiar face. All the same. . .

She cleared her throat. "There are any number of stops on this line. What if he gets off the train before Leeds?"

MacCallum was unruffled by the question, anticipating it, even. Which he probably had been. "Then we'll re-direct assets as rapidly as possible and bring in local Special Branch if necessary." His voice softened as he continued, "Take care of yourself, Mehr."

Behind her, the doors closed, gaskets sealing shut as the train jerked into motion.

No going back.

10:57 A.M.
Hadley Wood
London Borough of Enfield

Third coach from the engine. Harry resisted the urge to look at his watch again, glancing instead down the railroad tracks into the distance. The train would be here soon enough.

The Hadley Wood station seemed disproportionately large when compared to the town that played host to it—long platforms on either side of the rails.

Three security cameras that he had plotted on the dead ground map twenty minutes before, with a fourth inside the station itself.

"I have eyes on Tarik Abdul Muhammad."

Hacking the Bluetooth network of Mehreen's phone had been an afterthought, a precaution. *Insurance.*

He'd known they would bring her in, sooner or later. People with a command of the languages in that part of the world were a rare find, and the Western intelligence communities were still playing catch-up ball.

Finding her in the field was unexpected, though—he hadn't anticipated that. Mehreen had been a case officer back in the day, cut her operational teeth running assets for "Box" as MI-5 had been known in Northern Ireland in the late '90s.

But she had given all that up years ago. Or so he'd been led to believe.

Harry pulled his cap down lower over his eyes, glancing around at his fellow commuters. A college student talking loudly on her cellphone, a businessman staring absently down the train tracks into the distance—a middle-aged woman who looked as if she would have rather been anywhere else.

Lost in their own worlds, consumed by their own problems, their own dreams—unable to see how everything was changing around them. Crumbling into ashes.

And it was all for them. For them that his brothers had given their lives, fighting a war in the shadows, keeping the wolf from the door. So far from the door that most people preferred to believe there wasn't a wolf.

He tried to recall the first time he had felt this way and found himself unable to remember. Had it been his first time back Stateside from Iraq—feeling the tension of a country divided over something they didn't even begin to understand? Or had it been much earlier, before 9/11 even? The first time he had killed a man in the service of his flag, coming back into the country. . .the feeling of blood on his hands as he walked through the concourse at Dulles. Looking around at the people—at his countrymen, realizing that for them, *nothing* had changed. Not a thing.

It still hadn't. The Christmas Eve attacks on Vegas would soon be brushed into the past, forgotten just as 9/11 had been before them. *Not for him.*

The airhorn of the train resounded down the line and Harry glanced down the platform to see the locomotive a few hundred meters away, the long train moving out of the tunnel.

And it was time.

12:34 P.M.
Near the Masjid-e-Ali
Leeds, England

"What's our status?" Thomas asked, climbing back up in the surveillance van. He reached over to Norris, handing the analyst a covered cup of chai tea.

Darren glanced up from the surveillance screens lining the side of the van, popping off his headphones. "Hashim Rahman walked inside about twenty minutes ago, along with two others we've not been able to ID yet. Tarik Abdul Muhammad and his friend are still an hour out—the train's on schedule."

"Thank God for small miracles," Norris observed, running a hand across his forehead.

They were all weary, working on what sleep they had been able to grab in between briefing the DG and their return by helicopter to Leeds.

Thomas settled into a seat, popping the top off his cappuccino. "Did we find anything on the man I ran into on the street yesterday? How is he tied into affairs at the masjid?"

"We did." Darren reached down into a messenger bag for a thin folder, passing it over. "Ismail Besimi. Sixty-nine years of age, Albanian-born, he was the original imam at the *Masjid-e-Ali*. A pillar of the Islamic community here in Leeds for many years, according to what my contact at Special Branch told me."

"Was?"

"Got pushed out—perhaps sidelined would be a better word—when Rahman came to town. He couldn't match Rahman's charisma, his appeal to Muslim youth. The allure of the 'war hero.'" There was a sneer in the former Royal Marine's voice as he spoke the words.

Nothing heroic about any of this.

"A potential asset?" Thomas asked, flipping open the folder to reveal Besimi's passport photo staring back at him. There was no emotion in his voice, just the clinical detachment of someone who had been down this road before. You were always looking for something—for *someone* you could use. An edge.

Roth and the analyst just looked at each other.

"Thank you. . .we'll handle that end of things," Darren said finally, clearing his throat. "Now, if you'll excuse me, gentlemen—I need to leave for City Station. It's time to get our teams in place."

12:51 P.M.
East Coast Main Line
Doncaster, England

We're nearing the branch off, Mehreen tapped into her phone's keypad—glancing out the window as she pressed SEND.

East Coast's London trains came to a parting of the ways at Doncaster. North to Scotland by way of Newcastle—northwest to Leeds.

It was one of the biggest passenger interchanges in the UK, handling nearly four million travelers every year. More than enough traffic to lose a man, which was why she had advised strongly in favor of placing officers on the Doncaster platform, in case their target tried to give them the slip.

Tarik.

She closed her eyes, trying to shut out the memories of what Nichols had said. *Disassociate.*

As an analyst, you couldn't allow yourself to become personally involved in an op—allow emotion to enter the equation. Disrupt your analysis.

It was the same out in the field, as she had learned so many years ago. Except that people died if you got something wrong. Not just in theory.

In fact.

Harry could see her face from where he sat, a window seat across the aisle and three back. Just far enough back to be out of her direct line of sight when she rose—just close enough to where he could himself watch Tarik Abdul Muhammad. And the black man sitting on the outside, ostensibly to protect his principal.

To be this close.

The last time he had seen the Pakistani had been the night of the meeting with Andropov there in that Vegas strip club.

Just days before the attacks. Just days before his dreams had come crashing down.

He could feel the bulge of the Sig-Sauer under his jacket, riding against his hip, looked down to make sure it wasn't printing against the fabric. Carrying a weapon might have presented a problem in the tight security of London's Tube, but not here.

The doors opened as the northbound train came to a stop, passengers flooding in on off the Doncaster platform. His eyes narrowed as he tried to keep tabs on Tarik's position in the press of traffic.

It would be so *simple*, Harry thought, his mind flickering back across the years to another op. In Europe. A train station just like this one.

So simple to just raise his hand, the suppressed pistol concealed within his coat. Fire a single shot, walk on without stopping, without even pausing to give the cameras something to work with. Leave your target to bleed out. He'd done it before.

His bodyguard would be useless, he plainly hadn't been to this dance before. The crowd wouldn't help him—not in time. The first few people to see him fall wouldn't want to be distracted. The first person to see blood would be afraid to get involved.

People were like that.

And yet something held him back.

1:09 P.M.
The Masjid-e-Ali
Leeds, England

The Shaikh. They had only talked on the phone twice, Hashim Rahman thought—gazing down at the copy of the Qur'an on his desk, the flowing script beneath his finger. Twice, and for only a few moments each time. . .yet he had felt moved by the very experience of speaking with the man.

It was a power few men possessed, the power to lead men—to *unify* them under a single banner. Long had the house of Islam looked for such a man.

The imam's eyes fell upon the clock on the far wall, marking the time as he had been doing ever since he'd entered the mosque. Not long now.

8:24 A.M. Eastern Time
CIA Headquarters
Langley, Virginia

So beautiful. She'd had the eyes of her mother, David Lay thought, glancing at the picture which sat on his desk, a thin layer of dust cloaking the frame.

Untouched since the funeral.

The CIA director pushed back his chair, buttoning his suit jacket as he rose.

Tailored once, it hung on him now in folds of excess fabric, swathing a man who was but a shadow of his former self. The skin of his face loose, cheekbones prominently visible. He was in his early sixties, but he felt old.

Grief did that to a man. The grief of losing a daughter—a daughter one had known for such a short space of time.

Lay reached for the photo frame, a thumb brushing at the dust—azure-blue eyes staring back at him, a face framed by blonde hair. *Carol.*

He had known what it was to have a family once, a wife and daughter. In a different age, almost past memory.

The closing years of the Cold War, a time of tumultuous uncertainty. He'd been a field officer in those days, spending months away from his family at a time.

He'd given his life to his country, he thought, gazing sadly down at the picture. And in return, they'd taken away his family. Or had he done that to himself?

His wife had left first, weary of the long days—the nights laying there alone in bed. Just up and left, taking his daughter with him—taking back her maiden name for the both of them. *Chambers.*

He hadn't fought, although many times through the years that followed he'd wished that he had.

And when his daughter had showed up on the Agency's doorstep two years before, a twenty-eight-year-old analyst with a degree from MIT. . .well, he'd thought it was a chance to begin anew.

Two years. So short a time, filled with the missteps and awkwardness that inevitably came with long estrangement.

But they'd found each other, and in the end, that was all that mattered.

In the end. And the end had come, despite all his precautions, like a ghost in the night. The whiplash *crack* of the sniper's bullet that had ended her life.

He could still remember the phone call, hear the flat, almost robotic tone of the FBI agent. The voice of someone who had made too many death calls in one night—his daughter just another one of the many who had died in the terrorist attacks on Vegas.

Just another one.

A teardrop fell from his eye, splattering against the glass of the frame and he brushed it angrily away, leaving a smear of dust across its face.

Not a tragedy. A statistic.

The intercom on his desk blinked and he pressed it, swearing softly at himself. He had to focus, had a job to do.

"Yes?"

It was his secretary's voice. "Director, your meeting with Bernard Kranemeyer is within the hour. Conference Room #3."

War waited for no man, spared time for no grief. "Thank you, Margaret. I'll be there."

1:43 P.M. Greenwich Mean Time
Leeds City Station
England

So close now, Tarik thought, listening to the voice above him ring out, "Leeds City Station."

A mechanical, empty sound. Like so much of the West—lifeless, godless.

Together they rose from their seats, pushing their way forward. Tarik brushed into a woman in the press of the crowd, elbowing his way toward the opening doors. Through the herd.

He was half-way there when someone going the other way bumped roughly into him—man, woman—he didn't see their face, didn't even realize what had happened until they were well past.

Realized that their hand had slipped into the pocket of his windbreaker. Deposited something therein, the weight giving it away. A mobile phone, perhaps? But he hardly dared touch it, his hand beginning to tremble despite himself.

A *brush-pass*, it was called—or so he thought, a vague memory of a trashy American spy novel he had been given while at Camp X-Ray. He glanced behind him, unable to stop moving in the press, his eyes nervously scanning the crowd. He couldn't show fear—not in front of Nadeem.

But someone was there.

The next moment, the mobile in his pocket buzzed with an incoming text.

There. Harry saw Tarik's face in the crowd, moved to close with him, keeping an eye on Mehreen's position as he did so. The Pakistani's head was down as he stepped out on the platform, seeming to consult something in his hand. A phone?

You have watchers, the message read. *The mosque has been compromised.*

A simple, stark message displayed on the screen. *How could they. . .*

Tarik's face came up, once more scanning the crowd flooding out onto the platform—his eyes darting from face to face. He could feel the panic within him and struggled to suppress it. To keep his head.

I seek refuge in Allah from Satan, the Accursed, he breathed, trying and failing to calm himself. Nadeem's voice in his ear, distant and far away, lost in the noise of the crowd.

His fingers feeling clumsy as wooden stubs as he tapped back, *Who are you?*

"Something's wrong," Mehreen whispered into her earpiece, watching as their subject's demeanor changed completely, a suddenness like none she had ever seen. "I think he's on to us. . .tell me we have following teams in place?"

"We do," Roth responded calmly. "Webster and Saunders are on the platform with you—another pair of teams outside the station, with Victor elements split between Wellington and Aire Street, covering the public exits. What spooked him?"

"I don't know."

Who I am doesn't matter. There's a woman to your left, the new message read, the phone pulsing in his hand. *Dark skin, dark hair. Forties. She's with Five.*

And he looked back, his eyes resting on the face of someone who could only have been a countrywoman of his.

1:47 P.M.
The surveillance van

There was a burst of static, then the words, "I've been made" came over the speakers, punctuated by a curse.

Mehreen Crawford's voice.

Thomas exchanged glances with the Five analyst. What was going on?

Norris tapped a command into his keyboard, glancing up at the screens surrounding them—streaming CCTV footage of City Station. "Webster, Saunders—move in, move in on the target. We still have eyes. Darren, pick up Crawford and get out of there."

"Copy that," came Roth's response as Norris brought up the screens outside the station, marking the positions of their secondary teams.

Command and control was essential to any surveillance op, and despite Norris' initial reaction to Crawford's presence, he seemed to know his stuff.

"Victor One, Victor Two—hold your positions. Sierra elements, do not—I repeat, do not follow closely." He glanced up to see Parker watching him, waved a weary hand toward the monitors. "If we don't loosen up this perimeter before he exits, everything is going to go pear-shaped."

1:49 P.M.
City Station

Something was going wrong with Five's operation—very wrong, Harry thought, pushing his way through the crowd toward Tarik's disappearing form. He had seen it in the man's eyes, watched Mehreen's body language. This mission was going sideways on them, and it was impossible to say why.

He kept his head down, making out at least one MI-5 surveillance team as he made his way across the platform toward the concourse. They were good, but you learned what to look for over the years.

The signs.

And it was in that moment that he felt someone's eyes on him. *Almost safe.*

Nichols? Mehreen froze, Darren's voice in her earpiece fading away to a faint echo, her eyes fixed on the retreating back of the man she had just seen. The familiar profile of a face. The beard.

It couldn't be. How could he have known? She glanced up into the eye of a nearby surveillance camera. Would he have dared come *here?*

"Mehreen," Darren's voice repeated. "Can you hear me?"

"Yes—yes. Coming to you."

The mobile vibrated once more in Tarik's hand as he moved down the concourse, sultry-eyed women looking down upon him from the walls, sensuous ads for beauty products and leased cars, local hotels and mobile phone plans.

All of it being sold by women. By *sex*.

They have a man on the escalator with you, the message read, the faceless, voiceless reminder that someone was watching. *You'll need to lose him.*

His mind was screaming questions. Who was this? Why were they helping him? *Were* they helping him—or was it all a mirage, a fantasy designed to manipulate him?

Why? And yet he glanced back, saw the man just starting up behind him—felt the phone pulse again. *Turn at the top—follow the corridor to your left. There's a dead zone there.*

And then another message, right on the heels of the one before it. *Time for you to part ways with your friend. Baffle the hounds.*

Someone was guiding the man, Harry realized suddenly, taking in the way Tarik glanced down at the phone in his hand—then directly back at the MI-5 officer at the foot of the escalator. *Someone with access.*

He saw Tarik's hand grasp his companion's shoulder, hurried words exchanged between the two—a frown crossing the black man's face. A shake of the head.

He couldn't hear their words, not over the throbbing roar of the crowd, but he knew what they were saying. Knew he would have to make a choice, knew without hesitation what it would be.

He had to be careful in his pursuit, he thought—visualizing the station's layout in his mind. The surveillance cameras.

The British officer was half-way up now, no longer standing still on the escalator, but pushing his way up.

By the time the watcher had reached the top, Tarik Abdul Muhammad had disappeared down the corridor, and the black man was hurrying farther along the concourse, nearly lost among the crowd as the officer spoke into a barely visible earpiece, no doubt talking to his superiors.

Harry smiled grimly as the Brit hesitated, then quickened his pace.

A few moments passed, and then he moved down the corridor after Tarik. *Primary target.*

Darren gave her an odd look as she opened the passenger door of the BMW and slid in. "Are you okay, Mehreen? You look as if you've seen a ghost."

No. She had seen him, she knew she had. But too much was at stake here. Everything, in fact. "I'm fine," she replied, lying through her teeth. "It's just been a long time since I was in the field—maybe too long. What's our status on Tarik?"

"Saunders is still on him."

1:55 P.M.
The surveillance van

"I don't see him," Thomas observed, leaning over Norris' shoulder to look at the screens. "Just the African—not Tarik."

It was at that moment that a curse filled his earpiece. From the officer they called Saunders. "I've lost him—he must have separated from al-Qawi somewhere in the crowd."

Norris swore, his eyes flickering over the monitors above him, typing in commands to bring up more coverage. "Stay on al-Qawi, Saunders—he might be our last lead. All teams, our target is in the wind. I say again, our target is in the wind."

1:59 P.M.
Leeds City Station

There are two more teams waiting for you outside, the message read as Tarik hurried down the concourse past Sainsbury's toward the Aire Street entrance, moving as quickly as he could without attracting attention. *You'll need to avoid them.*

He almost stopped short before a second message pulsed onto the phone's screen. *Take the service door to the right. It's a dead end—but the second locker has a change of clothing. Do it now.*

9:02 A.M. Eastern Time
CIA Headquarters
Langley, Virginia

"Gentlemen, what do you have for me?" Kranemeyer looked up to see David Lay enter the conference room, shutting the door behind him. Out beyond the sound-proofed glass, they could see the nerve center of the Clandestine Service, the banks of screens lining the walls. Analysts hurrying by, folders in their hands.

"Good afternoon, David," Kranemeyer greeted, leaning over to grip the DCIA's hand. "Thanks for coming down."

Lay had lost weight during his leave of absence from the Agency, he thought leaving the man looking ten years older. Gaunt and weary.

"This about the Korsakov transfers?" Lay asked, glancing pointedly down the conference table at Ron Carter.

"It is," Kranemeyer replied. "We've traced the recipient of at least some of the funds. I asked Ron to step in and bring us up to speed. Ron?"

Taking a remote off the table, the analyst rose as Lay took his seat. "It took us most of the day just to get past the anonymizer they were using, but we finally traced the transaction itself to a user IP in West Sussex, the United Kingdom. As for the recipient, well part of the money ended up in Singapore. In an account under the name of Sean Blackburn."

He gave the men a look as if he expected to see recognition in their faces. *None.* "Blackburn was a known alias," he continued, aiming his remote at the TV screen on the wall, "for this man. Stephen Flaharty, former UK citizen. Current—or at least as of last intelligence—arms dealer. Former terrorist, went independent after the Provos decommissioned in '05. By that time, we had recruited him."

"He's one of ours?" Lay asked, looking at the picture displayed on-screen.

"Was," Kranemeyer interjected quietly. "Continue, Ron."

Carter looked from one director to the other. "Right. Well, as has been stated, Flaharty was an on-again, off-again CIA asset from '03 to '12, when a covert team from the Special Activities Division intercepted an arms shipment that was destined for Malian rebels. We realized a bit late—*late* as in, after the convoy was smoldering wreckage—that the weapons had belonged to Flaharty. He wasn't amused. Made contact, demanded that we compensate him for his losses."

Lay nodded, realization spreading across his face. "Of course, I remember that affair now. Didn't we give him the brush-off?"

"Indeed—and the administration needed new underwear when they found we'd been running a former terrorist as an agent," Carter chuckled. "Instructed us to sever all ties, which was relatively easy to do, considering that Flaharty took off for parts unknown the minute he realized he wasn't getting his money. Hadn't crossed our radar since."

"Until now," the DCIA observed. "And you're suggesting that someone familiar with our protocols may be responsible for this funds transfer to Flaharty. Perhaps trying to reactivate him?"

Carter nodded, glancing over to meet Kranemeyer's eyes. An unspoken message passing between them. "That's exactly what I'm suggesting—the amounts are too exact to be coincidental. Someone was trying to fly under the radar, and they would have done it too if that one account hadn't been flagged. As for someone trying to 're-activate' him. . .you pay me to analyze, not speculate. I can't say, the data just isn't there."

Lay nodded, seeming content with the answer—his gaze still focused on Flaharty's picture. When he spoke, his question took both men by surprise. "Who led the SAD strike team into Mali?"

The analyst paused a half-second too long before recovering. "I don't know, sir—I'd have to find out."

"Please do."

2:05 P.M. Greenwich Mean Time
Leeds City Station
Leeds, England

Someone was moving heaven and earth to get Tarik away from his minders, that much was clear, Harry thought—watching as the Pakistani came back out the service door, a black hoodie jacket pulled over his head.

Access. Planning. *Timing.* They had known Tarik was coming, known he would be followed, known how to get him out.

And judging by the look on his face. . .he hadn't been read in on the program. Which meant they weren't part of the group he had come to Leeds to meet.

You had to have training to pull something off like this. The type of training most people only found two places in life: the military and the intelligence community.

Which meant what, exactly?

He didn't have the answer to that question, so he just stayed behind his target as Tarik headed out through the doors, out onto Aire Street—right past an unarmed bobby at the door.

No surprise. Judging by the way Five was running this op, they wouldn't have read in local Special Branch—let alone the beat cops.

A sound call, but it was in this type of situation that "sound calls" came back to bite you and you had to learn to adjust, make up new rules as you went.

It was something at which bureaucracies did not excel.

There's a black Ford across the street, fifteen meters in front of you, the messages read. *A driver waiting for you. He will get you out of there.*

Somewhere, they were still watching him, Tarik thought—glancing about him as he prepared to cross the street. Wishing that he hadn't sent Nadeem away, sent him to make contact with Rahman at the masjid.

But it would not end here, not this day. He reached the side of the car, saw the man behind the wheel—whispering a quiet prayer as he reached for the handle of the door.

In the end it was too open, he was too exposed, Harry thought—measuring the distance between himself and Tarik as the terrorist disappeared into the interior of the Ford. The *passenger* door—someone had sent a driver to pick up the Pakistani. Another place, another time, his solution would have been simple. Break into another car, hotwire the engine—take up pursuit.

But an open street, filled with pedestrians. A police presence. Cameras.

He just stood there, bile rising in his throat as the door closed, the car shifting into motion, a flash of the license plate before it swung out into traffic. *Alpha. Echo. Zero. Five. Romeo. Yankee. Whiskey.*

And then he saw it, half-hidden between a pair of cars—a dark gray Kawasaki, a helmet hung loosely over the handlebars.

Quickening his pace, he moved across the street toward the motorcycle, never looking back. His walk brisk, confident. You had to look like you belonged, that was the key to remaining undetected. Always.

The Ford was nearly out of sight as he swung a leg over the Kawasaki's saddle, reaching down—fingers searching for the ignition cap.

There. . .

2:18 P.M.

"I want to know how he made me," Mehreen demanded, looking out at the passing traffic. The reports from the station had only gotten worse by the moment.

No sign of Tarik, and with their assets flailing to find him, Saunders had been left on his own to tail al-Qawi. Lost track of him in the crowd—surveillance wasn't a one-man operation. Never had been.

"It happens, Mehreen." Darren's face wasn't giving anything away as the former Royal Marine turned the car down a side street, accelerating as he did so. "You might have slipped up, revealed some tell—even just stared at him too long."

Her eyes flashed as she turned in her seat, looking back across at him. "I know what I'm doing. I worked Belfast, remember?"

"Belfast was a long time ago. We all change." There was no accusation in his tone, just the neutral statement. "I shouldn't have asked that of you, thrown you back out there—not without the time to prepare."

"I was *fine*, Darren," she snapped, swearing in frustration. "I would be the first to know if I couldn't do this anymore. And I would be the first to say it."

He didn't respond, not directly, but she could sense the skepticism, lingering there just beneath the surface. "We'll be at the van in just a few more minutes, can have Norris roll the footage then. It's going to be a long night."

2:59 P.M.
North of Leeds

The driver hadn't said more than five sentences since they had pulled away from the station, Tarik thought, glancing across at the man once again.

He had to be in his late thirties, an almost military bearing to the way he sat there ramrod-straight, his eyes constantly darting to the mirror to check their rear. An Englishman. . .there was no question of it.

"*Why?*" That had been his first question upon getting in the car, facing his driver for the first time. "*Why should I go with you?*"

There had been a long pause before the man responded, not a trace of emotion on his face. "*We can deliver you to Five as easily as we got you away from them.*"

It was a hard statement to challenge. Tarik took a deep breath, calm washing over him as the car rolled north. There was no changing the will of God, immutable as it had been from the foundations of the earth.

What will be—will be. . .

3:09 P.M.

Wind swept past his head as Harry leaned into a curve, guiding the Kawasaki up the road, the 118-horsepower engine throbbing beneath him. It was a powerful bike, he would give it that much. Powerful enough to have overtaken the dark Ford, had that been his objective.

But that wasn't in the cards—couldn't be, given the circumstances. You never tried a surveillance op with one vehicle the way they so often did it in the movies, it just wasn't done.

Three cars—that was a minimum. Even that was risky, going up against someone with training.

And the driver of the Ford had training, of that much he was certain. He'd been running the long leg of a surveillance detection route ever since picking up Tarik. That was the type of training you didn't pick up just anywhere, not even in the military.

It only served to further his caution as the Kawasaki thundered out into the English countryside. He was treading on a tightrope out here.

Don't look down. . .

5:37 P.M.
The moor
North Rigton, England

It was a strange feeling, walking to one's death. Tarik stepped out of the car—the door swinging shut under his hand.

He'd felt it first as a teenager, only days after his capture by the Americans.

Being marched down a long corridor—or that's what it had felt like—a hood over his head, arms shackled behind his back. But back then, he had not known this peace. Only sheer terror.

A smile crossed his lips as he looked up toward the rough outcropping of rock known among the locals as Almscliffe Crag. *His destination.*

And they'd called *him* a terrorist.

The sun was already fading in the western sky as he walked away from the road, its fading rays casting long shadows across the moor.

He didn't spare a glance backward at his driver. . .he had seen that look in the Englishman's eyes. That look of barely veiled hatred—an attack dog straining at his leash.

He was somewhere there behind him—perhaps with a gun trained on his back.

No matter.

5:53 P.M.

The crag. That had to be his destination, Harry thought, watching the moving figure from afar, the man walking out across the moor.

He'd hidden the Kawasaki a few hundred meters back—off the road in a rain-washed gully just out of the village, sheltered from view of the road by bushes.

Reaching into the pocket of his jacket, he pulled out a compact pair of binoculars, squinting as he adjusted them to his eye. Focusing on the Pakistani.

And it was *there*. A moment of blinding clarity and he could see it—a firing reticle holding steady on Tarik's head, just above the ear. His finger gently curving back, the hair trigger breaking beneath the pressure.

Not this time.

When he lowered the binoculars, his hands were trembling uncontrollably. The memories flooding back, the lust for revenge so strong he could taste it.

He collapsed behind the wall of old fieldstone, leaning back against rocks worn smooth by the wind, the rain—the passage of time.

Control. He closed his eyes, fighting against the sensation. Had to stay in control. Or it was going to kill him.

He rose up once again, leaning forward against the stone—glassing the top of the crag with the binoculars, jagged rocks glowing in the light of the setting sun—jutting out from the surrounding terrain like some sort of pagan memorial from a bygone age. Old as time itself.

There. He caught movement, something there among the rocks. The figure of a man, silhouetted against the sky for so brief a moment, he might have thought he had imagined it.

But he hadn't, he knew that. Someone was up there, someone that Tarik was going to meet.

Naked ground, he realized—looking out over the moor between his position and the wooded path that led toward the summit of the crag. Nearly two hundred meters of open terrain, not so much as a rock for cover.

Time to get moving.

6:05 P.M.

It felt like home. Tarik pulled himself up on the rocks, for a moment envisioning himself back in the mountains of his native Pakistan. The land of his birth. Of his love.

The land he had abandoned. . .to walk among this house of war.

He looked out over the moor, the English countryside spreading out before him—the village through which they had passed off in the distance, a farm across the road.

He felt eyes on the back of his head and turned to find a man just standing there. Watching him.

There was nothing remarkable about the man, nothing imposing. He couldn't have been more than 5' 8", his form cloaked in a long overcoat. Late fifties, perhaps slightly older.

Brown eyes smiling from a face that could have only been described as placid.

He walked quietly out to join Tarik on the edge of the rocks, gazing westward into the setting sun.

"A few ground rules," he said finally, breaking the silence. "When we are done, you are free to leave, should you wish to do so. We need never speak again. But don't think of playing me. My bodyguards are within the sound of my voice. . .and your driver?"

He gestured down to the moors below. "He's down there—with a sniper rifle aimed at your chest."

Despite his external calm, Tarik felt a chill run through his body. "Who are you?"

The man turned toward him. Smiled, the quiet, confident smile of a man who knew exactly what he was about to do.

"My name is Arthur Colville, and I believe we can be of help to each other. You have something I want, and I have something you need."

Chapter 6

6:19 P.M.

The gathering twilight was Harry's only cover as he worked his way across the moorland, his tall frame bent nearly double.

He knew there'd been at least one man at the top of the crag with Tarik Abdul Muhammad. One man—and possibly more.

The driver.

The half-frozen muck of the moor came rushing up to meet him as he threw himself flat, cursing himself for the oversight.

Tarik's driver was out there, somewhere in the darkness. He'd known that. How could he have been so *stupid?*

He lay there in the mud, eyes searching the growing darkness as he looked back toward the road—the lights of a farm glowing in the distance. *Nothing.*

All it would take was one good man with a rifle, he thought, rolling over on his side—feeling the bulge of the Sig-Sauer beneath his arm. A single shot.

He had made such a good target.

And still nothing—no gunshots. No shouts of alarm. But he'd allowed emotion to blind him, allowed himself to forget a threat he'd known all too well.

Walk away, a voice inside admonished him, the voice of caution. Of reason. *Turn back.*

He rolled up onto his elbow, glancing back along the path by which he had come, footprints in the slush.

Shook his head and began to pull himself forward by his elbows. It was farther back than forward to the treeline. Not that turning back had ever been an option anyway.

Not for him.

6:25 P.M.

"You know what I'm saying to be true," Colville continued, his voice lowering as he circled Tarik. "You see it all around you, in the faces of your own people. They are becoming complacent. Adapting, assimilating more by the day. You still try to rally the youth with your stories of Afghanistan, of Syria—of faraway Muslims butchered by the Western 'imperialists,' but those tales of atrocity grow more stale by the day."

He paused, meeting the Pakistani's eyes. "When the last Americans leave Afghanistan—when the Taliban retakes power in Kabul—when the Ayatollah dictates terms to his puppet government in Baghdad. . .how will you rally your people *then?*"

It was a long moment before Tarik responded, knowing that the words the Englishman spoke were the truth. He *had* seen it, both in the United States and here. Apostasy. . .

"The Lord of worlds will show us the way, as He has ever in the past," he replied evenly. "The faithful will not desert His struggle."

"Struggle?" Colville demanded, a derisive edge to his tone as he began to circle the top of the rock once more. "You think your 'struggle,' your faith, can compete against the allure of the West—all the ads promising fame, power? Wealth? The temptation of an English tart in a short skirt?"

Tarik turned to face him. "And why is it that you care what becomes of my faith?"

The English publisher shook his head. "I don't. The devil with you and your Prophet, for all I care. But you see. . .I have a similar problem."

6:27 P.M.

Voices. Faint and indistinct above him. Harry raised himself up from behind the boulder, glancing up the rocky face of Almscliffe.

There was one easy path up the side nearly to the top, but they would be watching that one—if they possessed half the professionalism they had displayed at the station.

He glanced back down toward the abandoned car there by the side of the road, his eyes once more scanning the darkness for any sign of the driver.

Still nothing. His eyes returned to the cliff, looking for handholds among the rocks. A way up. . .

There was something there. *Movement.* Conor Hale wrapped his hand around the scarred walnut stock of the L42A1 sniper rifle, his eye adjusting to the scope as he lay there, looking across the road toward the crag.

The rifle had been British Army issue up until the mid-'80s, back in the days when his father had carried one into Northern Ireland. Long time gone.

The face of the crag was picked out in stark relief in the night-vision scope he had mounted onto the old rifle, every rock visible. Every shadow. Could it have been his imagination?

He would have happily shot the Pakistani in the back as he crossed the field, Hale thought. He'd seen his kind before, fought against them in Afghanistan. Saw what they did to their own, let alone those they counted *khaffir*. Infidels.

To trust him was folly, despite Colville's assurance that he had no intention of doing anything of the kind.

There.

He sucked his breath in, a low sound in the stillness. There it was, a man's forearm stretched out along the rock face, as though to pull himself up.

And then a head, the profile of a face—a beard masking his features.

Who? Had their information been flawed? Had the Security Service managed to follow them out here?

The questions shot through his mind in the split-second before he rejected them angrily. It didn't matter.

All that mattered was what was to be done. He took his eyes off the scope, reaching for the mobile phone in his breast pocket.

6:31 P.M.

"England has gone soft," Colville said, gazing out through the darkness toward the few, flickering lights of North Rigton. The last faint rays of the sun were slipping beyond the horizon—the stars emerging in the sky above them. "We were a proud people once. The sun never set on the Union Jack and an Englishman bowed his knee only to his Queen and his God. Now?"

He shook his head. "The leaders of this country take their marching orders from Brussels, bow down before every sodding immigrant that washes ashore. Grovel in the dirt for fear of offending them or their precious beliefs, styling themselves 'multiculturalist' in so doing. They need to be shocked from their comforts—awakened to the danger of what they have embraced."

The hatred in the man's voice was so clear, so *real*, that it was all Tarik could do not to react. The embodiment of everything to be despised of the West. And yet. . .

"And this is what you would have me do? Provide your 'shock'?"

The Englishman nodded, his face sober in the darkness. It was impossible to doubt his sincerity, mad as it seemed. Was this it—the path pre-ordained of Allah—the answer he had sought?

"You would ask me to *use* my people to provide ammunition for your newspaper? For all the rest of the Zionist propaganda coming out of the media?"

"Not *just* that," Colville replied, shaking his head impatiently. "What I am offering us is a chance at destiny. We both know all too—"

Whatever he had been about to say was lost as one of the publisher's bodyguards called out, appearing for the first time from around a tall chimney of rock. There was a mobile phone extended in his left hand. . .and a drawn Beretta in his right.

"What are you playing at?" Colville demanded, gesturing for Tarik to remain where he was.

The Pakistani took a step back, but he could see the surprise in the Englishman's eyes. If this was a trap, it wasn't the way they had planned it.

"It's Conor," the bodyguard explained, barely glancing at Tarik as he handed the phone over. "We've got company."

Colville took the phone, his eyes meeting Tarik's as he listened for the space of a few moments. When he spoke, his voice seemed to tremble with emotion.

"Take the shot."

6:35 P.M.

He reached up, his fingers finding no purchase on the stone. His body weight shifting as he reached over, clawing for another handhold.

It saved his life.

The bullet came in over Harry's shoulder, smashing into the stone where his head had been only seconds before, blasting rock outward into his face.

He felt his fingers give way, felt himself falling—backward off the rock.

The impact pummeled the air from his lungs, his left leg twisting underneath him as he slammed into the hard ground. *Shock.*

It felt as if he were in a daze, the world seeming to shift around him. He could hear voices—shouts from above.

They were coming.

He rolled over onto his stomach, biting his tongue to keep from crying out as another stab of pain shot through his ankle. It didn't feel like a break, perhaps a sprain—but none of that was going to matter in a few minutes.

Not once they had his location.

Wincing as he began to put pressure on the ankle, he pulled himself behind a nearby boulder, leaning up against it. Keeping himself low as a second bullet whined overhead.

They'd keep the sniper in place, using him to provide suppressing fire while the people on the top of the crag moved in for the kill.

It's what he would have done.

And he hadn't a prayer of taking on the sniper himself—not even if he'd been completely mobile, he thought, digging the Sig-Sauer from its holster within his jacket.

A single pistol—a pair of magazines. Twenty-seven rounds. Little enough. . .

6:38 P.M.

Impossible to tell whether his target was dead, Hale thought, his left hand thrust out past the small sandbag as his cheek pressed against the rifle's buttstock.

The target had *fallen*, but that wasn't the same as a kill. Or even a hit.

He'd seen a friend make that mistake once. Iraq, his days before the Regiment. They'd kicked in a door in a small Iraqi village near Basra, his partner had moved inside—shot a *hajji* once and the man had gone down. *Next target.*

It had fallen to Hale, coming through the door behind him, to shoot the man again as he came back to life, a pistol in his hand.

"Murphy, get the principal out of there," he barked into his phone, never taking his eyes off the scope.

Protecting Colville—that took priority, getting him out of the area. Then, "Booth—I need you down in those rocks. Find him!"

He could walk, Harry determined, gritting his teeth against the pain. It wasn't a break, but he could feel the swelling—the flesh of the ankle already warm and inflamed.

Blood dripped into his eye from a gash on his forehead and he grimaced, reaching up to wipe it away. *Any moment now.*

They wouldn't be sure whether he had been hit—perhaps even killed—and he was counting on that uncertainty.

It was just about all he had.

And there was a noise, the sound of a foot kicking against a stone. Above him, maybe fifteen feet to the front. *Close.*

Moving silently through rocks in the dark was a feat few ever mastered, and the man stalking him clearly wasn't one of them.

Balancing himself against the boulder, Harry leaned forward, the Sig coming up in both hands, the tritium of the nightsights glowing before his eyes.

Three dots, all in a row.

Off in the distance, he heard a car door slam shut—his head turning toward the sound for but a moment.

A fatal reflex.

The sharp report of a pistol filled the night, a round ricocheting off the rocks near his hand.

He glimpsed a dark figure among the rocks maybe eight feet away as he hurled himself to the side, squeezing the Sig's trigger as he went down. Once, twice—the shots going wild into the night.

Close enough to make the man take cover.

The stones cut and scraped his outflung hand, but he ignored the pain, moving back into the shadows of the overhanging crag—straining to listen for movement, for anything that might offer him a clue to his opponent's position.

Their position, he corrected himself, only too aware that there might be more than one.

6:41 P.M.

"Who was it?" Colville demanded, turning on Tarik almost as soon as the doors of the Suburban had closed on them. "*Who* did you bring with you?"

The Pakistani's eyes blazed, gesturing up toward the driver. "No one—how could I have? Your man was with me all the way here."

It was impossible to tell whether they believed him or not. Even more impossible to know who it could have been. The Englishman glanced back through the tinted windows, swearing under his breath as gunshots rang out over the moor. Three shots, almost all together. Then silence.

"We need to get back to Leeds."

They had his position, Harry thought, listening as another heavy rifle bullet smashed into the rock above, shards of millstone showering down upon him.

He glanced down at the glowing screen of the mobile in his hand, the number he had tapped into the small keypad: *999.*

It was the emergency call number for the United Kingdom, their equivalent of *911.*

His finger moved to press *Send*, but he hesitated. It was one thing to take a life when it was necessary—another to place good men in danger.

The local constables wouldn't be prepared for the type of firepower his opponents had at their disposal. They'd be unarmed, most likely. Little more than targets, in the truth of it.

A distraction. That was all he needed. This couldn't end—not here. Not *now.*

He could have cursed himself for not taking the shot earlier, when he had Tarik in his sights on the train. Could have ended it right there. All of it.

And he pushed the button, raising the phone to his ear as the call began to go out...

6:48 P.M.
A Security Service safehouse
Leeds, England

It was their third time over the tapes, ever since they had secured them from City Station. Three times, no answers.

"He pulls out the mobile phone right—here," Darren said, pausing the feed as he indicated the spot on the screen with his index finger. "Doesn't answer it, but you can see the mobile's screen is lit up. And right here, as he exits the coach. . .he's typing."

He glanced over at Mehreen. "Can you get a request to your contact over at GCHQ—have him pull instant messaging data from around the area of the station at these timestamps?"

"Already done," she replied, nodding. "It's going to be in the thousands."

6:52 P.M.

"Negative," Hale whispered, the scope's reticle dancing over the face of the crag as he swiveled the rifle's position on the sandbag. "I've lost him."

"So have I," the response came back, punctuated by a string of curses. He could hear the nerves in the man's voice, feel the fear.

Their target was armed, and still mobile. It had been a long time since Iraq for all of them—security contracting only did so much to help you keep your edge.

"Well, he didn't just bloody well evaporate, Booth," the former SAS sergeant exclaimed in frustration. "Keep looking."

So much rode on this. *On the spin of the wheel.*

6:55 P.M.

Harry leaned back against the rocks, his eyes closed as he strained to pick up the slightest noise. The voices.

They weren't Arabs, not that he could tell. The accents sounded British, although that could have meant most anything, these days. And their radio discipline could have been better.

He'd panicked the North Yorkshire dispatcher—or maybe the reverberation of gunshots punctuating the call had accomplished that.

But the cavalry had yet to arrive. What was the old saying talk show hosts back in the States liked to repeat? *When you only have seconds. . .the police are only minutes away.*

Yeah, that was it. He shifted his weight, moving farther back into the shadows, wincing at the pain from his ankle.

It reminded him of the last week of Jump School, so many years before. He'd sprained an ankle then, a parachute landing fall that had been less than perfectly executed.

He'd gutted it out, kept moving—kept pushing. Right up to the end of the week—the plane back to Virginia.

He'd also been younger then, he reminded himself, ejecting the half-empty magazine from the Sig-Sauer. A *lot* younger.

And then he heard it, the wail of sirens from back off toward North Rigton— blue and white lights flashing through the darkness as a pair of white police cars came hurtling up the road.

He slipped the full mag from his pocket and rammed it into the butt of the gun, briefly brass-checking the Sig's chamber. *Loaded.*

It was time.

Hale lifted his eyes off the scope the moment he heard the sirens, a curse exploding from his lips. "You need to stop arsing about and get out of there, mate. *Now.*"

"Roger that." He saw the police cars as they pulled up abreast of the crag, the yellow-and-blue checkered paint scheme looking odd in the lens of his night-vision scope. They were between him and Booth.

The ex-sergeant brought the L42A1 up off the sandbag, reaching over for the weapons bag stretched out on the ground beside him. He could hear voices from the roadway, the shouts back and forth as constables piled out of their cars.

Perhaps they were armed, perhaps they weren't. No matter—he wasn't going to lift a hand against them. Not tonight.

He had just finished zipping up the soft case when he heard it. Two more pistol shots, crashing across the moor. Followed by a third.

"Booth?" he demanded, keying his headset. "Have you gotten clear?"

Silence. . .

7:01 P.M.

Harry just stood there, looking at the back of the man's head as he swayed, his knees giving way beneath him. Collapsing to the ground, face-down on the rocky ground.

He'd been facing away, Harry thought, the Sig-Sauer still drawn in his hand as he limped forward. And he had put three shots into the man's back—the first two between the shoulderblades, the final one into the base of the neck.

Mozambique Drill.

It hadn't been a fair fight, but he hadn't intended it to be. Honor was something for another era, a nobler time.

There was a Bluetooth headset in the man's ear, Harry noted, casting a glance down the slope toward the police vehicles. The gunshots would make the constables cautious, slow them down. But he still had only moments.

He reached down, gripped the dying man by the shoulder—rolling him over until he was looking up into the night sky.

Wide eyes gaping up into his.

Eyes he *remembered*. It felt as if someone had punched him in the stomach, the look on the young man's face transporting him back across the years.

To Iraq. To Basra. The years of the insurgency.

A squad of British Paras they'd worked with, a young, camouflage-painted face staring back at him across the troop compartment of a Blackhawk.

The same face he saw now, blood gurgling from between his lips—his body convulsing in the final throes of death.

No. His face tightened, hardening as he forced himself to focus—his hand moving up to the man's ear to remove the Bluetooth, removing the phone from the pouch on his belt.

There was no wallet in the dead man's pocket, no form of identification. Nothing. A pistol lay a few inches from the man's hand, a compact HK45, the type of sidearm favored by a lot of security types. He scooped it up, along with a holster and magazines from the man's belt.

Favoring his right leg, he staggered to his feet—adjusting the headset to his own ear.

Keying the mike.

Something had happened to Booth, Hale thought, the noise of the shots still echoing in his ears.

He paused, there on the moor—gazing back toward the looming face of Almscliffe Crag. You didn't leave a mate behind.

There was a brief crackle of static as if something was being rubbed across a live microphone and then a voice came over his headset. Cold, emotionless. A voice so familiar, and yet so hard to place. A voice from somewhere in his past.

"Your partner was a good man, but he's dead now. Be careful who you climb into bed with. . .*soldier*."

And then he was gone.

5:38 P.M. Eastern Time
Cypress, Virginia

There were no tire tracks in the slushy snow of the driveway, Kranemeyer observed, pulling his black Suburban over by the side of the country road.

Nothing in or out.

He let the engine idle as he stared down the lane, back toward the old antebellum plantation house known among the locals as Grove Manor.

The place Nichols had once called home, the property left to him by his parents at their death. A once beautiful place that now—as he looked back through the denuded branches of the towering oaks surrounding the house—looked desolate.

He hesitated a moment before reaching forward to switch off the ignition key, replacing it in the pocket of his trench coat. Pushing open the door of the Suburban, stepping out into the snow.

He knew what he'd find. . .had known ever since Carter had walked into his office with the report on the Korsakov account activity. Even before?

Perhaps he had seen it in Nichols' eyes that mid-January day he had asked for his resignation, standing there in the DCIA's office on the seventh floor. Known that he wouldn't give up.

And now. . .Kranemeyer let out a heavy sigh, stalking down the lane toward the house—a lone figure against the fields, the Virginian Piedmont stretching as far as the eye could see. Now the issue was how to handle it.

How to deal with the situation that he feared Nichols was creating. Before it blew up in all their faces.

There weren't any footprints around the house either—no light glowing from the windows in the gathering dusk of the evening. The entire place held the look of desertion, almost haunting in its emptiness.

He knocked anyway, the great brass knocker cold even through his gloves. Once, twice.

Nothing.

He turned, his booted prosthesis striking against something there, nearly buried in the snow on the portico.

It was a bag, he realized, grimacing as he stooped to pick it up. Just an opaque plastic bag, the type that zipped shut at the top.

There was paper inside—and he brushed his gloves against the fabric of his trench coat before reaching in. *Church bulletins.*

A smile touched his lips. Nichols had been devout, one of those rare men that lived his faith. Without apology. Without hypocrisy.

There was a note inside the top bulletin, from the pastor. Just a friendly note of concern. Of inquiry. And then his eyes scanned across to the date imprinted at the top of the facing page.

February 8th.

He raised his gaze from the bulletin, staring back down the lane toward the darkened SUV.

Nichols had been gone for a long time.

11:07 P.M. Greenwich Mean Time
A Security Service safehouse
Leeds, England

Mehreen knew something was wrong from the moment she re-entered the safehouse, kicking the door shut behind her—a tray full of cups of coffee filling her hands.

The mood of frustration that had characterized the team when she'd left on the coffee run had been supplanted. . .by one far darker. More somber.

"What's going on?"

Darren looked up from the head of the old wooden table, its surface pocked and scarred, discolored from cigarette burns that had to have dated back to the '70s.

He leaned forward, tenting his fingers as he looked across at Norris. "Four hours ago, North Yorkshire constables responded to a 999 call out in the countryside west of the village of North Rigton. Shots fired."

She swore, setting down the tray on the table. "Tarik Abdul Muhammad?"

"We don't know," Norris responded, seeming agitated. "The caller didn't identify himself—his voice was largely obscured by the gunshots. The dispatcher, a disabled Gulf War veteran, reported that it sounded like a quote, 'sodding firefight,' unquote. The responding constables found a bunch of empty brass and one John Doe, dead on arrival."

Darren shoved a glossy photo down the table toward her. "This man. He was shot three times in the back—9mm hollowpoints. Never had a chance. No identification on him, no weapon, though GSR was found on his hands."

Gunshot residue.

The photo had been taken in a morgue, that much was clear, the man's body lying on a cold white table—his eyes closed in death. His hair was cropped short, his face clean-shaven, his body lean and muscled. Naked under the harsh lights. "Any leads on his identity?"

"Just this," the former Marine replied, handing over another photo—this one taken close-in, of lettering tattooed on the man's bicep.

It took her a moment to make out the words—a half-second more to remember *why* she knew them. "*Utrinque Paratus*," she breathed, "Ready for anything."

Darren nodded. "The motto of the Parachute Regiment."

"I know," she replied impatiently, staring down at the lettering. At the body of fallen soldier. "Nick had a tattoo just like it."

Roth's gaze seemed to soften, and he reached for the photo. "We've forwarded everything to Thames House—have them run it against their databases. Speaking of which. . ."

He gestured toward Norris. "Simon found something on the station footage."

"Something else?" she asked, glancing between the two men. "We'd been over those tapes again and again."

Darren nodded. "It was on the sixth run-through. Throw it up on the screens, Simon."

The analyst typed a command into his laptop and a series of frame grabs came up on the screen on the far wall. "Look at this," he said. "Here. Here. Here. . .and here."

"What am I looking at?" she asked. She was tired, they all were—the fatigue getting to her.

"Right here, this man—almost on the edge of the screen in each grab," Norris said, indicating the area with his finger. "He's always just *there*. As if he was shadowing us while we shadowed Tarik."

Nichols. She found herself fighting to control her expression, all weariness gone in that moment. Hoping they hadn't seen the first flash of reaction. "Are you sure?"

The analyst nodded. "He's in too many frames for it to be a coincidence—and he seems to have training. Never once looks into a camera, that I could tell. As if he knew exactly where they were."

He had, Mehreen thought, her mind flickering back to the look on Harry's face in the park. The dead-ground map she had given him.

He'd played her—played them all. She picked up the photo once again, looking into the sightless eyes of the man lying there in the morgue. A growing fear gnawing at her heart.

That her information had been responsible for the death of a British soldier.

Chapter 7

12:01 A.M., March 26th
A hostel
Leeds, England

Sleep. It didn't come easy on nights like this. All of the years, all of the loss. All of the *killing*.

One would think that eventually it would all become easier. But it never did, Harry realized, rolling over on his back.

Not with the face of the young Para staring back at him every time he closed his eyes.

He couldn't remember the kid's name—had likely never known it. All he knew was that their paths had crossed during a mission in Iraq. . .and a vicious Fate had brought them back together on that moor nearly a decade later.

He knew what it was that had led *him* there—but what about the former paratrooper? It was an impossible question to answer, and equally haunting. It had been a justified kill, he knew that, but it was hard to process that reality when the nights grew dark.

He was still dressed, only his boots removed—an ice pack wrapping his swollen ankle. His Sig-Sauer was in the jacket under his head, the stolen HK45C tucked securely beneath his shirt. He'd already been over the dead soldier's phone twice, for all the good it had done him. It was a burner. Cheap, disposable. Only two numbers in the call history—one of them the number belonging to the sniper, no doubt itself a burner.

The second one. . .he recognized. And perhaps that was what kept him awake.

A hostel made up for in anonymity what it lacked in privacy—he'd known that for years, experience garnered from the times he'd run ops for the Agency in Europe.

And it lacked *everything* in privacy, he thought, glancing over to see bodies moving in the bed just across from him. A woman's soft moans coming from beneath the sheets.

Okay. . .that wasn't going to make sleep any easier.

5:34 A.M.
Colville's country estate
The Eastern Midlands

It was the type of place that had once been associated with the landed nobility, Hale thought, slipping off his boots in the mudroom.

The type of place that England's old blood could no longer afford to maintain, the global recession wiping out fortunes—destroying in the space of hours the accumulated wealth of the centuries.

Many of England's old estates had gone to the auction block of Lloyd's, most falling prey to developers, a few being scooped up by England's "new money."

Men like Colville.

The man who served as butler ushered him silently up the curving staircase and into a second-floor study—the last flickering embers of the previous night's fire casting a faint glow across the floor.

"He's dead, isn't he?" the publisher asked, not even glancing up as Hale entered. He sat facing away from the door in an armchair, a housecoat still wrapped around his body. Reading glasses on the stand inches from his hand.

He looked small sitting there, the ex sergeant thought. Small and uncertain, projecting none of his customary assurance.

"He is," Hale replied simply. Booth had been a good man, one of many that had tried to leave the Army after Iraq—only to find that the skillsets prized by the military were almost useless in civilian life, all the entry-level jobs taken by immigrants. By the same bloody Muslims they'd just been fighting.

You couldn't support a family that way, and Booth had had a kid, a little boy. And a wife—common-law, that is.

Hale swore under his breath. He had no idea how he was going to tell her. . .that had always been the padre's job.

How she was going to tell their kid.

"Where's our Pakistani?" he asked, suddenly realizing that he hadn't seen Tarik since the previous night—since Murphy had hustled the two of them away from the crag.

"Take a seat, Conor." Colville gestured with his hand. "He demanded to be taken back to Leeds."

"And you bloody *let* him?" Hale exploded, walking across the study until he could face the publisher. He didn't sit down.

"We couldn't very well keep him against his will," Colville replied quietly, seeming to recover himself. "The way this works—the *only* way it works—is if Tarik Abdul Muhammad is fully invested in the success of the operation. We need him to rally his people, to incite them into a fury—to throw petrol upon the fire we're stoking. He won't do that with a gun to his head."

"My God," Hale breathed, gazing into the fireplace. "This is really happening, isn't it?"

The publisher smiled. "This is history, Conor. History like man hasn't seen it made in decades—no, centuries. The world is being heated in the fire, and soon the time will come to place it upon the anvil. To forge a better world. If not for us, then for our children and the generations to come. Generations of *Englishmen*."

"And if he refuses?"

A shrug. "Then you and your men can, well, 'dispose' of him and we shall find ourselves another. Perhaps not as well-known, not as charismatic, but we'll find someone." He chuckled. "That is our root problem, is it not? Too many bloody Muslims."

Hale didn't laugh. "We have another problem."

"And that would be?" the publisher asked, glancing up.

"The man who took Booth out. . .I recognized his voice when he used Booth's earpiece to communicate with me."

"Who was it?"

The former SAS sergeant shook his head. "I can't place him—don't remember anything beyond his voice. An American, by the inflection. It has to be someone I worked with in the old days. Someone very dangerous. . .most of the people I knew then were."

It was a long moment before Colville spoke again, and when he did, it was to ask the same question Hale had been asking himself for hours.

"Then why is he *here*?"

6:23 A.M.
A small flat
Leeds

There is no God but God, and Muhammad is His Prophet, he repeated quietly, raising his forehead from the mat. *God is great.*

And truly He was, the boy thought. Great and faithful to those who followed

Him—who obeyed His call. Aydin rose to his knees, folding the *musallah* with reverent hands, his fingers tracing over the carefully embroidered mosque lamp at the head of prayer mat.

It was a symbolic reference to the Verse of Light in the Holy Qur'an, the words given to the Prophet. *God doth guide whom He will to His light. . .*

He laid the mat folded in a corner apart from the rest of his personal belongings, glancing back at the now-darkened screen of his computer. The Internet, his one source of solace from the world around him.

His father had threatened to take it away from him when he'd first begun talking of Syria—when he'd stopped partaking of the glass of wine the family shared at the dinner table. *Haram.*

But the disapproval of his family was nothing compared to what he faced at school—the private school that they paid for him to attend, as his father reminded him every evening. The heckling cries of *"Paki"* following him wherever he went. The abundant ignorance that was so characteristic of the *kaffir.*

Democracy. His teacher had called his father in for a meeting a few months before after he'd spoke out passionately in class against the corruption of the political system.

"What is democracy?" He'd demanded, his eyes flashing as he glanced around at his classmates. *"What is it but a system of government for those who believe they know better than that which is revealed unto us by God? For those who wish to shake their fist in the face of the Almighty?"*

He'd been shouted down at that moment as the classroom erupted—one of the footballers shoving him back into his desk, his head striking against the metal.

The teacher had come to pull him out of the scuffle, but he'd been bleeding by then, a gash to his temple which had to be sewn up at the local clinic.

And his father had told him it was all his fault, he remembered bitterly. That it served him right for causing trouble.

Trouble.

He glanced at his mobile before placing it in his schoolbags, checking the time. After school, the imam had promised—after school he was going to introduce him to a man. A very great man, one who had dedicated his life to the cause of Allah.

To His struggle. . .

7:45 A.M.
The MI-5 safehouse
Leeds

"His name was Evan Booth," Norris announced, setting the folder down on the scarred wood of the table. A dead man's face smiled back at them, close-cropped hair capped by a maroon beret. "Formerly Lance Corporal Evan Booth, of the 1st Battalion, Parachute Regiment, Special Forces Support Group. He was twenty-nine."

"The Sporting First," Darren mused, a tight smile creasing his face as he referenced the battalion's nickname. "Ran a lot of ops with those lads in the old days. Good mates, all of them. So what has our Para been up to since leaving Her Majesty's service?"

The analyst shook his head. "Hard to say. There are a lot of gaps in his employment records—doesn't seem to have been able to hold down a job for long."

From across the table, Mehreen could see the former Royal Marine wince. The old, familiar story. So many soldiers, coming home from a war to find that their world had moved on without them.

Lost.

It was half the reason Nick had stayed in, she knew that. Knew deep down that he was more afraid of life out of the military than he was of facing the guns once more.

Until finally it had killed him.

"Any indication of whether he's connected to any of this with Tarik?"

Norris shook his head. "Nothing definitive other than the timing and the fact that Booth's bank account has been. . .healthier of late. Local Special Branch isn't going to give us further access to the investigation without our being able to claim a valid national security threat at stake. And we don't have it."

"Any family?"

"Has a girl in Croydon—she works nights as a waitress. Been together for six years, have a little boy."

There was a long silence before Darren spoke again. "I'll have Thames House send someone over to interview her, see what she knows. Norris, I need you to focus on our stranger at the station—see if there's any camera angles we missed. And be sure to keep all of this from our American cousins."

"Parker's going to know something is going on," Norris observed. "And he's not going to like it."

Darren shot him a look. "He doesn't have to like it. No matter what some gentlemen at Whitehall seem to think. . .we are not America's bloody 51st state."

The analyst smiled, touching fingers to his brow in a mock salute. "Aye, aye."

Mehreen started to rise as Norris left the room, but Darren motioned for her to remain seated.

"We got a message last night—left for us in a dead drop. It was Ismail Besimi. He wants to set up a meet."

Ismail Besimi. The name brought back so many memories. He'd been her imam in the days before she had met Nick, before she had moved from Leeds to London to work for the Security Service.

He'd also been one of the first assets she had recruited after 9/11, as the priorities of Five shifted away from the Irish problem to more immediate threats. Corrupting those you knew from a past life was a peculiarly intimate affair. *Trust*.

"Why are you telling me this?" she asked, looking him in the eye. "I handed off control of Besimi years ago when I got my desk at Thames House. He isn't my responsibility."

Darren nodded. "I know. But this time. . .he asked for you. Personally."

"He used my *name*?" She still had family in Leeds, a brother, his wife, and son—a boy in his late teens. She couldn't believe he would have put them in danger.

"No. He was very discreet—and very clear that he would meet only with you. No one else."

"Then there's no other choice," she responded, rising to her feet. "I'll set up the meet. What are the current communication protocols with Besimi?"

He withdrew a small magnetic case from within his jacket, handing it over. "The deaddrop is in Woodhouse Moor," he said, referencing a small park near the city centre, "the second bench past the old Wellington statue where Moorland Road meets Clarendon. The message is already encoded on the paper within, you'll simply leave it on the underside of the bench. A white horizontal chalk line on the side of the monument itself will signal Besimi that the deaddrop is active."

She took the case from him. *Already encoded*. "You knew I'd agree to this, didn't you?"

Darren shrugged. "Like you said, there's no other choice."

8:01 A.M.
The hostel
Leeds

It was at moments like this that he realized the magnitude of what he had undertaken. Harry counted out the pound notes distractedly, shoving them across the counter at the hostel's manager as he listened to the voices in his earpiece.

If this had been a sanctioned Agency op, he would have had ears on Mehreen's phone 'round the clock, everything analyzed and passed back to him.

Granted, things rarely went that smoothly in the field. Theory, always so much better than practice. But the support network was there.

Now. . .well, he didn't have the capacity to record more than a few minutes of audio at any one time—he was restricted to listening to it live, taking what he could get in the moment.

Which meant that he had no idea what had preceded Mehreen's orders to visit the dead drop in Woodhouse Moor Park, he thought, tucking his wallet back into the pocket of his jacket as he limped toward the door of the hostel, favoring his weak ankle.

He just knew that he was going to need to meet her there.

9:37 A.M.
Thames House
London

"What are you telling me, Darren?" Julian Marsh asked, glancing back toward his desk. The secure phone unit was on speaker, the glass walls of his office soundproofed against any possible listeners.

"I'm telling you that I think you were right, sir," the field officer's voice came back, clearly audible. "I think the Americans are running an op on our soil."

There was a pause, punctuated by a snort of disgust. "They may even have gotten to him at the station—perhaps the man we picked up on our cameras was part of a grab team. A NOC."

Non-official cover. An "illegal," in the community parlance. The director-general ran a hand over his forehead. This all was shades of the Cold War, a reminder of the years when he'd first come to Five.

A junior officer fresh out of Cambridge, one of the prime recruiting fields for the Security Service.

The CIA had developed their own network of assets in the UK back in those days—one of those things that everyone knew and everyone denied.

It was their insurance, agents who would "stay behind" in the event of the Soviet overrun of Europe that everyone had expected to come. But like all good things, it had turned to other designs over the years. Other purposes.

"You think they already have him?" Marsh demanded, gazing out over the Centre. They were stretched so thin. . .but had that been the intention?

"I don't know, sir. All I can state with any certainty is that we *don't.* Almost twenty-four hours now. I'm firewalling off Parker's team from this end of the operation."

That was necessary, but it wasn't going to be good enough. "Are you making any progress on the man at the station?"

It was an impossible question, Marsh knew that. He'd seen the images—the man had done an incredible job of keeping his face off the cameras. The type of job that marked him a professional more clearly than anything else he could have done.

"Negative, sir. We've been looking for more camera angles ever since it went down, something that would give us a face—show us who he is. There's nothing."

10:13 A.M.
An Internet cafe
Leeds

He'd resisted the urge to go anywhere near the mosque, Tarik thought, glancing around the small café. He'd thought of finding a hotel—getting the sleep that his body craved.

But he couldn't have slept if he'd tried. He felt as if he had been taken up into the top of a high mountain, the world spread before him.

His fingers seemed to fly over the grimy, stained keyboard before him, his eyes burning with intensity.

Arthur Colville was no friend, that much he knew. If the bitter hatred glittering in the Englishman's eyes hadn't been sufficient warning, the pages upon pages of blasphemy that came up with a quick Internet search of the publisher's name would have served as proof.

And yet. . .was this the path God was showing him? The path for which he had prayed? *Fate.*

Was this the will of Allah? That the pride of the unbelievers be used against them as a weapon. To bring them down to the dust. Was not this so often His way?

A peace washed over him, the assurance which had been his stay throughout his years in Cuba and it seemed as if the path had been laid open before him. The future, naked and bare.

"*Mashallah,*" he breathed, ignoring a suspicious glance from the overweight, balding man at the computer beside him. *God has willed it.*

And who is truer to his covenant than Allah?

10:59 A.M.
Woodhouse Moor Park
Leeds

She was alone on this one, Mehreen thought, her feet pounding down the tarmac surface of the park path. Just like she had been so many times in Belfast, running agents for Box. They were overcommitted in their efforts to re-establish surveillance on Tarik, leaving her to take care of this on her own.

She'd changed into sweatpants and a light jacket at the safehouse, her dark hair pulled back from her face into a ponytail, snapping back and forth as she jogged. She knew what she looked like—a middle-aged suburban housewife desperately trying to stay in shape.

Just another one of a hundred women on any given morning in Leeds. She crossed the road, moving under the shadow of the trees.

There were mornings when she wished she *was* just another woman. But that wasn't where her life had led her—the decisions she had made, those years ago, now all coming to harvest. *Choices.*

She made the dead drop without incident, the magnetic strip securing the case against the metal framework of the bench.

The statue of Arthur Wellesley, Duke of Wellington, was just across the road—the bronze long ago turned green by the weather, the duke staring out across the park, one hand on his hip.

The Victorian-era statue was defaced now, paint smeared across the pedestal, crudely drawn graffiti.

It struck her that a single chalk line would be hard to make out before she realized that that was exactly the point. *Hiding in plain sight.*

Just a single line. A brush of the hand across the pedestal and she was already moving past it, picking up her pace.

She felt something—a presence. Brought her head up, sucking in a hard breath as she saw Nichols standing there, a few feet in front of her. In her path.

"*You.* How did you—"

That old familiar sad smile creased his face, a wordless acknowledgment of her anger.

"Walk with me, Mehr," he said quietly, turning to walk beside her. He was limping, she noticed, distracted by the sight.

"What happened to you?" The words were out of her mouth before she could recall them, finding herself suddenly unsure whether she wanted the answer to that question.

"I killed a man last night," was the response, confirming her fears. There was not a flicker of emotion in his voice.

Not a trace of regret. It was more a weather report than a confession. "North of here. Out on the moor."

No. She stopped short, turning to look up into his face. "That *man* was a British soldier."

A nod. "I know. Remembered him from the old days. Basra. But he wasn't a soldier any longer."

She didn't know what to make of that statement. Didn't care in that moment. "You were there at the station, weren't you?"

The truth was there, written in his eyes. She went on without waiting for an answer. "You *used* me, Harry—used me to destroy a joint op with the Agency. An op I was running. And now a former Para is dead because of it. For God's sake, Harry. . .he had a family."

"They all have families," he responded, seemingly unmoved. "And you have a mole."

The air around her suddenly seemed to grow colder, a chill prickling at her spine. "What are you trying to say?"

"I didn't destroy Five's operation, Mehr. Someone grabbed Tarik right out from under your nose—someone with *access*. I watched as they guided him right out past your watchers, past all the cameras. Tell me, how did they do that?"

She had no answer for that, nothing but the fear that it was all misdirection. Another attempt to manipulate her. He was so good at that. Always had been.

"I can't trust you," Mehreen responded, starting to move past him. "Not after this."

He reached out, gripping her arm just above the elbow. His eyes boring into hers—only inches away. "You never should have, Mehr. I never asked it of you. But none of that matters now, not in the face of all that's at stake. Not with other players taking a hand."

She met his gaze with her own. "Who? Give me a name, *something*, Harry. Some reason that I should believe you. Because I don't."

"A name?" Harry shook his head. "I don't have a name—I just know that Tarik was taken to meet with someone out on that moor. Someone with access to your people. Someone who would count a former Para among his bodyguards."

He could tell from the look on her face that she wasn't buying it. "I need something to go on. Something solid."

The Para's cellphone was still in his pocket, but he rejected the thought of giving it to her. *Not yet.* "You have it. You have the body."

"The body of a man you *killed!*"

"He's the key to all of this," he responded, not letting go of her arm. "I'm sure of it. And there's something else. The license number of the car that picked up Tarik outside City Station."

"You got it?"

"I followed it. It was a black Ford Fiesta, license number: Alpha. Echo. Zero. Five. Romeo. Yankee. Whiskey."

Harry turned before she could respond, walking away along the path, his tall form disappearing among the trees. He was maybe thirty meters away when he heard a curse escape her lips—then his headset exploded in static, the sudden noise hammering his eardrum.

Too bad, he thought, leaning heavily on his left leg as he gazed back toward the Wellington monument.

Mehreen had destroyed her phone. . .

8:09 A.M. Eastern Time
CIA Headquarters
Langley, Virginia

Ron Carter was already in the elevator when Kranemeyer entered, head down, dark thumbs moving over the keyboard of his phone. He looked the way Carter always looked—like he hadn't slept. More so lately.

Neither man said a word until the doors closed, the elevator shuddering slightly as it begin its ascent.

"What did you find, boss?" the analyst asked, tucking the phone back into the pocket of his jacket.

Kranemeyer shook his head. "Nothing. He wasn't there. Hasn't been there for a very long time."

"Do you think. . ." Carter's voice trailed off as he looked over at the DCS.

"It's thin," was Kranemeyer's response. And it *was* thin—but they were both used to that. It wasn't like they were trying to convince a jury. "But it's possible. Anything is possible. Particularly when it comes to Nichols."

The analyst swore under his breath. "This is beautiful. Just beautiful. I'll need to brief Lay."

"No," Kranemeyer said, reaching forward and tapping the button to hold the elevator doors closed. He gave Carter a warning look. "You won't."

Carter shook his head. "Look, I liked Harry as much as anyone else here. He was a good guy, but I am not going to lie to the DCIA for him. Or you. I can only stall so much longer on his request for the report on the Mali op. And we both know who led that team."

The analyst wasn't comfortable with any of this, and Kranemeyer knew why. He'd come to the Agency from Air Force intelligence, spent years at the Intel Directorate. Everything handled just so. By the book.

That was all before Kranemeyer had requisitioned his services for the ops side of the house—the Dark Side, as many of the Directorate's desk jockeys called it. All these years, and Carter still wasn't quite at home.

The DCS took a step closer, looking his head analyst in the eye. "Let me make something perfectly clear, Ron. This is my call. You work for *me*. And if I ask you to lie for me. . .you will."

The elevator doors opened.

3:48 P.M. Greenwich Mean Time
The hostel
Leeds, England

He'd come back to the hostel after meeting with Mehreen, stretched out on the bed, his leg propped up on a pillow. It wasn't a bad sprain, by his estimation—and he'd had ample experience with those—but his morning walk had done nothing for the swelling.

Harry looked down at the map spread out on the blankets, eyeing the crude markings he had made in red pencil. It was hard to find a paper map these days, with most people entirely dependent on their GPS.

The hostel was nearly deserted now, most of the tourists out seeing the city. The countryside.

He reached for the Para's mobile lying on the pillow beside him, the number displayed on-screen. The number he knew so well.

We need to meet, he typed, his fingers moving awkwardly over the keypad, punching each key until he had the letter he desired, reviewing the message for a brief moment before pressing SEND.

A minute went by, then two. Three. Four. *Nothing*.

It was a gamble, he knew that. He would only get one chance at this, and then it was gone forever. Mehreen could have done much more with the information on the burner—if she would have. *If*.

He sighed, unable to blame her for her words. She was right, even, but none of that mattered in this moment.

When the mobile pulsed in his hand it almost startled him, catching him off-guard as he slid the screen up to reveal the message. *Can't it wait till the delivery tomorrow nite?*

A delivery. The words sent a chill through his body, the fear that perhaps he had been played all along. It felt as if he had walked out into the middle of an empty room, the ceiling vaulted high above him—danger lurking in every shadow.

No, he tapped back, composing himself. *It's urgent. Tonight, the industrial estate north of the city. Midnight. Come alone.*

Another long wait, the minutes ticking by as he feared he might have lost him. Inadvertently warned him that everything was compromised.

There was no such thing as certainty in this game, you were always taking risks. Realizing that your life served as stakes in the gamble.

When the mobile pulsed again, the message was brief. Three words. *Will be there.*

He fell back against the pillows, wincing at the pain from his ankle, relief washing over him.

The bait had been taken, now all that remained was to spring the trap.

11:43 A.M. Eastern Time
Capitol Hill
Washington, D.C.

There was no such thing as "friendship" in Washington, Coftey mused, moving swiftly down the hall as he left the chamber of the Senate.

The sooner you came to terms with that reality, the longer you'd last. Take too long in the learning of it, you'd get cut off at the knees.

Left to bleed out by the same people who would smile across the table and bow their heads with yours at the prayer breakfast the next week. A game, all of it—played out for the benefit of the biggest audience in the world. The despised group of little people known colloquially as "the electorate."

A staffer moved at his side, hurrying to keep up with the older man—gesturing with the folder in his hand as he spoke.

No doubt something he felt was desperately important, but Coftey barely paid him heed. He was just like all the rest of the interns that came through these halls. Young, idealistic—enamored by their proximity to power, unable to grasp just how unimportant, how expendable they were. *Cannon fodder.*

He nodded to Greg Hunter as they passed, but the freshman senator from Pennsylvania just kept on walking, eyes straight ahead.

Coftey smiled tightly, an expression masking the cold fury within. *Gratitude is the disease of dogs* was a maxim people lived by in the Beltway.

He had *made* Hunter—campaigned hard to help the Pennsylvanian win the rural areas of his state, areas where Coftey's Oklahoma good ol' boy persona trumped that of a slick Philly lawyer any day of the week. And twice at Sunday family dinner.

He'd put him in office in what had been a nail-biter of a race, a victory by the narrowest of margins. And now. . .well, Cahill had gotten to him as well.

It wasn't that Coftey didn't understand the pressures the young senator had been placed under to distance himself.

No one had more connections in the party than Cahill—no one. And with word on the Hill that he was beginning to leverage influential donors against anyone foolish enough to stand with Roy Coftey, the Oklahoma senator was all too aware that his hold on his committee chairmanship was growing ever more tenuous with each passing day.

Oh, he understood the reasons for Hunter's disloyalty, all right. 'Understanding' didn't mean he had slightest inclination to forgive.

Or forget.

Continuing to ignore the staffer, he pulled a phone from his pocket, speed-dialing a number he could have dialed from memory. *So familiar.*

He smiled when a voice came on the other end. A genuine smile this time, his first of the day. "Melody," he began, "I want you to meet me for lunch. Bub and Pop's. I need to see a friendly face."

He listened to her response for a moment, then thrust his keys toward the young staffer. "Make yourself useful for a change, son. Bring the car around."

5:09 P.M. Greenwich Mean Time
The MI-5 safehouse
Leeds, England

The heavy door clicked shut behind her, an ominous sound in the silence, the emptiness of the entry hall. She'd been in dozens of safehouses over the years. . .all of them possessing the same lifeless sterility. You became accustomed to it, learned to ignore your feelings.

But now she could feel the oppression of the place, the chill of the surroundings permeating her very body.

Betrayal. It was a reality every spy had to understand, had to be prepared to experience. Be prepared to *wield.*

But the truth was you were never prepared. Not really. That you were was a lie you told yourself.

Hoping to sleep at night.

Mehreen closed her eyes, leaning back against the door of the safehouse, still struggling to process the events of the morning. She had known what Nichols was planning—had known better than anyone else what he was capable of.

And yet he had still found a way to blindside her, to betray what trust she had placed in him, those many years ago.

Perhaps she had never thought that he would go so far. That some things were sacred.

And she had known better, because that wouldn't have stopped Nick.

You have a mole.

He had said it with such conviction, such certitude, she thought. . .just the way Nichols would have told a lie. And yet.

A black Ford Fiesta. License number Alpha. Echo. Zero. Five. Romeo. Yankee. Whiskey.

The licence plate, perhaps that was the key. If there even was one.

6:49 P.M. Greenwich Mean Time
Leeds, England

"She's going into surgery tomorrow," the voice in his ear protested. "An' they don't know if she's going to come out the other side. I can't bloody well just *leave* her. You understand that."

"We've gone over this, Paul." Hale took a deep breath, accelerating the Nissan out into the next lane of traffic. One of Colville's men had disposed of the Ford the previous night—no sense in taking the chance that it might have been seen leaving the station with Tarik. "What are you going to be able to do for her there? Hold her hand? Pray?"

Silence from the other end of the phone. He hadn't intended the words to sound so mocking—hated pushing an old friend like this, but he didn't have a choice. This was happening. *Now.*

"Look, mate. I'm giving you a chance to hit back at these animals—in a way that makes a *difference*. Now stop arsing about on me, you're either in or you're out."

More silence, then Paul Gordon cleared his throat. "I'm in."

"Good. Then be up here tomorrow—I'll send you an address for the rally point."

Hale switched off his headset, turning off the main road down a side street, south of city centre. *Almost there.*

Gordon's words kept running through his head as he drove, the hesitation he'd heard in the man's voice. He'd told Colville that he trusted his old comrade with his life. . .but was that true?

It had been so many years since the war. So many years, and people changed.

The former SAS sergeant pulled the Nissan over by the sidewalk, glancing up at the buildings on either side of the street. All those years, and still the first thing that ran through his mind in a place like this was "chokepoint."

A grim smile touched his lips. Perhaps not that much changed after all. And Paul was a good mate.

The next moment, the passenger door of the Nissan opened and Tarik Abdul Muhammad slid onto the leather seat.

Hale didn't look at him, just plucked a small black square of fabric from the pocket of his jacket and threw it into his lap. It was a blindfold, the type marketed to suburban housewives with insomnia and often used for "other" purposes.

"Put it on."

8:57 P.M.
An industrial estate
North of Leeds

Harry had arrived early, hiding the motorcycle behind a building deep in the estate. He'd need to ditch it after tonight, should have done so before now but he just hadn't had the chance.

There was a massive truck bay beneath him, the windows of the small office offering a view out over the plant, an enclosed bridge connecting the building to its fellow across the main road.

The window gave him a clear field of fire on the gate, but he didn't have the weaponry to take advantage of that.

Not at hand, he thought, glancing at the pair of handguns he'd laid on the desk. He'd had to leave the Accuracy International in the boot of the car back in London—waiting for a moment that might never come.

No matter. If he came to need it tonight, it would mean things were already gone well beyond redemption.

He picked up the Sig-Sauer, tucking it into its holster as he palmed the compact H&K. When had it all changed? When had his mission turned from one of killing Tarik Abdul Muhammad to one of tracking down. . .whatever this was?

He'd lost sight of his objective, he knew that. But he'd been a soldier for far too long to turn his back on this. A soldier, lost in a war without end.

He brass-checked the H&K, tapping the luminous dial of his watch. *Three hours. . .*

9:03 P.M.
The surveillance van
Leeds

"Rahman's still in there," Thomas observed, turning his eyes from the bank of screens to glance at his companions in the van. "Working late tonight."

The brunette from the previous day had been rotated out, replaced by a gentle-faced, matronly woman in her late forties. He knew her only as "Meg", a name that seemed utterly suited to its owner.

She checked her wristwatch, a look of regret flitting across her face. "My son, Billy. . .his football game was tonight, wanted me to be there. Had to tell him yesterday that I had to work. His da' wasn't able to get off, either."

"Is he a good player?" Thomas asked absently, the headphones encircling his neck.

"One of the best." She smiled. "Or at least I think so. Do you have any children?"

A grin tugged at the corners of his mouth. "Not that I know of."

The grin was gone almost as soon as it appeared, a man's face appearing in his mind's eye. Grim, angry. Reproachful. The face of the FBI's special-agent-in-charge in Vegas. A man whose wife he'd once slept with.

"So it's true what they say about you boys at the Agency, after all? James freakin' Bond. . ."

He'd died ten minutes later, killed as the Las Vegas conference center exploded around him. Leaving behind his once-unfaithful wife and their unborn child.

There were some things you just couldn't take back. She hadn't been the first. Or the last.

He needed a drink, had needed one ever since his phone call with Jimenez that morning. Three days dry this time, and he could almost taste the need, it was so powerful. Thomas refocused his attention on the screens, just in time to see a slight figure walk in from off-camera, moving toward the mosque.

"Look alive, people," he said, gesturing to the second British intelligence officer sharing the van with them. "We have a visitor."

The door handle gave under Aydin's hand and the boy slipped into the darkened entrance of the mosque, kneeling to remove his shoes. He had been to the mosque earlier in the afternoon and received the same answer as the day before: "The *Shaikh* is not here."

There had been a shadow in the imam's eyes when he said it, as though there was something more. Something he wasn't willing to say.

He put his shoes on the rack, padding barefoot deeper into the building.

"Camera 3," Thomas announced softly, bringing it up on the mainscreen as the young Muslim entered the lens, moving along the corridor. He glanced back at Meg. "Make sure you send a screengrab to Thames House, maybe we can get an ID."

The woman just looked at him. "You honestly think he's a courier for Tarik?"

"Could be. I saw a kid no older than him walk up to a patrol near Kandahar," Thomas replied, no emotion visible in his eyes. "He had a vest strapped to his body—took out four soldiers. Three of them went home in caskets, the fourth will never recognize his wife again. So, yes, anything's possible."

He didn't look to see her reaction, his eyes focused once again on the screens as a tall figure emerged suddenly from the shadows of the mosque's corridor, its movements jerky in the camera feed. It seemed to move *at* the teenager, forcing him back against the wall.

"Tell me we have audio on that hall," he demanded, searching through the screens for another camera angle, anything that could tell them what was happening. "We need ears."

There was a pause, then the British intelligence officer shook his head. "Negative."

"Who are you?" the black man demanded, his hand around Aydin's throat as he slammed him back against the wall, towering over him in the darkness.

Munkar, was the thought that went through the boy's mind—glancing up at the intimidating figure, into his dark eyes. *The questioner.*

But he wasn't dead. Not yet.

"I—I—" he whispered, struggling to form the words, get them out past the fingers pressed against his throat.

"Let him go, Nadeem," came a calm voice from behind the black man.

He reeled against the wall, massaging his bruised vocal cords as the man stepped back, revealing the imam standing behind him.

"That's Rahman," the British woman announced, staring through the lens of the surveillance camera as a figure stepped from the shadows, moving forward to place a hand on the boy's shoulder. They could see the man's lips move, but without audio. . .

Thomas swore under his breath. This was the bane of any surveillance operation. You just couldn't have mikes *everywhere* you might need them.

"I am sorry, my son," Rahman continued, looking into the boy's eyes as he squeezed his shoulder. "We are all under a great deal of pressure in these days. You came to ask me about the *Shaikh*, yes?"

Aydin nodded, still rubbing his throat with his hand as he looked past the imam back to where the young black man stood, arms folded across his broad chest.

"It is as I told you earlier—I do not know where he is. No one has spoken with the *Shaikh*, God keep him in safety, since Nadeem parted company with him at City Station yesterday." The imam shot a dark look at his companion and once again it seemed as if there was something they weren't telling him. "I fear he may have been taken by the secret police."

"*Ya Allah.*" Oh, God. A whispered prayer that it might not be so. "No."

Rahman shook his head. "Our times are in Allah's hands—and the *mujahid* must always understand the price which may be required of those who have chosen to follow the green birds."

Green birds. The birds of paradise, in whose bodies the soul of a martyr could find eternal peace.

He glanced up to see the imam regarding him keenly. "We spoke of your dreams, of your devotion to God's struggle. . .but is this a price you are prepared to pay?"

The boy swallowed, feeling his fingers tremble in that moment. "*Insh'allah.*"

As God wills.

9:43 P.M.
The Colville estate
The Midlands

Light. The crackling flames of a fire, the sound of a log shifting in the hearth. Tarik's eyes shone with an unholy fire of their own as he leaned forward over the desk, tracing his finger over the papers laid out before him.

The plan was audacious, that much could not be denied. Almost to the point of madness.

Nearly as ambitious as his own strike against the United States, only months before. A strike which had been years in the planning.

But this. . .

"Do you honestly believe that this can be done?" he asked, glancing across the desk into Arthur Colville's eyes. "What you're envisioning—it would take an army."

The publisher smiled, a quiet, mocking smile. "Where is your faith in your god, '*Shaikh*'? I promise you this, and only this. If you can raise an army, we can arm it."

"*Insh'allah.*" It took everything within him not to respond to the unbeliever's arrogance, but Tarik merely nodded, looking from Colville back across the study to where the ex-soldier stood, his holstered pistol clearly visible on his hip—cold eyes never leaving Tarik's face. "And you're prepared to just stand by and watch this happen."

It seemed as if a look of sadness crossed Colville's face. *Regret.* "I am not a terrorist. The death of the innocent is not something I take pleasure in—unlike you people. But hard choices must be made, and this is necessary. . .it is a sacrifice which must needs be made. For the greater good. For a better world."

"A world in which *my* people have been 'cleansed' from your soil," Tarik spat, his lip curling up in contempt.

"Yes," Colville returned, his eyes narrowing as he leaned forward, knuckles pressed against the hard English walnut of the writing desk only inches away from a snifter of brandy. "In a hundred years, I want a British boy to grow to manhood without ever hearing the name of your child-molesting prophet spoken in the streets of England. *That* is what I want."

Blasphemy. "And you expect me to help you in your endeavor?" the Pakistani demanded, stabbing out a finger in Colville's direction. He saw the soldier flinch, the guard dog responding to a perceived threat to his master—but he didn't draw his weapon.

"I expect you to recognize the inevitable when you see it in front of you." The publisher gestured with his hand. "This cataclysm is coming, regardless of anything you and I might try to do. Two months from now, the year after next, a decade hence—this little island will be plunged into chaos. But, ah, what comes *out* of that chaos. . .now that is not nearly so inevitable. And that is what I am offering to you—to *us*—the chance to take that chaos and use it to forge the world we see in our dreams. The world we believe in. So, are you with me?"

A moment passed, and then Tarik nodded. "Yes."

Colville smiled, picking up the snifter from the desk and raising it, as if it were in a toast.

"Then may the best man win."

11:53 P.M.
The industrial estate
North of Leeds

A light rain had just started to fall as the Ford Explorer pulled up to what had once been the front gates of the industrial estate. One of the chainlink gates was bent and twisted, leaning drunkenly from one remaining hinge—illuminated in the harsh glare of the headlights.

Stephen Flaharty glanced out of the passenger window, gazing critically up at the abandoned structures looming as they did over the vehicle in the night. Dark. Foreboding.

"Are you sure about this?" His bodyguard asked from the driver's seat, his jacket gaped open to reveal his holstered FNX-45.

"Aye, Davey," Flaharty smiled, looking over at his old mate, his greying hair visible beneath the edge of his cap. "Of course I am."

They'd been friends since boyhood, throwing rocks and curses at British riot police in the streets of Belfast. And then they had grown older and traded in the rocks for pistols and pipe bombs. Pipe bombs. . .and car bombs, as Flaharty's talent for explosives had grown with his years.

Davey Malone had always had his back, saved his life more than a few times through the Troubles.

And now he was lying to his friend, Flaharty thought, tapping a message into his phone. *Where are you located?*

Because he wasn't sure about this at all.

He pushed open the passenger door of the SUV, stepping out into the loose gravel. Forcing a smile. "Wish me luck."

"We've always made our own luck, Stephen." Malone reached down, pulling a Remington 870 from beneath his seat and laying the pistol-gripped shotgun across his lap. "Thirty minutes—and then I'm comin' for you."

He took another step from the SUV and the phone buzzed in his hand, droplets of rain splashing against the screen as he opened it to reveal the message. *The building past the loading dock, the office at the top—come across the enclosed bridge.*

A second message, following on the heels of the first. *Lose the jacket.*

He was early. Harry laid down the phone, raising the binoculars once more to his eyes as his target took off the jacket, throwing it back onto the passenger seat of the Explorer. But that would be Flaharty.

The Irishman also hadn't come alone, he thought, marking the thermal bloom of a second man in the driver's seat. Not that he had really expected him to. One didn't get where Flaharty was in life by following other people's rules.

Rules. Everyone had them, things they just didn't do. Boundaries they didn't cross. And whatever gunrunning the Irish arms dealer had done in Africa—across the Middle East. . .Harry would have thought that Flaharty would have found arming homegrown Islamists in the UK to be one of those boundaries.

Up until the moment he had found one of Flaharty's numbers on the phone of the Para he had killed.

Perhaps it *was* all about the money. Perhaps some people did believe in taking a crap where they ate.

Footsteps on the bridge outside and Harry set the binoculars aside, moving back and to the side of the door, the HK45 out and in his right hand.

There had once been glass windows lining either side of the enclosed bridge—but they'd been smashed by vandals long before, jagged shards of glass protruding from the frame. It felt as if he was walking into a trap, Flaharty thought. He glanced out the window back toward the gate, the headlights of the still-running Explorer clearly visible through the specks of rain that had dotted his glasses.

He had seen the look in Malone's eyes. They both knew they weren't as young as they'd once been—knew that if things went pear-shaped, he didn't have a prayer of getting to Flaharty in time.

If only this deal hadn't been so important, if only so much hadn't depended on Booth—he wouldn't have dreamed of coming.

There was a 9mm Kimber Solo inside his waistband, concealed by the loose sweater he wore. He thought about drawing it as he neared the door, then pushed that aside. Whatever awaited him within, the pistol wouldn't be of much use.

Darkness met him as he pushed the door open, moving cautiously inside as his eyes adjusted.

He'd taken barely five steps into the office when he heard a noise from behind him and an oh-so-familiar voice announced, "You don't know just how sorry I am to see you here, Stephen. Keep your hands out where I can see them."

It wasn't Booth...

Chapter 8

12:03 A.M., March 27th
The industrial estate
North of Leeds

"Nichols?" the Irishman demanded, standing there in the middle of the office, his hands raised in the darkness. "What are you doing here, boyo?"

Harry snorted, covering Flaharty with the muzzle of the compact H&K as he moved to close the door. Staying well back, out of reach. "I had in mind to ask you the same thing, but I see you didn't come alone. Thought I made it clear that your invitation didn't read 'plus one', Stephen."

Flaharty shrugged. "So that was from you. I suppose I can assume that Booth is. . ."

"Dead," Harry finished, his face a grim mask. "You should pay closer attention to the news, old son. They found him out on the moor last night. Acute lead poisoning."

"He was a good lad."

"So people keep telling me." He kept the gun up, circling the weapons dealer until he could see Flaharty's face in the dim ambient light coming through the window of the office. "It doesn't explain what he was doing working with the jihadis. Or what your number was doing on his phone."

There was no faking the surprise that washed across the man's countenance. Whatever was going on here, Flaharty was not fully informed. He started to lower his arms. "I have. . .no idea what you are talking about."

"Keep them up," came the peremptory command as Harry gestured with the H&K. "Unless you want your reunion with Booth expedited."

Another shrug, but Flaharty raised his hands—keeping them well away from his sides. "What do you want me to say?"

"I want the truth."

7:09 P.M. Eastern Time
An apartment
Washington, D.C.

He'd crossed the line. That was the reason Nichols had been asked to leave the Agency, Kranemeyer thought, staring out the window of his apartment over the city, the glow from a sea of traffic lighting up the night sky—the towering obelisk of the Washington Monument dimly visible in the distance.

The reason that had been *given*.

Crossed the line. . .and yet where was that line drawn, really? Haskel's face flashed before his eyes and Kranemeyer could see the FBI director there again, laying face-down on the Persian rug in his own house, the room reeking of his own excrement. His eyes pleading for mercy.

Kranemeyer looked down at the shot of bourbon in his hand. Prince Badr would be landing at Dulles within the hour and he was supposed to be preparing for his meeting with the Saudi intelligence chief in the morning. But it was impossible to push this aside.

He had crossed lines of his own, done what was *necessary* to see justice for his men. Only a fool believed that justice and the law were one and the same.

So where did that leave Nichols?

The man had been a formidable operator, a brilliant team leader—easily the equal of anyone Kranemeyer had served with during his years at Delta. A born warrior. And yet he had seen the signs even before Vegas. The cracks appearing like spider veins.

Had it been Hamid Zakiri's betrayal in Jerusalem the previous October? The murder of Davood Sarami at Zakiri's hands?

The revelation that one of their own paramilitary operations officers was in fact an Iranian sleeper had been devastating to all of them, but to none more so than the man who had recruited him: Nichols.

He'd been the target of an internal investigation headed by the CIA's inspector general in the months that followed.

Internal investigation? "Witch hunt" was more apropos—all the members of the NCS strike team had come under scrutiny, but Nichols in particular. And then in the midst of it all had come the assassination attempt on David Lay—on his daughter—and all that had followed.

Nichols had left bodies in his wake. . .on American soil. The type of thing that couldn't have been swept under the rug, no matter how hard they might have tried.

He'd allowed emotion to cloud his judgment, placed innocent lives in jeopardy. An American teenager, dead. Lay's daughter, also dead—killed by a sniper outside the Bellagio on that dark Christmas Eve in Vegas.

And now he was out there—somewhere. Doing *something*.

Kranemeyer shook his head, turning away from the window of the apartment. He knew exactly what Nichols was doing—he was doing what the American government couldn't do. Couldn't bring itself to do.

Taking out the trash on an ally's soil. *Tarik Abdul Muhammad.*

He tossed back the last of his bourbon, releasing a heavy sigh as he placed the shot glass on the granite countertop.

He'd never been a praying man, never believed in anything he couldn't see—but he found himself praying now.

That Nichols would succeed.

12:11 A.M. Greenwich Mean Time
The industrial estate
North of Leeds, England

"I knew something was wrong—I just didn't know what. That's why I had Booth—he'd procured hardware for me before, when I saw him on their crew I knew I had someone I could use. He was my man on the inside. Until you up and shot him in the back."

"Why should I believe you?" Harry demanded, staring across the old metal desk at Flaharty.

He still hadn't lowered his weapon—the Irishman's face clearly visible through the iron sights of the H&K. "Booth said they were nationalist hard-liners or some such bollocks. He was going to have more information for me tomorrow night." He paused. "What do you think I am, bleedin' daft? Getting mixed up with the Muslims?"

Harry shook his head, unconvinced. Searching for an opening, an advantage. Anything he could seize. Exploit. "You've done it before. *Anṣār ad-Dīn* comes readily to mind, I'm sure there were others."

Flaharty favored him with a pained look. "Honestly, Harry? You're going to go and bring up Mali? Sure an' it's not the same thing—not at all. You and your sodding Agency knew I ran guns. . .if it weren't for wogs killing other wogs, there'd be no one to run guns to. It's what keeps men like me in business, so of course I did. Helping them *here*, that's another matter entirely."

"I've seen your Security Service file. You went to Libya in the '80s—the training camps at Zuwarah. Spent over a year there, near as Five could determine. That's a good long time."

"A good long time," the Irishman repeated, anger playing across his face. Real or feigned, it was hard to tell. "The longest year of my life—not a single drop a' liquor in the bloody place. Davey and I got back to Belfast after our training was over and hit the pubs so hard. . .I don't even remember the following day. Or the day after that."

David Malone. He'd been on the Agency's radar for nearly as long as Flaharty, a former PIRA enforcer long suspected in the execution of a pair of British soldiers in Armagh back in the early '90s. The two of them had been nearly inseparable.

"Is that who you brought with you?" Harry asked, inclining his head toward the window. Flaharty just looked at him, unanswering—which was answer enough in itself. He wasn't going to have much time.

Moving on. "You spoke of a delivery—tomorrow night. I want to know the when, the where. I want to *be* there."

"No," the Irishman retorted. "Not a chance. You've cost me enough—you're not costing me this deal."

Harry shook his head, not giving an inch. "That wasn't a request. You're going to get me in there, or—"

Flaharty cut him off, gazing at him keenly. "Or *what*? You'll get on the phone back to Langley and tell them one of their old assets is off the reservation? No, because you can't. Because you're farther out of bounds than I am, boyo. So what will you do?"

"Contacting the Agency never crossed my mind," Harry shot back, feeling the emotion rise within him, forcing himself to calm down. He was so close, and yet so far. Had to see this through if he was to stand any chance of success. When he spoke again, his voice was low and even. Calculating. "But what about Malone—the rest of your boys? They know about the work you did for us, back in the day?"

A very real fear spread across the Irishman's face, his voice trembling ever so slightly as he responded, "You wouldn't."

3:31 A.M.
The Masjid-e-Ali
Leeds

"Do you think he's deserted us?"

Rahman looked up to see Nadeem slouched there in the doorway of his study, his dark face almost masked in the early morning shadows.

He had the feeling that neither one of them had slept. He had spoken with confidence to the boy, but it was another thing to *feel* such confidence. And he did not. It would not be the first time the cause of God had found itself betrayed from within, and yet the reputation of the *Shaikh*...

"No," he responded, summoning up all of his strength. "I don't believe that."

"You don't believe it—or you don't want to?" the young man demanded brazenly. It entered Rahman's mind to rebuke him, but he went on without waiting for an answer. "I was there, man. He told me to leave."

"So you said."

"It's the truth, I swear it. He blanked me all the way from London, not so much as a bloody greeting. If he was threatened by the secret police, why didn't he want me to stay at his side? I could have taken 'em."

It might have seemed like a prideful boast, but it was hard not to believe him, Rahman thought, the muscles of the black man's chest and arms prominently displayed by the undershirt he wore.

Word was he had split his time in prison between the gym and the lectures of the visiting imam. Somehow, judging by his irreverence, Rahman doubted that it had been an even split.

And yet the questions he raised were impossible to answer. "He will be returned to us, *insh'allah*."

He turned back to his books, a tacit dismissal—but it was at that moment that the cellphone in his pocket rang. *Number Withheld*.

"Hold on," Meg announced, reaching over to grip her sleeping colleague by the shoulder. "Call the safehouse and wake Roth up. Rahman's getting a call."

7:07 A.M.
The MI-5 Safehouse
Leeds

"Shortly after 0300 hours this morning, Rahman's cellphone received a call from a blocked number," Roth announced, looking around the table at the faces of his team.

Most of them already knew that much, it having marked the time they had been roused from sleep. "GCHQ has their people attempting to run the number, but the phone has likely already been disposed of. It's immaterial—we got the voice-match. It was Tarik Abdul Muhammad."

"Do we know what was said?" Norris asked, looking haggard as he glanced up from his notes. Normally a neat dresser, it looked like he had barely had time to shower and throw on a sweater, his brown hair hopelessly mussed.

The American came in at that moment, a half-eaten muffin in his hand, and Darren acknowledged his entrance with a nod. "We were making progress on the translation. . .Mehreen? Do we have a final transcript?"

"The essence of what was being said, yes," she replied, gesturing to the print-out before her. She had been awake even before the call, working on Nichols' plate number. A dead end, as she had suspected from the beginning. Just a stolen car, nothing on the station's CCTV to support Nichols' claim of connection to the *Shaikh*.

She cleared her throat. "It's a rough translation—the best I could do in the time I've had. There are nuances to the Arabic. . ."

"Let's have it."

"They kept the call short, under two minutes. Just the normal greetings at first, and then Tarik tells him, 'The Day of Judgment is approaching.' Rahman responds, something in an undertone that isn't picked up, then demands to know where he has been. His tone. . ." She paused, her brow furrowing. "I don't know quite how to describe it. It's very accusatory, almost challenging his loyalty—as if Tarik has deserted them. That's certainly the way he takes it, responding, 'War can never frighten me to abandon the truth. I am not afraid of death. I will live for Islam and I will die for Islam.'"

Norris snorted, shaking his head. "And the religion of peace strikes again."

That earned him a sharp look from Darren. "Let's keep our focus, people. What is he trying to say, Mehreen?"

"It's actually a quote," she replied. "It's taken from the response of Ali ibn Abi Talib, the fourth of the 'rightly guided' caliphs, to the defiance of the rebel Muawiyah back in the seventh century."

"But what does he mean by using it?"

Mehreen tapped her pen against the sheet. "I think it's an affirmation. Of his loyalty—of his belief that God has chosen him to lead the fight against the West."

The look on Norris' face betrayed his skepticism. "And the 'Day of Judgment'?"

"Theologically, it's a common reference to the apocalypse used by the Prophet in the hadiths and the Qur'an."

Thomas Parker cleared his throat and eyes swiveled toward the American. "Sifting back through signals traffic out of Pakistan from before the Vegas attacks, the NSA picked up several references to a coming 'Day of Judgment.' Or 'Day of Reckoning,' as I believe their translation had it."

"Then an attack is coming," Darren murmured, his face grim. "It's only a question of how soon."

Mehreen nodded. "I concur. And it's an interpretation supported by references which are common among jihadists on the Internet. But coming from someone with the alleged background of Tarik Abdul Muhammad. . ."

The inference was clear to all. This was something to be taken seriously.

"Time to get to work, people," Darren announced, closing his folder of notes as a signal that the conference was over. "I'll run this up the flagpole to Thames House and see if we can secure additional resources."

He motioned for Mehreen and Simon to remain behind as the room emptied, waiting until the door had closed behind the American. "The meet is all set for tonight, correct?"

"It is," Mehreen replied. "I've arranged to meet him at the restaurant at 1900 hours."

"Good." The concern was clearly visible in Darren's eyes. "With these developments, Besimi's intel is going to be more critical than ever."

9:47 A.M.
A warehouse
Blackpool, England

"Are you out of your bleedin' mind? Bringin' him *here*?"

Flaharty pushed his glasses up on his nose. "Don't fret yourself, Davey. I know what I'm doing, as ever."

From the dark look on the big man's face, Flaharty knew he was unconvinced. It was a look he knew all too well—and Malone's skepticism had saved them both more than once over the years. *Not this time.*

He glanced down the length of the warehouse, eyeing Nichols' figure among the crates. "He's not a man I want as an enemy."

Malone snorted, unzipping his jacket to reveal his FNX-45 in its shoulder holster. "That's easily solved."

"Not as easily as you might think," Flaharty warned, placing a hand on the arm of his lieutenant. "And if half of what he has said is true, having him around could be useful in cleaning up the mess."

"And if it isn't?"

A shadow passed across the bombmaker's face. "Then things will have to be. . .*sorted*."

10:49 A.M. Eastern Time
The National Mall
Washington, D.C.

International relations. Kranemeyer grimaced, tucking his hands into the pockets of his windbreaker as he gazed up at the towering columns of the World War II memorial standing stark in the light of the morning sun. A reminder of a simpler time—a better world.

The niceties of diplomacy were not his forte. . .nor his job under ideal circumstances.

The circumstances of the last few months had been anything but ideal.

"Men everywhere walk upright in the sunlight," the man at his side intoned in heavily accented English, reading MacArthur's words chiseled into the granite. "The entire world is quietly at peace."

He paused, dark eyes hidden behind an expensive pair of Raybans as he glanced at Kranemeyer. "And how long did that peace last?"

"It never began, your highness," Kranemeyer responded, turning to look the Saudi intelligence chief in the eye. The man was dressed in Western clothes, as were his bodyguards. Nothing that would attract attention here on the Mall in the mid-morning, despite their relative solitude.

Aside from a few joggers, the Mall was largely deserted. Most public places had been in the months since 12/24, as the media had already started calling the Vegas attacks.

On the other hand, the prince's bespoke suit likely cost as much as Kranemeyer earned in a year, the DCS thought wryly. Just another reminder that the Kingdom had more money than it knew what to do with. Money for fine suits, fast cars, exotic women. . .and the widows of the martyrs. In all the years he'd dealt with Prince Badr, there had never been a suggestion that he was tied to the jihadists—but when it came to the House of Saud, certitude was an impossibility.

"That," Kranemeyer said, gesturing toward the inscription, "well, that was just flowery language from a general who knew better in his own heart."

He turned away from the monument, beckoning for the prince to follow him. "Because any old soldier knows that war never ends. Walk with me."

It wasn't a request.

"You know why I have come to Washington, Mr. Kranemeyer," Prince Badr announced suddenly as they began to walk across the well of the memorial toward the Reflecting Pool, his bodyguards fanned out behind them.

Of course he did—they both did, although they had been carefully avoiding the subject for the past three hours. It was the Arab way. . .and Kranemeyer had spent enough time in the Middle East to know that there was no hurrying it. No more than one could hurry the onset of spring.

"You wished to inquire further regarding the unfortunate death of Prince Yusuf ibn Talib al-Harbi, I believe?" Kranemeyer asked, glancing keenly at his counterpart.

"Indeed."

"Then why are you talking to me, your highness? I believe the police of Monaco might be able to give you more answers than I."

The prince inclined his head, his expression unreadable. "If I shared your belief, I would be in Monaco."

"To the best of my knowledge," Kranemeyer began, measuring his words carefully as he walked, "the prince died of natural causes."

The Saudi intelligence chief stopped stock-still, surprise washing across his swarthy face as he stared at Kranemeyer. "The *prince*," he began—almost spitting the words out, "was shot twice between the eyes."

The DCS shrugged. "Like I said. . .natural causes."

4:01 P.M. Greenwich Mean Time
The MI-5 Safehouse
Leeds

It had been years since she'd worn the hijab, Mehreen thought, looking down at the square piece of black fabric on the counter before her. Her parents would never have been known as fundamentalists, but growing up there had been the cultural pressures and she had begun to cover her hair in her early teens.

Then had come their flight to the UK, and everything once thought certain had been turned upside down. Lives spilled out as they fled the growing influence of the Taliban—the darkness of those who permitted no variance of conscience in the worship of God.

A darkness that had now spread itself over Britain. The island her parents had called "sanctuary."

"I want you to wear a wire," Darren announced, appearing in the doorway just as she finished adjusting the hijab around her face, glancing at her reflection in the mirror. *So many years.* Nick would never have heard of her covering her hair, but so much had died with him. And this was necessary.

"No," she replied firmly, meeting his eyes in the mirror. It wasn't the image of submission that the hijab had been meant to convey. The world she had left behind.

"That wasn't a suggestion."

"I knew it wasn't, and my answer is still 'no.' My recruitment of Besimi was built upon trust—mutual trust. The knowledge that he could speak freely before me and not have his words parsed and re-interpreted by some chair-warming boffin in London."

There was something small in his hand. "I had MacCallum send this up from Thames House. He'll never know you're wearing it."

She looked over at him. "I'll know. Which means he will as well. Look, Darren. . .Besimi was my asset. If you're going to ask me to run him again, we're going to do it my way. Otherwise, you can roll the dice and send in your own officer."

11:03 A.M. Eastern Time
The National Mall
Washington, D.C.

"So you're telling me that you had him killed?" Prince Badr asked, seeming to recover himself as they stood there, looking out across the Reflecting Pool toward the Lincoln Memorial.

Kranemeyer shook his head, only too aware that he was treading on dangerous ground. "Not at all. . .only that there is a certain level of risk that must be accepted when one makes the decision to finance terrorism. I trust you can appreciate the distinction?"

"Mr. Kranemeyer," the prince began, removing his shades for the first time so that Kranemeyer could see his eyes. The eyes of the desert dark. Enigmatic. "The stance of the Kingdom against terrorism could not be more unequivocal, as we have ourselves been victim. We stand with the West in solidarity against religious extremism of all kinds."

"The families of our dead appreciate your empathy," the DCS replied, his words biting, "but when *was* the last time your 'unequivocal stance' ended in you beheading a jihadist in Deerah Square?"

"The Kingdom has," Prince Badr paused, ". . .begun to move away from public beheadings. We prefer the firing squad."

Welcome to the eighteenth century, Kranemeyer thought, but he didn't voice the sentiment. There was only so far he could go in sending this message. "May I speak freely, your highness?"

There was no change in the eyes of the Saudi. "I believe you have been so speaking."

"There's an old saying—I believe it came to this country from Europe. 'If every man swept his own doorstep, the whole world would be clean.' What I am saying is that if the Kingdom does not sweep its own doorstep, it will be swept for them. Swept clean."

4:49 P.M. Greenwich Mean Time
The warehouse
Blackpool, England

There was a beauty to Semtex, Harry thought, molding the plastic explosive between his fingers as Flaharty looked on.

"Well, will it actually work?" the arms dealer asked, glancing at his watch. They were on the clock.

Harry ran his thumb across the top of the "brick", smoothing out the imperfections until even the closest inspection would have revealed nothing out of the ordinary. "Patience. . .we'll know in a moment."

"Patience?" Flaharty swore under his breath. "Patience, boyo, is me not putting a bullet in you for being a royal pain in the arse."

He picked up his phone, looking back toward the flatbed trucks, the crates Flaharty's men were loading aboard them. Pound upon pound of Semtex—along with Heckler & Koch assault rifles, old G3s that had been phased out by European militaries in the years before. They were military surplus now, being sold off to a score of little countries in the developing world. Still dangerous in the right hands—or the wrong ones.

And somehow Flaharty had diverted several hundred of them here.

It was enough weapons and ammunition to start a war. Letting such a shipment reach its buyers, it would have been categorized as "unacceptable risk" back in his days with the Agency.

Now. . .well, now nothing seemed "unacceptable" to him. Not any more. Not if it meant once again locating Carol's killer. *Stopping* him.

"Something you said last night," he began, hesitating ever so slightly. "That I couldn't reach out to Langley—what did you mean?"

The Irishman gazed keenly at him. "I mean you're out, Harry. I suspected it from the first, but I know now. The account of mine you transferred your payment into? Bloody frozen within twenty-four hours. Agency fingerprints all over the place, poking into my business. Costing me money."

The Korsakov accounts, Harry thought, struggling to conceal his surprise. They were flagged. They had to have been. He could have cursed himself for not thinking of it sooner. For taking the chance.

"There's blood in the water," Flaharty continued, "and I'm not doing myself any favors swimming nearby. But we're both low on options right now, aren't we?"

True enough. His phone powered on with a low buzz and he loaded the app, gazing intently at the screen as the tracking beacon came on-line.

There. He managed a grim smile as he turned the screen toward Flaharty. "The tracker's live—we're in play."

5:12 P.M.
Thames House
London

"Do we have a name?" Alec MacCallum demanded, glancing over his shoulder back at one of his analysts.

"Nothing yet—the mobile was purchased as part of a group plan. Hard to pin down exactly who is using it."

"Well, get on it. We need to know who he was talking to." MacCallum looked up to see the director-general standing in the doorway of the operations centre.

"My office," Julian Marsh instructed, turning back without another word.

MacCallum shook his head for a moment, setting down a stack of folders on the nearest workstation before turning to follow the DG. Marsh closed the glass door firmly behind him as he entered, transfixing him with a shrewd glance. "I just came from a meeting with the Home Secretary about PERSEPHONE. She was. . .unamused. Is there something more I should know?"

"There is." The head of analysis took a deep breath. "Rahman wasn't the only person Tarik Abdul Muhammad called. He placed five other phone calls over the same thirty minute window."

"And?" Marsh asked.

"We're working as rapidly as possible to determine the recipients and obtain transcripts of the calls."

The DG nodded. They both knew how this went—you could only move so fast. Some days, it just wasn't fast enough. *Don't let it be* this *day.*

"Put more people on it—anyone you can spare," Marsh responded, moving behind his desk and taking his seat. "Has there been any more progress in determining who contacted Tarik in City Station two days ago?"

"No, there hasn't. Even being able to narrow it down by the timestamps and likely keywords, there were thousands of texts. GCHQ Cheltenham has put their people on it—it's only a matter of time."

"And that," the old spook said, leaning forward on his desk, his fingers tented as if in prayer, "is something we have not a great deal of. The powers that be are in motion."

6:29 P.M.
Sheffield, England

Paul Gordon knew which building it was—Hale's instructions had been quite explicit, but it seemed if the former Para stood on the sidewalk forever staring across the street, his rucksack thrown over his shoulder.

Just looking on.

All those years, all the lives lost. *We're fighting them over there so that we don't have to fight them here.* That had been the bloody mantra of the politicians, every sodding one of them that had urged Britain to war.

And while his brothers had been bleeding and dying in Iraq, those same politicians had been busy giving away their jobs—their homes. Their *birthright*, usurped by immigrants and asylum seekers.

The same animals that had raped Alice.

Hot tears sprang to his eyes at the thought of her and he wiped them away with the back of a rough hand, moving quickly across the street. There was work to be done.

6:43 P.M.
A council tower
London

It seemed as if he had been waiting for this day all his life, the young man thought—staring into the broken mirror that hung over the washbasin.

It had been that way for the two years he had lived there since he had first started attending the university—maybe longer. Nothing got repaired in the council flats these days. . .the money simply wasn't there.

Or so they said. Perhaps it was just another example of the way the West chose to oppress the faithful. Another reality of the house of war. Money intended to help the impoverished, diverted into the pockets of the Jew.

As ever.

He laid aside the scissors, splashing water over his face, his now close-cropped beard.

A noise, footfalls in the corridor outside and he started, his body tense. Rigid, his gaze stealing back toward the small bed, the long knife—more of a machete, really—concealed beneath the mattress.

Another moment, and the footsteps moved on by. *Calm down*, he told himself, reaching for the razor at the side of the washbasin. The hour was coming. It was time to follow the green birds.

Insh'allah.

6:56 P.M.
The warehouse
Blackpool, England

"Flaharty says you're to ride with him in the lead SUV," Malone announced, a Remington shotgun held loosely in one hand as he came up to Harry.

Harry looked up from the cluster of tracking beacons on his phone's screen, into the shadowed face of the older man. "Good."

Malone started to turn away—then paused, as if there was something on his mind.

"Do we have a problem?"

"Of course we do," Flaharty's lieutenant responded, taking a step closer. *Too close*. He wasn't quite as tall as Harry, but heavier-built—a huge hand enclosing the receiver of the Remington as he looked into Harry's eyes.

An intimidating presence, but Harry didn't back up, his jacket open—hand at his side, only inches away from the holstered H&K. "Flaharty is a fool to let you go along on this run. Sod me if we oughtn't take you out there and dump you in the Irish Sea."

And he was right, Harry thought, meeting his gaze evenly. That would be the right operational decision, likely what he would have done if the situation was reversed. And yet there was something more here—something *personal*. "Do we have a history?"

By way of answer, Malone reached down with his left hand, briefly pulling up his sweater to reveal an ugly pockmark on his lower abdomen, the indentation purplish and discolored. *An old wound*. "Last time we met. . .you bloody well shot me."

Mali? It had to have been.

"Oh, well that can't have been me," Harry smiled grimly, clapping a hand on Malone's shoulder as he moved past the big man. "You're still alive. . ."

7:03 P.M.
A small restaurant
Leeds, England

"It's been so many years, Mehr." The old man smiled gently, motioning for her to take a seat across from him in the small, darkened booth. "Too many. And you look weary."

Mehreen nodded, gazing into Ismail Besimi's face as she slid into the booth. He looked troubled, despite the casual nature of his greeting. "They've not been easy years, father. Not since. . .Nick passed."

He closed his eyes reverently. "I had heard. He was a good man—may God receive him unto paradise."

An Asian waiter appeared at their table and she adjusted her hijab to veil her face in shadow, allowing Besimi to order her a cup of tea. It wasn't something he would have done for her under normal circumstances—but discretion was the imperative in these times. For his sake. And hers.

He waited until the waiter left before speaking again, his voice low. "The years have come and gone, and our community has only grown more divided with the passage of time. Here in this land where we came for freedom. For opportunity."

The imam paused, meeting her eyes. "If only we had *all* shared those reasons."

She knew only too well what he was referring to. "The Service is aware of Hashim Rahman."

"Rahman," he said, waving a hand, "is but a symptom of the larger problem. The dogmatists that have overrun our faith. . .insisting stridently that theirs is the only way by which a man can worship God and any other is *murtad*."

Apostate. As her own family had once been declared. It was an accusation that carried with it death in many parts of the Islamic world. "I've done what I can to stand against him, but he is a charismatic figure. And your people have tied my hands. One cannot at once be a reformer and an informer, and your Security Service places a short-sighted priority on the latter."

She shook her head, looking up as the waiter brought her tea. "We've gone over all of this in the past," she said, glancing cautiously at the man's retreating back. "Back when I first recruited you. We need sources inside the Islamic community if we are to stop these attacks."

"No," he replied, the sudden strength in his voice surprising her. "What you *need* is the ability to cut them off at the roots, where they begin. Not with the first purchase of fertilizer, the first theft of blasting caps—but with the innocent children sitting cross-legged listening to those who preach hate. Those who take away all their hopes and ambitions and fill their young minds with dreams of dying in Afghanistan, in Syria. Those who spread the perversion that being a *shaheed*—a witness for God—means blowing yourself up in a market crowded with innocents. Until you can counter *that*, people will continue to die, no matter what else you do."

Mehreen remained silent as the old man paused, only too aware of the truth of his words. The magnitude of that which they were attempting to fight. "The best solutions always seem to be the ones which are hardest to implement."

"Solutions?" There was a touch of bitterness in the imam's voice as he gestured toward her. "No one is interested in solutions, Mehreen. Not the street preachers who blaspheme Allah's name with their praises every time their sermons lead to the death of the innocent. Not the politicians in Whitehall, too timid to even name that which threatens them. Not the thugs of the British Defence Coalition, lashing out at anyone who looks like he might be an immigrant. Nor their backers in the press."

It wasn't what she had come to discuss, but she knew Besimi—as well as the culture from which they both had come. It would have been considered an insult to interrupt him.

He raised a long, bony finger as if something had just come to mind. "You know who Arthur Colville is, do you not?"

She nodded. "He's the right-wing publisher of the *Daily Standard*."

"The same. It was after the 7/7 bombings that he first put out his call for Muslim leaders willing to take a public stand against those he calls 'fundamentalists.'"

"I remember," Mehreen replied. *All too well.* Colville's offer of a column in his paper to any Muslim leader willing to denounce the Islamists had become a yearly ritual, every year on the anniversary of the bombings. Every year unanswered, hanging there like a taunt.

He smiled, a sad smile of resignation. "What you don't know is that I contacted him that first year—offered to take my stand, even if it meant being declared apostate."

"And?"

"And my calls were never returned that year—nor the next year, when I repeated my offer. Nor the next. He's learned the lesson of those he claims to despise, Mehreen. That there is money to be made in the peddling of hatred."

There were no words—the dishonesty of it all. Perhaps nothing should have surprised her, not after all her years with the Service.

Besimi started to speak, then seemed to think better of his words—regarding her with a strange look. *Something was wrong*, she thought, her hands wrapped around the steaming cup of tea in an attempt to warm herself against a sudden chill.

A feeling of foreboding.

"But all of that. . .it's not why I asked to meet with you tonight."

7:14 P.M.
Thames House
London

"Good God," Alec MacCallum breathed, glancing down at the sheet of paper in his hand. "This is confirmed?"

The analyst nodded. "GCHQ just sent it over with the hourlies."

Something like this should have been sent immediately, without waiting for the hourlies. Those *boffins*.

MacCallum swore loudly, drawing looks from around the Centre as he hurried toward the DG's office. This couldn't have been worse.

Marsh looked up as he burst in, not stopping to knock. "What's going on?"

"We have a problem, Julian," MacCallum announced, thrusting the sheet toward the DG.

"What am I supposed to be looking at?"

"It's the text message that was sent to Tarik Abdul Muhammad in City Station," the lead analyst replied, running a hand across his forehead as he began to quote the text. "Who I am doesn't matter. There's a woman to your left. Dark skin, dark hair. Forties. She's with Five."

"And the sender?" Marsh asked, his eyes still scanning down the paper.

"Ismail Besimi."

7:16 P.M.
The restaurant
Leeds

"Then what is it, Ismail?" Mehreen asked, her eyes searching his aged face.

He hesitated once again. "We have been friends for many years, Mehreen. Ever since you first came to worship at the masjid as a young woman."

Another pause, as he smiled sadly. "I remember those first weeks—your earnestness, your curiosity. Too many in our faith would disregard the questions, the searching of a woman, but I knew you were something special from the first time I saw you, *mash'allah*. And that's why, when all this began to happen, I knew I had to speak to you first."

"What?" she asked, a fear suddenly gnawing at her heart. Her phone buzzed in the inside pocket of her jacket, but she ignored it. "When *what* began to happen?"

He looked away for another moment, as if pained to meet her eyes. "It's Aydin. . ."

7:22 P.M.
The surveillance van
Leeds

"Come on, Mehr—pick up the bloody phone," Darren whispered, glaring at the screen of his mobile. "Sod it!"

"Special Branch is another five minutes out," Norris announced, looking up from his screens.

The field officer shook his head, still struggling to process all that had unfolded since the team had received the first red-flash. That they had been betrayed. "That's not going to be soon enough."

"It's going to have to be," the analyst replied. "We don't have tactical authority."

The former Royal Marine spat. "Oh, bugger tactical authority, we're talking about Mehreen."

Norris was right, but he could feel the bulge of the Sig-Sauer Marsh had given him against his side and he found himself fighting against the urge to draw it and go in alone. "We sent her in there with a traitor."

Dear God, Mehr, why wouldn't you wear a wire?

He looked up into the American's eyes, reading a cool appraisal written there. They'd both served in Afghanistan, both knew what it was like to lose people—all too well.

It was the moment of truth. "Parker, you're with me. Everyone else, stay here—man the cameras and keep your comms live."

He pushed open the back door of the van, jumping out into the darkened street with the American officer right behind him. "What's the plan?"

"You take the back door, I'll take the front. Whatever you do, mate, don't let anyone leave—we'll stage the assault once Special Branch arrives."

7:23 P.M.
The restaurant

"No," she whispered, looking into the imam's eyes. It couldn't be. "That isn't possible."

"But it is, Mehreen," he said gently, his eyes never leaving her face. He looked as if he might have reached out to touch her hand, but not even Besimi was that progressive. "I've seen the way he looks at the imam when he speaks of Syria, of those fighting and dying there—I've seen him and some of the others talking together after the lectures. I fear there can be no mistake. . .Aydin has fallen under Rahman's spell."

"He was such a beautiful boy. . ." She shook her head sadly, her words filled with regret. She hadn't seen her nephew since his eighth birthday, one of the last times she'd visited her sister's family. He'd just been a normal British boy then, ecstatic over receiving his gifts—unwrapping the *Harry Potter* novel she had given him. *The Prisoner of Azkaban*, if she recalled correctly.

Had it been *that* long? "We have to do something," she whispered, wiping a defiant tear away from the corner of her eye.

Besimi shrugged, spreading out his hands before her. "I've tried, believe me when I say that. But for all his claims of now being a 'true' Muslim, Aydin no longer has the respect for his elders that our faith would demand. I thought that perhaps with you being his aunt. . ."

Mehreen smiled, a bitter, angry smile. "An absent aunt that he probably only remembers for giving him a book he now no doubt considers blasphemous. But there has to be something—it would break Nimra's heart if he went to prison, or. . ."

She couldn't even bring herself to voice the alternative.

Her phone buzzed again—this time with an incoming text. Gesturing to Ismail to excuse herself, she flipped it open, reading the message displayed on the screen: two words. *Get down.*

She didn't have time to react, to process the meaning before she heard the shattering of glass from the front of the restaurant, heard something thrown inside, metal rattling against the tile.

Without hesitation, she threw an arm across the table, seizing the old man by the shoulder and pulling him with her as she hurled herself to the floor. "*Down!*"

The next moment, the room exploded in light. . .

Chapter 9

7:26 P.M.
The restaurant
Leeds

Darren turned his head away, cupping a hand against his ear as the stun grenade went off inside the restaurant, the explosion hammering his eardrums—light washing over him as the evening turned bright as the noon, the shouts of the tactical team sounding faint and indistinct, echoing dimly in his mind.

He would have given anything to have been on the entry team, he thought, staggering back, glancing into the depths of the restaurant as the light faded. But a tactical team was an organism unto itself, and there was no way they would have let a stranger—no matter how well-trained—lead the stack.

Come on, he whispered, silently cursing. They had to have been in time, a cold chill running once more through his body at the thought of the danger they had placed her in.

Screams. Her ears rang with the force of the explosion, her eyes half-shielded from the blast.

She felt, rather than heard, booted footsteps pounding against the floor—a gloved hand on her shoulder pulling her to her feet, helping her up.

A voice shouting in her ear and she looked up into a helmeted face, the insignia of the North Yorkshire Police on the shoulder of the man's uniform, a Heckler & Koch MP-5 slung across his chest.

It was a friendly. But *why?*

Ismail, she thought, glancing around herself for the old man, her vision still blurry and painful from the flash-bang's glare.

And then she saw the imam, lying face-down on the tiled floor of the café, a policeman's boot on his shoulder as another member of the entry team zip-cuffed his hands behind his back.

"What are you doing?" she tried to ask, but she could barely hear herself speaking the words as the officer took her by the arm, her voice sounding disembodied. *Weak.*

There was some mistake—something had gone wrong. She staggered toward the doorway with the officer holding her up, fearing the worst: that the local constables had blundered carelessly into their op, placing them all in danger, but Besimi most of all.

It wasn't until she saw Darren standing in the doorway of the café that she realized that wasn't the worst.

Far from it.

7:45 P.M.
Sheffield, England

Wait. That's what they had told him to do, Paul Gordon thought. Just sit and wait.

His eyes swept across the garage—the motor pool—for that's what it really was, taking in the four lorries parked before the doors. Conor had spoken of being able to strike back, to actually make a difference.

But what was this? What had he meant? He didn't recognize any of the other men in the garage, bustling around the trucks—but he'd spent long enough "in" to know soldiers when he saw them.

Even if he hadn't been a hero.

A side door of the garage opened at that moment and Hale came in along with a rush of cold air, a jacket cloaking his powerful frame.

"Paul," he said, smiling as he reached out a hand to draw Gordon into a fierce hug. "I couldn't be happier to see you here, mate. Right chuffed."

Gordon returned the smile, but with an effort. It had been hard to smile at anything these last few days. "What is it, exactly, that we are doing, Conor? They told me you would explain things when you arrived."

"You've not forgotten how to use one of these, have you?" Hale reached into his jacket, pulling out a Beretta Px4 Storm and handing the compact semiautomatic over, butt-first.

The former Para shook his head. "No, it's one of those things. . .you never forget. What's this for?"

"Tonight," Hale began, clapping him warmly on the shoulder. "Tonight we begin to make history."

8:09 P.M.
Thames House
London

"They have him," one of the communications officers announced, removing his headset to glance back over his shoulder. "Besimi is secured and Crawford is safe."

Thank God, MacCallum thought, trying to hide his emotion. He and Mehreen had worked together for so many years. . .for it to have ended this way. At the hands of a compromised asset.

"Where is Besimi now?"

"In Special Branch custody at Leeds," the man replied. "They'll be transferring him back to Paddington Green as soon as he can be processed."

"How long are we talking about?"

"Two, three days maximum."

Bureaucracy. The section chief shook his head, cursing softly under his breath. They'd simply have to make the most of it.

"Contact our Leeds office, have them send a minder over. Make sure any locals responsible for interrogating Besimi are fully cognizant that any information pertaining to this case falls under the Official Secrets Act *before* they're put in the same room with him." It was questionable how much they could get out of him, but perhaps this was the break they had been waiting for. He could only pray so.

"Sir," came a voice at his side, a young analyst standing there—extending a folder toward him.

"What's this?" MacCallum asked, taking it from him.

"We have a name on one of the numbers called by Rahman this morning. The mobile belongs to one Javeed Mousa, a Libyan national. He's here on a student visa, been attending the University of London these last two years."

"And?"

The analyst seemed to swallow hard. "And I just got off from talking with the headmaster. No one has seen Mousa in the last month."

9:25 P.M.
A flat
Leeds

Perhaps he had known it was inevitable, a risk of the path God had commanded him to follow.

Perhaps. But it didn't make the reality any easier.

EMBRACE THE FIRE

The hair on the back of Hashim Rahman's neck prickled as he stood there on the step outside his second-story flat, fumbling for his keys. His wife at work, pulling night shift at the infirmary—his daughter staying with her grandmother for the night. He felt naked, exposed in the glare of the light above him.

He'd only noticed the surveillance earlier in the day, making his way to the *masjid* for the first of his lectures—a dark-haired man in the driver's seat of a sedan across the street, taking pictures.

A man standing behind him on the bus coming home, close enough for them to have touched.

Another man at the corner market where he'd picked up groceries—just the necessities, as ever. He had always been a man of simple tastes, as a true follower of the Prophet should be—values he had made sure his family embraced. The decadence of the West was ever about them, but it did not have to permeate their own lives. *Insh'allah.*

The imam shifted the bag of groceries to his other arm, finally finding the key to the flat on his chain—his fingers trembling as he inserted it into the lock.

He pushed the door closed behind him, shutting out the street noise. . .and the watchers? Given the technology of the imperialists, it was impossible to say.

He walked across the small flat without turning on the lights, emptying the bag of groceries into the small refrigerator in one corner of the kitchen, struggling to push the paranoia aside. Perhaps he had been imagining—

"*Salaam alaikum,*" a familiar voice pronounced from the darkness, Rahman's heart nearly stopping in that moment.

His hand flew out, flipping on the lights to reveal the tall form of Tarik Abdul Muhammad leaning back in his armchair on the other side of the living room.

"What are you doing here?"

"Peace, my brother." The *Shaikh* smiled, the picture of calm as he rose from his seat to cross the room to the window, peering cautiously down at the street below as if looking for watchers. "Tonight. . .is the beginning."

9:39 P.M.
A nightclub
London

Lights. Pounding music, a sensuous rhythm washing over him—strobes swirling through the darkness as he pushed his way through the crowd of swaying men.

He had showed the bouncer at the door his student ID, Javeed thought, running a hand over his now smooth-shaven face.

That had itself been enough to get him in for free, a lustful look in the bouncer's eyes as he ushered him in.

Blue light hit him in the face, blinding him for a moment as he felt someone grab at his buttocks.

Heaven. That's what they called this place, but it was more a vision of hell—his mind bringing back to memory the words of the Prophet. *If you find anyone doing as Lut's people did, kill the one who does it, and the one to whom it is done.*

Kill. He jerked himself away from the groping hand, unable to tell to whom it belonged, the darkness punctuated only by blinding flashes of light.

It was time. He shoved his way past a pair of men kissing up against the wall, their hands roving over each other's bodies. The stage was just before him, a heavily tattooed DJ calling out to the crowd, the turntables spinning beneath his fingers.

"*Allahu akbar!*" Javeed called out, his heart pounding against his ribs as he heaved himself up on stage. *God is great.*

There was nothing—none of the fear he had expected, no terror, no reaction at all—his words swept away by the beat of the music. He began walking toward the DJ, unzipping the front of his hoodie as he moved—screaming the battle cry at the top of his lungs.

The DJ saw him then, a puzzled look crossing his face at the young man's approach. Bewilderment turning suddenly into shock as the jacket fell open, as Javeed brought the machete out.

God is great. . .

9:49 P.M.
A pasture
Off the M6, Near Claughton

"Don't make me regret this," Flaharty announced, breaking the silence between them.

Harry leaned back into the rear seat of the SUV, glancing out the window at the darkness—at the pickets Flaharty had thrown out to await the arrival of his buyers. "I never make promises. It's bad business."

Never again. He could hear Carol's voice, a whisper from the dark corners of his mind. *"Promise me that you won't hurt him. Swear it."*

His own voice in reply: *"Before God."*

And it had been a broken promise in the end, a bitter echo of the inevitable. Perhaps he had known that from the beginning, he didn't know. All he knew is that he would have promised her anything: that's what she had meant to him. And now she was gone as well.

Flaharty shook his head. "Oh, sod this for a game of soldiers, Harry. You know I'm not doing this because you aimed a gun at me."

"I do."

And he did. Stephen Flaharty had lived his entire adult life in the cross-hairs of Her Majesty's government. One more gun pointed in his direction wouldn't have swayed him for an instant.

The Irishman paused, adjusting his glasses. "I wouldn't mind seeing a few bombs blowing up in old London town—Mother Mary knows I spent years trying to do just that. But these jihadists. . ."

A pause, as his voice trailed off. It was ironic, Harry thought, one terrorist passing judgment upon the actions of another. But those were the ironies of this world, and the quicker you learned to reconcile yourself to them, the better.

No one was virginal in this business.

"If they *win*," Flaharty began again, a curious intensity creeping into his voice as he glanced at his watch, "it will mean the end of the world as we know it. That's not what I fought for—I fought for a free Ireland."

"And your bombs killed women and children," Harry replied quietly. "All for your free Ireland."

"Aye, that they did," the arms dealer replied. He didn't look at Harry, just stared out the window into the night. "And what. . .you'd ask me to regret it? To repent of my sins?"

Harry didn't reply, and Flaharty went on without waiting for one. "The world has been sold a fiction, boyo. . .that wars can be waged without the deaths of the innocent. A sterile affair. Everything kept neat, tidy—all so people can sleep at night, secure in their belief that their cause is just. Ours is the only era that's believed it. Our fathers and grandfathers knew different, when they flew Lancasters over Dresden, when they dropped *the* bomb on Hiroshima and Nagasaki. And you know different, too."

And perhaps he did. But there had to be some *right* in this world, some place where you drew the line and said, *"This far and no farther."*

Even if he hadn't found it yet.

Headlights filled the empty pasture before he could reply and Flaharty smiled. "Time to get cracking, so."

10:07 P.M.
Thames House
London

". . .shockingly graphic footage tonight from a mass stabbing which has taken place at Heaven, one of London's most prominent gay nightclubs. Police are reporting five fatalities. . ."

Julian Marsh pressed the "mute" button before the Sky News reporter could continue, suppressing a bitter oath.

It was a truism in the intelligence committee—no matter how good your sources were, no matter how hard you tried, there was going to come a day when you found out about a threat from watching the news. Those were the days that had always haunted him, but it was worse now.

Back in the Cold War, when he had come up through the ranks of the Security Service, there had been no 24-hour news cycle. A blessed thing of memory.

This time, though, it was worse than the reporters had yet discovered. What they were calling a "stabbing" had, in fact, been a beheading—with the head of the DJ, an East Londoner named James Brent, nearly hacked from his torso with a machete before his attacker had turned on the crowd. Shouting, *"Allahu akbar!"* as he did so.

That was another tidbit that hadn't yet made its way onto the news. There was no doubt that if the Security Services had the information, the press had it as well, but in a world where competition to "break" stories was fierce, no reporter wanted to be the first to suggest that there was a religious motivation behind the atrocity. More specifically. . .*Islam.*

And so they waited, in anxious indecision. Timid. Uncertain.

Marsh flipped the folder open on his desk, staring down at the University of London student photo of Javeed Mousa.

A two-year-old photo of a young man looking into the camera, a faint glimpse of uneven white teeth against his swarthy face. A smile, easy—confident even, betraying no hint of the darkness beneath. Of what he would become.

No resemblance to the man taken out by CO-19 as they descended upon Heaven in response to the dozens of panicked 999 calls.

A man who had been activated by Tarik Abdul Muhammad. Just like the man whose folder that lay beneath, one Muzhir bin Abdullah. A Moroccan, and a college student just like Mousa. They hadn't found him yet, not even a trace.

The DG's face hardened as he rose from behind his desk, buttoning his suit jacket.

A visit to the Home Secretary was in order, the first thing on the morrow. The time had come to remove the Pakistani from the equation.

Cull the herd. . .

10:12 P.M.
The pasture
Off the M6, Near Claughton

Flaharty was good, Harry thought—moving abreast of the arms dealer as they walked out into the open pasture to meet his buyer. Malone was just back of them, shotgun at the ready, the only one of the three of them displaying a weapon.

The rest of the men were fanned out back by the trucks, deployed against trouble. Not close enough to be their salvation if things went sideways.

Yeah, Flaharty was an old hand. . .but no matter how many times you had done this, it could still go so wrong. In so many ways.

He moved closer to the headlights, staying about three meters to the right of Flaharty, the cool night breeze rustling the tall pasture grass around them. Felt eyes on the back of his head and turned to meet Malone's baleful gaze, only a few paces away.

So very many ways.

"Thought there for a moment you lads weren't going to show." The words were cheerful enough, but there was no mirth in Flaharty's voice, Hale thought, coming around the front of the SUV, a heavy leather briefcase in his left hand. The Irishman wasn't any happier to be here than he was.

Had he joined the Regiment twenty years earlier—or even ten—it might have been his duty to track down men like Flaharty. Track them down and kill them, for that had once been the Regiment's job. Back when England had possessed the courage to call her enemies by their rightful name.

By the time he'd come through Selection, however, old enemies had been changed for new. An enemy the politicians, safely ensconced in their comfortable offices in Whitehall, didn't even dare whisper.

The path that had led him to this night.

"And miss this?" Hale responded, smiling tightly as he moved forward. He was armed, but it wouldn't be enough to save him. Moments like this, you had to rely on your mates. Having Paul Gordon in the darkness behind him with a rifle aimed at Flaharty's chest was insurance enough. Together, Paras once more.

Utrinque Paratus. Ready for anything.

"Wouldn't dream of it. This is the 'liquidity' you asked for. The rest of the payment has been transferred to your account."

The *voice*. It was so familiar, echoes of a time long past. Hard to place. Harry edged to one side, trying to get a better look at the buyer, his form backlit against the glare of the headlights.

It was destroying his night vision, making it hard to get a look at the man's face without drawing attention to himself—without moving out of the shadows and directly into their beams.

The man reached out, standing there just a few feet away from him as he handed the briefcase over to Flaharty and Harry heard his voice once more.

It all came back, washing over him. Memories of that night in Lebanon. *Operation LODESTONE.* It was the sounds that were the most prominent in the dreams. Always the sounds.

The gunfire—the thunder of a minigun sawing through the darkness, the screams of the dying. Nick Crawford lying there in the cabin of the Blackhawk as the helicopter lifted off from that rocky Lebanese hilltop, his eyes glassy, an IV stabbed into his arm.

The *second* SAS sergeant. He could still hear that voice in the night. *"Chalk it up, mate. Two more dead* hajjis.*"*

Hajjis. A term of honor in the Islamic world for those who had completed a pilgrimage to Mecca, it had become a slur among soldiers fighting in Iraq and Afghanistan. A term of derisive contempt for people who had tried to kill them times beyond count.

Impossible to forget. But what had been his name? Heller? Hall?

Names hadn't been so important on that night, he thought, his eyes scanning the darkness around them, a chill prickling at his spine. They were so exposed.

He glanced back to see the buyer staring directly at him, a strange look on his face. "One of your men, Flaharty?"

10:20 P.M.
KillingBeck Police Station
Leeds

"No." Mehreen swore, tearing the hijab from her head and stuffing into the pocket of her jacket with a quick, angry motion. Memories of a former self. "I'm not listening to this, Darren."

She turned on him, her dark eyes flashing. "I have known Besimi since I was a child. There is no way he's in with the jihadists."

"It's true whether you want to believe it or not," the former Royal Marine retorted. Roth didn't flinch, just stood there, looking at her sadly. "We have the proof of his communication with Tarik Abdul Muhammad. He sold you out, Mehr."

No. Her hand balled into a fist, knuckles whitening against dark skin. First Aydin, now this, the last vestiges of her old life seeming to crumble about her. Her life before. . .Nick.

"I need to see him."

EMBRACE THE FIRE

Roth shook his head. "That's not happening."

"I know him better than anyone in the Service," she protested. If Roth wouldn't listen to her, no one would. "He was *my* agent. If anyone can get to the truth, it would be me."

A sigh. "And that's why I asked you to go under this evening—to meet with him. And it didn't work out. I'm not putting you in the same room with him again, not taking that risk."

She started to speak, but he cut her off. "It's out of my hands, Mehr. He's in the custody of Special Branch now—not my jurisdiction any longer."

10:21 P.M.
The pasture
Off the M6, Near Claughton

"Yes," Harry heard Flaharty reply from a few feet away. He didn't look over at him, his eyes still locked with those of the buyer.

There was nothing to be gained by looking away—and everything to be lost. "He's a PMC, been with me for years."

Private military contractor.

There was cool appraisal in the former SAS sergeant's gaze, along with something else—something far more dangerous. The nagging tendrils of recognition there, just below the surface.

All of the years, the darkness of the night—then *and* now—that was all that was holding him back. *Uncertainty.*

"Then why haven't I seen him before?" the man challenged, turning away from Harry to focus his attention back on the arms dealer.

Hale. The name struck Harry suddenly, burning itself into his memory. That was it—that had been the sergeant's name. *Conor Hale.*

"We're here to make sure you don't get buggered, mate." Nick's voice, once again, as it all came back.

But Flaharty was speaking now, a curiously righteous indignation in the Irishman's voice as he responded. "An' that's because he was in Latvia up until three days ago, on a sodding job. For *me.*"

It was a performance that could have earned an Oscar, Harry thought—watching as Flaharty drew himself up to his full height, glaring at the soldier. "Now, boyo, if you've vetted my personnel to your satisfaction. . .shall we proceed to business?"

Acting and directing. A command performance.

Hale paused, glancing back into Harry's eyes for a long moment. Then, "Very well. Let's do this."

Chapter 10

12:17 A.M., March 28th
The M6 Motorway

Silence. Fifteen minutes of it, ever since Flaharty had re-entered the vehicle.

The arms dealer's convoy had split up upon leaving the pasture, fanning out in all directions and now they were alone. Alone, speeding north on the motorway.

There wasn't much traffic at this hour in the morning, Harry thought, glancing out the tinted windows of the SUV. Not much at all.

"You bloody well knew him."

It wasn't a question—more of an accusation, by the sound of it. "I did," Harry responded, turning to look Flaharty in the face. "His name's Conor Hale—former Regiment. We served together once, long time ago. A black op in Lebanon. A dark and bloody night."

"Did he know *you*?"

"Hard to say." There was movement, catching his eye in the night back of them along the motorway. Just a moment, and then it was gone.

The Irishman swore loudly, hammering his fist against the door. "You knew he would be there."

Another accusation.

Harry shook his head, keeping his voice level as he responded. "No. I knew the risks I ran—the chance of crossing paths with someone I knew from the bad old days. Nothing more. I judged it an acceptable risk."

"*Acceptable*," Flaharty spat, another curse escaping his lips. "Not your sodding decision to make, Harry. Not yours—mine. This was my deal. My rules. And you broke them."

Another flash of movement and Harry looked back through the rear window of the vehicle to see another SUV behind them. Moving up fast. Then again, a lot of people drove fast at this hour of night.

Not with their lights off. "Yeah, well. . ." he replied, reaching inside his jacket, "it looks like they're about to get broken—again. Malone!"

The big man jerked his head around, his eyes falling upon the drawn Sig-Sauer in Harry's hand. "What the—"

"We have company."

The words had barely left his mouth before the SUV was alongside, coming up hard on the left, as if to force them off the road and into the guardrails of the median. Harry saw the muzzle flash of a rifle on full-automatic, felt and heard the first bullets strike the armored side of the Ford Explorer.

"What's going on?" Flaharty's pistol was out now, small in his hand as he slid down, crouching on the floor of the Explorer. "Stop arsing about and get us out of here, Davey!"

It wasn't going to be enough, he thought, throwing a critical glance down the motorway. *No exits.*

The ballistic glass crystallized over his head, weakening under the impact of the rounds. *Bullet-resistant.*

Bulletproof didn't exist. Not outside of Hollywood. And given enough time, the effectiveness of ballistic glass was degraded by sunlight.

They weren't going to hold for long.

The next moment, Harry felt the vehicle lurch drunkenly to the left, the hideous groan of metal against the surface of the road. He knew what it was without asking. They'd just lost a tire—their last mobility leaving them in that instant.

He saw Malone wrestling with the steering wheel, struggling to bring the Explorer to a controlled stop on the edge of the median without overturning the vehicle.

Out of time. Switching the Sig-Sauer to his left hand, Harry reached across Flaharty, throwing the door open as the vehicle ground to a stop. "Out, out—*out!*"

He shoved the Irishman from the vehicle, following him closely as they both jumped out onto the median—a bolt of pain shooting its way through Harry's body as the loose gravel gave way, his bad ankle betraying him in that moment.

There was no time for weakness. Not now.

He risked a glance back through the damaged windows of the shot-up Explorer, just in time to see the SUV pulling to a stop on the other side of the motorway—men fanning out from the vehicle. At least four, perhaps five—shadows moving quickly in the darkness. *Military training.* They were outnumbered.

And outgunned, he realized, making out the outline of assault rifles in the men's hands. Long odds.

"What the devil is going on?" Flaharty repeated, punctuating his words with a flurry of curses. "Who are they?"

"They're not Special Branch," Harry said, hissing the words through gritted teeth as he leaned back against the side of the armored SUV, his eyes scanning the terrain around them. The ground they'd have to cross. "My guess? You did business with the wrong people this time. . .outlived your usefulness."

Too much open ground—not enough cover. Not enough time. *There*. There was an overpass running above the motorway, perhaps a hundred and fifty meters off. A windbreak of tall pines back of them, across the southbound lanes—some concealment there, but nothing that would stop a rifle bullet.

Either was a long sprint under fire on the best of days—and he was in no shape for a run. "If you can make it to that road above us," he began, "you should be able to grab transportation and get out of here."

Flaharty measured the distance with a practiced eye and obviously came to the same conclusion Harry had only moments earlier. "You're bleedin' insane."

"Give me your shotgun," Harry spat out, glancing back over his shoulder at Malone. "I'll cover you."

"Sod that," the arms dealer retorted, a look of disbelief in his eyes, "now I *know* you're insane."

A burst of full-automatic fire ripped through the night, followed by another. And another. Harry knew what it was—suppressive fire, designed to keep their heads down. They were being flanked.

And all he could remember was another night—lying on his belly in a California oil field with a rifle in his hand, waiting for Korsakov's mercenaries to move in. Baiting a trap with himself. Gambling his life to protect Carol's.

It hadn't saved her in the end.

He shook his head. "You want to stay here and die arguing over my mental state if you want, makes no difference to me. But if you want to *live*. . ."

He paused, as if lost momentarily in thought. "Do you have any more plastique?"

12:25 A.M.
Outside Claughton

The wounded man was lying there on the ground in the darkness, moaning helplessly as Conor Hale walked up to him, weapon drawn in his hand.

"Please. . ." A bloody froth bubbled around the man's lips as he mouthed the plea. "Don't."

The former SAS sergeant shook his head remorselessly from behind the black balaclava mask, his arm coming up. "Fortunes of war, mate."

The Sig-Sauer coughed twice, 9mm slugs spitting from the barrel—smashing into the skull of the fallen Irishman. It didn't matter that the man was scarce old enough to have remembered the Troubles, let alone participated in them. . .killing him was a good feeling.

Justice. For all his brothers killed through the years.

Hale safed the pistol and holstered it, glancing across at the bodies of the other men they had killed, sprawled near the truck—blood pooling around the corpses.

He saw Paul Gordon out of the corner of his eye, the former Para clutching the Beretta Px4 in both hands, head up, his eyes still scanning the area around them.

Ever the soldier.

"How you doing, mate?" Hale asked, noticing that his old comrade was breathing heavily, his hands trembling ever so slightly. It had been a long time out of the saddle for all of them.

"Fine," Gordon replied, his eyes hollow as he looked toward the bodies of the men they had killed. "They never stood a chance, did they?"

"No they didn't," came Hale's ready retort, his voice even as he stared keenly into the face of his old friend. "Do you have a problem with that?"

There was no reply for a moment and Hale took a step closer to him, lowering his voice. "If you want out, tell me now. It doesn't get any bloody easier from here. We both lost good mates in Iraq—I trust you to leave without turning tout on us."

Another moment passed, and then Gordon swallowed hard, seeming to calm down. "No," he responded at length, holstering the Beretta, "I'm staying. It was all about the money for them—they would have sold those weapons to anyone, even the Muzzies. Deserved what they got."

"Good man," the former SAS sergeant smiled, surreptitiously easing his hand away from his own weapon. "Then let's get this mess cleaned up."

They were committed now. No going back, no retreat for any of them. He had taken a step past Gordon back toward their vehicle when the phone on his hip buzzed.

"Is it done?" a voice demanded as he flipped it open. *Arthur Colville.*

"Nearly." Hale looked back to see Gordon and another of his men rolling one of the bodies into a black body bag. "His men are down, here and at the crossroads. Just waiting for a sitrep from Baker Element on the primary."

"Good. Call me when it's been taken care of."

12:29 A.M.
The M6 Motorway

Gunshots. Short, controlled bursts, the sporadic flicker of muzzle flashes in the night above him. They were up against professionals, Harry thought—the type of people a man like Conor Hale would have surrounded himself with.

He was leaning up against the side of a shallow ditch in the very center of the median, cold, slushy water seeping through his pants. The chill, clammy touch of death.

Harry pressed himself back against the rough-cut gravel, holding the Remington 870 across his chest. It was a good weapon for an enforcer like Malone—a tool of intimidation—but the pistol grip made it almost impossible to aim with any degree of accuracy.

He would have been a fool to rely upon it. He waited another moment, hearing the gunshots grow louder as the hostiles moved closer to his position—waiting for his opening.

Whether Malone and Flaharty had made it across the southbound lanes, whether they had made it up to the overpass, he had no idea—had never intended to cover their retreat. They were bait, drawing the kill team into his own trap.

A wince crossed his face, and this time it wasn't from the pain of the ankle. This was a concept foreign to him—out in the field you lived and you died for the men beside you. For your *team*. And trusted that they would do the same for you.

But now. . .there was no more place for trust. And they weren't his team. *Now*!

He raised himself up on one knee, eyes sweeping the darkness, the detonator Flaharty had given him clutched in his left hand. *Target. Target. Target.*

Dark figures fanned out around the van—two of them clustered together. First mistake, but their fire was more deliberate now, more purposeful. Aimed shots, not suppressive bursts, as if they'd found their targets.

He risked a glance in the direction of their fire and nearly slammed his fist into the gravel in frustration.

Flaharty and his enforcer hadn't gone for the overpass—they were pinned down just across the motorway, just short of the treeline. Their deaths were a matter of time.

Movement out of the corner of his eye—off to the left—and Harry wheeled, finding a fifth man almost on top of him. Man? No. *Target*.

He dropped the detonator. . .an unavoidable reflex, his left hand closing around the shotgun's forearm—bringing the barrel up. He saw surprise register on the man's face, his lips opening to scream a warning. Too late.

The Remington's trigger broke under the pressure of his finger, the recoil of the twelve-gauge slamming back into his unsupported right hand as a deafening blast ripped through the night.

Chaos.

The load of buckshot struck his target full in the stomach and the man staggered back, his mouth opening and closing in silent spasms. His legs going out from under him.

He had already crumpled to the macadam by the time his screams found their voice. An ungodly, bestial sound.

Harry's left hand came back, a spent shell flying from the chamber as he racked the action. Chambering another round in the work of a moment.

Not soon enough.

The night exploded around him as two of the gunmen near the Explorer turned, opening fire. He pulled the trigger, the Remington slamming back once more into his palm as he got off a second shot, but it went wild in the darkness.

Lights from an oncoming vehicle along the motorway swept over his position, silhouetting him against their glare. *Perfect target.*

He threw himself backward down the slight embankment, dropping the shotgun. His hand clawing blindly in the darkness for the detonator.

It had to be there. Had to be. Could it have fallen into the water? He considered the possibility for a moment, then dismissed it. *No.*

Had to find it while he still had mobility. Before the gunmen moved to flank him.

Before they moved outside the blast radius. He heard the stutter of gunfire—the screech of car tires. Had they fired on the hapless motorist?

There was no time to think of that now. No time to consider the loss of an innocent life. His outstretched fingers touched the hard plastic of the detonator, his hand closing around it—flipping open the cap.

Pain. It was a curiously numb feeling, Flaharty thought, his eyes opening and closing as he lay there—his breathing labored. More heat than anything else, as if someone had slammed him in the ribs with a hot anvil. "Bugger," he announced simply, his fingers coming away from his side sticky with blood. "I'm hit."

He glanced over to see Malone lying there beside him, the enforcer's FNX-45 recoiling into his hand as he got off a wild shot into the dark.

Across the road, Nichols' weapon had once again fallen silent—the American might have been dead, for all Flaharty knew.

He *did* know that their fate was sealed as soon as their assailants moved across the road, as soon as they could enfilade their position with fire. A round slammed into the rocks near his head even as he thought it, stone spalling away and peppering his face.

"We're not making it out of this one, Davey," he hissed, gritting his teeth against the pain in his side.

His old friend shook his head and Flaharty could have sworn he saw a smile there. Malone had always been one to laugh at death.

"Sod that," the big man snarled back, wrapping his right arm around the arms dealer's torso even as he got off another shot—the explosive report hammering Flaharty's ears. "I'm not leaving you here."

Together, the two of them staggered to their feet, Malone covering him with his body as they limped back toward the treeline. *So exposed.*

Flaharty heard the whiplash crack of bullets in the air around them as if through a dream, the bark of Malone's pistol as he returned fire. They'd made it only a few steps when the night exploded around them. . .

12:33 A.M.
Charing Cross Hotel
London

Terror. It was all over the news, the "stabbing" at Heaven—with more of the gruesome details emerging by the hour.

It wasn't a surprise, Daniel Pearson thought, shaking his head as he glanced at the television screen. He had sensed it in the manner of the news anchors, an unspoken fear of something they dared not name.

More importantly, he'd known for years that this day was coming, had warned of it.

Had been called a "radical" himself for his warning, been accused of hate speech—of being an "Islamophobe." Had nearly lost his seat in the House of Commons in the resulting furor.

And now Priam trembles. A curse escaped his lips, sounding unusually loud in the empty hotel room. Futile. He was past grief, long ago—now the reality of what had happened filled him only with anger, a fury cold as the night outside his hotel room window.

The lives which could have been saved had his warnings only been heeded.

His mobile buzzed from where he had placed it on the nightstand and he walked over to the bed, a grim smile crossing his face as he read the name displayed on-screen.

They'd been friends for years, allies in the fight against all that was coming against Britain. Standing alone.

He hesitated only a moment before answering, his eyes still fixed on the television. "An evil morning, Arthur. I was expecting you to call."

Evil. That was such a complex notion, Colville thought, staring into the fireplace as he listened to the MP.

Good and evil. Right and wrong. How would history remember what they were about to do? How would they be judged?

Ungratefully, of that he had little doubt. Few would ever understand the sacrifices which had been made for them. The English blood spilt for the preservation of their way of life.

Which was of no consequence, so long as it *was* preserved. "You've been watching the news from Heaven?" he asked after a moment. It was a rhetorical question. They both had.

"Ever since the story first broke," was Pearson's response. "It was a Muslim, wasn't it?"

Colville snorted. "The disk jockey was *beheaded*, Daniel. His assailant wasn't Church of England."

"Do you have details?" He could hear the note of caution in the man's voice. Ever the politician and at his heart, little different than the rest of his kind.

A useful mouthpiece, little more.

"His name was Javeed Mousa," the publisher responded. It struck him then, the incongruity of a newspaperman leaking information to a member of government, and he was forced to stifle a laugh. *The world turned upside down.* "A twenty-three-year-old Libyan national here on a student visa. The Security Services are investigating his ties to homegrown Islamic terrorism."

It was a moment before Pearson spoke again. "That information hasn't been on the networks, anywhere. Do I want—"

"No," Colville replied, cutting him off before he could even voice the question. "You don't. Now you'll be wanting to get some sleep—I've secured an interview for you on Sky News in the morning. Do us proud."

12:35 A.M.
M-6 Motorway

Light. The heat washed over him in a wave, the ground rushing up to meet him. Flaharty swore, the breath knocked from his body—the noise of the explosion still reverberating through the night.

He rolled onto his back, shielding his eyes as he looked back toward the roadway—flames leaping into the night sky from the burning shell of the Ford Explorer.

"He did it," the arms dealer breathed, glancing over at Malone. "He sodding did it."

Flaming pieces of the Explorer rained down from the night sky above him, burning metal hissing as it landed in the water of the drainage ditch.

Harry pulled his head up, drawing the Sig-Sauer from within his jacket as he rose up on one knee—scanning the area for threats, the flames casting eerie shadows over the motorway.

Devastation. He saw the bodies of the shooters sprawled along the roadside near the burning SUV, one man's mangled torso draped over the guardrail, his right leg sheared off north of the knee.

No signs of life.

The bomb had done the work for which he'd intended it, more completely than he had even dared to hope.

A moan seemed to rise from the earth at his feet and he glanced down into the eyes of the soldier he had shot, only moments before. It seemed like an eternity.

He was young, couldn't have been out of his twenties—eyes wide and staring, a face distorted in agony. He was lying there on his side, nearly disemboweled by the load of buckshot, trying to hold his entrails inside him with a bloody hand.

Bleeding to death there on the cold, hard asphalt.

Dying, Harry thought dispassionately, placing a hand on the young man's shoulder and gently rolling him onto his back. Nothing he could do about it. Nothing at all.

"Listen to me," he began, his voice low against the crackle of the flames in the background—the noise of a car speeding by on the southbound lanes. No doubt dialing 999 in a panic. "You were military, so you know you don't have long. . .five, six minutes at the most before you bleed out. That's all. So make it count."

Tears ran down his cheeks as he stared up into Harry's face, fighting to maintain his defiance, his body trembling with silent sobs. Struggling to speak, his lips forming an obscenity. ". . .you, you Provo sods."

"We're not that different, you and I," Harry continued, his expression almost regretful as he reached up to smooth back perspiration-slick hair from the dying man's brow. The man *he* had killed. "Soldiers, the both of us. Trapped on opposite sides of a war we haven't even begun to understand."

He paused. "I know the man you work for, his name's Hale. Formerly of the Regiment. Served with him in the sandbox, good man then. Maybe even yet. Nearly three hundred Heckler & Koch G3 assault rifles—more than a hundred charges of plastique. Who is the shipment intended for?"

"I. . .don't know," the man gasped out, and Harry could read the truth in his eyes. He had no idea, probably didn't even know what was in the shipment, let alone whom it was for.

He glanced down at the man's forearm then, briefly revealed in the flickering flames—the tattoo of an upward slashing dagger nearly hidden amidst the wiry hair. *A Para.* "So you're doing what. . .just following the lead of an old comrade, eh? A man you fought side by side with in Iraq? I know the way that goes—the right man, you'd follow straight to hell. Problem is, that's right where Conor Hale is taking you."

Movement behind him and Harry wheeled, his weapon coming up until he saw Flaharty's bloodied form stagger from the darkness—Malone at his side.

"Easy there, old son," the arms dealer said, putting up a hand, "You've done well. What does he know?"

A grim shake of the head. "Not near enough."

The soldier was slipping in and out of consciousness now, nearly overcome by pain and blood loss. Harry leaned down, his lips only inches away from the dying man's ear. "You had your weapons. . .why come after us? Why the hit on Flaharty?"

His eyes flickered open momentarily, his breathing tortured. Yet there was something else besides agony distorting his features. It took him a moment to place it. *Hatred.*

". . .said he'd killed our mates. Time to take the—the *justice* our government wouldn't give us."

A phone buzzed at that moment and Harry reached up, digging a mobile from the man's jacket pocket. A feeble hand was raised to stop him, but he was far too weak—it fell limply away at his side.

"Has our Irish problem been dealt with?" were the first words Harry heard as he pressed the button to *accept call.*

Hale's voice. From off in the distance, he could hear the first discordant wails of emergency sirens coming down the motorway. Time was short.

He straightened without answering, extending the phone in a bloody hand to Flaharty. "It's for you."

5:47 A.M.
The MI-5 safehouse
Leeds, England

THRUSH. That was Besimi's codename, given to him back in the years when she had first recruited him, Mehreen thought—double-clicking on the file folder to open it.

There wasn't much there—the Service was obsessed with the idea of a security breach compromising the identities of their assets and kept all the important files off-line. A hacker successfully breaching the numerous active firewalls protecting the Thames House intranet was well-nigh a statistical impossibility, but Five had always found itself run by classicists like Marsh, not statisticians.

Man himself was fallible.

THRUSH had been a Five asset for thirteen long years. An unlucky number in a world where luck counted for far more than anyone cared to admit.

Over a decade of turbulence as Britain's Islamic community swelled with refugees and asylum seekers from the wars in the Middle East. As the Security Services struggled to contain the threat posed by radical preachers like Anjem Choudary.

Such a narrow line between liberty. . .and death.

And Besimi had remained faithful all through those years—to his congregation there in Leeds, to his faith, to the country he had adopted as his own. One of their most reliable assets.

He'd been directly responsible for Five's breaking up of a terror cell in Leeds in 2004, the seizure of a massive stockpile of fertilizer that the terrorists had stored for use as a truck bomb aimed at Whitehall. One of the Security Service's many unsung coups in the years since 9/11.

Had it all been part of a plan? To earn the trust of the Service, to get a man on the "inside." *Sacrifice a pawn.*

It was an impossible question. A question which had kept her awake all through the night—along with a hundred others.

And the file before her held no answers. No clues. She would have to ask MacCallum to pull Besimi's jacket from the Registry upon her return to London. Until then. . .

She looked up from the computer to see Darren standing there in the doorway. "How long have you been there?"

A weary smile creased his dark face. "Long enough to know that if you didn't hear me you had to be exhausted, Mehreen. Did you get any sleep?"

A shake of the head. "No." And yet it seemed as if she was still sleeping. . .trapped in a dream with no escape.

"Have you seen the news?"

Another "no", but a growing sense of foreboding gnawed at her heart. What *news?*

The former Royal Marine walked over to the table, leaning forward on its hard wooden surface until he could look in her eye. "A Libyan student stormed a gay nightclub in London last night and beheaded the DJ with a machete, killing several bystanders. He's believed to have had communication with the *Shaikh.*"

Mehreen just sat there, struggling to process it all. There were just no words.

First Besimi. . .and now this. The inescapable feeling that wheels were already in motion.

The wheels of something they couldn't stop. "I need you on your game, Mehr," he said quietly, his eyes never leaving hers. "Or I need to find someone who is. That means that Ismail Besimi will have to wait for another day. Let the quizmasters do their job, and let's do ours. Understood?"

He was right, that was the worst of it, she thought, her face betraying none of her emotion. And yet it was so hard to turn your back on a friend. Harder still to believe that they had betrayed *you*. She met his eyes for a moment, then responded, "Understood."

She had barely stopped speaking when Thomas Parker entered the main room of the safehouse, his brown hair still tousled from sleep, buttoning his shirt.

He looked from Mehreen to Darren as if perceiving that he had interrupted something, then proceeded, "I'm going to need transport to City Station. In the wake of last night's attack, the powers that be have summoned me back to Grosvenor Square."

Darren rounded the table to face him. "Your people will remain with us to continue our effort to reacquire the *Shaikh*?"

The American nodded. "Of course."

"Very well. I can arrange for your return to the embassy—Norris is leaving for Thames House by car within the hour."

7:08 A.M.
Colville's estate
The Midlands

"At least tell me the shipment has been safely dispersed?"

"Yes, sir," Conor Hale replied, his face impassive as he stood there, hands clasped behind his back. At attention, or so he felt. "They arrived at the predesignated locations an hour ago, and I've detailed my men to secure them."

"Good." The publisher turned slowly back from the open window, the cold breeze playing with his greying hair. Behind him, dark, wind-driven clouds rolled across the face of the morning sky, nearly shutting out the dawn. "So tell me, sergeant. . .what went wrong?"

Hale shook his head. "I'm afraid I don't fully yet know, sir. The NCA has the scene locked down—it looks as if they used a VBIED, to be honest with you."

"English, please."

"A vehicle-borne improvised explosive device. Essentially, a car bomb. Dealt with enough of them in Iraq to know one when I see one."

"Well, I haven't had the benefit of your vast military experience," Colville said dryly, "but I've been around long enough to know a cock-up when I see one. Tell me again what he said to you?"

"He said," Hale began, biting back an angry retort, "that we should have made sure of killing him. Because he would bring us down."

A snort from the publisher. "And I bloody well agree with him, but it's an idle threat. We pulled his fangs—didn't we?"

"We did. From our best intelligence of his operational strength, he can't have more than half-a-dozen men now. All that's left of his organization after last night."

"Yes, well I trust that 'intelligence' is more precise than your estimates of the force required to take out Flaharty," Colville announced, turning his back on the soldier.

"There's still the matter of our potential asset. . .our actions last night may have made recruiting him more difficult, but not impossible—not with the right approach, the evidence we have of Flaharty's activities with the Americans. He might be willing to give him up."

"Do it," Colville responded coldly. "There is no more time for uncertainty, for hesitation. The die is cast."

He glanced out the window, across the windswept green pastures cast in shadow, faint rays of the morning sun stabbing their way through the dark clouds. "A storm is coming. . ."

Chapter 11

7:12 A.M.
A safehouse

"Are you sure you haven't been compromised here?" Harry asked, glancing around the kitchen of the small flat.

It looked as if it had been deserted for years—dropcloths covering most of the furniture, dust lying thick on the countertop.

Flaharty gritted his teeth, painfully shrugging his shoulders out of his torn jacket. "I'm sure."

Harry moved over to the next door, his Sig-Sauer in his hand as he pulled it open, sweeping the dim interior of a living room. "You were sure last night and they still nearly got us. They had intel. Good intel."

"You think I don't know that?" the arms dealer spat back angrily. "You don't think that's what's been runnin' through my mind every bleedin' moment since the ambush? Davey and I are the only ones who know about this place. . .we're secure."

"All right." Harry returned the pistol to its holster inside his waistband. Time to move on to the next problem. "I need to take a look at your side. You're looking pale."

"When Malone gets back from ditching the car," Flaharty warned, grimacing even as he did so. "Not before."

"Fair enough," he responded, moving to check the windows. "It's your blood."

Blood. It had been hours, but try as he might, he couldn't get the face of the British soldier out of his mind. Lying there in the road, bleeding to death.

"No," he could hear his own voice saying, *"there's no point to it. He'll be dead before they can get here."*

"And if he's not? It had been Flaharty who asked the question, a dark assurance in his voice. *"Do you want to run the risk that he'll talk—tell Five about the shipment? You're relying on those trucks to get to their destination, I know you are. Can't have the wrong people knowing they're in-country."*

And he had been right. Didn't make what he had done any easier. Didn't make it feel any less like murder.

Nor was it. He'd taken the Sig-Sauer and put two rounds into the young man's temple, killing him instantly.

Or as nearly as ever it was. An act of mercy, in reality—but mercy had had nothing to do with his reasons for doing so.

No, this was all about preventing the mission from being compromised, he thought, moving like a dark shadow from one window to the next—most of them boarded up, the glass without long-ago shattered by vandals.

The *mission*. He could feel his face harden, anger rising within him. That word—it had been to him what the mantra was to a Buddhist priest. The only thing that mattered—the only truth.

For so many years. And now all that was gone. He'd spent all his adult life fighting for a flag, those blood-red stripes unfurled to the breeze—white stars against a field of blue. A righteous cause.

But now. . .what was his cause? He closed his eyes once more and this time it wasn't the young soldier's face who rose before him—but Carol's.

Vengeance. . .

7:05 A.M.
Sky News Studios
Isleworth, West London

"To answer your question—no, I'm not surprised by the nature of the attack," Daniel Pearson responded, looking gravely across at the Sky News anchor on the opposite couch. "Not surprised at all. I've been warning of this for years—when Drummer Rigby was butchered in the streets of Woolwich, I warned that if we did not take active measures to deal with this threat, it was only a matter of time before it happened again."

The anchor paused, glancing off-camera as if he expected some help from his producer. "By 'this threat,' Mr. Pearson. . .you are referring to the threat posed by. . .jihadists?"

He could see the jaded skepticism in the anchor's eyes, mixed there with the confusion. Allowed himself an inner smile. "Of course I am. Under the umbrella of this "conservative" government, we've seen a flood tide of immigrants and asylum seekers come rolling into this country—and why, I ask you? The 1951 United Nations Convention on Refugees is very explicit—refugees may only legitimately seek refuge in the *nearest* safe country. I don't know if you've looked at a map recently, but the UK is far from a neighbor of the Middle East and we have no legitimate responsibility in the affair. But what do my fellow members of parliament care about legitimate responsibilities?"

The anchor held up a hand to stop him. "And that's all well and good, Mr. Pearson. . .but what exactly does all of *this* have to do with the stabbing at Heaven? There's been nothing made public about the identity of the assailant—nothing to connect it with religious extremism of any kind."

"No?" Pearson asked, reaching inside the pocket of his tailored suit to retrieve a morning copy of the *Daily Standard*. "Then perhaps, sir, it's time for your people to get off their posh couches and do some journalism."

He threw the paper onto the table between them, Arthur Colville's headline clearly visible above a picture of panicked club-goers streaming out of Heaven: *"The Religion of Peace Is Back."*

7:28 A.M.
A bookstore
Mayfair, London

All of the planning, Sayyed Hassan thought—staring up at the TV on the far wall of his store, its screen displaying the news coverage of the attack on London's den of perversion—all of the work, all of the times he had risked his life for God's struggle.

And someone else had been chosen in the end. The leader of the London cell dug the burner phone he had been given out of his pocket, looking almost wistfully at the darkened screen. It had been days since Tarik Abdul Muhammad had made contact. Days since he was to have returned from Leeds.

A sharp rap came at the door of the bookstore and he glanced up, startled—moving through the stacks of used and rare editions surrounding the counter until he could see the door, shuttered as it always was in the morning—his *Closed* sign still hanging in the window beside it.

He thought of ignoring it, but the knock came again. Harder and more insistent this time. "I'm sorry," he began, opening the door just a crack. "We're still closed. . .please come back—"

Nadeem was standing on his doorstep, the young black who had been recruited by the cell while still in prison. "*Salaam alaikum*, brother."

Blessings and peace be upon you.

"*Wa' alaikum salaam,*" Sayyed stammered out. And unto you peace. Visiting his place of business like this, unannounced. . .something was wrong. "Please, come in."

He closed the door behind the two of them, turning to the young man. "What news do you bring me from—"

Nadeem's big hand flew out without warning, closing around his throat and forcing him back toward the wall—cutting off what he had been about to say. "Quiet," he whispered, fire flashing from his dark eyes as he placed a finger to his lips.

Shaken, the store owner nodded his assent, massaging his bruised throat as Nadeem released him. *What was going on?*

He watched as the black man stalked through the shop—*his* shop—finally moving behind the counter to where Hassan kept a small radio. He turned it on, working with the dials until he found a rap station and turned the volume up.

All the way up, until vulgar, licentious music poured from the speakers, filling the store.

"What are you doing?" he demanded, finally finding his voice.

"I don't know, bruv," was Nadeem's calm reply, coming back to stand before him, his voice low and nearly drowned out by the throbbing backbeat. "You notice anything different these last few days?"

"No, no—nothing," Sayyed responded, still baffled by his demeanor. "Why are you asking all this? Who sent you?"

It was a moment before Nadeem responded, his eyes roving across the walls—the shelves of books. As if searching for something. At last he turned back, "The *Shuikh*. He has reason to believe that Five's got you under surveillance. . ."

7:35 A.M.
The M1 Motorway
Near Towchester, England

"We've known this was coming for years."

Thomas half-turned from the passenger seat, glancing across at the British analyst. "What was?"

It was a moment before Norris responded, threading the small Volvo through heavy work traffic on the southbound lanes. "The Islamic threat, the attack on Heaven last night. It's been building for more than a decade—Tarik Abdul Muhammad is only a convenient catalyst."

"But he's at their head," Thomas observed quietly, watching his counterpart's face. "With his connections to both AQ and *Lashkar*—his ability to unite Arabs and Pakistanis under one banner—he's perhaps the most charismatic leader the jihadis have seen since the death of UBL, certainly after the success of the Christmas Eve attacks."

"Oh, he's a leader," Norris replied, his eyes darting from the road in front of him to his mirrors as he pulled out into the next lane. "I'll give him that. But this didn't start with him, and we'd be fools to think the threat would end with him either."

Another moment, and the analyst's drawn face relaxed into a smile. "But why am I trying to convince you of something you already know to be true? You joined the Agency because of 9/11, as I recall."

"Indeed," Thomas replied, knowing all too well that there was no "recall" about it. "You've done your research. . .well."

He paused. "Not opposition research, I trust?"

"Opposition?" The look on Norris' face was that of a man who just hadn't had enough practice lying. "Perish the thought. We're allies after all, remember?"

Yes, of course, Thomas thought. *Allies*. And his allies were keeping something from him. The only question that remained was how to find out what it was.

8:17 A.M.
Thames House
London

"I want to know how in the name of *God*, Alec, they got this," Marsh announced, his face dark as he stormed into the conference room. He picked up the remote from the conference table and aimed it at the screen on the wall, ignoring MacCallum for the moment. "Pearson was on Sky News an hour ago, and gave this interview."

The MP's face appeared on-screen the next moment, caught in mid-sentence. "—attacker's name was Javeed Mousa, a twenty-three-year-old Libyan here in the UK on a student visa. Right here in our country, living as one of us. Eating our food, attending our schools, plotting to murder us in the name of his god."

MacCallum watched as the news host struggled to find his footing in an interview suddenly spun out of his control. "Since, uh, entering the House of Commons, Mr. Pearson, you've been marked for your strongly anti-Muslim rhetoric, and—"

"No." On-screen, they could see Pearson lean forward, an unmistakable intensity marking the MP's features. "I am *not* anti-Muslim, though that is how you would tar me. I am against those who have embraced democracy only to destroy it—against those who have come to this country with no desire to learn that which once made it great. Those who bring with them their ideology of hate. And in the interests of stopping this Islamist threat, I will stand with anyone—Christian, atheist, Muslim, Sikh—who believes as I do in the greatness of Britain and is willing to rise up, to take a stand in her defense."

"He's a passionate speaker, I'll give him that," MacCallum acknowledged, clearing his throat. "But how did the *Daily Standard* get that name? That type of information, it hasn't been released to the public."

Marsh held up a hand for silence. "There's more."

"Your name has long been associated with right-wing nationalist groups like the British Defence Coalition," the host interjected, finally getting a word in. "How do you feel that the extremist rhetoric of such groups helps your cause? Is this not an issue to be addressed with cool heads, not the anger of protesters in the streets?"

Pearson leaned back into the couch, clearly incredulous. "Their *rhetoric*. . .are you serious? The bodies of our countrymen are scarce cold—the Security Services are investigating Mousa's connections with the Islamic State here in Britain—the body count of our failed multicultural experiment grows by the day. . .and you're concerned about rhetoric? About anger?"

He paused, holding up a long index finger to cut the anchor off. "I'll tell you why there's anger—why people have taken to the streets. People see the images on their telly, they see their countrymen blown up, beheaded by these Islamists, all in the name of some 'holy war.' And in response to these atrocities, they find their own government passing laws to protect—no, not them, but the hurt feelings of the very people who share common creed with the terrorists. They feel helpless, impotent, betrayed. Angry."

Another pause, Pearson glancing directly into the camera as he spread his hands. "And I ask, can you blame them?"

Marsh threw the remote down upon the conference table with an angry gesture, the screen going black in that moment. "This is only going to fan the flames."

"Even if he's right?" MacCallum asked, glancing over at the DG.

"Especially if he's right," the Cold War veteran glared back, one hand poised on the edge of the table. "We are officers of the Security Service, Alec. Public servants. We do not weigh morality in the balances, we do not presume to place ourselves in the seat of God. That is, after all, what we have Whitehall for."

The DG's index finger tapped against the polished wood of the conference table—a hard, insistent drumbeat. "Somewhere. . .we have a leak. Find it. Plug it. Tell me when it's done."

9:34 A.M.
The safehouse

"The trackers are still on-line?" Flaharty demanded. He looked pale from loss of blood, unsteady as he stood to his feet, shrugging his jacket back on over the bandages—the torn shirt.

Harry nodded, watching as the arms dealer reached for the bottle of Bushmills sitting there on the counter and poured himself a shot—the whisky splashing into a glass far too large for the purpose. "They were when I checked an hour ago. Do we have a plan?"

Malone snorted from his position across the room, near the door. He hadn't been back from his recce of the area more than a few minutes "What do you mean 'we', boyo? You're not one of us."

"I'll take that as a 'no,'" Harry responded coolly, not even glancing at the bodyguard. "But *we* will need a plan if we're all to make it out of this."

"Stephen and I," he began again, an edge to his voice, "were dodging the British Army in Belfast years before you were even a leer in your da's eye. We don't need your help getting this sorted."

This time, Harry turned, transfixing Malone with a cold, hard stare. Only too aware that he was baiting the man.

"Perhaps I was misinformed. . .I wasn't aware that you were in charge here, Malone. You would have died in that ditch last night if it weren't for me." He shrugged. "Maybe I should have let you."

"Why, you—"

Flaharty slammed his glass down into the countertop, his hand trembling as he pushed it away from him. "Enough! We're all in this together now whether we like it or not. Don't need to bloody well do their job for them. Davey—were you able to establish any contact with the lads?"

A reluctant, almost sullen nod. "Aye, I did—finally, after calling up Éamon's bird. She put him on the phone."

"And?"

Malone sighed, a heavy sound. "Everyone's dead, Stephen. They caught up with the trucks outside of Claughton—our boys never stood a chance. Every last bleedin' one gunned down."

The color seemed to drain from Flaharty's face, a curse escaping his lips. "Even Sean?"

A nod. "Dear God," the arms dealer whispered, "Sean was a good man. One of the last from the old days."

"Éamon said he'd be letting his widow know as soon as he could put his head up."

Flaharty's face twisted in anger at the memory and he poured another shot of the Bushmills into the glass, tossing it back. "They are not going to get away with this. They are not going to bloody get away with killing my men."

"No, they're not," Harry interjected, looking from one man to the other. "And I'll help you bring them down, so long as I get what I want in the end."

"Which is?" the arms dealer asked, steadying himself against the counter.

"Tarik Abdul Muhammad. *Dead.*"

Malone shook his head angrily. "Bugger off. We can handle this ourselves."

"Easy there, Davey," Flaharty said sternly, shooting his subordinate a warning glance. "We're going to need all the allies we can find. You. . .have your deal."

Harry acknowledged his words with a simple nod. "Then it's time we were to work."

"Indeed." The arms dealer raised his glass, as if in a toast, a grim smile playing at his lips. "To the confusion of *our* enemies."

9:58 A.M.
Leeds Central Police Station
Park Street, Leeds

Confusion. Light and darkness, swirling together, a cacophony of noise filling the small, windowless room. Loud music broken every few seconds—or so it seemed—by the wail of a siren.

He no longer had any idea how long he had been alone, but it had to have been hours. At least. It felt like weeks. He put his head down on the small table, struggling to move his manacled hands up to shield his ears against the noise.

God suffices me, he breathed, struggling to focus long enough to finish the *dua'a*. *There is no god but He. On Him do I rely and*—

All the noise ceased abruptly, the silence hitting him with the force of a physical blow—light flooding through the room as the lights came on above him.

Then the sound of a chair being dragged back over the floor—an almost unbearable noise in the wake of the sudden stillness. "Your name is Ismail Besimi, am I correct?"

Head throbbing, the imam raised his eyes from the table to stare into the face of a British officer perhaps half his own age. "Yes," he managed, his throat dry.

A photo was slid across the table until it rested against the knuckles of his shackled hands. "Tell me about your communication with this man."

It was the face of a young man. . .Pakistani perhaps? Dark hair, a close-cropped beard—and blue eyes that stared out of the photo with mesmerizing power. "I've...never seen this man before in my life," Besimi stammered, struggling to think.

An indulgent smile. "That's not what I asked."

10:58 A.M.
Thames House
London

"Ah, there you are," Alec MacCallum observed as Norris entered the operations centre. "And just in time. How was your visit with the cousins?"

"Unproductive," was the analyst's response. "They don't have anything on Muzhir bin Abdullah—or rather if he's ever showed up on their radar, they're not saying."

That meant they had nothing, and both men knew how dangerous that was. A trail that was already several months cold, dating back to the time when Muzhir had left his flat in East London, never to return.

The *Shaikh* had placed five phone calls, one of which had already resulted in a terrorist attack. The remaining three were as yet unidentified.

Which left them with Muzhir.

Norris went on after a moment, "Didn't learn anything from Parker except that he's good at his job. Very good."

"And we already knew that." MacCallum came around the edge of Norris' desk, laying a plain, unmarked folder before him. "I need you to look into something for me," he said, lowering his voice, "and keep it off the radar."

"What is it?" Norris asked, not moving to take the folder.

"We have a problem...someone leaked details about the nightclub attack to the *Daily Standard*."

"The *Standard*?" The analyst's brow furrowed. "That's Arthur Colville's paper, isn't it?"

A nod. "It is, and he's using this to stir up a firestorm. A bomb went off on the M6 last night in Lancashire, north of Claughton. The blogs are going crazy saying that it was another Muslim terrorist attack."

"Was it?"

MacCallum pursed his lips. "No idea—Roth was sending someone up, but the NCA is spearheading the investigation. I need you to focus your attention on this—find out exactly who was read in on the attack details and who could have leaked them to Colville."

"Anyone could do that—you need me on the search for Tarik Abdul Muhammad."

"No," the department chief replied, tapping the folder with his finger. "Marsh needs this prioritized. . .and I need someone I can trust. Get back to me when you have answers."

11:37 A.M.
The M6 Motorway
North of Claughton

Slushy snow met Mehreen's boots as she stepped out of the BMW, closing the car door behind her. It was a desolate stretch of roadway, wind blowing across the open meadows—through the towering pines that lined one side of the motorway.

"Mehreen Crawford, military intelligence," she announced, flashing her identification at the edge of the tape. "I need to speak with the officer in charge."

"That would be Inspector Haverson, ma'am," the young policeman responded, lifting the edge of the crime scene so that she could slip under it. "He's over there—beside the burned-out Explorer."

And she saw him, a short, balding figure standing by the blackened hulk gesturing to the man at his side—his form cloaked in a light windbreaker with the letters *NCA* on the back.

National Crime Agency.

It looked American—and indeed, there were many in the UK who resented the NCA as an American import, echoes of the powerful Federal Bureau of Investigation, with its power to supersede local constabularies. A state police.

She walked up and introduced herself, showing the identification once more. "What are we looking at?"

"A spook, eh?" Haverson asked, looking at her keenly. She didn't respond, just stared back, her eyes never leaving his. Five was an insular service, guarding the identities of its employees far more closely than most other Western intelligence agencies.

"Right," he said finally, seeming to quail under her gaze. "Well, ma'am. . .let me know how I can be of help."

She glanced across the pavement, taking in the multiple chalk outlines. "How many bodies are we looking at?"

"Five," came the taciturn reply. "Four of them clustered around the van here—another one ten meters away, above the median ditch. Everyone else was killed in the explosion, by the looks of it, but not him."

"Oh?" she asked, hands shoved into the pockets of her coat. Nothing made sense here.

"He was. . ." the NCA inspector paused, as if choosing his words carefully. "Well, he was nearly disemboweled by a shotgun blast, ma'am. That type of wound—I was never military, but I've never seen anything like it."

Mehreen grimaced.

"That's not what killed him, though," Haverson went on after a moment's pause. "He was executed—a pair of 9mm rounds to the temple. In and out. Mitchell dug one of them out of the macadam."

It had likely been a mercy, she thought, staring back along the roadway at the chalk outline marking the place where the body had once lain—the faint stain of blood. "Any ID on the bodies?"

The inspector shook his head. "Nothing in the way of formal identification on them, no—no driver's licenses. One of the men had a military tattoo on his arm, though and judging by their kit. . ." He gestured toward a pile of spent rifle casings still lying on the roadway. "I've made inquiries with the MoD."

The Ministry of Defence.

A sudden chill ran down her spine at his words—a premonition? A feeling so familiar. "The tattoo. Can you describe it?"

He ran a hand across his chin, shaking his head. "Almost—I don't know—a winged dagger?"

It wasn't wings, but rather a wreath of flame—but it was no moment for quibbling. "Yes. With Latin underneath it?"

"Something like that." Haverson looked up suddenly, realizing the import of her question. "You recognize it?"

But she was already on her mobile, holding up a finger for silence as she listened to it ring.

This was happening. . .again.

11:52 A.M.
The flat
Leeds

". . .as you can see behind me," the Sky News reporter said, looking over her shoulder at a line of riot police, "violence has erupted this morning in the Washwood Heath ward of Birmingham as men wearing the armbands of the British Defence Coalition clashed with police, assaulting members of the majority Muslim community here in Washwood Heath and setting fire to several Muslim-owned shops. The BDC has. . ."

She was pretty, Tarik Abdul Muhammad thought, gazing absently at the screen. In the blatantly sensual way of the West.

The way her dark hair framed her face. . .those red lips. The soft white column of her neck as it descended into her blouse.

It reminded him strangely of one of the prostitutes there in Las Vegas, on the eve of the attacks.

A curse broke from behind him and he looked up from the couch to see Hashim Rahman standing there, the imam's eyes fixed on the telly.

"And all across this country," he hissed, waving a hand, "Muslims grovel and scrape the ground in an effort to be accepted by these. . .*animals*. We have to do something."

"We have been," Tarik replied calmly. He had known that Colville would retaliate, even if he had not known the target. Muslim women being beaten in the streets—one nearly half-strangled with her own *niqab*—it was the perfect trigger. "And there is more to come."

"Small attacks," the imam spat, pacing back and forth across the floor in front of Tarik. His fist clenching and unclenching as if of its own will, his body trembling with anger. "Mourned today and forgotten by the next news cycle. They took Imam Besimi last night, took him right out of a restaurant here in Leeds."

"Besimi," Tarik shrugged, "was an apostate. You told me that yourself."

"That's not the point, God will judge his soul, not this corrupt government. We need to make them *pay* for what they have done to our brothers, our sisters. Not just here—but all across the Middle East."

"They will, *insh'allah*."

"Truly?" He gestured toward the darkened window, the shades drawn shut. "Ever since December, the name of the *Shaikh* has been on every faithful lip—the name of the man who had been used of God in the humbling of the Americans. You were compared to Usama, to Saladin. . .even to the companions of the Prophet. Lofty praise for one so young."

Tarik spread his hands. "Does the age of a man matter in the sight of God? We are all but His slaves, the instruments of His will. Nothing more."

Rahman went on without acknowledging his response, his voice growing with intensity—seemingly heedless of his sleeping wife only a few rooms away as he glared over at Tarik. "And when I heard that you had arrived in the UK, when you responded to my request for a meeting, I felt that God had sent us a messenger. A man to rally the faithful to our cause once and for all. And yet here we cower."

The *Shaikh*'s gaze never wavered, his voice calm when he spoke again. "For the moment. For those who fight in Allah's struggle, no retreat is final. No failure permanent. Even the Prophet, peace be upon him, was once forced to flee the persecution of the unbelievers. Our time will come."

"When?"

The Pakistani smiled, answering the question with one of his own. "How many men can you give me?"

1:35 P.M.
The United States Embassy
Grosvenor Square, London

It was something about Kranemeyer's eyes, Thomas thought, staring at the screen on the wall of the station chief's office. The type of eyes that could look straight through a man, piercing orbs the color of anthracite.

He'd known the man for years—in point of fact, it had been Kranemeyer that had recruited him, long ago at a Heritage Foundation dinner in Philly. A snowy evening, as he remembered it. But he'd never once felt comfortable in his presence.

And today was no exception, even with the man Parker called "boss" over a thousand miles away.

"The 'day of judgment' to which Tarik Abdul Muhammad referred in the intercepted call with Rahman—there is no likelihood in your mind that it was a reference to the attack on the nightclub?"

A shake of the head. "No. Our analysts here at Grosvenor Square have gone over it—the verbiage is the same as was used before the Vegas attacks. My assessment, and that which I have conveyed to my counterparts at the Security Services, is that we are looking at an attack equal or greater in scope."

"Crap," Jimenez observed quietly, summing up what they were all thinking in a single word.

"Your liaison officer—this Darren Roth," Kranemeyer began again after a brief pause. "What can you tell me about him?"

Thomas glanced over at Jimenez as if looking for guidance, but there was none to be found there. The former Marine's face was impassive. "He's an extremely. . .competent officer. Good in the field—clearly more comfortable there than behind a desk. He—"

On-screen, Kranemeyer held up a hand. "I can learn all that from Roth's jacket, which was compiled by the purportedly knowledgeable people over at the Intel Directorate. Give me something they can't."

There was no room for hesitation. "He's very close to a Five intelligence officer on his team," Thomas replied, his mind moving back to the previous night. The takedown of Besimi.

The look on Roth's face—his angry retort. *"Bugger tactical authority. This is Mehreen."*

"Do you have a name?"

"Mehreen Crawford—she's Pakistani, fluent in Pashto, Arabic and Urdu."

"I know her," Jimenez interjected quietly from his seat behind the desk. "Top flight officer, one of Julian's best people."

"And the nature of the relationship between her and Roth?"

"I have nothing solid," Thomas replied, spreading his hands as he glanced up at the screen. He could still remember the look in the former Royal Marine's eyes when he'd thought she was in danger. It had gone beyond concern for a team member. "I can also tell you that he's carrying."

That got the station chief's attention. "No way. The Security Service doesn't issue sidearms." He laughed, a short, barking sound. "They leave that for us cowboys."

A flash of annoyance passed across Thomas' face at the attempt at humor. "I know what a gun looks like when it prints. Legal, illegal—I don't have the answer to that, but Roth has a gun. And he's keeping us in the dark."

2:48 P.M.
The Home Office
2 Marsham Street, London

"I'm sorry, Julian, but my hands are tied. They truly are." Kathleen Napier pushed back the chair, rising to her feet.

Only the third woman to hold the office of Home Secretary, she was a tall, stately woman just a few years younger than Marsh—graying hair framing a face the years had not left untouched. "Even assuming you could find Tarik Abdul Muhammad—which is itself an uncertainty at this moment—to incarcerate him on no more evidence than we have now, evidence obtained by methods that the Prime Minister has officially denied utilizing. . .it would be a media firestorm."

"A media firestorm. . ." the director-general mused, leaning forward in his seat as he gazed at her. He had known Napier for years, but had never expected that she would be one to climb so far. So fast. "Are you quite sure the avoidance of that is worth risking a bona fide firestorm?"

"What are you saying?"

"I'm saying that despite these political considerations, it is the opinion of the Security Service that the danger of allowing him to retain his freedom is no longer outweighed by the dangers posed by the backlash from the Islamic community, of the civil liberties groups. We don't need 'evidence'—the man is here illegally. That will suffice for our purposes, much as Capone's tax evasion did for the cousins last century."

Napier turned back, her hands resting on the back of her chair. Fixing him with a keen gaze. "Is that the opinion of the Security Service, Julian—or yours?"

"I was twenty years old when Five recruited me, still just a lad studying the classics at Cambridge—Pliny, Ovid. Homer. I've been a spook ever since." He shrugged, not a trace of irony in his voice. "The opinion of the Security Service. . .mine? I fail to see how there is a measurable difference between the two."

She sighed, a heavy, weary sound. "Then you've been in the government long enough to understand *realpolitik*, Julian. The sacrifices which must be made so that the ship of state sails on. Perhaps last night what you're asking would have been possible, but after Pearson's disastrous interview on Sky News this morning, after the riot at Washwood Heath. . .we cannot be seen as standing alongside such Islamophobia—as condoning such hatred for the thousands of innocent Muslims who live and work among us on a daily basis."

A pause before she went on, as if she was giving time for her words to sink in. "I need you and your people to find Tarik Abdul Muhammad and monitor his movements, as before. That is all—do you understand?"

"Of course," Marsh replied, buttoning the center button of his suit as he rose to leave. "'The Assyrian came down like the wolf on the fold. . .'"

"What?"

"It's Lord Byron—just a relic of my misspent youth."

"Ah. . ." was her only response, seeming to accept his answer. "One more thing: you were in Cambridge with Arthur Colville, were you not?"

It was an odd question. "The publisher? I was an upper classman when he first entered the university, but yes. Why?"

Napier gestured to the front page of the *Daily Standard* lying there on her desk, the headline still screaming out defiance. "I want you to set up a meet. Find out what he knows. See if you can convince him to take a step back."

10:12 A.M. Eastern Time
CIA Headquarters
Langley, Virginia

"I copy you loud and clear, Bravo-Actual," Ron Carter heard the comms chief say, staring up at the imagery on the screens lining the north wall of the Op-Center, a slate-gray landscape as stark and bare as the surface of the moon. "We're getting the Reaper's feeds coming through now."

This was bad, he thought, eyeing the panorama spread out before them. No matter how carefully you planned a mission, you could never account for *everything*. And it was what you hadn't accounted for that came back to bite you.

"What's going on?" Carter glanced back to see Kranemeyer standing a few feet away, clearly just arrived on the floor.

"Bravo Team in the Sinai," he said, turning away. "They were planning to go in on the compound tonight—got surprised in the hide by a pair of Bedouin shepherds shortly after 1600 hours local time."

The DCS swore under his breath. "And. . .?"

"And the *Sa'ka* lost their heads," the analyst replied, referencing the Egyptian special forces. "Cut both men down in a hail of automatic weapons fire."

Alerting everyone within five miles, he didn't say. "Coordinating" with local forces was ever a gamble at best—most days a roulette wheel would offer better odds.

"With the mission compromised, Nakamura was left with no choice but to order the assault. The result was nine *Ansar* militants KIA, with another five taken prisoner. The Egyptian commandos lost three men—at least one injured in their own fire on entry. Bravo Team, however, suffered no casualties."

Kranemeyer grimaced, shaking his head. "What about Umar ibn Hassan?"

"Nowhere to be found," Carter said grimly. "No evidence he had ever been there. A dry hole."

It happened. Intel was bad. People lied. Best you could do was pick up and move on. *Chase another shadow*.

"Make sure I'm fully briefed on where the operation proceeds from this point," the DCS said, eyeing the drone imagery with a critical glance as he turned to leave.

He paused a moment, suddenly extending a folder in his hand. *A personnel jacket*. "Oh, and Ron. . .with regards to what we discussed the other day. The Mali operation."

Carter took the folder from him, a chill running through his body as he opened it—his eyes scanning down the page. "You can't be serious. You don't honestly expect me to—"

"Oh, but I am," Kranemeyer responded, his dark eyes never leaving Carter's face. "And I do. . ."

4:30 P.M. Greenwich Mean Time
The M6 Motorway
North of Claughton

"I understand, Alec. Just get me the results as soon as you can get the data from the NCA." Mehreen sighed, rubbing a dark hand across her forehead as she stared out through the windshield of the BMW. Shows on the telly made DNA look so magical, so *instant*. The reality was that they wouldn't have a positive ID on the charred bodies from the bombing for weeks. And she knew that. "I have a bad feeling about this, remember just a few days ago—the Para shot dead in the countryside north of Leeds?"

"I do," MacCallum replied. "Are you saying that they're connected?"

Was she? She hesitated, remembering Nichols' face. The way he had looked when admitting to Booth's murder. *No remorse*. But MacCallum couldn't be told the truth of that, couldn't learn what she herself had done.

This was no time for her to find herself pulled into the type of internal investigation that would inevitably ensue. Not with Besimi being held on suspicion of conspiracy with terrorists. Not with her own nephew in danger.

"I don't know." It was only half a lie.

"Mehreen," the section chief began again, a distinct note of hesitation in his tone. "there is something more. Something I was able to pull up."

"What is it?" There was something strange about his voice, a dark sense of foreboding that chilled her to the bone.

"It's the charred-out Explorer. . .I got a partial from what was left of the plates—ran it through our database. Got a hit. It's registered to one Sean Dugan, a citizen of the Republic of Ireland."

"So?"

Another pause. "Sean Dugan is a suspected alias of Stephen Flaharty."

She turned away for a moment, her eyes shut tightly, struggling against the emotion that threatened to overwhelm her. "Oh, God. . ."

6:07 P.M.
A warehouse
Ashton-under-Lyne

"That's where they are," Harry announced, sliding back into the car and handing the binoculars across to Flaharty. The man didn't look good, the pallor of his cheeks almost impossible to disguise.

"Are you sure?" the arms dealer asked, wincing as he shifted his position in the passenger seat.

He nodded, his eyes still focused on their target across the road. The view from the parking lot wasn't as good as the one he'd had from the top of a nearby overpass only a few minutes before, but he could still make out the front gates. "It's the only warehouse within a reasonable radius of the tracker beacon. They have two men out front, both with sidearms, probably another one or more in the back. There's a utility vehicle fifty meters back of the main gate, near the sentries. Even money they're keeping the long arms in there, under wraps."

"Likely," Flaharty responded. "It's the way I'd play it."

"Another car's there now, couldn't make out the full license plate, but I think I got enough before they pulled it into the warehouse itself."

Harry brushed back the sleeve of his jacket, revealing a row of letters and numbers scrawled onto the winter-pale skin of his wrist.

"So, how do we get in?" Malone asked, casting a shadow over them as he came up beside the car. That was always the question of any op, after the reconnaissance had been done, after you had all the intel you could garner. *How?*

But not today.

"We don't," Harry replied calmly. "This was a recce, nothing more."

The enforcer swore, placing a meaty hand on the edge of the car's lowered window. "They butchered our lads, Stephen," he said looking across Harry into the arms dealer's eyes. His voice low, earnest. "Good men, all of them. Can't let that stand. We need to hit back, fast and hard."

It was the wrong move, and Harry knew it—but he could see Flaharty beginning to waver. *Revenge.*

It was a thirst he knew all too well. . .the desire that had gnawed at his heart since Vegas.

"If you do this," he countered, trying to stay one step ahead of the demon, "you're going to throw it all away. Every chance we have of getting to the bottom of their play. They'll *know* that we're tracking them—they'll know we're out here. And they will come for us with everything they have."

"Do you have a better plan?" Flaharty asked, glancing between him and Malone.

Harry tapped his wrist, indicating the license number. "We watch. And wait."

It was dark inside the warehouse, fluorescent lights providing only pale illumination among the stacks of crates—the last faint orange-red rays of sunlight making their way through the skylights above.

"Are you sure no women or children will be killed?" Paul Gordon asked, perspiration glinting on his forehead as he straightened, reaching over to take another bag of fertilizer from Conor Hale.

A weary shake of the head as the former SAS man handed it over, his sleeves rolled up above his elbows. "This is war, Paul. There's never any way to be *sure.* We both know that."

Hale seemed to sense his hesitation and leaned in closer. "Look, mate, this isn't hard. Your grandfather flew for the RAF over Germany, didn't he?"

Gordon nodded reluctantly. "Aye, that he was. The bombardier on a Halifax."

"And tell me honestly," Hale continued, "when he opened those bomb bay doors. . .how did he know—how could he be *certain* that the people he dropped those bombs on were grown men wearing Wehrmacht grey? It's no different for us."

"But we're going to time the blast to minimize the collateral damage?" Perhaps it was a useless question, Gordon thought, wiping his brow with the back of his hand. Perhaps they all deserved it in the end, but he had to ask. *For Alice.*

"Of course," came the reply. "The bomb will go off hours before it's even open to the public. All we're doing here is sending a message, mate. That's all."

He took a step back as Hale placed the final bag of fertilizer in the boot of the car, watching as the former sergeant spread a tarpaulin over the load. "We'd be safer using the Semtex," he cautioned, his gaze drifting over to the smaller crates by the rifles. "It's more stable, easier to reliably time to go off when we want it to and not before. Or after."

"And," Hale straightened, a hard look in his eyes, "it points a great big bloody arrow right back at us. You go using plastique—that's the mark of professionals. Of funding. It compromises the mission."

He could sense that he was on dangerous ground, but he had no other choice. "Then why did we go to all the trouble of getting it if we're too afraid to use it?"

Hale pushed past him, drawing car keys from his pocket as he moved. "Oh, don't you worry. That time will come."

"We have movement—they're coming out." It was Malone's voice coming over Harry's Bluetooth headset. The Irishman had taken up an overwatch position about five hundred meters to their west, with a better line of sight on the warehouse itself.

"It's the sedan?" Harry asked, his mouth still full of potato crisps. Or chips, as he would have called them in the States. He dropped the half-empty bag onto the seat beside him as he reached for the binoculars.

"Aye." And sure enough, there it was—the two guards he had observed earlier moving to swing the gates open, allowing the car to depart. *Swinging inward*, he thought, mentally noting it against future need.

An inward-opening gate was vulnerable to a ramming attack. An assault would be counterproductive, as he had warned Flaharty, but he'd been at war for too long for the observation to escape him.

"I want you to get in your car and follow them," he ordered calmly. "See if you can stay on them—see where they go."

"Is that a fact? And what will you be doing in the meantime, boyo?"

Harry glanced over at Flaharty, his lips forming something that could have barely passed for a smile. "Waiting. . .for the changing of the guard."

7:45 P.M.
Leeds

She had been in the car for two hours, just watching—absorbing the sights and sounds of the neighborhood as night fell. The place she had once called home.

Not much had changed, by the looks of it—still the old flats dating back decades, the time-worn red brick that had characterized Leeds ever since its days as a center of the wool trade.

Mehreen sighed, running a hand across her face. She'd lied. Told Darren that she was following up on a lead in the city.

It couldn't have been farther from the truth, she thought, remembering his final words. *"Be careful, Mehr. No telling who might have seen you with Besimi—who he might have told. He knows your name, he knows who you really are."*

As did the people in the house across the street from where she sat in the driver's seat of the BMW.

She took a deep breath, looking down at her watch. Knowing that she was only postponing the inevitable.

Her hand moved to open the door and then she was out, rounding the front of the car to head across the street, her jacket pulled close around her body. The wind tousling her dark hair.

So many years. She stopped by the ground-level door of the flat, hesitating as she lifted her hand to knock. It was a strange feeling, the reluctance. The dread.

That what Besimi had said might even be true.

Another moment, and her hand rapped against the metal. Once, then twice.

It was on the third knock that she heard the sound of a chain being unfastened—a bolt slid back. A woman appearing in the opening, silhouetted against the light coming from the hall—her face framed by the familiar shape of the *hijab*. "I'm sorry, we—"

The woman stopped suddenly, recognition filling her eyes. "Mehreen," she began hesitantly, backing away from the doorway as it swung open. "It's been so long. . ."

Chapter 12

8:06 P.M.
A mosque
London, England

The street was dark—and good reason for it, the man thought, kneeling by the back entrance of the mosque.

He'd shot out the light only moments before with a scoped pellet rifle, the shot only a whisper in the night.

Conor Hale removed the second lockpick from between his teeth, a smile crossing his face as the tumblers moved beneath the steady pressure. *There.*

A glance back toward the darkened sedan assured him that Gordon was still in place. Keeping watch.

Trust. Hale grimaced, going to work on the deadbolt. It was such an uncertain gamble.

He'd told Colville that he would trust any of the Paras with his life—more importantly that he *had*. Once upon a time, in a godforsaken place called Iraq.

But Gordon's questions at the warehouse. . .it begged the question whether any of them truly had the stomach for what was coming. What was *necessary*.

Another *click* and then the bolt gave, the door opening as he pushed in—revealing only darkness within. No flashing lights, no alarms. Their intel had been good.

He straightened, waving a hand to signal his partner to come on in. It was time to get to work.

8:17 P.M.
The house
Leeds

"And your work in the city goes well?" Mehreen smiled, glancing up at her sister-in-law's question. Her family, they believed that she was a low-level functionary at a government agency in London. A clerk, nothing more.

"It does, Nimra." She took a sip of the steaming tea as the younger woman bustled around the kitchen, seeming nervously busy, only now having removed the hijab from around her face.

Two women alone, in the sanctity of the home. "And your family? How is Aydin?"

It was a long moment before Nimra replied, and when she did, she didn't meet her eyes. "He is well, thank you. So big now, we are very proud of him."

"I'm sure you are." Mehreen waited until her sister-in-law had finally taken her seat across from her. "This late, I had almost thought I might see him. Is he out with friends?"

"Yes, he is with friends." Once again, she looked away, her reply almost mechanical. It was so unlike the woman her brother had married, the sprite of a girl whose laughter had captured the hearts of her parents in the years before they had passed.

A replacement for the daughter they had. . .*lost*.

Her lips pressed together into a tight line at the memory. They had never forgiven her.

"Friends from the school?" she asked brightly, trying not to push too fast, struggling with the thought of using her training *here*, with her own family. Something within her rebelling at the very idea.

"Yes," her sister-in-law replied after yet another moment of hesitation, a shadow passing across her face. "He's a good boy. . but so serious."

Mehreen forced a smile, lifting the cup of tea to her lips. "Serious? It's hard for me to think of him like that—he was such a child when I saw him last. Do you think I will see him tonight?"

"Probably not. And I don't know what he would think if you did."

"What do you mean?" It was hard to maintain this expression of innocence, this naivete—in the face of what Besimi had told her. If it was true. Was anything true?

The younger woman paused, stirring her tea with a spoon. "Aydin, he—he does not believe that his father and I—that we are good Muslims, that we take our faith as seriously as we should. If he were to see you. . ."

Her gaze swept over Mehreen in an almost embarrassed manner—taking in the jeans, the stylish blouse beneath the unbuttoned jacket. The message clearly and painfully written in her eyes. "Please, I don't like talking about it. He is good at heart, just. . .too passionate. It will pass."

It was a statement made utterly without conviction, a mother trying to convince herself of something she knew wasn't true. Of something they both knew wasn't true. "I-I warned him to be careful this evening, after the riots in Birmingham earlier—they were all over the telly. My cousin knew one of the women who was beaten, it was just horrible."

"The tensions are only building," Mehreen responded, sincerely enough. Feeling her way along. "It is a difficult time to be one of the faithful in this country, with all that surrounds us."

Nimra's eyes widened and she leaned forward, as if sharing some great secret. "Did you hear—the police took Imam Besimi last night?"

"No," she breathed, closing her eyes against the lie. She could still see the shock written on his face, the bewilderment as the stun grenade exploded almost on top of them, nearly blinding them with the blast. "I had no idea. What are they charging him with?"

"No one knows—no one has heard from the imam since they took him away. Not a single word."

"That's just. . .wrong," she said, replacing the lies with the utmost of conviction. "He was a good man."

And she believed it. She looked up to find Nimra looking finally into her eyes, something of despair in her gaze—and looked away, lest her own eyes betray something of what she knew. "May I use your loo?"

A nod, a few directions. *At the top of the stairs, the first room on the right.*

Mehreen turned on the light over the sink—glancing at her own reflection briefly in the mirror as she turned both faucets on full, closing the door behind her as she stepped back into the darkness of the upstairs hallway. *Three rooms*, she noted, trying the handle of the first door.

It gave under her hand, opening into darkness. She flipped out her mobile, the glow of the screen revealed a room cluttered with odds and ends—a broken ironing board propped in one corner, a deserted exercise bicycle in another, a bag of clothes strewn on the floor. The detritus of a normal life.

She closed the door as gently as she had opened it, hearing Nimra moving about in the kitchen downstairs. It felt as if she were invading their privacy.

Betraying something. . .sacred.

8:25 P.M.
The mosque
East London

It seemed strange to be doing this, after all those years in Iraq—after all the mates they had lost to roadside bombs, to the ever-present IEDs. As if a bomb was a weapon of evil. . .but he knew better. Evil was what *they* were fighting, just as they once had overseas.

Just different weapons, that was all.

"This will bring down the whole bloody building, won't it?" Paul Gordon asked, watching as Hale finished wiring the detonator. It was a timed device, set to go off hours before the mosque opened for morning prayers.

The former SAS man grimaced, glancing up at the steel beams above them supporting the ground floor of the structure. "That's the idea—we'll see how they like arriving to a hole in the ground in the morning."

Another moment passed, and both men heard a faint *beep* as the device armed itself. Hale rose, his smile faintly visible in the darkness. "It's time for us to be leavin', mate. Go home, get some sleep. Visit your sister in the morning. Might be your last chance for a while."

Footsteps faded away across the floor of the basement, lights flickering out into darkness.

And within the mechanism of the bomb, an internal clock began ticking down to the moment of detonation. *15:59:05. . .15:59:04. . .15:59:03. . .*

The hour of the noonday prayer.

8:26 P.M.
The house
Leeds

There was data. A lot of it. Mehreen ran a hand over her face, staring at the glowing screen of the laptop in the darkness of Aydin's bedroom. Watching as the program mirrored everything on his hard drive off onto the thumb drive she had slipped into the side of the machine.

Internet search history, blog posts, saved files. . .the little she had seen of it so far was painting a far different picture of her nephew than Nimra had portrayed. Withdrawn, sullen—passionate? Angry would have been a more apt descriptor.

Eighty-five percent complete. Someone was going to need to sift through all of this—and it would have to be her. There was no one she could trust at Thames

House with a matter of this delicacy. Not and be assured that it would stay out of official channels. . .for now.

Looking at the screen, at the sites her nephew had visited—at the messages he had sent—she had to admit that there might come no other choice. But not yet.

"Mehreen!" Her heart nearly stopped, the sound of her sister-in-law's voice coming from downstairs. *Eighty-nine percent.*

Come on. . .

The hallway was dark when Nimra mounted the stairs, the sound of running water coming from the bathroom. *No response.* It had always been a challenge for her to understand her husband's sister. The woman was just so. . .different.

Her way of life so alien from theirs, even as Western as Ahmed tried to be in his dress, in his business.

"Mehreen," she began, pausing at the door of the bathroom. "Is everything all right?"

A moment passed and then the door opened, revealing her sister-in-law standing there. "Yes," Mehreen smiled, wiping damp hands on the legs of her jeans. "It is."

Mehreen's smile faded as Nimra turned to lead the way back downstairs, her heart still pounding against her chest. She had come so close. . .so close to jeopardizing everything that she held dear.

She slipped a hand into the pocket of her jeans, feeling the data-filled thumb drive against her fingers. Knowing the secrets it could hold.

Knowing that day might yet come.

10:03 P.M.
The warehouse
Ashton-under-Lyne

Surveillance. It was the most boring and simultaneously most common job in the business—the one no movie director worth his salt would dream of showing his audience.

The plan, if you wanted to call it that, was to monitor Hale's people—to wait for the security change and follow one of the guards home. Get an address, get a name.

Slow work, but it was the best they had. They needed more intel, needed it badly.

Unless Malone got lucky and found something by tailing the sedan.

Harry shifted in the driver's seat of the car, wincing as pain shot through his ankle. His legs were cramped from sitting for so long, the used water bottle lying on the floor between him and a sleeping Flaharty now nearly a quarter full with urine.

As with the other, you used what you had.

He'd known many such nights over the years—most of his adult life had been spent just like this, endless hours cramped up in tight spaces. Watching dangerous people.

The life he had once thought he could leave behind. What was it he had told Samuel Han, standing there in that cabin in the mountains of West Virginia?

Don't kid yourself, Sammy. No one's ever out of the game.

Oh, he had known. . .but he'd lied. To himself. To *her*. It had seemed the thing to do at the time.

And now this. There had to be something, some connection they were missing. It felt as if they were wandering in a maze, the darkness closing around them.

"That's why I had Booth. . .he was my man on the inside. Until you up and shot him in the back."

Flaharty's voice, coming back through his memories—conjuring up the image of the young Para lying dead on the hard ground beneath AlmsCliffe Crag.

It was just possible. . .he tapped a finger absently against the steering wheel, lost in thought. "What did he know?" he asked softly, staring out at the night.

"Who?" Flaharty demanded and he glanced over to see the Irishman staring at him. No longer asleep.

"Booth. We're missing something here. Could he have known who was bankrolling the shipment?"

"I've no idea what he knew." Flaharty snorted. "Never will, either, thanks to you."

"It's not Hale," Harry continued, as if he hadn't spoken, "ex-SF NCOs don't have that kind of money."

He could see Mehreen's face before him the last time they had spoken, the look of reproach in her eyes as she spoke of the soldier. What had she said? *"He had a family."*

"Booth was a family man?" he asked aloud, returning his attention to Flaharty.

"Had a woman," was the short reply. "Down near Surrey somewhere. Doubt she would know anything."

"She doesn't have to," Harry said, running a hand over his beard. Not if there were financial records. Intel still stored on the dead man's hard drive. "Still worth our while to pay her a visit. Can you get an address?"

A slow nod, Flaharty's eyes suddenly fixed across the road. "As soon as we're done here."

Harry looked over to see movement from the warehouse, lights flashing across the yard, and he reached down, shifting into Drive. "Showtime."

11:19 P.M.
Abbey Road, London

He'd had two wives—well, three. . .if you counted his first, a marriage which had only lasted a few months.

And now he was old and the terraced house was empty, his footsteps hollow on the stairs as he threw his coat across the bannister—shrugging off his suit jacket.

Telling them had always been the hard part, Julian Marsh thought, grimacing as he walked into the kitchen, turning on the lights as he went.

Telling them that the man they had grown to love, was a spy. He'd had more than several back out on him at that point, some angry at the deception, the rest simply realizing that his life was not to be theirs.

The others had forged ahead, swearing their loyalty. Their "undying" love. Yes, well that had been a lie—like so much else in his line of work.

Regnum Defende. Defend the realm.

It was late, but Marsh pulled down a glass from the cupboard over his head anyway. The rum should help him sleep—it was about the only thing that did these days.

Perhaps enough sleep to prepare him for the meeting Napier had asked him to arrange with Arthur Colville in the morning. *Perhaps*.

The phone rang before he could pour it, a discordant sound in the empty house. "Marsh, here."

It was MacCallum—his tones urgent. Clipped. "We just got a face off CCTV in South London. . .one of the OSIRIS cameras. It's Muzhir bin Abdullah. And he's not alone."

11:28 P.M.
A nightclub
Southeast London

"She's not going to miss you at home—last night and all?" The man had to raise his voice to be heard over the beat pulsating through the club, but Corporal Dunne heard him.

"We don't do good-byes, Michael," he replied—glancing over at his mate. "She's had enough of those."

"Fifth time, right?"

He nodded, draining the last of his beer—wiping away a few droplets of the warm liquid away from the corner of his mouth with his sleeve. He'd be in uniform by morning, huddled in the back of an RAF Hercules.

On his way to Afghanistan for his fifth deployment. And the last one, or so the politicians said. They'd said it before. All he knew was that he'd had enough of it. And so had Sally—they'd been together through the last three.

"I wish I was going back with you," his companion said regretfully, looking out over the swaying crowd.

"Don't, Michael," Dunne responded, with more heat than he had intended. "Just bloody don't. They don't have a clue what we're doing over there, mate. Never did."

"Politicians. . .they never do." The man smiled, tapping his right leg with his empty glass—the action producing a curiously dull sound. "Of course, I couldn't even if they'd let me. No room in the army for a gimp."

They both laughed at that, though there was little humor in it. "You sure you're not drinkin' too much, mate?"

Dunne arched an eyebrow. "I'm not the poor sod that has to be flying that plane in the morning. But you have a point. Let me find Billy and Todd and we'll be going."

The night wasn't cold, at least not by London standards—but the temperature didn't matter so much when you were wet, Muzhir thought—grimacing as rain dripped from his black hair to sluice down the back of his neck.

Impatience threatened to overcome him as he shifted his weight from one foot to another, glancing at his companions—the three who had come with him this night. True brothers. They couldn't afford to wait much longer.

"Do not fear death," he began, repeating the words of *Inspire* as he moved from one man to the next in an effort to strengthen them for this moment, "whoever does not die by the sword will die by other means. Various are the means, but death, it is one. Provided that there is no escape from death, it is of weakness that you die in a cowardly manner."

He was the only one in the group with a gun, the only firearm they had been able to obtain. An old Smith & Wesson revolver. . .an American gun. *Irony*.

And then he saw the doors of the nightclub open, light and music spilling out—saw their targets emerge into the street—a group of men laughing and singing. A group of *soldiers*.

11:35 P.M.
Thames House

"The threat *is* imminent," MacCallum repeated, swearing under his breath. "Do whatever you have to do."

He replaced the phone in its cradle, looking up to see Simon Norris standing there. "Do you have anything on the identity of Muzhir's companions?"

The analyst shook his head. "Nothing yet, facial recognition isn't coming up with anything on the men with him. They're not in our systems."

"Then expand your search parameters and find them." It wasn't as simple as that and both men knew it, but it was their only option.

"What's going on now?"

MacCallum gestured to the phone. "CO-19 is on-scene and beginning their sweep of the area." He stared up at the screens on the wall before them, the timestamp of the first CCTV images clearly visible. "Forty minutes. They could be anywhere now."

11:37 P.M.
Southeast London

"I think you were right," Dunne laughed, an arm thrown around his old comrade's shoulder as the two of them staggered down the street toward the bus station.

"About what?"

"I think," the British Army corporal began again, his words slurring as he lifted one finger for emphasis, glancing around at his friends, "that I may. . .have been drinking too much."

That brought a laugh. They had seen so much together, been through so much hell since the day they had first met on a FOB in the Helmand—so many years before. "But what's a last night for if you can't spend it getting royally. . ."

A shout interrupted Dunne's words, the sound taking a moment to penetrate through the haze surrounding his brain. A single man standing perhaps ten feet in front of them, his face cloaked by a hooded jacket. ". . .killed our brothers in Iraq, in Palestine! And if God had willed, He could have taken vengeance upon you Himself. But—"

"Oh, bugger off, Paki, what are you on about?" Dunne responded, still not full grasping their danger.

And then he saw the gun.

The wood was slick against Muzhir's palm—slick with sweat he realized, bringing the heavy revolver up in one hand. Squeezing the trigger.

Squeezing and squeezing. . .he hadn't cocked the hammer back, panic seizing hold as he struggled to pull the heavy double-action trigger. This wasn't how he had envisioned it, the glory of this moment turning to sheer terror in his heart.

He saw the British soldiers start to move toward him—the sights of the Smith & Wesson wavering from one to another.

And the trigger broke, the night erupting in fire. . .

11:58 P.M.
M40 Motorway
Near Birmingham

It had been the right thing to do. The necessary thing to do if she hoped to extract her nephew from the danger that he had placed himself in. She knew that, but it didn't change the way she felt. Dirty, as if she needed to bathe.

If she had known that working for Five would one day pit her against her own family—her own community—how would she have responded to their efforts to recruit her? Mehreen shook her head, staring straight ahead as the car sped down the motorway back toward London.

It was a question she had asked herself time and again in the years since 9/11. A question she still didn't have the answer to. Hadn't seemed relevant back in the '90s.

All she knew now was that the personal was rapidly overwhelming the professional, despite all her efforts to the contrary. Nichols, Besimi. . .now her nephew.

She felt the slight bulge of the drive again, tucked into the pocket of her jeans. Knowing that the data on it could incriminate her family—could even bring her down, if it went that far.

But for the moment, all that mattered was saving Aydin from himself.

All that mattered. That had been Nick, once. Their love the only thing in life she had cared about. Until it had been ripped away from her.

If she closed her eyes, even for a moment, she could hear MacCallum's voice saying, *"Sean Dugan is a suspected alias of Stephen Flaharty."*

A name from the past, she thought bitterly, struggling to push aside the anger. To *focus*. She couldn't trust MacCallum with this—he was far too loyal to the Service. The same went for everyone else at Thames House, the people she had worked side by side with for years.

And yet. . .there were too many variables at play, too many things that could go wrong. The risk of losing her nephew far too high, her family the only thing left to her. She wasn't going to be able to do this alone.

Her hand stole within the unzipped front of her jacket, closing around the mobile in her inner pocket.

She pulled it out, hesitating as she glanced at the screen. The moment of decision, doubt plaguing at her mind. What would Nick have done had he faced this?

Mehreen swore under her breath. She knew, because she knew who Nick had been. *What* he had been.

She punched in the number from memory, waiting as the phone dialed, its ring the only sound in the darkened car as she sped south. *Pick up.*

An automated voice came on as the call went to voicemail—no name, just the number, which was as she might have expected. The phone was a burner, no doubt.

She opened her mouth to leave a message, but found herself hesitating once more even as she did so, Nichols' face rising before her.

The way he had looked in the park, lifeless blue eyes staring back. *"They all have families."*

Did she dare trust him. . .again? With this? The seconds ticked by, just the tone in her ear as the car continued to roll south.

The phone vibrated against her fingers in the next instant with an incoming call, MacCallum's number displaying itself on-screen as she turned the screen toward her face.

"Mehreen here," she responded, struggling to pull herself together. Perhaps she should have left a message on the burner. *Perhaps.* But the opportunity had passed.

"Where have you been?"

"Following up on a lead," she responded, repeating the lie she had told Darren with an ease that unsettled her. "I'm driving back to the city as we speak."

"Come directly to Thames House—I need you here." She could hear the tension in his voice, didn't understand it.

"What's going on?"

"There's been another attack."

Chapter 13

7:03 A.M., March 29th
A flat
Failsworth, England

"Did you see the news?" Harry asked, kicking the door closed behind him as he entered, bearing a steaming cup of coffee in either hand. Everyone in the small market had been clustered around the television, watching the reports out of London.

Reports of a shooting, British soldiers on the eve of deployment—gunned down outside a London nightclub.

Flaharty was leaning back on the dirty, tattered sofa, his pistol lying there beside him, within easy reach. "I did. There's nothing bloody else on the telly. Just people bawling their eyes out over a few dead Brits."

He looked up as Harry set the coffee down on the table, catching his sharp glance. "What—you thought I'd be sorry for them? I killed my first British soldier when I was fifteen, boyo."

And yet. . .there was something there in Flaharty's voice. Was it regret? "You never forget your first," Harry replied, a perverse irony in the words.

Flaharty took his glasses off, holding them up to the light as if seeking smudges on the lens. "I can still see his face if I try—the look in his eyes when I put the knife in. The way he struggled, trying to scream against my hand." The man's voice grew softer at the memory, a note of hesitation entering his tone. "He wasn't much older than I. . .just a boy, really. And how about you—who was your first? A wog?"

Harry shook his head, unzipping his jacket to reveal the Sig-Sauer holstered on his hip. "No," he replied, the memories of that night in Istanbul flooding back. So many years ago.

John Patrick Flynn sitting there in the driver's seat of the Passat, handing over a Ruger Mark II, a round already chambered, a suppressor screwed into the long black barrel. *"You're going to kill two men in there, son. Your target. . .and the man you* were before tonight. There's no road back from this." "He was a Berliner, a scientist. A family man. Selling the wrong thing to the wrong people."

Nuclear components to Saddam's Iraq, as he recalled—thinking back. An eternity ago. "But that's something you would know all about, wouldn't you?"

Flaharty replaced the glasses on the bridge of his nose, picking up his coffee and taking a long sip of the steaming liquid. "Did he deserve to die?"

Harry didn't reply right away, shrugging the jacket off his shoulders and tossing it over the back of a chair. There wasn't a clean spot in the apartment, bags and wrappers strewn over the floor—the torn wallpaper stained yellow from cigarette smoke. He'd seen far worse over the years, known long months when being "clean" was an unaffordable luxury.

"Someone believed that he did," he replied finally, remembering the pleading fear in the man's eyes, the way his own fingers had trembled as he raised the pistol—the long barrel wavering. *The moment of truth.*

"And you?" Flaharty pressed. "What did *you* believe?"

"That it was the wrong question to ask," Harry said, unable to get that face out of his mind. It was one thing to take a life when your blood was up, reacting in your own defense in the heat of the moment. But they never told you how it really was to kill a man, kneeling before you, begging for his life. How hard it became to pull the trigger in that moment.

"And that would be?"

"That in the end, it didn't matter whether he deserved to die. Only whether others deserved to live."

Only silence followed the statement, the grim weight of memories bearing down. They'd both made their choices, so long ago. No turning back.

At length, Flaharty leaned back into the thin cushions, extracting a slip of paper from the breast pocket of his shirt. "I found the bird," the Irishman said simply.

He reached out, taking the slip of paper from Flaharty's hand. Unfolding it to reveal the address scribbled thereon.

Their last lead, unless Malone had known more success than they. Following the guard the night before had ultimately given them nothing, just a cheap hotel on the outskirts of the city.

One room among a hundred others. No name, no way to pursue it further without rousing more suspicion than they could afford. "How soon do we leave?"

"As soon as Davey gets here."

"You've heard from him?

A nod. "He lost the car in the city last night."

"Leeds?"

The Irishman shook his head. "No, trailed them to London." He caught Harry's look of disapproval at the news and scowled. "Look now, Davey's a good man—none better—and I'd trust him with my life. That doesn't mean he's had all your spook training, teachin' him all the latest sodding methods of surveillance and counter-surveillance. We learned on the streets of Belfast, and lived to tell the tale. That's bloody good enough in my book."

Fair enough. It was hard to argue against, in light of their own failure. *But London. . .*

8:43 A.M.
The Richmond Footbridge
London

Three soldiers dead. Eventually, no matter how hard you tried, you became numb—a little piece of your soul slipping away with each casualty report.

Except this wasn't Baghdad. This was London.

Julian Marsh folded the newspaper in his hands, staring out over the Thames, the gathering high tide rushing through the opened sluice gate below him.

Muzhir bin Abdullah.

The Moroccan was dead now, beyond questioning, his brains bashed out against the pavement by a British Army corporal who had since succumbed to his own wounds in a London hospital. *Dunne*, he believed the man's name had been. It got so you couldn't remember all the names.

And they were no closer to finding Tarik Abdul Muhammad. *Failure.*

The stone faces of dead soldiers stared back at him from the front page of the *Daily Standard*, underneath the headline, "*Never Have So Many Been Betrayed By So Few.*"

A figure emerged from the light mist along the footbridge, pausing by the rail a few feet away—near an ornate lamppost dating back to the bridge's construction in the late Victorian era.

"Where did you get the death photos?" Marsh asked, looking over into the eyes of Arthur Colville. "They haven't been released to the press yet."

The publisher smiled, the damp breeze toying with his greying hair. "Like any journalist worth his salt, I have my sources inside the MoD."

"And apparently, the Security Services," the director-general countered grimly. "What are you playing at, Arthur?"

"Play? I'm not one for games. Never have been—we didn't know each other at Cambridge, you were so much older than I. But discussing my past, that's not why you asked me to meet you here this morning, is it?"

"No indeed." A shrill steam whistle shattered the morning stillness and a small tug broke through the mist up-river, its rounded prow seemingly aimed directly at the two men. Marsh turned, his back to the river as he faced the publisher. "Life could become very difficult for you, you know that. Whomever your source for the Mousa story might have been, he's in clear violation of the Official Secrets Act. Given the right barrister. . .I imagine we could find you in violation as well."

"You brought me out here to threaten me?"

"I'd prefer to think that wouldn't be necessary," Marsh replied calmly. He'd been in this position before—so many times. Blackmail, it was part of his trade.

"All this. . ." he continued, indicating the front page of the *Daily Standard* with a forefinger, "I need to ask you to reconsider your position and that of your paper. For the good of your country."

"My country." Colville's grip on the rail tightened, his knuckles whitening for a brief moment. Beneath them, the whistle sounded again as the tug passed over the barrage, ripples fanning out from its churning wake to touch both sides of the Thames. When he spoke again, his voice was barely above a whisper. Laden with a curious intensity. "All that I have done. . .I have done for my *country*." He paused, gazing keenly into the director-general's eyes. "And what of you?"

Marsh saw the riposte coming, just rapidly enough to meet it with a parry of his own. "I have dedicated my life to the service of this country."

"No, no," Colville held up a hand in remonstrance, "you dedicated your life to the service of the state, to 'defend the realm.' They're not the same thing, you know."

Semantics. The debate was pointless, Marsh thought. Not the time—or the place. "This country is like a tinder box, Arthur. People are desperate, ready to lash out at the slightest provocation. And the *Standard* is pouring on the petrol."

"We are telling the *truth*." There was an unmistakable passion flaring in the man's eyes. The look of a true believer. "That's the job of the fourth estate—or do you not believe that? Do you believe that people only deserve the 'truth' your state wants them to know—the 'truth' that you've deemed them capable of hearing?"

The honesty of the press and the secrets of the realm. Freedom of speech and the security of the state. The knife's edge upon which a free democracy balanced. It was an old argument. . .and irrelevant to his purpose.

"We've had two terrorist attacks in the last forty-eight hours," Colville continued without waiting for a reply. "Two *Islamic* terrorist attacks, and the *Standard* has been the only paper with the courage to name the threat."

The intelligence chief held up a hand. "We've had two terrorist attacks in the last forty-eight hours and a reprisal—and that is exactly why I'm asking you to take a step back. Don't fan the flames."

Colville seemed to consider his words for a moment, standing there with one hand upon the parapet. "Is that a request?"

"For now. . ."

8:56 A.M.
The safehouse

"This isn't bloody well going to work."

Harry looked up from the GPS map on his phone to see David Malone staring at him. There was something different about the man this morning, something. . .*beyond* the usual hostility. Hard to properly identify. "What do you mean?"

"All this waiting—watching," the enforcer spat. "Trying to follow up on 'leads.' We don't have the manpower for that and you know it."

The worst part of it was that he was right, Harry thought, glancing over at Flaharty.

Sending Malone to shadow the car leaving the warehouse had been a dice roll, nothing more. Making the best of a bad situation. A five-car surveillance team would have been hard-pressed to run a tail in the urban environment he'd found himself confronted with.

"You find this woman," Malone continued, gesturing to the address on the paper lying there on the counter. "You get her to talk. Or you don't. Or she knows sod-all *nothing to talk about.* And what have we gained? Nothing. But they have—they've gained time."

"That's a risk we have to take," Harry returned evenly.

"No, we don't." Malone met his gaze for a moment before turning back to Flaharty, making his outlook on the chain of command all too clear. "I can reach out to Éamon, get a couple of the lads that are left with us. We strike while they're still recovering from their losses on the motorway, hit the warehouse tonight."

"We've been over this once before already," Harry shot back. "It doesn't *work.*" But there were no loyalties like old loyalties, he thought, watching Flaharty's face, the indecision written there. The two Irishmen had fought shoulder-to-shoulder against the Queen for years, trusted each other implicitly.

It was a relationship he couldn't hope to match, an argument he couldn't counter. Emotion overpowering reason, a desperate feeling he knew all too well.

Malone ignored him. "You and me, Stephen. . .we've been together a long time. And you didn't get where you are by letting people betray you. They have to *pay.*"

"Wait," Harry interjected, holding up a hand as Flaharty began to turn toward him, his mouth opening to speak. It was a desperate play, made all the more so in light of the last time he had parted with her.

But there had been a call placed to the burner the night before, a blocked number. Could it have been her?

He'd rolled the dice on far longer odds. "They will pay, for all they've done. For the lives of your men. And it will be done today. But not like this."

"Then how?" It was Malone, still pressing his advantage.

The moment of truth. "I've been in contact with a friend. . .at the Security Services. I can—"

"Five?" Flaharty demanded, his eyes flashing. "What have you bloody told them?"

"About you, Stephen? Not a thing." Harry shook his head. "But this can be to our advantage. I can call in a favor. Let me set up a meet, tell her about the weapons shipment—not its provenance, but its location. Special Branch sweeps in, seizes the shipment and arrests Hale's men. You have your revenge, I still have my trackers—and we're all in the clear."

9:01 A.M.

"Look, Paul, I don't know what to tell you," Conor Hale responded, staring out the windows of the Vauxhall, toward the footbridge. "It must have been a dud—these things happen, mate. You know that."

And that was a lie, as he knew all too well. He heard Gordon swear in frustration on the other end of the line, knew that he couldn't take him into his confidence. Not on this.

Not yet.

"We lost another three last night, Conor," came the bitter rejoinder. "Good men—what are we going to do about *that?*"

It had been hard to read their names in the paper that morning, even though he had known what was coming. What was. . .necessary. For the greater good.

"I'll do what I can to check on the project after work tonight," Hale replied, choosing his words carefully to avoid any keywords that might trigger the listening ears of GCHQ. "Our debt will be paid in full."

They were always listening.

From where he sat, he saw Colville's form emerge onto the stairs leading up from the footbridge to the street. On his way back. "I need to go, Paul. Stay with your sister and get some rest. I'll let you know if I need you."

He saw the look on the publisher's face as he covered the ground between the bridge and the car in quick, purposeful strides. The look of a tempest.

There was silence between the two men as Colville slid in onto the passenger seat of the Vauxhall, leaning back against the smooth leather.

"Is Five going to be a problem?" Hale asked finally, turning the key in the ignition.

He could still remember their first meeting, over a year earlier—the first opening steps of the mating dance known as recruitment. He had known even then the reality of where it would lead—the risks that they would have to take.

Sometimes he wondered if Colville had.

"No," the publisher replied after a moment's pause. "Not in time. Is everything on schedule?"

"It is." The former sergeant glanced at his watch. "Less than three hours now."

9:48 A.M.
Thames House

"So what you're telling me is that we really have nothing more than we did before the shooting?" Marsh demanded, leaning back in his chair as he cast a baleful glance around at his team.

"Essentially," MacCallum replied grimly from his seat at the end of the conference table. "There is no known connection between Muzhir bin Abdullah and Javeed Mousa. Nothing we can find to tie the two men together."

"Other than Tarik Abdul Muhammad," Norris interjected.

"Yes," the section chief replied. He looked haggard, his eyes ringed with darkness. "Other than Tarik Abdul Muhammad. They know how to compartmentalize their operation. Mehreen?"

She glanced up to find both MacCallum and the DG looking at her. "We're still trying to get an ID on Muzhir's companions—it has proved problematic."

Even Muzhir had been challenging to identify—his face disfigured almost beyond recognition.

As near as London Metropolitan had been able to piece together from witness statements, he'd only fired the revolver twice—had been trying to get off a third shot when the wounded corporal had tackled him, forcing him to the ground and bashing his head repeated against the stone of the street until his skull cracked from the impact.

"Metro is saying they may have been illegals, in which case they're not going to be in our systems." Her mobile buzzed in her pocket with an incoming text, momentarily breaking her train of thought. "I. . .sent the faces to Interpol two hours ago."

Norris seemed to examine his notes before glancing over at MacCallum. "Is it possible that any of the other three numbers called by Tarik Abdul Muhammad belonged to the men with Muzhir?"

"We should be so blessed," the section chief intoned, shaking his head wearily. "Anything is possible, but I consider it unlikely. Certainly nothing we can count ourselves assured of. No, the odds are that three more cells have been activated."

Marsh swore softly under his breath. "Then it's time we were about our business. Let's get back to work—find me what you can."

It was hard to escape the sense of impending doom that hung over the building as Mehreen made her way back from the conference room into the Centre. The feeling that their defenses were being probed, that the two attacks were just the beginning. Of something much, much larger. They were too small, too insignificant to be anything else.

And Aydin was mixed up in all of it, as the information on his hard drive had proved all too thoroughly. How seemed almost irrelevant now after reading his blog posts about Syria. About Afghanistan. *About jihad. . .*

She reached into the pocket of her jeans to retrieve the phone just as she reached her workstation, running her thumb over the touchscreen to reveal the message. MUST PASS ALONG INTEL. MEET ME AT THE OLD PLACE. 1130 HOURS.

It was Nichols. . .*the old place*. Regent's Park. It had to be.

"Mehreen." She covered the phone quickly with her hand, looking up to see MacCallum standing there in front of the desk. "Were you able to learn anything from your source?"

"My source?" she asked, regretting the words the moment they escaped her mouth. A night without sleep.

"Roth said you went out last night to talk with a source there in Leeds—one of your contacts from your time in the city, I believe?"

Mehreen nodded, recovering herself with an effort. "I did, but he knew nothing of value. It was a wasted evening."

"It happens," MacCallum replied, a note of understanding in his tone. They both knew how the intelligence game worked—sources came up dry more often that not.

Except this time, she thought, looking away as if he could read the truth in her eyes. She was lying.

"We're missing something here," the section chief added after a moment. "I want you to focus on Ismail Besimi—work on background, any anomalies you can find. Any gaps. The quizmasters aren't getting anywhere with him."

Because he's innocent, she wanted to say, but didn't. Objectivity was the watchword of any analyst. And after the previous night, she no longer considered anything certain.

"Of course," she replied instead, running a hand over her forehead. "I'll let you know what I find."

And then he was gone, winding his way among the workstations—calling out to another analyst as he went.

Somewhere, somehow, they needed a lead. Anything. She glanced again at the message, reading Nichols' words once more as she began to type a reply.

5:46 A.M. Eastern Standard Time
The White House
Washington, D.C.

"Director Lay," the President greeted, rounding the edge of the *Resolute* desk and extending his hand. A tall, wiry man with sandy hair and green eyes set deep within his face, Norton's athletic build served as a reminder to Lay of what he saw as a disturbing trend. . .American presidents seemed to be getting steadily younger.

Or perhaps he was just getting old. Richard Norton was fifteen years Lay's junior, making the age gap between President and DCIA even more pronounced than when Hancock had taken office.

And he knew all too well how that had turned out, a disaster that even he could never have envisioned. Blood and fire. . .

Never had a President posed such a danger to the American intelligence community as Roger Hancock, Lay thought, handing over the folder containing the daily brief.

Unless it was the man that now occupied the office.

"I had hoped that Lawrence would be able to join us this week," the President said, gesturing for Lay to take a seat, "but I understand that he's still under the weather."

Indeed, Lay grimaced. The Director of National Intelligence, Lawrence Bell, was a hold-over from the Hancock administration—a good man who had found himself in the wrong place at the wrong time. And now in poor health.

The rumors were cancer, but it wasn't his place to pass along rumors to the President. Reality was hard enough to digest.

He suppressed a heavy sigh as he sank back into one of the chairs opposite the desk, eyeing Norton carefully as the President opened the folder, signaling his willingness to begin the morning's briefing.

Remembering his speech to the American people, the promises he had made.

Transparency. . .the god to which all bureaucracies paid token obeisance.

Except this man meant it—and somehow, that was even more frightening.

10:43 A.M. Greenwich Mean Time
Thames House
London, England

"I understand, I don't need what was sent over with the hourly reports—I need the raw data." Mehreen paused, listening to the man on the other end of the line for a moment before adding, "All of it."

Mehreen ran a hand over her forehead as she replaced the phone in its cradle, glancing around the operations centre. She'd already been over the hourlies in question twice since her arrival earlier in the morning, and something wasn't adding up.

The evidence against Ismail Besimi hadn't originated at Thames House, but with GCHQ's analysts at their headquarters in Cheltenham—drawing from thousands of message intercepts during the operational window during which they had lost Tarik Abdul Muhammad.

They had been able to trace the sent messages to Besimi's personal cellphone—an incredible lapse in operational security, if indeed that's what it had been. No evidence of the use of encryption the like of which had characterized jihadi comms ever since the first development of *Asrar al-Mujahideen* encryption software back in 2007.

The mistakes of an amateur, she thought—the imam's face appearing in her mind's eye—the look in his eyes when she had first approached him about working for Five.

No. . .all those years he had spent undercover, either working for the Security Service or the terrorists. Whatever else he was, Besimi was no amateur.

11:03 A.M.
Leeds Central Police Station
Park Street, Leeds

The loud, seemingly endless wail of the sirens had been replaced by silence now, ever since his interrogators had left. . .the previous day, was it?

There was no longer night or day for Ismail Besimi, the fluorescent lights shining down relentlessly overhead, keeping him from sleep. He eyed the nearly empty water bottle at the edge of the table through tired, bloodshot eyes, only too aware that what was left would have to last until they returned, whenever that was.

The door flew open suddenly, the British officer from the day before appearing in the opening.

The man crossed the distance between door and table with slow, deliberate steps. Fire flashed in his eyes, gazing at Besimi as he leaned forward, knuckles pressed against the table.

"You heard my proposition. Have you had enough time to think it through, Mr. Besimi?"

He'd had nothing but time, Besimi thought, meeting the younger man's gaze. And it didn't change anything. "Everything I know about Hashim Rahman and potential terrorist activities in Leeds," he began slowly, "I have reported to my handler as per Security Service protocols. As I was trained. If I had more information, why would I not give it to you? I was never his confidant."

The interrogator seemed not to have heard him as he circled around the table, drawing a picture from the inside of his suit jacket and throwing it onto the table before Besimi. The face that stared back was young, looking grimly into the camera as if alive to the danger he faced. *Alive.* "Colour Sergeant Michael Galloway, British Army. Awarded the Military Cross for gallantry during action in the Helmand Province in 2006, during which action he lost his right leg. *Killed* last night outside a London nightclub by one of your people. A man activated by Tarik Abdul Muhammad."

"As God is my witness, I do not *know* this man you speak of."

Another photo landed on the table, another face staring up at him as the interrogator continued, "Corporal Anthony Dunne, British Army. Four tours in Afghanistan. *Killed* last night. . ."

11:06 A.M. Greenwich Mean Time
The mosque
London, England

The protestors were already outside, Ibrahim Khattam observed, glancing from the window of his office. After the attacks, after the violence in Birmingham the previous day, he had been expecting them. . .the blood-red cross of St. George prominently displayed on white armbands sprinkled throughout the gathering crowd.

He turned, running a hand through his dark hair as he adjusted his *kufi*, his only concession to traditional dress. They were in England after all, the country of his birth—not Pakistan.

Too many of his fellow Muslims forgot that. And too many of their countrymen, he thought, taking another look out the window—were all too ready to remind them.

He reached over to one side of his desk, picking up the *tasbih* from where it laid atop his leather-bound copy of the Qur'an. Running the prayer beads through his fingers, each of them representing one of the hundred names of God. Whispering a prayer. For surely they would be protected through this time.

And in the basement, the bomb's internal timer continued to tick down. Fifty-one minutes. . .

11:13 A.M.
The 274 Bus
London

There had been a day when he would have given up his seat to the British woman standing three feet to his left—shifting from one foot to another as she held onto the pole at the edge of one of the seats, very obviously pregnant and far along.

It was the way he had been raised, so long ago.

Now. . .Harry stayed in his seat, head down, eyes apparently fixed on the blank screen of his phone, cap pulled low over his forehead to avoid the security cameras he knew would be near the bus stop.

How many pieces of himself had he lost through the years, he wondered, glancing briefly out the window of the double-decker bus as it slowed, approaching Regent's Park. Moving from one cover to the next, assuming new identities—altering himself to match them, until the man he had once been was nearly lost in the metamorphosis.

I am made all things unto all men, came the verse of Scripture to his mind, something obscene about the thought.

Indeed.

The bus came to a stop and Harry rose, pushing past the woman as he made his way down the steps, hands shoved into the pockets of his jacket. It was nearly time.

11:27 A.M.
The Colville estate
The Midlands

To be this close. It was a strange feeling, somewhere between fear and anticipation.

An intensely physical thrill, Colville thought—staring out the window of his den out over the spring green fields. It had to be something like the sensation of going into combat for the first time, or so he imagined, glancing down to realize that his fingers were trembling.

He walked back to the desk, pouring himself a snifter of brandy. It was early in the day, but this was no ordinary day.

"Sir," came Hale's voice from the door, Colville smiling at the military choice of words. Then again, perhaps it was appropriate—considering the war upon which they had embarked.

"Yes?" he asked, turning to face his subordinate, glass in hand. "What's our status?"

It was the closest he had ever seen the former sergeant come to a smile. "I just got off the phone with Lucas," he replied, gesturing to the mobile in his hand. "They're outside the mosque, with a larger crowd gathering by the moment."

"And the media?"

"Sky News has a van on-site, interviewing BDC activists and streaming live coverage of the protest on their website."

It couldn't have been more perfect. The publisher poured two fingers of brandy into a second glass, passing it over to Hale as he raised his own. "To England."

"To England."

11:38 A.M.
Regent's Park
London

He was late, Mehreen thought, glancing briefly at the screen of her phone as she leaned back against the wrought iron of the park bench. Or perhaps he wasn't coming.

And she couldn't wait forever.

Perhaps he was out there even now, she thought, raising her eyes to scan the park. Out there weighing his decision to come in.

Nothing. Just a few joggers, the usual crush of people in the park heavily reduced by the attacks, the resultant unrest.

She wouldn't see him, though—she knew that. Nichols was far too careful, always had been.

But what if he wasn't coming? She swore under her breath, knowing it was all too possible. This meet was so very risky for both of them now, with London on high alert.

And if he didn't show. . .if she failed to persuade him—where did that leave her with Aydin?

It was a question she knew the answer to. The *only* answer.

If she couldn't find a way to extricate her nephew from the situation he had created for himself, she would be left with no choice but to report his activities to the authorities. To inform on her own flesh and blood.

It was a decision she had demanded of others countless times while running assets over the years—from Northern Ireland to Leeds.

Somehow it looked so. . .different, now that she found herself staring it in the face.

Movement out of the corner of her eye and she turned just as he sat down beside her on the bench, as if he had materialized out of nowhere.

He just sat there for a long moment, never so much as looking at her, hands buried in the pockets of his jacket—staring out at the park, at the joggers. Lifeless blue eyes, actively scanning the crowd without seeming to move at all.

"I wasn't sure if you would come," he said finally, still not glancing in her direction. It was tradecraft, she understood that. They were two strangers in a park, nothing more.

She paused, trying to read him. "I'm not sure why I did. Or why you asked for it. If intel on Tarik Abdul Muhammad is what you're wanting, you came to the wrong place. We haven't been able to place him since your stunt at the station in Leeds."

No reaction to her words. "I figured as much," he replied, a curious inevitability in his tone. "That's not why I'm here."

He paused, as if measuring his words, determining his next move. And Mehreen let him. Years of running agents for Box had taught her that you didn't push an asset in a meet like this. Didn't pressure them unless you had to.

Was that all Nichols was to her now? Her asset? A friendship gone horribly wrong.

Or, an even more troubling thought: was she *his*?

"I came to bring an olive branch. . .a token of goodwill." His left hand came out of his pocket, placing a folded slip of paper on the wood of the bench between them.

She waited a moment before placing her hand over it, unfolding it to reveal a series of numbers scribbled in black ink. GPS coordinates, she realized a moment later. "What is this?"

"Someone's brought an arsenal into the UK—military surplus assault rifles and Semtex. Someone connected with Tarik Abdul Muhammad."

It took a moment for the full import of his words to sink in. "My God. Then these last attacks. . ."

". . .are only the beginning," he finished for her. "Prelude to a requiem."

"Who was responsible for bringing the weapons into the country?"

"I don't have access to that intel," he responded, without a moment's hesitation. "I do know that any attempt to maintain surveillance on them—to *use* them to trace back to Tarik Abdul Muhammad—will be futile."

"What are you saying?" She knew even as she asked. *You have a mole*, the words that had haunted her consciousness for every waking moment since he had uttered them by the side of the walking path in Leeds.

"Like I told you," he said, eyes still straight ahead, "you've been penetrated. How I don't know, but he has help, likely the same people that helped him escape your surveillance teams in Leeds. You need to keep the circle tight, take them out of play—now, before he can use them to arm his people."

He was right—she knew that. It was the nightmare scenario: jihadist sleeper cells armed and equipped with modern weaponry and explosives. Planted throughout Britain.

There were dozens of them that Five knew of, and like any iceberg, the majority were still beneath the surface. Aydin's e-mail account had convinced her of that much.

And yet. . .

She took a deep breath, preparing herself for what she knew she had to do. She had joined the Service to protect her country, but what good was all this—any of this—in the end, if you couldn't protect the ones you loved. "I can pass this intel along to Thames House, can recommend to the DG that we move at once to seize the arsenal. But I'll need something from you in return."

He turned to look at her finally, cold blue eyes meeting her gaze—a wary caution in their depths. "Cut to the chase, Mehr. . .what are you trying to say?"

11:51 A.M.
Barnet Hospital
North London

". . .crowd of protesters grows behind me at the Madina mosque in North London as faithful Muslims gather for worship at the noon prayer."

Faithful Muslims. Paul Gordon closed his eyes, fighting against the bile rising in his throat. Like the ones that had. . .he looked down to see his sister's small white fingers interlaced with his, her skin cool.

She lay there in the bed beside him, her thin body swathed in a hospital gown, the steady, rhythmic hum of the oxygen filling the room. Helping keep Death at bay.

On the screen of the telly, the Sky News reporter droned on, camera panning back to reveal the figure of a short man standing beside him, hair cropped into a military buzzcut, a nose that looked like it had been broken more than once and set, badly. "Here with us is Lucas Sanders, member of the British Defence Coalition and organizer of today's protest. What would you like to say to us today, Mr. Sanders?"

The man seemed surprised, looking back and forth between the reporter and the flickering red eye of the camera as if uncertain of his ground.

"What I have to say to you," he said, a stubby finger jabbing outward from his fist toward the camera, "I will say to everyone here in a few minutes. So that everyone can hear precisely why we have come here—without you lot taking my words and editing them, twistin' them to make us out to be something we're not."

11:54 A.M.
Regent's Park
London

There came a moment in the life of every spy when the job became personal. It was that moment that killed you, even if your body might not know it yet.

For him that moment had come for him on a dark night in Vegas, the red and blue lights of emergency vehicles washing over the face of the woman he had loved, sightless eyes staring up into his face. Her blood soaking his hands.

For Mehreen. . .that moment was now. Harry looked up at the sky as she continued speaking in the same low undertone, the sun struggling to peek through slate-gray clouds hanging low over the city.

Knowing what he should say, knowing he should refuse. Talk her out of it.

"So those are your terms?" he asked quietly, glancing over as she finished.

A nod. She leaned back against the back of the bench, her dark eyes fixed on his face. Almost unreadable. "You were Nick's friend, you were mine"—he winced at her choice of the past tense—"but I've put everything on the line this last week to help you, without asking anything in return. No more. I can make sure Special Branch hits the warehouse this afternoon, but I need you to promise me that you'll help me get Aydin out of this."

"And if he doesn't want to come?"

11:56 A.M.
Barnet Hospital
North London

"They asked me what I'd like to say," the man called Sanders said, gesturing to the gathered crowd of protesters as he stood upon the rude stage the BDC had erected in the middle of the street before the mosque. "Asked me what I wanted Britain to hear—that lot over there with their cameras, their microphones. Asked me why we were all here today. And what do we tell them?"

It somehow seemed like he should be there, with them in the crowd, Paul Gordon thought—his gaze shifting from the screen of the telly back to the comatose body of his sister. He was useless here, Hale's words coming back to mind.

"What are you going to be able to do for her there? Hold her hand? Pray?"

On-screen, Sanders took the microphone, raising his free hand as he gazed out over the crowd. "They call us racists—but Islam is not a race. They call us haters, but we're not here because of what we hate, but what we love—*England*. All that it has been in the past. All that it can yet be in the future, if that future is not stolen from us. The boffins up in Whitehall, they go on TV—all dressed up in their sharp Italian suits—usin' fancy words like "multiculturalism" to describe what they've done to this country."

The crowd roared their displeasure and Sanders paused, his voice trembling with passion. "An' it sounds so good, so noble. So bloody holy. But do you know what it means? It means men beaten for selling a bottle of wine. It means young women groomed by paedos old enough to be their gran'fathers, plied with money and drugs until there's no way out and they're sold as sex slaves. It means a beautiful nine-year-old girl comin' to her da' in the middle of the night—as mine did not a week ago—asking if she should cover her face at school. *My* daughter. Here. In *England*. Is that what you want?"

Gordon could feel his breath catch short at the plain, rough oratory—the protestors' thunderous *"NO!"* echoing down the streets. The Sky News camera zoomed in on Sanders' face until you could see the tears shining in his eyes as he waited for the crowd to subside.

"And that's why we're here today—to speak for those who can no longer speak—for those who have given everything to defend this country against those who have threatened it, from without and within. But first things first." He paused, taking a step forward on the stage, lowering his head like a prizefighter bracing for a rush, sharp eyes searching the crowd. "Yesterday, a band of soddin' thugs wearing the armbands of the BDC attacked and beat Moslem women in the streets of Birmingham. . .listen to me and listen to me well—that was not us.

We do not *support* that. There is no room in our movement for thugs, for the beaters of women, not an inch will I give to cowards like that. Do you want us to become like *them?*"

This time Sanders didn't wait for the shouts from the crowd to die out, but continued, raising his own voice with theirs. "I am a soldier. *Am*, not was. It has been twenty years since I raised my hand and swore an oath before my God an' my Queen to defend this country, but they told me sod-all about it expiring, 'cept with my own life. If you swore the same oath, repeat it with me now."

"I, Lucas Sanders," he began, the swelling volume of the crowd nearly drowning him out, "swear by Almighty God. . ."

And in the darkened hospital room, Paul Gordon squeezed his sister's limp hand, a tear sliding down his cheek as he repeated, ". . .that I will be faithful and bear true allegiance. . ."

11:58 A.M.
Colville's estate
The Midlands

"He's a good man," Colville observed, watching the live coverage on Sky News. Arranging for the entire protest to be carried live had required calling in serious favors, but it had been necessary. For what was to come.

Hale nodded, his face nearly expressionless—his eyes never leaving the screen. "Maybe too good a man."

"How many of our people will be killed?" The publisher asked. It was the hard question he had asked himself time and again in the planning of this.

Hard questions, harder decisions—the kind of decisions no one in this government had been willing to make for decades.

But now *he* had.

"Impossible to say," the former sergeant responded, shaking his head. "It's a big bomb."

Hale glanced at his watch. "We'll know, soon enough."

12:00 P.M.
The mosque
London, England

"In the name of God, the Most Gracious, the Most Merciful," Ibrahim Khattam intoned, his eyes closed as men's voices swelled around him, repeating the words of the *zuhr*. "All praise is due to God, Lord of all that exists. The Most Gracious, the Most Merciful, Master of the Day of Judgment. . ."

"You remember the words," Lucas Sanders cried, raising a clenched fist toward the sky, his gaze sweeping the crowd. "Now it's time to ask if you remember their meaning? England needs men who remember their oaths. Men willing to stand and *fight* for all they hold dear. Men who—"

In the basement beneath the prayer hall, beneath the carelessly folded tarpaulins. . .the bomb's internal timer reached 0:00.

12:00 P.M.
Regent's Park

"You may not be able to save him. You know that, don't you?"

Mehreen nodded at Harry's words, gazing out over the placid waters of the boating lake—absently twisting the wedding ring around her finger. "I know," she responded, hardly daring to voice the words. "But I can't stand by and do nothing. He is my family."

"I can remember having a family." There was a curious resignation to his words. A finality. As though speaking of something which once had been. . .and would never be again. He looked over to meet her eyes, an intensity creeping into his voice. "And I would have done anything for them."

He reached over, pressing a phone into her palm. "Use this and only this to contact me from here on out. Let me know when you're ready to move and I'll do whatever I can to assist you. You have my word, Mehr."

Before she could respond, a muffled *crump* from the north struck their ears. An odd sound, faint and indistinct like the far-off rumble of thunder.

Except it wasn't, and they both knew it.

Nichols sprang to his feet, eyes scanning the park as if searching for danger, his right hand burying itself in the folds of his jacket. . .as the first wail of sirens began to ring out over the city. The next moment, her phone started to ring.

It felt as if she was moving in a dream as she ran her thumb across the screen to accept the call, heard MacCallum's voice on the other end of the line.

His words clipped, peremptory. *No.* This couldn't be. Mehreen ran a hand over her forehead, as if she could clear her mind by so doing.

"What's going on?" She heard Nichols ask as the call ended.

"It was. . .a bomb." It seemed strange to hear herself speak the words, everything still seeming in a daze. Memories of her childhood flashing past. "They bombed a mosque—in North London."

They. The Taliban had burned down the mosque in the small town where she had been raised. Men with guns, carrying torches.

And now it was happening here. "I have to get Aydin out of this—we have to move faster than I had even thought. Harry?"

Silence. "Harry?"

Nothing. Her eyes jerked up from her phone, realizing suddenly that she was alone. "Harry!" Her head swiveling, searching back and forth along the walkways crisscrossing the park, trying to pick out his tall form among the joggers and pedestrians.

But he was gone. . .

Chapter 14

12:09 P.M.
Barnet Hospital
North London

"My God," Paul Gordon breathed, the same two words he had been repeating over and over again—his eyes fixed to the screen of the telly, the flames rising from the devastated ruins of the Madina Mosque, bloodied protesters limping away from the scene. A woman, her hijab torn, tears streaming down her exposed cheeks as she screamed for her son. "My *God*. . ."

Devastation. It hadn't been supposed to happen this way, not like this—with the loss of innocent life. It was far too soon to expect casualty estimates, but he had been to war. He knew the power of a bomb like that.

The type of weapon that had been used against him and his men in Iraq, time and again.

He found his hands trembling as if in the grip of a fever, a fear seizing hold as he glanced from the carnage on-screen back to the helpless, broken form of his sister.

Nausea building in his stomach, threatening to overwhelm him with the enormity of what they had done. A *mistake*, the like of which could never be undone.

He made it as far as the sink in one corner of the cramped hospital room before he retched, his stomach emptying itself into the basin.

How long Gordon stayed there, on his knees, he would never remember, the raw, acid taste of bile filling his mouth—tears running down his face. *God. . .what have I done?*

A prayer with no answer but the one he dared not face. A question for which he knew the answer far too well.

At length, he pulled himself back up on unsteady legs, trying to pull himself together. His hand found the mobile in his pocket, Conor Hale's number the only one listed under *Recent Calls*.

Three rings, and the former SAS man came on the line. "I'm here at the hospital with Alice," Gordon began, trying to settle down as the words came pouring out." I was watching the protest—the mosque."

It was a moment before Hale responded. "A tragic mistake. I have no idea how it could have gone this. . .wrong, Paul. I'm sorry."

Perhaps it was the calm, contrasting so strongly with his own overwhelming emotions. Perhaps it was the flat monotone in which the statement was delivered.

But Gordon could hear his old comrade's voice echoing through his mind. *"This is war."*

And in that moment of numbed shock, he knew the truth. There had been no mistake with the bomb, no malfunction of the timer. Everything had gone exactly. . .according to *plan*. The massacre of the innocents.

He caught sight of his own visage in the mirror over the sink—a haunted glance. But he knew what he must do.

"No, you were right, mate," he lied, a grim resolve entering his voice. "We didn't begin this war, they did. I—I only hate them the more for what they've made us do. What is necessary."

12:19 P.M.
Colville's Estate
The Midlands

"He's ours," Hale smiled, tucking the mobile back into its pouch on his belt as he re-entered the den. "This with his sister. . .it's devastated Paul, but I knew all along he was one of the good ones. I shouldn't have doubted him."

"No," the publisher countered, looking up from where he sat behind the desk. "Suspicion will be our salvation—I picked you from the start because I recognized you had solid instincts. Don't ignore them."

Colville rose from his seat, pacing across to the window, the pastoral scene lying behind giving no hint of the devastation they had just unleashed. "Still, I am of course glad that we are not short a valuable man. Now, regarding the other matter?"

A shadow passed across the sergeant's face. "My men are soldiers, not murderers. Finding a man to do it was difficult."

"But?" The publisher asked, an eyebrow raised as he glanced expectantly back at Hale. It was no hour to be developing a conscience.

"But, it is being dealt with as we speak. Getting everything moved will be another story. I have the lads working on it."

"And as for our source?"

"Once we have the all-clear, he'll be taken care of. Until then, he's still of value to us."

"Good."

12:33 P.M.
London, England

The mark of any good spy was the ability to stay one step ahead of a situation. To predict, to *anticipate* the moves of your opponents. Don't react, *act*.

But no matter how good you were, you could never predict everything. "Getting to you will be the problem," Harry said into the phone, raising his voice to make himself heard above the sea of people flooding around him, nearly trampling him in the press. "They've shut down the Tube—along with most of the bus system."

"Sod it," Flaharty exclaimed, exploding into a string of curses. *Agreed.* He shifted the phone to his other ear, moving with the crowd as someone bumped into him from behind, the sharp end of their elbow catching him in the side.

Markov. It had been on a similarly crowded street in this very city that Bulgarian dissident Georgi Markov had been assassinated in '78—long before his time, Harry thought—a ricin pellet jabbed into his thigh with an umbrella.

A long time ago. . .but he found himself moving even more cautiously now, scanning faces in the press. It was something only a spy would have remembered.

"I'm not going to be able to reach you, old son," the Irishman added after a long pause. "Getting into central London is dicey for someone like myself on the best of days. Today. . ."

Harry cast a long look up the street as he moved toward the crosswalk, taking in the sight of uniformed bobbies on horseback moving along the outskirts of the hurrying crowd. Trying to maintain control. "Copy that," was his terse response, pulling his cap down lower over his eyes. "I'll find my own way out."

12:47 P.M.
Thames House

"Where's Alec?" Mehreen asked, entering the Centre out of breath. With London's transportation system closing down, getting back had been more problematic than she could have imagined. It was like 7/7 all over again—the panic in the streets.

"He's in conference with Marsh," Norris responded, giving her a look as he moved back and forth between workstations, monitoring his screens. "We have a claim of responsibility."

She winced. It was something that had been conspicuously absent from the previous two attacks. "Tarik Abdul Muhammad?"

He shook his head, a strange look on his face. "No. . .it's a web video from a group calling itself the Infidels of St. George."

"A far-right group?" Her brow furrowed in bewilderment. "Is the claim legitimate or just opportunism?"

"You be the judge." He waved a hand at the screen, motioning for her to come over. "This hit the Internet three minutes after the blast—it's spreading like wildfire. No way they could have gotten something this sophisticated up that fast if they weren't involved."

"The bombing of the Madina Mosque is only the beginning," a synthesized male voice announced from the screen as the video began to play—revealing a dark, seemingly featureless room, the plain white wall in the background draped with a large flag of St. George. *Red cross on a field of stark white.* "For years," the man's voice continued, as a masked figure dressed in dark clothing moved into the view of the camera, "we have been invaded, by an enemy our elected leaders are too cowardly to even name. They have taken over our schools, bombed our buses. Assaulted our women. No longer. This is where England takes a stand, for all that is right in this world. They call us infidels, and so we are, for we have not forgotten our oaths. We are coming."

The figure turned, walking off into the shadows as the instrumental strains of "Rule, Britannia" began to pour through the speakers and the video faded to black.

"The Infidels of St. George," Mehreen repeated thoughtfully, staring at Norris' screen. "What do we know of them?"

He shook his head. "Nothing. Absolutely nothing. No chatter, no Internet noise. They're like a ghost."

"Or they don't exist," she retorted.

"Or they're just very good. Look here." He reached forward with his pen, indicating a portion of the video. "That's not plaster, that's plastic sheeting."

"They masked the room." It was something the jihadists had learned after years of hard experience—even a glimpse of the wall in the room where a video had been taken could provide valid intel on the location of a terrorist cell. The solution had been to drape the walls in dark cloth—or plastic, as here. "Any clues on origin of upload?"

Norris winced, shaking his head. "GCHQ is working on it, no substantive leads so far. The reference to the remembering of oaths is nearly a duplicate of something said by Lucas Sanders, a mid-ranking BDC captain who was leading the protest."

"Have we spoken with him?"

"He was critically injured in the blast," the analyst replied. "CO-19 has him sequestered in a ward at Barnet, under armed guard."

She saw MacCallum leaving the conference room at that moment, his steps quickening as he moved toward the elevators and she hurried to catch up with him. Calling out as she did so.

"Where have you been, Mehr?" he asked, his voice low as he turned to meet her. "This whole day is exploding out of control—I can't afford to be a man down."

There was nothing for it but to take the plunge. "I was contacted by an informant earlier this morning—a source I hadn't heard from since my days in the field," she lied, looking him in the eye. Trying not to oversell it. "They were always very reliable. Solid intelligence."

"And?"

"They gave me this," Mehreen responded, handing over the slip of paper with the scrawled coordinates. "It's the GPS coordinates of a warehoused weapons cache in Ashton-under-Lyne. . .apparently a significant stockpile of illegal weapons and explosives. High-end stuff. Plastique, even."

She paused, considering her options before adding, "I think it could be connected to today's attack."

1:27 P.M.
Barnet Hospital
North London

Sirens were still wailing as Paul Gordon walked out of the hospital, the emergency wards flooded with bombing victims. A man screaming in agony, clutching at a leg no longer there, a young woman lying on a stretcher—half her face burned away.

She had reminded him of Alice.

He'd seen the death count on the telly before leaving his sister's side. Thirty and climbing—their bomb had taken out the support beams of the Madina Mosque, collapsing the building in upon itself. The news reports said emergency personnel were still pulling people from the rubble.

Dear God. What had he *done*? He could see it all now, the truth revealed in

Hale's voice. This had never been about sending a message—unless it was one written in blood.

And perhaps he had known the truth all along. Known and refused to see it, blinded by his own lust for vengeance. By grief.

He kept his head down as he made his way down the street, hands shoved into the pockets of his jacket—moving past uniformed officers interviewing survivors.

Now what? A germ of an idea—a dangerous idea—had begun to form in his mind when he had been talking to Hale. . .but it was just that, an idea. Not a plan.

And not nearly enough.

1:35 P.M.
The United States Embassy
Grosvenor Square

"Of course, sir," Carlos Jimenez replied, speaking into the phone "We'll do everything within our power. Understood."

There was a *click* on the other end of the line and he leaned forward, replacing the Secure Telephone Unit in its cradle on the desk.

There were few things more stress-inducing than being chief of station when your host country had just suffered a terrorist attack, Jimenez thought, staring at the phone. And with the UK having suffered three in the last three days, calls like the one he had just hung up from were becoming an all-too-frequent occurrence.

His door opened to admit Parker. "You called for me, Carlos?"

A nod. "I did. Have the Marines get you a car, my authorization. I want you at Thames House directly." He gestured toward the phone. "That was Director Lay—the President wants us to lend the Security Service our full support in the wake of this terrorist attack on the Madina Mosque. Everything we have. As usual. . .the special relationship, 'hands across the sea' and all that."

"I understand that," Thomas replied, "what I don't understand is what I'm going to be able to accomplish at Thames House?"

Jimenez got up, rounding the desk to look Thomas in the eye. Lowering his voice. "Honestly? A threat against the UK is a potential threat against the US. I want you to find out what they know. *Everything* they know."

2:43 P.M.
A school
Leeds

It wasn't real. It just *wasn't*—the images, the video. Cameras had been rolling at the moment of the explosion, and now the footage was being replayed for all the world to see—streamed over the Internet by thousands of users.

Thirty-eight of the faithful dead. Aydin looked down at the screen of his iPhone, a tear running down his cheek as the news coverage of the carnage continued.

At the front of the classroom, the teacher rattled on—her shrill voice drowned out by the sounds of death in his ear. The sirens.

The chatrooms were already alive with the word, spreading like wildfire across the web. . .the attack had been carried out by right-wing fascists. The type of men behind the riots in Birmingham. The type of men who had oppressed Muslims in the Middle East for years.

And now it had come back here to kill those at prayer.

He choked back a sob, leaning back in his desk as he glanced around at his classmates—finding himself repulsed.

Remembering the words of the imam, sitting there in that café. *"It is truly as the Prophet has said. . .everyone will be with those whom he loves."*

He didn't love them. Didn't belong with *them*. When Aydin next raised his head, the tears had been replaced by an angry defiance—his youthful face hard as he glared forward toward the young teacher.

He glanced down once more at the message he had typed, hesitating for only a moment before pressing *SEND*.

And it was done.

2:51 P.M.
The apartment
Leeds

Had he not known in advance what must happen, the events of the day would have come as a devastating shock.

Even so. . .Tarik Abdul Muhammad found his gaze drifting back to the television screen—the images of destruction replaying themselves continually in an effort to satisfy their Western audience's appetite for horror.

And horrifying it was, but the imam of the Madina Mosque had disgraced his faith in his appeasement of the West. And had not the Prophet himself cleansed

Arabia of the apostate Muslims before turning his attentions outward?

He turned his attention back to Hashim Rahman, to the phone in the imam's hand. "Can he be trusted for the work we are going to perform?"

"He is a pious young man," Rahman nodded. "Completely unskilled, but true of heart. He would never betray us."

Tarik smiled, placing a hand on the older man's shoulder as he moved past him into the kitchen of the small apartment. "*Insh'allah*, it takes no skill to detonate a suicide vest—only the courage to wait for the right moment."

3:06 P.M.
Thames House
London, England

It was an unmarked Embassy car that dropped Thomas Parker off at the door of Thames House, the Marine driver letting it idle as Thomas pushed open the passenger door, flashing open his ID toward the nearest guard. With the city on high alert, Jimenez had wanted to keep things as low-key and unobtrusive as possible.

Marsh had doubled down on security, he thought as he was waved in, passing beneath the barrel-vaulted entrance—noting the unusual sight of H&K submachine guns slung at the ready.

The door closed behind him, shutting out the street noise as he moved farther into the building, his eyes sweeping from one side of the corridor to the other—beginning to empty his pockets as he approached the metal detectors.

Time to be a good ally.

"I talked with Marsh," MacCallum announced as soon as Mehreen entered the conference room. Papers were strewn about the section chief at one end of the table—and his usually impassive face bore the marks of stress. "He's approved the seizure of this arms cache."

He paused. "Any other time we might hold back—conduct surveillance, monitor the situation. Move in only after we've identified all the players. Perhaps that would still be best, but we're stretched thin and the Home Office is calling for blood."

"I understand. Desperate times," she began, but MacCallum finished the sentence for her.

". . .require desperate measures. And this couldn't be more so." The section chief shook his head. "The levels of Internet chatter have exploded—on both sides. The jihadis are holding this up as an example of the futility of Muslims attempting to curry favor with the West and the web views of Enoch Powell's old 'rivers of blood' speech have tripled in the last two hours."

She shook her head. "We're on the brink." Perhaps they had been for a long time, but the reality was hitting home. And all it would take was another push.

"We are. But like I say, we're short on men. Parker is on his way over here, on loan from the cousins." MacCallum's eyes seemed to move past her, out through the glass of the conference room. She looked back to see the American just entering the operations center—as casual as ever, a light jacket over jeans.

"Speak of the devil. Take him with you, there's a helicopter warming up on the pad at Battersea," he continued, hopelessly dating himself by using the old name for the London Heliport. "You'll be liaising with the Lancashire Constabulary's Firearms Unit—they're in charge of operations on the ground."

3:47 P.M.
Hammersmith
West London

"I nearly thought you weren't going to show, boyo," Flaharty snarled, reaching across to unlock the door as Harry rapped loudly on the window.

Harry slid into the passenger seat of the BMW, favoring his ally with an exasperated glance. "Have you ever tried lifting a car in central London? Cameras everywhere."

The OSIRIS map data he had downloaded onto his phone had saved him, but only barely.

The Irishman shook his head. "I was always too sodding smart for all that."

Harry snorted. "Booth's flat—you've already been and done a recce?"

"About ninety minutes ago," Flaharty responded, nodding. "Everything was quiet. She might be out to pick up her tyke from school now. . .we can always go in and wait for her."

It was likely for the best, Harry thought—his mind flashing back to the picture he had seen of Caitlyn Murray as he'd gone over her Facebook account earlier that morning.

Pictures of the two of them, relaxing. A day at the beach—their son building sand castles in the distance.

How did you look a woman in the eye and tell her that you had killed the man she loved? Shot him in the back. There was no honor in that, but he had left honor far behind, long ago.

Yet another casualty of the years, like all the rest. He swallowed hard, feeling the bulk of the dead man's gun under his jacket. Steeling himself for what was to come.

"So," Flaharty began, glancing in the mirror as the car pulled out into the narrow street. "The meeting with your contact at Five—what came of it?"

"It's on," Harry replied, checking his watch. He had received a message from Mehreen barely twenty minutes before, confirming everything they had agreed upon. "They should be hitting the warehouse within the next half hour."

4:12 P.M.
Ashton-under-Lyne

As helicopter flights went, Thomas Parker thought, it had to be one of the calmer ones of his life.

He looked out the window of the police Eurocopter as the city flashed past beneath them, remembering other flights.

Coming in low over a desert bathed in the green of his night-vision goggles, feet dangling from the door of a Little Bird, the pilot flying nap-of-the-earth up a wadi. A scoped Remington rigged across his chest, ready for action. He'd always been the team's sniper.

But he was unarmed now, he thought—looking over at Mehreen. Unarmed and vulnerable. They both were.

A fact that didn't seem to bother her in the least. Perhaps you got used to it after a while.

He heard the pilot's voice over his headset, felt the helo bank sharply to the right, pulling into a hover.

A glance at the ground and he spied the large open parking lot the Lancashire Constabulary had set up as a staging area—the strips of fabric laid out to form a massive "H" in the middle, amidst the emergency vehicles.

H marks the spot.

"There's been no activity observed in the last hour since my men arrived on site," the constable announced, glancing from Mehreen to Thomas. He ran a thumb across the screen of the tablet, opening up a satellite overlay of the area.

It was from a commercial geosat, with dated imagery and less detail than Thomas had come to expect from his years of receiving support from the National Reconnaissance Office. Still, it would do for their purposes.

Mehreen shook her head. "Our intel indicated that the cache was under guard. You may be facing opposition once you breach the perimeter."

"We'll be deploying a team here—and here," he said by way of reply, indicating the points on the screen with the worn-down eraser of a stubby pencil. "We'll be ready for them."

A familiar mix of old technology and new, Thomas noted absently, his gaze taking in the constable's equipment. A Glock 17 holstered on the man's hip, a Heckler & Koch G36 carbine lying there atop the safe in the back of the Ford S-Max armed response vehicle.

The rest of the Firearms Unit was similarly equipped, and looked. . .competent enough, Thomas thought—assessing them with a critical eye. He'd seen better, and he had seen much worse.

Whether they were good enough for today was yet to be seen. His attention shifted back to the constable just in time to hear Mehreen ask, "How soon can you have your men in position?"

4:17 P.M.
Hammersmith
West London

It was a quiet neighborhood—at least as quiet as things got in the city. Nicer than he had expected, Harry thought, shoving the car door closed behind him—for a lance corporal's pension.

Whoever had been paying Booth, they had done so sufficiently to enable him and his family to live in a measure of comfort. The flat was one-half of a terrace house, the white stucco distinguishing it from the pale blue-green of its neighbor—a low brick wall surrounding the small courtyard in front.

"Stay here and keep watch," he instructed quietly, putting a hand on the iron gate and swinging it open.

Flaharty nodded, taking a pack of cigarettes from his pocket and shaking one out. Harry had never taken up the habit himself, but he acknowledged its worth.

No one ever gave a man out for a smoke a second glance.

A child's red bicycle lay abandoned in one corner of the courtyard, its training wheels still on. He noted its presence with a twinge of sadness—envisioning in that moment a father with his little son, guiding him along the street as his legs found the pedals for the first time.

A father that would never be coming home.

Fortunes of war. His face tightened, forcing an unfelt smile to his lips as he lifted his hand to knock.

Once. Twice. Then again, a hard rap this time—and still nothing.

He raised his hand, signaling back to Flaharty as he drew a set of lockpicks from the pocket of his jacket, selecting two from the small pouch.

Come on now, he thought, slipping them into the lock as he knelt down by the door—listening as the tumblers moved under the careful pressure.

EMBRACE THE FIRE

He had done this so many times over the years. Despite what they showed in the movies, many times picking a door was more expedient than kicking it in.

Speed. Surprise. Violence of action. The balance of those core principles, ever so delicate. Often, as now, the need for surprise outweighed all other considerations.

There. The lock gave, turning in his hand—and he stood, pocketing the lockpicks as he pushed the door open, motioning for Flaharty to follow him in.

The small entrance hall was empty—a staircase there before them leading up into the second story of the flat.

He heard the faint sound of voices in that moment, and Harry gestured for Flaharty to stay at the foot of the stairs as he moved deeper into the house, unzipping his jacket to have access to his pistol.

There was a living room immediately off the hall to the left—a bay window facing the street. *Empty.*

Another room to the right, and Harry prodded the door open with his foot. A washing machine and half-filled laundry basket greeted his gaze. Laundry room.

The next doorway to the right opened into a kitchen, the voices becoming clearer as he stepped across the threshold.

A radio. The smooth, polished accents of the BBC announcer coming from across the room.

He could feel himself relax, his hand easing away from the butt of his Sig-Sauer. *False alarm.*

Another step, rounding the edge of the kitchen's island—and he stopped stock-still, his breath catching in his throat.

Caitlyn Murray lay at his feet. . .her body splayed out across the tile of the kitchen floor—long brown hair fanned out around her head in a grotesque caricature of a halo.

Her snow-white tank top was torn and stained with blood—the hilt of a steak knife protruding from her belly as if it had pinned her to the floor.

Eyes open and staring vacantly toward the ceiling. Eyes which would never see anything. Ever again.

4:28 P.M.
Ashton-under-Lyne

There was something eerie about watching the assault unfold this way, Mehreen thought, staring at the laptop in the back of the armed response van. The split screen displaying the jerky, streamed video from the helmet cams of each team's point man.

There was no sound beyond the shuffle of men in riot gear moving into position—they'd be communicating solely by hand signals at this point, and she knew that.

Nichols had warned that there would be guards out. Had told her to expect resistance.

And there was no one. She cursed under her breath, half-fearing that she had been played once more. It couldn't be. For Aydin's sake. . .and her own.

She glanced over to see the American regarding the screen intently, remembering Darren's warning about Parker. *"He's ops, not an intel officer. No idea why they sent him."*

If that was true, no doubt he had seen assaults like this before. *Participated* in them, even. His advice would have been invaluable.

But Jimenez had introduced him as an intelligence liaison, and so they were stuck playing out this little charade.

They were closing in on the central building now, she saw, taking a step back from the laptop as she looked around the parking lot. As if she could glimpse the raid on the warehouse going down, nearly a mile distant.

There was a mighty crash from the laptop's speakers as the entry team's Enforcer battering ram smashed into the side door of the warehouse—taking the door off its hinges. There was a reason Special Branch referred to it as "the big key."

The camera shuddered, then came up once more—the point man's H&K entering the frame as he swept back and forth, reveal the vast open expanse of the warehouse floor.

The *empty* expanse of warehouse floor. She could hear the shouts as the teams converged. "Clear. . .clear. *Clear!*"

Another moment passed, dragging on with painful slowness. Then the constable's face appeared on the screen—the visor of his tactical helmet pushed back. "Ma'am, there's nothing here."

4:32 P.M.
Hammersmith
West London

She'd been dead for. . .maybe thirty minutes, Harry thought, sliding his gloved hands beneath her in an instinctive check for a improvised explosive device.

Not even long enough for her body to cool.

"Any sign of the kid?" he asked as Flaharty came back into the room from his check of the upstairs.

The Irishman shook his head, leaning heavily against the counter as he gazed down at Caitlyn Murray's body. "Not a trace. My guess is tha' he's still at school." He winced. "He's gonna be there a long time."

"Someone got to her before us," Harry observed, slowly rising to his feet. There was nothing they were going to be able to do here, their best lead lying dead at their feet.

He glanced back toward the hall, his mind racing. The door had borne no marks of forced entry. No damage to the lock. "Someone she knew."

"Or had reason to trust," Flaharty added ominously. "What did you tell your friend at Five?"

"About this? Not a word." Harry looked back at the body of the murdered woman, the blood-drenched clothing, the knife still protruding from her stomach. Her assailant would have had to have been looking her in the eye to deliver the blow, he thought—knowing all too well from experience. It was an intensely intimate manner of killing. "Even if I had...the Security Services wouldn't do something like this."

"Oh, sod off, boyo," Flaharty snapped. "What do you know about this? Any of this?"

His index finger jabbed out toward Harry, eyes flashing with a dark fury as he continued. "You haven't seen what I have, so don't you *dare* stand there and pretend to lecture me on what that lot is capable of. I knew Mairead Farrell well..." his voice faltered, trembling with emotion. "She was a beautiful woman, one of the finest—the *bravest*—women I have ever had the honor of knowin'. And the Regiment killed her that day on Gibraltar. Gunned her and the lads down like dogs in the street."

"The shoot was justified," Harry fired back, only too familiar with the story. Operation Flavius had been long before his time, but it was still used at the Farm as a textbook example of what covert units did *not* do. "She was there to bomb the changing of the guard."

The murderous look in Flaharty's eyes never wavered. "So was I."

The next moment—before Harry could respond—his cellphone began to ring.

4:36 P.M.
The warehouse
Ashton-under-Lyne

There was little mistaking the tone of Nichols' voice for anything other than genuine surprise, Mehreen thought. But he was an old hand, and she had been wrong about him before.

It was so hard to escape the fear that he had been one step ahead of her the whole way. "What do you mean they're not there?"

"You tell me," she retorted, an edge of anger in her voice. Reminding herself not to use his name on an open line. "The constables just finished sweeping the warehouse, for the second time. It's empty—no sign of anything ever having been stored there."

There was dead silence from the other end of the line for a long moment and she felt the anger boil over. "This *nation* is in the middle of a crisis today, and I diverted precious assets away to deal with this intel. Intel you assured me was credible. If this is all part of some elaborate ploy of yours—if you've been playing me, so help me I'll—"

The flat
Hammersmith
West London

"I'm not playing you," Harry responded honestly, shooting Flaharty a look. And he wasn't. . .but he knew where her mind had gone. Knew why.

He'd said it so many times through the years—you had two choices in life when it came to dealing with people.

Never lie to them—or never get caught.

Because once you'd been caught, they would have no reason to ever trust you again.

With Mehreen, both of those choices were firmly in his rear-view mirror. It was the price you paid for being a spy.

It was why he had never been able to bring himself to lie to Carol—a desperate attempt to keep those parts of his life separate. To keep some things holy. Until the night they had smashed irrevocably together, leaving everything in ashes.

Looking down at Caitlyn Murray's butchered corpse, it all came back.

Focus, he thought, his hand balling into a fist as he struggled to think clearly. As powerful as the desire for vengeance had become, he couldn't let it overcome him. Not now.

"The weapons *were* there—I saw them being moved with my own eyes."

"I want to believe you," she responded after a moment, "but I have nothing to go on—no reason to. There's no evidence anything was ever here."

He shook his head. He had been prepared for this from the beginning. Would never have risked the weapons being delivered without the safeguard of the trackers.

And that was all he needed now.

The warehouse
Ashton-under-Lyne

"I don't ask that you trust me, I only ask that you give me the chance to prove that what I've been telling you was true. I can set this right."

Words. Mehreen shook her head—glancing back down the alley toward the warehouse. Her foot kicking absently at a rusty tin. It seemed surreal that she was even considering trusting him.

And yet she was. Another moment, and she sensed movement from behind her. Turned to see the American standing there at the end of the alley, maybe twenty feet away. His eyes searching her face.

"Look," she said, lowering her voice, "I can't talk about this any further right now."

"I understand," he replied, clearly picking up on her tone. "When I have updated intel, I will send it to your phone. Keep it with you and turned on."

"It will have to be soon." She ended the call without saying good-bye, shoving the burner phone back into her pocket as she walked back toward Parker. "Have the constables completed their final sweep?"

"They have," Thomas nodded, watching the woman as she moved by him. There was something. . .his British counterparts had been keeping him in the dark ever since his arrival—that was to be expected. But this was different.

The phone. He closed his eyes, replaying the scene through his mind. It was different—black, not the grey case he had seen earlier on the flight in.

He looked up, staring as she moved back toward the warehouse, accosting the lead constable as she neared the trucks. Crawford would bear watching.

4:41 P.M.
The flat
Hammersmith, West London

No. He ran a hand over his face, standing in the flat's small bathroom—looking up to see his own reflection in the mirror.

Dead, lifeless eyes stared back at him, sunken deep into a face he scarce recognized as his own. Perhaps it wasn't, perhaps that too had been lost along the way.

He reached down, checking the phone again as if to assure himself that it wasn't true.

But it was. And they were gone.

He had gambled on vengeance and lost the roll of the dice. *If you set out for revenge, dig two graves.*

But this. . .there were going to be far more than two graves. The blood on his hands now far too deep a stain to be erased.

The disappearance of the weapons, the murder of Caitlyn Murray before they could question her—it was all falling into place.

Somewhere, somehow. . .something was going very wrong. It was a sick feeling, like sliding off a cliff.

"We need to get out of here," he said to Flaharty, walking back out into the kitchen. They were being set up—he could feel it in his bones.

"What's going on, old son?"

"I'll explain in the car," Harry replied, casting one final glance back at the young woman's body. The blood on the floor. They couldn't cover her up, couldn't leave any trace of their presence. Everything just as they had found it.

He could only pray that her son never had to see her—like this. He shook his head. Lately, answers to prayer. . .it hadn't been a good batting average.

"That was your contact at Five, wasn't it?" the Irishman demanded as Harry led the way out into the entry hall.

He didn't answer, his mind racing—trying to stay one step ahead of an opponent he couldn't even begin to name. His hand closed around the doorknob, started to pull it open.

And then he stopped, a sudden premonition washing over him. *Something.*

"You stayed on that call too soddin' long," Flaharty continued, not waiting for an answer he apparently didn't need. "They could have traced your position in—"

"Eighteen seconds," Harry responded, cutting him off. He motioned for the Irishman to stay where he was, moving carefully into the living room of the small flat, its bay window giving a view of the street. The cars parked without, all of them exactly as they had been when they'd entered the flat. Except *one*—a dark grey Toyota Camry across the street from them, two men visible inside. "I know what I'm doing—I've worked their side, remember?"

"Sure an' it's hard for me to forget," Flaharty retorted from the hall, an edge of menace in his words.

Suspicion.

Distracted, Harry turned back from the window, his eyes locked with the Irishman's, seeing the look of skepticism written there. *Stabilize the asset*, he thought—old instincts rising to the fore past the surge of emotion that had overcome him at the sight of Caitlyn Murray's body. The instincts that had kept him alive for a decade and a half in the field.

Prioritize. *Compartmentalize.* If he lost Flaharty. . .he lost control of this mission. It was that simple.

"The weapons were gone, Stephen," he announced with all the calm he could muster. "*And* the trackers."

The surprise in Flaharty's eyes couldn't have been more genuine. Surprise, along with a nameless fear. They *both* knew that the Security Service hadn't been told about the trackers.

He glanced back to the window in time to see the driver's side door of the Camry come open, the driver seeming to glance down at something in his hand before looking up. Directly at the flat.

"And we've got company."

4:46 P.M.

Go in, the text read—confirming his query of a few moments before. He didn't like this, but they had waited long enough.

The man paused, glancing once more across the street as his partner pushed open his door of the Camry. As three more men came walking up from just down the street where they had parked the second car.

"Lewis, Taylor—Collins," he began, addressing the new arrivals as he pulled a Sig-Sauer P226 from a holster beneath his jacket and screwed a suppressor into the threaded barrel, "you three take the back—go through the alleyway. Rogers and I will take the front."

He said nothing more, briefly brass-checking the chamber of his pistol as they began to advance across the street. Nothing more needed to be said—he'd led these men into battle before. And now, as then, they had their orders.

They weren't going to have much time, Harry thought as he hit the heavy steel door at the back of the flat—his pistol coming up in both hands as he stepped out into the fading afternoon light, eyes sweeping the surrounding rooftops.

Nothing.

"Who are they, and how the devil did they find us?" Flaharty demanded, wincing in pain as he hurried out the door behind him.

Harry ignored him—those would be questions for a later time. If there *was* a later. Whoever was coming for them. . .they'd had training. Not in counter-surveillance, or their monitoring of the flat would have been significantly less sloppy. But he couldn't count on them slipping up again.

"Go," he hissed, motioning to Flaharty and gesturing down the alley. It was tight, long and narrow, high terrace houses on both sides—a kill box. And neither of them were in shape for a long run.

He found their drive to the flat replaying itself through his head. There were railroad tracks perhaps a kilometer to the west—he thought.

It could be their salvation. Or a fatal dead end.

And then he heard a shout from out on the street and knew their time was up. "*Go!*" he repeated, giving the Irishman a shove down the alley as he stepped back, taking up his position to one side of the back door. *Calm down.*

He leaned back against the wall, his fingers sweaty against the pistol grip. Trying to slow his breathing. To find that place deep within—that cold, dark place every fighter knew. *You didn't know her*, the voice admonished. *She was just a woman, in the wrong place at the wrong time.*

Like Carol.

He shook his head angrily, furious at himself for the weakness—his fingers clenching around the butt of the gun. *Get a grip.*

The next moment, a man in dark street clothes came around the edge of the building from the side alley, taking the corner wide. His pistol already raised.

Harry shot him twice, high in the chest—the cycling slide of the Sig-Sauer making more noise than the report itself.

And there was no rage—not anymore. No anger. Just nothing. A dangerous calm, like that in the eye of a hurricane.

His target staggered back, but didn't go down until Harry put another bullet in him, the 9mm slug ripping through his throat and out the back of his neck.

He went down in the dirt of the alley, legs kicking—blood pouring from the throat wound as he strove to staunch the flow with his hand.

That was the idea, Harry thought coldly, squeezing off another round as the man's partner tried to break cover to retrieve him. Slow them down, give them casualties.

Wounded talked. It was a risk they weren't going to be able to afford.

And then the door came open beside him, movement out of the corner of his eye. The muzzle of a suppressed pistol leading the way out.

No hesitation—pivoting on the balls of his feet, he threw his body weight against the steel door, slamming it back on the man's gun hand with a sickening *crunch*.

A *scream*, an unearthly sound barely muffled by the door—the clatter of a pistol falling to the concrete.

Harry kicked it away, ripping the door back open to reveal his assailant just within, his face twisted in anguish—his right arm hanging useless at his side.

He glanced up, giving Harry a brief look at the face of a man perhaps ten years younger than himself—hard eyes, the close-cropped hair of a man not long out of the military. Perhaps he was still in.

The type of man he had spent the last fifteen years serving beside, Harry thought, the Sig-Sauer coming up in his hands. Sights framing his opponent's face.

He saw the hardness turn to fear, saw the plea begin to form on the man's lips.

And he shook his head.

When death came, it was with a suppressed *cough*.

Chapter 15

4:53 P.M.
Colville's Estate
The Midlands

". . .Pearson, in your interview with Sky News yesterday, you issued an angry call for British citizens to 'rise up,' to 'take a stand' against what you called the Islamist threat. In the light of these provocative comments, what do you have to say regarding today's bombing of London's Madina Mosque by a right-wing group whose rhetoric seems to take a page from your friends at the British Defence Coalition?"

The camera zoomed in on Daniel Pearson's face as the reporter finished asking his question, and they could see the MP falter, sweat showing on his face. "Well, I think it's too soon to know who was genuinely behind the attacks, uh, anyone can post anything on the 'Net. But speaking for myself and the BDC—not that I speak for the BDC, of course—but their stance, and mine, on violence has always been, uh, exceptionally clear. The type of carnage that wreaked havoc in London earlier today is unconscionable and I—"

"Pathetic," Colville snarled, flicking the television off before returning the remote to his desk. He glanced across his den to where the former sergeant stood, arms folded as he leaned against the door. "But I could have told you he would fold the moment there was *real* pressure. Our nation's 'leaders'—spineless cowards, the lot of them. Which is why it falls to us to do what needs to be done."

He paused, pacing back to the window. "How long has it been?"

"Ten minutes since I got the text from Martin," Hale replied calmly. "Three minutes since you last asked."

The publisher halted his pacing for a moment, stabbing a finger in Hale's direction. "It's been too long. I told you we should have used a sniper to handle things with Flaharty. It would have been simple."

"On the telly," the sergeant snorted, waving a hand to the now-darkened screen. "In real life. . ."

He walked over to the desk and poured himself a finger of brandy. "Nothing is ever simple. And a sniper? That was one thing they taught us in the Regiment—most of the world over, eliminating a target with a marksman sends a clear message: state sponsorship."

"Or in our case," he added, draining the glass, "state *training*. I have good men, but we don't need to draw any more scrutiny than absolutely necessary, sir. Not yet. Leave the operations end of this to me."

4:56 P.M.
Hammersmith, West London

Feels good, feels good. Fired up.

Harry's boots pounded into the broken-up asphalt of the alley as he ran, the words of the old cadence song replaying itself through his brain as he forced himself to move past the pain, ignore the throbbing of his ankle.

Conjuring up memories of Agency training. Of the endless nights and longer days at Camp Peary—later in the mountains of North Carolina. SERE School.

Survive. Evade. Resist. Escape. The mantra that had preserved him. . .and survive he had.

He'd also been fifteen years younger then. Hard to believe the difference that made.

Shouts. They'd caught sight of him, a thought which found confirmation a moment later in the form of a bullet creasing the air past his head. He ducked to one side, his leg nearly giving out from under him.

Gotta run. Feels good.

Just another lie you told yourself in an effort to stave off the inevitable.

And he was coming to the end of his rope. Another few minutes. A lucky shot. That's all they'd need.

Time to end this.

He could see the end of the alley ahead, light shining through from the street as he slipped, boots sliding in mud left by the previous day's rain. Twisting, weight hard on the sprain.

He threw up a hand, catching himself against the wall of the adjoining building even as another round caromed into the brick only inches away from his hand. Bits of mortar spraying outward, peppering his face. Drawing blood.

Pain. He reeled, staggering blindly toward the end of the alley as he struggled to clear his vision. Hearing the rush of footsteps behind him—certain that the next moment he would feel a slug bite into his back.

He made the corner and rounded it, breath coming in heavy gasps—wiping the blood from his eyes as he leaned back against the wall, getting his bearings.

The lot was empty—or nearly so, converted at one time into a makeshift basketball court, a few young Asian men shooting baskets in a pick-up game. Opening out onto a busy London street, filled with pedestrians and cars. If this became a shooting gallery. . .

There didn't seem to be much way to avoid it.

He saw one of the players look his way, appearing to react to the sight of the limping, bloodied man. He ducked his head to avoid further attention, carefully drawing the Sig-Sauer and holding it within his jacket.

Then the sound of running footsteps focused his attention back on the alleyway. He'd expected them to come out slow—"cutting the pie" to cover their angles, eliminate blind spots—but it was easy to lose sight of your training in the heat of the chase.

To make mistakes. And in this life, you only got one to a customer.

The foremost pursuer took the corner tight, feet pounding against the gravel and broken asphalt. He sensed the presence there a moment too late—looked up, just as Harry's left elbow smashed into the point of his chin.

The ex-soldier's head snapped back under the impact, body crumpling to the ground in a heap.

He heard one of the Asian kids yelling, something incoherent amidst the curses as the players realized something was wrong. Very wrong.

Harry's hand shot out, fingers twisting in the man's collar as he pulled him close—wrapping an arm around his waist to keep him from falling as he dragged the soldier backward into the open lot, bringing the pistol up in his free hand as the final two pursuers exploded out of the alleyway, weapons leveled.

He could dimly hear the curses, the shouts of fear from behind him as the lot emptied, players scattering. It could be only minutes until the police were alerted. Minutes he didn't have.

The two men seemed to hesitate at the sight of him standing there, using the limp body of their comrade as a human shield—then the leader nodded and they began to separate, going right and left. Circling, their weapons never leaving him.

He shifted the muzzle of the Sig-Sauer up, until the cold metal of the suppressor pressed firmly into the young soldier's temple. "Take one more step," he warned, "and I blow out his brains."

5:07 P.M.
The warehouse
Ashton-under-Lyne

Come on, Harry. . .where are you? Mehreen glanced at the still-dark screen of the burner phone and shook her head, glancing from the warehouse back to the churning rotors of the Eurocopter. It was time to leave, she knew that.

The Lancashire firearms unit was already packing their gear back into the S-Max vans, their multiple sweeps of the property complete.

Nothing. A dead hole. Her eyes swept the buildings once more, searching. Nichols had led her out here for *some* reason.

What was it? What was his agenda?

But there was no answer to that question, and she could delay no longer in the hopes of intel that clearly wasn't coming.

Mehreen tucked the burner into the pocket of her windbreaker and turned back toward the helicopter, ducking as rotor wash whipped hair into her eyes.

Levering herself up into the seat beside the American, she leaned forward, her hand on the pilot's shoulder. "Get us in the air. It's time to get back to London."

5:08 P.M.
Hammersmith
West London

"We have no fight with you, mate," the man with the gun said, a faint accent of Yorkshire tingeing his words, the muzzle of his H&K never leaving Harry's face. "Our orders were only for your boss. Just put down the gun and walk away."

"My boss?" A taut smile tugged at the corner of Harry's lips. "I don't have one—not anymore. As for walking away, afraid I can't do that either."

He nodded at the leader, taking the measure of the man in a sweeping glance. The close-cropped sandy hair, the hard eyes. The military bearing, the way his hands wrapped around the H&K, anchoring it in a rock-steady two-handed grip.

Time to stall. Every second he could buy until the bullets started flying. . .

"Who were you with? The 1 Yorks, Prince of Wales's Own? I worked with A Company at Shaibah back in '07. Good men, all."

"No." A shake of the head, but he could tell from the startled look in the man's eyes that he had hit uncomfortably close to home. "The Green Howards."

"Ah," he replied, keeping an eye on the second gunman out of the corner of his eye. He was getting antsy, his gaze continually shifting between Harry and his own leader.

The Yorkshire Regiment's 2nd Battalion had been deployed to Afghanistan, not Iraq. Helmand Province to be exact. "I was up north on temporary deployment when you lads went into Musa Qala. . .three days of some of the toughest fighting that'd been seen down there in years, or so I was told."

The ex-soldier nodded, a grimace passing across his face at the memory. "It was."

A curse exploded from the lips of the gunman. "Enough of this, Martin—he's stallin'."

The oath seemed to bring the leader back to his senses, the distant wail of police sirens punctuating the words. Harry saw him rock slightly forward on the balls of his feet, finger tightening around the H&K's trigger.

The next moment, a shot shattered the London air.

5:11 P.M.
The surveillance van
Leeds, England

"What's our status on Rahman?" Darren Roth asked, sliding the van's side door closed as he deposited the tray of coffees onto one of the seats.

"He went out for a walk," came the response from the officer sitting in front of the screens lining one side of the van, the bright glow casting his pale face into dark shadows. "He's down at the mini-mart—likely picking up a packet of crisps."

Roth slid into the seat beside him, handing over a coffee. "Do we have a visual?"

Given the lower traffic of the area surrounding the imam's flat, they had been forced to fall back on the local CCTV. Any tails would have been made on the first day. Not to mention that the ethnic make-up of the neighborhood was. . .unforgiving. All these years into the War on Terror and Five's recruitment efforts in the Asian community were still lagging.

"Negative," came a woman's voice from behind him and he looked back to see the second officer sitting there. She was one of the Americans, on loan from Jimenez as part of Parker's team. Her name, what was it? Traeg, something. "We've got a camera—there—on the corner across the street from the market covering the entrance, but the angle's wrong to see inside the store."

Something felt wrong about this, a vague sense of disquiet lurking in the dark corners of his mind. *Instinct.*

Roth shifted in his seat, watching the screen the woman had indicated as the minutes passed.

"How long has he been in there?"

His officer shrugged. "Ten minutes, maybe a little more."

"He left the apartment at 4:51," the American cut in, her hands moving over the keyboard in front of her to bring up the footage. And there it was. Hashim Rahman exiting the flat dressed in a light blue hoodie and jeans, hands shoved into the pockets of his jacket as he made his way down the street. Taking his time, stopping at one moment to tie shoes that hadn't come untied—one of the oldest countersurveillance tricks in the book.

This guy was good. . .which once again led him to ask: *What was he doing in the mini-mart?*

"I'm going to go take a look," he said, running a hand over his shaved scalp as he reached for a hat. Of any of his officers, he stood the best chance of blending in.

"No—wait, hold up—he's coming out," his man announced, pointing to the screen as Roth got to his feet. "Heading back to the flat."

He could see him on the screen, hurrying along the sidewalk in the fading light of day. Hurrying—and something was. . .

"There," Roth said, leaning forward to tap the screen. "Take that back."

Tapping a command into the keyboard, the field officer rewound the footage, showing Hashim Rahman leaving the mini-mart—moving down the street.

"And now from earlier," he ordered, dark eyes flickering from one screen to the next as the earlier footage came up.

Only a few seconds of the tape rolled before a low curse escaped Roth's lips. "Those are two different men, that's not Rahman. Red-flash Thames House—he's done a runner."

5:12 P.M.
Hammersmith
West London

The first rule of a gunfight. . .was that there were no rules. No secret tricks. No magic words. Just chaos, raw and bloody.

And the man who could ride that chaos—that was the man who lived where others died.

The echoes of the unsuppressed gunshot hadn't even died out over the streets of West London before Harry was moving, taking in a sweeping gaze the sight of the gunman reeling backward—clutching spasmodically at his chest.

Flaharty. It had to be him, but there was no time to process *that* as another round came whining in almost simultaneously with the first, ricocheting off the brick.

Harry put a second bullet into the falling man, the round striking him high in the chest. *Insurance.*

His eyes locked with those of the man still standing before him, saw the surprise written there at the sudden gunfire—saw the ex-soldier's eyes tighten, his trigger finger taking up the slack, a movement born of instinct.

The muzzle of his own gun moving to cover him. *Ride the chaos.*

But it was too late, the pistol recoiling into the man's hands even as Harry's Sig-Sauer came to bear.

He didn't hear the sound of the pistol firing—the suppressed *cough* of the H&K drowned out by the screech of car brakes, a cacophony of horns as the shots brought traffic grinding to a standstill in the street behind him.

But he felt the bullet striking home as if it were a hammer blow slamming into the limp body in his arms—the sickeningly wet sound of a bullet ripping through flesh, shattering bone.

Sirens.

He fired the Sig-Sauer off-hand, moving backward and letting the man's body crumple to the asphalt of the vacant lot—his shots going wild as the soldier ducked for cover.

Live to fight another day.

It was past time for him to follow the same advice, Harry thought, the muzzle of his weapon covering his retreat as he moved back on the street, working his way among the stalled cars.

Break contact. Forcing himself into a limping run, he threw his free hand out, vaulting himself over the crumpled hood of a Nissan Micra compact that had smashed into the rear of the delivery van in front of it.

The airbags had deployed—the driver's seat empty, he saw, staggering painfully as he regained his feet.

There was a little girl crying in her car seat in the back of the Micra, her mother nowhere in sight. Pistol still extended in front of him in both hands, his head came up—eyes searching the once-quiet city street, picking out the figures of bystanders running in terror. *Fear. Chaos.*

Like they had that night in Vegas.

And then, in the space of a moment, he was back there—standing outside the Bellagio—the sound of the approaching sirens ringing dimly in his ears, a cold sweat breaking out on his forehead. His legs felt suddenly rubbery from the run, his breath coming in sharp, shallow gasps.

He could feel Carol's hand on his arm, hear her voice. *"You thought I was going to leave you?"*

He closed his eyes, trying to shake the paralysis that seemed to have overcome him, but he could only see her face—white and gasping for breath. Struggling to form those last, painful words. *"I'm. . .sorry."*

Gone.

Movement—off to his right—and he swung, bringing the muzzle of the Sig up to cover the threat.

Flaharty. The Irishman was standing there, his own weapon drawn as his eyes searched Harry's face, questions written in their depths.

Questions with no answers. And no time to look for them.

"It's time we were leavin', boyo."

6:17 P.M.
A bus stop
Leeds

It seemed hard to believe that he was this close, after so many months. He had been so bold on-line, yet so afraid of actually taking action. . .and that was to his shame. Even now, it seemed hard to believe that the imam had welcomed him to their ranks so readily.

Aydin collapsed into a seat near the back of the First Leeds bus, digging into his jacket for his phone. Pulling it out as he did so, to check Rahman's message one more time.

A single endeavor in God's Cause, he thought, recalling the words of the hadith, *is better than the world and whatever is in it.*

For surely it was. And his young eyes shone with an unholy fervor as they scanned down the screen, burning the address into his memory.

The hour was at hand.

6:24 P.M.
Thames House
London

No asset was ever 100% reliable—that was the first thing you ever learned as a case officer. People were wrong. People lied.

Which was it with Harry?

"Marsh wants to see you in his office," were the first words that greeted Mehreen as she walked back onto the floor of the Centre. The tone of MacCallum's voice betraying the strain they all were under.

She responded with a nod in his direction, too consumed by her own thoughts to muster a reply. *Which was it?*

Impossible. She ran a hand across her forehead, struggling to shut out the emotion.

To distance herself, analyze the situation objectively.

The worst of it was that she *needed* to trust Nichols—had to, if her plans to extricate her nephew were to proceed. And yet, deep down, she knew. . .the odds of him being wrong were much worse than of him having lied.

He was a spy, after all.

6:26 P.M.
The M40 Motorway
North of London

Run. Farther and deeper into the night, voices echoing in the darkness of his mind. You always tried to escape your past, but it was like trying to outrun a tsunami, a towering wall of water growing higher with every step you took.

Come crashing down to sweep you away.

He was driving too fast, far too fast and he knew it, the speedometer needle of the stolen Audi pegged at almost ninety miles per hour. Harry put the wheel over hard, knuckles white, sliding around a utility van as he moved into the far right lane of the motorway. *Slow down.*

He caught a glimpse of his own face in the rear-view mirror above his head, the red brake-lights of a car ahead casting a hellish reflection into empty eyes.

Trying to outpace the demons. Knowing the futility of it.

He could feel the bulge of the Sig Sauer under his jacket, knew all too well the consequences if they were stopped.

Consequences. It seemed impossible that they could be any worse than for what he had already done. Sins for which there was no atonement to be found.

"*Don't* call," he said abruptly, a faint electronic glow warning him that Flaharty was looking at the screen of his phone.

"Easy there, lad—I wasn't plannin' on it."

It was the first words Flaharty had spoken since the bus in London, since Harry had laid out the harsh truth of what they were facing. He could see the pain in the Irishman's eyes, the searching for answers.

Betrayal.

"Do you really think you're right?" Flaharty asked after another long moment, wincing as he shifted position in the passenger seat—tucking the phone back into the pocket of his jacket.

Harry eased off the gas finally, marking the time on the Audi's dashboard clock. "We'll know in a few hours, won't we?"

"Aye," the Irishman replied, running a hand across the lower half of his face. "That we will."

Another few moments passed, the noise of the traffic the only sound as the motorway flashed past in the night.

Then Flaharty cleared his throat. "So what happened to you back there?"

Silence.

6:31 P.M.
Thames House
London

The TV was on in Marsh's office—the audio a dull murmur, flames flickering on-screen, footage of an unknown scene of chaos.

"Birmingham, forty-five minutes ago," the DG intoned by way of explanation, his eyes never leaving the screen as he stood there in the half-darkness of the office. "Someone threw a Molotov cocktail onto the front seat of the No. 9 bus as it was taking on passengers. The driver didn't make it out—over a dozen others are being treated for serious burns."

She whispered a curse under her breath, the darkness seeming to close around her—thick and oppressive.

"We'll be liaising with West Midlands on the investigation," Marsh continued without appearing to notice, "but all they have right now is uncorroborated eyewitness reports of a group of Asian youths harassing women at the bus stop in the minutes before No. 9's arrival. Metro's searching for three gunmen in Hammersmith—found one man shot dead in the midst of what bystanders are calling a 'gun battle.'"

"What are we looking at—retaliation for the attack on the worshipers at Madina?"

"God knows," he responded, a bitter edge to his voice. "And we'd all best be praying one exists. Hashim Rahman eluded his surveillance team an hour ago—used a decoy to get out from under."

We all fall down. A house of cards collapsing in upon itself, the dust and rubble obscuring the road ahead.

And the timing couldn't have been worse. He looked at her finally, asking, "Ashton was a dry hole?"

"It was," she responded. "My intel was. . .faulty."

It was more than that, but it seemed the best way to describe what had taken place. The *cleanest.* "What do you need to me to do?"

"Right now?" Marsh threw a look back at her over his shoulder. "Go home, get some sleep. Roth has his people out scouring Leeds for Rahman, I'm going to need someone fresh to work on Besimi. He's the last lead we have."

9:42 P.M.
The flat
Failsworth

Home. The flat in Failsworth had been many things in the ten years since Flaharty had purchased it, but home had never been one of them.

These days, it was hard to even say where that was. Ireland? The land of his birth? He hadn't dared return there in three years—his parents long dead, his older brother fallen years before in the Troubles.

Now. . .well, Davey was the closest thing he had to family. Brothers in all but blood.

Davey. There were lights on in the flat as Flaharty mounted the stoop, inserting his key in the lock.

He pushed it open, wincing as the movement of the arm pulled at his injured side.

The wound. He needed a stiff drink—and fresh bandages. In that order.

Footsteps from the hall and he looked up to see Malone standing there, pistol already drawn in the big man's hand.

"Oh, it's you," the enforcer said, a strange shadow passing across his face as he lowered the weapon. "Glad to see you stopped arsin' about and got back here—I was beginning to think something had happened."

Flaharty gritted his teeth, shrugging the jacket off his shoulders and tossing it onto the back of a chair. "Bugger me if it didn't, Davey."

"Oh?"

"Things went completely pear-shaped. . ." The arms dealer shook his head. "I could use a drink."

He followed Malone into the flat's small kitchen, watching as his old friend took down the bottle of Bushmills from an upper cabinet, along with a pair of glasses.

"The whole thing was a sodding ambush," Flaharty began, throwing back the shot of whisky. He felt the fire race down his throat, searing his vocal cords. "Like they knew we were comin'."

Delay. It was a dangerous game he was playing, hard as it was to believe, even yet. He set the glass back down on the counter, pushing it toward Malone and gesturing for him to refill it. "I barely made it out of there alive—had to ditch the car and take a bus out of London."

"And the American?"

Flaharty picked up the tumbler and turned, making his way back to the couch in the living room. "No idea—last I saw him was when the shooting started. After that, everything got muddled. Gets precious hard to keep track of everyone once the bullets start flying."

"I bloody well told you he couldn't be trusted. Doin' business with him wasn't worth the money."

He stared down into his drink, his own reflection staring back from the whisky. "I don't know. I've known Harry for a long time. Maybe he caught a bullet, maybe he *was* part of it. All I know is they've been staying one step ahead the whole way—like they knew my every move before I made it. Even he didn't know that much, so how?"

And that was the question, wasn't it? *How?*

Flaharty tossed back the second shot of whisky, feeling the liquor begin to warm him—take the edge off the pain. "I think I could do with another, Davey. . .Davey?"

Silence.

He looked up to see Malone standing there, not five feet away. A drawn pistol in the enforcer's hand.

Pointed straight at Flaharty's head.

9:46 P.M.
A warehouse
Leeds

"Are you sure he will be here?" Aydin asked, hesitation in his voice as he moved over to where the imam stood near the edge of the room, checking the screen of his phone.

"Aye," Rahman replied, seeming distracted. "He will be, *insh'allah.*"

Of course, the boy reminded himself, looking across the warehouse at the small knots of young men gathered together in conversation. *As God wills it.*

He had to be the youngest of those gathered, he thought—all the others in their early twenties, at least. College students, many of them. All wearing at least the semblance of a beard.

His own chin was painfully smooth to the touch as he ran a hand across his lower face, trying to hide the awkwardness he felt as he sized up his companions. The inescapable feeling that he couldn't have been more out of place.

And yet. . .

There was a noise from without, and he looked up to see the large black man from the mosque enter through a side door, his eyes sweeping those assembled with a suspicious glance.

Aydin's eyes took in the long dark case strapped to the man's back before spotting the second man entering behind him.

A man tall as a tree and slender as a woman—his form cloaked in a light windbreaker, a cap pulled low over his forehead.

But his *eyes*—blue and piercing—Aydin knew from the moment he gazed into them. They were the eyes of a prophet.

The Shaikh.

9:51 P.M.
The flat
Failsworth

"What in the devil are you playing at?"

"I didn't want for it to end like this, Stephen," Malone responded, a sad smile creasing his face. "So help me, I didn't—but you're not leavin' me with any choice."

"He's sold you out—sold both of us out." Nichols' words, ringing in his ears. *"It was you, me, and him. The three of us—the only ones who knew about the trackers."*

Even now, staring into the barrel of Malone's .45, it didn't seem real. "Why did you do it, Davey?" he asked simply, leaning back into the threadbare sofa—staring into his old friend's face. "Was it the money? I thought you were better than that. . .we were brothers, you and I—went through the Troubles together. Back to back, the two of us against the world. I—"

"Oh, don't act so sodding righteous," Malone cut him off, anger flaring in the man's eyes as he took a step closer, the pistol still trained on Flaharty's head. "The Troubles were a long time ago—we both played our patriot game and found the pay piss-poor. But I believed. . .and you, you didn't, did you? You saw the handwriting on the wall—knew what was coming for all of us—that's why you turned tout, wasn't it? Did you tell yourself it was better somehow because you sold out to the Americans? Washington, not London—as if they didn't pass along every last thing you gave them to the Security Services?"

That was the way, wasn't it? A long-ago admonition filtering back through his mind—the words of his parish priest back in Belfast. *Be sure your sins will find you out.*

He had been an altar boy back in those days—before his life had exploded into violence, before he had thrown the first flaming bottle of petrol at a British troop-carrier.

Mea culpa, mea culpa, mea maxima culpa, he thought, recalling to memory the words of the Mass. Through my fault, my most grievous fault. *Ideo precor beatam Mariam semper virginem.*

I beseech the Blessed Mary ever-virgin. . .

A faith that had been forever lost in the fires of Bloody Sunday—thirteen unarmed boys and men gunned down in the street by the murdering thugs of the Parachute Regiment.

The Holy Mother hadn't stopped the bullets on that day any more than she was going to stop this one—the hammer back on Malone's .45, his voice trembling with fury as he continued.

"Gerry Adams and the bloody council surrendered and you sold out—so don't you *dare* sit there now and preach to me of loyalty. Of betrayal. Not after all that you've betrayed."

The big man paused, sorrow in his eyes as he gazed down the pistol's barrel at Flaharty. "I didn't want to believe it when they showed me the proof of what you'd done, Stephen. Didn't want to have to kill you myself—for the memory of all the years. But maybe this is the way it was meant to be. Good-bye. . .old friend."

The end of the road. His Kimber was only inches from his hand, but he would be dead before it could clear the holster. He saw Malone's finger tighten around the trigger, closed his eyes in resignation.

Fate. The end of every man.

The next moment, a pair of suppressed gunshots rang out, the sound reverberating through the small flat.

He heard a strangled cry of rage and pain escape the enforcer's lips, felt a bullet bite into the sofa between his legs.

His eyes came wide open just in time to see Malone crumple to the dirty grunge of the carpet, pistol falling from his fingers, his legs going out from under him—shot through both kneecaps.

The figure of Harry Nichols emerged from the semi-darkness of the flat behind Malone, the suppressed Sig-Sauer still in his outstretched hand.

"You took your own good time," Flaharty swore under his breath, finding himself trembling as he staggered to his feet. "Thought you were never going to show up."

The American shrugged coldly. "You wanted to know the truth. Now you do."

"Well sod you," Flaharty shot back, eyeing Malone as the man struggled to pull himself forward on the carpet, moaning from the pain of the shattered kneecaps.

Ignoring the pain in his side, Flaharty reached down, scooping up the FNX just before Malone reached out for it, a final, desperate gesture.

"Davey, Davey, Davey. . ." he whispered reproachfully, taking a step back as he aimed the weapon down at the man who had saved his life so many times. "What in the devil's name has become of us?"

He glanced up, saw Nichols standing there. "Give us a moment."

Harry's eyes met with those of the Irishman—eyes filled with pain. Remorse. Over friendships betrayed.

Past sins.

After a moment, he nodded—tucking the pistol back underneath his leather jacket as he went out into the hall.

It was quiet outside as he gazed through the window, a thick layer of grime and automobile exhaust doing its best to obscure his view. No one visible in the street.

"Did he deserve to die?" Flaharty's question of the early morning, only hours before—though it seemed like an eternity.

The unanswerable question, Harry thought once more, standing there in the darkness of the hall. He had spent over a decade watching men die. Good men, bad men—made no difference, they died all the same. No rhyme, no reason.

Just *death*.

Two minutes later, a single gunshot rang out from the living room.

10:35 P.M.
The warehouse
Leeds

"The spark has been lit," the Shaikh announced, his voice low and trembling with intensity. His gaze sweeping the assembled men as they pressed forward—straining forward to hear every word that fell from his lips. "In the martyrdoms of Javeed Mousa, of Muzhir bin Abdullah and his companions, names which shall be forever remembered throughout the *Ummah*. And it will burst into flame here, in the midst of the house of war, spreading across the very land from which the crusaders first set forth."

Aydin felt the eyes rest upon him, piercing his very soul. "And you," the Shaikh continued, seeming to speak directly to *him*, "will be the spreaders of that flame."

It was a moment before he realized that the Shaikh was beckoning to him. *Ya Allah.*

He felt everyone's eyes on him as he took a step forward—saw the muscled black man at the side of the Shaikh bend down, unzipping the soft case and extracting a long, black rifle—its barrel gleaming in the harsh glare of the utility lights which illuminated the warehouse floor.

The Shaikh reached out a hand and took the rifle from his bodyguard, holding it up like a mujahideen would. Defiantly. *Proudly.*

"This and many more—the arms of the crusaders—brought into our hands by Allah's aid, that we might finally take the fight to the *khaffir*. For too long the enemies of God have laid desolate the lands of Iraq, of Sham. Now, it is their own streets which will run red with blood."

He reached out, motioning for Aydin to take the rifle as he continued. To stand at his side.

The rifle was heavy as the boy hefted it in trembling hands, cold and black as death itself.

Power.

But the Shaikh was speaking again, the index finger of his right hand raised as his piercing gaze swept the crowd of assembled men.

"One third of them shall flee," he began, his voice washing over Aydin, holding him in thrall as he repeated the words of God's Messenger, "And Allah shall never forgive them. One third will be killed; they shall be the best martyrs with God. And one third, shall conquer them, and never be afflicted with temptation."

"*Allahu akbar!*" a young college student exclaimed, his eyes shining with fervor, his fist raised in the air. Then those around him began to join in the chant. "*Allahu akbar! Allahu akbar!*"

And Aydin joined in, tears of pride streaming down his cheeks as he looked out at the men. His *brothers.*

For every man will be with those whom he loves. "*Allahu akbar!*"

Chapter 16

3:02 A.M., March 30th
A flat
Rochdale, United Kingdom

"You knew—*you* knew." *Carol's voice so familiar, so reproachful. Haunting him even as the mists seemed to part—the figure of a blond woman kneeling there on the bloodstained tile, cradling a shattered head in her lap.*

Her hand stroking the lifeless arm of a boy. Pyotr. *An American college student, dead before his time.*

The sins of the father.

And there was nothing he could do—helpless, trapped. He felt himself reach down, fingers searching for her wrist, seeking to pull her close to him, keep her safe. . .and the face of the boy seemed to melt away, even as he did so. The weathered visage of Davey Malone in its place, hollow and staring. Carol's voice, harsh and bitter. "Does this look like 'no harm' to you?"

And then she looked up at him, and in place of her blood-streaked countenance appeared the stricken face of Mehreen, dark eyes gazing back into his own. A look of condemnation, of—

Fear. Harry came awake with a start—finding himself back in California in that moment, staring down at the body of Pyotr on the bathroom tiles of the abandoned mansion.

His hand flew out, clawing for his pistol. Fingers closing around the checkered grip. *No.*

It wasn't happening—not again, he wouldn't allow. . .he gazed up at the darkness of the ceiling in the bedroom of the small, second-story flat—realizing only then where he was.

But it had been so *real*.

He slowly rolled into a sitting position, knees drawn up, leaning back against the head of the bed. *Calm down*.

Post-traumatic stress. That's what a doctor would have called this—except there was nothing *post* about it.

Just demons which came in the night, nightmares that wouldn't flee with the approach of day.

Because the reality was worse.

Flaharty was on the couch when Harry came out into the main living area of the flat, just sitting there staring off into nothing.

Malone's pistol was lying on the coffee table in front of him, inches away from a bottle of Bushmills.

He glanced over at Harry in the dim light, a bitter smile slowly creasing his face. "So, you couldn't sleep either, boyo," the Irishman observed, slurring the words drunkenly. "There's a kind of justice, there."

He lurched forward in his seat, reaching with unsteady fingers for the Bushmills and up-ending it into the small tumbler.

The resulting trickle of amber liquid barely enough to cover the bottom of the glass.

A curse exploded from Flaharty as he pulled back his hand, throwing the empty bottle against the wall.

The crash broke the silence of the apartment, fragments of glass cascading to the floor as he buried his face in his hands, seemingly overcome.

"I don't know how I could have. . .*missed* something so sodding obvious," he said finally, downing the last of the whisky with an angry gesture.

Friendship. *Trust*. That most perilous of human actions.

"It happens," Harry replied after a long moment, unable to escape the memories this had awoken. Of Jerusalem. *Hamid Zakiri*.

The beginning of the fall.

Flaharty snorted, staring down into his glass. "The worst of it is, he was right. I sold out to your people. I'd spent my youth fighting for a free Ireland—had bugger-all to show for it—nothing but the ashes of dreams. Along came one of you Americans—a smooth-talking sod with a suitcase of money. And I thought I'd seen my way out. A way to make a fresh start for myself."

Fresh start. The chance to begin again—start over. Lay aside the sins of the past. Live free.

The chance he had glimpsed ever so briefly with Carol, Harry thought, leaning heavily against the counter. A man would do most anything for such a chance. Beg, borrow, steal.

Kill.

"But you know what, boyo? You can't escape from who you are," Flaharty continued, a sort of morose honesty coming through the whisky. "Because no matter how hard you run, you always catch up with yourself in the end—like a bleedin' dog chasing his tail. And tonight. . .tonight I put a gun to the head of a man I'd loved like a brother ever since we were young, and I blew his brains out—all to save me from my sins."

"You had no other choice." It might have even been true, but that was less than relevant. Right now, nothing was more important than stabilizing the asset. *Nothing.*

The arms dealer just smiled. "That's what we like to tell ourselves, isn't it? 'No choice.' It was him or me. Kill or be killed. The lies we tell ourselves so we can sleep at night. Because everything we *do* is a choice."

And so few of them can be undone. The older you got, the more evident that became. The more frightening.

Flaharty set his empty glass down on the coffee table and stood, swaying uneasily. "So," he began, "Davey's no longer with us. And the weapons are in the wind. What are we goin' to do now?"

"I don't know."

12:17 A.M. Eastern Time
KramerBooks
Washington, D.C.

"You know, I wouldn't have really thought this was your kind of place."

"Oh?" Senator Roy Coftey asked, his eyebrows arching in more than a trace of amusement. He glanced briefly around the interior of the Dupont Circle bookstore before looking back across the cafe table at the junior senator from Florida.

A heavy emphasis on the *junior*. At thirty-four, the oldest son of Cuban immigrants, Daniel Acosta was the new face of a party that was still trying to remake itself in the eyes of an ever-hostile media—in the vanguard of the new Republican near-majority that had swept into power along with Norton the previous November. Seizing the White House along with a commanding majority in the House of Representatives. And forty-nine seats in the Senate, falling just short of majority.

So very close to the kind of power the GOP hadn't seen in nearly a decade. *And yet so far.*

"And what precisely did you think was 'my kind of place'?" Coftey continued, lifting his half-empty lager to his lips.

The young man shrugged, seemingly embarrassed. "I don't know—didn't really see you as much of a reader."

"I'm not," Coftey laughed, tapping the thick hardcover sitting there only inches from his plate. The political memoir of the erstwhile Vice President—an eminently forgettable book from an eminently forgettable man which had been written as the lead-in to a presidential run that didn't have a prayer of coming to pass. "But Kramer's gives me the opportunity to peruse the latest political tell-alls without ever wasting good money on my colleagues' bilge. And that, my friend, can be *invaluable*."

"Friends?" Acosta leaned back in his chair, a skeptical look on the young Republican's face. "Is that what we are now?"

Coftey smiled. Say what you would, the kid had sand. That could be. . .useful. "Well," he said, gesturing to the slow-roasted duck on Acosta's plate, "that's a question I suspect we'll know the answer to by the time you've finished your cassoulet."

5:34 A.M. Greenwich Mean Time
The house
Leeds, United Kingdom

In another hour, he would need to be up and readying himself for school, but Aydin hadn't been able to sleep, just lying there awake, staring up at the ceiling of his small bedroom.

Too much adrenaline still pumping through his veins to even think of rest.

He'd been back in his family's house for two hours, letting himself back in through the rear door with a spare key.

It had been three long hours since he'd left the company of his brothers, he thought. *The mujahideen*.

Brave men all, ready to die in Allah's struggle. *Ready to die*. And yet he had never felt more alive.

Aydin rolled over onto his side, slipping a nervous hand under his pillow.

Cold metal touched his fingertips, the metal grip of the pistol Rahman had given him. *Keep this. Our day is coming soon*.

And it was impossible to resist the urge to look at it once more, his eyes shining as he dug the small Czech semiautomatic from beneath the pillow, holding it up to the dim light filtering into his room from the street.

All praise be to God, he breathed, a single .32-caliber round falling from the weapon to strike his bare chest as he racked the slide—the cold sound of metal on metal loud in the silence of his room. *The Lord of worlds*. . .

12:51 A.M. Eastern Time
Kramerbooks
Washington, D.C.

"No." His long-forgotten cassoulet pushed to one side, Daniel Acosta raised a hand, shaking his head at Coftey. "That's simply not going to happen. Not going to happen. The American people want transparency, and that's what I promised to give them if I was elected. It's a promise I intend to *keep*."

Coftey leaned back in his chair, skepticism written in his eyes as he gazed at the junior senator. "What your average American voter," he began, "knows about the intelligence community—the actual *facts* they know—would fit in a shot glass. With plenty of room for ice."

"Laying aside the patronization," Acosta countered, "that's an argument for hiding less, not more. What do you think the Founders would think of the unaccountable system of surveillance that has been put in place?"

Unaccountable. Coftey swore softly under his breath. Well-nigh hamstrung by bureaucracy and endless layers of oversight, the intelligence agencies could hardly have been *more* accountable, even if that wasn't how they were portrayed in spy movies and the news media, the second portrayal even more fictitious than the first.

He glanced around the café before responding, taking the measure of the few remaining patrons at this late hour. A college student with a stack of books piled beside his laptop as he typed furiously away. A couple barely out of their teens, drinking coffee and hopelessly lost in each other's eyes.

A middle-aged blonde with earbuds in her ears, sipping on a latte as she perused a book on. . .Tantric sex. *Well.*

"Look, son," he began, lowering his voice and leaning forward, placing a heavy elbow on the table, "I don't think you understand how any of this works. I've been in this town since before you were born."

"Which is precisely what some people would say is the problem," came the swift retort.

"And they might not be all wrong," Coftey shot back. "But that's not the point here—the point is that the types of 'reforms' the House is pushing for will put out America's eyes—on the basis of information that simply isn't true. And it's not going to pass the Senate, not if I have anything to say about it. It's not even going to get out on the floor. You're on the Select Committee now. . .I need to know that I have your support."

Acosta didn't look at him for a moment, idly toying with his fork. "Why are you talking to me—why not your fellow Democrats?"

"My party?" Coftey snorted. "They've been gunning for the IC ever since Frank Church. And now you fools have joined them."

EMBRACE THE FIRE

7:03 A.M. Greenwich Mean Time
Thames House
London, United Kingdom

". . .acrid smoke from burning tires is forming a haze over the city this morning, restricting some flights in and out of Birmingham Airport. Mayor Janice Harding has issued a call for calm and police presence in Birmingham is expected to. . ."

All the televisions were on in the Centre, as usual. Like any intel agency the world over, they learned about far too much from watching news reports.

And this morning, none of the reports were good—riots in Birmingham overnight, leaving shops smashed and looted. A police officer in critical condition after she was stabbed in the midst of the riot.

A West Midlands Armed Response Vehicle had been overturned and set aflame, injuring two more officers. She hadn't yet seen credible intel on which side had started the fighting, but the dawn seemed unlikely to bring calm.

She'd been unable to reach her sister-in-law the preceding night, her text messages going unanswered. Normally that wouldn't have worried her—Nimra was notorious for not checking her mobile and their contact had been sporadic, at best, through the years. *But now.*

Mehreen shrugged her coat from off her shoulders, forcing herself to filter out the continuing drone of the news host as she dropped her coat over the back of the chair.

There was a thick stack of folders sitting on the desk of her workstation—along with a pair of USB thumb drives.

She reached down, brushing a hand across the cover sheet, the logo emblazoned at the head. Four letters beneath a blue diadem.

GCHQ.

The "raw data", the intercepts she had requested from Cheltenham the previous day. The data that could prove Ismail Besimi innocent. Or damn him completely.

To hold the fate of an old friend in your hands. . .

Enough. There was no place for any of that in this—an analysis had to be objective if it was to be worth anything.

Time to get to work.

9:35 A.M.
Failsworth

". . .neighbor thought they heard the sound of a shot. Of a car leaving shortly thereafter." Conor Hale paused, gazing through the windshield of his car.

"They're taking the body out now. Yes, I'm sure. It's Malone."

There was a long silence for a moment on the other end of the line, then Colville responded, "That's the end of it, then. We can't allow ourselves to be distracted with this any longer. Time to cut our losses."

Cut our losses. The former SAS sergeant flinched as though he had been slapped. He didn't care about Malone—would have happily put the bullet in the Irishman himself, but the men who had died in Hammersmith. . .well, it was enough to say that they were his brothers.

The Green Howards—as fine men as this world had ever seen.

Hale listened for a couple more moments in silence, then responded with a curt, "Yes, sir. Understood."

Did he? He closed the mobile, tucking it back into its pouch on his belt as he watched the emergency personnel moving in and out of the small flat.

Perhaps. He had lost men before, in Iraq. In war. And this *was* war—a little fact that none of his country's so-called leaders had the courage to admit.

That's why they were doing this, after all. Laying down their lives once more for the nation they loved—for the England their fathers had known. For the England that was being stolen from them, bit by bit. Day by day.

It didn't make the losing of them any easier.

Hale ran a hand across his face, the stubble of his beard scratching against the rough calluses of his palm. A hard road, and it was only just beginning. It wasn't going to get any better from here.

He glanced away from the flat in which Malone had died, down to the terrain map he had been studying, spread over the passenger seat beside him.

Marked heavily in red pencil—lines of sight marked out, paths of movement. Potential firing positions.

He would only have one shot.

High treason. That's what this would be called—he knew that. Once, it would have seemed unthinkable, but now it seemed that nothing was beyond the pale.

Desperate times. Far more desperate measures.

1:56 P.M.
The US Embassy
Grosvenor Square, London

"Birmingham, Leicester, Manchester, Luton, the Tower Hamlets. . ." Carlos Jimenez waved a hand at the wall map, shaking his head. "The whole country's on fire this morning."

That was an understatement, Thomas thought. An attempt to summarize a situation that was spinning out of control faster than anyone could keep up with it.

The death toll from the mosque bombing had climbed by five this morning, with another eight worshipers still barely clinging to life. Among them Ibrahim Khattam, the imam at the Madina, and one of the few strong voices of reason left in the Islamic community.

A voice now *silenced*.

"What are we picking up on our end?" he asked, taking his seat in the station chief's small office. Jimenez never had been one to stand on ceremony.

The former Marine gestured at the secure telephone unit on his desk. "I've spent the morning on the STU back to Langley. If they're getting anything actionable, they're not sharing it with me."

"And locally?"

Jimenez rounded the desk, cocking his head to one side as he gave Thomas a hard stare. "You know there's nothing for me to say there. . .we get all our information locally through Thames House, as per our intel-sharing agreement."

Officially. The CIA wasn't supposed to run sources on British soil, unofficially, well they did what they needed to do. And everyone knew it, even Jimenez wanted to play coy.

The whole situation called for a drink. Or two. Or more. Three days dry, this time.

Nothing to write home about.

Funny thing about AA, no one told you how hard it would become when work prevented you from going to the meetings. When your sponsor was four thousand miles away.

"And when it comes to Thames House," the station chief continued after a moment of awkward silence, "they just re-acquired Hashim Rahman."

Thomas glanced up. "Where?"

"Apparently still in Leeds. We're not getting any further details as of yet. Which is why I want you to get back up there, STAT."

2:04 P.M.
The M62
West Yorkshire, United Kingdom

Flaharty had been snoring when Harry left the flat, finally sleeping off the whisky.

No telling how long he would be out.

And there were more important things to be concerned with. The rolling fields of West Yorkshire flashed past as the Audi sped down the motorway, waves of grass as far as the eye could see, towering white clouds hanging low over the foothills toward the north, their bases dark and threatening.

Such a vastly different landscape from the terrain where he had spent so much of his life, where so many of his brothers had bled and died. The snow-capped mountains of Afghanistan—the searing, arid heat of Iraq.

And yet now the war was here. Hard as it was to believe, staring out across these pastures.

Ashton-under-Lyne had been the location of the first weapons cache—a cache now long gone, according to Mehreen's report.

The West Yorkshire town of Huddersfield, thirty minutes due east from Rochdale along the M62 Motorway, was the second—the coordinates on a slip of paper in the pocket of his shirt.

A sign for Junction 24 alerted him that he was approaching A629 into the town, and Harry glanced to the right as he shifted lanes, taking in the sight of Castle Hill far to the south, the granite silhouette of the Jubilee Tower standing tall against the sky.

It was a sight he remembered well, from a visit to the area with Nick and Mehr. In happier times. A hill fort dating back to the Iron Age, Castle Hill's slopes were now littered with the fragments of shell casings from a WWII anti-aircraft battery.

This land. . .was no stranger to war.

2:13 P.M.
Thames House
London

"Rahman showed up at the council estate shortly after noon, walking in right past a Yorkshire Special Branch surveillance team at the estate on an unrelated investigation," MacCallum said, glancing up from his notes. "Roth and his people were on-scene within the hour, and re-acquired him as he was just leaving for the bus station. He's currently in Bramley, just across the river, still under MI-5 surveillance."

"Do we have any idea of his purpose in going there?" Mehreen asked, her mind still revolving through the GCHQ intercepts she had spent the day going through. There was something wrong about the message—something very wrong, but she couldn't put a finger on what it was.

The section chief responded with a shake of the head. "None—the council estate is massive, nearly four thousand inhabitants. We're liaising with local authorities. Should have the tenant list by tonight so that Norris can run it against our database."

He shrugged, the message clearly written in his countenance. They had gotten lucky, Mehreen thought. Very lucky. It would be unwise to rely on that luck holding, and as for the tenant list. . .considering the state of council housing in the UK, it was unlikely to hold the answers they needed.

But they had Rahman, and that was something.

She saw MacCallum stand to his feet, signaling the end of the meeting—a nod and a word or two to Norris as the analyst disappeared back to his workstation.

"Where are we on Ismail Besimi?" the section chief asked as Mehreen also rose, moving toward the door of the conference room. "We need to pull together whatever we can to use as leverage. The quizmasters are getting nowhere with him."

She paused, turning back to face him. "There may be a reason for that—he might be telling the truth."

MacCallum shook his head, sadness in his eyes as he looked at her. "Assets turn, Mehr. It's the reality of our world. No matter how well we feel we *know* them. You can't ask someone to betray everyone around them and assume that they're incapable of doing the same to you. Besimi sold you out—the GCHQ intercepts confirm that."

He was right, she knew that. It had been a truth hammered into her from her first days with Five in Northern Ireland.

A truth she had come to realize first-hand, staring down the barrel of a tout's gun one dark night in Belfast. *And yet.*

"But that's just the thing," she began, finding her voice as she stared back at MacCallum. "Do they?"

She had his attention, Mehreen could tell that. He had always taken her seriously, the respect tendered by one veteran officer to another. "Go on."

"There are. . .inconsistencies in the message headers as received from Cheltenham. As though someone spoofed Besimi's phone—planted the messages, essentially." She shook her head. "I'm going to have to ask Norris to have a look at it, his technical expertise is far beyond mine in this arena. Whoever did this worked very hard to erase any evidence of tampering."

"*If* it was done," her colleague responded. Alec came around the edge of the conference table, placing a gentle hand on her forearm as he looked down at her. "I know you think this is something you have to do, Mehr, but this country is on fire. We're stretched to the breaking point—and I need you to ask yourself a question: are you trying to investigate Ismail Besimi? Or exonerate him?"

The one question she couldn't face. Not now. "I should speak to him in person, at least sit in on the interrogation—I know him better than anyone at Five, better than the quizmasters at Leeds could dream of."

"He's not going to be at Leeds much longer—they're moving him to Paddington Green tonight." MacCallum shook his head wearily, adjusting his glasses with a forefinger. "But go ahead and give me what you've compiled on the message headers. I'll task Norris with it, see what he can dig up."

5:42 P.M.
Leeds

"You'll stay close to me, bruv, and do exactly what I tell you to do." There had been an edge to the man's voice when he said it—a tone that would brook no disobedience.

The man introduced to him as "Farid" would have drawn no attention on any city street—slight in stature, an unremarkable face. The accent of a South Londoner. But he was a veteran of the jihad in Syria, one of many British Muslims who had returned home from fighting with the Islamic State against the *safawi* of Iraq.

A man who knew what it was to slay God's enemies.

Aydin pulled his coat tighter around his body against the chill of the evening, feeling the bulge of the small automatic in his pocket as he made his way down the sidewalk, a can of petrol in his left hand—staying three steps behind Farid, abreast of a young college student named Nisar who rounded out their trio.

The synagogue was a large building, pale blue domes surmounting the structure above a façade of brick. Three cars in the parking lot, the lights above shining down into the faces of the young men as they advanced silently on the building.

Let this serve as a message, the man had said, the final words he had spoken before leaving the car two blocks back. *To those who have rejected the word of Allah's Messenger.*

The side door was locked and Farid reached wordlessly back to the college student, who pulled a small crowbar and a hammer from within his sports jacket.

The hammer blows resounded loudly, echoing off the surrounding buildings. Aydin stood there, his free hand shoved deep into the pocket of his jacket, clutching the butt of the automatic.

His palms were slick with sweat, eyes darting around them as Farid and the student worked—heart pounding against his chest as though it threatened to break through.

Come on. He found himself praying, whether from excitement or fear, he didn't know which.

Five sharp blows of the hammer and the door came open—Farid leading the way inside, opening into a small, dark hallway.

Doors lined the corridor, the English lettering identifying them as classrooms, but the men ignored them—moving toward the faint red *Exit* lights marking the door leading to the stairs.

12:47 P.M. Eastern Time
CIA Headquarters
Langley, Virginia

"I understand, Khaled. I truly do. We've known far too many of our own losses in this War on Terror." *Borne the burden of most of them.* David Lay bit his tongue as he fell silent—listening to the *Mukhabarat* head on the other end of the phone. "And the death of each is a tragedy. Please convey our regrets to your president, along with my gratitude for your continued cooperation in the Sinai."

For as long as it continued was more like it, the CIA director thought—the buzzer on his desk going off even as he returned the phone to its cradle. Their status with the Egyptians was ever one of uncertainty.

His secretary's voice. "Ron Carter to see you, sir."

"Send him in," Lay replied, the door opening a moment later to admit the analyst.

"What's this about, Ron?" he asked, glancing up at Carter's entrance.

"The report on the Mali operation—as you requested, sir," the analyst replied, placing a folder on the desk and taking a step back. An unnatural tension seeming to pervade his body as he stood there, hands clasped behind his back. From the rigidity of his posture, one could almost imagine a younger Carter—dressed in the Air Force fatigues he had once worn—standing at attention before his superiors.

It had been a stressful week for all of them, Lay reflected, dismissing it as he opened the folder, his eyes scanning down the sheet. Between the end of the successful operation against TALISMAN and now the ongoing situation in Egypt, it was taking its toll on all the ops people.

"Brian Fornell," he said, his eyes narrowing as they fell on the name near the bottom, "he led the SAD strike team into Mali?"

"He did."

"And have you contacted him about the connection there with Flaharty?" Lay asked, looking up.

A shadow seemed to pass across the analyst's face. "Brian Fornell. . .was killed two years ago in Afghanistan. A VBIED—he died instantly, along with an SF liaison officer."

Lay grimaced, remembering the attack. "All right, then. See if you can hunt up any of the other members of the Mali team, as time permits. Egypt takes priority."

"Understood, sir."

The elevator doors had closed behind Carter by the time he dug the phone from his pocket, his fingers trembling despite himself as he punched in Kranemeyer's number, cursing under his breath as it rang again and again before finally being picked up.

"It's done."

5:51 P.M. Greenwich Mean Time
The synagogue
Leeds

There were only dim lights on in the main sanctuary of the synagogue, enough to make visible the outlines of the Torah ark at the far eastern end of the room—the almemar, or pulpit, in the center of the steps before it.

"The can," Farid ordered gruffly, motioning for Nisar to take the petrol from Aydin's hand.

He watched, excitement building within him as the fuel was thrown over the canopy of the Torah ark, drenching the scrolls beneath—the stench of it filling the air as the student began to spread it around the room, soaking the furnishings.

He had seen the images from Paris, protesters in support of Palestine clashing with French gendarmes—the broken glass, the synagogues in flames. And he had dreamed of being there. *Now. . .*

All at once the room was flooded with light, Aydin's heart nearly stopping—the fluorescents above them flickering to life. A dark silhouette in the shadows near the door issuing the challenge. "What are you doing here?"

He glimpsed Farid turn, the gleam of metal in the mujahid's hand as his pistol came out. And then flame exploded from the gun's muzzle.

There was a difference between watching the leaked videos on the Internet and the real thing. The *panic* of it.

He had never heard a gun fired before—not *here*, right beside him—and he found himself stumbling backward, falling to the carpet, trying desperately to protect his ears as the explosions hammered his eardrums.

One, two, three, four, five—the gunshots seemed to go on forever, the form of Farid visible moving amongst the chairs, firing as he went.

And then. . .silence. Heart still racing, the boy pulled himself aright—shaking his head as if he could by so doing clear the ringing from his ears.

He saw Nisar rising from where he had crouched for shelter, took in the sight of the Jew lying at the back of the room, a dark, viscous liquid pooling beneath the body. Farid standing there, just a few feet away, the slide of his pistol locked back on an empty magazine.

A scowl on his weathered face as he glared at Aydin, the look in his eyes speaking louder than words his appraisal of his companions.

"Enough," he said finally, cursing under his breath as he came over to take the can of petrol from Nisar's hand, upending it over the curtains of the windows, the heady fumes rising about them.

He threw the can at the foot of the pulpit and turned, leading the way to the door, Aydin stepping over the body of the Jew as they reached it.

Looking down into his face, the kindly eyes of a middle-aged man staring back from above his Orthodox beard, eyes now filled with pain. He was still alive, but barely—his breath coming in short, tortured gasps.

Farid turned back, kicking the wounded man in the belly, eliciting an anguished scream.

"Zionist scum. . ." he spat, pulling a lighter from his pocket. Eyes impassive, the fighter flicked it until flame spurted from the tip, tossing it without a moment's hesitation into the petrol-soaked room. "As the Prophet has surely spoken, may they taste the punishment of burning."

And behind them, as they turned to leave, the room exploded into fire. . .

7:08 P.M.
Huddersfield, Yorkshire

There. The final tumbler gave within the lock, an audible *click* striking Harry's ears.

He withdrew the lockpick and placed his hand on the door of the warehouse, pushing it open as his flashlight led the way inside, held in his weak hand, the Sig-Sauer in his right.

Into the vacant space of the floor—just emptiness stretching across the concrete floor like the breadth of a cavern, no matter where he flicked the light.

He had known there would be nothing here. Talking with the local color earlier had been enough to confirm that—reports of a tractor-trailer backed up to the loading dock late in the afternoon of the previous day, loading up crates from the warehouse.

Known, and yet he'd needed to see it for himself. Confirm his own worst fears. All the weapons Flaharty had brought into the country—enough weapons to start a war—*gone.*

Two of the locals said that the trailer had been white, a third that it was gray. No matter, it was far from here now. . .and he didn't even begin to know where to look.

He sank to one knee on the cold concrete, shaking his head as if attempting to clear it of the fog. He had made mistakes over the years—mistakes that cost lives, that haunted him in the night.

But nothing like this. "My God, what have I done?" he breathed, the words coming out as more a prayer than a question.

A prayer. He hadn't prayed since Carol's death, a yawning hole left where his faith had once been.

A hole? No, that wasn't true either. Anger and pain, bitterness rushing in to fill the void. *Horror vacui.*

Nature abhors a vacuum.

"God," he began, his voice rising as he gazed out across the warehouse floor, up to where light from the town filtered in through a high skylight. "Answer me. . .where *are* You?"

And back across the floor came only the repeated, weakening echo of his voice. Anguished and haunting.

"Answer me. . .where are You. . .where are You. . .*Are You?*"

8:34 P.M.
Westminster Tube Station
Central London

Routine. It was the sworn enemy of any spy—the danger of becoming too comfortable. The perilous illusion of security.

Westminster had been a part of Mehreen's workday for years, she thought, pushing past a businessman in a tailored suit on the crowded escalator as they descended into the deep-level station.

As near a constant as anything in her life. Twice a day, five days a week. And ever a sea of people, moving in and out of the city.

She was moving down the final few steps before they could reach the bottom—gazing up at the station around her as she moved toward the next escalator, spotting a short, bearded Sikh just ahead, his bright orange turban marking him as it bobbed along through the crowd.

The thing that had always struck her about the deep station was its harsh modernity, stainless steel and concrete—cross-bracing support bars running over her head to support the staggered banks of escalators, stacked one atop another as they descended to the Jubilee Line below.

It was a building devoid of humanity, cold. Austere.

Something prompted her to look up and back, half-turning on the step—catching just then the glimpse of a tall, sturdily-built man stepping onto the escalator above her, a small ruck slung over his shoulder, accessible to his weapon hand.

Their eyes met for just a moment, an almost perceptible *click*—and then he looked away quickly. *Too quickly*, Mehreen realized, a sudden chill running through her body.

Recognizing all the signs. Somehow. . .she had picked up a tail.

She's a threat, the former soldier thought, studying his target from above. That's what Hale had told him, their phone call hurried and veiled, as always. *"Take care of her."*

It wasn't an order he was comfortable with. Killing a woman, a civilian—it hadn't been what he had signed up for. Not those many years ago, raising his hand to swear the Queen's oath. Not now, serving once more with Conor Hale.

But getting out now, that wasn't an option. They were *all* committed.

The woman glanced back suddenly, catching him off-guard—their eyes locking for a brief moment in time. *Sod it.*

He looked away hurriedly, cursing himself under his breath—knowing that she would have had to have realized he was looking directly at her.

Knowing she wasn't young or attractive enough to have passed his gaze off as casual interest.

As if to confirm his fears, she picked up her pace, pushing past her fellow travelers as she moved ahead of them down the escalator. His gaze flickered to the bottom of the escalator, the sea of people moving toward the platforms.

She could lose herself in seconds amidst that press, their opportunity gone. There was a part of him that prayed for her to do just that—the part of him that didn't want to commit murder this night, to cross that line.

But he already had. *Trapped*. The decision already made for him, no way out.

His head swiveled, catching sight of one of his team members on the opposite escalator—a man he knew only as "Henderson", formerly of the Rifles—standing there, his hand on the rail as they moved down.

Their eyes met and he inclined his head toward the woman below them, the message clear. *Move in, move in.*

Take her now.

He began moving quickly down the escalator, pushing a small Asian man out of his way—squeezing past a woman with a stroller—his hand slipping beneath the flap of his ruck, closing around the narrow wooden shiv within, its tip hard and nearly as sharp as metal.

Out of the corner of his eye, he could see Henderson slightly ahead of him, shoving people aside as he went.

But by the time they reached the platform below, Mehreen Crawford had vanished.

Chapter 17

9:17 P.M.
Westminster Station
London

The cold night air struck Mehreen full in the face as she exited the tube station out onto the street—forcing her to wrap the scarf she wore more tightly around her throat. Her coat was gone, discarded in the stall of a women's restroom far below.

Anything that might change her appearance enough to avoid detection.

There had been three of them, she thought, eyes continually scanning the street—the familiar sight of one of London's double-decker buses off in the distance.

At least three, maybe more, fanning out across the platform in an effort to intercept her. And she had seen it their eyes.

They weren't there to follow her. They were a kill team.

It was like being back in Belfast all over again—more than one officer of Five had fallen there, been found lying face-down in a ditch, brains blown out.

But there she had known *why* people were trying to kill her. Why, and who. Here. . .

It was Ismail Besimi, she thought, joining a crowd of Japanese tourists leaving the station, weaving in among them as they crossed the street. The information she had uncovered in the intercepts from Cheltenham. It had to be.

He *had* been set up, just as she'd suspected.

And yet—she stopped stock-still in the middle of the crosswalk, frozen by the realization. The only person she had told about the problem with the intercepts was MacCallum. *Alec.*

Nichols' voice, suddenly echoing through her mind. *"You have a mole."*

A Japanese woman bumped into her from behind and Mehreen started moving again, walking faster this time. As if trying to escape from the reality. *No.*

It was as impossible to believe Alec was the mole as it had been to believe Ismail was a traitor.

But if he was—if *anyone* at Thames House was—she glanced up full into the eye of a surveillance camera and ducked her head quickly, realizing the danger.

She jerked her Security Service mobile from its pouch on her hip, fingers working feverishly to pull off the back, extract the SIM card. Another moment, and both phone and card fell from her hands to the pavement, to be crushed underfoot only moments later.

Still, it was only going to be a matter of time until they were after her again. London wasn't safe, not anymore.

London. She stopped again, her mind racing. Remembering one of the last things MacCallum had said about Ismail Besimi. *"He won't be there much longer. They're moving him to Paddington Green tonight."*

They hadn't hesitated to come after an MI-5 officer in the middle of a city station. Besimi wouldn't stand a chance.

She ducked into the doorway of a closed shop, pulling out the burner Nichols had given her. She had to get in touch with Roth. If anyone could help, it was him.

9:24 P.M.
MI 5 Regional Office
Leeds, West Yorkshire

Having the Americans did help.

Even Darren had to admit, however grudgingly, that Parker and his team had been an asset. With the escalation of violence since the bombing in London, the local Security Service team was overwhelmed, never mind assisting Darren's people with tracking targets and the continuing search for Tarik Abdul Muhammad.

It didn't mean he liked giving them this level of access, he thought—moving out of the SCIF into the main part of the office. It was becoming ever harder to firewall them off from sensitive information, and he suspected that was exactly what Jimenez had intended.

The Agency station chief was always working an angle. *Always.*

But then, nothing came free in this world. His mobile buzzed in his pocket and he opened it, not recognizing the number. "Roth here."

EMBRACE THE FIRE

"Darren." It was Mehreen's voice, nearly obscured by traffic noise. He could almost feel her pause, as if uncertain of her next words. "I need to ask you to do me a favor."

He glanced at his watch. "We're just about to rotate teams, Mehr, and I'm trying to keep a close eye on the Americans. If it's something I can manage—of course."

"I understand," she began, a strange urgency in her tone. "Ismail Besimi—he's being transferred by Special Branch from Leeds to Paddington Green. What time are they leaving?"

"They just did. Five, maybe ten minutes ago. I supervised the hand-off myself."

Dead silence from her end of the line, broken only by the horn of a passing vehicle. "Mehreen?" he asked finally. "Are you still there?"

"Yes," came the reply. Slow, hesitant. "Thank you, Darren. One more thing—two, if I might. I need the map of the route the transport is taking to reach London."

"Why do you need something like that?" The question was instinctive, alarm bells going off inside his head at her request.

A long pause. "Something is going on down here, Darren—I'll read you in when I can. We've worked together for years, and I'm going to have to ask you to trust me. I wouldn't ask if I didn't need it."

It was his turn to hesitate, looking back along the corridor to the office where he had set up shop for the duration of this operation. They'd both served their country for a exceedingly long time and Mehreen Crawford had given more in its service than most could even fathom. If she couldn't be trusted. . .well, no one could.

"All right," he said, re-entering the office and throwing his coat over the chair. "Just give me a moment, I'll send you what you need. And the second thing?"

"I need the list of Thames House personnel who have accessed the route files."

He tapped in his log-in access, opening the route data in a separate window. "That's strange. There's only one name, Alec MacCallum."

9:27 P.M.
London

"Thank you. That's. . .all I needed."

MacCallum. Mehreen shut the phone, heart pounding against her chest. She had wanted to trust Roth—wanted to tell him everything, enlist his aid.

But if Alec could be compromised, so could anyone else. Even one of Nick's old mates. *Moscow Rules.*

The watchword of British spies long before her time. *Anyone could be suspect.*

If she wanted to save Besimi—if she wanted to save *herself*, she was going to have to work outside the system.

And that was going to mean placing faith in someone she couldn't begin to trust—turning to the last man she wanted to rely on. *Nichols.*

She kept moving—only too aware that the kill team was still looking for her, that someone at Thames House could even now be tracing her position—doing her best to look like just another normal Londoner as she made her way down the street.

She raised the phone, hesitating for a moment before pressing speed-dial. Cursing her own uncertainty.

Under optimal conditions, it was scarcely more than a three-hour drive from Leeds to London.

There was no time to be wasted.

9:31 P.M.
The flat
Rochdale, United Kingdom

Nationalists, Harry thought, parking the car on the street down from the flat where he and Flaharty had spent the night before. That's who the Irishman had said bought the weapons—members of the British far right who had apparently made the decision to move beyond political activism and demonstrations into the realm of the euphemistically termed "direct action."

The same kind of people who had claimed responsibility for the bombing of the mosque in London.

The British far right. Tarik Abdul Muhammad. *Sworn enemies.* Or something, he knew not what.

It was the same feeling he'd had the previous December as the plot against Vegas unfolded, the sick sensation of being one step behind the pace. Only glimpsing a piece of the puzzle.

And people were dead because of it. Because of *him*. The guilt of failure.

He feared they were far from the last.

The flat was dark as he approached—shades pulled, no lights visible—but that wasn't a surprise. Neither of them had been keen to announce their arrival in the neighborhood.

"Nearly thought you had scarpered," Flaharty observed as Harry entered, letting himself in with the spare key. "And you with my brand new car too."

"Right," he responded, detecting the slur in the Irishman's voice as he laughed at his own joke. "You've been drinking again, haven't you?"

"And why not?" came back the demand as Flaharty lurched to his feet from the sofa. "Man's got to do something with his time. Nobody to talk to. Ah, whisky, you're my darling."

Another laugh, louder this time. Harry shook his head, about to respond when the phone in the pocket of his jacket rang. *The burner.*

There were only two people who knew that number connected to him. And with one of them standing before him—it had to be Mehreen.

"Yes?" He asked, ignoring the dark look of suspicion in Flaharty's eyes as he answered the call.

"We need to meet," she responded, careful not to use his name on the unsecured line. Burner it might be, but you still couldn't be too cautious.

Now wasn't the time. Not with so much hanging in the balance.

"Is this about your nephew?"

"No, it's not. This is," she hesitated, "more important. You were right about. . .Box."

Box. The old nickname for the Security Service. His words to her about the mole.

"Go on," he said, looking back at Flaharty and motioning for him to remain silent.

"I know who it is—and it's no longer safe for me here in London," she continued hurriedly. "An hour ago, three men tried to kill me in the middle of Westminster Station. And they're going to kill another man tonight. A good man. A man who could be the key to all of this."

He flinched as if he'd been slapped, surprising himself by his own reaction to the news of her peril.

There were so few people he had ever permitted himself to become close to—fewer still who were yet living.

He had betrayed the friendship they once had known from the moment he'd set foot in her door, and yet. . .she was still one of the few who meant anything to him.

For the memory of better days.

"Where do we meet?"

"At the old shooting grounds," she responded cryptically. "In the woods north of the cottage. You know the place."

And he did.

Harry shut the phone, sliding it back in his pocket as he turned away, gesturing to the Irishman. "Get yourself sobered up and ready to move—I'm going to need your help with this."

"Boyo," Flaharty began, his voice no longer sounding nearly as drunken as it had when Harry first entered, the look in his eye suggesting that it had been all an act.

He gestured toward the Sig-Sauer on Harry's hip, just visible through the open jacket. "Where you're going, you'll need more than that. There's an AK and a pair of NODs in the closet."

10:57 P.M.
The fields off the M1
North of Leicester

Timing. That was going to be everything, Paul Gordon thought, stuffing the black balaclava back into the front pocket of his tactical mask.

He picked up the G3 assault rifle, one of a handful retained from the shipments by Hale for their own use, and moved out beyond the treeline to survey the road.

It had gone without saying that the Special Branch transport would stick to the motorway. Side roads in England were. . .less than well maintained.

A good plan—on a normal day. Today, it just made them more predictable. Not that it would have mattered.

He hadn't asked Hale how he had such precise intelligence on the prisoner transfer—how he even knew it was taking place tonight in the first place. There had been enough for him to suspect that Hale had someone inside the Security Service.

"They're going to bloody well let him go, Paul," he had said, the anger playing across his features. *"Years this man has been preaching hate against our country, and now with all this hell raining down around us, they're just going to let him go."*

And that was the problem, wasn't it? The British legal system had been letting these people go for decades—judges frightened of their own shadow, afraid of being accused of racism or anti-Islamic prejudice.

And yet to execute an unarmed man this way. To run the risk of a gun battle with the British officers guarding him. Of killing *them*, men with families just like he once had known.

Sisters like Alice. He had thought of refusing the order—of walking away from it all, the carnage of Madina still weighing on his soul.

Walk away. Somehow he knew his old comrade well enough to suspect that wasn't an option.

The road lit up in the hazy green glow of the NODs as he raised them to his eyes, standing there on the knoll—the lights of speeding cars glaring brightly in the night-vision.

They were going to have to time this so *sodding* precisely.

11:14 P.M.
Outside St. Albans

"This the place?" Flaharty asked as the Audi rolled slowly down the narrow gravel access road, headlights piercing the darkness of the woods ahead of them.

Harry acknowledged the question with a terse nod. It was. He could remember it as if it was yesterday, coming to these woods with Nick and Mehr—a crisp fall weekend spent in the little cottage perhaps two hundred meters to their south.

The two men had gone out for pheasant, armed with a pair of old double-barrels borrowed from a friend of Nick's.

Tramped all day through these woods, with not a bird to be found. Two highly trained warriors, and only empty bags to show for it when night came.

The old shooting grounds, as she had called them. A brief smile touched his lips at the memory, but it vanished as quick as it had come.

Those days. . .were gone forever. And now Mehreen was in danger.

The headlights picked out another vehicle parked on the access road—a dark blue Toyota Camry just sitting there, lights out.

He could feel Flaharty stiffen beside him. "Is that your contact from Five?"

Harry shrugged, shifting the Audi into park and unzipping his jacket as he reached for the door handle. "I guess I'll just have to find out, now won't I?"

Stepping out of the vehicle, he stripped off his jacket, tossing it onto the driver's seat. He let the car door slam shut behind him as he walked out into the small clearing in the woods, arms spread open and away from his sides—allowing himself to be silhouetted against the Audi's headlights.

"Harry," a voice called from the darkness and he turned to see Mehreen walking toward him out of the woods from off to the side—in the opposite direction from the sedan. "Thank you for coming. I'm sorry I couldn't say more over the phone."

"You said more than enough," Harry responded grimly. "Are you certain you weren't followed here?"

She nodded quickly and he didn't press any further. No question in his mind that if she had been, she would have known it.

But there was a haunted look in her eyes that he hadn't seen before. "You mentioned the mole. . .what's going on, Mehr?"

"We don't have much time," she responded, glancing at her watch. "There's a prisoner transfer going down tonight—already en route—an old asset of mine, an imam named Ismail Besimi, is being transported from Leeds to Paddington Green on trumped up terrorism charges. He's never going to reach London—the same people who tried to kill me are going to take him out on the road before

Special Branch can deliver him."

"How do you know all this?"

Mehreen hesitated, and he could see the anguish written on her face. The night seemed to close around them, the woods quiet but for the low hum of the Audi's engine. "The mole—it's a man named Alec MacCallum. My section chief at Five."

Shades of Hamid Zakiri. He winced, shaking his head at the folly of it. *Traitors amongst us, foes without.*

Perhaps none of this meant anything, in the end.

But she was still speaking. ". . .Alec was the only person I told about my suspicions that Ismail Besimi had been framed. He said he'd handle it. Six hours later, I was targeted by a three-man team—former military, professionals—in the heart of Westminster Station. And I checked our systems remotely. His Thames House ID was used to access the route information for Besimi's transfer. The only one to do so."

A court would have called it circumstantial evidence, Harry knew that. Flimsy, even. Perhaps that's precisely what the barristers at Old Bailey *would* argue.

But this. . .was no court. There was no jury to render a verdict, no judge to pass sentence.

Just the two of them, groping in the dark. And that would have to suffice. "So, you have Besimi's route?" he asked, getting to the point of the matter.

"If they're on schedule," she replied by way of an answer, "they should be nearing Coventry now."

"And *if* they haven't already been intercepted."

A grim, tight-lipped nod, the sadness in her eyes visible even in the night. "*If.*"

"Do you have a weapon?"

She gave him a look. "You know good and well that the Service doesn't issue sidearms to its officers."

"I do," Harry replied, reaching into his waistband beneath his shirt for the compact H&K. "Thought Nick might have squirreled away a piece over the years. He never was much of a one for the rules."

"You're right," she said, a sad smile creeping across her lips as he handed it over to her, butt-first, "he wasn't. But I couldn't return to the flat. Not with Five compromised."

"Then it's a good thing I came prepared." He turned, starting to lead the way back to the car, his boots crunching against the wet, icy leaves, when he heard her come to an abrupt stop behind him.

"Who did you bring with you?"

He looked up to see Flaharty standing guard there beside the Audi, the Kalashnikov held loosely in the crook of his arm. "There's nothing to worry about, Mehr," he said, motioning for her to stand down. "He's with me. The type of people we're going up against, we can't take them on by ourselves. I thought I would bring back-up."

Harry gestured for the Irishman to step forward, his face becoming visible in the glare of the Audi's headlights. "Mehreen, I'd like you to meet—"

"*Stephen Flaharty*," she finished for him, eyes opening wide in a mixture of surprise and anger, the words exploding from her mouth in a hiss.

Harry heard the faint metallic *snick* of a safety being thumbed off, saw the Heckler & Koch come up in both her hands.

Aimed straight at Flaharty's head.

11:23 P.M.
Colville's estate
The Midlands

"You know," Tarik Abdul Muhammad said, glancing over at Arthur Colville—still blinking like an owl caught in the daytime from the blindfold the bodyguard had removed only moments before, "you really can dispense with the theatrics. I know who you are. Which means I also know where you live."

He could feel the ex-soldier tense behind him, the English bulldog sensing a threat to his master. But the publisher simply smiled, turning away from the fireplace to face him. "Fair enough. We should treat as equals, in truth." He extended the sheet of paper in his hand. "Your men did good work."

It was a mock-up of the *Daily Standard*'s front page, a lurid photo of the synagogue in flames filling the page above the fold. The article below lamenting the murder of Rabbi Chaim Ariel, his gunshot-riddled body found amidst the charred ruins by firefighters.

One less Jew. It was hard to find something to lament in that, the Pakistani thought, passing the paper back to Colville without comment.

"The PM's position is becoming tenuous," the publisher continued without waiting for an answer. "Two days of rioting, and there seems to be no end in sight. However, we need to up the ante. More precisely, *you* need to."

Tarik shook his head, at once affronted and amused by the Englishman's arrogance. "Do I now?"

"If we are to succeed...yes. I need you to launch a suicide bombing against a target here in the UK. A single bomber. Nothing elaborate, nothing high-profile—frightening in its very simplicity."

The boy. Tarik listened expressionlessly, the face of the young man from the night before clear in his mind's eye.

Rahman's words from earlier. *"He is a pious young man. Completely unskilled, but true of heart."*

And so young. The perfect candidate. And yet. . .

"Why?" he asked, his eyes never leaving Colville's face.

The publisher looked nonplussed. "We need the pressure to build of course, to foment a public outcry for the government to crack down harshly. That's exactly the wrong move, and Whitehall, for all their cowardice, knows it—which is why we can leave them with no choice. I think the reasons are fairly obvious, and—"

"You've explained how your plan is to your advantage," Tarik said coldly, cutting him short. "I have yet to see how following it is to mine. What are you prepared to give me?"

Colville nodded, glancing behind Tarik to his bodyguard. "I think, Conor, that it is time we discussed the endgame."

11:25 P.M.
The wood
Outside St. Albans

There were moments in one's life when you realized, in a flash of blinding clarity, just how badly you had miscalculated.

Even if you didn't yet fully grasp *why.*

"Put the gun down, Mehr," Harry warned, thrown off balance by the suddenness of her action. The burning hatred emanating from her dark eyes as she gazed at Flaharty. "I know this man's history of action against the Crown, but that's in the past. He's a CIA asset—he's working with me."

"No." She shook her head, a single tear leaving her eye and streaking down her cheek, glistening fiercely in the glare of the headlights. "I can't."

He moved as if to step between her and Flaharty, but something in her eyes warned him back. A glance over to Flaharty showed him that the Irishman hadn't moved since Mehreen had spoken his name, just standing there frozen in place—his assault rifle still held at the ready.

Harry shook his head. "Could someone be so kind as to tell me what is going on here?"

"Harry," Flaharty began, moving slightly forward into the light, "I'm afraid that—"

"Not another *step*," Mehreen warned him, spitting the words out from between clenched teeth. Harry heard another *click* as she thumbed back the HK's hammer to full-cock. "You. . .killed my husband."

Nick. Harry's heart seemed to turn to stone within him at Mehreen's words, his eyes flickering back and forth between Mehreen and Flaharty—her face full of anguish, his full of. . .guilt.

"Is this true?" he demanded, finding his voice in that moment. Glaring at the Irishman as if he could have killed him himself. He and Nick had been more than comrades, closer than brothers.

"Your husband," Flaharty began, staring earnestly at Mehreen, "was not the target. *You* were. And yes, I built the bomb."

"You *sodding*—" she spat, her finger tightening around the trigger, her hands trembling with anger.

"Wait," Harry said, cutting her off. The mission—*his* mission—had to come first. Anything that brought him one step closer to bringing down Tarik. *That* was priority. "Mehreen. . .you can take your revenge, but if we're going to intercept the Special Branch transport before they can be ambushed—if we're going to rescue your asset—we need to move, right now. You know I loved Nick like a brother, but you know as well as I what he would do in this situation. He'd see this mission through to the end."

Was that even the truth? Harry asked himself, watching her face in the night. Reading the indecision written there. The rage. The pain.

Would Nick have been able to lower the weapon had the situation been reversed? Had it been Mehreen's body lying beneath the stone there in Hendon? Had her killer stood before him?

No. No more than he would have spared—far less *allied* himself with—Tarik Abdul Muhammad. And yet he heard himself speaking once more, "You *know* what Nick would have done, Mehr."

11:35 P.M.
Colville's estate
The Midlands

The Shaikh was impressed, Colville could tell that much—though the man was trying hard to hide it. This is why he had made such an effort to locate him, risked so much to extract him out from under Security Service surveillance. He was a man of vision, a man whose sense of destiny was only equaled by Colville's own. That was what made him a man they could use—what made him dangerous to them.

Colville shook his head. *May God defend the right.*

"The River Dee serves as a natural barrier on the north," Conor Hale continued, gesturing with his pencil across the map. "On the west, there's nothing but barren Highlands. . .empty country. No place to run to, to seek refuge. No help coming from that direction. Control the bridges to the east, and you effectively control access—in and out."

"And how do you propose that I do that?" the *Shaikh* asked, his eyes searching Hale's face keenly.

"Riflemen, roadside IEDs—I don't suppose I bloody well need to tell you how to set up this type of thing. You sods did more than enough of that in Iraq. Provided you have men with the experience."

He could see the anger in his subordinate's eyes, the hatred festering there just beneath the surface. But Tarik seemed to ignore it, focusing instead on the map spread out before them on Colville's desk. "I have the men. Men who fought in the jihad against the Americans in Iraq, against the apostate in Syria."

"Brave men all, I'm sure," Conor observed, the sarcasm fairly dripping from his words.

Colville shot him a warning look, but the *Shaikh* was already replying, not a trace of irony in his voice. "Brave enough. . .as God wills. When will all of this take place?"

"The Queen will arrive at Balmoral on the morning of the 4th."

11:31 P.M.
The woods
Outside St. Albans

She had spent so many nights lying awake, alone in her bed. . .envisioning this moment. Flaharty's face framed by the sights of a pistol in her hands.

For Nick.

She had known they would come for her one day, had always feared what might happen to those around her. But Nick, had always seemed invincible.

Even now, she could feel his strongly callused hand gently caressing the nape of her neck, pulling her in close for a kiss as he prepared to go out the door—his tongue slipping teasingly within her mouth, a bit of the devil dancing in his bright eyes.

Less than two minutes later, she had heard the car's motor falter as it came to life—and then the flat's windows had exploded inward, shards of glass turned into flying daggers from the force of the blast.

A life—a *love*—extinguished, in the space of a heartbeat. *Less.*

She heard Nichols' words, saw the pallor of the Irishman's face in the darkness.

Nick. Ismail. *Aydin*. Loves warring within her, the dead vs. the living. Nick. . .could not be saved.

For the other two, there was yet hope.

Mehreen nodded finally, lowering the pistol—her heart still beating fast against her chest, her hands trembling with emotion.

She met Harry's eyes and looked away, scarce able to trust herself to speak. "Then let's be going."

Chapter 18

12:06 A.M., March 31st
Somewhere along the M1 Motorway

He was being moved. That's all he knew, arms shackled before him, a hood drawn tightly over his head.

Ismail Besimi leaned back against the partition of the van, feeling the road rush past beneath him—hearing the low murmur of the guard's voices from the front.

"Our Lord," he whispered, his parched lips breathing the words of the *du'a*, "place me not among those guilty of evil-doing."

There had to have been some mistake. Something which would be sorted out, as God willed. In God's time. That was something he had been telling himself for. . .days, was it?

Or *weeks*? The nights and days running together in a disorienting fog.

Don't lose faith. . .

12:11 A.M.

They had taken both cars, Harry thought, eyes fixed on the red taillights of Mehreen's Toyota ahead of him. Hand clenched in a death grip on the steering wheel, foot down on the accelerator as he did his best to stay with her in the midst of the late night traffic out of London.

And they had a location, or thought they did. This wasn't a sanctioned op—he no longer had Carter's team backing his play, providing him with intel in real-time.

What he did have was the long years at war—hard-earned experience in reading terrain.

Setting up ambushes of his own.

He'd looked over the route using terrain data from a commercial geosat—the type of information that had been the stuff of military secrets twenty years before, but now could be accessed by a teenager in his parents' basement with a five-second Google search.

Three locations showed promise—three locations that *he* would have chosen if this was his op, rather than one he was attempting to thwart.

They were marked north to south on the Audi's GPS—waypoints shining in the darkness along the M-1.

The first two were manageable in the time they had left. The third, well there was no chance they were going to reach it ahead of the transport.

He glanced over at Flaharty, sitting there in the passenger seat—staring out the window at the passing cars. They hadn't spoken a word since returning to the vehicle.

"I served with Nick Crawford," Harry said finally, breaking the silence. "From Iraq, to Lebanon, to Afghanistan. . .what seems like a score of god-forsaken places in between. I would have given my *life* for him. Nearly did, more than once. What she said back there—is it true?"

"It is," the Irishman replied, not looking at him, "every word of it."

Good men die. Harry's knuckles whitened around the steering wheel as he moved in on the sedan, closing the gap before a truck could change lanes and cut them off—the bellow of an airhorn filling the night around them. "You were a CIA asset then, your days with the Provos were over. Why?"

Flaharty sighed, an impatient sound. "You honestly think Davey was the first to suspect that I'd had a change of loyalties, boyo? He wasn't. This game we're all in together—you, I, the widow Crawford—you can stop playing, if you want. Give up. But you never get to *leave*. I had to prove myself, prove to them that nothing had changed. That everything was as it had always been."

"So you built the bomb."

"Aye," Flaharty responded, shaking his head. "I built the bomb. Tell me, Harry—tell me honestly. . .did you ever hesitate to kill an enemy?"

No, came the response to his lips, the instincts that had kept him alive all those years in the field rising to the fore. *Never*. And yet something stopped him. "This was different."

"How?" the Irishman demanded, a short, barking laugh escaping his lips. "She was with Five in Northern Ireland, her kind have been hunting me and my brothers for decades. Her husband—your sodding 'mate'? He was a Para."

His voice grew low and cold. "Many's the time I put on the gloves and went round after round with Jackie Duddy when we were both lads. He was like a brother to me. . .up till that fine Sunday morning when the Paras shot him down in the car park. Shot a seventeen-year-old boy in the back as he was a-runnin' away. I can still see Father Daley out in front of us as we tried to carry him to safety—his handkerchief stained red with blood—waving it before him as a flag of truce. But the Paras were having no truce, and Jackie wasn't the only friend I lost that day."

"Nick wasn't there on Bloody Sunday," Harry said quietly, his eyes focused on the road ahead.

"No, he likely wasn't," Flaharty conceded, "and that's not the way war is, you know that. You may never get the man who shot your brother in the sights of your rifle, so you shoot the sod next to him and tell yourself it's justice. That's *war*. And you're not going to ask me to regret what I've done."

Silence. Harry glanced up at the GPS, eyeing the first waypoint. *Five kilometers.*

"So, boyo," Flaharty began after a long moment, "after all this is over an' done with. . .are you going to let her kill me?"

Harry looked over at him, their eyes meeting in the darkness of the car. "I haven't decided yet."

12:31 A.M.
The Special Branch transport

Eight years, Dennis Tomlinson thought staring through the bullet-resistant windshield of the transport van at the night, the far off red taillights of the cars ahead of them. Traffic had been light tonight, but that was bound to change the closer they got to London.

Eight years. That was how long he had been with the West Yorkshire Police, ever since he had come home from Iraq. Come back from the war.

He'd started off on the street—working the beat as he watched the face of Leeds change from the city he had known growing up as a lad. Long nights away from his family, his wife and two young sons. Dealing with everything from domestic violence to the ever-pervasive drugs.

Tomlinson leaned back in his seat as his partner drove, feeling the butt of his holstered Glock dig into his ribs. He'd been an Authorised Firearms Officer for three years, and he was still spending long nights away from his family.

His partner was similarly armed, and there was a SIG 553 assault rifle in the secure weapons locker behind the seat—that last only to be deployed upon the receipt of authorization from their controller in Leeds. The same protocols that applied to armed response vehicle personnel.

In three years, he'd only had to seek that authorization twice—and prayed that he'd never need it in a hurry.

"What is *this*?" Tomlinson looked up at his partner's words, closing the mobile on his wife's text. And then he saw the road before them.

"Oh, bugger me. . .it's an artic."

An articulated lorry—what Americans would have called a semi—had jackknifed into the median, its trailer turned on its side, well-nigh blocking all four lanes of traffic. Flares sparked brightly in the night, the figures of men casting strange shadows as they moved about the scene of the accident.

One of them, a big man wearing a reflective vest, seemed to spot the transport and waved, running over to Tomlinson's window as he rolled it down. "Bloody mess," he said by way of explanation, "sodding fool of a driver was on his mobile."

Tomlinson snorted. Who wasn't, these days? "We're trying to get this cleaned up and out of the way," the man continued conversationally, "at least get one lane of traffic flowing again."

But. . .that seemed to be the exact opposite of what they appeared to *actually* be doing, the police officer thought, his eyes narrowing even as he realized there were far too many men there for an accident which had just taken place.

Tomlinson jerked around in his seat, finding himself staring into the barrel of a pistol clutched in the big man's hand.

"I'm sorry," the man said simply, a curious look of regret in his eyes.

And then the night erupted in fire. . .

12:43 A.M.
The M1 Motorway
South of Luton

They had passed the first two waypoints with no sign of the prisoner transport. *Nothing.*

And now their time was running out. Harry tapped the gas, sliding around a panel truck as he glanced back up at the GPS. Another five minutes to the final waypoint. The sickening feeling that he had been wrong gnawing within him.

And if he had, well Mehreen's asset was gone, forever.

It was then that he saw it, a looming shape across the southbound lanes—a low curse breaking from Flaharty's lips as they both recognized the overturned semi for what it was in the same instant.

A roadblock.

Harry saw the brake lights of Mehreen's Toyota flicker and he hit his own brakes, sliding into the far left lane—up against the median—shoving the door open almost before the car had stopped moving.

A twinge of pain shot through his ankle as he put weight on it, drawing his weapon as he moved toward the wrecked tractor-trailer. A doctor would have prescribed rest, but he'd had no time for anything of the sort.

He could hear Flaharty behind him, saw Mehreen out of the corner of his eye, silhouetted in the headlights of a passing truck, her pistol also drawn as they closed in.

There. His hands tightened around the Sig-Sauer as he spotted the darkened prisoner transport on the far side of the semi, just stopped dead in the middle of the road—the passenger window rolled down.

"Take the back," he ordered crisply, flicking on the tactical light in his left hand as he moved up to the side of the van.

Sightless eyes stared back at him from within the van—a look of shock frozen on the face of the Special Branch officer who had been riding shotgun.

An obscenely tidy round hole in his forehead marking the cause of his death. *Execution.* He'd never even had time to reach for his Glock, still securely fastened in its holster at his side.

The driver had been shot multiple times—center-of-mass, his blood staining the shattered glass. Now he just lay there, his crumpled body supported only by the seatbelt.

"Besimi's gone," Mehreen's voice announced from behind him, grim and resigned. "They've taken him."

He shifted the Sig-Sauer to his left hand and reached up, pressing his fingers against the dead officer's throat. *Still warm.*

Hadn't been dead long.

And that was when he spotted the dash-cam.

12:49 A.M.

It wasn't supposed to have been this way. Gordon shook his head angrily—glaring across the back of the van at one of his men as their driver turned off the motorway onto an access road, the vehicle shifting from side to side as it hit the gravel.

He had known from the beginning that it could happen, but somehow had still thought he could avert tragedy.

"You were supposed to hold them there," he snapped, looking away—down at the hooded and bound form of the imam lying there on the floor of the van between them. "They were serving their country just like you and me. . .killing them was a *last* resort. Those were my orders."

"And you're not the one giving the orders," the former soldier, a man named Davies, retorted. "Hale's orders were clear—the mission was not to be compromised, at all costs."

Hale, the ex-Para thought, burying his face in his hands. It always came back to him. All the darkness.

He'd always been the stronger of the two of them, the better soldier. But something had changed.

They were doing this for their country—for a better England, but what were *they* going to be at the end of it all? Murderers?

He closed his eyes and could see the footage from Madina, the figure of a small boy being pulled lifeless from the rubble.

Perhaps that's what they were already. He felt the van lurch as the going became rougher, knew they were approaching their destination.

The end of the road for the man who lay at his feet.

12:51 A.M.
Hertfordshire

Too late. That was what kept running through Harry's mind, an endless, haunting refrain. The dash-cam images of a hooded Ismail Besimi being dragged away from the vehicle and toward a waiting panel van.

They hadn't executed him on the spot, that was something. More importantly, it was all they had.

He knelt down at the entrance to the access road along the motorway, hearing the wail of emergency sirens growing louder in the distance. *There.*

A vehicle had passed this way within the last few minutes, the gravel still splashed with spray from a puddle left by the morning's rain. The panel van?

Harry straightened, looking off into the English countryside, fields stretching almost as far as the eye could see on both sides of the road, the dark shadow of trees in the distance.

"What are we looking at?" he asked, sliding back into the driver's seat of the Audi and looking back at Mehreen. They had ditched her car back at the scene.

She shook her head, flashlight playing over the paper map spread out before her. Low-tech, old school, the ways that actually *worked* when you found yourself out in the cold.

Cut off.

"There's nothing for miles. A few farms, nothing major."

"So. . .a dumping ground." He saw her flinch, but they all knew the reality of this. Of what was likely to happen.

He reached down, darkness settling around them as he killed the Audi's lights.

"No point in making a target of ourselves," he said, pulling the pair of NODs from within his jacket and handing them to Flaharty. "I'm going to need you to be my eyes."

The Irishman shook his head, his eyes opening wide as he grasped the plan. "You're bleedin' crazy."

"You've said that before."

1:02 A.M.
Surveillance van
Leeds

"And lights out." Roth turned at the American woman's words, glancing across the street at the Rahman's flat. *Sure enough.*

"Looks like all the family is tucked in for the night," Parker observed, leaning back in his seat. "Snug and cozy."

They hadn't expected the imam to return home—not after having given them the slip once. Perhaps he feared that they would take his family into custody, perhaps. . .

Well, there was nothing to be gained from speculation.

His mobile buzzed in that moment and he flipped it open. "Yes?"

"Darren." It was Norris, from Thames House. "We've got a situation. . .just got a red-flash from the Hertfordshire Constabulary. A prisoner transport was found abandoned near the wreck of an artic on the M-1. Both guards were shot, no sign of their prisoner. West Yorkshire has confirmed, it's theirs. It was Ismail Besimi."

Mehreen. He could feel the blood drain from his face, the news striking him like a blow. *There was no way that she. . .*

1:12 A.M.
Hertfordshire

I seek refuge in God from the outcast Satan. Ismail felt the vehicle lurch beneath him as it came to a stop, the voices around him growing in volume.

What was happening? He struggled against his bonds as rough hands hauled him to his feet—swaying drunkenly, the hood disorienting him, robbing him of sight and balance.

Was this extraordinary rendition? He knew the stories—

darkened airplanes flying out of the UK under the cover of night, off the radar—no flight plans.

Ferrying suspected terrorists to black sites in the Middle East, where they could be tortured for information under the auspices of regimes for whom "human rights" was little more than a cruel joke.

He knew the stories. . .and had dismissed most of them as the stuff of Islamist propaganda during his time with Five. But now.

Nothing was certain.

"Move," a rough voice hissed in his ear, nearly shoving him from the back of the vehicle, his legs wobbly as they hit the ground—stumbling and nearly going down.

The imam felt the barrel of a pistol jab into his back, prodding him forward, and suddenly he knew.

He was walking to his death.

1:15 A.M.

"Hard right in thirty," Flaharty intoned, holding the night-vision goggles pressed tight against his face. The tension palpable in his voice as the darkened Audi shot down the narrow country road, sending gravel flying from beneath its wheels.

Seconds, not meters.

Three. . .two. . .one. Harry put the wheel over, sliding into the turn.

"Sodding chancer," the Irishman exploded as the car corrected, fishtailing in the gravel. "You nearly put us into the ditch. Straight-away for forty, curve left."

Perhaps he *was* crazy, Harry thought, feeling the turbo-charged V6 rev beneath his foot as the car accelerated, the fields surrounding them only barely visible in the faint moonlight. It took a certain madness to drive with night-vision. . .let alone night-vision attached to someone else's eyes.

But wearing it himself wasn't an option, the headstraps of the old AN/PVS-5 long since broken.

You played the cards you were dealt.

Five. . .four. . . "Hold up," Flaharty ordered abruptly, throwing up his hand. "We've got the van."

1:17 A.M.
The surveillance van
Leeds, West Yorkshire

"This mobile user is no longer in service." Roth lowered the phone, staring at the screen in the semi-darkness of the van.

"Is there something wrong?" Parker asked, glancing at him from the other end of the vehicle.

Mehreen's mobile was dead. More like it no longer existed. And her former asset was in the wind—the pair of constables guarding him murdered in cold blood. Only hours after he had given her everything that she would have needed to intercept the transport.

"Thank you. That's. . .all I needed." There had been a curious finality to her voice as she had spoken the words—almost as if she was saying good-bye.

"No," he lied, tucking the phone back into his pocket as he straightened, turning his attention back to the screens before them. "Everything is fine."

Nothing could have been farther from the truth.

1:17 A.M.

Wet, icy leaves crunched under Gordon's combat boots as he led the way into the woods, the bare trees providing no shelter from the chill of the breeze. The loaded Glock heavy in his hand, a round in the chamber. Only awaiting his finger on the trigger to send it on its deadly way.

Don't do this. It seemed as if it was his sister speaking, her voice echoing in the dark shadows of his mind. Trying to pull him back.

But there was no way out of this one, he thought, glancing around at the faces of his men, visible in the light of the torch one of them carried. There were only four of them now—three with him, the other back at the van.

On Hale's orders they'd split up following the ambush, with most of his team heading back to London for. . .something.

And now he was left to finish this.

He paused in a small clearing, glancing up at the heavens above, the stars shining down out of the black. *How many lines did you cross? How far did you go?*

He turned, motioning for his men to stop—stepping in front of the imam and undoing the hood, jerking it off the man's head in one swift motion.

The eyes of an elderly man stared back into his own, dazed and bewildered. *Dear God.*

It was a look so familiar, memories of a granda' with Alzheimer's flickering through Gordon's mind. The same look of utter disorientation, brought on this time by the sensory deprivation.

"On your knees," the former Para said, struggling to even utter the words. Besimi didn't seem to understand him, and one of his men placed his hands on the imam's shoulders, roughly shoving him to the ground.

The old man fell to his hands and knees, looking up into Gordon's eyes. "Don't do this, my son," he whispered, hoarse words from a parched throat.

Don't do this. Alice's face appearing before his eyes.

He shook his head, bringing the pistol up—finger taking up the slack of the Glock's trigger as the sights centered on Besimi's forehead.

And then he heard it. A small sound from the direction of the van, faint—indistinct. Nothing more than a shallow cough in the night, the tinkling of glass.

But he knew it for what it was. *Death.*

He ducked to one side, bringing his weapon up as he moved, hissing at the man with the flashlight, "Kill that *torch!*"

1:21 A.M.

And the light was gone, as quickly as he had glimpsed it. Extinguished in the space of a moment. Harry stopped dead in his tracks, holding up his hand for a halt.

He glanced back to see Mehreen and Flaharty fanned out behind him, the Irishman's Kalashnikov held at the ready.

The first man had gone down without a fight—a single round to the temple killing him instantly, sitting there in the driver's seat of the van.

But now. . .just silence filled the woods, not a sound—not even the birds.

Another moment, and he began moving toward the spot where the light had last been seen, stepping over the log of a fallen tree—motioning for Mehreen to go left and Flaharty to go right.

He could already be dead. It was all too real a possibility, Harry knew that. They wouldn't have brought him out here for any other purpose. Wouldn't have wasted any time.

He certainly wouldn't have.

The NODs were stuffed in the pocket of his jacket, but he left them where they were as he stalked forward—his eyes already adjusted to the darkness.

There. It was a faint noise, a rustle among the leaves. He turned, bringing the pistol up as the shape of a man appeared beside the trunk of a tree, a shadow in the night.

Besimi? He hesitated for only a moment, long enough to see the long silhouette of the rifle barrel in the man's hands.

A pair of rounds spat from the Sig-Sauer's barrel, the two shots coming almost as one, the pistol recoiling into the palm of his hand—the bullets finding their mark high in the target's chest.

And then all hell broke loose.

No matter your training, it was hard to ever be prepared for that moment of first contact. That split-second of sheer panic as the rounds started coming in.

Gordon saw Turner stagger back as though hit, but the man didn't go down—the sharp supersonic *crack* of his rifle splitting the night as he returned fire.

Targets. He needed targets. His Glock came up, muzzle sweeping the woods around him, but there were none—nothing but the darkness of the night.

He saw Davies' face, white and drawn, his own pistol out—his free hand entwined in Besimi's collar as he stood over the imam.

Then Turner crumpled into the wet leaves and the firing stopped as quickly as it had begun, silence falling once more over the woods.

No more than fifteen seconds passing from first shot to last.

The former Para heard a noise to his right and turned, his weapon up—just in time to see the figure of a man emerge from the darkness, the pistol in his hand aimed at Gordon's head.

"Lay down your weapons and hand over Ismail Besimi," he said coolly, the accent ever so faintly American. Reminiscent of his days in Iraq, working alongside Coalition forces. "No one else needs to die tonight."

Gordon heard the familiar rough *klatch* of an AK's safety being flipped off from behind him and glanced back to see another, older, man standing there leaning against the trunk of an oak, Kalashnikov leveled.

He had started to lower the Glock when suddenly Davies moved off to his right, jerking the form of Ismail Besimi up against him—the soldier's dark eyes shining with a murderous intensity, the muzzle of his pistol pressed against the imam's temple. "Not another step. . .or I kill him first."

Chapter 19

1:24 A.M.
The forest
Hertfordshire

In combat, advantages were won and lost in the space of a heartbeat. A touch of the trigger—a life forever gone in the time a cardiac cycle took to complete.

"Not another step," the gunman repeated, his face pale as he gazed back at Harry through the night. "Drop your pistol and kick it over here, or I kill him now."

He could see the fear in the imam's eyes as he struggled against his captor's arm across his throat. The knowledge that death was only seconds away.

"Don't do it, Harry." He could hear Mehreen behind him, her voice trembling with resolve. "He'll only kill him anyway."

He shook his head, never lowering his weapon, arms forming a perfect *v* in front of him as he stared through the Sig's iron sights into the face of the gunman before him in the clearing.

He had no intention of doing anything of the sort. It might have been what everyone did in the movies, but this wasn't Hollywood. Putting down your weapon did nothing more than ensure your death and the death of the person you were trying to save.

Times like this, you went with your training.

"You don't want to do this," he warned, centering his sights between the man's eyes—just visible over Besimi's shoulder. "Just let him go, and you can go home tonight."

"Let him go. . .why?" The man demanded, almost spitting out the words. "So he can go back to preaching his hate—plotting to kill my comrades, destroy my country?"

"This man has been doing nothing of the sort, soldier," Harry said, picking up on his use of the word *comrades*. "You've been lied to."

"What bloody difference does it make?" the man demanded, a curse punctuating his words. "These Moslems are all the same—followers of their murdering prophet."

"Nothing could be farther from the truth," Harry shook his head, talking to keep his attention as he shifted from one foot to the other, moving to the left to get a clearer sight picture. "The woman who came with me tonight is a Muslim, and an officer with the Security Services. She's given more for this country than you could begin to imagine. The man you're threatening to kill is her asset."

"Five? A bloody civil *servant*?" The man laughed. "Our government—they're the ones what's done this to us. Sheltering these murderers. Putting them back out on the street."

"And if you take the life of this innocent man. . .what does that make you?"

Like the lives of the innocents at Madina, Gordon thought—standing there with the Glock held loosely in his hand, looking from Davies to the American as the man continued, the guilt stabbing into him sharp as the thrusts of a knife. Had Hale lied about this imam, the way he'd lied about the bombing of the mosque?

And in that moment, he could see the faces of the murdered constables staring back at him from the inside of that transport. The faces of men just like him—men who had laid down their lives to defend their country.

Men dead, all because of what he had done. Because of the man who now stood beside him in the clearing. *No more.*

"Enough, Davies," he said, taking a step forward. "Put up your weapon."

"No—can't you *see* what he's doing?" the soldier hissed, his eyes wild and desperate, the muzzle of his pistol pressing hard against Besimi's temple as Harry edged toward him, the Sig still leveled at his head. "One more sodding step and I kill him. . .I know what you're playing at."

Take the shot, a voice from within him warned—the man was losing control of the situation and he knew it. Cornered. On the brink.

He could do it—he'd done it before, he told himself, a chill sweat growing on his palms. Harder shots than this.

But he found his hands trembling with the thought, the face of the old man looming large in his sight picture. The terror. There was no margin of error in this. No room for mistakes.

Vegas.

"I gave you an order, soldier," the second man continued, his eyes locked on the face of the man he had called "Davies." "This is the end of this—lay down your gun."

But his own weapon was still clutched in his right hand—not raised, not pointed—but still there. *Still a threat.*

What was his game?

Movement—something off to the far right distracted Harry, the figure of Flaharty in the darkness on the edge of the clearing.

"Oh, sod off," came back Davies' reply, angry and bitter. "You're not in the army anymore, mate."

Circling, moving in for the kill. Flaharty was running his own play—improvising in a game where improvisation got people killed more often than not. A roll of the dice.

Snake eyes.

A fallen branch gave under the Irishman's foot a moment later, snapping with a loud *crack*—shattering the nervous tension, the stillness that had fallen over the clearing.

The world seemed to blur around him, leaving the target revealed in startling clarity as Harry struggled to regain his sight picture—seeing the man's finger tighten around the trigger.

No shot, no shot. Not even close.

The thunder of a single pistol shot echoed through the night and the figure of Ismail Besimi pitched forward, crumpling to the ground like a marionette with its strings cut.

Mehreen's scream pierced the darkness, a high-pitched, keening wail he had heard so many times before. *Afghanistan. Pakistan.*

Harry stood there, seemingly frozen in time, finger still curled around the trigger of the Sig-Sauer as he watched Davies topple, as if slow-motion, the side of his head blown half-away.

His head jerked right, taking in the sight of the other British soldier standing there—tears running down his shadowed cheeks, the Glock still extended in his outstretched hand.

"I'm sorry, mate," he whispered bitterly, looking down at the body of the man he had slain. "So bloody sorry."

1:49 A.M.
An Internet café
Leeds

The café was nearly empty when Tarik Abdul Muhammad entered, ordering a cup of coffee black, with no sugar, before taking his seat in a far corner and firing up the laptop he had dug from a messenger bag.

He still hadn't slept, the dark circles forming under his eyes and the dress shirt giving him the look of an overworked office functionary.

To kill the Queen. It wasn't an impossible feat, at least not from what the British soldier had showed him of her security.

No. He shook his head, running a weary hand over his face as the laptop's browser opened. *Nothing was impossible with Allah.*

It was a faith that had carried him from the mountains of Afghanistan—through his humiliation at the hands of the Americans at Camp X-Ray. Perhaps even that humiliation—that *humbling*—had been of God, to prepare him for the coming struggle.

For had not the Prophet himself, peace be upon him, indeed known humiliation at the hands of the idolaters of Mecca?

A map expanded in the browser and he used the mouse to zoom in on the location, eyeing the topography carefully as the satellite overlay refreshed.

They had the men. Not just the zealous, untrained college students that had rallied around him at the warehouse earlier in the week, but hardened *mujahideen*—British citizens who had answered the call of jihad and traveled to Syria to fight against the apostate regime of Bashar al-Assad.

And more would rise, as the rights of the faithful across the UK continued to be trampled upon—as the government cracked down. Of that he was sure.

The men. . .God had supplied. *Insh'allah*, he thought, a shadow passing over his face at the memory of the British soldier's words. *"Be careful who you trust, Shaikh. What you tell your men. Better to give them a form of the plan, if necessary, rather than the plan itself."*

Sound advice, even coming from a proud and wicked man. Tarik fished the mobile from his shirt pocket, glancing once more at the last text he had received from Hashim Rahman.

Who to trust?

2:12 A.M.
The forest
Hertfordshire

Money. Ideology. Compromise. Ego. Cold War intelligence officers had coined the acronym "MICE" to summarize the four most common reasons a man decided to betray his country. *His cause.*

Harry stared through the windshield of the van, letting the silence do its work. *Which was it this time?*

He suppressed the urge to glance at his watch. Mehreen and Flaharty would either be safely away by now, or they wouldn't—and there was nothing he could do to aid them in either case.

And the imam...Harry grimaced. The old man hadn't been so much as touched by the bullet that had ended his captor's life, but the strain of what he had gone through had been another matter entirely. He'd had to help Mehreen carry him back to the Audi.

"The bombing at Madina," the former soldier began again, his voice trembling with emotion, "wasn't meant to kill *anyone*. Or at least that's what I was told. It was only supposed to destroy the building. Send a message."

Send a message. He shook his head. *Mission accomplished.*

"But when I saw that building explode," the man's body shuddered at the memory, "I knew it wasn't an accident. Perhaps I'd known all along, perhaps I was just blinded by what had happened to Alice."

Revenge. You gaze into the maw of a gaping chasm, and it gazes back into you. A man becomes that which he has beheld. He knew something about that.

Harry put his hand on the edge of the lowered driver's side window, feeling something wet and sticky between his fingers. *Blood.* From the driver he had shot an hour earlier, the man's body lying scarce five meters from where they now sat.

"I've been prepared to die for my country," the man continued, staring off into the night. "For a long time. And I've had to kill for my country—more than once, there in Iraq. But the bombing of the mosque, the killing of civilians. That's what *they* did. I can't be a part of it, and I can't bloody well stand by and watch it happen."

Assessing the credibility of a potential asset...it was one of the most difficult tasks of any intel officer, and the one you never *stopped* doing.

Not if you were doing your job.

"So," he began, glancing over at the man who sat in the passenger seat, his hands bound in his lap with a zip-tie, "if I call Barnet and ask for an Alice Gordon, what will they tell me?"

A shake of the head. "Alice Thompson—she was married—sodding chav left her after six months, but she still carries his name."

Made sense. It was either the truth, or a detailed lie. The best always were. "If I'm going to let you go back in there—run you as an agent against the nationalists, I need to know that I can trust you."

There was no such thing as trust, never would be—no matter what happened. But there was often an advantage in allowing people to think otherwise.

He paused, measuring his words carefully. "Conor Hale...what's his endgame?"

Gordon flashed him a sharp look, surprise spreading across his face. "I didn't—"

2:15 A.M.
Hertfordshire

"Drive." That's what Mehreen Crawford had told him, her eyes betraying the truth. She'd as soon have put a bullet in the back of his head and driven the car herself.

Flaharty grimaced at the thought, glancing up at the rear-view mirror to catch a glimpse of her in the back seat. Speaking gently in a foreign language of some sort as she held a bottle of water up to the imam's parched lips.

"How's he doin'?" the Irishman asked finally, a gruff edge to his voice.

"Why?" She demanded, looking up from Besimi's recumbent form, anger playing across her features. *No truce.* "What concern is it of yours?"

"Because I was bloody well nearly shot rescuing him, that's why," Flaharty retorted in exasperation. But the words rang hollow even in his own ears. *Why?*

He could feel the bulge of the small Kimber pressing against the waistband of his trousers, knew that if he wanted to save his own life, he should have killed the intelligence officer the moment she entered the car.

Didn't know why he hadn't. *"You turned tout."* Davey's words, ringing in his ears, a reminder of all he had betrayed.

No. And he could feel himself standing there over his old friend's body—the checkered grip of the pistol biting into his palm. A wave of nausea threatening to overcome him as he realized what he must do. *"Davey, Davey, Davey. . .what has become of us?"*

What, indeed? Years of betrayal and lies, culminating in a single pistol shot. The execution of a friend.

A part of himself dying there on the floor of that flat with Malone. In the moments that followed, he had nearly turned the pistol on himself.

Ended it all. Right then, right there.

He met the intelligence officer's eyes in his rear-view mirror, saw the grief, the loss written in their depths. Knew that this road ended only in death. . .his or hers. Sooner or later.

But that was something that would have to be decided at a later date. He cleared his throat, weighing his words carefully. "You have a bolt-hole handy?"

2:21 A.M.
The forest

"You didn't give me his name," Harry cut him off. "You didn't have to. I served with Hale a time or two in the sandbox. He was Regiment—not a man to be taken lightly, as I remember him."

Gordon nodded, a distant look entering his eyes. "That hasn't changed. We were in 1 Para together—he made it through Selection. I didn't."

Old comrades, Harry thought, watching the man out of the corner of his eye. As if this wasn't dicey enough already. "Is that going to be a problem?"

There was a long pause, as the soldier seemed to consider the question. Then, "No. Hale has to be stopped. The people I helped him kill at Madina, the constables that were executed out on the highway tonight—they're only the beginning."

"And the endgame?"

"A race war in this country. . .how he intends to achieve it, I don't know. But I can find out."

Promises. He had heard it all before. Langley would never have approved an op like this—would have judged the danger far too high. The risk of blowback.

But when you found yourself staring down the muzzle of fate, sometimes risk was all that was left to you.

Harry pulled the Sig-Sauer from within his jacket, briefly brass-checking the chamber in the darkness of the vehicle. "If you're going to sell the story of your escape to Conor Hale," he said, noting the look of alarm in Gordon's eyes, "you're going to need to have something to show for it."

A few moments later, the muffled *cough* of a suppressed gunshot came from within the van.

3:09 A.M.
Thames House
London

"How did it happen?" the DG asked, dropping his overcoat across the back of the conference room chair before taking his seat—tenting his fingers before him as he gazed down the table at his people.

He'd known far too many of these nights throughout the years. Asked that question more times than he cared to remember, found it answerless more often than not. *How did it happen?*

"The prisoner transport was ambushed on the M-1 in Hertfordshire just south of Luton," Alec MacCallum said wearily, looking up from his notes. Like Marsh, he had been in bed when the attack happened.

"They stopped the transport using an overturned artic to block the motorway. . .we're still looking into how they acquired—"

"No," Norris interjected, cutting his section chief off as he entered the conference room late, dropping a stack of folders onto the table. "We found the owner of the lorry—a shipping company out of Sheffield. I just got off the call with them. The artic was stolen two days ago, we've confirmed their report with South Yorkshire."

"But?" Marsh pressed, sensing hesitation in the analyst's voice. Or perhaps it was just weariness.

"But, South Yorkshire has no suspects. The way things have been blowing up with the riots, they're stretched thin—haven't even begun to look."

"And we've lost Ismail Besimi," the DG mused. There was something about the way this had played out, the precision with which the transport had been targeted. The *timing* of it all. "Get ahold of Mehreen Crawford, if she's not already on her way in."

Norris and MacCallum exchanged an awkward glance, the silence seeming to swell and fill the room.

The section chief spoke first. "Mehreen has dropped off the grid. No one's seen or heard from her since she left here last night—her phone's been either destroyed. . .or deactivated."

3:09 A.M.
The harbor of Grimsby
Lincolnshire

He had always felt most at home on the water, Hale thought, feeling the spray-slick deck of the ship move beneath him as it rode at anchor within the breakwater. Ever since he was a lad in Liverpool, growing up on the docks.

In retrospect, it might have seemed strange that he hadn't found his home in the Royal Navy—but fate had had other plans. And it wasn't as though the Regiment had exactly been opposed to infiltrating their target from the sea, wherever possible.

From the sea. He smiled. It was the best way to get anywhere unnoticed and without warning, as the Vikings who had first come to the marshes of Grimsby in the 9th Century had known all too well.

And now they were about to implement the same strategy. He paused, his hands resting easily in his pockets as he stared up at the superstructure of the ship he had pressured Colville to buy, its containers looming large against the harbor lights, the stark silhouette of Grimsby's Dock Tower visible in the distance beyond them.

Built and launched from Barrow-in-Furness by the now-defunct Vickers

Shipbuilding & Engineering, Ltd. in 1972, the MV *Percy Phillips* had started life as a cargo vessel, the type of small container ship known as a "feeder."

Now. . .well, now the *Percy Phillips* was their transport, command center, and storage facility rolled into one. Inconspicuous, and above all, mobile.

And soon to set sail.

He gazed back across the water, toward the wharfs filled with offloaded cargo and fish—lights shining in the darkness, heavy equipment at work even at this hour. Toward the sleeping town beyond All of England encapsulated in that scene. . .all that he loved.

All that he was about to lose—forever.

He had no illusions about what was to come, the devastation their actions would unleash. Perhaps Colville did. . .

War. Only those who had seen it could understand it. Could grasp the enormity, the evil of it. The parts that never made it into the history books, the movies.

He had.

But the war, was already here—whether they wanted it or not. The war he and his mates had waged in the desert, following them home.

Inevitable as the tide. He started to turn, to go belowdecks, but the vibration of his mobile against his hip arrested him.

Gordon. "Yes?" Hale began, flipping the burner open. "Have you taken care of the package?"

The voice on the other end was weak, strained. Almost unrecognizable. But it was Gordon. "Negative," he managed, "the mission was a failure, a bloody cock-up. I'm wounded—on foot. The lads, they're dead."

Dead. The words struck Hale with the force of a physical blow, staggering him. *How?*

"All right," he said, struggling to pull himself back together. There was no time for grief—there never was, in the middle of a war. All of it locked away, until you got home. Except this time, there was no going home. "Give me your location, mate. I'm comin' for you."

3:17 A.M.
Hertfordshire

"Right you are," Gordon breathed as his old friend acknowledged the directions, the words escaping through gritted teeth as he leaned back against the utility pole by the roadside—his hand pressed firmly against the wound in his thigh, his torn undershirt forming a compress. "I'm not goin' anywhere."

He closed the phone, nausea nearly overwhelming him as he looked down at his bloody hand in the darkness, the wound beneath.

It was a straight in and out—through the meat of his thigh, missing the bone but leaving a nasty hole.

The American knew his business. *Something to show for it.*

He looked down the long road—not a house or a car as far as the eye could see. He had already come two miles. Perhaps he could move, get to a better vantage point. *Perhaps.*

His head swam as he tried to rise once more to his feet, finding himself weakened from the blood loss.

He had to stay lucid—had to keep it together. *Had to.* It was the only way to pull this off, to successfully regain Hale's trust. To betray a friend.

Davies' face loomed large before his eyes as he slipped in and out of consciousness. A look of shock, betrayal—frozen in time as his broken body toppled to the ground.

And this. . .was only the beginning.

6:49 A.M.
The bus station
Sheffield

Mingle with the crowd. Just keep moving forward. Don't draw attention to yourself.

Anymore, most people avoided eye contact, so you did as well. Observe without being observed.

Remain faceless.

Harry pushed his way to the back of the Leeds-bound bus, taking his seat across from a kid who looked fresh out of college, dressed in business attire, his eyes focused on the screen of the mobile phone in his hand.

The mood was nervous, he noted, reading the body language of those boarding behind him. As well it should be—with cars overturned and set on fire only hours before following clashes between police and rioters who seemed to have mostly been drawn from Sheffield's Somali community.

He'd ditched the van an hour before, more than a few kilometers to the south, its upholstery still spattered with blood and brain matter. DNA evidence all over—none of it his.

He had no illusions. They would find it soon enough. That was a given. In this game, you rarely got to stay more than one step ahead of your opponent.

And you had to pray that one step would be enough.

Ahead of him, the doors closed and the bus jerked into motion. Another few hours, he'd have linked back up with Mehreen and Flaharty.

Time to regroup.

8:38 A.M.
Thames House
London

"...as rioting continues for a third day following the bombing of the Madina Mosque in Northern London, the Security Services seem incapable of stemming the tide of violence. The Home Secretary is scheduled to deliver a statement at noon on the developing—"

Marsh punched the *mute* button on the remote, shutting off the droning voice of the reporter on the telly.

The twenty-four hour news cycle was going to be the death of them all. In the old days there had been time to react, to tamp things down before they hit the papers, the evening news.

Now, everything was instant. And it was only fueling the madness.

He looked out over the floor of the Centre, taking in the sight of the map thrown up on the big screen. A map of the UK, each red dot representing a flashpoint.

It looked as though the country had developed a serious attack of the measles.

The door opened and he turned to see MacCallum standing there, a folder in his hand. "Yes?"

"They found the van," the section chief responded, pulling a photo from the folder and handing it over. "It was abandoned in Stavely, about nineteen kilometers south of Sheffield."

Marsh took it from him, wincing as his eyes scanned across the image. It had been decades since he had been in the field, but he remembered Northern Ireland, and the picture was reminiscent of what he had witnessed there.

The seats of the van were stained with fresh blood, flecks of it spattered across the windshield, spider veins radiating out through the glass from a single bullethole.

"Ismail Besimi?" he asked, the meaning behind the question only too clear. They had been working off the premise that Ismail Besimi had been rescued by sympathizers—by friends. But what if that *wasn't* what they were looking for at all?

Question everything.

MacCallum shook his head. "No. Besimi's blood type is AB—rare, that one.

Preliminary swabs of the bloodstains in the van came back O. . .and B."

"Two victims?"

"That's Derbyshire's working theory. Impossible to say who—or *why*."

Indeed. The DG ran a hand over his chin, turning over the scenario again and again. "What do we have from the scene of the ambush?"

"Not enough. No eyewitnesses that we've been able to locate—no nearby traffic cameras."

"Satellite?"

"Nothing in the area," the section chief replied, hesitating for a moment. "We could see if the cousins had anything in the sky at the time."

"Oh, they probably bloody well did." Marsh swore softly, pacing across the floor of his office. "How is it we always find ourselves going to the Americans, hat in hand—asking for help?"

His subordinate didn't respond, just stood there in silence holding the folder. And he knew. This was necessary. "Fine," he said after a moment, "do it. But make it count—they never forget a favor."

MacCallum acknowledged his words with a brief nod, but made no move to leave the office.

"There's something else, isn't there?" Marsh asked, transfixing the section chief with a keen glance. They had known each other for years, and when he had been appointed to the post of director-general, bringing MacCallum over from SO-13 had been one of his first official actions.

A half-nod served as a reply, a torturous uncertainty playing across MacCallum's face.

The DG stepped to the door of the office, the noise of the operations centre without fading away as he closed it firmly. "Then out with it, man."

"I think we have to consider the *possibility*," MacCallum began, seeming to choose his words with the utmost of care, "that Mehreen was involved in Ismail Besimi's escape."

9:01 A.M.
A studio flat
Leeds

It was the smell that brought Aydin awake, the smell of spices, of bread cooking.

A smell like that of home. . .but *different*, somehow. He raised himself up on one elbow and nearly fell off the couch, realizing suddenly where he was.

"You're not going back." Farid's words from the night before, the look in the mujahid's eyes brooking no debate. And he had offered none.

He hadn't wanted to go back to his home, he realized with a start. Even knowing that he would never see his parents again. But *they* would hear of him.

He swung his legs off the couch, looking over into the flat's small kitchen to see Farid standing there by the stove, molding the roti in his hands as he prepared to cook it over the flickering blue flame of the burner.

Trash was littered around the small flat, faded bags of take-away stuffed into an overflowing rubbish bin in the corner.

It was only when he saw the sun streaming in through the window, when he felt Farid's baleful gaze fall upon him, that it occurred to the teenager—he had slept through the *fajr*, the morning prayer.

He flushed red, making his way to the flat's tiny loo to prepare himself for the performance of the *salat*.

Cleanliness is half of faith, Aydin thought, recalling the words of the Prophet as he turned the tap on full and cold—splashing the water over his face in the start of the ceremonial washing.

His head came up, water dripping down his cheeks as he stared into the mirror—and it was though he could see the form of the rabbi standing before him, his hands covered in blood, his lips forming the question: *Why?*

He could feel his hands begin to tremble, the memory of the Jew's eyes flooding back over him. The way he had looked, lying there helpless.

Knowing he was about to die.

Aydin's hands seized the edges of the washbasin, his stomach heaving as though he were about to retch, the ice-cold water continuing to splash unheeded below him.

No. It should have felt good, but it didn't. Even as triumphant as he had felt last night, now. . .he could feel only emptiness. It shouldn't be like this—the Zionists were the *enemy*, he told himself, struggling to regain control of his emotions.

The fear he had seen in the man's eyes, it was the fear of judgment. A believer need not know such fear.

But he *did*.

He raised his head slowly, as if he feared the Jew would continue to haunt him. But the apparition had vanished, and he began to slowly run the water over his bare forearms as he continued the ritual, willing his hands to stop their trembling.

Trying to once more find his faith.

He heard Farid's voice from without, felt the door open without a knock.

"Enough of that, bruv," the older man said gruffly, beckoning with his hand for Aydin to follow. It was only as he turned to go back toward the kitchen that Aydin saw the mobile phone in his hand, pressed close against his ear. "Of course. . .we'll leave at once. I'll have him to you by then."

9:12 A.M.
The MV Percy Phillips
Grimsby, Lincolnshire

"What happened out there, mate?" Gordon took another long pull of the brandy, leaning back against the bulkhead with his game leg stretched out before him.

He didn't remember very much about Hale coming to retrieve him or the journey back, drifting in and out of the haze of unconsciousness induced by the pain and blood loss. All he knew was that they had headed east—the rising light of dawn shining brightly through the windshield of Hale's car—and that they were now aboard ship.

Had to be at anchor at some port on the east coast of England. Ipswich maybe?

He shook his head, half to himself. "I don't rightly know," he began, lifting his eyes to meet Hale's. "We were all right after the lads split from us, all the way to the forest. Grimes was driving, I left him with the van. Took Turner and Davies into the woods with me."

The best lie was always the one that stuck closest to the truth, Gordon thought, nursing the brandy. And it was a good thing. . .because lying had never been part of his job description.

"We were just going to kill him and leave him there—like you said, no need to bury the body. That was the plan. But before we could do that. . .I heard a shot off toward the van. It was suppressed, but there's no mistaking it."

Hale nodded his understanding. They both knew that sound all too well. "I'm guessing they got Grimes then—I don't know. All I know is that the next moment rounds were flying through the trees. Davies went down before he could fire a shot, I caught a bullet in the leg—Turner got off a mag before I saw him fall. There were at least four of them, maybe more. I got away through the trees and back out to the road."

"Your attackers," the former SAS sergeant began, seeming to mull over all that he had said, "any idea who they were?"

Gordon shook his head. "None. Special Branch, maybe? SO-13? No bloody inkling how they could have been on to us so fast, though. Didn't see anyone tailing us out into the country."

And that was the truth of it.

"No," Hale replied slowly, "it wasn't Special Branch."

There was an odd, unnerving certainty to the way he spoke the words. "An' you know that how, mate?" the Para asked, feeling as if he was stepping out on the narrow ledge above a chasm.

His footing perilously uncertain.

And yet not to ask would have been just as unnatural. Hale looked at him for a moment, then smiled. "I'm sorry that I've not taken you more into my confidence, Paul. We were brothers, fought and bled together in those godforsaken sands not so long ago. But I've had to be very careful—what we're attempting is so perilous. If we fail. . .we'll all be sodding lucky to see the Tower. Dead, more than likely."

"We've faced those odds before," Gordon said, grimacing as he attempted to sit up straighter in the bunk. "No one ever guaranteed that we were coming back from Iraq."

Hale laughed, setting a hand on his friend's shoulder as he rose to leave. "That's a truth there. But this time we have an advantage on them. We have a source inside Five."

And a chill cold as ice ran down Gordon's spine as a vision of the scene in the woods rose before him, the American standing there—a pistol leveled in his hands. Remembering his words. *"The woman who came with me tonight is a Muslim. . .and an officer with the Security Services."*

9:34 A.M.
Luton, Hertfordshire

Nothing. Roth holstered the Sig-Sauer, feeling the pistol ride awkwardly on his hip beneath the jacket—an unaccustomed feeling, despite the brief time he had worn one in Somalia with Six. Perhaps Afghanistan had been too long ago.

Nothing whatsoever. The black man took a final look around the empty flat before closing the door, the chill morning breeze washing over his bare scalp as he moved back to his car. Bringing with it the acrid smell of burning rubber from the piles of tires torched in the riots the night before.

It was the third safehouse he had visited since leaving Leeds in the wee hours of the morning. The third to come up dry.

Perhaps he had known better than to think that Mehreen would use a Five safehouse for. . .whatever she was doing. Perhaps he'd run out of other options.

It was only a matter of time before Thames House began to tie her to the disappearance of Ismail Besimi—only a short time longer before they put together who had given her the information.

Information that had led to two deaths, he realized, sliding into the driver's seat of the BMW. He could still see the faces of the murdered constables if he closed his eyes.

The faces of their families. *Dear God.*

He sat there for a long moment, staring out at the street, the small English town just now beginning to awake.

It seemed impossible to fathom that Mehreen could have been involved in *murder*, but there seemed no other explanation for it.

You never truly *knew* anyone, such was the reality of their world. A wilderness of mirrors, a masquerade gone horribly wrong.

With death the only prize.

10:13 A.M.
The flat
Rochdale, United Kingdom

"How is he?" Harry asked, brushing the crumbs of toast from his fingers as Mehreen came out of the back room of the small flat. It was the only thing he'd had to eat since the preceding night, assuming you didn't count the coffee. Flaharty's safehouse wasn't particularly well-stocked.

Or its owner happy to have them. Flaharty was out at the moment on business of his own, leaving them alone with Besimi.

"Exhausted," she responded, looking as if she could have been referencing herself, "but he'll be fine. Given time."

And *time* was something they didn't have much of. "So Besimi is your asset?"

"Was," she replied, a distant look entering her eyes. "When I left the field, he was issued a new handler."

"And yet here you are."

She smiled grimly, taking a seat across from him and reaching for a now cold muffin. "Old habits die hard."

They did. One might even say that they never died at all. He leaned back in his chair, favoring her with a careful glance. "You said last night that Ismail Besimi could be the key to all this. . .how?"

An asset was only an asset so long as they could provide something of value. *That* was the truth, cold and hard though it was.

And they both knew it.

"I don't know," she admitted after a long pause. "Ismail has been a leading member of the Islamic community in Leeds for decades—all of my life, really. He's been an invaluable source of intel ever since I first recruited him. And last night, someone went to a great deal of trouble to have him killed."

And that's what it came down to, so often. . .you moved heaven and earth to keep someone alive simply because the opposition wanted them dead. Even if you didn't know why.

It worked for him. He drained the last of his coffee, sifting through what she had told him. All that had unfolded in the space of the last few days. "So how soon can I speak with him?"

It was only then that he realized Mehreen was no longer paying attention to him. Her dark cheeks taking on an unaccustomed pallor as she stared down at the phone in her hand.

"It's about Aydin. . ." she said slowly, lifting her eyes to face him. "I heard back from Nimra. She says they haven't seen him for two days."

11:46 A.M.
A terrace house
On the outskirts of Leeds

It was strange how at times you could see the echoes of yourself in the young, Tarik Abdul Muhammad thought, turning away slowly from the window.

He had not yet seen his thirtieth birthday—there were times when he questioned whether it would be God's will for him to ever see it—and yet he felt already old. His youth given in Allah's service, as would the youth of the young man before him be so given.

If far more quickly.

He smiled, brushing at an imagined spot on the sleeve of his white dress shirt as he motioned for the boy to take a seat. The television was on in the background, in advance of the Home Secretary's speech, the volume muted. "How old are you, my son?"

"I, uh, turned sixteen on the last day of December," he stammered, seeming overawed in the presence of the Shaikh.

Sixteen. Tarik smiled. That seemed like such a very short while ago. "Then God granted you an early birthday gift in the form of the blow struck against the homeland of the imperialists."

"A blow you struck," came the reply, the young man's eyes glowing with fervor. *Excitement.*

So young. "No. Allah strikes all blows against the unbelievers. At times and places of His choosing. You, I—all of the faithful you saw the other night—we are nothing but instruments in the hands of Allah. I was your age when I first fought against the Americans in the mountains of Afghanistan. And when I was captured, I found myself questioning God's will. . .doubting all that I had been taught. All that I believed."

He could see the disbelief in the young man's eyes, and he went on after only a brief pause. "But I came to realize, there in that prison overlooking the sea, that it was all a part of a plan. The path He had chosen for me to take, a weapon forged to be of service in His struggle."

Tarik rose from his seat, his penetrating blue eyes searching the young man's face as he continued, "As it is the path He has chosen for you, is it not?"

12:01 P.M.
The flat
Leeds

"Mehreen," her sister-in-law exclaimed, drawing her into her arms at the threshold of the door of their flat. "Thank God you could come."

"Of course," Mehreen responded uncomfortably, disengaging herself from Nimra's embrace as she moved into the house. "I was in the area, had to see if there was anything I could do."

"What can anyone do?" She looked up to see the form of her brother leaving the kitchen, wiping his big hands on a towel as he approached. The sadness in his eyes unlike anything she had seen before.

"Ahmed," she began uncertainly, finding him as difficult to read as ever. "I had expected that you would be at the market."

He exchanged a glance with his wife, shaking his head slowly. "No, I haven't been there. Last night. . ."

"Last night, with all the rioting—a gang threw rocks through the windows," Nimra finished, stepping to her husband's side.

He looked at Mehreen and grimaced, the pain visible in his eyes. "We were targeted," he corrected, "I went to open up this morning, found the floor covered in shattered glass. The walls spray painted in black graffiti. *'Go back to where you belong, Muzzie.' 'Don't buy from paedos.'* Others I'm not even going to bloody well repeat."

He shook his head, something of despair in his voice. "I just don't know what to do anymore, Mehr. I've lived in this country for so many years. Our parents sacrificed so much to bring the both of us here. I raised my son to be *British*. Yet I'm still a foreigner to these people, and our world has gone mad. And my son. . ."

Her brother paused, glancing at his wife as if uncertain whether he should go on.

"What about Aydin?" Mehreen asked, choosing to press the issue as she saw her sister-in-law insistently shake her head "no."

Ahmed's head came up, his face twisted in anger as he spat, "He's become one of *them*."

12:04 P.M.
The offices of the UK Daily Standard
London

"...I must lend my voice with that of the Prime Minister in enjoining calm throughout these troubled times," Kathleen Napier intoned, looking up from her prepared statement as she stood behind the lectern in the press room within the House of Commons. The high-resolution cameras did nothing for the middle-aged woman, Arthur Colville thought, regarding the telly with a jaundiced eye. Then again they did very little for anyone, which was why he ran a paper. "At this time, the United Kingdom finds itself embattled, under assault from forces both within and without. Her Majesty's government condemns, without qualification, the cowardly attack made upon the innocents of the Madina Mosque—men, women, and children—British Muslims, whose only 'crime' was to worship God in the way they saw fit."

The Home Secretary paused to adjust her glasses on the bridge of her nose as she continued, "An attack carried out in the name of a misguided and perverse 'patriotism' by a group claiming to represent the true soul of Britain. They do not."

"And still more representative than you lot," Colville growled, the publisher's eyes narrowing as he glared at the screen. Napier had been working her way up for years, advancing herself the way politicians always did. By carefully concealing whatever spine she once had until it atrophied away to nothing.

"The British people have known what it was to welcome immigrants for decades, and they appreciate all that Muslims have brought to the UK, the way multiculturalism has strengthened our country. Islam is an ancient and noble religion, and not to be judged by those who have perverted it—extremists like Javeed Mousa, the Algerian-born lone wolf who carried out the murder of the club-goers at Heaven earlier this week."

The phone on Colville's desk buzzed with an incoming call and he punched the mute button on the remote before picking it up. "Good morning, Daniel," he said, recognizing Pearson's voice. "Are you watching this?"

12:11 P.M.
The terrace house
Leeds

"For it is written in the Holy Qur'an," the woman said, appearing to consult her notes, "whosoever kills a man without reason is as though he has killed the whole world. And whosoever saves a single life, it is as though he has saved all the people."

She raised her head, staring directly into the cameras as she continued, "Is there one among us who cannot appreciate the simple majesty of these words? Who cannot agree with their message? This is Islam as it truly is—not as it has been distorted to serve the political agendas of murderers and cowards. And the British people will not succumb to the rhetoric of those who wish only to balkanize and divide us, to answer violence with violence until it consumes us all. Those who have perpetrated these attacks will be brought to justice, and the Security Services—"

The Shaikh turned off the television, cutting the Home Secretary off in mid-sentence. "They think that they can sit in their comfortable halls," he began, a dangerous edge to his tone as his eyes locked with Aydin's, "and smugly lecture us on the 'real *meaning*' of Islam. Telling us to remain silent—to be 'good Muslims.' Lull us into submission, all the while they support those who would oppress our brothers and sisters in Gaza and across the rest of the Middle East. Do you think this is what the Prophet, peace be upon him, would have desired?"

Aydin shook his head, swallowing hard. There was something mesmerizing about the Shaikh's eyes, the intensity of his gaze as he went on. "'Whosoever kills a man without *reason*.' Is not the cries of the oppressed reason enough? The West loves their 'democracy', the ability of every man, every woman, to make their voice heard in defiance of God. And the result? The blood is on *all* their hands—there is none innocent."

The door opened, admitting the young black man Aydin had seen at the warehouse. The bodyguard. "But this. . .is what you already know," the Shaikh concluded, drawing himself up with a grim smile. "Or you would not be here. And now the time has come for you to carry out your part in God's struggle. To follow the green birds."

He walked over to a small sideboard, pulling out the top drawer. When he turned once more to face Aydin, he was holding a suicide vest in his hands.

"Tomorrow morning," he said, extending the vest toward the boy, "you will be welcomed into Paradise."

12:13 P.M.
The flat
Leeds

Even after all that she had seen on Aydin's laptop—all of the websites, the blog posts—Mehreen found that her brother's words hit her with the force of a physical blow.

"How long have you known?" she asked, sinking down there beside him on the couch.

He shook his head. "Long enough. Aydin was such a good lad. Honest, obedient. Happy. All that a man could ask God for in a son. And then everything changed—it was as though he had withdrawn inside himself, as though the son I knew had died. He no longer laughed—he spent long hours on the computer, watching videos. Devouring every scrap of news he could find from the Middle East, from Syria. And then that *man* came to the mosque. . ."

"Imam Rahman," Nimra added quietly, as if by way of explanation.

"We came here to *escape* from all the suffering, Mehr, the fear of those willing to kill their neighbors over a difference of faith. I told him that if I ever heard him speak of Afghanistan, of Syria, again—he would no longer live under my roof." Her brother paused, his face hardening. "Perhaps that is the choice he has made, so be it."

Words so familiar. Echoes of an earlier time. She could see their father in him in that moment—the way he had looked on the night she had announced her intention of marrying Nick. The obstinance shining through the grief.

But now, lives were hanging in the balance. And she had no intention of giving up so easily. "Whatever I can do to save Aydin. . .I will."

Her brother looked up, the incredulity visible in his eyes. "I am his father—and I wasn't able to do a thing. You are the aunt he barely knows. . ."

The moment of truth. The moment when lies were shattered—and faiths along with them. Mehreen took a deep breath, looking her older brother in the eye. "I'm also an officer with the Security Services."

12:56 P.M.
The safehouse
Rochdale, West Yorkshire

Open source intelligence. It was at once the greatest blessing and the greatest curse of the modern spy.

Information was *everywhere*—most of it completely unprotected—streaming live from a million cameras and just as many keyboards. Flooding over the Internet in a never-ebbing wave.

Trying to properly analyze it all was like trying to drink from a fire hose.

Harry's Sig-Sauer lay on the table before him, beside the open laptop—his chair positioned to face the flat's entry hall.

There were already thousands of photos on-line from the riots, he thought—most of them uploaded directly from mobile phones onto social media.

People capturing what they saw in real-time, all across the UK. And no sign of the Shaikh.

Not that that was surprising. He leaned back in the folding metal chair, clicking through yet another image. One of hundreds he had looked at since the morning.

The people rioting would be nothing more than rank-and-file—if that. Expendable.

Pawns.

Even most of the Islamist imams were staying back from the fray, let alone someone of the stature of Tarik Abdul Muhammad.

But in the absence of any good leads, you followed up on the bad ones. Perhaps someone had captured. . .*something*.

Find him. If he closed his eyes, he could see Tarik once more ahead of him on the train out of London. Could imagine the iron sights of his pistol centering on the back of his head—the trigger breaking beneath his finger.

Shoot. *Don't shoot.* Pick one.

You could drive yourself mad thinking of opportunities lost. Of choices that could never be unmade. *Carol.*

He shook his head, clicking angrily through the next few photos. The UK was going up in flames—and somewhere, somehow, Tarik Abdul Muhammad was behind it.

Using the riots as a cover for something much larger. Far more dangerous.

It's what he would have done.

He felt someone enter the room almost without a sound, and looked back to see Ismail Besimi standing there in the doorway. "I understand I have you to thank for my life," he said, a faint smile creasing his lips.

Harry shook his head, rising in the presence of the older man. "Without Mehreen, I wouldn't have even been there." He gestured toward the stove, closing the lid of the laptop. "Would you care for a cup of tea?"

1:07 P.M.
Lambeth Bridge
London

One of London's famed red double-decker buses swung past Alec MacCallum into the roundabout—the breeze tousling the intelligence officer's greying hair as he moved out onto the bridge, shouldering his way through a crowd of businessmen returning from lunch.

The City was never at a loss for foot-traffic, even at the slow times of day. It made the job of blending in, going unnoticed, so much easier.

The American was standing at the middle of the bridge, elbows resting against the parapet as he gazed out over the water toward the House of Lords down-river. He was toying with the sandwich in his hands, absently tearing off bits of the crust and throwing it to the gulls below.

"I never did like the crust," he said as MacCallum came alongside him. "Used to throw it in the trash at school as a kid—you'd think the Corps would have cured me of that wouldn't you? I guess there's some things even the Marines can't do. Least the birds make good use of it."

MacCallum shook his head, continuing to scan the crowd of passers-by. *Americans.* "The information I mentioned to you earlier—were you able to secure it?"

Carlos Jimenez nodded, tossing the rest of his sandwich into the Thames in an unexpected motion. "I was indeed," he replied, a canny look entering the CIA liaison officer's eyes as he turned to face MacCallum. "There something going down that I should know about, Alec?"

Jimenez had always possessed all the subtlety of, well, the Marine he was. "What are you suggesting?"

"Come on now," his counterpart said with a smile that suggested he felt he held all the cards, "playing dumb isn't going to get you anywhere. I saw the local news out of Luton this morning, all about a pair of constables found murdered on the M1. You ask me to share highly classified imagery from a spy sat in geosynchronous orbit above that highway from the night before. . .I can connect the dots."

MacCallum shoved both hands into the pockets of his overcoat, leaning back against the parapet. "You found something, didn't you?"

"Yeah, you might call it that, brother." Jimenez grimaced, his face nearly unreadable, eyes hidden behind his Oakleys. "But if you want a line on it, you're going to have to give us a seat at the table."

That wasn't unexpected—you gave the Americans an inch, and they did their best to take a mile. It was worse when they had something you *needed.* "You already have one," he responded, still not looking at the liaison officer.

A snort of disbelief served as his reply. "Right."

1:13 P.M.
The safehouse
Rochdale, West Yorkshire

The guerilla must move amongst the people like a fish swims through the sea. Chairman Mao's dictum on insurgency, every bit as true for the spy.

For him in Afghanistan, it had meant countless meetings so very much like this one—a cup of steaming tea warming one's hands, sitting cross-legged across a small fire from a tribal elder. Those quiet moments, far more important to the success of his mission than any door he had ever kicked in.

Ismail Besimi reminded him of so many of those men—seemingly aged beyond time itself, the skin of his face weathered and leathery above the beard.

And now, as then, he held his peace—waiting for the older man to speak first.

"You're an American, are you not?" Besimi asked finally, an enigmatic smile creasing his lips as he stirred the tea idly with a spoon.

Harry answered the question with an almost imperceptible nod. This was a dance he knew so well. "A friend of Mehreen's," he added, by way of elaboration.

The imam nodded his understanding, raising the cup of Earl Grey to his lips. "I have known Mehreen for many years, ever since she was small. And I know that in her line of work, you only make friends among your own kind."

Your own kind. It was a good way to put it, strange as it seemed. The brotherhood of lies.

"She speaks highly of you," Harry observed, choosing to ignore the implication of the imam's words.

Besimi spread his hands, leaning back in his chair. "There is nothing to be spoken of. I am only God's humble instrument, *insh'allah*. . .nothing more."

"You've been in Leeds for a long time." He was probing, if ever so gently—and they both knew it. The old man was no one's fool.

"Long enough," Besimi mused, sipping slowly on his tea—long, bony fingers curling awkwardly around the cup. "I've seen men grow old and die, watched others drift from the faith of their fathers, never to return."

"Faith is a tenuous thing." Hard to hold onto, no matter how much you wanted to. A truth he knew far too well.

He half expected Besimi to respond, but the old man seemed lost in his own thoughts. "And there have been yet others. . ."

His voice trailed off, almost sadly. "Perhaps I always knew it would end this way."

Harry just sat there, the warmth of the tea seeping into his body, waiting for him to continue. There was a time to press and a time to pull back—an art to all of this.

"I grew up," the imam said finally, the ghost of a smile passing across his face, "in Albania—perhaps Mehreen has told you this, no? My father was a shepherd in the mountains in the years after the war, like his father before him, and *his* father before that. It's a simple life, really. Uncomplicated, if you know what I am saying. It gives a man time to think—to be alone with God. I learned more of the true nature of Allah from my father out on those hillsides than I have from grandly esteemed clerics in all the years since. But the life of a shepherd. . .is not without its perils."

And here it was, Harry thought, his eyes narrowing. If you worked long enough in the Islamic world, you learned that no story was told without purpose. And Besimi had just arrived at his.

"Most of all, I remember the wolves. How they would prey on the flock—harrying the edges, pulling down the stragglers. Rarely ever venturing within range of my father's Mosin. Just always *there*, always waiting."

He raised his eyes to meet Harry's. "Men like Hashim Rahman remind me of those days—wolves come to raven the flock. Pulling down the weak, and the vulnerable. The young."

"Like Mehreen's nephew."

The old man's eyes grew shadowed. "Yes. Like Aydin. My people were at peace before they came, at one with their neighbors. Muslim, Christian, Jew—all of them alike, the People of the Book, living together as brothers should. Now?"

He shook his head sadly. "They have set every man at the throat of his neighbor, baying for his blood. Children rise up against their parents in defiance of every precept of Allah, declaring that they and they alone know His *true* will."

"And a man's foes shall be they of his own household," Harry added quietly, finishing the last of his tea.

A light shone briefly in the old man's eyes, recognizing the scripture. "Truth. And what of you?"

1:25 P.M.
Thames House
London

"I was right," Alec MacCallum announced as the Marsh entered the conference room. "The Americans had eyes in the sky."

"And?" The director-general looked worn, an impatient edge to his voice. "Now that the Home Secretary has helpfully assured our fellow citizens that we are 'following up on leads', the pressure from on high is. . .building."

Politicians and their assurances. MacCallum shook his head. "And, their satellite overpass begins two minutes after the Special Branch transport was hit."

Marsh swore beneath his breath, an exasperated sound. "So we have nothing?"

"Not precisely." He turned toward the screen mounted at the far end of the room, thumbing the remote in his hand. "They picked up this."

The imagery began to play, dark and grainy—zoomed in from low earth orbit, three hundred and forty kilometers up. The M1 Motorway displayed in stark relief, each car clearly visible in the thermal imaging.

A moment later, three figures moved in from the northbound lanes—their movements jerky, hurried. But they were clearly converging on the transport.

Fanned out like a tactical team. And you could just make out the assault rifle in the one man's hands—raised tight against his shoulder.

"What am I looking at?" Marsh asked after a long moment, his brow furrowing as he stared at the screen.

MacCallum held up a finger, waiting as the satellite continued its pass, the camera focusing in on the far lane—a dark Audi pulled off to the side by the median barrier, doors thrown wide open.

"We're clearly not the only ones interested in the ambushed transport. There were several vehicles abandoned near the scene in the wake of the accident, but judging from the angle of approach, I think we can conclude that whomever these three were, this was their transportation. When the satellite makes its succeeding overpass ninety minutes later—after emergency personnel are on the scene—the Audi is gone." He fanned out a series of photographs on the table, displaying the same dark black Audi, its plates clearly visible. "From traffic cameras five and eight kilometers south of the ambush, respectively. I've already sent the licence number on to the NCA."

The DG acknowledged the information with a careful nod. "Do I want to know what Jimenez asked for in exchange for this?"

"A seat at the table."

"You realize," Marsh responded, acid dripping from his voice, "you could have simply answered that with 'no.'"

1:27 P.M.
The safehouse
Rochdale, West Yorkshire

"What do you mean?" Harry asked, staring across the table into the imam's eyes.

Besimi shrugged expansively, stirring his tea once more with the spoon. "You're an American, in this country doing things which could result in you being sent to prison for the rest of your life. And you find it strange that I would ask why?"

Why, indeed. Questions became hard when you scarce knew the answers yourself. A dangerously vulnerable feeling of uncertainty.

Time to go on offense. "Tarik Abdul Muhammad," he said finally, pushing his empty cup away from him. "That's why I'm here. The *Shaikh*, as he is known to his fellow Salafi. What do you know of him?"

"*Ya Allah*," the older man breathed, shaking his head wearily. Oh, God. "The name that seems to be on everyone's lips. . ."

"So you know him?"

"I know that British intelligence is even more *eager* to learn of him than you are."

Oh, I doubt that very much, Harry thought, but didn't say—his eyes never leaving the imam's face as he waited for him to continue.

"I was kept in solitary for three days at Leeds—I believe it was. Deprived of sleep, given only minimal food and water. All so that I would tell them what I know of this '*Shaikh*', as you call him." Besimi favored him with a rueful smile. "But as you and I both know—a man can only reveal that which he knows. And I know nothing of Tarik Abdul Muhammad beyond what I read in the news."

The old man was telling the truth, Harry realized, unable to disguise the disappointment washing over his face as he leaned back in his chair. There was no doubting it—when you worked in a world where deceit was the currency of the realm, you soon learned how to discern truth when you found it.

Or you soon were dead. It was that simple.

Besimi drained the last of his tea and set the cup before him, watching Harry carefully. "I know that for the last few months, there has been talk in the mosque. Whispers among the young, the followers of Hashim Rahman, of a man who was to come. A wolf, like all those who preceded him. Perhaps they were speaking of the *Shaikh*. . .only God knows."

A bitter laugh escaped Harry's lips. "And He hasn't been in the intel-sharing business of late."

"And you are interested in Tarik, because?"

The imam was probing, his eyes seeming to look right through Harry. "The man killed hundreds of my fellow Americans in the attacks on Vegas," he retorted, taken momentarily off-guard. "And *escaped*. I want to see him brought down."

"No," Besimi said after a moment's reflection. "If that were the whole truth of it, you would be here with the rest of your countrymen. Working with the Security Service. Instead, you are all alone. Taking incredible risks. Would I be wrong in thinking there is something more. . .personal, to all of this?"

Deceit. If you allowed it to go on long enough, it became second nature. The urge to lie more powerful that any impetus to tell the truth ever had been. And yet. . .

"No," Harry shook his head finally, finding it painful to even speak the words. "One of the Americans who died in Vegas. . .was a woman named Carol Chambers."

"Ah," the old man nodded, his voice soft as if with remembered sorrow. "And this woman—you knew her, no?"

Harry glanced toward the shuttered window of the safehouse, the faint rays of afternoon sun making their way in against all odds. "I loved her."

More than life itself. That was the truth of it, raw and bitter. In a way he hadn't loved *anyone* in a very long time.

"You can't bring her back to you, no matter what you do," Besimi said slowly. "No matter whom you kill."

"But I can bring *justice*," Harry shot back, feeling the old angers surge within him.

Besimi shook his head gently. "No. Only God can render justice. It is far beyond the power of you, or I. As He spoke through the voice of the Prophet Musa, 'To Me belongeth vengeance and recompense.'"

Enough. Harry shoved his chair back in a rough motion, metal scraping across the floor as he rose, turning toward the door. "I will do what *needs* to be done."

The old man just looked at him as he stood there, sadness filling his eyes. "I must warn you, those who seek to take that which belongs to the Lord of worlds. . .do so at their peril."

Harry paused with his hand on the door, a bitter smile playing at the corners of his mouth. The Sig-Sauer visible beneath his open jacket. "You grew up among shepherds—you know what you do when a wolf has come to ravage the flock."

He went on without waiting for Besimi to respond. "You bring in a hunter."

A moment later, the phone in his shirt pocket began to vibrate with an incoming call. . .

1:35 P.M.
Leeds, North Yorkshire

"Pick up," Mehreen whispered angrily, hearing Nichols' phone ring through her earpiece as she spun the wheel of the Audi, backing into a side street.

The city center of Leeds was shut down by a protest—police deployed in full riot gear to attempt to forestall a riot. It wasn't working, as the thin haze of smoke from torched cars bore painful testament.

She shook her head. As much as she had thought it could help—could calm their fears over Aydin, telling her brother and his wife of her employment by Five after all these years had been the wrong decision to make. *"How could you do this to your family?"* The pain in Ahmed's eyes had been all too real, along with the anger. The *betrayal*.

"How could you lie *to us all this time?"*

Perhaps she had known that all along. Her family, like so many immigrants from Muslim countries, came from a world where intelligence services were tools of oppression, of terror.

Instruments by which many a man had disappeared in the middle of the night, never to be seen again by his family.

Nothing like the Security Service, but it was difficult for some to differentiate emotionally between the two. Particularly in the years since 9/11, as the Service's resources had become increasingly focused on the Islamic community.

To have become one of *them*. . .it was an act of betrayal. Even more than her marriage to a British soldier.

A click as the phone was picked up. "Yes?" Nichols' voice, careful not to identify himself. Cautious as ever.

She hesitated for a moment, still wrestling with the emotions of having seen her brother once more. Of having parted with him in such a manner.

"We're on our own."

Chapter 20

10:47 A.M. Eastern Time
Russell Senate Office Building
Washington, D.C.

"That'll be all for now, Mark," Senator Roy Coftey said, handing a thick sheaf of papers from the upcoming appropriations bill to one of his staffers and placing a hand on the young man's shoulder. Glancing past him to where Melody sat behind her desk in the outer office. "Please, give the senator and me the room."

A nod, and then his aide was gone—the door closing behind him as Coftey turned back, his eyes falling upon the tall, muscular black man standing in the middle of the room watching the exchange with an amused smile written across his dark face.

Senator Lamar Daniels. Perhaps more pertinently where Coftey was concerned—*Captain* Lamar Daniels, United States Army, Retired.

"Always underfoot, aren't they?" Daniels asked, his voice thick with the drawl of his native Mississippi. His face breaking into a full grin.

"Always," Coftey smiled, reaching out to grip his colleague's hand in a firm handshake. "Staffers. . .they're a lot like women, Lamar. Can't live with them, can't live without them."

A laugh broke from Daniels' lips, his dark eyes twinkling with humor. "You know, Roy—my grandmother had the same thing to say about men."

"Fair enough," Coftey chuckled, opening his desk and retrieving a square box. "Care for a cigar?"

"In here?" Daniels raised an eyebrow in amused skepticism. The Russell Senate Office Building, like all federal buildings, had been smoke-free by law since 1997.

"That takes care of most of it," Coftey said, indicating an air purifier sitting unobtrusively in one corner of the room. "As for the rest, well you know good and well I've always been one to make my own rules. Chew on it if it bothers your conscience."

"My conscience has never been that frail," the man smiled, reaching out as Coftey used a guillotine cutter to trim the end of the *Romeo y Julieta*, handing it over. "But you didn't bring me here to discuss my misdeeds—so what's this about? The President's NSA bill?"

"After a manner of speaking." Coftey fished an engraved lighter from the inside pocket of his suit, briefly touching flame to the freshly-cut tip of his cigar before tossing the lighter to his colleague. "I'm sure you've heard that I'm to be primaried."

"*No. . .*" Daniels paused stock-still, his dark hand wrapped around the lighter, the cigar half-raised to his lips. A look of shock spreading across his face. "Are you serious, Roy? I had no idea."

And he believed him, Coftey realized, fragrant smoke curling from the end of his cigar as he looked into the man's eyes.

Even if he wouldn't have believed it from anyone else.

Lamar Daniels was the closest thing he had to a friend in the Senate, ever since the man had come to D.C. back in '98. Fresh off a victory over the Republican incumbent, in his early forties a decorated Gulf War veteran and the first African-American senator from Mississipi since Reconstruction.

And Coftey had found himself warming to the younger man, drawn together by their common brotherhood—despite the reality that Daniels had still been passing notes in grammar school when he'd been wading waist-deep through the rice paddies of Vietnam.

In 2002, they'd stood together leading the fight in the Senate against the Iraq War resolution. Arguing that the last thing the United States needed to do was embroil itself once more in the quagmire that had ever been the Middle East.

Well over a decade later, with the United States deploying more "advisors" with each passing month to combat the rise of the Islamic State—that argument was looking more prescient all the time.

He seemed to vaguely remember another war which had started with "advisors". . .

"Dead serious," Coftey said, rising from his seat. "The party wants me gone, Lamar. Put out to pasture? More like sold to the glue factory."

Daniels shook his head, tendrils of smoke escaping from between his lips. "Who's pushing?"

"Ian Cahill."

A nod of understanding. You didn't work on the Hill two months without realizing the influence the veteran party operator wielded there. "My guess," the older man went on, circling the desk, "is that he's been talking with the leadership. Feeling them out. Getting ready to make his next move. But I'm going to need something solid to work with if I stand a prayer of beating him—to say nothing of the NSA bill."

"And that's where I come in?"

"That's where you come in," Coftey nodded, leaning back onto his desk—the solid oak easily supporting his bulk. "I want to know who they're going to try to use for the primary attempt. The shortlist at least, their choice if they have one. Can you find out for me?"

There was something there in the man's eyes, a hesitation he hadn't expected to see. *Et tu, Brute?*

"I know it's not an easy thing to ask," he began, his eyes searching Daniels' face. Wondering if he had caved, if they'd gotten to him first. "Going up against Cahill like this. But—"

"No, it's not that," the Mississippi senator said quickly, the moment passing as quickly as it had come. "It's just that I may not be the right person to ask, Roy. I'm too close to you—the people we need aren't likely to let their guard down around me."

"If you'd rather I. . ."

"No." Daniels shook his head, the cigar still clenched in his left hand as he rose, offering his right to Coftey. "You asked me, and I'll find out what I can. I give you my word."

The word of a soldier, Coftey thought, clasping the man's hand firmly. It would have to be good enough.

4:05 P.M. Greenwich Mean Time
Leeds

"Sierra, Echo Five, subject is a kilometer from your position. Maintaining following position—he just received a phone call."

Thomas leaned forward in his seat, scanning the screens before him with weary eyes. *Nothing.*

Day after day of this—he had never been cut out for surveillance work. A necessary evil. He looked over the relevant screens once more to make sure he wasn't missing anything. He wasn't.

"I thought we were up on Rahman's mobile?" he asked, turning to the British intelligence officer at his side.

"We are," she responded, her brow furrowing as she reached forward, adjusting one of the microphones. "But we're not showing any calls."

"He must be using a burner."

She shook her head in frustration, running a hand through her greying hair as she picked at the half-empty box of crisps beside her computer. "Another one. . .sod it."

"Of course," Hashim Rahman responded carefully, looking both ways as he moved onto the crosswalk, crossing the street as he neared his flat. There had been a woman behind him for a block or more, but now she was replaced by an older man in a business suit, eyes down on the phone in his hand as he hustled along.

Were they following him? Was it his imagination—paranoia overcoming him in the wake of the last few days' events?

Impossible to say.

"The date of the wedding has been moved up. . .I understand. The suite will be prepared, as promised," he said after listening a few more moments. Knowing only too well what the *Shaikh*'s words meant.

The boy was going to become a martyr. A young life, given in God's struggle.

"*Mash'allah*," he whispered beneath his breath, mounting the steps to the front door of the terraced house. How beautiful a thing.

Now all that remained was how best to take advantage of his sacrifice.

He closed the burner and turned it over, quickly stripping out both the battery and SIM before returning them to his pockets, the footfalls coming ever closer behind him.

Rahman half-turned at the door, watching as the man walked on by with no hesitation—his steps never slowing. Perhaps it had only been his imagination.

The door closed behind him as he entered, making his way up the flight of stairs and to the entrance of his second-floor flat.

He could smell the savory aroma of his wife's cooking even through the door—heard the footsteps of his little daughter running to meet him as he removed his shoes.

The sound of her voice serving to wash away all the care. The stress of the last few days.

The imam smiled to himself there in the semi-darkness, feeling himself at peace. *Mash'allah*.

"Sierra, Echo Five, we have lost visual. Subject has entered residence."

"Echo Five, Sierra—loss of visual confirmed. Establishing audio surveillance presently."

"Are we getting anything?" Thomas asked, leaning forward in his chair as the woman typed another command into the workstation before her.

She listened for another moment, the frown deepening across her face until finally she removed the headphones. "Just our lad talking with his wife. He's no longer on the call."

That figured. Rahman was leading a double life. The family man, the good Muslim—the "pillar of the community."

And the terrorist. Or the inciter of terrorists, which amounted to the same thing.

Not under UK law, he reminded himself. "What about the phone?"

"We can narrow it down a three-block radius," she replied, favoring him with a weary glance. "A city like Leeds? That's easily north of five thousand calls at any one moment. If Rahman was careful to avoid keywords. . .it could take GCHQ days to identify his number."

Intel. Anymore, it was an embarrassment of riches. The door of the van slid back unexpectedly and the figure of Darren Roth entered, clad in one of the Yorkshire Gas & Power uniforms they all wore.

"Thought we'd lost you," Thomas said, eyeing his counterpart skeptically. "Where have you been?"

"Following up a lead on the *Shaikh,*" the British intelligence officer responded, but said no more as he took the empty seat at the back of the van before the surveillance feeds.

"Dry hole?"

It was a moment before Roth spoke, his hesitation palpable. Finally, "You might very well say that, mate." He went on without giving opportunity for further comment.

"Is Rahman giving us anything actionable?"

5:31 P.M.
The safehouse
Rochdale, West Yorkshire

"You told your family what you really do," Harry observed quietly. It wasn't a question, just a sober assessment of the facts at hand. One bearing more than a hint of reproach.

She turned from the stove, her eyes settling on his face. "I did. What would you have done if *you* had been in my situation?"

He shook his head. "I don't know. It's been a long time since I knew anyone I cared about enough to tell them that much truth."

There had been Carol, but she had already known more than he could ever have brought himself to tell her. Already a part of this world, no matter how much he might wanted to have kept her out.

No matter how high the walls he attempted to build between the two.

For in the end, all the walls had come crashing down. *The rubble of dreams.*

Mehreen swore softly under her breath. "That's how things are for you, aren't they? Truth is whatever you tell people—whatever you decide they *deserve* to hear. A web of lies, twisting and entwining about you until you realize that you're trapped too. I can't live my life that way."

"Then you should never have joined Five." And *that* was truth, cold and brutal. The way truth so often was.

He could see the angry reply forming on her lips, but she seemed to suppress it with an effort. They had both been at this long enough to know he was right. The realities of the life they had chosen for themselves. And those around them.

No man is an island.

"So where does that leave us with Aydin?" Harry asked, breaking the awkward silence that hung between them after his statement.

"I wish I knew." She shook her head, seeming to pull herself back together. Re-focus on the objectives before them. "If I had Five's resources, I'd at least have a starting point, but with MacCallum's defection. . .even accessing them is impossible. Let alone diverting them."

That would have been hard to do in any case, he thought. Not without drawing down the kind of attention none of them could well afford. "As it is," she continued without waiting for him to comment, "I don't know where to begin. I'm his estranged aunt. I don't know his habits, his routines—where he spends his time. I don't even know who his friends are."

"But I do," a voice announced from the doorway and Harry swung around to see the imam standing there. "There was a young man from the university—one of Rahman's young wolves. A good friend of Aydin's. I have been trying to think of his name. It was Nasir. . .I believe."

"One who gives victory," Harry mused. It was a fitting name for a *shahid*. "Do you know where he lives?"

"No," Besimi grimaced, running a hand across his beard. "But I once visited his parents shortly after he came to the mosque, and I believe I could locate them again. Perhaps he is still with them."

Harry stood, reaching for his jacket and pulling it on over the holstered pistol. "It's enough."

7:01 P.M.
A studio flat
Leeds

"You can sleep over there," Nasir said, indicating the worn, faded couch with a gesture. "I have to make sure you get to that bus in the morning."

Aydin nodded mutely, his eyes taking in his surroundings—there was scant room for even the most basic furniture in the small, dimly lit flat. Loud rap music came pounding through the thin walls from the neighboring flat, each lewd profanity only too distinct—reminding him of why he was here.

The corruption of the West, spreading across the earth like a stain. Contaminating all it touched. *Even the faithful.*

"The loo is back there—through the bedroom." He glanced back at the college student, acknowledging his words with another nod. They had met the previous summer at the mosque, in one of Imam Rahman's classes. Kindred spirits, despite the difference in age. *Brothers.*

Nasir smiled, as if sensing Aydin's disquiet. "You should be proud, bruv," he said, coming over and drawing the teenager into an embrace. "The *Shaikh* is placing a lot of faith in you. Remember the words of the Prophet, right? 'A single endeavor in God's Cause is better than the world and whatever is in it.'"

And that was all he was to have. *A single endeavor.* He smiled with an effort, withdrawing from Nasir's embrace. "*Alhamdullilah,*" he murmured. Praise be to God.

Turning away, he pulled the explosive vest from within the duffel bag he carried, laying it on the low table before the couch. Where it would be easy to put on when he dressed in the morning.

He ran his hand gently over the front of the vest as the music's insistent beat continued to pulsate through the walls around him, feeling its bulk—the hundreds of ball bearings embedded in a sheet of plastic explosive beneath the fabric.

It was time to follow the green birds. . .

9:25 P.M.
A pub
Leeds

"*The wedding gift has arrived.*" Tarik Abdul Muhammad read the message twice before sending a message of acknowledgment. The boy was now safely under wraps until the moment he boarded the 6:40 AM bus to London.

A bus filled with businessmen headed for the city. For London's bustling Victoria Station.

Once Aydin had boarded that bus, it would be too late for anyone to stop him. Too late for him to stop himself, the *Shaikh* thought, eyeing the one unused number filed under Contacts.

The number which would detonate the vest.

He closed the phone and tucked it into the pocket of his jeans, catching the eye of a young British woman sitting on a stool by the bar, her skirt riding perilously high on smooth, bare legs. Blonde hair falling over her shoulders.

She had been there for nearly an hour, clearly working. He met her bold gaze for a long moment, then looked away, feeling the ache keenly. It had been three long weeks since he had been with a woman—the teenage daughter of one of the families with whom he had sought refuge.

A beautiful girl, if completely inexperienced. Her innocence so very. . .tempting. He smiled at the memory.

"Having a good night, luv?" a feminine voice asked from above him and he looked up to see the woman from the bar slide into the booth across from him. A challenge dancing in her eyes.

So bold. He reached forward across the table, his decision made in that moment—taking her hand in his, his eyes searching her face. "Oh, yes."

10:39 P.M.
Allerton Bywater, West Yorkshire

This was England, Harry thought, scanning the quiet village street as he sat behind the wheel of the darkened Audi. The way all the tourist websites described it.

Rows of modest brick dwellings, gated courtyards facing the street. The tranquil waters of the Aire, wending its way through the village only a few hundred meters from his position.

They had been inside for over an hour, he realized, checking first his watch and then the burner phone. *Nothing from Mehreen.*

You stayed alive in the field by knowing when to press and when to hold back. The art of fieldcraft.

She had persuaded him to stay outside—gambling that a known face and a woman from the community might succeed where the mere presence of an American could doom them to failure.

It was the voice of experience. . .she knew her people. As did he. There was nothing more sacrosanct in the Middle East than a man's home.

The phone buzzed in his hand and he glanced down to see an incoming call glowing on the screen. It wasn't Mehreen. "Yes?" he asked, keeping his eyes on the house.

"We need to meet," came the abrupt response. No greeting, and no identification, although neither was necessary. *Flaharty*. "I'm on the coast."

He thought about asking *which* coast, but decided it didn't make a difference. Either coast was hours away.

"It will have to wait—I'm in the middle of something."

"Aren't we all?" came the Irishman's caustic response. "Heard anything from your soldier boy?"

Paul Gordon. "That's a negative." It wasn't surprising—whatever Hale was planning, he was clearly playing it all very close to the vest. It would take time for the former Para to fully gain his confidence, even longer for him to pass the word along.

Developing assets wasn't something you expected to pay off within hours. Not in the real world.

"When Hale contacted me the first time, he did so through a cut-out. I've had a...talk with them."

"And?" Harry asked, his face impassive. He knew only too well what that "talk" might have consisted of, wondered for a brief moment if the cut-out had survived. The Provos had been one of the most brutal Republican groups in the years of The Troubles, and Flaharty had learned his craft well.

"And they gave me a lead on Hale. He's tied to a feeder that's lying at anchor in the port of Grimsby. The MV *Percy Phillips*."

"What's his connection?"

"He didn't know," Flaharty responded, an ominous certainty in his tone. "But it's worth looking into."

"I'll meet you in Grimsby come morning."

"No. We need to do this tonight. Bugger whatever else you're up to, Harry, I stuck my bleedin' neck out for you."

Harry shook his head in the darkness. Never allow an asset to play you—the moment you let that happen, you were dead. It was a delicate line.

"That was about you extricating yourself from a very bad situation." A situation the Irishman had gotten himself into, he didn't add. He had to have known just how hazardous dealing with those who sought to bring weapons into the UK could be—hazards he was sure had been reflected in Flaharty's price.

"Sure an' now it's about revenge," came the response. He wasn't giving an inch. "They butchered my lads and they've come after me. All I need to know is if you'll be there."

"Not tonight. There's an attack imminent." He hadn't voiced it to Mehreen, but if Aydin was involved with one of the *Shaikh*'s cells, there was only one reason they would have pulled him from his family, and it was one they both knew. *It was coming soon.*

"So?" Flaharty challenged. "They've been hunting me and mine for decades—do you honestly think I *care*? I want Hale."

"And we'll both get him. In good time." Movement out of the corner of his eye and he glanced over to see Mehreen coming out the front door of the house. "I have to go."

Flaharty started to speak, but Harry cut him off, closing the phone without another word. There was no *right* call. . .he needed both Flaharty and Mehreen. And he bid fair to lose one of them no matter what decision he made.

It was a choice you didn't get to make twice.

"What do we have?" he asked Mehreen as she slid into the passenger seat of the Audi, the back door opening to admit Ismail Besimi.

"An address for Nasir's flat."

11:06 P.M.
Thames House
London

He should have gone home two hours before, but no one at Thames House had been keeping regular hours for the last week. And it wasn't as though he had anyone waiting for him.

"Come on," MacCallum whispered, rubbing his forehead as he sifted through another series of images from Westminster Station—the security cameras overlooking the deep platform, the escalators from the surface. *No sign of her.*

He checked the timestamps once more—the cameras had clearly captured Mehreen's descent into the station. Then nothing.

She had boarded no trains, that was clear enough. She hadn't gone home. And she had disappeared off the grid only fifty minutes after entering the station.

The only thing that remained to be answered was *where.* "Working late?" He glanced up to see Norris standing there, a question written in the analyst's eyes.

"Earlier this evening," MacCallum said, minimizing the open windows with the surveillance feeds before Norris could see them, "North Yorkshire Special Branch took into custody five men suspected of organizing the riots in Leeds. All of them Moroccans. I need to get their names, photos off to the DGSE before I leave. See if they recognize any *kunyas.*"

When it came to Morocco, they were heavily dependent on the French—and whatever they could pick up from M.I.-6's people on Gibraltar.

Sometimes it was easier to get information from the French.

A *kunya* was the component of an Arabic name meant to denote the name of a man's eldest child, but fictitious *kunyas* had crept into use by Arab terrorists as far back as Yasser Arafat.

"Need any help with them?" Norris asked, shrugging the sling of the messenger bag off his shoulder.

The section chief shook his head. "No, almost got it wrapped up. Just a couple more things to run."

He waited until Norris had disappeared through the doors of the Centre before he brought the feeds back up, guided by a sudden impulse as he shifted his focus to the cameras on the street outside Westminster.

A sea of faces in the illumination of the streetlights. And then. . .he paused the feed, rewinding it a few seconds. *There.*

Mehreen Crawford's face, staring up into the very eye of the CCTV camera. He checked the logs once more and then the timestamp on the video. The picture had been taken ninety seconds before her phone went off-line.

"*Got* you. . ."

12:08 A.M., April 1ˢᵗ
A hotel
Leeds, North Yorkshire

Tarik Abdul Muhammad rolled over onto his back, letting out a contented sigh as he leaned into the pillows.

Sated, that was the word for it, he thought hearing the water of the shower come on from within the suite's small bathroom. The blonde had been good, perhaps even more skilled than the Russian whore he had enjoyed in Vegas the night he had met with Valentin Andropov.

The bodies of women. . .the taste of fine wine—pleasures he permitted himself. Were they sins? Perhaps, but he had confidence that they would count as nothing when the deeds of his life were weighed at the end of time.

Grains of sand in the balances.

Nothing to be compared with the work he had done to advance the cause of God. The holy jihad.

He could be allowed a few sins.

12:24 A.M.
The Seacroft council estates
Leeds

"What do you think?"

Harry didn't answer for a long moment, continuing to scan the face of the tower block with the NODs Flaharty had loaned him. *It wasn't good.*

"I think we only get one chance at this," he replied slowly. And not a good chance, at that. To do this right, he would have needed a tactical team—*his* team, preferably.

Mehreen was a good intel officer, but she wasn't an assaulter. Didn't even have the benefit of the minimal firearms training CIA case officers received. This would have been a crapshoot even with Flaharty.

"What's the demographic makeup of the council estates like?" he asked, the building showing up as a dark green in the view of the night-vision. Lights from a few of the flats, glowing bright splotches that distorted his view.

"Young, poor. Heavily Asian." He winced. Hostile territory, possibly gang turf—assuming nothing more formidable. That meant they were going to need to get out quickly once they had secured Aydin.

"Nasir al-Kutobi's flat," he began, "where is it located in the tower block, precisely?"

"The top floor."

He swept the NODs from the bottom of the tower block to the roof. *Ten stories up.*

This just kept getting better.

12:37 A.M.
The studio flat
Seacroft council estates

He should have been sleeping—he knew that. He would need all his strength for the morning. Aydin rolled over onto his side, eyes wide open as he squirmed deeper into the cushions of the couch—struggling to get comfortable to rest.

He had never felt more alert in his life, every fiber of his body seeming to hum as if with electricity, with excitement.

They had stayed up late, making a video to be released over the Internet once he had given his life—the black flag of the Prophet unfurled across one wall of the flat, an index finger raised to the camera in recognition of the *tawhid*, the belief in the singularity of God. And it was only as he had stared into the unblinking electronic eye of Nasir's small video camera that it had hit him. . .this was *real*.

He had watched so many such videos over the last year, read so many testaments of faith.

And now, it was to be his turn. Bringing the war home to those who had raped the house of Islam. The justice of God upon the *kaffir*.

He reached over the suicide vest for his phone, briefly checking the glowing screen in the darkness. Only a few more hours.

Insh'allah.

12:49 A.M.

Almost there. Harry rounded the landing of the dimly-lit stairwell and took the final remaining flight of stairs two at a time—his hand resting on the butt of the suppressed pistol within his coat.

The pungent smell of *khat* permeated the building, evoking memories of his time overseas. The mild narcotic was to the natives of the Middle East what coffee was to Americans—a well-nigh ubiquitous stimulant.

They had passed a group of young Asian men on the landing two stories below—their cheeks bulging with the leaves, regarding them with suspicion as they moved toward the next floor.

"Are you ready for this?" he asked, turning to Mehreen as he paused just within the door leading out of the stairwell.

Once they were out there, they were committed. No way back. She nodded quickly, not looking him in the eye, and Harry reached out, putting his left hand on her shoulder.

"You know that I will do whatever is within my power to ensure Aydin's safety," he said, his voice low and urgent, "but there is no way for me to guarantee it."

She nodded her understanding, her face drawn and pale in the faint light, and he went on, "Stay behind me when we go in—and do *not* fire unless you're forced to."

His Sig was the only suppressed weapon they had—the moment she fired the HK, their advantage of surprise was going to go straight out the window.

And depending upon the reaction of the tower block's residents, they might go out the window right along with it.

He looked past her to the imam, who had paused on the steps just below them to catch his breath. "I'm going to need you to remain in the hall."

12:51 A.M.
Thames House
London

There had been no signs of Mehreen on any of the other cameras beyond the station. Nothing that he could confirm was her.

It was as if she had vanished into the darkness of the London night, like the trained spy she was. Like the spy *they* had trained her to be. And only hours before Ismail Besimi had vanished as well.

MacCallum shook his head. It was the moment any intelligence officer dreaded—when he found himself facing off against one of his own. *A friend.*

And so much that remained to be answered. *How could she have* known?

But there was no more to be done tonight. He stood, gathering his coat and briefcase before checking once more to make sure his workstation was closed down and secure—his evening's work under wraps.

He had nearly made it to the keycard-access doors that sealed off the operations centre from the rest of Thames House when he heard a man's voice calling his name.

"Yes?" he asked, looking back to see an analyst hurrying after him.

"We just got this in from North Yorkshire," the man said, handing him a grainy print-out of a photo. "They picked up the Audi on traffic cameras entering the city an hour ago."

MacCallum released a heavy sigh, taking the print-out and dropping his coat over the back of a nearby chair. So much for the night being over.

12:53 A.M.

Thirteenth flat from the stairwell, the west side of the building. Harry could feel his heart pounding against his chest as he led the way down the hall, the Sig-Sauer extended before him, a small flashlight cupped under the barrel in his left hand. Everything now depended upon speed.

Surprise.

It probably only took them thirty seconds to traverse the length of the hall, but it felt like an eternity before they stood before the door of the flat—the rusted numbers indicating the address they had been given.

This was going to be dangerously far from textbook. . .but in the absence of any good plans, you rolled with the best bad one.

He paused, eyeing the lock—then motioned for Mehreen to step to one side. *Time to do this.*

Footsteps. The sound of movement in the hall without. He had been hearing noises from the neighboring flats all night—the paper-thin walls blocked out nothing—but this was different, somehow.

And then they seemed to stop. *Just outside the door.*

Aydin sat bolt upright, feeling within the pocket of his jacket for the small Czech semiautomatic Rahman had given him only a few days before.

His fingers had just closed around the cold metal of the grip when the door came crashing inward.

The door splintered around the lock, flying back on its hinges and Harry followed it into the room, stumbling forward, weapon up—a dull throb pulsing through his injured ankle from the force of the kick.

Left. He swept the room to his left with the muzzle of the Sig, the flashlight's beam traversing the same arc. A television mounted against the far wall, a small, empty couch—a blanket lying discarded over one arm. As if its occupant had been there only moments before. He could feel Mehreen entering the room behind him, but he pressed forward.

He was alone in this.

He could only hope that she would hold her fire as he had instructed—in the confusion and darkness, someone with her lack of weapons training was as likely to shoot him as anyone else in the flat.

The long dark barrel of the pistol tracked right, the light revealing a small kitchenette, a refrigerator and stove—dirty dishes piled high in the sink. A door leading toward. . .the bedroom?

He inclined his head toward it, nodding silently for Mehreen to cover the door.

Left. Nothing—no sign of Aydin, or Nasir al-Kutobi, for that matter. The abandoned couch the only tell that anyone within had reacted to the intrusion.

But there was something. Weapon extended before him, he moved closer to the couch, his eyes narrowing as the light flicked across the cushions.

It was a nearly fatal distraction. He heard the *click* of the door opening behind him, heard Mehreen scream a warning.

And he was turning, but not nearly fast enough. He glimpsed a figure in the doorway of the bedroom out of the corner of his eye, the glint of metal—just as the muzzle blast of Mehreen's pistol lit up the darkness of the room.

Once, twice. Three shots. The sharp reports battering his eardrums, reverberating through the tower block.

He saw her target stagger, but the man didn't go down—the pistol in his hands still coming up. A slow, painfully inevitable arc.

The flashlight beam hit the young man's face, framing it between the posts of

Harry's iron sights. Three dots, forming a perfect triangle. *Sight picture.*

A pair of bullets spat from the suppressed muzzle of the Sig—the first catching the target in the upper chest, the second going higher—tearing into his throat.

The college student went down, hard—crashing into the bedroom door, the pistol falling from weakened fingers.

Harry kicked the weapon away from him, looking remorselessly down into the young man's face as he lay there, blood gurgling from his throat. *Dying.*

No more fight left in him.

He glanced over to see Mehreen standing a few feet away, her eyes wide and staring, the HK still leveled in her hands. The shock of seeing a man killed right before your eyes—of having had a *hand* in his death.

Keep moving. That was the imperative now—the sound of shouts coming from somewhere deep in the building. They weren't going to have much time.

He stepped over the dying man and into the small bedroom, the light playing before him as he swept each corner in turn. Kicking open the door of the small bathroom. *Nothing.*

"He's not here," he announced grimly, feeling Mehreen enter the room behind him. He turned, seeing the devastation, the loss written in her eyes.

Faulty intel was the reality of their work, more often than not. Perhaps deep down she had known this was a fool's errand from the very beginning.

Like he had.

"Aydin!" He grimaced she began to call her nephew's name, her voice ringing desperately through the flat. "*Aydin!*"

He turned away, ejecting the magazine from the butt of the Sig-Sauer and replacing it with a full mag from within his jacket. Out in the field, you learned that reloading was just like sleeping.

You did it every chance you got, because you never knew when you might get another one.

"Where is my nephew?" He looked back to see her kneeling over the body of the fallen college student, her hands wet with his blood—her face distorted in rage. "Tell me—what did you do to him? *Tell me!*"

The shadow of a death's-head smile passed across the young man's face as he attempted and failed to respond—his vocal chords shredded by the hollow-point round. The contempt, the hatred in his eyes only too visible.

"Leave it, Mehr," he cautioned, shifting the Sig to his left hand as he placed his right on her shoulder. Knowing that look all too well. Even if he could have spoken, they would get nothing from him.

She shook her head, glaring up at him through the tears shining in her eyes. "Is that what you would say? If it was *your* family?"

"That's been far too long ago," he replied simply. No going back there, not for him. He swept the light around the bedroom, its beam picking out a laptop.

That was going with them.

And then it happened—movement out of the corner of his eye, from behind them in the main living area of the flat. The crash as a lamp fell to the floor, a figure stumbling toward the broken door.

He turned, bringing his weapon up in an instinctive movement. Hearing Mehreen cry out, rising to her feet as if she would have taken the pistol from him. "*No!*"

Aydin.

And the figure was gone, a shout from Ismail Besimi in the corridor without heralding his departure. Harry shook her off and moved quickly into the corridor, finding only the imam leaning there against the wall—his eyes wide with fear. The door leading to the stairwell was swinging open, as if someone had passed in a hurry.

"Aydin?" Harry demanded, the Sig-Sauer still drawn in his hand.

The old man nodded a mute "yes" and Harry was moving on, his steps quickening as he reached the stairwell. It was then that he heard Ismail's voice calling after him, arresting him where he stood. "He—he is wearing a vest."

1:04 A.M.

Ya Allah. Oh, God. He could feel his heart pounding against the wall of his chest as if it threatened to break through, tears streaming down his cheeks as he flew down the stairs—feet slamming into the hard concrete. *Oh, God.*

Nasir was dead. *They* had killed him, and they were coming for him.

He took the steps two at a time, the panic nearly overwhelming him as he struggled to zip up his jacket over the hastily thrown-on vest.

His aunt's voice echoing in his mind, calling his name. The look on her face when she had shot Nasir. *She was one of them.*

There were moments when fresh intel changed the very nature of a mission—irrevocably. Learning of Aydin's suicide vest was one of those moments.

They had come to rescue him—to save him from those who had turned him against his family, his community, but now. . .Aydin's life was no longer the priority.

Stopping the bombing had become their primary objective—whatever that took. Even if it meant killing the boy he had come to save.

Harry slowed as he reached the landing, his face a cold, expressionless mask—the Sig-Sauer extended before him as he pivoted, slicing the pie as he turned to face the next flight of stairs down.

Once, Aydin's age would have given him pause, but that was far in the past. You didn't work long in the Middle East without learning a fundamental truth: Age counted for nothing—a sixteen-year-old was every bit as capable of detonating an s-vest or pulling a trigger as an adult fighter.

All that mattered was the innocent lives which could be lost.

He hurried down the stairs, favoring his ankle awkwardly as he moved. From below him, he could hear the sound of the boy's running footsteps—growing more distant by the moment. He was losing ground. Come on, *move*.

Harry rounded the next landing and stopped short, hearing the sound of voices below—the unmistakably rough, guttural sound of Pashto transporting him instantly back to the mountains of the Hindu Kush.

It was too low for him to make out what was being said, but he knew that harsh, barking tone. Knew what it meant. An order was an order in any language.

And they were fresh out of time.

He hesitated for only a moment, the long black suppressor of the Sig still pointing the way down the next flight—then turned, heading back upstairs.

They were going to have to find some other way to stop Aydin. For now, it was past time to be leaving.

Lack of sleep amplified everything. Stress. Injury. He hadn't truly slept since. . .he couldn't remember.

He saw Mehreen as he exited the stairwell into the corridor—the question written so clearly in her eyes. "No," he said simply, shaking his head. "Toss the flat—take everything you can. Anything that could yield us actionable intel."

"What are you saying?"

He cast a glance backward toward the stairs. "I'm saying we have a minute and a half to clear this floor."

1:12 A.M.

Once again. The rock swung awkwardly in a downward arc, the impact shuddering through Aydin's arms. But the lock held, holding the bike in place.

Ya Allah. He nearly swore, throwing the rock away in frustration. If he'd had even a knife, he might have sawed through the cable lock—but as it was, there was nothing.

He straightened, breathing heavily—his cheeks still stained with tears. It couldn't be more than few miles to the bus station. Still more than five hours remaining until his bus departed for London.

He could make it.

1:23 A.M.

The tower block itself might have been stoutly built of reinforced concrete, but inside the walls were thin.

That had worked against them earlier, but *now*—he pressed himself up against the wall just inside the corridor door, hearing the footsteps pounding up the stairs without.

The rough sound of Pashto fading away as the men moved up the stairs to the level above. He pushed the door open slowly—the muzzle of his pistol tracking to cover the flight of steps below them. *Clear.*

Six stories down, four to go. He glanced back at Mehreen and Ismail, motioning them out the door with his left hand. *Go, go, go.*

It wasn't going to be long before the searchers figured out they were no longer in the upper half of the tower block. And once that happened. . .

"Have any luck getting into that phone?" he asked quietly, throwing the question back over his shoulder as he led the way once more down the steps.

"Just now," she nodded, looking up from the screen of the Samsung Galaxy she had found beneath Nasir al-Kutobi's pillow. "Not seeing anything actionable yet. More than a fair bit of rather. . .kinky porn, but nothing we can use."

That figured. For all their presumed piety, most jihadis were only true believers up to a point. Sex tended to be that point—he had seen more stashes of porn scattered across the Middle East in his years with the Agency than he ever had in college.

They rounded the landing and were headed down the next flight of stairs when he heard Mehreen murmur, almost as if to herself, "*Wait.* Just a minute."

He started to turn back to face her, to ask her what she meant, but at that very moment the door below them opened, a young Pakistani appearing in the opening.

There was no time to take cover, to go back up the stairs. The young man's eyes widened as he saw the long black barrel of the Sig-Sauer in Harry's hand—his mouth opening, but not a single sound coming out.

And then Harry saw the glitter of steel in his left hand, the gleam of a switchblade extending from his fist. "*No*," he breathed, his eyes locking with those of the young man's across the railing of the stairs. *Don't even think it.*

Law enforcement were trained to the Tueller drill—a knife-armed attacker within twenty-one feet presented a lethal threat to an officer. One and a half seconds to engage.

He'd seen things go south far faster than that, and he wasn't law enforcement. *No rules.* Except survival.

The hesitation was ever so clearly written in the young man's eyes—the uncertainty. *Don't try to be a hero, son,* Harry thought—his eyes never leaving the young man's face as he shifted his weight, bringing the pistol ever so slightly forward. *Don't make me do this.*

As many men as he had killed—as many times as it had been *necessary*—it never got any easier. Any less haunting.

And then he heard Mehreen's voice from behind him, the Pashto sounding strangely foreign, unpracticed on her tongue, despite it being her native language. Speaking words of caution, reassurance. *Warning.*

A long moment passed, and then the young man turned, retreating back into the corridor. The door closing behind him.

It was only then that Harry realized he had been holding his breath ever since the appearance of the Pakistani.

But they weren't out of the woods just yet.

"Go back, go back," he gestured—pushing both of them back toward the floor above. If the young man got on the horn to the gangs, they needed to be elsewhere, or he was going to regret not putting a bullet in his head when he had the chance.

Mehreen paused on the landing, her eyes still focused on the phone in her hand. "What is it?"

She turned it so he could see the screen, the fear written so clearly across her face. "Al-Kutobi purchased a ticket for the morning bus from Leeds to London. One-way."

He took it from her, noting the departure and arrival times. "Then we know the target. And you know what you have to do."

1:27 A.M.
The MV Percy Phillips
Grimsby, Lincolnshire

The night was strikingly clear—the stars above shining down, pinpricks of light against the dark sky.

Paul Gordon leaned heavily on his good leg, feeling the waters of the North Sea gently lap against the vessel's hull as he moved to the rail. Gazing out toward the town.

What in God's *name* had he gotten himself into? He had been to war—had allowed himself to be convinced that this was just a continuation of the same fight.

It wasn't.

"I thought I heard you come out." Hale's voice behind him, freezing him where he stood. "Couldn't sleep?"

It was impossible to know the intent behind that question, he thought—the tone giving away nothing. Even during their days together in the Parachute Regiment, Hale had always been a hard one to read.

And they had a man inside the Security Service. . .if Hale *knew*, then he was dead. Simple as that. The phone seemed to burn a hole in his pocket, reminding him of his danger.

Nothing to do but play this through. Gordon nodded, turning slowly to face his old comrade. "Yeah. Can't stop thinking about the lads. I knew Grimes—he and I went through training together, so many years ago. How many more do we have to *lose*, Conor?"

"It's war," the former NCO responded, walking out of the shadows to join him at the rail. "You and I both know that. We've been there before."

"We have. And we buried a lot of good mates—for what? We didn't win. There was no 'victory.' The politicians said it was over and brought us home. I won't—I *can't* do that again." Gordon's voice shook with emotion, wavering there on the brink between what he knew was right. . .and the cause the former SAS man had laid out before him.

He believed *in this*.

"You're not going to have to, mate," Hale said after a long moment. "That's why we're doing this. And there are no sodding politicians going to hold us back this time. We see this through to the bitter end, whether that end lies in victory—or every last one of us dead in the grave."

He smiled, an odd, bitter smile as he continued, clapping a hand on Gordon's shoulder. "We're Paras, remember? *Utrinque Paratus.*"

And Gordon felt himself begin to smile in return at the memory of their old unit motto. *Ready for anything.*

"If I remember from Iraq," Hale went on, his tone changing abruptly. "You were every bit as good on a long gun as you were kicking in doors. Do you think you still are?"

Taken by surprise, Gordon nodded. "It's been a long time, but I did it for so many years. . .I'm certain I could again. Why?"

A shadow seemed to pass across the sergeant's face, as if even he was yet coming to terms with what they had set out to do. "Get some sleep, mate. There's work to be done come morning."

The figure standing in the shadow of the Grimsby Dock Tower stood there for a long time after the two soldiers had disappeared below-decks.

Sod you, Harry. Stephen Flaharty lowered the binoculars to let them hang about his neck, using a small rag to wipe the gathering mist from his glasses. *There's your bleedin' mole. At Conor Hale's right hand.*

1:35 A.M.
Seacroft council estates

Almost there. Harry glanced back along the streets of Seacroft as Ismail and Mehreen hurried behind him, the stark outline of the tower block overshadowing the terraced rows of newer council flats like a grim omen in the night.

Their egress from the tower block had taken longer than he could have predicted—going floor by floor, dodging the gang members looking for them. You never wanted to leave behind more bodies than you absolutely had to. Even Nasir al-Kutobi had been unfortunate, if inevitable.

He picked his way past a man lying there by the side of the street—a muddy jacket wrapped around him, his body reeking with the familiar smell of *khat*.

Aydin was somewhere out here, in the night. Running scared. Or hell-bent on accomplishing his objective.

In his experience, the latter was the more likely of the options. Faith and indoctrination were powerful things. When you could convince someone that death was something to be *desired*—they could be well-nigh unstoppable.

But doing just that had been his job for years. And he was still alive. . .and more than a few of them were dead. Powerful though it might be, faith wasn't something that stopped bullets.

"Clear," Harry announced, approaching the Audi from the passenger side—his light flickering through each of the windows in turn.

It hadn't been compromised. *Yet*.

Mehreen slid into the front seat across from him—the engine humming to life as he turned the key in the ignition. He didn't even look at her, just checked his mirrors as he pulled out into the street.

"Make the call," he said abruptly, his tone brooking no opposition. *It was past time*.

But he could feel her stiffen beside him all the same—her heart and mind locked in a death struggle over the fate of one she loved. "He has a vest, Mehr."

"I know," she said quietly, looking out the window of the Audi as it accelerated down the street. "But he's just a *boy*."

"No." He shook his head. "He's not—not anymore. That changed the moment he started listening to Hashim Rahman, the moment he put on that bomb vest. You have to accept that he's already made your choice for you. Call in Special Branch."

"He's right," Ismail Besimi added from the back seat of the car. Harry's eyes flickered up to the rear-view mirror to meet those of the imam. Glimpsing a face full of sadness. . .and yet grim resolution.

"And what if he spends the rest of his life in prison because of me? What if. . ."

Mehreen hesitated as if unable to form the words. "What if they have to *kill* him?"

Then that's what will happen, he thought—eyes on the road ahead. The cold laws of cause and effect, brutal and unforgiving.

Aydin had chosen his path.

"We can get to him," she went on after a moment, a raw edge to her voice. "We know where he's going to be—we can stop him."

He caught Ismail's glance once more in the rear-view, saw the sympathy there. But they both knew the truth, as did she.

Math.

That's what it came down to in the end. One of the hardest lessons any officer ever had to learn in the field. The grim necessity of weighing the one life against the many. Human lives reduced to numbers, nothing more.

Think of it any other way, and it would paralyze you. Like it was paralyzing Mehreen.

"And if we fail?" he asked, finally glancing over at her—her face shadowed in the darkness of the car, eyes staring straight before her.

He had seen the aftermath of a bus bombing once, in the Middle East. Could still remember the pall of dark smoke hanging over the scene. The raw, anguished screams of the injured and dying. The smell of burning human flesh.

The bodies, scattered like broken dolls. *Never again.*

There was no response to his question, and after a moment he went on without waiting for one. "No matter how hard this is, Mehr, you can't allow it to become personal. The moment that happens, people start dying."

"You mean the way they have been," she began slowly, her voice brittle, "ever since you lost Carol?"

Chapter 21

4:31 A.M.
Thames House
London

"I got in here as quickly as I could after your call—things were light on the Tube. Early yet," Norris added, looking suddenly to where MacCallum stood at the head of the conference table. "You've been here all night?"

The section chief nodded slowly. "Aye. One brushfire after another. And now we have a real problem developing. Seen anything of Marsh?"

"He was on his way in when I came up. Should be here right soon. What's going on—any further leads on Ismail Besimi?"

"No, North Yorkshire's scouring Leeds for the Audi after it was picked up on traffic cameras entering the city last night. Nothing thus far."

"They're stretched thin." Norris shook his head. "Radio on the way in was full of the riots. . .an officer in Birmingham was stabbed to death last night. The British Defence Coalition is organizing a march on the Tower Hamlets for this afternoon."

MacCallum murmured an obscenity under his breath at the news, glimpsing the form of the DG out in the operations centre. "Oh, that's exactly what we bloody need."

"Given that you've called us all in here hours before dawn, Alec," Marsh began icily as he came through the door of the conference room—dropping his overcoat over the back of a chair, "I think we can assume that there is something of grave importance to be addressed?"

"There is," MacCallum responded, turning with the remote in his hand and aiming it at the TV on the wall as a grainy CCTV image came up on-screen.

"This man landed at Heathrow this morning, arriving from Zurich on Swiss Airlines Flight 327. Our systems are giving us an 84% match with a man known as Mirsab Abdul Rashid al-Libi."

The DG nodded. "'The Libyan'. . .and?"

"And last fall," MacCallum continued with a glance at Norris, "al-Libi was fighting in Syria alongside the Islamic State. He's a trained marksman—Libyan Army—deserted and joined *al-Harakat al-Islamiya* when the civil war broke out and Quaddafi was overthrown."

A light seemed to dawn in Norris' eyes. "Of course. Is he the one—"

"One and the same," the section chief replied, using the remote to bring up a second picture of the man alongside the first, this one showing a bearded man dressed in combat fatigues, holding a Russian-made sniper rifle. "Al-Libi became an Internet sensation after his amateur videos of his kills spread across Salafist jihadi sites last November. Hundreds of thousands of views in Europe and the UK alone. He's known as the "Sword of the Prophet", which is the literal meaning of his first name."

"And now he's here," Marsh observed grimly, running a hand across his forehead.

"That appears to be the case." He didn't need to say anything more. Computer matches were an. . .inexact science at best, and to the naked eye, the comparison of the clean-shaven man on screen with the heavily-bearded rebel fighter left something to be desired.

In this business, you went with what you had—and could afford to leave nothing to chance.

"Anything to indicate why he's come to the UK at this time?"

"None. Safe to say it's not for the Earl Grey."

6:17 A.M.
Leeds City Bus Station
North Yorkshire

Where was he? Trying to pick a face out of a crowd was ever difficult, no matter how good your training. Harry moved down the concourse, taking in the bus station, the queue of people forming to buy tickets. His eyes scanning each face before passing on, struggling to focus on the mission. Suppress the growing sense of disquiet within him.

The on-line ticket confirmation Mehreen had found on al-Kutobi's phone had been for National Express—whose coach buses occupied the western side of the station.

More specifically the No. 19 bus, now boarding. With scarce twenty minutes to go. "Mehr, what's your sitrep?"

"Still no sign of him. Ten people on the bus so far." He ran a hand over his beard, ducking his head as he moved back toward the ticket counter, Ismail Besimi following behind him as he went.

The decision to take up positions within the station itself had been one of dangerous necessity, made even more so by the presence of security cameras.

They simply didn't have the manpower to cover all the entrances to the single-story brick structure—preferable as that would have been.

That left them with. . .only the bad options. Harry stopped at the end of the concourse—leaning back against a timetable display as he turned to watch the bus itself, perhaps thirty meters away. The first morning rays of sun streaming into the station through the glass roof above their heads. "You *were* right, you know," Besimi said quietly, standing there beside him. "Mehreen's heart is full of love, but this will not end as she hopes."

Harry didn't reply, taking a sip of his coffee as he scanned the concourse. The old man was speaking the truth, of course. . .but he *needed* Mehreen—needed her help in a crusade that couldn't have possibly been more personal. His texts to Flaharty hours earlier had gone unanswered, nothing but dead silence from the Irishman.

She was all he had left.

And what did that make him? He asked himself, glancing around at the faces of the travelers flowing through the station. Gambling with their lives. Their futures. For what?

Justice?

"When I was a young man," the imam went on after a long pause, "perhaps not much younger than Aydin—my father had a dog that he took with him into the mountains to help herd the sheep. He was one of the ugliest beasts I had ever seen, but a good and faithful animal."

A man jostled into his arm as he moved past on his way toward the bus, pulling a carry-on—and Harry felt himself react instinctively, his free hand falling toward his waistband, his eyes searching the man's face for any sign of a threat. *Nothing.*

"But one night—my father never knew why—that dog attacked the flock. Somehow, somewhere he had grown to a taste for blood. It has been over fifty years since that night, and I can still see the gore dripping from his maw—the mauled body of the sheep lying there dead on the side of the mountain. After that. . .well, my father was left with no choice."

The moral of the old man's story couldn't have been more clear. Once a dog crossed over that line between protector and predator, he had to be put down.

There was no help for it. And the same held true for people, too.

Aydin.

"I remember the sorrow in my father's eyes," Besimi went on earnestly, "as he loaded that old Mosin and went out into the night. But he did what *had* to be done. And so will you."

Harry nodded, his eyes still searching the crowd of people ahead. "Let's just pray it doesn't come to that."

"*Insh'allah.*"

6:32 A.M.
The offices of the UK Daily Standard
London

The city lights were going out one by one, replaced by the gathering light of the rising sun streaming over the Thames as Arthur Colville stood on the roof of the office building—looking out over the city that he had called home for so long.

Centuries of English history spread out before his eyes, hidden only by a cloak of fast-fading darkness.

He could remember first visiting the city as a schoolboy—standing there in Trafalgar Square gazing up at Nelson's Column with eyes full of wonder as his father recounted the story of England's one-eyed hero.

The four facing reliefs depicting the admiral's victories, themselves cast from the melted-down bronze of captured French cannon. *That* was victory.

He shook his head as the burner phone in his hand vibrated with the call he had been expecting. *One more time.*

"I trust you've called to report success?" he asked, unlocking the phone with a flick of his thumb across the screen.

"I have," replied the voice of his man inside the Security Service. "Marsh is convinced that the Sword landed at Heathrow four hours ago. They'll have resources tied down for days—chasing a phantom. And you're now free to proceed."

Colville smiled to himself. The man had been part of his inner circle almost since the beginning of this, and even he did not know the plan in its entirety. "And our stand-in?"

"Is staying at a hostel in South London. No one from Five is going to find him there. He's being paid good money to stay in his room and watch the telly."

While the world burns around him. It was hard to find fault with the ambivalence of a foreigner—so many of his fellow Englishmen were no better.

"Make sure they don't. And stay close to Marsh. We underestimate him at our peril." *Marsh*. Given the choice, he would have far rather had the old Cold War warrior as an ally than an enemy, but that was not the hand Fate had dealt them.

The publisher ended the call without waiting for a response and strode to the edge of the roof, standing there with his hands resting on the parapet as he stared down at the city below.

He had walked hand-in-hand with his father through the streets—riding high in the open top of a double-decker bus as he heard of how many times through history this city had been destroyed, only to rise once more. The inferno of 1666. . .the German Blitz.

And each time London had passed through the fire, she had risen from the ashes, a phoenix reborn.

Purified. Her dross purged away.

Colville turned over the burner in his hands and pried open the back, extracting the SIM card and the battery and returning both to his pocket. He hesitated for only a moment before tossing what remained of the phone over the parapet, leaving it to fall fifty stories to the streets below as he turned away, heading back toward the stairwell that led from the roof.

Seven long decades had come and gone since the Blitz. Time once more for this city to be baptized in flame. . .

6:37 A.M.
Leeds City Bus Station
Leeds, North Yorkshire

"No. 19 now boarding for Victoria Station, departing in three minutes."

Three minutes. And no sign of Aydin, Harry thought—glancing down once more at the photo of the boy displayed on his phone's screen. His head coming up once more to scan the crowd. The imam stayed behind him as he moved, just a few paces away. And he could see the same questions in his eyes.

Perhaps they had the wrong bus? Perhaps he had bought a ticket for another line after seeing al-Kutobi gunned down?

Questions without answers. . .that seemed to be all he had these days. The price one paid for being out in the cold, operating without a network. Without sanction.

Without backup. After fifteen years in the Agency, he knew just how wrong the intel could be when you had all the support structure in the world.

But without it—it felt like crossing a chasm on a thin wire. Just putting one foot in front of the next, ever groping for the next step. *Never look down.*

And then he saw him—just passing the ticket counter, the hood of his grey jacket pulled forward, but his face clearly visible as he moved. Hands shoved into the jacket's pockets. *A detonator?*

He keyed his earpiece, his right hand falling to his waist as he began to make his way through the press of travelers, elbowing one man aside. "Mehreen, I need your twenty."

Silence. A cold chill ran through his body, his mind refusing to even consider the possibility. His head coming up to once more search the crowd. *No.* "Mehreen, do you copy?"

Still nothing. It was as though she had dropped off the grid completely. And there was no time to look for her, not until they had secured the suicide vest. Strange, but that was how he thought of it. Not a boy, but a vest. *Depersonalize. Prioritize.*

He turned to look back toward Aydin, now only feet away from boarding the coach bus—and that was when he saw her, pushing her own way through the crowd on an interception course.

The situation crystallized for him in that moment—her intentions becoming only too clear. "Stand down, Mehreen. I say again, *stand down.*"

Too late. He saw the flash of recognition in Aydin's eyes at the sight of his aunt, the fear. *Fight or flight*, conflicting emotions warring within the boy's mind.

And he was too far away to intervene, his hand resting on the butt of the Sig-Sauer within his jacket—but he didn't have a clear shot. Any shot at all, really.

A small form bumped into his leg and he glanced down reflexively, the wide blue eyes of a little girl staring back into his. An almost surreal innocence reflected in their depths.

If that s-vest was triggered. . .he didn't even need to finish the thought. He had seen the bodies of mangled children before—watched helplessly as they died.

His head came up, taking in briefly the sight of the girl's mother—distracted on her mobile. Oblivious to the danger so close at hand.

As were they all.

He pushed past the two of them, circling to avoid detection—his eyes fixed on the spot where Aydin was still standing, seemingly rooted in place. His weapon free from its holster, trying to get an angle. A shot.

The boy broke just then, running for the back of the station like a frightened deer. *Flight.*

A shot impossible in that moment. Harry jammed the Sig-Sauer back into its shoulder holster and launched himself after him, hearing curses explode from a bystander as he elbowed the man out of his way, nearly knocking a woman to the floor as he rounded the front of the coach—glimpsing the grey hoodie flying in front of him, perhaps just ten feet ahead.

Let him reach the door, he thought, struggling against the anger surging within him. Mehr had blown everything by not staying on comms—by trying to go it alone. *Talk* him down.

Now the last thing they needed was to corner him in the crowded station. He heard a woman shouting behind him, thought he recognized Mehreen's voice—but there was no time to stop, to slow down.

Harry hit the door of the station just a few paces behind Aydin, slamming it open as they raced out into the open, the boy's form disappearing behind a parked bus. *Don't lose him.*

He'd already gotten away from them once. They weren't going to get a third chance.

6:43 A.M.
The MV Percy Phillips
Grimbsy Harbor, Lincolnshire

"Four hundred and twenty-eight meters," Paul Gordon observed, feeling Hale's eyes on him as he noted the distance marked on the terrain map spread out on the table in the bridge of the motor vessel. *A heavily wooded slope. A river on the east, curving around to the north.*

An open area with buildings and a road in between. He didn't recognize the area, and suspected that he wasn't meant to. "Looks like it will be a relatively simple shot—what need do you have of me?"

"Insurance," the former SAS man replied simply. "We both take the shot simultaneously, positioned on a line about fifty meters apart. If one of us doesn't hit his mark, the other will."

"Fair enough." It *was* a simple shot—or would be for someone who had handled a long gun more recently than Iraq. He hadn't. "And our target?"

Hale held his gaze for a long moment, eyes boring into his own—not responding, just looking at him. Finally, "It's natural that you'd ask, mate. And you wouldn't be standing here if I didn't trust you."

"You said we were going to take the fight to them—and no politician was going to stand in our way this time. What is this," Gordon asked, indicating the building markers on the terrain map, "some sort of training camp?"

"Not exactly."

6:46 A.M.
Leeds, North Yorkshire

Fired up, feels good. Harry's feet slammed rhythmically into the pavement as he ran through the carpark, trying to ignore the exhaustion—the pain still pulsating through his weakened ankle.

He could hear Aydin ahead of him, breathing heavily as he vaulted over the hood of a parked Nissan—heading for an alley between two towering brick buildings of the type that characterized the center of Leeds. He might have been two decades younger, but youth had its limits and the boy had already hit the wall.

This wasn't a videogame. And it wasn't Harry's first foot chase.

The buildings above cast strange shadows in the morning sun down upon the runners as they entered the alley, never slackening their pace. He didn't know if Mehreen or Ismail were behind him—whether they had been able to follow him from the station.

Or whether this was where it was all going to end, here in this alley. All alone.

It had to end soon—he could feel himself tiring, his breath coming quicker as he ran, his body protesting against the demands he continued to pile upon it.

And then he saw it, before Aydin did—perhaps ten meters farther on, the alley widening out into a vacant lot. . .backed by a chain-link fence perhaps eight feet high.

Dead end.

Harry dropped to one knee in the gravel and drew the Sig-Sauer from within his jacket, his heart still racing with adrenaline as he struggled to catch his breath. Never taking his eyes off Aydin.

Stay alert. A dangerous animal was never more so than when you had successfully run it to ground.

He heard a string of curses break from Aydin's lips as the boy saw the fence—only then realizing that he was cornered. Turning to face his adversary, his back to the wall.

"Don't come near me," he screamed, unzipping his jacket as Harry staggered to his feet—the bomb vest just visible in the dim light of the dawn. "Not another step or I blow us both up—I'm not joking, man. I'll do it, I'll bloody do it."

6:48 A.M.
Thames House, London

"North Yorkshire has the Audi," Norris said, appearing in the door of MacCallum's office. "Located it two kilometers from the city centre."

"And?"

"They're trying to isolate prints—match what they can against the legitimate owners and then work from there. Also, they found a loaded assault rifle in the boot—wrapped in cloth along with three spare magazines. It's a Kalashnikov."

"Good God," the section chief shook his head. "Do we have *anything* on where the driver or drivers could be?"

"They've begun conducting a sweep of the area—based on traffic cameras, the Audi can't have been parked there more than two hours ago."

"Keep me apprised."

6:49 A.M.
Leeds, North Yorkshire

"No, you won't," Harry replied, advancing slowly as he stared at the boy through the iron sights of the Sig. Seeing the detonator clutched in Aydin's sweaty, trembling left hand.

He was in the blast radius, he knew that. He also knew his terrorists. "If you really wanted to blow yourself up," he continued, his tone even, almost conversational, "you would have done it back in the station. So close to your target, surrounded by dozens of the *kaffir*. Out in a blaze of glory—fulfilling God's will just as Rahman told you. But you didn't, did you?"

An anguished sob escaped the boy's lips as he shrank back against the rough chain-link of the fence. "Stay away from me."

"You lost your nerve, Aydin. That's all there is to it. It's why you didn't press that detonator back in City Station, and it's why you won't do it now."

Watch the eyes, not the hands. The eyes always gave the game away, signaled what was to come.

"I will if you come any closer—I swear to God, I will!" Fear was a weapon, but one to be wielded carefully. It wasn't altogether unlike talking down a bridge-jumper, but a *shahid* had been convinced that death was *desirable*. All that remained was to play upon what every man *did* fear.

"Men do not fear death, only the thought of death", as Seneca had put it millennia ago.

"Have you ever seen what happens when one of those vests is triggered?" Harry asked, pressing his advantage. His words slow and deliberate. "I have. It isn't like they show you on all those martyrdom videos—a quick flash of light and it's all over. Neat. Clean. Nothing like that. The bomb shreds you into raw, screaming meat, takes your head right off your torso like it was done with a sword. You don't want to die that way."

Another stifled sob as the boy looked away, the desperation only too visible in his eyes. "Give me the detonator, Aydin," Harry said—taking his support hand away from the Sig and extending it toward him. "Just give it here, and this can all be over."

6:51 A.M.
Thames House
London

They were being overwhelmed, MacCallum thought—casting a critical eye toward the crisis point map displayed on one wall of the Centre. Slowly but surely.

Drowning in noise.

"I need to show you something," Norris announced, hailing him as he passed the analyst's workstation.

He gestured to the screen of his unclass computer as MacCallum leaned in, taking in the assortment of windowed webpages. "What am I looking at?"

"We've been monitoring Twitter traffic out of Leeds ever since the riots began. Looking for patterns, coordination. . .it's all open-source. Ten minutes ago, we started getting a bunch of tweets from the area immediately surrounding the bus station. Reporting some sort of disturbance—to be honest, none of them are overly cogent. Bleedin' chavs."

Not far from where the Audi was found, MacCallum thought—making the connection instantly. "Get local police on the phone, make sure they devote resources to the area. And CCTV from within the station when you can."

"Already sent in the request—I'll get on North Yorkshire."

Another analyst came hurrying across the floor in that moment, making straight for MacCallum.

"We just got this in from Leeds," he said, handing over a print-out of a surveillance camera image. "It's Tarik Abdul Muhammad. Last night, he checked into the Queens Hotel in City Square. Along with this woman. We've not been able to ID her as of yet. Possibly a working woman."

A prostitute. *Got you,* MacCallum thought, looking at the grainy image of the terrorist. Every man had his weaknesses. "Is he still there in the hotel?"

The analyst shook his head. "No visual confirmation at this point."

"Have Darren get a team over there at once and alert CO-19," MacCallum ordered. They couldn't risk losing him again, not with so much at stake. "Where's Marsh?"

"On his way to meet with the Home Secretary. He's to brief her prior to her meeting with the PM later this morning."

"Make sure they're both informed—we'll need her to sign off on any direct action." He paused, struck by a sudden thought. "How far is the Queens from City Bus Station?"

"Not much over a kilometer." The analyst shook his head, seeming baffled. "Why?"

6:52 A.M.
Leeds, North Yorkshire

There was hesitation there, a flicker of surrender. And then Harry heard a shout from the alley behind him. "Aydin!"

Mehreen. Aydin's head jerking up at the sound of her voice.

"Stay back," he warned her, his voice sharp as a knife's edge—but the damage was already done, all the boy's defiance rushing back in the space of a moment.

"Aydin, how can you *do* this?" she cried out, her voice torn with agony. "To your family, to your *faith*. I spoke with your mother yesterday, her heart would break if she knew that—"

"And what do you know of family, *kaffir*?" the boy hissed, his face glistening with perspiration as he leaned forward, spitting on the ground toward his aunt. "How can you call yourself a Muslim and work with. . .*them*?"

He was on a dangerous edge, Harry thought, watching him carefully. Caught between his fears and his pride—now brought to the fore in the presence of a woman.

And they were losing control of the situation.

He caught Mehreen's eye just as she began to respond, motioning for her to remain silent. "If you are truly a follower of the Prophet," he began, looking the boy in the face, "then you know that declaring *takfir* on a fellow Muslim is a prerogative reserved to the *ulema*. To make an accusation like this without such authority is to tread on dangerous ground."

Aydin shook his head, the knuckles of his hand whitening around the detonator. "You're an infidel yourself—you know *nothing* of my faith."

"Not an infidel," Harry corrected him, "but a follower of Jesus. One of the 'people of the Book', as your Qur'an so clearly states. Tell me. . .what reward awaits he who has slain the faithful?"

The wail of emergency sirens could be heard in the distance in that moment, before Aydin could respond. *Had the alarm been raised back at the bus station?* There was no way to know, no time to find out.

"*No*," the boy breathed desperately, the word sounding more like an anguished plea than anything else. On the brink.

He lifted his tear-stained face, glancing wildly back and forth between Harry and Mehreen. "I told you I wasn't bloody joking around—I will *do* this if you try to take me."

Take the shot. Harry's finger curled around the Sig's trigger, taking up the slack. *The eyes.*

"Don't do it," came Ismail's voice from behind him and Harry glanced back to see the imam standing there, breathing heavily from his exertion.

"But you said—"

"I know," the old man said, holding up a hand as if to cut him off. "But 'whoever saves one'. . ."

"'It is as if he had saved mankind entirely'," Harry quoted, finishing the verse. A difficult truth.

Ismail nodded. "Please, give me the chance to talk with him."

6:54 A.M.
The Queens Hotel
Leeds

"What were you possibly *thinking?*" were the first words Tarik Abdul Muhammad heard as he answered his mobile.

He didn't recognize the voice.

"Who is this?" he demanded, throwing the covers aside and rising from the bed. He knew better than to stay on the call. . .and yet.

"A friend, that's all you need to know—the friend who helped you when you first came to the city."

The railroad station. And it all came flashing back, the text messages—coming out of nowhere. Guiding him out from under the Security Service's surveillance and to Colville.

"The woman—where is she?" the voice asked, pressing on without a pause.

They knew. "She—she's gone. I paid her and she left." There was a long silence and for a moment Tarik thought the line had gone dead.

"And you need to as well—don't leave through the lobby. Five just found out you're there. Picked you up on CCTV."

Ya Allah. He reached for his pants, pulling them on hastily as he cradled the phone against his shoulder. "How long do I have?"

"Eight, ten minutes. No more."

6:55 A.M.
Leeds

"I need you to lower your weapon," Ismail said, placing a hand on Harry's shoulder as he moved past him toward the boy. He met Harry's eyes, clearly seeing the doubt written there, and squeezed his shoulder, adding, "Please...grant me this."

De-escalate. It was a strategy not without merit, but one which held its own dangers.

"Give him a chance, Harry." He looked over to see Mehreen standing there, her eyes pleading with him.

Mercy. Justice. Weighed in the balances, and found wanting. He had never warmed to the roles of judge, jury, and executioner. As many times as he had assumed them.

"If I do," he said slowly, returning his focus to the imam—his voice low and terse, "I won't be able to protect you."

Besimi smiled, peace seeming to settle over his countenance. "I seek refuge in God from Satan the accursed...if He chooses not to protect me, neither will your skill."

Fair enough. The old man had guts, that was undeniable, Harry thought, carefully lowering the Sig-Sauer until it rested at his side.

Fearless, even—but if something went wrong, his life wasn't the only one on the line. All of them were going to die.

The minimum evacuation distance protocol dictated with an s-vest was thirty-four meters, a number seared into his memory from years of hard-earned knowledge.

They couldn't have been more than ten.

"Look at me," the imam said, speaking softly as he advanced toward Aydin. "The words this man has spoken to you, they are truth. You are very young, and I pray that God, *subhanahu wa' ta'ala*, may even yet reward your zeal—but you have strayed far from His paths."

"That's a lie, all of it is *lies*," the boy spat angrily. "You've taken for friends the enemies of God."

Besimi shook his head, moving closer. *Steady now*, Harry thought, his body tensing involuntarily. *Tread carefully.*

"Is that what they have been teaching you, my son, distorting the words of the Prophet to serve their own ends?"

6:56 A.M.
M.I.-5 Regional Office

If he hadn't known better, he might have thought the Americans had them all bugged, Darren thought—favoring Parker with a skeptical glance. Perhaps he *didn't* know better.

That or the CIA operations officer was just an exceedingly light sleeper.

"We just got the red-flash from Thames House a few minutes ago—they've tracked the *Shaikh* to a hotel in City Centre," Roth said, grimacing as he inserted his earpiece. "If we're lucky, we'll be able to re-establish surveillance on him there."

"Re-establish surveillance?" Parker asked, an incredulous look playing across his face. "Your country is on fire, the level of civil unrest you're seeing between the far right and the Muslim community is unsustainable. Someone like the *Shaikh*—you know he has to be stoking the flames from behind the scenes. We both know that."

"We do," Roth replied, briefly testing his comms unit before shrugging on his jacket. They were short on time. "But you and I, we don't make policy. We execute it."

The American smiled. "Ours not to reason why. Mind if I join you for the ride-along?"

6:57 A.M.

No, Aydin breathed, his heart pounding against his chest as though it threatened to break free. Hugging both arms close to his body, desperation threatening to consume him. It wasn't supposed to end like *this*.

He looked up into the bearded face of the aged man, standing there now only feet away, the small *kufi* resting atop his white hair. The face of a man who had been a part of his life. . .for as long as he could remember.

But now he was one of them. "The Prophet himself," the imam went on soberly, "peace be upon him, warned that such would come—dividing the *ummah*, setting brother against brother. Son, against father. They recite the Noble Qur'an, but alas, it does not pass their throat. In the day of reckoning, they will rise with the *Dajjal*."

The false messiah.

The old man moved closer, placing his right hand on Aydin's trembling shoulder. Extending his left toward the boy. "Just give me the detonator—you don't want to die this way. Taking your own life and those of your fellow believers."

He closed his eyes, fighting against the emotion that surged over him. It was so *tempting*, so seductive.

He could put all of this behind him, go back to life as it had been—go back to his family, his parents. . .no. *Never.*

The fingers of his right hand closed around the butt of the small semiautomatic within his jacket, the touch of the metal reminding him of his purpose.

Follow the green birds.

The pistol came back out in his hand, its muzzle swinging inexorably toward the old man—his finger tightening around the trigger.

A moment later, a pair of shots shattered the dawn.

6:58 A.M.
The MV Percy Phillips
Grimsby Harbor

The Queen. The success of his mission—his very *life* depended on falling in line with Hale's plan, but now that it was unveiled, he couldn't begin to suppress his reaction.

"Are you bloody serious? We swore a sodding *oath*, mate," Gordon said, shaking his head as he stared across the ship's small wardroom at the former sergeant. "Do you need me to be repeatin' it to you? 'I swear by Almighty God that I will be faithful and bear *true* allegiance to Her Majesty—'"

Hale held up a hand to cut him off, but there were no traces of anger. Instead, he was smiling. "I remember it well, and I'm glad to hear it from your lips. Had your reaction been otherwise. . .I would have feared you were trying to play me, brother."

It was a test. Only a test. Gordon could feel himself relax, the shock beginning to fade away. Only to return with Hale's next words.

"It was *my* reaction when the plan was first proposed to me, over a year ago. But with all I have seen of the fall of this country, I have come to believe that it is *necessary*. Not that the Queen should lose her life, but that she be put at *risk* of losing it. At the hands of those who would be the death of us all."

7:00 A.M.
Leeds, North Yorkshire

No! Harry heard the shots—their echo ringing again and again off the canyon of buildings surrounding them. *A death knell.*

Time itself seemed to slow down, every movement sluggish, but revealed in startling clarity. He heard Mehreen scream, saw the imam stagger back, then go down. Crumpling into the muddy gravel of the vacant lot. *Gun.*

His own weapon coming up instinctively, his left hand moving to support it. Aydin's face coming into focus through the iron sights of the Sig-Sauer. *Target.*

There was no hesitation, no time for thought. Training taking over. The trigger broke under his finger, a small red hole appearing in the middle of the target's forehead as the pistol recoiled into Harry's hands.

The boy's head snapped back, his legs going out from under him as Harry put two more rounds in his upper chest. *Target down.*

It was only then, as Aydin's body collapsed into the dirt like a broken doll—the detonator falling from his nerveless fingers—that everything snapped back into focus. Time breaking from its ennui.

Harry stalked forward, the pistol still clenched in his right hand, until he stood over the corpse—looking down into those young eyes, now staring sightlessly up at the sky.

Threat eliminated.

A human life reduced, in those final moments, to a target with a gun. And a detonator. Put down like a rabid dog.

He glimpsed Mehreen's face as she pushed past him, dropping to her knees beside her nephew's body.

Heard her keening wail of anguish, such a familiar sound. Agonizing, unearthly. He'd heard it far too many times in his years across the Middle East.

Been the *cause* of it, far too many times.

Ismail Besimi lay a few feet away, his leg twisted beneath him—his breathing heavy and labored. His crisp white shirt sodden red with blood. His eyes beginning to glaze over, death waiting in the wings.

"Just hang in there," he whispered, kneeling over the old man, clasping his limp right hand in both of his. "We're going to get you help—you're going to pull through this."

It was a lie, and they both knew it. He was far past any help. The imam coughed, blood flecking his beard as he struggled to speak. "Don't risk. . .yourself, my son. It's too late f-for that."

Logic told him the old man was right, but everything in him warred against the decision. Logic could be such a liar. "I'm sorry."

Survivor's guilt. His turn, by now long overdue and nowhere in sight.

Besimi grimaced, suppressing another cough with a mighty effort. "Don't be—death is something that comes for every man. And it has found me as I lived, in the service of my God. I am ready to face the Questioners."

Munkar and Nakir. Angels who came to test the faith of the dead. *"Who is your Lord? Who is your Prophet? What is your religion?"*

Harry started to respond, but the old man cut him off. "Your sorrow—save it for Aydin. Mourn a life lost before it could begin. A life *stolen*."

His left hand came up, seizing Harry's wrist with what remained of his ebbing strength. His eyes shining with a peculiar intensity. "You were right, after all—and I wrong. The wolves have preyed upon my people for *far* too long. The time has come. . .for a hunter. Pr-promise me you won't fail."

He looked down, feeling the anger burn within him as he watched the old man's life slip away, his hand falling from Harry's arm. "I promise."

7:03 A.M.
The Home Office
2 Marsham Street, London

"You're asking that I give you authorization to bring him in." The Home Secretary stopped pacing behind her desk for a moment, staring across to where Marsh sat.

"Precisely," the DG replied, adjusting his suit as he sat there—watching her closely. In all the years he had known her, decisiveness never had been Napier's strong suit. She had risen to the top by carefully gauging the political winds, ever making sure they were in her favor.

But which way do you tack when *no* wind is favorable?

That was the one question no politician ever wanted to face. . .and also the one that he faced on a daily basis at Thames House.

"The political climate has only worsened since we last spoke of this, Julian," she began, seeming to measure her words with the most extreme of care. "The bombing at Madina, the rioting that has followed all across the UK—it took many previously available options off the table."

"The flames of which the *Shaikh* has almost certainly had a hand in fanning," Marsh observed coolly.

She turned back to look at him. "'Almost certainly' isn't something I can take to the PM."

7:05 A.M.
Leeds, North Yorkshire

No. Harry shook his head, gazing down into the lifeless eyes of the imam. His broken body sprawled in the muddy gravel, his blood mingling with the rainwater. It had happened once more, despite all his efforts. Despite *everything*. In a world full of evil, the good were ever taken first. Leaving behind those. . .far less worthy. *Like himself.*

"*Jazak'allah khair,*" he whispered in Arabic, reaching up to brush his hand across Ismail's leathery face, closing those unseeing eyes for one final time. That most futile of prayers. *May God reward you goodness.*

He rose to his feet, hearing once more the sound of approaching sirens. His face hardening into an implacable mask. There was no more time for any of this. He had been keeping to the backbeat ever since he had arrived in the UK.

Watching, waiting. *Reacting.*

No more. It was time to cut off the head of the snake. He walked over to where Mehreen still knelt, cradling Aydin's shattered head against her chest—his blood staining her hands. Her clothes.

She was staring off into the distance past the chain-link—a vacant look he knew all too well. Her dark cheeks wet with tears.

"It's time we were going." He knew how the words sounded, but he was too far gone to recall them. The anger welling up within him seeking a target.

Any target.

"That's how it is for you, isn't it?" She asked after a moment, her voice sharp. Brittle as ice. "He meant nothing to you. . .did he? Just another pawn in your *bloody* great game. A piece to be played. Like you have me. Tell me, did your 'friendship' with Nick mean anything to you—or was he just a piece too?"

Enough. Her words a knife, stabbing deep into his heart. Again and again.

She shook her head when he failed to respond, rising to her feet as he took a step away, unscrewing the suppressor from the Sig's muzzle and tucking the long black cylinder into an inner pocket of his jacket. "Is it even possible for someone to be more to you than that? Are you even *capable* of such a thing?"

"*Stop it.*"

"You just turn your back and walk away from everything you've done—the lives you've destroyed," she continued, her eyes shining with tears. "As if they never existed, as if they weren't even real. Aydin was *real*, and now he's dead. Because you killed him. You have to face that."

"You want to know who killed your nephew?" Harry demanded, almost spitting the words out as he wheeled to face her—his face dark with barely-restrained fury. "*You* did—the moment you made the decision to go cowboy at the station. We had a plan that might—just *might*—have kept things from going sideways, but you knew better, didn't you? And he was dead from that moment on."

She just stood there, seemingly stunned into silence as he stooped down, pushing aside the folds of Aydin's hoodie and fumbling for the straps securing the suicide vest to his young body.

It was a moment before they pulled free, and then he brusquely pushed the boy's limp, lifeless arms away, stripping him of the lethal garment. "What are you doing?"

He straightened, vest in hand, his face hard as he stared into her eyes. "Something that should have been done a long time ago."

Chapter 22

7:14 A.M.
The Home Office
2 Marsham Street, London

The phone vibrated within the inner pocket of Marsh's suit for the second time, but he ignored it, his attention focused on Kathleen Napier.

"I can offer my recommendations to the PM, Julian," she said, spreading her hands as she turned to face him. "That's really all I can do."

And that was a lie, he thought, his face neutral. She had the capacity to authorize the *Shaikh*'s detention on her own, but not the will. Ever seeking cover. Paralyzed in the face of hard choices.

He inclined his head to one side, smiling tightly as he rose, buttoning his suit jacket. "Thank you, Home Secretary," he said, reaching out to take her extended hand. "Your support is. . .ever appreciated."

Her hand grasped his with all the warmth of a dead fish, her best politician's smile plastered to her face. "And I trust you know that you will always have it—to the extent that I am able."

She had mastered the art of the caveat long ago.

"Of course." He too could play the politician, when necessary. "I will keep you apprised of developments."

The DG didn't touch his phone until he was well away from Napier's office—moving down the broad corridor Home Office natives referred to as "the Street", the morning rays of sun shining down on him through the colored glass above his head.

Two missed calls. He sighed heavily, punching the call-back button and listening to it ring. "Talk to me, Darren. What is your status on the *Shaikh*?"

It was a moment before his field officer's voice came on the line. "He's not here."

7:16 A.M.
The MV Percy Phillips
Grimsby Harbor

"You're right," Gordon said slowly, looking over to where Hale sat, the field-stripped L42A1 laid out before him as he pushed a rod down the barrel, a still-white cleaning patch emerging from the breech. A single brass 7.62x51mm NATO cartridge stood upright beside the sniper rifle's bolt. "Everything with Alice—I suppose I just haven't been able to wrap my head around all of it. That it's really come to this."

That you would ask me to betray my country, he thought but didn't say.

It was a moment before his old comrade looked up from the gun. "But it has. . .look, mate, I don't blame you for your reaction to what I've asked of you. If I had told myself this five years ago, I would ha' sworn I was taking the piss. But our country has fallen a long way in five years."

That it had. He couldn't have argued with that, even if he had wanted to. But facilitating a terrorist attack like this, even if the Queen's life was to be spared by dint of their own marksmanship in the end—it was unspeakable. The lives that would be lost before this was all over.

"And they're doin' sod-all to stop it," Hale continued, shaking his head. "From the Queen to the PM, all the way down. Not a thing. Cowards, the lot of them, holed up in their bloody halls of power, trembling and hoping the hajjis come for them last. They fill the moat of the Tower of London with red poppies, speak of the 'brave soldiers' who have 'defended the realm'—but all they have for us is words. And that leaves us to save what we can. As ever before."

He paused. "I wouldn't have asked this of you, Paul, if I thought I couldn't trust you. Or if I didn't *need* you. I have a lot of good lads. Most of them infantry, precious few marksmen among that lot."

Gordon laughed despite himself. Despite the fear clawing at his heart. The Army's standard-issue rifle—the "Politician", as British soldiers had once derisively dubbed the SA80 bullpup—was hardly a tool that lent itself to the skillset of a sniper.

"And I'm not going to be lyin' to you. This is like to be a one-way trip. The odds of us coming out of those woods any other way than in a body bag—or a lorry headed to Paddington Green. . .they're not ones I'd take to Monte Carlo.

But I need to know, Paul—more than I've ever needed to know anything in my life—are you with me?"

"Yes. *Yes...I am.*"

7:57 A.M.
Leeds City Station

So this is how it will go, Harry thought—his own reflection staring back at him from the men's room mirror. Hard eyes the color of gunmetal, anger simmering just barely concealed beneath the surface.

Alone. He wasn't, really—the sound a toilet being flushed behind him reminding him of that reality. The distant sound of the PA system announcing departing trains from the platform without. But in terms of his mission, he had never been farther out in the cold.

On his own.

The past two hours bearing stark testament to just how badly that could go wrong. *Let me count the ways.*

He thrust his hands beneath the faucet and felt the warm water cascade over them, scrubbing away Ismail Besimi's dried blood.

"You just turn your back and walk away." He closed his eyes, trying and failing to shut out Mehreen's reproach.

He'd found the Audi swarmed by constables when he tried to return to it—a part of him hoped that she had known enough to stay away.

The other part no longer cared. *Walk away.*

The dangerous part was he had known better, allowed his exhaustion to override his judgment. Stolen vehicles had a shelf life—and they had pushed the Audi far past the limit. Which meant the authorities might well have been able to trace their steps farther back than he was comfortable with.

He needed sleep. He needed a plan.

And he needed the means to execute it, he realized—pushing his way into an empty stall and latching it as he leaned back against the partition, dropping the new duffel bag containing Aydin's vest—its remote detonator now safely deactivated—onto the tile of the floor and unzipping his jacket.

The Sig-Sauer came out in his hand, his thumb hitting the magazine release. Only six rounds left.

Not nearly enough.

From without, he could hear the faint voice of the PA system, calmly announcing, "The next train at Platform 8 is the 08:05 East Coast Service to London Kings Cross, calling at Wakefield Westgate, Doncaster. . ."

Three minutes left.

It was time to regroup.

8:19 A.M.
Thames House
London

"The *Shaikh*. What can you give me?" Marsh asked, coming back through the doors of the Centre.

MacCallum shook his head. "I have Kirkpatrick running CCTV on City Square and the surrounding area—she has nothing yet. Room service was requested thirty minutes before Roth and his team arrived on-site. By the time it was delivered, the room was empty."

The eternal danger of playing defense. *Reacting.* The director-general's eyes narrowed. "So you're telling me he was warned?"

"There's currently no evidence to reach that conclusion," the section chief replied. The DG found himself smiling despite their circumstances. . .the Scotsman was ever the analyst. Never willing to overreach beyond what could be directly inferred from available intel.

It was a valuable, if at times frustrating, trait. "And we have another problem," MacCallum went on, pulling a picture from one of the folders in his hand. The stripped upper torso of an old man, lying flat under bright lights, his eyes closed. "Just before seven, North Yorkshire had a report of shots fired less than a mile from the hotel. Responding constables found two bodies, both dead of gunshot wounds. Casings from at least two different handguns."

"But this is—"

A curt nod. "Ismail Besimi."

Marsh shook his head in disbelief, staring at the man's body. "What was he doing there?"

"We don't know. The other body," the section chief said, pulling another photo from the folder, "was that of a young male, Asian—maybe 15-16. Too young for a licence. . .no other forms of ID found on him either, just a few pound notes and a ticket for National Express from the City Centre Station, a bus which departed about twenty minutes prior for Victoria Station. We're still working to establish whether there's any connection to a reported disturbance this morning *at* the station."

Marsh nodded. "Good man—stay on it and let me know when you have something. And if anyone from the Home Office reaches out regarding the status of our operation with the *Shaikh*, stall them."

11:34 A.M.
The offices of the UK Daily Standard
Central London

"...are swelling the crowd of protesters—estimated by Metropolitan Police Commissioner Andrew Mayne-Thornton at five thousand—as the far-right British Defence Coalition prepares to march upon the Tower Hamlets at noon today. Also present, to counter the BDC, are members of United Against Racism..."

The Sky News television cameras instinctively panned to the figure of an overweight young college student standing in the middle of the street clad in only her underwear—what remained of her cropped hair dyed orange and spiked—rubbing a graffiti-desecrated flag of St. George provocatively across her bum.

The fall of the West. Summed up in a single image, Arthur Colville thought, turning his eyes away from the screen and checking his phone once more.

Nothing.

No messages, no news alerts. Nothing trending on social media. He checked his watch once more against his computer screen to make sure one of them wasn't wrong. The *Shaikh*'s bomber was to have struck Victoria Station by now.

The *coup de grace*, driving the Tower Hamlets march into the type of violence the police would be unable to contain—violence stoked by Hale's men in the crowd.

But everything depended upon that *bomb*.

11:41 A.M.
The Queens Hotel
Leeds, North Yorkshire

There was nothing like being a liaison officer to drive a man to drink, Thomas thought—eyeing Roth across the hotel suite. The Brits' operation was going sideways and there wasn't much he was even permitted to do about it.

The bed looked decidedly well-used and was no doubt a treasure trove of Tarik Abdul Muhammad's DNA, but that didn't solve any immediate problems.

Their dilemma wasn't identifying the man, but *finding* him. He stepped out into the hall, rubbing his forehead. The hotel bar was two floors down. Just a quick elevator ride away, a few short steps.

No, he shook his head. He'd been two days dry now, and found himself absurdly proud of such a small victory. *Don't blow it.*

He turned to go back into the room, nearly running into a hotel maid as she moved down the corridor, pushing her cart before her. "Please, sir. . .I am sorry," she exclaimed in broken English, a distinctively Slavic accent to her voice. *Russian?*

He started to turn away, then stopped, pulling his phone from his pocket and brushing his thumb across the screen until he brought up the picture of the prostitute who had accompanied the *Shaikh* into the hotel. "Excuse me," he began, holding the phone out toward the maid. "Do you know this woman?"

11:45 A.M.
Middleton Park, outskirts of Leeds
North Yorkshire

Mobile number out of service. Tarik Abdul Muhammad looked down at the phone in his hand, a chill pervading his body. He glanced across the green of the park, spotting a young boy playing football with his father. A woman walking a dog.

There had been no detonation at Victoria Station, he thought, checking the phone's browser once more. That much was certain.

The Jews might have had tight control over the world media, but there was no way even they could have prevented a bombing from leaking out onto the Internet.

And although the boy might have lost his courage, there was no way he possessed the skill to actually disarm the vest.

He could feel his heart begin to beat more rapidly, his eyes darting from one point of the park to the next. First the Security Service discovering his location at the hotel. . .now *this.*

Ya Allah. Taking one final look around, Tarik turned toward the woods, making his way hurriedly down one of the many trails. The phone seeming to burn a hole in his pocket.

Unable to escape the question repeating itself again and again in his mind: had it been a lie ever since the beginning? Was Arthur Colville setting them up?

12:38 P.M.
Thames House
London

The phone was still silent from the Home Secretary, Marsh thought—turning his attention briefly away from the ongoing television coverage of the march on Tower Hamlets, a haze of tear gas obscuring the cameras' view as protesters clashed with police on horseback.

No matter. She would be calling soon enough and he had nothing to give her. Politicians tended not to be accepting of reality.

A knock at the door of his office and he looked up to see McCallum standing in doorway. "I need you to take a look at something, sir. We have fresh intel on the boy."

"We confirmed his presence at the station off CCTV," the section chief said when Marsh joined him on the operations centre floor a few minutes later. "And this. . .was uploaded to an Islamic State-affiliated web forum just forty-five minutes ago."

His finger found the button of the remote and the video began to play, its shaky image showing a young man clad in a suicide vest standing before the black flag of jihad. His face easily recognizable, even through the low-resolution camera, as that of the teenager found in Leeds.

La illaha illa Allah, the DG mused ironically—recognizing the familiar lettering of the *shahada*. *There is no God but God*. But no. . .of course religion had nothing to do with this.

". . .message to the *kuffar* that as you bomb, so will you be bombed," the boy's voice continued, trembling with nerves. "As you kill, so will you be killed. Enough is enough. The seeds of war which you have sown in Palestine, in Iraq, in Syria, now bearing fruit in your own streets. In your own homes. . .where you have felt secure in defiance of God and His laws. Where—"

"So, we're dealing with the body of a martyr who didn't reach his target," Marsh observed dryly, raising his voice to talk over the audio. "Did they find a vest?"

The analyst shook his head. "No sign of one."

None of this made sense, but then again, when had it ever? Not since the end of the Cold War at least, when all the rules had come crashing down along with the Wall. The uncomfortable détente of superpowers replaced by the chaos of a world gone mad.

Once more unto the breach, dear friends, once more. Marsh grimaced, remembering only too well how that particular line of *Henry V* ended.

But the boy hadn't finished, his voice growing higher as he stared into the camera. ". . .who will say that I abandoned my family, but for years I hid my faith, tried to be 'normal'—and found only emptiness. Those who know me know that I have never been happier than I am now, more secure in the guarantee of *Jannah*. Truly was it said of the Prophet, every man will be with those he loves. My brothers are those who war in the cause of—"

"Look at this," Norris interrupted from several feet over, an unusual urgency in the analyst's voice. "The CCTV from Leeds Station. . .we've got a face."

"Who is it?" Marsh asked, circling around the workstation until he could see Norris' screen.

"Mehreen Crawford."

8:29 A.M. Eastern Time
Russell Senate Office Building
Washington, D.C.

The leadership, Coftey mused, casting a sidelong glance at his reflection in the mirror which hung on the far wall of his office. The early morning call from the Majority Whip hadn't come entirely as a surprise, but he hadn't expected it to be this soon.

Cahill was making his move. He paused, attempting to straighten his tie. That was the only explanation for it, the only thing that could necessitate such a meeting.

"Here, let me," Melody said, brushing his hands aside as she stepped in close, fussing with his collar. "You're nervous."

"Am I?" he smiled indulgently, the smell of her perfume filling his nostrils as he looked down at her. "I hadn't noticed."

"You are such a terrible liar," she whispered, suddenly pulling his tie tight. He winced, rubbing his throat.

"And you, well you're actually rather pretty when you're mad," he responded, his hand wrapping around the back of her neck and pulling her in for a fierce, passionate kiss. Her body soft and yielding against his.

She pulled away after a moment, doing her best to frown at him and failing. "Are you sure you want to be wearing my lipstick when you walk into Fuentes' office?"

"Why not?" he chuckled, turning for the door. "Might do the old girl some good."

"Roy," Katherine Fuentes greeted, not a trace of warmth to be found in her voice as she gestured toward the chair facing her desk, "sit down."

The Majority Whip didn't even look up at his entrance—as he took his seat. Just kept looking through the papers on her desk. Pausing at one point to adjust her glasses before continuing to read. A power play, as so much was with her. Making him wait.

Putting him in his place.

He smiled, leaning back in his chair as he waited silently for her to finish.

Southern charm might have kept him in office for over three decades, but it wasn't going to help him here. Not with her.

Fuentes had grown up in the barrios of Eastside Los Angeles, the daughter of an illegal immigrant mother and an absentee father who'd walked out of her life never to return when she was five.

She might have stayed there, found herself stuck behind the counter of a bodega—living from one paycheck to the next. More of a subsistence than a life. But Fuentes was nothing if not a fighter, and made of sterner stuff than her parents. She'd graduated from UC Berkely with a law degree at the age of twenty-seven and gone on to become a highly successful LA defense attorney before running for elected office, first in the California Assembly—then on the federal level, becoming the first Latina ever elected to the US Senate. And now, at the age of sixty-two, majority whip.

She hadn't made it this far by being the kind of woman you crossed.

"I'm going to get straight to the point, Roy," she said finally, closing the folder and looking up. Her eyes cold and hard as they met his. "It has come to the attention of leadership that you're lobbying hard against the NSA legislation, attempting to use your influence to sway other senators to vote 'no' on the Senate's version of the bill."

He shrugged, his eyes never leaving her face. "I don't think I've made any secret of my opposition."

"It needs to end," Fuentes replied, seeming to bristle at his tone. "Now. The moment you leave this room."

Coftey shook his head. "I'm sorry, but that's not going to happen."

She broke eye contact for a moment, flipping open a folder on the desk before her. "You have a bill coming to the floor next week, I believe. Further appropriations for disaster relief in Oklahoma in the wake of last fall's devastating tornadoes."

"That's correct," he replied, knowing all too well what was coming next. The way this game was played.

"You've been in the Senate a long time, Roy," she said, adjusting her glasses once more as she looked up. "And you've always been a team player. . .until now. We can make sure that there's more there than you asked for. You can be the hero again, just like you have been so many times over the years."

The carrot and the stick. Her unspoken alternative, so nakedly obvious.

He smiled, shaking his head. "Or else it will die an untimely death? I'm sorry, Katherine, but I'm not so easily bought. People where I come from? If the government won't help them, they'll help each other. They'll live."

"Perhaps I've failed to make myself completely clear," Fuentes said after a moment, clearing her throat. Her dark eyes meeting his in a steely, unwavering gaze. "The party is invested in the passage of this bill. You can either get onboard, or we will be finding a chairman who is."

2:04 P.M. Greenwich Mean Time
MI-5 Regional Office
Leeds, West Yorkshire

"She's known to the local police," a woman's voice announced and Roth looked up to see a middle-aged Security Service officer standing in the doorway. She walked forward, placing a folder on the desk he had commandeered upon his arrival in Leeds. "As might have been guessed, her name isn't 'Eve'. It's Sarah Russell, a twenty-five-year-old native of Kent. She was first picked up for solicitation as part of a sting operation in 2011—someone paid the fine and back she goes. Two more arrests since, both went exactly the same way."

It was a familiar story, Darren thought, idly opening the folder. Prostitution was legal in the UK—although not Northern Ireland as of recently—but soliciting for sex in a public place on the part of either prostitute or john was punishable by law. A piece of paper about the size of a brochure fell from the folder as he did so, landing face-down on the desk.

A "tart card", he realized, turning it over to find a voluptuous brunette staring back at him. *Not*, he suspected, Sarah Russell—if experience was to be any judge.

"They're up in phone booths all over the city," the woman added, a slight air of disapproval about her, as if she had read his thoughts.

That too, was common—however anachronistic it might have seemed these days. "The police. . .do they know how to find her?"

She nodded. "They're familiar with the areas she's known to frequent—particularly at night."

"Then have them pick her up." They were grasping at straws at this point, but this woman was better than nothing. And according to Parker, the *Shaikh* was known to have a weakness for prostitutes.

A bit of intel the Americans might have been better off sharing a month earlier, in Darren's opinion.

"On what charge?"

He waved a hand. "We're dealing with a known tart. Tell them to get creative."

5:45 P.M.
Thames House
London

Forty injured, a half dozen critically. That was the report out of Tower Hamlets in the wake of the afternoon's march.

MacCallum shook his head, looking at the screens displaying BBC, Sky News, CNN. . .in any normal week those casualties would have headlined every evening broadcast.

Now they were barely even granted a passing mention, brushed over in favor of the unfolding horror out of Birmingham—a young mother who had taken the wrong turn into the middle of a riot. She had been dragged out of her car and beaten to death before her six-year-old's eyes by what the BBC was euphemistically calling an "Asian street gang."

He was getting far too old for all of this.

"Look at this," came Norris' urgent voice from a few workstations over.

"What do you have?"

The analyst gestured excitedly toward his computer screen. "I was going over the tapes from the bus station again. . .once the commotion starts, there's a man who goes out the door right after the would-be bomber. As though he's in pursuit. So I went back to see if I could find him earlier."

"And?"

"And that man is all over that station in the hour leading up to the incident, once at Mehreen Crawford's side—and they appear to speak for a moment. But not once does the camera capture his face. Not even a decent profile shot."

"He's had training." That was the only reasonable conclusion you could draw from it. Any normal person would have been picked up a score of times in that window.

"He has," Norris responded, using his mouse to bring up another window beside the first, "and something about it all seemed very familiar—so I went back and grabbed the CCTV from the *Shaikh*'s disappearance on the Leeds train platform. Remember the man who was always just *there*—right at the edge of the screen whenever he had to be looking toward the cameras, out of focus. Never a clear shot of his face?"

"I do," MacCallum responded, feeling a cold fear begin to creep down his spine. The fear that he knew exactly where this was headed.

"I put the two CCTV feeds side by side and ran stride analytics on them. There's not much room for doubt—it's the same man."

"So you're saying. . ." *No. It wasn't possible.*

The analyst nodded grimly. "I'm saying that Mehreen Crawford knew the man at the station that day with Tarik Abdul Muhammad—was perhaps even working with him. And chose not to tell us. Which means we have to consider the possibility that—"

"That she was the one who blew the op," MacCallum finished for him, finding himself in disbelief. *Denial.* "Alerted the *Shaikh*. Deliberately. . .good God."

6:57 P.M.
Leeds Central Police Station
West Yorkshire

"No," Darren managed, finding his voice at last as he stared at the blank wall of his small office. Remembering the call from Mehreen, her insistence on obtaining the route information for Besimi's transport. "That's not possible."

"I found it hard to believe myself," came MacCallum's voice from the other end of the line at Thames House. "Mehreen has been more than a colleague, she's been a friend."

"You're not hearing me," Darren snapped back, anger boiling over. "I didn't say it was hard to believe—I said it wasn't sodding *true*. I served with Nick Crawford in Iraq, had him pull my arse out of the fire more than a time or two. If it wasn't for him, I might not be standing here today—least there'd be a lot less of me here. No way his wife is one of *them*."

And yet he could see the faces of the murdered constables who had made up Besimi's escort. Silent, haunting condemnation in their eyes.

My God, what have I done?

11:04 P.M.
Outside the Rahman residence
Leeds, North Yorkshire

"Lights just went off in the front room," Jan Traeg announced, monitoring the screens before her in the back of the surveillance van. "Looks like he's home to stay."

They should be so lucky, the American intelligence officer thought—massaging her neck gently with both hands. But they weren't. She was missing her daughter's anime convention for this. All because some madman wanted to set the world afire.

Then again. . .a wry grimace passed across her face, envisioning her husband amidst a sea of twenty thousand screaming teenage girls. Perhaps she *was* better off here.

"Dennis should be almost back by now, shouldn't he?" she asked her counterpart, glancing at the screen of her phone to confirm the time. The second British officer had gone out for a coffee run quite a while before.

"Nearly," the man replied, seeming unconcerned. "Pretty near time for check-in with McBrien's crew."

The other van was parked on a flanking street, watching the exit of an alley that stretched behind Rahman's flat, finally coming to a stop in a dead end behind the row of buildings.

"Echo 1," he began, picking up the radio, "calling Echo 2. How copy?"

"Loud and clear, Echo 1," a thick Cockney accent came back in reply. "All's quiet."

There were two vans, the watcher thought—aiming his binoculars through the Vauxhall's windshield. Unmarked, but clearly identifiable if you knew what you were looking for. Standard protocol for the Security Services on a surveillance op like this one.

Two vans, three officers in each. *Two*, he corrected himself, glancing back at the barely visible form of the British officer lying unconscious and bound in his backseat.

The van watching the front of the residence was now down a man.

He pushed open the driver's side door of the Vauxhall, his balaclava-masked face visible in the glow of the streetlight for only a moment before he raised a gloved hand from his side, casually putting a single bullet through the light.

Fiery sparks fell to the street, soon consumed in darkness as he moved around to the rear of the car, removing a messenger bag from the boot.

He took another look down the street toward the van as he unzipped the bag, his fingers closing around a metal cylinder. *Time to do this.*

11:09 P.M.

Boredom was the most formidable enemy you faced on any surveillance operation. It dulled the senses, took off the edge.

The only solution was to rotate personnel incessantly, Jan thought—scanning the screens once more in an effort to keep herself alert—but that was getting more difficult as time wore on. As the civil unrest in the UK continued to build.

Her counterpart's mobile rang suddenly, the noise unexpected and startling in the stillness of the van. She glanced over to see him checking the phone for a message. "It's Dennis," he said, reaching over to unlock the van's side door from the inside. "He's back."

The door slid to the side as Jan leaned back in her seat, stretching to keep her legs from falling asleep. The coffee would certainly help.

Her first indication that something was wrong was the metallic sound of something striking, then rolling across, the floor of the van. Accompanied by an ominous hiss. *Gas.*

It was a surreal feeling, the realization of being under attack. Something strangely disembodied about it all.

She could hear her voice screaming a warning, her eyes already watering as the CS gas began to tear at her throat, a cloud of it filling the van. *Fight or flight.*

They had no means for the former—she turned, unable to find the British officer amidst the smoke—desperately hoping to reach the open door. *To escape.*

Eyes burning, she staggered across the van just as the door slid shut, her fingers unable to find a purchase in the metal. *Weakening.*

It occurred to her far too late that their only hope was to reach the other van, her comms headset still on the ledge by her chair. *Abandoned.*

She turned back to get it only to find that she lacked the strength, her body convulsing into wracking coughs. Collapsing to the floor, nearly unable to breathe.

Unable to speak.

Harry could hear the bodies of the British officers fall to the floor of the vehicle—waiting another moment until he wrenched the door of the surveillance van back open with a gloved hand. His eyes beginning to water through the black balaclava as he plunged unprotected into the cloud of gas.

The memories flooding back. Training at The Farm at Camp Peary, Virginia. A CS grenade being tossed into a room full of recruits, the booming, distorted voice of a masked instructor counting slowly from amidst the haze.

Thirty seconds, a minute. . .a minute and a half. Then, and only then—eyes burning and nearly choking from the gas—were they permitted to begin putting on their own masks.

He had ninety seconds.

Removing a riot baton from within his jacket, he stepped over the incapacitated woman lying on the floor—smashing the computer screen with the tip of the baton. Ripping out the wires of the van's comms system.

He spotted a cellphone by the computer and brought the butt of the baton smashing down into its screen, the time frozen beneath the shattered glass. *11:13.*

His eyes flickered up to the screens, the surveillance imagery showing the interior of the imam's flat—and inserted a thumb drive into the USB port of the terminal, uploading a worm into the system.

Sixty seconds.

11:16 P.M.
The Rahman residence

The boy had failed them, Hashim Rahman thought, running a hand over his beard as he stared at the screen of his computer. The martyrdom video pulled up in a window.

There was no way to avoid that truth. . .not now, not in the light of the hours that had passed since he was supposed to have martyred himself.

A curse upon him, Rahman breathed, his face darkening. *And all those who fled in the day of battle. One third of them shall flee, and Allah shall never forgive them.*

Truly had the Prophet spoken.

He felt his wife's presence in the doorway and quickly minimized the video. "Are you coming to bed?"

"Soon," he replied, not looking at her. "I have been talking on-line with a student from the university. A very perceptive young man. He has many questions about Islam, about how it would be possible for him to revert."

"*Mash'allah*," she exclaimed, coming up behind him and resting her hands on his shoulders—her eyes visible in the reflection of his screen, her hair unbound in the privacy of their home, now framing her face. *So beautiful.*

A gift from God, in reward for his faithfulness. He took her fingers in his, pressing his lips against the back of her hand. "Is Huma asleep?"

"She is," his wife smiled. "Long ago. And you?"

A sound struck his ears before he could respond, faint and indistinct—coming from somewhere toward the front of the flat. He froze, his body suddenly rigid and tensed. "What was that?"

"I heard nothing."

"Stay here," he warned, pushing her to one side as he moved toward the hall. *Could it be Special Branch?*

No. The British special police would have come in loudly—battering rams and bullhorns. Striking terror into the hearts of all around. Intimidation.

This was something different. He made it to the end of the darkened hall, almost to the kitchen—his hand groping out for the light switch.

There.

The blow came without warning out of the darkness, an elbow catching him on the point of the chin and snapping his head back.

Stars exploded in his brain from the force of the impact, a thousand points of dizzying light as the floor rushed up to meet him. He heard a man's voice roaring out, "Where is the *Shaikh*? Tell me the location of Tarik Abdul Muhammad!"

And then his wife began to scream.

Speed. Surprise. Violence of action.

"On the floor. *Now!*" Harry bellowed, aiming the suppressed Sig-Sauer at the woman cowering ten feet away. The anger, the rage he had suppressed for so *long*, now flooding out of him—his gun hand trembling.

Aydin's face rising before him, along with that of Ismail Besimi. Victims of *this* man, both of them. *No more.*

"What do you want from us?" she screamed, falling to her knees, her hands raised—tears streaming down her cheeks, unable to take her eyes off the prostrate form of her husband. "*Ya Allah*, what do you *want?*"

"Ask your husband." He kicked Rahman in the ribs with a booted foot as the man attempted to rise, the blow connecting with a sickening *crunch*—sending him back against the wall, doubled up in pain.

Cowering like the dog he was, as if fearing another kick. He dropped to one knee, the Sig-Sauer in his right hand as he quickly frisked the imam—running his free hand over his body. *No weapons.*

As he had expected. Out of the corner of his eye, Harry saw the woman start to rise, to flee—turned to stare at her through the black mask. "If you so much as stir from that spot," he warned, his voice as cold as ice, "I kill your husband where he lies."

11:19 P.M.
The surveillance van

God. The pain. . .the *burning.* She tried to open her eyes, but it felt as though they were on fire—her throat raw and inflamed.

Rolling onto her stomach, Jan groped blindly for the edge of the open door—finding it and using it to pull herself forward. She fell out of the van to the curb, the fall knocking the breath from her body.

Fresh air. She lay on her back, staring up at the night through her burning, tear-drenched eyes. Drinking in the fresh air in massive gulps, desperate for the pure oxygen.

They had been attacked. But why? *Who?* The intelligence officer rolled to her knees, still struggling to breathe—feeling the rough pavement cut into her skin.

Had to get to the other van. Had to get help.

11:20 P.M.
Rahman's residence

"I don't...*know* the man," Hashim Rahman whispered, his face contorted in pain.

The man was a bad liar, Harry thought—and he had known many good ones. The imam's eyes never met his own, darting all over the place like a caged animal seeking any route of escape. He knew *far* more than he was saying.

But he was running out of time. The MI-5 surveillance teams would recover soon enough, and then there would be hell to pay.

He forced himself not to glance at his watch, to give Rahman any idea of the constraints he was under. *Maintain control.*

Use every ounce of leverage.

"Look at me," he began, lowering his voice so that only the two of them could hear, "you can tell me what I need to know and I'll leave. But if you refuse, you are going to sit here and watch while your wife's brains decorate that wall. And then I will go upstairs and kill your daughter while she sleeps."

He watched impassively as Rahman recoiled at the words, his face growing pale with fear—his wife's sobs filling the silence between them. And then it passed as quickly as it had come, a dark acceptance in the imam's eyes as he glared at Harry. "I—I will see them once more in *Jannah*."

Paradise.

Bluff called. Harry reached out, his free hand entwining in Rahman's collar as he stood, pulling the man with him. He jammed the suppressor of the Sig-Sauer into his damaged ribs, his face expressionless as the Imam grimaced in pain.

"Skin for skin," he spat, his face only inches away from Rahman's, "yea, all that a man has will he give for his life. You're coming with me."

Chapter 23

1:07 A.M., April 2nd
Outside Rahman's Flat

"It's a N225 CS grenade, standard police issue," the North Yorkshire constable announced, holding up the evidence bag to the glow of the lights now set up around the perimeter of what was now a crime scene. "No prints on the casing."

"Sod it," Darren Roth murmured, taking a step away. None of this made sense. *Nothing.*

He walked over to where the American woman was sitting in the back of an ambulance, a cup of water in her hand. She was drinking it down desperately, as though she couldn't get enough. Parker standing beside her, his hand resting on her shoulder.

There was something about the man, the ease with which he carried himself with women.

But that wasn't relevant. "We have a Security Service helicopter inbound on our location," he said, walking up to the two of them. "About twenty minutes out. Ms. Traeg, I'm going to need to ask you to go with the officers back to Thames House for a full debrief on what happened here."

Parker shook his head, a challenge in his eyes. "That's not the way this is going down, Roth. My officer, my rules. And Jimenez has already ordered us both to return to Grosvenor Square just as soon as medical clears Jan for travel."

Roth glanced back toward the terrace house to see Mrs. Rahman being escorted out by a pair of female constables. "You can't be serious, mate—the *Shaikh* is in the wind, our second-best lead was just dragged from his house by parties unknown—and you want to start a sodding turf war with me?"

"Those are the breaks," Parker retorted, not giving an inch. "Maybe next time we tell you someone needs to be taken out of play, your people will pay it some heed. I'll make sure Thames House receives a full summary of Ms. Traeg's report."

Americans. Roth swore under his breath, shaking his head in barely suppressed fury. *So bloody helpful.*

The worst part was that Parker was right. His personnel, his playbook. Not much he could do about it. The uncomfortable feeling of being held hostage on his own ground.

Roth turned away after a moment, retrieving his mobile from its pouch on his belt. Time to get on the horn to Thames House—he needed more manpower.

6:05 A.M.
The industrial estate
North of Leeds

Torture. It wasn't as unreliable as the media made out, Harry thought, glancing across the room at the unconscious form of his prisoner, hanging by his wrists from the steel support beams of the ground floor. That was a polite fiction designed to preserve the veneer of civilization. Keep everyone sleeping peacefully at night.

In truth, everyone had a breaking point. It was just a matter of finding it.

He should know—he'd once been on the other side. Held a prisoner by the Taliban back in 2008, tortured on an almost daily basis. They hadn't broken him. . .but they'd come close. So *very* close. Closer than he'd ever admitted to anyone at Langley.

You didn't talk about things like that, not any more than you had to. Say the wrong thing to the wrong person—someone might get the idea that you were a liability to the team.

Which is what had happened, in the end. He leaned back in the rusty metal chair, taking a sip from the bottle of spring water in his hand as he gazed at his prisoner. It was curious how little emotion he felt about that now—his firing from the Agency.

Perhaps he had known it was coming, sooner or later. Some things were unforgivable.

Like this. He screwed the cap back onto the bottle and set it aside, eyeing Hashim Rahman critically—his form starkly visible in the glare of the utility light Harry had placed on the floor a few feet away. He had passed out from the pain of his broken ribs nearly an hour before, his screams and curses fading away as he slipped from consciousness.

Harry closed his eyes, feeling the anger build within him once again at the memory of Aydin's face. Lying there in the mud, the panic frozen in his eyes at the moment of death.

Rahman's young wolves.

Time for their master to pay the price for his sins. He rose from his seat and moved toward the small table at one end of the room, the duffel bag sitting atop it.

Never use the same place twice. That was the conventional wisdom in his business. You never wanted to establish patterns, anything that could be used against you.

But returning to the abandoned industrial estate where he had confronted Flaharty six days earlier had been a matter of necessity.

Taking out the Security Service surveillance team was going to bring down more heat than he fancied dealing with, rendering a long drive with Rahman stuffed in the boot of the Vauxhall inadvisable, at best.

And frankly, he was running short of boltholes. Which was all the more reason to bring this to an end.

Harry unzipped the duffel bag, lifting Aydin's suicide vest out and laying it to one side, harmless and inert for the time being—its remote detonator disabled.

Another moment, and he found what he was looking for, a length of rubber hose about the length of a man's forearm, from elbow to fingertip. His face hardening at the sight of it. *The memories.*

He seized it in his right hand, moving back to stand before the suspended Hashim Rahman. Reaching up to pass his hand over the man's face. Slapping him across the face when he did not immediately wake, first gently—then a second time, harder.

Rahman's eyes flickered open, wide and staring.

"Time to wake up, Hashim," Harry began, his face a death mask as he stared into the imam's eyes. He drew his arm to the side, the hose describing a brutal arc as it came crashing back into Rahman's broken ribs.

The scream resounded off the walls of the small room, an anguished, terrorized sound. Harry seized Rahman's chin in one hand, holding it in a vise grip as his entire body trembled, sobbing uncontrollably through the pain. Forcing the man to look at him. "You can make all this stop any time you want. . .just give me the location of the *Shaikh.*"

And then the hose came slicing through the air once again. . .

10:46 A.M.
Leeds Central Police Station
Park Street, Leeds

This had been a bad idea. Which didn't even begin to cover highly irregular.

Darren shook his head. It had taken a special dispensation from Umar Hussein, the Chief Superintendent of the North Yorkshire Police, for him to be even permitted to question a detainee, despite the fact that her detainment had been orchestrated by the Security Services. He closed the folder, glancing across the table at the prostitute as he mentally prepared his plan of attack. Struggling against the exhaustion, the frustration of watching leads slip away over the last twenty-four hours. *Mehreen.*

He had tried to get some sleep, but it had eluded him despite his best efforts. Lying there awake, staring up at the ceiling through the darkness. Questions without answers, haunting him.

Sarah Russell might have been beautiful, even charming—when she wanted to be. When her *business* required her to be, he thought—staring into the woman's eyes.

But none of that was on display now, sitting across from him in the small room. He cleared his throat. "Do you know why you're here, Miss Russell?"

She shrugged her shoulders, the same dead look in her blue eyes. Knowing everything, admitting nothing.

"Same as the other times, I expect," she said finally, meeting his gaze with a look that tried to rise to the level of defiance, but failed miserably.

He shook his head. "While it's true that you've not been always the most. . .discreet in your business affairs, that's not why you're here this morning."

Her eyes narrowed, registering surprise and suspicion. *Distrust.* He opened the folder again, extracting a single picture of Tarik Abdul Muhammad and passing it to her across the metal tabletop.

"I don't care about how you make your money, and the constables won't either, not once I give them the word. I'm only interested in this man—your john from the other night at The Queens. What can you tell me about him?"

11:34 A.M.
Woodhouse Moor Park

She didn't know why she had come back, Mehreen thought, gazing up at the weather-worn statue of Arthur Wellesley, bronze-greened eyes staring impassively ahead as a light rain fell from the heavens, dripping from the feathers of the Duke of Wellington's doffed bicorn.

Her finger tracing the nearly washed away line of chalk which had signaled the dead-drop.

It felt like returning to the scene of the crime. The place where her life had intersected once more with that of Ismail Besimi, only a week before.

More like an eternity.

Would he have asked for the meeting, had he known it would end in his death? One domino crashing into another, and another, and another. Until they all fell down.

Ismail. Aydin. *Nick*. You were never prepared for the death of the ones you loved, no matter how much you attempted to steel yourself for its inevitability.

And you couldn't save them from themselves, in the end. Couldn't even save them from. . .*you*.

12:05 P.M.
Thames House
London

". . .fresh clashes have erupted between police and rioters as marchers carrying signs reading 'Stop Moslem Immigration' and 'End Multiculturalism Before It Ends Us' attempted to march upon the House of Commons this morning. In Birmingham, the investigation continues into the savage beating death of Sally Hines, the young mother dragged from her car in the middle of the riots. We go live. . ."

Julian Marsh thumbed the mute button, cutting off the BBC news host in mid-sentence. Chaos in the streets. New violence seeming to spring up every day. The nights, even worse. And in the midst of it all, a trained Islamist sniper.

There had been no new intel on Mirsab Abdul Rashid al-Libi since the Libyan's arrival at Heathrow a day before. It was though the man had never even existed.

Norris appeared at that moment in the doorway of his office, seemingly out of breath. "We just heard from Leeds."

"Any answers regarding the attack on our surveillance team?" The after-action report from the British officers involved had been less than illuminating, to put mildly. If there was another player out there—he had left nothing that could have identified him. A troubling new reality.

Norris shook his head. "The prostit—the *woman* Roth located—she claims to have intelligence on the location of the *Shaikh*."

"And?"

"She wants money."

MICE. The director-general shook his head, almost smiling despite himself. *Money. Ideology. Coercion. Ego.*

It didn't take the seventh son of a seventh son to predict which one of those a whore would choose. "How much?"

"Twenty quid."

"Twenty thousand pounds. . .is that all? For a moment, I feared we might become a burden on Her Majesty's exchequer."

12:34 P.M.
The industrial park
Outside Leeds

"*Ya Allah, ya Allah,*" Rahman sobbed through the pain, well-nigh incoherent. Tears streaming down his face, shining among the coarse black hairs of his beard. *Oh God, oh God, oh God.*

The strain of the suspension showing in every fiber of his body, sinews stretched taut. A ghastly sight in the harsh glare of the utility light, a man reduced to a wreck.

Begging, pleading helplessly for his life. For an end to the pain. After all that he had *done*. The lives he had destroyed.

No. Harry's eyes flashed with a murderous fire, the rage of all the months finding a righteous target. There could be no mercy, no forgiveness. Only a reckoning.

"God doesn't seem to be listening to you, Hashim. Why could that be?" He backhanded Rahman across the cheek, watching him recoil against the ropes securing him to the ceiling, his helpless body dancing in the glare of the light. His hand wrapping around the back of the man's neck as he brought him in close, staring him in the eye. "Surely is it not written in *Surah an-Nisa*? 'And whoever kills a fellow believer intentionally, his punishment is Hell. Let him abide in it.' You sent Aydin Shinwari out to die—to commit suicide in defiance of all God's laws—you *killed* Ismail Besimi."

"Besimi," Rahman began weakly, summoning up what little defiance he could muster, "was an *apostate*."

"Ismail Besimi," Harry breathed into his ear, holding him in a close embrace, unable to move away as he drove a punishing blow into the man's damaged ribcage, "gave his life in the service of his god, true to the faith of Islam to the very end. Would that you could say the same."

He took a long step back from the man's swinging body, his face dark as he picked up the bloodied hose once more. "Welcome to hell, Hashim. . ."

12:57 P.M.
Leeds Central Police Station
Park Street, Leeds

"You're not police, are you?" Darren looked up from his phone at the sound of the prostitute's voice, finding her eyeing him carefully.

"Why do you ask?"

She smiled, but it never reached her eyes. "I was out on the streets doing this at sixteen. Known lots of police. And I know men."

Fair enough. It *was* her stock-in-trade, after all. He shook his head, unsure where this was leading. Giving her room to talk.

"It's in your eyes, I think," Sarah Russell went on after a long moment. "That look, I've seen it before. Lads that came back from the Middle East, found their world had bloody well moved on without them. Sometimes their wives too—which is where I came in, of course. You're. . .what, military? Security Services?"

There was no comment he felt inclined to offer. Or that would have been safe to do so. "I knew it," she continued, something of triumph in her face. "You're with Five."

Before he could form a response, his phone vibrated against the metal of the table with the buzz of an incoming message. MacCallum.

We have a deal.

He picked up the phone in one hand, turning it around so that she could see the screen. "You'll get your money. Now, what can you give me on Tarik Abdul Muhammad?"

His words seemed to bring her back down to earth, focusing her attention once more on the reality of their situation. "He paid for me to meet him tonight. *All* night. I was given the address of a flat."

"Then that's exactly what you're going to do."

8:01 A.M. Eastern Time
Russell Senate Office Building
Washington, D.C.

"Pruitt?" Coftey asked guardedly, stepping to one side as a Capitol Police officer scanned his briefcase. "Has he even hit puberty yet?"

"He's thirty-one, Roy," Lamar Daniels responded. "Not much younger than you were when you were first elected."

True enough, the senator thought, acknowledging the officer with a curt nod as he retrieved his briefcase. He'd been young—very young for a US senator.

But by the time he'd come to the Senate at the age of thirty-three, he'd already been to war. Led patrols deep into Viet Cong territory, where the least mistake—the slightest error in judgment—could have cost the life of every man with him. Not to mention his own.

Brian Pruitt, on the other hand, was rumored to have still been living in his parents' basement in Lawton five years earlier when he'd begun making a name for himself as a blogger—quickly establishing himself as one of the Hancock campaign's fiercest partisans. And now, if Daniels' information was correct, he was being groomed as the man to take Coftey's seat in the Senate.

Not without a fight.

"Thanks for looking into that for me, Lamar," the senator responded distractedly, hearing the Gulf War veteran's hearty acknowledgement as he signed off, returning his cellphone to the inside pocket of his suit.

He caught sight of the statue of Senator Richard Russell as he moved through the rotunda—pausing, as he did ever, to regard it with a mixture of admiration and disbelief. Hard to believe that they hadn't torn it down by now.

In his day, Russell had been the most powerful senator on the Hill. . .and a segregationist until the bitter end. Caught on the losing side of history. Last advocate for a lost cause.

Was this what it felt like? Coftey shook his head, glancing up at the high, vaulted ceiling of the rotunda as if he expected to find his answers written somewhere up there among the Corinthian capitals. But this cause wasn't lost. *Not yet.*

You didn't gain power in a single night—and outside of being caught in bed with a live boy or a dead girl—you didn't lose it in a single night either.

Which meant that you could still wield what power you had while it lasted. The weak would use it to strike at once in desperation, lash out at their enemies with what remained of their ebbing strength.

The strong, would remain in the shadows. Gathering strength.

He felt his phone buzz suddenly against his ribs as he mounted the stairs to the upper floor, digging it back out to see a brief message displayed on-screen. The response to a text he had sent nearly an hour earlier.

Central span, Key Bridge. 1840 hours tonight. Be there.

1:04 P.M.
The offices of the UK Daily Standard
Central London

"And there's *nothing* you can do?" Arthur Colville shook his head, glaring across the office at the painting hanging upon the far wall. Richard Caton Woodville's depiction of the charge of the 21st Lancers at Omdurman. British grit and steel cutting its way through a sea of Muslim fanaticism.

Would God that doing so today were so simple, so straightforward. After all they had sacrificed, all they had *risked*—the months of planning—it seemed well-nigh unbelievable that it would come down to this. Everything ruined by one man's stupid lust for a whore.

"Nothing," came the voice of his contact at M.I.-5. "Special Branch is already on their way. They'll have the flat surrounded within fifteen minutes."

"And we have no way to contact him," Colville demanded, careful not to mention the name of the *Shaikh* over an unsecured line, "to *warn* him?"

"None. My last instruction to him, as we discussed, was to go to this safehouse after disposing of his last burner and stay there. Stay out of sight after the fiasco of yesterday morning. Our friend was supposed to visit him this evening with another supply of mobiles. You will be needing to warn him off."

Conor Hale. "I will handle it. In the meantime, see what you can do there to. . .adjust the situation in our favor. We *need* him free if things are to move forward as planned."

"I assure you, I know the stakes."

1:24 P.M.
The US Embassy
Grosvenor Square, London

"The text message, it was from the British officer," Jan Traeg responded, taking another sip from the bottle of spring water. Despite all the hours that had passed, she could still taste the CS gas deep within her throat. "At least it was supposed to have been."

"It was," Carlos Jimenez confirmed quietly, glancing at Thomas. "Or at least his phone. The Security Service has verified that. They recovered both phone and officer, about five miles west of the flat—he was roughed up and disoriented, but otherwise fine. And what happened after that?"

Otherwise fine. *No casualties*, Thomas thought, a growing sense of disquiet gnawing at him as it had ever since he had first heard the story from Traeg hours earlier. Something was wrong with all this. He glanced at his watch, mentally calculating what time it would be in the States.

"My partner opened the door to let him in—and the next thing I heard was the grenade. I-I didn't see—it all happened so fast."

It would have.

"If you'll excuse me, Carlos," Thomas interjected, forcing a bland smile to his face as he rose from his seat. "I'll be back in just a moment. . .have to take a leak."

The station chief barely even looked up. "Of course."

"Look, Ron, don't give me that. This isn't a social call." Thomas swore into the phone in exasperation, wishing for the hundredth time in the day that he had a drink.

Or a woman, he thought. . .momentarily eyeing the State Department attaché who had just stepped from the elevators down the hall. Tall and blonde, with a tan that certainly hadn't come from the climate around here.

Focus. He closed his eyes, forcing himself to address the matter at hand. "Something's come up—with the op here in the UK. I need to talk with Richards."

There was a brief pause before Ron Carter responded, a thousand miles away in Langley, Virginia. "I can't do that. Not right away. Not on an unsecured line."

"But you *can* do it?"

"I didn't say that," the analyst responded. "I'll do what I can. Richards is off-CONUS at the moment. I can't say anything more, you know that."

"I do." Deployed with Bravo Team, no doubt. In the months since Harry's departure, Tex had become Nakamura's right-hand man over at Bravo. "Get in touch with him and get back to me soon as you can."

"I'll see what I can do."

"Make it a priority, Ron. I'll owe you one."

He signed off and ended the call, shaking his head as he gazed down the hall at the gracefully retreating form of the attaché. The hit on the surveillance van was. . .familiar.

Very familiar.

5:47 P.M.
The industrial estate
North of Leeds, North Yorkshire

Exhaustion. Harry passed a hand over his face, unscrewing the cap on his bottle of water and taking a long, deep swallow. There was only so much longer he could keep this up. Interrogation, torture, if you wanted to call it that—and he had no problem with doing so—was as much emotional as physical.

And it took as severe a toll on the interrogator as the man being interrogated.

Okay, maybe not, he thought—eyeing Rahman's suspended, bloodied form. Memories of his first rendition flight coming back to the fore. *As a man sows, so shall he also reap.*

It had been him and John Patrick Flynn—just the two of them—flying into Queen Alia late one night in the fall of '03 in a blacked-out Agency 737. A bound-and-hooded senior Taliban field commander in their custody. . .try as he might, he couldn't even remember the man's name now.

He could never forget what had happened after they landed. After King Abdullah's *Mukhabarat* met them on the tarmac. All smiles and Savile Row. *"Welcome to paradise."*

Hell, more like.

"Don't look away." That had been Flynn, his soft gray eyes turning hard as a flint. *"If you do, you're no better than them."*

Them. The Agency bureaucrats back at Langley, reading their intelligence reports and averting their eyes from the truth of how that intel had been obtained. The politicians on Capitol Hill, pushing for "something to be done", then claiming utmost innocence when something was.

The American people, snug in their beds.

"A man does what has to be done," Flynn had gone on, watching through the glass as the Taliban commander was stripped naked and chained to the wall of the darkened room, the only illumination coming from the fire pit at its center, the glowing pokers resting in the coals. *"And he doesn't pass it off to others, he does it himself. He accepts that responsibility. And everything that comes with it. The demons."*

His own reply, haunting in the ghostly silence that preceded the screams. *"Is that why we're on this side of the glass?"*

9:45 P.M.
Leeds

"Are you sure you want me to do this?"

"Of course," Darren responded, looking over at Sarah Russell in the passenger seat of the darkened BMW. A transformed woman from the way she had appeared before him in the police station only hours before, the sparkle of diamonds in her ears, the dress well-nigh open in the back—her neckline dipping perilously low.

It wasn't nearly so hard to see how she commanded the prices they'd seen on the 'Net. "We've been over this a time or two."

She shook her head, biting her lip in the darkness. Not looking at him, the nerves on full display. "I don't know if I even *can*. What if he suspects?"

Right. "Just do what you've always done," he said, no emotion in his voice. "Fake it. All these years. . .how many of your clients have suspected?"

Russell laughed, but it was a laugh as fake as the diamonds in her ears. Brittle, sharp. "Not a single one. Men, they're all the same."

"There you go, then. Nothing to worry about." She unbuckled her seatbelt, her hand on the door when he stopped her. "And one final thing. We'll need you to wear these."

She looked back, her eyes fixing on the black lace in his hand. "What do you mean, I..."

"It's important. And I need you make a gift of them to him when you leave."

Seeing the puzzled look on her face, he went on. "There's a miniature transmitter in the gusset—transmits location and audio back to us in microbursts. We'll have ears in the room."

She reached out and took them from his hand, favoring him with a look of disgust. "So you're going to be enjoying the show, is that it? Bugger you—if everything was as it should be, I'd be charging you lot for the entertainment."

"If everything was as it *should* be, Miss Russell, I'd be arresting you rather than sending you in," he replied, the ghost of a smile flitting across his dark face. "But that's not the way the world works."

She could feel her heart beating loudly against her chest as she walked up to the door of the terraced house, steeling herself not to look back—not to attempt to find the police surveillance team she knew was somewhere on the street.

And then she was inside, her eyes adjusting to the dim light of the entry hall—stilettos tapping against the weathered wood as she made her way to the door of the flat, her hand lifted to knock.

Calm down. She'd had dangerous clients before. This one wasn't even particularly rough. Or at least he hadn't been.

She heard the bolt slide back, and then he stood there before her in the doorway. "I was hoping it would be you," the Pakistani said, favoring her with a charismatic smile as his gaze swept over her body. "You really don't know how much I've been looking forward to this."

The sound of a passionate kiss came over his headphones, followed by the unmistakable noise of fabric tearing.

A woman's laugh, nearly pitch-perfect...but somehow vaguely discordant. *False.*

Roth leaned back in the chair of the surveillance van, raising his eyebrows as he glanced at the other British officer. "She's in."

He waited a moment before toggling his earpiece. "Are you getting this, Thames House?"

"Loud and clear," came MacCallum's voice unexpectedly. The section chief should have gone home hours before, but none of them had been getting much sleep of late. "Voice-print analysis has been confirmed, it's the *Shaikh*."

Thank God, Roth thought. Would have been a rum thing if they'd gotten the wrong john, after all this. "And our status on the assault?"

"Marsh is on his way to meet with the Home Secretary."

6:37 P.M. Eastern Time
The Francis Scott Key Bridge
Washington, D.C.

Darkness. Kranemeyer leaned forward, his elbows resting on the parapet of the bridge—hands clasped before him as he stared out toward the city, the towering obelisk of the Washington Monument just barely visible in the night, nearly two miles to the east. That was what this city represented, its thousand glittering lights notwithstanding.

The dark, corrupt heart of a country that was slowly rotting from within.

"I'd applaud your sense of irony, Barney," a voice said from off to his right, the traffic flowing over US Route 29 behind him masking the sound of approaching footsteps. "If the whole thing weren't so unspeakably. . .macabre."

He glanced over to see the figure of Roy Coftey standing there a few feet away, the senator's face shadowed in the glare of passing headlights.

He was right, Kranemeyer thought, his eyes following Coftey's down to where the dark waters of the Potomac lapped against the arches nearly a hundred feet below. It was from almost this very spot that CIA Deputy Director Michael Shapiro had plunged to his death scarce three months prior. *Just before Christmas.*

A suicide—that's what the FBI had ruled his death. And so it had been, after a manner of speaking. A last honorable act from a man who had long since forfeited any claim to "honor."

Kranemeyer pressed his lips together into a tight, bloodless line, remembering that night. *All too well.*

"What do you have for me, Roy?" he asked, shoving aside the memories with an effort. Bringing them both around to the reason for their meeting here this night.

"Here," Coftey responded simply, handing over a massive sheaf of papers secured with a binder clip. "Thought you could use a look at what's bearing down on us."

"What's this?"

"SB286, the Senate version of what is being colloquially referred to on the Hill as the 'NSA bill'—although I'm sure some intern will be dragooned into coming up with a cute backronym for it before this is all over. All six hundred and seventy pages of it."

Bureaucracy. Kranemeyer snorted, flipping through the first few pages in the dim light—his eyes scanning down the sheet.

"I'd need five days and as many lawyers just to understand what I'm reading," he said finally. "Why don't you give me the highlights?"

"Highlights?" The senator looked as if he might laugh, but there was no mirth in his eyes. "There are none, just a laundry list of goals from starry-eyed idealists who have spent their political careers communing with the good idea fairy and whom the voters have, in all their omnipotent wisdom, finally entrusted with the power to bring their vision to pass."

He turned to look out across the river, his face solemn—his voice raised scarce high enough to be heard above the sound of the passing traffic. "They're going to tear the Clandestine Service apart, Barney—dismantle the Special Activities Division—fold its capabilities back into the DoD. Force the Agency to come calling on JSOC for whatever they need in the direct action arena, Title 10 the whole of it. Just like the 9/11 Commission recommended back in '04. Just like they've been doing with the drone program."

Madness. Kranemeyer shook his head, his eyes flickering back toward the lights of the city. The capital of the nation he had defended for so very long. But Coftey wasn't done.

"And they intend to extend the Fourth Amendment beyond the borders of the United States—to the 'citizens of the world', to use the President's language. You want to spy on anyone, anywhere, for any reason—you're going to need a FISA warrant. With the Select Committee granted far broader powers of oversight over the entire process."

"Something like that, it's going to virtually destroy SIGINT-enabled HUMINT," Kranemeyer responded, struggling to keep the anger out of his voice. It was a rare Agency recruitment these days that wasn't facilitated by—if not originated from—a targeting package developed by Fort Meade. *Identifying potential assets.* And it worked the other way too—or *had.*

The senator just nodded. "That's not by accident, but by design. People on the Hill are frightened of the power wielded by an intelligence community working together in the way it has since the 'walls' came down post-9/11, even as limited as we both know that to have been. Rendition. . .enhanced interrogation, it's all going to be a thing of the past. And they're talking about pursuing retroactive prosecution against officials and officers who have been involved in such activities."

Kranemeyer swore under his breath. "That's not even constitutional."

"If you think any of this is about the Constitution," Coftey said, a grim, hard smile crossing his face, "you haven't been paying attention."

He paused, a clear note of regret entering his voice as he continued. "And there's nothing I can do to stop it. Had a meeting with leadership—their message couldn't have been more clear. If I oppose the bill, they'll strip me of my chairmanship."

The most unkindest cut of all, the DCS thought, turning toward his old friend. "Wouldn't have thought that would stop you, Roy."

"It wouldn't," Coftey replied sharply, meeting his gaze, "but my hands are tied. My influence as chairman is what enables me to mount an effective opposition. Without it. . ."

"How does the Vice President feel about all this?" Kranemeyer mused. Nearly twenty years the President's senior, Kenneth Havern had himself been a part of the intelligence community back in the '80s, a CIA deputy director for two years before leaving that world to enter politics, becoming the governor of his home state of Ohio.

And when Norton had received the nomination, he had tapped Havern as VP in a gesture to the Republican establishment. A gesture that was, in retrospect, increasingly resembling a middle finger.

"Like his pitcher of warm piss just got emptied over his head. But his hands are tied. He can't come out and publicly oppose the President. Not this early."

Because the political costs are too high, Kranemeyer thought, the unspoken message all too clear. *Politicians.*

"The devil take all of them," he snarled—tossing the bill over the bridge with a sudden movement. Hundreds of white sheets of paper fluttering in the darkness as they descended toward the river below.

His eyes flashed as he turned on Coftey, the senator standing there in shocked disbelief as Kranemeyer's finger jabbed out toward his chest. "There has to be a way. *Find it*. Or else this is war."

11:59 P.M.
The industrial park
North of Leeds

"I really don't enjoy doing this, Hashim," Harry said, his tone almost conversational as he stared across the table into the imam's half-closed eyes. The man was barely strong enough to sit upright, moaning in agony as he leaned back into the metal of the chair. "It goes against everything I believe—violates every precept of my faith. But I do it all the same. . .why? Because there are men like you in this world. And no amount of peace and righteousness is going to stop you. So instead, there's me."

He took Rahman by the wrist and pulled his hand across the table-top until it was resting palm-down on the metal, fingers spread out. He saw the man's eyes flicker nervously to the hammer lying a few inches away, and nodded.

"The human hand is such a fragile thing, Hashim—surprising, really, when you think about it. The bones splinter so easily. And are so very difficult to repair."

Sniveling sobs escaped Rahman's lips as he began to tremble, trying to pull his hand back, but finding himself helpless in Harry's grasp. "No, no, no. . .please. *Don't.*"

"That's not my decision, it's yours. All this stops, the moment you give me the location of the *Shaikh*. You'll be free to leave—go back to your family, your wife and baby girl."

"I don't *know* where he is."

"So you've said," Harry responded coldly, reaching for the hammer. "What do you say—start with the little finger and work our way in?"

"*No, no,*" Rahman whispered desperately, jerking against Harry's grip. "Please, please, *no*. I don't know where he is, I swear it before Allah. . .but I know where he is *going* to be."

"You have my undivided attention."

Chapter 24

3:03 A.M., April 3rd
The council estate
Seacroft, West Yorkshire

There. He felt the last of the tumblers click into place, the handle of the access door giving under his hand as Harry pushed outward, holding his breath for a moment. *No alarm system*. Or at least none he had been able to detect.

No doubt considered pointless, given the neighborhood.

He tucked the lockpicks back into their pouch and stepped out onto the roof of the tower block, taking in his surroundings for a moment—the dull roar of the ventilation systems filling his ears.

The cool night breeze struck him in the face as he set the case to one side, moving to the parapet of the roof, a chest-high balustrade made of the same stark concrete as the rest of the building.

He pulled out Flaharty's NODs and began a scan of his surroundings, sweeping down to the street seventeen stories below, leading in from the bus station—back to the west and the other two, smaller, council blocks.

From the vantage point of the rooftop, he had a clear field of fire on either approach from the bus station, sweeping back along the roads into the council estate.

Fire. He lowered the binoculars and walked back from the parapet, stooping down to unzip the long soft case he had brought up with him, pushing it open.

His fingers finding the long, thick barrel of the Accuracy International L115A3, closing around the buttstock as he pulled—lifting the heavy rifle in both hands and unfolding the bipod, setting it aright.

He took the single magazine and the box of ammunition, leaning back against the parapet as he began to feed one 8.59mm round after another between its steel lips.

No rush. Once he got started, Rahman had been eager enough to talk. Telling the truth? Well, that had taken another two hours and three fingers—along with the realization that his release was only going to happen after the *Shaikh* was dead.

Or not. Harry shook his head, grimacing as he forced the final long brass cartridge into the mag, feeling it spring into place.

Over time, lying became as natural—as effortless—as breathing. You lied to enemies, to allies, to friends, family. . .to yourself.

Until you found yourself alone at the end of it all, standing on a windswept roof with a rifle in your hands. *The end of all dreams.*

It seemed fitting, somehow.

He removed the compact range-finder from the case and walked back to the edge of the roof, aiming it down at the entry roads as he calculated the range.

Wouldn't be much over a hundred and fifty yards, still south of two hundred if the other road was used. Could have made that shot over open sights, let alone with the British army rifle's high-powered optics.

He lowered the range-finder and looked out into the darkness, allowing himself the faintest shadow of a smile. His first in months.

If Rahman's intel had been correct, Tarik Abdul Muhammad would come walking down that road at 0700 hours, to meet up with a small Islamist cell in the tower blocks behind him.

At 0701 hours, he would be dead. *Blood for blood.*

4:12 A.M.
The MI-5 surveillance van
Leeds

"I understand, sir," Darren said as he listened to Marsh's words, glancing over at his fellow intelligence officer, their faces lit by the glow of the electronics. The Home Secretary had given authorization for the apprehension of Tarik Abdullah Muhammad. Finally. *This is it.* "And your orders?"

"A pair of SO-15 Firearms Units are inbound on your location via helicopter from Battersea," the DG responded over the phone. "Upon arrival, Scotland Yard will assume operational command of PERSEPHONE."

And we fade into the backdrop, Darren thought. That was ever the way. Gathering the intel and turning it over to others for action to be taken. Five didn't have powers of arrest. "How soon will SO-15 be with us?"

"Within the hour."

4:28 A.M.
Seacroft Council Estate
West Yorkshire

The uniforms were laid out before him on the small table, the inner linings removed as he worked with needle and thread, securing the wires tight against the fabric—wires leading up to the crude pipe bombs now concealed within the front of the bulky uniform jacket.

There was little heat in the small flat—it only worked sporadically—but he was sweating. His brow beaded with perspiration as his fingers arranged the wiring, his eyes flickering back and forth between the jacket and the small tablet at his side, the wiring schematics he had downloaded weeks before displayed on its screen.

"*Alhamdullilah,*" the young man breathed, leaning back in exhaustion, feeling his fingers cramp from the tedious work. God be praised, the worst was over.

"You already up, bruv?" came a sleepy voice from the sofa, a form stirring beneath the blankets. "What time is it?"

"Time for us to be about our work," Jawid reproved as his roommate emerged from the semi-darkness, rubbing his eyes. They were both students at Leeds Trinity, with Jawid in his second year of a journalism degree. Second and final, he thought grimly. "The *Shaikh* will be here in a few hours."

A smile spread across his roommate's face. "Tomorrow morning. . .we will wake in Paradise."

"*Insh'allah.*"

4:42 A.M.
The MV Percy Phillips
Grimsby Harbor
Lincolnshire

No plan survives contact with the enemy. Hale shook his head, staring out over the water out past the quay toward the North Sea, Colville's voice coming through his earpiece.

That was the reality of any war, but the more he listened to the publisher—the more it became apparent that he hadn't grasped that. *Civilians.*

He cleared his throat. "Do we have an alternate plan to execute, should he be taken out of play?"

Only silence answered his question, in itself answer enough. He swore under his breath. "We're in too far to turn back now—have to bloody well *find* a way to go through with this, come what may."

"The Sword," Colville said after another long moment. Clearly referencing their deception ploy with the Libyan sniper. "It might be time to offer a demonstration of his talents. Our friend on high. . .may have outlived his usefulness to us."

Friend on high. Daniel Pearson, the nationalist MP. Their ally. Hale's breath caught in his throat. "Are you serious?"

"If our piece is taken off the table," Colville replied, referring to Tarik Abdul Muhammad, "yes. You've seen the interviews he's been giving these last few days, as the violence has grown. He's lost his nerve—and there's no place for that in the world to come. He's giving a speech in Birmingham this afternoon."

The implication was all too clear. "If you wait to make this decision, it won't give me the time I need to do a proper recce."

They had never intended to play this card more than once. To do so twice—was an unlooked-for gamble.

And he could hear the indecision in Colville's voice as he replied slowly, "Go to Birmingham, take up positions. I'll keep you informed as this develops."

5:05 A.M.
The flat
Leeds

It wasn't the first time she had stayed with a client through the night—some men valued the physical contact afterward as much as the sex itself. And were prepared to pay for it.

That was the most important thing, of course, Sarah Russell thought—the sleeping man's arm draped around her waist as they spooned, his breathing low and rhythmic. Such a contrast with the animalistic passion he had displayed only a few hours before.

Men. . .they were all the same. If she'd wanted love, she would have bought a dog.

She just laid there, wide awake but motionless, staring at the wall, feeling his breath against her neck. A part of her wanting to get up and leave—to run, to be anywhere but here.

Only too aware that the police outside were listening to every word. Every *sound.*

The clangor of mobile's loud ringtone startled her, piercing the stillness of the room. She heard a muffled groan from her client, his hand sliding back across her bare stomach as he roused, sitting upright in the bed.

Stay still, her mind warned—something in her subconscious deadly afraid of this man knowing she was awake. Stay *very* still.

5:08 A.M.
The surveillance van

"Hold up a minute. He's getting a call," the British intelligence officer announced suddenly, motioning with his hand.

Darren reached for the headphones, slipping them on as he heard the jangle of a ringtone, followed by the *Shaikh*'s voice—sounding distant, muffled. *Sod it.*

This was the part of the spy business they never showed on the telly. Your bug was never placed *quite* where you needed it. . .God only knew where that thong had ended up.

His face twisted into a grimace of concentration, focusing on the words in an effort to make them out. The *Shaikh* was speaking Arabic, but he was painfully rusty and this was a different dialect than he remembered from Iraq. *Mehreen, this is when we needed you.*

But he couldn't let himself think about that, not now. Not in the aftermath of her betrayal. Her *collaboration* with these people.

He grabbed a piece of paper and began scribbling down words, his face changing as he listened.

Another moment and he ripped off the headphones as the call ended. "What's going on?"

Darren ignored his partner's question, keying his mike to bring in Thames House. "What's our status on SO-15?"

"On the ground at the heliport," MacCallum's voice responded, "They'll be staging on you in fifteen."

He shook his head. "Negative. We may want to hold back on the assault. . .our man just got a call from another cell, confirming a meet this morning. My Arabic's not what it was, but I believe he was referencing an attack. *Today.*"

"I'll brief the DG. Parker and the Americans are on their way up from Grosvenor Square—Washington requested a presence on-hand when the *Shaikh* was taken into custody."

Roth's face darkened as he remembered his confrontation with the CIA officer only the previous morning, after the abduction of Hashim Rahman. The *arrogance* of the man. He brushed it aside with an effort. There was no time for any of that. "Good," he managed, "we're going to need the manpower."

1:23 A.M. Eastern Time
Coftey's residence
Vienna, Virginia

This is war. Coftey rolled over onto his back, his massive frame shifting restlessly against the pillows. Gazing up through the darkness of the bedroom at the ceiling, Kranemeyer's words from hours before still playing through his mind.

There has to be a way. Find *it*. There had been a frightening intensity in the man's voice, haunting echoes of the last time they had found themselves in this place—trying to protect their country from those who sought to undermine its security, to betray those who defended it.

The lengths to which they had both *been forced to go.* Coftey's face twisted into a grimace, still remembering their meeting in Foxstone Park that cold December night, the look on Kranemeyer's face sending a chill through his body. A look he hadn't seen in a man's eyes since Vietnam. A look he had prayed he would never see again.

"Shapiro and Haskel are dead."

They couldn't go down that road, he thought, shuddering despite himself. *Not again.*

"You're still awake," he heard Melody whisper, her voice suddenly breaking the stillness of the night. A statement, not a question. *She knew him well.*

"I'm sorry," the senator responded, glancing over at her in the darkness. "Didn't mean to wake you."

"You didn't." She raised herself up on one elbow, her form silhouetted against the dim light coming in through the window. "Is there something bothering you?"

Leave the politics on the Hill. That's what he'd told her on their first date, taking in the symphony at the Strathmore.

Their relationship, a sanctuary from the strains and pressures that politics inflicted on everyone who chose to engage in it. They didn't bring it home—didn't bring it to bed. *Yet all the same. . .*

She was the only one he could trust.

"The NSA bill," Coftey responded finally, a heavy sigh escaping his lips as he leaned back into the pillows. "It has to be stopped. *Somehow.*"

He ran a hand across his chin, his mind still churning. "But the leadership, they're tying my hands. The meeting with Fuentes—she made their position clear. If I obstruct the bill, I'm gone. The chairmanship, everything."

Everything I've spent three decades achieving. Three decades, clawing through the muck of the D.C. swamp. Surviving. Accumulating power. *Gone.* But what was any of it worth, if he couldn't stop this? "And yet, I can't just stand aside."

It was a moment before she replied as she rolled over onto her side, her warm body pressed against his in the darkness—her hand gently caressing his arm. "Why does it have to be you?"

"Because there's no one else," he responded, his face grim. The same reason he had gone to Vietnam. *The same answer as it always was.* Age-old and unchanging. "But even so, I can't see a means of doing so. The Republicans may not have a majority in the Senate, but with Fuentes and the leadership determined to give them this. . .seems like the only way out would be to convince the Republicans that they don't want it. But *how*?"

"You should try to get some sleep."

He shook his head, scarce hearing her—still lost in his own thoughts. "There are security hawks in the GOP, even in their leadership. But you'd have to have something they wanted bad enough to go up against their own POTUS, as improbable as that. . .*wait.*"

Her hand stopped. "What?"

"What did I say?" he asked, the realization flooding over him like a tidal wave as he sat up in bed, reaching over to turn on the lamp. "What did I just say?"

"I don't know, I—"

"The Republicans tried to take a majority in the Senate last November," Coftey replied—his words coming quickly, his face animated as he looked at her—her blonde hair still tousled from sleep, her eyes betraying confusion. "They failed, they fell short. But by how much?"

"A single seat, of course. What are you saying?"

"That's right," he said as he pushed aside the covers, rising to his feet. A smile creasing his face as he looked down on her. "That's exactly right. A single seat."

She laid there until she heard the bathroom door close behind him, heard the water come on in the shower. Her mind racing through what he had just told her. *The implications.*

And he would do it, of that much she was certain. She might not have loved him, but after six months of sharing his bed, she *knew* Roy Coftey in more ways than one. Well enough to know that he wasn't the kind of man who was going to back down.

Melody pushed away the covers, brushing her hair back from her eyes as she reached out to where her phone lay charging on the nightstand.

Her fingers quickly swiping across the unlock screen, chewing her lip slowly as she tapped in a number from memory, beginning to compose a text.

We need to meet. As soon as possible.

6:47 A.M.
The council estate
Seacroft, West Yorkshire

Thirteen minutes. Harry tucked the half-eaten bar of chocolate back into the pocket of his shirt, gazing out over the council estate into the morning sun, its rays striking him full in the face. He'd known so many mornings just like this over the years. . .full of peace and stillness. Waiting for a rifle shot to split the dawn.

Thirteen minutes and then this would all be over. Over and done with. Behind him.

It didn't feel like he had imagined. No anticipation. No joy. No anger.

Just *nothing*. Emptiness, a void rising within him. Ismail Besimi's words circling around and around in his head. *"Those who seek to take that which belongs to the Lord of worlds. . .do so at their peril."*

But this was *justice*.

He lifted the heavy sniper rifle in both hands, once more unfolding each leg of the bipod so that it rested upon the parapet of the tower block—its long black barrel aiming down into the street below.

The stock of the rifle came up, nestled against his cheek as he reached forward, the fingers of his right hand finding the bolt—working it back and then forward again, bringing a round into the breach.

Ten minutes.

6:54 A.M.
Seacroft Bus Station
Seacroft, West Yorkshire

"Echo Lead, he's getting off the bus. You should have eyes-on any moment."

And sure enough, Thomas Parker thought, his eyes scanning the people emerging from the open door of the bus. . .there he was. "Solid copy, Zulu. I have a visual on CERBERUS, taking advance position."

"Tailing" from in front was ever a challenging proposition, but he'd done it before. And with the benefit of modern technology. . .

His radio crackled with static once more, the British officer's voice announcing, "Standing by to launch Raven-4."

You're welcome, he thought, smiling briefly to himself as he turned, walking on toward road leading into the council estate. The CIA team had brought the man-portable UAV with them from Grosvenor Square, one of several the Marines used for perimeter security at the Embassy.

He glanced back and over to the right, catching sight of another one of the British officers—a middle-aged woman who looked like a social worker. Maintaining a loose following position on the *Shaikh*.

Another few moments, and they were going to have eyes in the sky.

6:57 A.M.

It was a beautiful morning, the sun streaming through the clouds from the east to warm his face as he walked down the road curving into the council estate, moving past red-brick buildings worn by the years.

Tarik lifted a hand to stroke his beard and smiled. Even after a shower, the smell of her perfume was still on him. The feel of the whore's body against his lingering in the forefront of his memory.

She had left after he'd paid her and he had watched her go—knowing that he would never see her again. Not after the destruction which was about to rain down on this country. *The judgement of God.*

Judgment that he had been chosen to deliver, back behind the chain-link and barbed wire of Camp X-Ray.

He lifted his face to the horizon, finding the pair of smaller tower blocks in the distance that served as his destination.

Where a pair of brave *shahid* prepared to meet their deaths.

6:58 A.M.

"He's turned down Bailey's Hill," Darren announced, comparing the map overlay in the van to the live feed streaming in from the UAV, hovering at an altitude of nearly fifty meters over the council estate. A noiseless, almost ghostly presence. "Still moving west-southwest. Echo Lead, maintain your current heading. Victor One and Two, assume eyes on, take over pursuit."

"And my men?" a voice asked from behind him, and Darren looked back to see the SO-15 commander standing there.

"All in due time, Inspector Howlett," he responded icily. "This is still the Security Service's operation. And will remain so until we have confirmed the location of the second cell."

The police officer shook his head. "If my men are to play any role at all in this, they need to start moving into their positions *now*."

"Look," Darren replied, using his pen as a pointer as he gestured to the map overlay, pointing out the towering council blocks. "Here, here, here—and here. The *Shaikh* could have sympathizers, allies anywhere. If one of them is on one of these upper floors, they have command of the whole estate. They see Special Branch moving in, he's going to rabbit before any of us can stop him."

6:59 A.M.

There he is. Harry picked out the figure of Tarik Abdul Muhammad in the Accuracy International's scope as he turned into the cross-road, occasionally disappearing between buildings. *Two hundred meters.*

The man was playing it cautious, working his way toward the tower blocks on an indirect route. The way *he* would have done it. Only a fool came straight in.

It was going to cost time, but none of it was going to make a difference in the end, Harry thought, spotting him again as he came out on the other side of the building—his form easily recognizable despite the rest of the foot traffic through the estate. A tall, almost regal figure.

About to be laid low. *At last.*

Was this the way it had felt to be up on the roof of the Caesar's Palace that night in Vegas? Aiming down at the sea of first responders and survivors emerging from the entrance of the Bellagio. *Picking out one.*

Carol. He felt anger surge within his heart, seeing her face before him once more. She had stayed behind. . .trying to ensure that he got out before the bombs blew   the scent of camphor in the air as soman nerve gas began to fill the casino

Her voice, desperately earnest. *"And you thought I was going to leave you?"*

If she only had, she'd have lived. Her life for his.

"You can't bring her back to you, no matter what you do. . .no matter whom you kill." The reproach in Ismail Besimi's eyes as he'd spoken the words. And now he was dead too, cut down by his own compassion.

Mercy had no place in this world.

7:02 A.M.

There. Jawid rubbed sweaty palms against the legs of his uniform slacks, trying to calm his nerves. He'd had to take a break from it for an hour, but now he was cutting it close.

The plan was for both of them to strike at the crowded bistro where they worked as waiters. The height of lunch hour—his roommate detonating his vest in the middle of the restaurant—then he would hit the first responders as they arrived. Maximum carnage.

Double-tap.

"You about done with those, bruv?" his roommate asked, grunting as he rose from the grungy carpet where he had been doing sit-ups, his feet tucked under the sofa.

"*Almost*," Jawid breathed, glancing nervously at the dimmed screen of the tablet, its battery now running low but still displaying the diagrams. All that remained was to connect the detonator switch.

If everything was wired properly, this should be easy. If he hadn't—he dismissed that thought with a shudder. He *had*.

Insh'allah.

7:05 A.M.

"Come on in," Harry whispered, the buttstock of the sniper rifle tight against his shoulder—the figure of Tarik Abdul Muhammad centered in the firing reticle, high on the chest. Nearly every hair of his beard revealed in the high magnification of the scope.

He was out in the open now, coming down the street at the foot of the hill as he came back in toward the tower blocks. Nowhere to run, nowhere to hide. Just a few cars and the open street.

Trees beyond—out of reach. He could put three shots in him in the time it took a man to run that far. And it wasn't going to take three shots.

"*'Vengeance is mine, I will repay,' saith the Lord.*" An admonition as old as time itself. Harry shook his head, calculating for the breeze—a gentle crosswind. The drop of the bullet, almost nonexistent at this short range.

"For the blood of man," he breathed, nestling his cheek against the cool polymer of the stock, "shall man's blood be shed."

He took a deep breath and held it—his gloved finger curling gently around the rifle's match trigger. A lover's caress.

The explosion came without warning, ripping the morning air asunder, reverberating across the council estate. A fireball bursting from the fifth floor of the T-shaped tower block to the west. Blowing out the eastern wing of the "T" in a blossoming pall of debris and smoke.

Startled, Harry's eyes came up, off the rifle, his finger jerking the trigger back in a rough, reflexive movement—the Accuracy International's stock delivering a punishing blow as it recoiled into his shoulder.

The unmistakable supersonic *crack* of a rifle shot ringing out in the moment of deathly silence following the explosion.

A miss. He knew without even checking the scope. The sickening realization hitting him like a punch in the stomach. *Not even close.*

7:07 A.M.

Sniper. That was the first thought through Thomas's mind, lying flat on the asphalt of the road running under the shadow of the tallest tower. There was no mistaking that sound for anything else in the world, even coming as it did in the wake of an explosion.

A burst of static came through his earpiece, along with Roth's voice. Urgent, but even. Unflappably calm. "Echo Lead, Victor Element—we just lost the UAV—what in God's name is happening out there?"

Nichols. That thought came following close on the heels of the first, as it had been ever-present in his mind ever since the attack on the MI-5 surveillance van. The inescapable belief that his former team lead was *here*, in this country—seeking vengeance for Carol Chambers' death.

This had his name written all over it.

"It's like a sodding bomb went off," came the voice of the British officer known as "Victor Lead." His tone that of a man stunned, well-nigh struck dumb. *Would Harry have gone that far?*

Thomas glimpsed the form of the *Shaikh* slipping behind a parked vehicle, debris from the explosion still raining down over the street—saw Victor Element closing in, the four British field officers taking cover themselves even as a second shot lashed the dawn. But where was it coming from?

The roof of the tower. His mind supplied the answer almost as quick as he asked it, rolling onto his back to stare up at the looming council block above him. It was the vantage point he would have chosen—the one Nichols would have gone for, almost certainly.

"We've got CERBERUS making a run for it," he exclaimed, toggling his mike in response to Roth's query. "And someone's doing their best to kill him. Send in Special Branch—send in Special Branch right *now!*"

He didn't wait for a response from the command van, grimacing as he thrust himself to his feet—deliberately muting his earpiece as he measured the distance between his position and the ground-floor entrance to the tower block.

Time to boogie.

7:08 A.M.

The Security Service. Harry hammered the palm of his hand against the concrete of the parapet, swearing at himself in frustration as he watched the officers take shelter. Sweeping the street with the scope, trying to find Tarik once more. A fool's errand.

He had known there would be a police response—had known he'd only have time to take the shot and move immediately to E&E. He hadn't anticipated Five being right on the *Shaikh*'s heels. Shadowing him.

How could he have missed it? The signs, so painfully obvious, that his target was himself under surveillance.

Tunnel vision. His grief, his thirst for revenge blinding him to what was right before his eyes. Right *there*.

The Accuracy International swiveled on its bipod, its long muzzle traversing slowly as he endeavored to pick out his target amidst the smoke and debris from the tower block, trying to slow his breathing—to calm down—his hands sweating despite the chill of the morning air.

Go now, his mind screamed, every instinct that had kept him alive across fifteen years warning him to leave.

Before it was too late.

No. He had come so far, there was no going back now. He glimpsed a figure, movement in the haze near where Tarik had disappeared. *Target.*

He pulled the stock of the rifle snug against his shoulder, his finger slipping inside the trigger guard. *Good-bye. . .*

The next moment, the form of a middle-aged woman emerged from the smoke before his eyes, staggering—her clothing torn and bloodied.

His reticle centering on her face, almost perfectly between her eyes. *My God.*

He found his hands trembling suddenly as if seized with malaria, his face ashen as he realized what he had almost done.

The *life* he had so nearly taken. A nameless fear overwhelming him.

Glancing over his shoulder, he glimpsed a Special Branch team moving in from the road to the northwest in full tactical gear, weapons shouldered.

He straightened, laying the rifle aside—taking one final long look down toward the burning building, the spot where Tarik Abdul Muhammad had disappeared.

Dark disappointment twisting inside him, along with a grim realization.

If he was going to get out at all, it would have to be now.

7:09 A.M.
The command van

"Echo Lead, what is your sitrep? I say again, what is your sitrep?" Nothing but static filled the comms net, the uncanny silence gnawing at Darren. The American had just completely fallen off the grid. *Vanished.*

Just like CERBERUS.

And they were now utterly blind in the command van. . .the American UAV had been flying too close to the tower block when the explosion took place and had gone down, crashing into the roof of a nearby house. "Victor Element, what can you give me? Do we have a visual?"

7:15 A.M.

Nichols would take the stairs—of that much he was sure. No operator of his experience would risk being caught in the closed-in shooting gallery that an elevator could become. Not with this much on the line.

Thomas came around the landing and bounded up the next flight of stairs, heading toward the eighth floor. Wishing for what seemed like the hundredth time that he had a gun. *Anything.*

He shook his head at the very thought—it was surreal. He had served with Nichols for years. Fighting back-to-back in one godforsaken country after another. Never could have envisioned a day when the two of them would be on opposite sides.

Even in this.

A sudden thought struck him as he reached the next landing and he shouldered open the heavy fire door—scanning the hallway which ran down the length of the building to the other stairwell, straight and linear. Displaying all the architectural creativity of council housing the UK over.

Nichols could already be making his way out of the building down the other staircase, and he'd never know the difference. Could be hiding in any one of a hundred apartments.

He reached up to his muted earpiece, almost prepared to read Roth in on this—to bring Special Branch in to sweep the tower block.

But no. . .if it was Nichols, this was an Agency matter. Their man, *their* problem.

Even as he hesitated, he heard a fire door slam shut from above him—one, perhaps two flights up.

7:17 A.M.
The MV Percy Phillips
Port of Grimsby, Lincolnshire

"Seen anything of Hale?" Gordon asked, passing another former soldier in the passageway 'tween decks. The man was stripped to his shirtsleeves, the word *Sapper* inked in flowing script across the length of his forearm.

"Not lately. Check for'ard—he might be going over our course with the cap'n."

The *Percy Phillips'* captain was a former warrant officer from the HMS *Bulwark*—the rest of the crew being former Royal Navy as well. Hand-picked by Conor Hale, all of them.

Which is why he was going to have to be so careful. "I'm this far," he replied, knowing all too well where Hale actually was, "might as well check his quarters."

He moved past the man, hurrying his steps as soon as he was out of sight. Didn't have much time—the former sergeant was out on the docks, readying the car.

"We set sail as soon as we get back."

Pausing outside the door to Hale's quarters, he withdrew a pocketknife and a sturdy paperclip he had taken from the bridge—testing the door briefly to see if it could already be unlocked.

No such luck.

7:19 A.M.
The tower block
Seacroft, West Yorkshire

They might only have a couple teams in the field from the looks of it, Harry thought—his right hand tucked into the folds of his jacket gripping the suppressed Sig as he hurried down the stairs, his eyes flickering ahead of him to the landing below. Enough to take down a terrorist—not enough to cordon off a council estate.

That left him with. . .*what?* Eight, nine minutes? You never had as much time as you wanted.

He crossed the landing hurriedly, cutting the pie as he turned to face the next flight of stairs. *Going down.*

The door above him opened without warning, and he heard a familiar voice announce, "Harry."

His hand was a blur, the pistol coming out—his left hand sweeping up to support it as he aimed it back up the stairs, a man's face coming into focus between the sights. "*Thomas.*"

7:21 A.M.
The MV Percy Phillips
Port of Grimsby, Lincolnshire

There had to be something, somewhere.

The American had been right. Hale might have been running this operation, but he wasn't funding it.

Paul Gordon turned from the small desk back to the bunk, spotting a rucksack tucked into the shadows near its head. *There.*

He laid it on the bunk and unzipped it, noting the Kahr PM9 tucked securely into one of the side pockets along with a pair of spare mags. A tactical light. A few chocolate bars. And a mobile phone.

It wasn't the phone Hale usually carried, but it was the one he had seen him using several times—including just this morning, a few hours before.

He slid it open to reveal a darkened screen, pressing the Power button. It came on with a loud tone that caused him to cast a worried glance back over his shoulder to the still-closed door.

He was a soldier, not a spy. None of this came naturally to him. Not a bit of it.

A log-in screen came up before him and he felt himself panic, trying to shut the phone back down, but it didn't work—prompting for the password once more.

Come on. And then he remembered. . .a girlfriend of Hale's from back in the day. *Iraq.* Remembered him Skyping with her late at night, the packages from home. She'd had an unusual name—what was it?

Shay. That was it. He tapped the four letters into the phone, his thumbs moving awkwardly across the touch-screen. *"Password incorrect."*

He started to delete it all and start over, then thought better of it, changing first a single letter, then two. *$h@y.*

And there it was. The screen opened, his fingers quickly bringing up the menu—a series of numbers displayed under "Contacts." No names, just a log full of calls. Incoming and outgoing—several daily, each number seeming to have been used sequentially. Stretching back weeks.

There was the sound of footsteps in the passageway without as he tried to memorize the numbers and his breath caught in his throat. Time to get out of here.

7:22 A.M.
The tower block
Seacroft, West Yorkshire

"You're here with Five," Harry stated simply, lowering his weapon ever so slightly. "I remember now—Kranemeyer was planning to send you over as liaison officer."

He paused, his eyes searching his old friend's face for a long moment before he added, "Congratulations."

The New Yorker shrugged easily, keeping his hands away from his sides. In plain view.

"It's a dirty job, but somebody had to do it." It was a moment before he went on, gazing keenly at Harry. "And you?"

It was a question they both knew the answer to.

7:24 A.M.
The harbor
Grimsby, Lincolnshire

To take the life of one of their own. Hale shook his head, tucking the rifle case into the boot of his car and covering it over with a tarpaulin. But was he *really*?

The MP had paid lip-service to their cause, had been one of their leading voices for years. But since the outbreak of the violence—since being called out by the media for the role his own rhetoric had played, Pearson had quailed.

Like the politician he was. Securing his own future while better men than he bled and died for what he claimed to have believed.

Enough. His face darkened. Colville was right. . .there was no place for such men in the new world. In the world they were prepared to sacrifice themselves to secure.

He closed the boot with a heavy sigh, only too aware of the reality of that which he was about to do. Looking up, he saw Paul Gordon standing there on the gangway from the *Percy Phillips*, something of a shadow marking the former Para's face.

"You ready, mate?" he asked, walking toward him. "I have some. . .business to take care of inland—but I can get you on a bus into the city first. Take what time you have. Go see Alice."

Time they all had their affairs put in order. "I'll do that, thanks."

"No worries," Hale responded, putting a hand on his old friend's shoulder. "Go ahead and get in the car. Just need to grab my mobile."

7:25 A.M.
The tower block
Seacroft, West Yorkshire

"I had a feeling you were over here," Thomas went on after not receiving an answer. Harry's gunmetal blue eyes never leaving his, his weapon lowered now, but still clutched in the gloved fingers of his right hand, hammer back. "Hunting down the *Shaikh*. Just like we were. The attack on the surveillance van night before last—that was you, wasn't it?"

"I don't know what you mean." The lie was delivered perfectly. Nothing, not even a flicker of reaction in his former team leader's eyes. He could have laughed, if the situation hadn't been so dire. *Quintessential Nichols.*

"My officer is still in the hospital," he continued, forcing a note of anger into his voice to carry the lie. He had to know, to *confirm* the truth of what he suspected, or they were looking at a far bigger problem than he had even imagined. "They got her in intensive care. She had really bad asthma before all this, had an attack in the midst of all that CS. Barely got to her in time. She might pull through, might not—hard to say."

7:27 A.M.
The MV Percy Phillips
Port of Grimsby, Lincolnshire

He needed to be on the road already, Conor Hale thought, pushing open the door of his cabin and moving toward the bunk. All the moralizing in the world wasn't going to change anything if he wasn't in position to take the shot.

But it wasn't like leaving his mobile was an option. Not with awaiting word from Colville. And he had left it *right*. . .he found himself reaching, his hand finding only empty space as he groped for the phone inside the side pocket of the rucksack.

Nothing.

He jerked the ruck up onto the bunk, popping open clasps until he located the phone tucked in the pocket just across from where he thought he remembered leaving it.

But he *had*. Acting on a sudden impulse, he tapped in the password to unlock the screen, bringing up the *Recent* tab. Someone had opened his call logs.

A cold chill ran through Hale's body. He had personally chosen *every* man on this boat—a hand-picked few from the ranks of those he had served with in Iraq and Afghanistan. Men chosen for their loyalty, for their love of the country they all called "home."

And yet one of them had to be playing him false. *Who?*

He replaced the mobile and slung the ruck over his shoulder, locking the cabin door behind him as he moved quickly out into the corridor and toward the stairs, his mind racing.

Preoccupied with his thoughts, he nearly ran into a soldier descending from the upper deck, the man taking a step backward with a curse.

Hale registered the elaborate, flowing *Sapper* tattoo on the man's arm, recognizing him. *Delaney*. The two of them had spent time together in Basra, gotten drunk together more than once on leave in Kuwait. "Sorry about that, mate. Wasn't lookin' where I was going."

The man's next words stopped him dead in his tracks. "Did Gordon find you?"

Hale turned on heel, his eyes transfixing the former sapper. "He was looking for me?"

"Just a few minutes ago," the man nodded. "He was headed to your quarters last I saw him."

7:28 A.M.
The tower block
Seacroft, West Yorkshire

No. It wasn't possible, Harry thought, only too aware that his face had betrayed him in that moment. Regret and surprise, intermixed. He could see the woman even now, doubled up on the floor in the middle of the gas attack. It hadn't been *meant* to take her life.

Consequences. You tossed a stone into the water, watched as the ripples arced out from the point of impact, folding and unfolding until they were out of sight. A big enough stone could sink ships.

Destroy worlds.

Innocents damned. He felt the old bitterness wash over him in a storm surge, looking away down the stairs toward the next landing. "I'd pray that she makes it. . .but lately, almost think she might be better off without my prayers."

Wait. There was something there, behind the words. His head came up suddenly, eyes burning as he glared at Thomas. "But you're lying."

A shrug, the CIA officer still careful to keep his hands visible. "Am I now?"

"I should know," Harry fired back, seeing his friend's game in that moment. "I trained you."

Thomas had always been good. *Too good.*

His face twisted into a grimace, the Sig coming back up in his hand. Leveled at Parker's head. "You're stalling for a reason. Special Branch is on their way up the stairs even as we speak, aren't they?"

"Not that I know of," came the calm reply. "I turned off my comms set when I entered the building. No one knows I'm here."

"I don't believe you."

"Don't be ridiculous." Thomas shook his head. "What was it you once told me, Harry? Not long after I joined the Agency. 'That thin line between distrust and paranoia they warn you about. . .what they never tell you is that to do this job right, you're going to have to make crossing it part of your daily commute. The trick is not to set up shop on the wrong side of the tracks.'"

"I haven't," Harry replied, a cold certainty in his voice. "But this is where we part company."

He reached forward with his left hand, the Sig in his right still covering his friend. "Your earpiece. Take it out and hand it over. *Slowly*."

7:33 A.M.
The command van

"Negative, sir. I say again, we do not have a visual on CERBERUS." It was happening again, Darren realized as his earpiece crackled with static, staring at the map overlay in a measure of disbelief. Once more, they had *had* him—and once more he had made fools of them all.

Firefighters were on-scene now, trying to put out the flames even as West Yorkshire arrived in force, attempting to establish a cordon.

And the media. . .oh, yes, the media had been johnny-on-the-spot as well—in response to reports of the explosion, their news cameras aimed all over the place, sticking microphones beneath the noses of policemen.

It was a sodding *circus* out there.

He glanced back to see the SO-15 commander standing there with arms folded across his chest. "If you'd taken the advice I gave, Roth, my tactical teams might have been better placed to respond to the situation as it unfolded."

And so the bureaucratic scuffle begins.

"Save it, Inspector," he ordered brusquely, sunlight striking him in the face as he rolled the side door of the van back and stepped out onto the street.

There were people at Five—people like MacCallum—who excelled at the art of commanding from behind a computer screen, finding their skillsets best utilized in an office far removed from the heat of the moment. Working the 'big picture.'

He'd never been one of them.

His eyes roved the council estate as he moved forward along the street, assessing angles. Fields of fire. Someone had tried to take out the *Shaikh* before he could be taken into custody, that much was clear—his mind flickering back to Marsh's warning of the previous week.

"The Americans have placed a member of their Special Activities Division in charge. A paramilitary."

Which itself raised another question, in the midst of all this chaos. . .where *was* Parker?

The mobile in his pocket vibrated with an incoming call as if in answer to his question, an unfamiliar number displayed on-screen. "Hello."

"This is Parker," came the American's voice in reply. "I've found the sniper's perch—roof of the big tower, north corner. The rifle's still here."

Darren's head came up, shading his eyes against the dawn as he stared up at the looming tower block to the south. "And the sniper?"

"No sign of him."

7:40 A.M.
Seacroft Bus Station
West Yorkshire

Failure. It was a feeling you soon became acquainted with out in the field. The bitter taste of defeat. You couldn't win them all.

Couldn't save the world.

But somehow despite all of that, you always believed you could save the ones you really *cared* about. That your protection was enough to render them invulnerable.

Only to find them furthest beyond your grasp.

"Alpha now moving to clear south-east quadrant," came the voice through the stolen earpiece as Harry moved out along the roadway leading away from the council estate past the bus station. His pace brisk, but unhurried. Nothing that would have served to attract attention. "Going house to house. We have confirmation, I say again, we have confirmation on the sniper. Keep your head on a swivel."

But they were too late. Not only for him, but the *Shaikh*, most likely.

Too late. It was a feeling he knew all too well—the moment when you found yourself a moment too slow, a hair's-breadth behind the pace. Left avenging the ones you hadn't been able save.

And sometimes. . .failing even in that.

He picked up his pace, hands shoved into the pockets of his jacket. Two more kilometers to where he'd stashed the Vauxhall. Assuming it hadn't been compromised, which was unlikely.

Time to regroup, he thought. To reevaluate. There had to be an endgame to all of this. Finding that would be the key to finding Tarik once more. To *killing* him.

The bruised, bloodied face of Hashim Rahman rose darkly before his eyes. He'd nearly killed the man before he'd left this morning—put him out of his misery. Now he found himself glad he hadn't acted on that impulse of mercy.

They weren't done just yet. Not even close.

Chapter 25

9:43 A.M.
Thames House
London

"I am to meet with the PM and the Home Secretary an hour from now," Julian Marsh announced, taking his seat at the head of the conference table as he swept each member of his team with a critical, piercing gaze. "What, precisely, am I supposed to be telling them?"

"The operation to take down CERBERUS was an unadulterated failure," MacCallum began, clearing his throat. "The *Shaikh* has once more given us the slip, and to compound our problems—if he didn't know we were tailing him before, he does now. He will either go to ground, or this will only move things up."

"The 'reckoning' of which he spoke in his call to Rahman."

"Precisely. He'll try to strike hard and fast—act before we can locate him again."

The DG spread his hands, glancing around the table. "Does this storm cloud *have* a silver lining, gentlemen?"

"The terror cell in Seacroft that the *Shaikh* was on his way to meet," Norris interjected. "They're dead—casualties of the explosion, which is believed to have resulted from a malfunction with their own explosive vests. Final confirmation is waiting on the arrival of 11 EOD's 521 Squadron from Chester. They're in the air as we speak, twenty minutes out."

"The Lord be praised for small blessings," Marsh intoned, looking down at his tented fingers. "And the sniper?"

MacCallum shook his head. "Nothing as of yet, SO-15 recovered an Accuracy

International L115A3 from a nearby rooftop. Someone was clearly set up and waiting. We weren't the only ones who knew the *Shaikh* was going to be there."

He let that statement hang there for a long moment, its implications only too clear. They weren't just being outplayed, they hadn't even identified all the players at the table. A perilous oversight.

"And we have no idea who it is, do we?" the DG asked finally, voicing what they were all thinking.

"No idea," Norris replied. "We've pulled all the available CCTV footage from the area around Seacroft—I have my people sifting through it even as we speak."

"Get back to me the moment you have something. The *moment*."

10:56 A.M.
The industrial estate
North of Leeds

Killing a man in the heat of a firefight was one thing—the mind rationalized it easily enough.

No choice—him or me. Like Flaharty had said, they were words you told yourself to get to sleep at night. To escape the reality that you had taken the life of another human being. And escape it you could, given time. . .and practice.

But to take a man's life slowly, deliberately—using his pain as a weapon against him until it finally became too much for his mind or body to withstand. That was something different entirely.

The line between men and monsters.

The metal chair gave off a loud, unearthly scraping noise in the silence of the underground room as Harry dragged it across the floor, taking his seat across from Hashim Rahman. The man was slumped in his chair, his bloodied head resting on his chest—the zipties securing him to the chair the only thing keeping him aright.

Harry unscrewed the cap of the water bottle in his hand and tilted it back, taking a long sip. Letting the silence build until the tension was unbearable.

It was a feeling he remembered all too well from his captivity in the Hindu Kush. Sitting across from one of his interrogators in a room not so much different than this—beaten with a wooden club every time he made eye contact with the man, before they lapsed back into a silence broken only by his moans of pain.

Hours of it. Days, even. Until it came to that dark place where even the beatings were more welcome than the silence. Nothing more than a broken shell remaining where a man had once been.

He'd come so *close*. . .

His body shuddered, unable to even finish the thought. To relive the memories brought back by what he was about to do.

But he didn't have days. Or hours, really. Not now, with Tarik on the run.

Rahman's head came up slowly, fearfully—his eyes gazing out through blood-matted hair. "I. . .gave you what you wanted," he began, his voice hoarse and trembling.

The things that I want. Carol alive, the *Shaikh* dead. A house in the Virginia countryside. A wife, children coming home from school. Peace.

The American dream.

It wasn't a dream for men like him. Never had been. He replaced the cap of the water bottle, screwing it on with a painfully deliberate motion as he rose to his feet, walking over to where the terrorist sat.

"Please. . .I *helped* you. You promised. Please, just let me go. I swear, I—"

His hand drew back without warning, describing a sweeping arc until it met the side of Rahman's head, connecting with enough force to rock the chair back on two legs.

It hung there in the air for a single, agonizing moment, then crashed backward—a scream of pain and fear escaping the man's lips as he slammed into the concrete floor.

Harry stood there for a moment, looking down at him. A pitiful sight.

Probably the way he had once looked, lying there on the dirt floor of that house in Pakistan. But there was no place for pity this day.

He bent down on one knee beside Rahman, his face devoid of emotion. "You couldn't be more wrong, Hashim. You and me. . .we've only just begun."

11:07 A.M.
Thames House

"The crowd of counter-protesters is building as the British Defence Coalition gathers in Birmingham's Victoria Square at noon today for what has been advertised on the group's Twitter account as their 'largest rally to date', sparking fears that the strong nationalist presence may only incite further violence as Birmingham shop owners continue to sweep up broken glass from Monday's riots. MP Daniel Pearson is scheduled to address the gathered. . ."

And in the midst of it all, the Queen was departing for what was traditionally her late-summer residence in Balmoral, Scotland, Alec MacCallum thought—reviewing Her Majesty's route on the screen before him. SO-14's Special Escort Group had sent it over for Five to conduct a threat assessment.

He looked up at the sharp, insistent knock on his office door—reaching for the TV remote and hitting "mute" as he saw Norris standing there. "What is it?"

"It's CCTV from the council estate. You need to see this—it's the sniper."

MacCallum tapped a brief command into his computer, locking his workstation as he rose to follow Norris out into the corridor.

"He was careful," the analyst went on excitedly, "but not sodding careful enough. This time, we got his face."

"What do you mean, 'this time'?"

"I mean," Norris said, glancing back as he led the way into the Centre, "that we've run stride analysis on the CCTV feeds. It's the same man who was with Mehreen Crawford in City Station just before the deaths of Ismail Besimi and the young suicide bomber. The same man who was at the train station the day we lost the *Shaikh*."

He retrieved a folder from his desk and handed it over to the section chief, the heading "TOP SECRET—CANUKUS EYES ONLY" clearly visible at the top.

Canada. United Kingdom. United States. Three of the "Five Eyes."

"This man."

MacCallum took it from him without a word, pulling back the cover sheet impatiently to reveal the thin jacket beneath—a single photograph and a typewritten page—his eyes widening as they scanned down the paper.

"My God," he whispered, scarce able to believe what he was reading. "Get the DG on the phone at once."

11.34 A.M.
The council estate
Seacroft, West Yorkshire

So this was how it happened, Darren thought—walking to the edge of the roof and glancing out over the parapet, down to the street where Tarik Abdul Muhammad had last been seen.

It had been a couple years since he'd had a long rifle in his hands, but it was an easy shot. Or should have been. He could tell that.

The Accuracy International and the three ejected shell casings still lay where they had been discarded by the sniper—a West Yorkshire constable now snapping photographs of their placement. Reconstructing it all. This was a crime scene now, whether they liked it or not.

He shook his head. The number of people who would find themselves receiving a refresher on the Official Secrets Act after all this, it was going to be endless.

Movement off to his left and he saw Thomas Parker standing there, looking off toward the bus station. "We didn't have the eyes-on we needed after the UAV went down," he began, catching the American's eye. "If you had radioed in the sniper's position instead of deciding to play cowboys and Indians, we might have taken him."

"As I told you," Parker responded quietly, "I hit the ground hard when that freaking bomb went off. Damaged my comms unit in the process. Couldn't make contact over the network. Besides, it was a hunch, nothing more."

"Based on what?"

The CIA officer came over to the parapet to stand beside him, his eyes hidden by the polarized Wayfarers. "I. . .spent some time in Afghanistan, few years back. Rotated out to Kabul Station. Lost more than a few good men to sniper fire. You get a feel for where they're hiding."

At least part of that was true. "And you saw nothing of him on your way to the roof?" Darren pressed. "No one who looked or acted suspiciously?"

"Do I count the teenagers chewing *khat?*" The American shook his head. "Not a soul. It took me several minutes to even get to the building, he likely took the shots and made his egress immediately. That's what training would dictate."

Darren's eyes narrowed, trying to read the man's face. "Who said he had training?"

"No one. But that," Parker shrugged, gesturing toward the Accuracy International, "isn't something you use unless you do."

The man had a point. Darren started to respond to him when the phone in his pocket began to vibrate. *Thames House.*

"Roth here," he began, turning away from the American and walking to the far side of the roof. "Talk to me."

"Darren," came Julian Marsh's voice from the other end of the line, snapping him to full attention. *The DG.*

For Marsh to contact a field officer personally, in the middle of an ongoing operation—it was nothing short of unprecedented. "I just left a meeting with the Home Secretary. We've had a rather unexpected. . .development. I need you to listen very carefully."

11:40 A.M.

Thomas left the roof through the access door, drawing his Agency cellphone from his pocket as he moved down the stairs into the top floor of the tower block, which had been evacuated and sealed off by SO-15.

He listened for a moment, then entered an eight-digit alphanumeric authentication code—looking back over his shoulder. It was the first time he had succeeded in breaking away from his minders in hours. Roth suspected something, that much was clear.

And to be expected.

Langley had to be notified—brought into this. Stopping Harry on the stairs had been beyond his power, alone and unarmed, but it wasn't an end they could afford to leave loose.

A rogue officer operating on the soil of an allied country was a nightmare—the surest recipe for an all-night bender he'd ever heard.

An uncomfortably long moment passed before the call connected, Lasker's familiar voice answering. Not even zero-seven hundred hours back in the States. . .someone was in early.

"Listen, Danny," Thomas began, casting another wary glance down the corridor. Unable to escape the feeling that time was running short. Which was why he was going straight to the top, devil take protocol. "We've got a situation. Next few hours, give or take, it's going to get very delicate over here. I need to speak to the DCIA."

"He's not in-country at the moment," came Lasker's terse response. "Flew out of Dulles yesterday for a meeting with Anaïs Brunet in Paris."

Brunet. The head of the DGSE, France's foreign intelligence service.

"All right, then," he replied, his mind racing. There had to be a way to get ahead of this, to shut it down. He'd known Harry for a long time. Had never known him to stop. "Have Kranemeyer give me a call as soon as he—"

Thomas looked up suddenly to see Darren Roth standing there a few feet away, flanked by Howlett and two of his men. There was no mistaking the look in Roth's eyes—or the stance of both SO-15 officers, their hands resting on holstered weapons. *Crap.*

"I'm going to have to give you a call back, Danny. Something's. . .come up."

He closed the phone, turning to face the British officers with a half-smile. "Is there something I can do for you gentlemen?"

"Inspector," Roth began, his eyes never leaving Thomas' face, "have your men take Mr. Parker and his team into custody, by order of the Home Secretary."

It was hard to look surprised, but he managed it. He'd bluffed his way out of worse situations before—but this wasn't a Third World country. The chain of command here was all too clear. "On what charge?"

"Conspiracy to carry out an assassination in the UK."

12:16 P.M.
Victoria Square
Birmingham

He was positioned too far away to hear the words coming from the stage at the foot of the steps leading to the Council House, but no matter. He had heard them all before, many times. That's all they were. . .words. Stirring up the crowd for a passing moment before they would retreat to the comfort of their flats and fancy themselves warriors on-line.

The time for them was past.

Hale sank down behind the long gun, resting its barrel on a pair of sandbags he had brought for the purpose, glancing momentarily at the cloned burner phone lying there on the floor a few feet away, its screen still dark. Gordon had made contact with no one since they had parted ways, his location data showing him to be going exactly where he'd said.

Barnet.

Time to put all those suspicions—all thoughts of Gordon's possible betrayal—out of his head, for this moment.

He had a mission to perform.

The twenty-eighth floor of the office building was available for lease, but he had let himself in. He wondered absently if the small circular hole he had cut in the glass with a handheld saw—the aperture just wide enough to admit the L42A1's muzzle—would impact the property values.

Probably not as much as what he was about to do, the former SAS sergeant reflected, glancing back toward the black flag of jihad he had spread across the far wall, the thick copy of the Qur'an—all green and gilt—lying beside the sandbags. *Mirsab.*

The Sword of the Prophet. . .their mythical Libyan.

His scope swept the square nearly three hundred meters away to the east, making out the hideously modern "sculpture" known as *Iron: Man* rising high above the sea of protesters.

And there he was. He glimpsed the MP making his way toward the stage, escorted by an honor guard of former soldiers wearing BDC armbands.

Striding up onto the stage with the air of a conqueror, feeding off the energy of the crowd. Like the sodding politician he was.

His reticle centered on Pearson's temple as he moved, just to the front of the ear. *Easy, now.*

Right *there*. His finger slipping within the trigger guard. Ready to take up slack.

The primary phone in his trouser pocket vibrated with an incoming call in that moment, jarring him from his concentration and he reached back to withdraw it without taking his eyes off the scope. "Yes?"

"Our pawn," Arthur Colville announced, something of relief clearly audible in the publisher's voice, "is still in play. You can stand down."

12:24 P.M.
Barnet Hospital
North London

There was never any quiet in the hospital—the shrill sound of unattended alarms in the corridor mixing with that of authoritative voices over the intercom. The moans of patients.

And then there were those who would never speak again.

Paul Gordon reached out, taking his sister's limp, warm hand in his as he scooted closer to her low bed. His eyes taking in once more her bandaged face, the slow rise and fall of her chest the only sign that she was still alive. If just barely.

Lost in his own thoughts. Knowing their visit must come to an end soon. Knowing he couldn't leave without making his final confession.

She was no priest, but her hospital gown was more sacred to him than any cleric's robes in this moment.

"This last week," he began slowly, a single tear escaping the corner of his eye to leave a salty trail down his cheek, "I've done a lot of evil. I've betrayed my oaths, been responsible for the deaths of innocent women and children. And I told myself. . .I was doing it all for you. I was wrong."

His fingers found the burner the American had given him in his pocket and he took it out, turning it over and over in his hand. Staring at its darkened screen as he chose his next words carefully. As carefully as if she could have actually heard them.

"But I swear by the memory of our parents—by all that's holy in this world— that I'm going to do all I can to set this right. Even if it means I don't come back." He paused for a moment, forcing himself to face the reality of the choice. What he was about to do.

"Truth is, Alice," he went on at last, gazing earnestly at her sleeping form, "I'm not coming back."

He rose from his seat, leaning forward to kiss her forehead through the bandages. Fingers tousling a lock of what remained of her hair. "Now be good, luv. Get your rest."

And he was gone.

12:37 P.M.
MI-5 Regional Office
Leeds, West Yorkshire

"We've identified the man Mehreen Crawford was working with at the train station the day the Shaikh disappeared. At the bus station the morning the young suicide bomber was found dead. He's a CIA officer."

And a bloody good one by the looks of it, Darren thought, MacCallum's words filtering through his head as he scanned down the sheet. *Harold Nichols.*

Five didn't have much on him—only a single photo, dated 2008. Taken at Heathrow, judging by the backdrop.

That was impressive, in and of itself. And somehow. . .he had gotten to Mehreen. *Recruited* her.

One of their officers, a CIA asset. Unfathomable as that seemed.

"We have to face reality, Darren. Helping the CIA might be morally less repugnant than aiding the Islamists, but it's no less treason." The section chief had paused, as if suspecting he knew more than he was letting on. *"Mehreen was a friend, but she must be made to answer for this."*

The worst part of it was, MacCallum was right. And if Five even suspected that he had helped her, he'd be brought to book as well.

He opened the drawer of his desk to reveal the Sig-Sauer Marsh had given him—glancing carefully around the office to make sure no one was looking his way as he removed the pistol, holstering it on his belt beneath the jacket.

Slipping out in the middle of the renewed search for Tarik Abdul Muhammad—a search he was still, technically, in charge of—was hazardous, but leaving her out there was more so.

He still knew of a place or two to look.

12:43 P.M.
North London

Third call. *Straight to voicemail.* The American wasn't picking up his phone—no indication that it was even on.

Gordon swore under his breath, his head coming up as a passer-by jostled him on the crowded kerb. There had to be some way to stop this—to put an *end* to it.

The bus station was just ahead—forty minutes and he could be in Millbank. At the front door of Thames House.

It would be so simple. They would know how to handle this, they would know how to protect him.

Or would they? Hale's words, running back through his mind. *"This time. . .we have an advantage on them. We have a man inside Five."*

No. The American was his only option—the only solution for this. He hit SEND once more, listening as the voicemail came on once again.

"If you've abandoned me," he hissed when the tone came through, his voice trembling with anger and fear, "so help me, I'll see the end of you yet. Call me back as soon as you can."

12:48 P.M.
The industrial estate
North of Leeds

"The Queen," Harry whispered, using the remnants of Rahman's torn undershirt to wipe the blood from the tip of the hammer's claw, his hand moving with exaggerated care. "So what you're telling me is that the *Shaikh's* plan is an attack on the Queen—the royal family?"

"Yes, yes—*yes*," the man sobbed, his head buried in the crook of his arm, nearly incoherent from the pain. His fingers smashed, bloody stumps. Harry turned away for a moment, unable to maintain his composure—the memories flooding back. The pain, the *torment*.

He couldn't keep doing this much longer—the darkness threatening to reach out and overwhelm him. Swallow him whole.

Get a grip. It was an audacious idea—the kind of thing you would expect from a man who had brought an American city to its knees.

But that attack had to have been years in the planning—this one? It felt different, somehow. "And this attack," he began once more, turning on the moaning terrorist, "when will it take place?"

It took a moment for Rahman to respond, his breath coming in short, sharp gasps. "Her motorcade will be ambushed. . .on the road—on the road to Balmoral. *Tomorrow morning.*"

Dear God. It was happening, all over again. The moment when you looked up from running and realized you not only *weren't* ahead of your opponents. . .you weren't even running in the same race. Out of time.

"Is that the truth?" Harry leaned forward across the table—grasping a fistful of Rahman's coarse black hair and using it to roughly jerk his head back.

"Look at me," he commanded, his face scant inches from the imam's, "look me in the *eye*. Are you *sure*, Hashim? Are you sure this is the plan? Because you don't have enough fingers left to be lying to me this time."

"It is—it *is!*" Tears streamed down the man's face, mingling with the grime.

The blood. "I swear it before God."

Harry shook his head, reaching for the hammer. "That means nothing. You have broken so *many* of His laws—why should your oaths be any different?"

"No," Rahman gasped, the panic only too visible in his eyes. The look of a man who had been pushed so far past his limits he no longer even remembered what they had looked like. Desperation, raw and visceral. "No, *no*—please don't."

He was telling the truth. Harry released the man's head, watching him suck in great gulps of air—hyperventilating. "The plan was to hit. . .her motorcade, with a—with a bomb. Tarik said we'd disable the escort vehicles—kill the guards. Take her."

And butcher her on live camera. That was the way such things went—he'd heard this song before. He closed his eyes, fighting against the rage welling up within. His fingers finding the butt of the Sig-Sauer in its shoulder holster.

It was so tempting to just draw the weapon, put a single round through Rahman's forehead. *End it all, right here and now.*

But no. He eased his hand away from the pistol, his vision clearing. He had to get clear, think this through. *Plan.*

12:53 P.M.
Leeds Central Police Station
West Yorkshire

Enough of this. Thomas leaned back in his chair, glaring across the holding room table at the SO-15 officer standing there. "Protocol clearly dictates that Ambassador Cullen be apprised of any situation such as this one."

"And he will be," Howlett replied, with a smile that signaled more clearly than words how thoroughly he believed himself to be in command of the situation. "All in good time."

He pulled a photo from the folder in his hand and placed it on the table, sliding it across. "Do you know this woman?"

It was a picture of a woman in her mid-forties, dark-skinned—Pakistani, maybe? Dressed in Western business clothes, hair cascading over her shoulders. Dark waves shot with silver. *What was going on here?*

"I've never seen her before in my life."

Howlett shook his head. "I asked if you *knew* her, not if you'd ever met."

"Not biblically, no," he shot back, unable to repress the smile pulling at the corners of his mouth. "Haven't had the pleasure."

"The woman's name," the SO-15 man responded, controlling himself with a visible effort, "is Mehreen Crawford. She's an MI-5 intelligence officer—and a CIA asset."

"Well then. . .I'd hate to be you."

1:01 P.M.
The industrial estate
North of Leeds

It was a truism of the intelligence business. Everything you needed *was* out there, somewhere. On any attack, just as it had been on 9/11.

But intel was worth nothing unless you could get it into the hands of those who could make use of it.

And that was his current dilemma, Harry thought, pushing open the service door at the top of the stairs and walking out into the sunlight, finding himself blinking like an owl caught in the noonday sun.

The Agency was off-limits. Thames House was compromised. And Mehreen? She was as far out in the cold as he was, now.

Nowhere to turn. He felt a sudden vibration from his jacket pocket and reached within, fumbling for his phone.

Four missed calls. And a voicemail. He hadn't heard a thing—the cell's reception no doubt blocked by the building. He entered the brief passcode, the Para's voice coming over the phone only a moment later—his words hurried, clipped. Fear in his tone.

It was no reflection on the man's bravery. It was one thing to keep your head in a firefight—with death whining about your ears and men falling all around you.

It was another to take a step out on a tightrope, balancing above a chasm of lies. Knowing every single step could be your last.

Three rings, and then Gordon's voice answered cautiously, "Yes?"

"You had something for me, I believe?"

1:05 P.M.
New Barnet Station
North London

"Nearly thought you'd scarpered on me," Gordon exclaimed, feeling anger along with the relief that washed over him at the sound of the American's voice.

"I'm right here. Talk to me."

Gordon glanced down the tracks, hearing the sound of an approaching locomotive. Orders had been to rendezvous with Hale in Leicester, and he had already delayed far too long.

"There's going to be a jihadist attack, in Scotland. They're not just *letting* it happen, Hale's bloody well putting it together. It will—"

"Target the Queen's motorcade," the American finished coolly. "I know."

But. . ."I-I don't—how?"

"How I know doesn't matter. Give me the details—something I can work with. What is Conor Hale's endgame in the attack?"

The train was closer now, more people moving onto the platform. "He wants to turn public opinion in this country against the Muslims once and for all. Drive them out—start a war."

"And he believes that when the Queen is killed by the *Shaikh*'s men tomorrow morning, all that will be accomplished?"

"She's not to die in the attack," Gordon responded hurriedly, lowering his voice as if he feared being overheard. "The two of us will be set up on the ridgeline with sniper rifles—covering the motorcade. The *hajjis* won't get near her."

"Then why are you going to the risk of calling me?" The American asked, the same even calm in his voice. "It sounds like Hale has everything in hand."

Why, indeed. What had driven him to turn informant on an old comrade? His back on men he had fought beside. Was it still the screams of the innocents at Madina? The knowledge that he had betrayed everything he once fought for in that moment?

The train was pulling in, its loud whistle piercing the afternoon air. "If Hale gets his way, tens of thousands will die. Not just the animals we've been fighting over in the sandbox, not just thugs like the ones that. . .*raped* Alice. Thousands of women and children too. Theirs, ours, all of us together. I can't have any part in that." Something hit him just then and he paused, his mind racing. "Wait just a sodding moment—why did you say tomorrow?"

1:09 P.M.
The industrial estate
North of Leeds

"Because that was the nature of the intel I received," Harry replied cautiously. *Where was this going?* Rahman couldn't have been lying—or could he?

And the answer to that was *yes*, as he knew all too well.

"Then someone's been playin' you, mate," came the Para's response. "The attack is to take place as the Queen leaves Balmoral on the 11th. Hale an' the rest aren't anyways close to being in position. The ship with the arms—still at harbor in Grimsby."

And he could see it all in that moment, dark anger rising once again to the fore. Understanding what had so nearly happened. It was an old trick and a clever one.

There were few things an intelligence officer feared more than being wrong, having passed along bad intel. Being discredited.

And that was exactly what the imam had tried to do—strike a final blow for his cause by feeding him disinformation.

Dezinformatsiya, the Soviets had called it. Few things more deadly. *Enough of this.*

"And the man behind Hale?" he pressed, hearing voices in the background. The shrill piercing whistle of a train. His contact was on the move. "What have you learned?"

A pause, filled by the pneumatic hiss of doors opening and closing. A muffled apology exchanged. "I got into his phone," Gordon continued, his voice coming through clearly once more. "Had a series of numbers he's been calling for weeks. First one, then the next—and the next. Dozens of calls."

"Give them to me. I'll have it run." Somehow—he didn't know how, but there had to be a way.

The former soldier read it off the numbers twice, adding, "They were in his contacts under the label *Artorius*."

The Latin name of the man who had faded into the mists of British history as "King Arthur", Harry thought, inscribing the series of numbers into the back of his hand with a pen. It had to mean something, but what was unclear. *Misguided nationalist fervor?* Something more?

"And what are you wanting me to be doing now?" There was hesitancy there in the man's voice, but underneath it a resolve of steel. The resolve of a man who had looked into the abyss and turned his back upon it. "I don't have any training for this sort of thing, you know."

"None of us do," Harry replied, honestly enough. There was no training in the world that could prepare you for the reality.

The only way to learn this game was to play it, win…or die. "Stay with Hale—keep close to him. And keep me in the loop. Do it by text if you have to, and remember what I told you if you do."

Make sure not to forget the authentication code, he didn't add, unsure whether to assume the connection was secure.

He'd set it up to be simple—easy to remember. Hard to say if it would be easy enough. The stress of the spy business played games with a man's mind. Even when you were used to it—and the Para wasn't.

"I will."

It would have to be enough.

1:12 P.M.
Birmingham New Street Station
Birmingham

Conor Hale heard the call disconnect, lowering the cloned burner phone from his ear and watching the screen slowly fade to black as he leaned back into the threadbare seats of the train carriage. The doors sliding shut as the train began to move.

"They're not just letting it happen—Hale's bloody well putting it together." Those words, ringing in his ears. Again and again, a bitter echo. Barely-controlled anger distorting his face.

Betrayal. He'd told Colville that he could trust every man he had approached. Trust them with his *life*. . .but Paul Gordon more than most. They'd been mates, nearly made it to the Regiment together until Paul had collapsed that day on the slopes of Pen y Fan. A good man.

Or he once had been.

1:14 P.M.
The industrial estate
North of Leeds

Everything was quiet when Harry descended once more into the darkness beneath the abandoned industrial complex. The ninth circle of Hell.

Treachery.

The stench of excrement and fear filled his nostrils as he moved to one side of the room and switched on the utility light, its harsh glare illuminating the scene.

Hashim Rahman lifted his head from the table where he was handcuffed, moaning with the effort—his eyes filled with fear at the sight of the Questioner come to torment him once more.

Munkar. Nakir.

Not this time. Harry reached within his jacket, pulling out the Sig-Sauer and screwing the suppressor into the end of the threaded barrel. Slow, deliberate movements.

"*No*," he heard the man gasp, his voice weak, dehydrated. At the end of his strength. "Please, I did—I gave you *everything*. Please, my family. You said—"

"Shut up," Harry ordered brusquely, turning to face the man with the weapon in his hand—brass-checking the Sig's chamber to assure himself it was loaded.

Flaharty's words filtering their way back through his mind.

"You may never get the man who shot your brother in the sights of your rifle, so you shoot the sod next to him and tell yourself it's justice."

Was that what this was about? His inability to eliminate Tarik—to take vengeance for Carol's death? No matter. . .this *was* justice. And Flaharty had been right. It *was* war.

Eternal, unchangeable.

Chapter 26

2:04 P.M.
Thames House
Millbank, London

"The CIA team is being brought back to Paddington Green under armed escort," Norris announced, coming over to MacCallum's workstation. "They should arrive within the next couple hours."

"Has Grosvenor Square been notified of their detainment?" the section chief asked, glancing at his subordinate.

Norris shook his head. "Not yet."

"Well, we can't put off doing that forever," MacCallum acknowledged, running a hand across his face. "Have Hoskins draft an official memo and get it sent over. Nichols himself?"

"Nothing yet. The man's a professional, he'll have gone to ground." The analyst paused. "We suspected him of involvement in the 2006 murder of Ibrahim al-Qawi, a radical Islamist preacher in Marseilles—a man believed to be instrumental in recruiting young French Muslims to wage jihad in Iraq. Someone strongly resembling Nichols had been caught on CCTV boarding a Chunnel train from the UK to France only five days before, but we were never able to confirm the match with reasonable certainty, and that's where the trail went completely cold."

The type of man who was bloody impossible to find, MacCallum thought, gazing at his computer screen. They didn't have the resources to conduct another manhunt of this size—not with the *Shaikh* still in the wind. Had to narrow it down somehow.

"And Mehreen Crawford. . .what's his connection to her?"

Norris took a deep breath. "Crawford has foreign intelligence contact reports filled out as far back as 2002—it appears that he and her husband were friends up until the sergeant's untimely death."

"Served together?"

"I think that's a reasonable assumption—I don't have the clearance necessary to access the relevant files."

That told the whole story, right there. "Make sure Roth is apprised of that information."

"I tried," the analyst replied. "He's not answering his phone—no one at the regional office has seen him in over an hour."

Bugger.

2:17 P.M.
The offices of the UK Daily Standard
Central London

"I have eyes on our man," the man announced without preamble when Arthur Colville picked up the phone. The voice of his contact within the Security Service. "He's at the train station in Leeds—mingling with the crowd. Probably deciding on a ticket. Picked him up on CCTV twenty minutes ago."

The publisher swore. "And you're just now getting around to calling me? If he bolts—if Five gets their hands on him—it's the end. We'll have to start this whole bloody thing all over again."

"And I'm of no use to you if my cover is blown," the man replied coolly, "I called as soon as it was advisable to do so."

"Is there any way you can contact him?"

"Not reliably, no. You're going to need to get a man there—to make contact with him in person. Make sure he's still on-course. Guide him back if he's not. A call won't accomplish that, even if we had the means."

And there it was, the fatal flaw. "I don't have any people close enough. No one I trust."

Conor Hale was the only man he had entrusted with the entire plan, from start to finish. The only man that could be sent to meet with the *Shaikh*—to bring him back to the fold.

And he was on a train bound for Leicester—too far away to do what needed to be done. Unless. . .

"Once he buys a ticket," he ordered tersely, "get me his destination."

His man at Thames House just snorted. "That's not even possible, it's not like we're dealing with a bloody airline. Best I can do is give you the train he's on through CCTV once he boards. No way of telling where he intends to stop."

"Fine. Do it."

Colville ended the call, walking to the window of his office overlooking the city—weighing his options, none of them good.

At length, he pulled out the mobile once more, dialing a number from memory. "Brian," he began when the other end came on, "how soon can you have the Agusta in the air?"

2:23 P.M.
The industrial estate
North of Leeds

And it was done. Harry stripped off the bloody latex gloves one at a time, dropping them into a plastic bag and placing it in the boot of the Vauxhall. Every last shred of his presence removed from the industrial estate, only the battered and bloodied body of Hashim Rahman remaining in the underground room that had borne witness to his torture and execution.

No matter. By the time anyone found the corpse, it would be far too late for them to do anything. And there was nothing to connect him to the death.

Except the Agency. Or Thomas Parker, which was effectively the same thing. They knew now for a certainty what they might have only suspected before—it only remained to be seen what they would do with the knowledge. Whether they would inform the Security Service.

Not very likely, he thought—moving around to the driver's side door. He had spent most of his life in their employ. He knew how they worked, how they thought.

The millstones of bureaucracy might grind exceeding small, but they ground slowly. Slowly enough for a man to roll out of their way, if he kept his wits about him.

If. The burner phone vibrated within the pocket of his jacket and he reached for it, glancing at the screen. *Number unknown.*

"Yes?" he answered cautiously, his hand on the open door—eyes scanning the abandoned industrial buildings surrounding him. Searching for vantage points. Any sign that he was being watched.

"I've been watching the news out of Leeds," Mehreen's voice responded. "That was you, wasn't it?"

The accusation was there—beneath her words. He didn't know how many people had died in the tower block, that ball of fire exploding from the eastern wing. How many *innocents*.

"The explosion. . .wasn't my doing," he responded slowly, "but I was there."

And that was always the way, wasn't it? Samuel Han's words to him—that night in Vegas.

"After this, Harry, after all of this is done—I never want to see your face again. Where you go, Death follows. . ."

And scant moments later, it had followed him straight out the door of the Bellagio and claimed Carol's life. Like it had followed him here.

Sammy had been right.

Silence. No response from the other end of the line, just the faint sound of her breathing. "I'm afraid I'm going to need to make this short, Mehr," he said after another moment, forcing the emotion to subside, "so what can I do for you?"

"I called. . .to apologize," she began, clearly struggling to speak the words. "You were right, and it was wrong of me. Aydin left you with no choice."

No choice. He shook his head, still seeing the kid's face. *If there had been another way, do you think I wouldn't have taken it?* He wanted to ask, but the words wouldn't come out.

"No, he didn't," he responded finally. Leaving it there, the silence hanging once more between them.

"If you were there at the council estate this morning," she went on, an edge to her voice, "then that means you tried to take the *Shaikh* out of play. And it means you failed, because the news would have had that report. If not them, the bloggers. I want to help. I know this country, Harry. Better than you ever will. If you want to find him again. . .well, there was a reason you showed up at my door when you came to the UK. You need me."

That much was true, but there was something else. Something she wasn't saying. "And in return?"

"When all this is over, when the *Shaikh* is dead—I want Stephen Flaharty."

3:31 P.M. Local Time
A chateau in the Gironde Department
Aquitaine, France

"It's a beautiful place you have here," David Lay observed quietly, glancing about him at the grandeur of the old chateau—one face of the western wall covered in climbing ivy, similar growth providing a shroud for the iron gate ahead leading down the path toward what would have been, in the 17th Century, the servant's quarters.

A beautiful place, and one far beyond the salary of a public servant. But "public servant" seemed an insufficient descriptor for the likes of Anaïs Brunet.

A former chief executive of the now-defunct Astrium—a French aerospace manufacturer—the fifty-four-year-old Brunet had left the private sector over a decade earlier to pursue a second career in French politics, one that had led her to the head of the General Directorate for External Security. The DGSE, to use the acronym taken from the French.

Clearly, Lay thought, her career choices had agreed with her.

"*Merci*, David," Brunet responded, ushering him through the gate ahead of her. She was an attractive woman if one chose to think of her in such terms—short dark hair and piercing black eyes. "Back when all of this was built in the 1600s, in the years following the devastation of the Thirty Years' War, its owners were producers of some of the finest Bordeaux reds in all of Aquitaine. Left Bank vintage, of course—with proportionally more Cabernet Sauvignon than Merlot."

"You know your wines, Anaïs."

"Could I rightly call myself French if I did not?" She laughed, her dark eyes never leaving his face. A moment passed before she spoke again, her expression softening as she did so. "I am only glad that you could come and pay me this visit. Only a few months ago, there was speculation that you might not return at all. That you might not make a full recovery."

Full recovery. What did that even look like? The CIA director asked himself, forcing a false smile to his face. How did you "recover" when everything that made life worth the living had been ripped away from you? Your one chance at redemption—forever lost.

"I lived," he responded simply. *Honestly.*

She favored him with a sidelong, searching glance—as if suspecting there was more he would not say. "And that is good. But this trip, David, out here away from the trappings of our respective offices. . .and the listening ears that go along with them. You did not come to France to discuss my wine or the Islamists' attempt on your life."

Ah. . .yes. It was reassuring to know that even a rival intelligence service had bought into the cover story surrounding the attempted assassination. The truth was far too devastating.

"You're right, of course." He stopped, casting a look back toward the chateau as he turned to face her. They were not alone, of course—their bodyguards back there, keeping a careful overwatch. "The Agency's involvement in Alliance Base is coming to an end."

"Effective *when*?" Brunet demanded, turning on him, her dark eyes snapping like coals of fire. Unable to conceal her surprise—her inexperience in the intelligence world never more visible than in that moment.

Lay shrugged. "Six months. A year, maybe. If we're lucky. I'll do what I can to drag my feet, to slow things down, but it's not going to change anything in the

441

end. The new President is committed to bringing a new 'transparency' to the intelligence community."

And the kind of veiled, secretive intelligence-sharing efforts that had led over a decade earlier to the creation of the joint CIA-DGSE Counterterrorist Intelligence Center in Paris had no place in this brave new world.

"'Transparency?'" The woman sneered, shaking her head in disbelief. "Every politician promises that."

"This one means it."

Brunet just looked at him incredulously, whatever she might have been about to say lost as Lay's phone began to ring. He took it out, intending to silence it—until he saw the identifier code displayed on the screen. *Langley.* "Excuse me," he said apologetically, "I have to take this."

2:33 P.M.
Leeds, West Yorkshire

"No," Mehreen heard him say, his tone brooking no opposition, "that's not going to happen. If it wasn't for him, I wouldn't have gotten this far, wouldn't have even had a shot at Tarik. I'm not going to step aside at the end of it all and let you put a bullet in his head."

"But he was responsible for my husband's *death!*" she hissed, closing her eyes to envision Stephen Flaharty standing before her once again. There in the wood of St. Albans, her pistol aimed at his head.

To have taken that shot. "The two of you were mates in the sandbox. . .Nick loved you like a brother."

"And giving Flaharty over to you to be executed, it's not going to bring him back, Mehr."

Mehreen laughed, a bitter, mirthless sound as she pushed open the door of the small Toyota—stepping out onto the street. "Are you even bloody *listening* to yourself? The hypocrisy of what you're saying? You have only one sodding reason for being in the UK—to avenge the death of someone you loved more than life itself. That's what Nick was to me, Harry—life itself. And that *man* took him away from me."

Her hand came up, angrily brushing away a tear from her cheek as she continued, the torrent of words pouring out of her. "Who do you think you are, God? You and you alone get to decide who lives, who dies? You don't have the *right* to seek your own vengeance—and then deny me mine. No right at all."

There was a long silence from the other end of line before Harry's voice came back on, "You're right. I'm sorry, Mehr. . .that was unfair of me."

There was something strange in his voice—a curious note of resignation. *Defeat?*

"I've secured intel on what Tarik's planning," he went on after a long moment, changing the subject, "not something we can discuss over an open line. Where can we meet?"

She glanced down the street toward her destination, a nondescript terraced house near the end of the row, its windows boarded over. "There's an old safehouse in north Leeds, abandoned about six years ago in the restructuring of Five's network. I'll text you the address. And Harry—about Flaharty—do we have a deal?"

"We have a deal," he acknowledged, his voice cold, emotionless. "I'll meet you there."

The old passkey still worked in the front door of the abandoned safehouse, the hinges creaking as Mehreen let herself into the hall—closing it behind her.

Her eyes adjusting to the dim light—the familiar sight of a place where she had worked more than one asset over her years as a case officer.

Case officer. That's what her conversation with Nichols had reminded her of, an exchange between a case officer and an asset.

Perhaps that's really all this was to him—an operation. Her, an asset. In which case. . .could she trust him to do what he had promised?

Trust. It was a concept as alien to her as to him, both of them inhabitants of a world where lies were the currency of the realm.

But Harry had been Nick's closest friend—more of a brother, really. There was no way he'd let his killer walk free in the end. No way she would *let* him.

Mehreen shrugged off her jacket and hung it on the bannister of the stairs, revealing the HK45C holstered at the small of her back as she moved into the kitchen. Might as well take inventory—they were going to be here awhile.

She was stooped down by one of the cabinets when she heard a noise from behind her—the sound of a footstep against the floorboards, her heart almost stopping.

Moving with exaggerated slowness, she rose from her crouch, her hands kept away from her sides as she turned to face the doorway. Darren Roth was standing there in the entrance, an unreadable expression on his dark face—the suppressed Sig-Sauer P229 in his hands aimed at her head.

"Lose the gun and have a seat, Mehr," he ordered, indicating one of the dust-covered kitchen chairs with a jerk of his head. "We really need to have a talk."

10:57 A.M. Eastern Time
The Russell Senate Office Building
Washington, D.C.

"Understood, ma'am," Melody responded, cradling the office landline against her shoulder as her cellphone buzzed with a text message. "I'll have the Senator give you a call as soon as he's available. Yes, I understand."

Can't meet today, the text read—the number withheld on-screen. *Perhaps tomorrow?*

She hung up the phone and started to tap a reply, but the door from the inner office came open in that moment. Coftey himself emerging from within—his suit and tie discarded for a light windbreaker. His snow-white hair covered by a Longhorns ball cap.

"See if you can re-schedule my lunch with Senator Pressman," he said, a smile crossing his face at their eyes met. "Give him my regrets. I'm going to need to slip out."

"You got through?" she asked, genuine surprise in her voice. She hadn't expected. . .

"Ellis is going to meet me for lunch," Coftey nodded. "They're taking it seriously."

And then he was gone, her face changing almost as soon as the door had closed behind him. Twisting into a frustrated grimace as she swiped her thumb across the phone's screen, tapping in a brief message.

Too late.

4:12 P.M. Greenwich Median Time
Leicester Railway Station
Leicestershire, United Kingdom

Plans have changed, the text message from Hale had read, Gordon thought, glancing out the window as the diesel train moved slowly out of the Victorian-era station, gathering speed as it headed north. *Business to take care of. Stay on the train*—*msg me when you get to Leeds.*

Return to boat? Had been his query in response, a question answered simply with: *No. Establish comms when you reach Leeds.*

Something was wrong—he could *feel* it, somehow—a nervous tension pervading the air. The way it had before more than one ambush in the sandbox, the massive explosion of a roadside bomb taking out the lead vehicle—the chatter of weapons on full-auto filling the air.

He glanced over at the young woman sitting beside him, her earbuds firmly in place, oblivious to everything around her—her thumbs moving swiftly over the screen of the mobile in her hands.

Ease up. Another few days and this would all be over. Come what may.

11:27 A.M. Eastern Time
Bob & Edith's Diner
Arlington, Virginia

"You're serious," Scott Ellis said, a skeptical look in the minority leader's eyes as he leaned back into his seat, his back against the wood.

"You know I am," Roy Coftey responded, putting down his sandwich and dabbing his fingers on a napkin. "Otherwise you wouldn't be here."

Ellis shook his head, glancing around the nearly deserted diner. The lunch crowd hadn't arrived just yet, and they all but had the place to themselves. "And I probably *shouldn't* be. If we're seen in public together, Roy—the rumor mill, it's never going to stop."

Coftey just smiled at his Republican counterpart. "If you think anyone is going to recognize me wearing a Longhorns cap, you're kidding yourself."

Ellis didn't laugh, his blue eyes never leaving Coftey's face. A searching, penetrating gaze—the look of the prosecutor he had been before leaving the criminal justice world for politics.

"So you're actually prepared to come over?" he asked, lowering his voice as he leaned forward, his elbows on the diner table. "You understand the ramifications of doing something like this?"

"Don't patronize me, Scott," Coftey replied, his voice taking on a harder edge. "I've been in this town for over thirty years—was already on the Select Committee when you were putting away small-time drug dealers in Albuquerque. So I can assure you that when I offer your party the chance to seize the majority in the Senate, I know what I'm doing."

"In exchange for killing the President's signature first-year legislation. And it's not a real majority you're offering us," Ellis countered, "but a technical one. It'll be split straight down the middle, 50-50."

"Just like it was in '01-'03. And just like with Dick Cheney back then, you've got Vice President Havern on hand to split any tie votes." Coftey shook his head. "Norton has a lot of big battles coming up. The budget, entitlements. . .those are all going to be party-line votes and you know that as well as I. What I'm offering you is the chance to deliver on all those, big-time."

"But in return, we have to ensure that the NSA bill never makes it through the Senate."

Coftey nodded. "Dead on arrival. I don't want it even coming to the floor for a vote."

"That's going to be—"

"Don't give me that. You have the clout to do it, Scott. And the votes. Norton's people may have made inroads, but you're not the only security hawk in the party—and you're no more interested in seeing this bill pass than I am. The only difference between us is that I'm willing to lay my entire career on the line to stop it—and I'm giving you a way to ensure you can without having to."

"All right," Ellis said quietly, rising from the table. "Let me see what I can do."

4:35 P.M.
Leeds, West Yorkshire

"I understand, I do, Stephen—but that is why I'm calling," Harry said, his eyes scanning the city street as he continued, leaning back into the driver's seat of the Vauxhall. "If we're going to have any shot at stopping this, I'm going to need the weapons to do it."

It was a brutally delicate business leading a man to his death. *One false step*.

But those were the terms of his agreement with Mehr. He closed his eyes, shaking his head. That it would come to this. Bartering lives to obtain his objectives. It wasn't as though he hadn't done it before, a hundred times. Even so. . .

"And in return," Flaharty began, the skepticism clearly audible in his voice, "I get. . .what?"

"We *both* get what we want," Harry retorted, his face hardening, "revenge. You for the lives of your men. And I for the death of the woman I loved."

There was a harsh laugh from the other end of the line. "And your friend the widow Crawford? What about her? There's no way this ends with all of us getting what we want, boyo."

And there it was.

"You just leave that to me." He took a deep breath, glancing down the street toward the abandoned Security Service safehouse where she had requested the meet. "I've known Mehreen for a very long time. I can *handle* her."

It was hard for him to even know which of them he was lying to.

The door of the safehouse was unlocked, just as Harry had expected it to be—the knob giving beneath his hand with a moan of protest, the entry hall dark as he entered.

Light came from a doorway off to one side near the end of the hall, its rays illuminating the thick dust cloaking the bannister of the stairs to his right.

Safehouses were ever the same, all over the world. Desolate and sterile, devoid of warmth. The hollow shells of lies, just like the people who used them.

Lies, like the one he had just told Flaharty. Telling the man what he needed to hear, what *he* needed him to believe, more importantly.

The Irishman was in—on his way to retrieve the weapons Harry had requested from a cache. . .somewhere. That didn't matter.

What mattered was that he believed he would be protected at the end of all this. *Safe*. When nothing could be further from the truth.

Harry stepped through the open doorway and into the light, finding himself in the kitchen. Glancing over to see Mehreen sitting at the table half-way across the room, just sitting there. Looking straight at him. The whistle of the teapot on the stove the only sound breaking the silence.

There was something wrong. . .he could see it in her eyes, he could *feel* it, a sixth sense warning him of danger. He took another step into the room, clearing his throat. "Mehreen?"

He sensed the presence there even before he heard the footstep against the floorboards behind him—turning on heel to find himself looking down the barrel of a Sig-Sauer, nothing but steely resolution in the eyes of the black man holding it. He was shorter than Harry by four or five inches, his head shaved clean. His bearing unmistakably that of a soldier.

"Keep your hands where I can see them, Nichols," the stranger instructed, the pistol's cold, dark muzzle never wavering. "No sudden moves."

4:48 P.M.
Thames House
London

"Sir." Julian Marsh looked up to see Alec MacCallum standing there in the doorway of his office, a strained look on the section chief's face. "We may have a problem."

"If there proves to be *only* one," Marsh observed, a biting sarcasm in his tone, "it will be a delightful change of pace. Spit it out, man."

"Word just came in. The CIA director has landed."

"David Lay is *here*?" The DG shook his head incredulously. "In London?"

"Came into Heathrow on a private business jet an hour ago—we picked him up on CCTV. I would assume he's on his way to the embassy even as we speak."

"That didn't take long at all," Marsh observed, his face twisting into a grimace. They had informed the American ambassador of the team's detainment scarce two hours before.

He hadn't expected Lay to show up in person. "There's no other reason he could be here, is there?" he asked, glancing up suddenly.

"None that we are aware of. It wasn't a scheduled visit."

Bugger-all. Well, there was no help for it now. Time to do what must needs be done.

"Reach out to Grosvenor Square on my behalf," Marsh began slowly, "and arrange a meet. And make it clear to Lay. . .this isn't a request."

4:52 P.M.
The safehouse
Leeds, North Yorkshire

"Why are we spying on our allies?" Harry had once seen a TV news anchor ask in the wake of the Snowden leaks, self-righteously ignorant outrage burning from her eyes as she stared into the camera.

His own mind supplying what was, to him, an only too obvious answer: *"To make sure they're still our allies."*

Alliances. . .nothing more than shifting sands in the world of the spy. And salvation belonged to the man who stayed one step ahead of the quicksand. Moved his feet in time.

Like he had just failed to do, he realized, keeping his hands away from his sides as he glanced back at Mehreen.

Sold out. There was an irony there—in that only an ally could betray you. Only a friend get close enough to put a knife between your ribs.

"Your friend?" he asked, indicating the armed man with a small gesture. "I don't believe we've met."

She didn't meet his eyes. "Darren Roth. He's with the Security Services. Formerly of Her Majesty's Royal Marine Commando, Special Boat Service."

SBS. That told him what he was working with—gave him his odds of winning if this went completely pear-shaped.

Slim to none.

"Thames House." He shook his head, gazing reproachfully over at her. "So that's what this was about, Mehr. Telling me you were willing to help me get the *Shaikh*, to bring him down before he could launch his attack. . .all of it just a game, a ruse to get me here. Turn me over to Five—get yourself back on the inside."

"*Enough,*" she whispered, nearly spitting out the words as she rose from her seat. "This has *never* been about me. And you've been lying to me since the very beginning."

His eyes shifted from Mehreen to Roth and back again, his mind racing. Searching for a way out. *Finding none.*

The accusation was true enough, but what did she *know*? "I have no idea what you mean."

"Come off it," Darren Roth ordered, his weapon still leveled as he stared Harry down. "All the lies, all the deception. It ends here. *Now.* No point to it anymore—your team has already been taken into custody."

"My team?" Harry asked, shaking his head in confusion. And then it hit him.

4:57 P.M.
The train station
Midlands

Even now, hours later, Tarik could still feel the panic-fueled adrenaline coursing through his veins as he stepped from the coach onto the platform—glancing about him at his fellow passengers.

It reminded him of the first time he had been shot at, coming under fire during the ambush of an American infantry platoon in the mountains of Afghanistan.

Those first moments of sheer, unadulterated terror when the rounds began flying.

Had the British publisher sold him out to Five? He thought, moving through the station toward the entrance. His eyes catching sight of a bus for Northamptonshire just starting to fill up on the street without.

Had this all been a set-up from the very beginning, some ploy of theirs to trick him? To lure him into exposing his people?

When he closed his eyes, he could still see the way Colville had looked at him that night of their first meeting—the unadulterated hatred burning from the Englishman's eyes.

He had never dreamed of trusting the man, but he had thought their meeting might well have been ordained of Allah.

A clear pathway laid out before him, down which the faithful could advance.

And now everything which had then seemed so clear was clouded once more. Had he misjudged God's will? Mistaken it for his own plans?

It felt as if he was standing on the brink of a precipice. . .so close to launching an even more devastating blow against the West than he had struck in Vegas. And yet so uncertain.

He boarded the bus, still lost in thought as he took a seat toward the back—closing his eyes as he leaned into the cushions, the bulk of the Beretta within his light jacket pressing against his ribs. The time had come to confront Colville. To get at the truth.

Then, and only then could they proceed with the attack. To bring the justice of Allah to one who had so long defied him.

"This seat taken?" A strangely familiar voice asked and he looked up just as Colville's second-in-command—the British soldier—took the seat beside him. His eyes boring into Tarik's own for a brief second.

Ya Allah. He could feel his heart pounding against his chest—just as it had when the crack of the sniper's bullet had split the air past his head in Leeds only hours before.

5:00 P.M.
The safehouse
Leeds, West Yorkshire

"Listen to me, Mehr," Harry began earnestly, looking her in the eye. "Think about it. If I still had the Agency's backing when I came to the UK—*if* I had a support network in place *inside* the surveillance operation—why would I have shown up on your doorstep? Asked for your help in tracking down the *Shaikh*?"

Everything—*everything* depended on bringing her over. On her *believing* the truth. Because that's what this was. But when you made for yourself a life of lies. . .the day came, sooner or later, that even the truth wasn't enough.

And you found yourself against the wall, with no way out.

"I don't know," she replied, shaking her head as she seemed to consider his words. "Because I don't know *you*. I don't know who you are anymore, Harry—it's not like you trust anyone. Did you suspect that the Security Services would keep the Agency team in the dark, that they wouldn't have the access you needed? Did you just need someone to take the fall when you took out Tarik? Was it because using Agency assets was too much of a risk?"

"Too much of a risk?" She recoiled as he took a step toward her, ignoring Roth's weapon—his eyes flashing. "As if contacting a foreign intelligence officer *wasn't*? Do you think the Agency would have *ever* sanctioned anything remotely like that? That they—"

"You've said enough," the former Royal Marine interrupted, cutting him off. "Let's say you're telling the truth. If Parker isn't still working with you, then why didn't he—"

"Take me in?" Harry spread his hands in an expansive gesture. "How precisely was he supposed to do that? Not like you Brits let him carry a weapon—though I see you've managed to lay your hands on one, Roth. Hardly standard issue with Five, now is it?"

The man shook his head, his face hardening as he glared at Harry. "The patronization isn't going to get you where you want to be, Nichols. I'm asking why didn't he report it—give you up as soon as he could reach SO-15? We had tactical teams in place, could have pinned you down before you had gotten a hundred meters."

That last was an open question, but there was no point in arguing. "Hard to say. Might have been loyalty. . .to me, maybe—to the Agency, more like. If you've ever worked with Langley, you know they prefer to clean up their own messes." His eyes narrowed, shifting between the two of them. "Or maybe he just knew what I know."

"And what would that be?" He could see the gears turning in the man's mind—trying to figure out where he was going. Stay one step ahead.

"That Thames House is compromised," Harry replied evenly. "Like I'm sure Mehreen has already told you."

5:04 P.M.
The bus
Midlands

"You're a long way from where you need to be, *Shaikh*," Conor Hale observed in a low voice, his eyes facing straight ahead. Showing no sign of knowing the man he had just sat down beside.

"You tried to have me *killed*," the Pakistani hissed, his voice equal parts anger and fear.

"I assure you. . .that wasn't us."

"I give *that* for your assurances," the man shot back, spitting angrily on the floor of the bus. "How do you expect me to believe you?"

This is what it had been like in the Middle East, Hale thought—conducting "joint operations" with the rabble who called themselves the Iraqi Army.

Like trying to reason with a child. "Because," he began slowly, with exaggerated patience, "if it had been us, you *would* be dead. And we wouldn't have needed a sodding sniper."

The *Shaikh* lapsed into silence, seeming to consider that for a long moment. "And our plans?"

"Still on track," Hale responded. "The motor vessel will dock in the port of Aberdeen later this night. Your men began arriving in the city a few hours ago."

A nod, as if in acceptance. "All they await," the former SAS man continued, "is the arrival of their leader. And that starts with both of us getting off this bus."

5:07 P.M.
The safehouse
Leeds

"We've already been through all that," Darren replied, an edge of ice to his voice, lowering his weapon at long last. "Well before you walked in."

Indeed they had, Mehreen thought—for the better part of two hours, with her laying out every bit of evidence she'd been able to obtain of MacCallum's treachery.

And she still didn't know if he believed her. Or if he still somehow suspected her of responsibility in the deaths of the British officers who had formed Ismail's escort.

As reluctant to trust her as she now was to trust Harry. Perhaps there was an ironic justice there, somehow. As little of it as could be found in this world.

"I don't know what to think," he continued finally. "It just doesn't add up."

"Are you sure about that?" She saw Harry's eyes flash with intensity as he pressed his advantage. This was Nichols in his element, and trust him or not, there was no denying his skills. "Nine days ago, you had Tarik under surveillance at Leeds Station—you had that place blanketed with personnel, officers all over. And he walked out, right past you. How did he do that—a man who had never been to Leeds before in his life—without help? And that hasn't been the only time he's been able to pull that off, has it?"

There was a moment's pause before Darren responded, and then he nodded. "No, you're right. It's happened more than once. We had tracked him to the Queens in City Centre yesterday morning. By the time we had a team on-site, he had vanished."

"Because he was warned," Harry continued, not letting up. "Warned off by someone with access to Five's internal networks. It couldn't have been Mehreen, not then—she was no longer on the inside at the time."

He could see the man waver, pressed on. "I don't ask that you trust me, I only ask that you recognize that the stakes we're playing for couldn't be any higher. And in this, we're *both* on the same side."

"But Alec. . .it just doesn't make any sense. I've worked with him for a long time—years. He's a good man."

"A 'good man'," Mehreen spat, unable to contain herself for any longer, "who attempted to have me killed. I considered Alec a friend as well—the closest of friends—but you have to face the facts, Darren."

"The facts?" He turned on her, ignoring Harry for a moment, his face distorted with raw emotion. A dark anger, boiling there beneath the surface. "You mean like the facts that show you were turned by *this* man? That you became an Agency asset? Those *facts*?"

"My *life* has been devoted to the Security Service," she retorted, her voice trembling—her dark eyes glittering as she met his gaze. "I lost my husband in the defence of this sodding *realm*. Turned my back on my family. You can't honestly believe any of that."

"Frankly, Mehreen, I don't know what to believe. Not anymore." Darren just looked at her for a long moment, shaking his head sadly. "But if anything you've told me is true. . .we're in a very dangerous place."

He turned back toward Harry, his face grave. "I'm told you're in possession of intelligence concerning an impending attack. Here, in the UK."

Harry nodded, adding, "An attack on the Royal family."

She could feel the blood drain from her face, the shock in Darren's eyes mirroring her own. "My God. . ."

Chapter 27

5:13 P.M.
The United States Embassy
Grosvenor Square, London

"Let me know the moment he arrives. The *moment*," Carlos Jimenez emphasized, replacing the phone in its cradle on his desk. He needed a drink, but that hardly seemed the best of ideas, with the director set to arrive.

David Lay's Agency transport was still fifteen minutes out, caught in heavy traffic that had snarled in the wake of five young "Asian" men rolling tires out into the middle of the A4 and setting them on fire.

This was turning into a career-ender of a nightmare.

Having your officers detained on the soil of an allied nation was bad enough. Having the DCIA come in to resolve the situation personally was even worse.

It implied incompetence, even where none existed. That he had, as yet, been unable to ascertain *why* his officers had been detained only furthered the perception.

Jimenez sifted through the stack of folders on his desk as if hoping they might contain the answers he sought. Parker's last reports had been made nearly twelve hours before and indicated that the British had greenlighted the closing down of the surveillance operation—moving in to take Tarik Abdul Muhammad into custody pending the apprehension of another terror cell.

And then. . .silence. Social media had been awash all day with news reports of a bomb blast from the council estate where the operation had been conducted, but MI-5 itself had never been more close-mouthed. All the usual back channels closed down. An intelligence officer was well-nigh useless without access to intel, and he had never felt more useless than in this moment.

This wasn't the 'Stan, either—not like he could send out a patrol kicking down doors to get the information he needed.

He was still sitting there, lost in thought, when the phone rang a moment later. The voice on the other end informing him, "You have an incoming call from Thames House. Alec MacCallum."

Jimenez was bolt upright in an instant, immediately alert. "Put him through."

"Was any explanation given?" David Lay asked brusquely, one of the uniformed Marines leading the way past the security barriers as they entered the Embassy. There had been no pleasantries, the DCIA descending upon London Station like Christ come to cleanse the temple.

"None," Carlos Jimenez responded, glancing cautiously over at the director. The two men had only met once before, three years earlier at Langley, but in that time Lay had aged. . .a decade, maybe more. "He simply relayed the request from Marsh for you to meet him at his club tonight at 2300 hours."

"Julian Marsh," Lay mused aloud, his expression unreadable. "That old warhorse. Tell him I'll be there."

5:47 P.M.
The port of Aberdeen
Scotland

He'd been fifteen when he first saw the open sea, Nadeem thought, hands shoved into the pockets of his hoodie as he strode along the quay, the gigantic gantry cranes casting hulking shadows in the harbor lights. Strange, that—for a lad raised in South London.

But that had been the reality of his life, growing up. Skipping school whenever he could, running with the gangs. Getting into trouble.

It wasn't like his mum had anything to say about it, drifting in and out of alky-clinics all through his childhood. Lost in her bottle and pills, unable to find the peace that had eluded him until those darkest of days in prison.

The peace of God. The path that had led him to this place, prepared to give his life for something *greater*.

Nadeem glanced up at the warehouse looming large in the semi-darkness ahead, then back toward the chain-link fence surrounding the complex. One of the brothers standing guard by the wide vehicle gate he had entered only minutes before, a pistol concealed beneath the man's jacket.

Brothers. The like of which he had never had before. A sense of belonging. Of *purpose*.

Making his way along in the shadow of a towering stack of shipping containers, Nadeem moved toward the side door of the warehouse, taking in the sight of a second man stationed there. "*Salaam alaikum*, bruv," he said softly as he approached.

"*Wa' alaikum salaam*," the older man responded, his dark eyes never leaving Nadeem's face. "But among God-fearing men were two on whom Allah had bestowed His grace. And what did they say?"

The briefest of smiles touched the lips of the young black man as he recited the pre-arranged response to the challenge. "When once you are in, victory will be yours."

6:09 P.M.
The safehouse
Leeds, West Yorkshire

"The scope of an attack like that," Darren Roth mused, leaning back in his chair as Harry finished talking. "The resultant fallout if it could be pulled off, if the Queen's life was even placed in jeopardy. . . it would be unimaginable. I don't understand what they can hope to *gain*."

"What do they ever hope to gain?" Steam drifted upward from Mehreen's tea as she sat there, stirring it idly. Her eyes vacant, the eyes of someone who had seen far too much.

"I don't mean the *Shaikh*," Roth shot back, gesturing impatiently with his hand. "I spent years fighting against his kind in the mountains of Afghanistan. I mean the nationalists—men like Conor Hale. The kind of men I *served* alongside."

"Your country is on the brink," Harry offered, leaning back against the faded linoleum of the counter. "The violence of the last couple weeks, the bombings. All it will take is one push to send everything over the edge."

Over the edge, and hurtling headlong into the abyss.

"And what then?"

"What then? What's ever the aim of the revolutionary—from Robespierre to Mao Zedong? To ride the chaos, remake the world in their own image. It takes a special kind of hubris to throw the world into the fires and believe you can pull it back out without being consumed yourself."

"So that's what this is all about?" Roth asked, the irony clear in his voice. "A 'better' world?"

"Isn't it always?" Harry allowed himself a grim smile. A nameless wag had once observed that the reason history repeated itself was that no one had been listening the first time around. Not that they ever did. "They believe they can accomplish with this what none of the wars they bled and died in ever have—eliminate the Islamist threat to the UK, once and for all. A 'final solution', you might call it."

Echoes of more history. Repeating itself, again and again and again. And ever to the accompaniment of the cry, *Bring out your dead.*

It was a moment before the British officer responded, sitting there shaking his head as if struck dumb by it all. "It's madness. And yet he's getting men to follow him. In God's name, *how?*"

"We both went to war," he continued after a moment, "look around you. Do *you* recognize the country you came back to? I never did—and the longer I spent at war, the less of a bond I felt with those I had left behind."

Between the protector and the protected. . .a great gulf fixed. A chasm washed in blood.

"War teaches a man that he has only his brothers." And sometimes not even them, Harry thought—feeling anger swell within him at the memory of brotherhood betrayed. *Hamid Zakiri.* "That they are *all* that matters—because at the end of the day, they're the only ones comin' for you. And it's that brotherhood that Conor Hale is leveraging to achieve his objectives. The sacred trusts of men who have been through the fire together."

"But who is backing his play?" Roth looked up, his eyes searching Harry's face. "An operation of this magnitude—a former NCO isn't funding it off his bloody pension."

He pulled a slip of paper from the pocket of his jeans and extended it to Roth. "We have this. . .a list of phone numbers Hale has been in communication with over the last week. Can you see that they're run—discreetly?"

A nod. "I believe so—there's an officer I know at GCHQ. Owes me a favor or two."

"Call them in," Harry responded simply. It was no time to be holding back. *Go for broke.* "We only have eight days to get to the bottom of this. Less if we stay here—by now Five has to be wondering why you haven't brought me in. They'll be sending back-up, might already be on their way."

Roth exchanged a glance with Mehreen before clearing his throat, drawing a disassembled cellphone from an inner pocket and laying it out on the table. Shell, battery. SIM card. "Thames House doesn't know where I am."

The admission caught Harry off-guard, his eyes narrowing as he stared at the intelligence officer. "Then do you mind telling me what are you actually doing here?"

"You spoke of brotherhood," Roth said, pausing for a long moment before continuing. "And from what Mehr tells me. . .you and I both passed through the fire with the same man. Nick Crawford."

9:58 P.M.
Brooks's
St. James, London

It had been as a young intelligence officer that he had first set foot in one of London's famous gentlemen's clubs, Lay thought.

Back in the '80s, before the Wall came down. When the biggest enemy—near the *only* enemy—on anyone's radar was Russia, and Usama bin Laden was nothing more than a failed guerilla fighter.

But then, as now, he had come to meet with an opposite number in British intelligence. The more things change. . .

The passage of nearly thirty years, and yet the unmistakable feeling of entering the Old World remained, the Great Subscription Room's barrel-vaulted ceiling rising high above him as he strode purposefully among its clustered tables—brushing past a waiter in formal attire carrying a silver tray upon which balanced a decanter of brandy and a pair of crystal tumblers. A room in which the fortunes of English nobility had once ridden on drunken wagers, the stakes ludicrous even by modern standards—thousands of pounds sterling changing hands in a night over games of whist or ribald bets.

Nowhere near as high as the stakes this night.

The stern countenance of Pitt the Elder gazed down from a marble bust of the long-dead statesman as Lay mounted the stairs to the suite of rooms on the second floor of Brooks's, finding himself standing a few moments later in a small, dimly-lit room, towering oaken bookcases filled with gilt-bound volumes stretching toward the ceiling—the portrait of some 18th Century English lord hanging over the mantel.

"It's been a very long time, David," a voice announced, the slight form of Julian Marsh rising from a dark leather wingback chair just across the room. "Too long. . .please, have a seat."

"I can just as easily stand," Lay responded coldly, pausing where he stood—his bulk framed in the open doorway.

"If that's how you prefer it." The Cambridge graduate shrugged—his eyes keenly searching Lay's face. The eyes of a man who had spent years at this game, grown old in the playing of it.

And there was nothing more dangerous than an old spy, as they both knew.

"We've known each other for what, nearly three decades?" Marsh asked, taking a bottle of Glenlivet off the small endtable by his chair and deftly pulling the cork—watching as the aged single malt splashed into a glass. "Drink?"

Lay shook his head in the negative. "Very nearly. It was the fall of '88, if I remember correctly. West Berlin."

"Ah, yes. . .that was during the Medinsky affair, wasn't it?" Marsh smiled faintly. "A rum show, that."

More like a case study in how quickly and completely an operation could go awry, from his memory of it. Even with his experience running assets into Castro's Cuba—Berlin had been a league unto itself. "Rather."

"Hardly, I dare say, a high point of Anglo-American cooperation," Marsh observed, returning to his seat. "But you and me—we saw it through."

"You, me, and Beecher."

The DG smiled, taking a sip of his whisky. "Right, Frank Beecher—how could I forget?"

We three spies. Two Americans and a Brit—him freshly divorced, Marsh and Beecher fighting over the same woman.

"Best case officer Berlin ever saw," Marsh went on, "leastways the best on our side of the Wall. Any word from him of late?"

"No, I'm sorry," Lay shook his head, feeling a pang. "I thought you knew—Frank passed away back in '09. Prostate cancer."

Marsh winced. "A shame. He was a good man. And Jacqueline?"

"By his side to the end. They were always good for each other. But you didn't arrange this meet to discuss old times and dead spies, Jules—so why don't you just cut to the chase?" Lay advised sharply, knowing it had been a mistake almost as soon as the words had left his mouth.

Never blink first.

But he was running short of patience with. . .all of this. This godforsaken world of shadows that had claimed first his marriage, then his only child. Perhaps him, as well—when it really came down to it, not that it seemed to matter. Not anymore.

Marsh leaned back into his chair, his elbow resting on the polished leather, drink poised delicately between the fingers of his left hand.

"You know, David," he began finally, extending a long forefinger toward the CIA director, "I could almost bring myself to admire, even respect, the audacity of what you've done—if this was playing out in some sodding Third World backwater. But this isn't Afghanistan, this isn't the Bekaa. This is *Britain*. We are a nation of laws, and I will *not* sit idly by and let you run them over roughshod."

He had known the situation was serious. The detainment of an entire team was unprecedented in the history of relations between the Agency and the UK intelligence community—on either side the Atlantic. But this. . .this was something far graver.

"Perhaps it would help both of us," Lay responded, his words clipped and low, "if you explained precisely what you believe I've 'done', Jules. And why you've now ordered the detainment of my team—a team tasked with *aiding* your service, on the dime of the American taxpayer."

The DG just sat there for a moment, regarding him silently. As if deciding what to say next. At length, he picked up a folder lying there on the endtable beside the bottle of Glenlivet and extended it to Lay. "This man. . .do you know him?"

There was something in the way he asked the question, and in that moment Lay knew. He just *knew*, a premonition seizing hold of him as he took the folder from Marsh, flipping it open to reveal an oh-so-familiar face staring back at him.

The face of the man he had once entrusted with all that was dear to him—the safety of his daughter, her protection against the men who had tried to take his life. *A sacred trust.*

A trust betrayed.

"Harold Nichols," Lay acknowledged, lifting his eyes from the folder. "I know him."

10:14 P.M.
The safe house
Leeds, West Yorkshire

"You still don't trust him, do you?" Mehreen asked, breaking the silence as she glanced across the table toward Roth. Harry was out, recovering his equipment from the boot of his vehicle—the two of them alone once more.

"No," her colleague responded after a moment, meeting her eyes with a steadfast gaze. "Do you?"

An impossible question to answer, easy as it would have seemed just weeks before. *God, how do these things get so complicated?*

"No," she admitted finally, the words coming out with painful reluctance. How had they ended up in this place? "But I believe him. And that's the more important thing, in this moment. You don't?"

Roth let out a long heavy sigh. "I believe there is another agenda at play, whether it's his or the Agency's."

"Then what do you intend to do now?"

"Head back in to the regional office," he responded, pushing back his chair and rising to his feet, "make my best excuses for my absence and do what I can to trace these mobile numbers. Best case, I get myself recalled to Thames House. If I can get back to London, I have a direct line to the DG. I can go around MacCallum, or anyone else. But this isn't something to be dealt with over the phone. Keep me apprised of developments here—anything you find out. As soon as you find out."

"But you said. . ."

"I don't believe Nichols." Roth took a step toward her, placing a big hand on her shoulder as he looked into her eyes. "But I believe *you*. And if you believe this is what needs to be done, then we're going to let it play out. We have eight days."

Relief. Stemmed only by the fear that somehow she might be wrong—that her own thirst for revenge could be blurring her vision, blinding her to the truth. "I thought earlier that—"

"I had to be sure," he replied, drawing her close—his arms enfolding her. "But those times in Iraq. . .all Nick could talk about was you. You were everything in life to him, and I'd be betrayin' his memory if I let you down now."

Memories. It was hard to think of them now. Now, when all they represented was grief.

"What time is Stephen Flaharty supposed to arrive here with the weapons?" he asked quietly, holding her in a gentle embrace.

"Sometime in the morning—I don't know the exact time. Neither does Harry."

Or didn't seem to, she corrected herself silently. The two were not the same.

He looked down at her, concern written across his dark face. "Are you *sure* about this, Mehr? I can pull you out right now—you don't have to go through with this."

"But I *do*," she replied, taking a step back from him. This was more important than her own life. Justice, finally served in Flaharty's death. *For Nick.*

"All right, then," he nodded, turning to leave. "We let this play out. But understand at the end of all this, Mehreen. . .Tarik, Flaharty, Nichols—MacCallum, if he's as guilty as you believe—we're taking them all down. Every last one of them is going to prison."

"I understand."

10:19 P.M.
Brooks's
St. James, London

"And you honestly believe that I *authorized* an operation of this nature?" Lay took a seat on the couch opposite Julian Marsh, tossing the folder on the coffee table between them as he sank back into the smooth leather. "Are you out of your mind, Jules?"

"What I choose to believe doesn't alter the facts," the DG responded calmly. His words even, measured. Ever the epitome of the unflappable Brit—exactly as Lay remembered him from those days back in West Berlin. "Or the reality that our alliance now hangs by the most tenuous of threads. We do *not* spy on one another, David. . .it is that imperative that undergirds the very existence of the Five Eyes. A trust now broken."

Australia. Canada. New Zealand. The United Kingdom. The United States. The five countries whose intelligence-sharing had coordinated efforts against the Warsaw Pact throughout the darkest days of the Cold War. And these days, against the threat of international jihad. No partnership more vital.

Marsh drained the last of his single malt and set the glass back on the table beside him, his eyes coming back to rest on Lay's face. "You understand, I don't hold you personally responsible for any of this. If there is one thing I realize all too keenly, it is that you and I are the instruments of policy—not the architects of it."

The eternal dilemma of the spy, as it was that of the soldier, Lay thought—considering his next words. Tasked ever with executing the will of other men. Threading the needle between the objective desired and that which was possible. Understanding that no politician who mouthed the words *"Do whatever it takes"* ever really meant them. Or would stand behind them when the butcher's bill came due.

But Marsh wasn't done.

"After all, the last time your nation was attacked on such a scale you responded by going to war—twice. Is it inconceivable that you would launch a covert operation to assassinate the one man responsible for the attack on Las Vegas? Hardly. If anything, that's rather restrained by the standard of you Americans."

It made sense, he could see that. And was precisely the course of action he would have presented to the President. . .if Tarik Abdul Muhammad had sought refuge anywhere but the UK. Not that there was any guarantee *this* President would have given his authorization.

"You might very well want to believe that, Jules," Lay responded finally, measuring his words with care. "But nothing could be further from the truth. Nichols resigned from the Agency over two months ago."

"How convenient."

10:27 P.M.
London Bridge
Central London

London bridge is falling down, Arthur Colville thought—a smile touching his lips at the memory of the old children's rhyme as he stood there by the concrete balustrade, staring up-river at the unmistakable silhouette of Tower Bridge, lit against the night. *Falling down, falling down. My fair lady.*

A man materialized at his side, all sound of his approach covered by a passing automobile—and Colville glanced over to recognize the face of his man inside the Security Service.

"The Thames is beautiful at night."

"Indeed it is," the man replied, delivering the pre-arranged response, "but you'd have a better view from the Tower."

Colville leaned back against the concrete, his eyes searching the man's face for any sign that he was playing them false. *None.* "Hopefully, we shan't all end up there in the end."

"You know," he went on, gesturing toward the southern bank of the Thames, "hundreds of years ago, there was a gatehouse at that end of the bridge—it was where they'd mount the heads of traitors. William Wallace was the first, followed by countless others over the centuries. Now? The traitors to England can be found in the House of Commons. Did you bring the drive?"

"I did," the man said, pulling a small thumb drive from his pocket and holding it up, visible in the glow of the streetlight above them. His hand trembling ever so slightly as he passed it over. "It contains. . .everything. Five's files on PERSEPHONE, in their entirety. Every last piece of intel, laying out the history of the operation from its beginnings. Every time Thames House could have brought the *Shaikh* in—and didn't."

The keys to the kingdom.

"When you go to press with this following the attempt on the Queen's life," the intelligence officer continued, "the British people will be finally forced to wake up, to *face* how our national security has been jeopardized in the name of political correctness—of this sodding 'multicultural experiment.' It's going to bring down the government."

"You are going to be safe from reprisals?"

The man nodded slowly. "I have taken precautions. But what of you?"

"I'm prepared to go prison for publishing these documents, if necessary," Colville replied, looking the man in the eye. *True believers.* In reality, the Security Service was going to be kept far too busy to worry about him. . .the next twenty-four hours would see to that. "If that is the price that must be paid. *For England.*"

"It's really happening, then," the man breathed, seeming almost overawed by the realization.

"It is." The publisher smiled, reaching out to clasp his informant's hand. "England confides that every man will do his duty."

"Godspeed." And the man was gone, vanishing into the night almost as quick as he had come.

Colville stood there by the balustrade for a moment longer, gazing down into the Thames—its waters glittering a blood-red hue in the lights of London Bridge, lights lit every night in memoriam of England's fallen.

For that was what one did in the modern world. Mourned one's dead, but left them unavenged. *No more.*

He felt the phone on his hip vibrate with an incoming call and he plucked it from its pouch, taking in the sight of an unfamiliar number. "Hello?"

"Our piece has taken its place on the board," Hale's voice responded, speaking carefully. "As of twenty minutes ago."

"Good," the publisher said, tucking the phone closer to his ear as a vehicle passed by on the bridge, its engine noise drowning out all other sounds. The *Shaikh* had arrived in Scotland to take command of his men. Behind schedule, but he was there. And that would have to be enough. "And the shipment?"

"Arriving in the port of Aberdeen in the next two hours. I'll be flying up later tomorrow."

That came as a surprise. "You haven't left?" Colville asked, glancing quickly at his wristwatch. Hale was supposed to already be in Scotland, leading their team—to deviate from the plan at this critical moment. . .

"Not yet. Still wrapping up a few things on this end."

And that could mean anything, the man's tone giving him nothing to work with. "Anything that I should be made aware of?"

There was a barely-perceptible pause before the former SAS sergeant responded, "No."

It was impossible for Colville to determine whether there was anything there beneath the man's words, but Hale had been his first recruit, and he trusted him. Trusted him to carry out the work they had both committed themselves to. Knowing that death or imprisonment could well lie at the end of this road. "Very well," he responded. "Communications will be kept at a minimum from this point in, but do not hesitate to apprise me if the situation necessitates it. Understood?"

"Of course, sir."

Colville returned the mobile to his belt, turning away from the balustrade and walking back along the bridge toward north London. Less than twenty-four hours now.

Cry havoc. . .

10:31 P.M.
Brooks's
St. James, London

"No," Lay began heavily, looking across toward the painting over the mantel. He was starting to regret not having accepted that drink. "Nichols was *forced* to resign from the Agency after his actions leading up to the Vegas attacks."

A skeptical raise of the eyebrows was Marsh's only response for a moment, oppressive silence continuing to reign in the small upper room of the club. Finally, "And what actions might those have been, that you would have forced out a senior field officer?"

"He went rogue. Executed a young college student, the son of a Russian arms dealer, in the process of trying to obtain intel to stop the attacks. The kid was an American citizen."

Marsh winced. In a world where they broke the law on a daily basis, there were some lines you could never cross.

"And," Lay went on, his voice trembling with emotion, "he was responsible for the death of my daughter that night in Vegas."

The DG's face registered shock, complete and unfeigned. "I'm sorry, David. . .I had almost forgotten that you had a child. Forgive me."

"Don't apologize," Lay responded, his voice sharper than he had intended. "She wasn't much more than a toddler when we were in Berlin together, Jules—right after her mother left me. Had only been back in my life for a couple years when she died outside the Bellagio that night. A sniper's bullet. Nichols was supposed to have *protected* her."

He took a deep breath, attempting without success to collect himself. "You're right if you believe I want to see Tarik Abdul Muhammad brought down. But if you think for one single moment that I would trust that *man* to do it. . ."

"I believe you," Marsh responded after a long moment, reaching for the bottle of Glenlivet and pouring himself another drink. "All these years—but from what I see, they haven't changed you that much."

He leaned back in his chair, shaking the single malt gently to loosen the ice. "But this former officer of yours—he murdered a citizen of your country. Why isn't he in prison?"

"Such a prosecution," Lay began, shaking his head slowly, "would be. . .problematic, to say the least. There are aspects of the case which would be in the best interests of no one to have dragged into the public eye. You can appreciate the delicacy of such a situation?"

"What I can appreciate," Marsh replied caustically, pausing for a moment to drain his glass once more, "is that had the American justice system worked properly, Tarik Abdul Muhammad would still be cooling his heels in Guantanamo Bay and Nichols would be in federal prison. Instead they're *both* here, on UK soil. And your problem has become mine."

That much was inarguable. "Perhaps there is a way we can help each other."

The DG set his glass on the endtable and leaned back in his chair. "And that would be?"

"Arrange the release of the officers you detained this morning. Do what you need to—declare them *persona non grata*, put them on a plane back Stateside, I really don't care," Lay said, gesturing impatiently.

"And in exchange?"

"And in exchange, I'm prepared to offer you the full cooperation of the US intelligence community. In tracking down and effecting the capture of Harry Nichols."

Chapter 28

*3:07 A.M., April 4*th
The safehouse
Leeds, West Yorkshire

"*Promise me.*" *Low, desperate words. Soft lips melding into his, bodies pressed close together—her back against the door. His rough, callused fingers caressing her cheek.* "*Promise me this won't be the end. That there will be a future—for us. Beyond all the fighting. All of the war.*"

"*Yes. . .did you really think I would leave you?*" *A voice filled with tears, her words punctuated by the sharp* crack *of a rifle. The sound of a bullet breaking the sound barrier—smashing through soft flesh.*

And she was falling. Falling. Falling—

Harry's eyes flickered open, his breath coming fast—his shirt soaked with sweat as he came off the sofa, his hands finding the butt of the Sig-Sauer and jerking it from its holster. The muzzle coming up as he brought it to level, a faint metallic *snick* as the safety was thumbed off.

Only the shadowy outline of the door met his eyes through the semi-darkness, and he found his hands trembling. Carol's voice still ringing in his ears, haunting in its recrimination. *"You knew. You* knew.*"*

Get a grip. He safed the pistol, laying it on the low table as he stood—struggling to calm himself, his heart beating against his chest as though it threatened to break free. The weight of memories bearing down upon him. A crushing load.

There had never been a future. Not for him, no matter how much he had tried to deceive himself otherwise. There was only *this*.

Harry stumbled from the living room and down the hallway to the small bathroom, flicking on the light and turning the faucet on, full-blast. Splashing cold water into his face with both hands, eyes gazing back at him from the mirror. Haunted and staring.

Enough. He glanced at his wristwatch—Flaharty was due to arrive with the weapons in less than five hours. Time to get what rest he could, while he could. *If* he could.

God only knew what the dawn would bring. Roth. . .it was impossible to know whether the British officer was going to follow through on what he had promised—or give them up to Five.

Which is what he would have done. Back when he'd been with the Agency. Fighting for a flag.

But those days were over. Fallen to ashes. Just like the dreams of something more.

5:37 A.M.
The port of Aberdeen
Scotland

Salt water from the North Sea splashed over Tarik's bare feet as he rubbed them vigorously up to the ankles, first right and then left, washing them carefully three times in the performance of the *wudu*, the ritual cleansing that ever preceded prayer. "O Lord," he breathed, whispering the words of the *du'a*, "Keep me firm on the Bridge to Paradise on the day when feet will slip. . ."

A day when men's hearts will fail them, he thought, reaching forward to take a small cloth from Nadeem. *A day like unto today. I seek refuge in God from the outcast Satan.*

He could feel his body fairly hum with nervous excitement as he stooped once more, drying his feet. A spiritual ecstasy the like of which he hadn't experienced since Vegas, preparing to strike at the heart of the infidel. "I bear witness that none has the right to be worshipped save Allah alone, Who has no partner," he said, reciting the *shahada* as he handed the damp cloth back to the black man. "And I bear witness that Muhammad is His slave and His messenger."

The first of the five pillars of Islam, he thought, padding barefoot out across the cold concrete of the warehouse floor toward where his men had begun to assemble. The creed of his faith.

A faith which had become his stay through the long years at Guantanamo Bay, locked away behind razor wire on those cliffs overlooking the sea. A vision of God appearing to him in those darkest of hours. Setting him back on the path.

Keep me firm on the Bridge to Paradise. . .

He strode to the front, gazing out over the assembled company gathered in front of the vehicles they would use to mount their assault—the body of a delivery van already stripped in preparation for the packing of plastic explosive along its frame.

The *mujahideen*, nearly forty strong, some of them already armed—the rest awaiting the final shipment of weapons in a few hours. College students mixed in with grizzled veterans of the wars in Iraq, in Syria. The dark hijabs of a few women mingling amongst the men. Martyrs, all—the sight of the faithful overwhelming him with emotion.

Eyes shining with tears, he raised both his hands beside his head, whispering the *takbir* in a voice of awe and hearing the thunderous shout of "*Allahu akbar!*" in response.

For truly. . .God is great.

8:07 A.M.
Thames House
London

". . .the cause of two more deaths overnight in Ipswich, as police continue to investigate the apparent murder of Sheik Ajmal Rafik, the imam of the Argyle Street mosque, who was found dead in his Priory Heath flat early yesterday morning. While no motive has been ascertained, Rafik's death has stoked violent protests in the once quiet town, as rioters converged on city hall and burnt tires in the street. The mayor. . ."

Another day, Alec MacCallum thought wearily, pulling his eyes away from the BBC news report as he began to sort through the hourlies. Another day, and the violence showed no sign of abating. If anything, things seemed to be getting worse.

As if all it would take was a *push*. To send them hurtling over the brink. Into the abyss.

"You look bloody knackered," Norris' voice observed from behind him and he glanced back to see the analyst standing there, setting a steaming cup of coffee down on the edge of his workstation as he dropped his jacket over the chair.

"Didn't go home last night," MaCallum conceded, running a hand across his forehead. "Too many fires to put out. Not enough time, not enough personnel. My *God*, Simon. . .it's getting mad out there."

The younger man just nodded soberly, taking his seat. "There was a fight on the Tube last night—I had to get off a station early and walk. Some drunk footballers decided to mix it up with a group of young Pakistanis. One of the

Pakis pulled a knife. Things got a little crazy after that."

Insanity. Stories like that were becoming more and more common as the Met struggled to hold the line even in London itself. Places like Ipswich, the local constabularies didn't even begin to have the resources to handle the storm bearing down upon them. "We're nearing a breaking point."

"And in the midst of the whole cock-up, a Yank on the loose. A Yank who's managed to turn one of our own." Norris took a sip of his coffee, pausing as he began to scan the cover sheet of the folder lying on his desk. "What in the devil's name is *this*?"

MacCallum turned around, taking in the sight of the folder in the analyst's hand. "That, is our solution to the 'Yank.' A directive from the DG—we're to liaise with Grosvenor Square on this one."

"Are they having a laugh?" Norris demanded incredulously, shaking his head as he opened the folder.

"Not so you'd notice it. The Agency has burned Nichols as a rogue—disavowed any connection to his activities here in the UK. And, frankly, we need their manpower."

Norris raised a skeptical eyebrow. "What are they getting out of it?"

"Their team is being released from detainment at Paddington Green within the hour. Beyond that. . .ask Marsh. That's well above my pay—" the phone on MacCallum's desk rang at that moment, cutting him off. He reached for it, pausing as his eyes fell on the authentication codes flashing on the small display screen. "It's Roth."

8:12 A.M.
MI-5 Regional Office
Leeds, West Yorkshire

"Thames House."

MacCallum's voice. So familiar. Darren hesitated, glancing around the nearly empty regional office. It was hard for him even now to believe that the man could be playing them—could have betrayed an oath they'd all held so dear. *Regnum defende.*

"Are you all right?" the section chief asked after the silence hung in the air for a moment. *What a question.* "We lost contact with you yesterday not long after the incident at Seacroft, there was concern—"

"I'm fine, Alec," he replied, "met up with an old asset last night on a possible lead regarding the Nichols affair. Had to go dark, no comms."

Another pause. "And?"

Was it probing? Twenty-four hours, the thought wouldn't have even crossed his mind. But now. . .

"And it was a dry hole," Darren lied, cursing himself for the thought. Was this exactly what Nichols had wanted? To have them turn on each other? Peter Wright all over again, tearing Thames House apart looking for a mole. *Chasing shadows.* "I need to speak with the DG."

"He's at a meeting with the Home Secretary, briefing her on the situation with the cousins. Is there a message I can give him upon his return?"

And there it was again—cautious probing? He couldn't take the chance. "No, I'll just try back later. It isn't important."

He just sat there, staring at the phone in his hand as its screen faded to black. Going to Marsh with what he had now—it wasn't going to be enough to convince the DG. Not even close, not unless the Thames House intranet bore the electronic fingerprints of MacCallum's tampering.

Sod it all. Darren reached into his shirt pocket for the scrap of paper Nichols had given him, spreading it out on the desk before him until the phone numbers were clearly visible. Was one of these the key?

Only one way to find out. Another number, dialed from memory—he raised the phone to his ear, listening as it rang once, twice, three times before a man's voice responded. "Neil, I need you to do me a favor."

8:45 A.M.
The port of Aberdeen
Scotland

Driving from one end of the harbor to the other. That's all this was, Delaney told himself, tapping the artic's brakes as the stolen lorry rolled to a stop at the traffic light—the former sapper's muscled, tattooed arm hanging out the open window. Slate-gray buildings dating back to the late 1800s rose across the street from him, their color blending in with the low clouds moving in overhead, blocking out any sign of the sun.

Just driving from one end of the harbor to the other—with the most dangerous load he'd ever carried in the three years since leaving the Royal Engineers and obtaining his HGV license to drive these lorries.

A load that would put him away behind barbed wire in Category A until the day he died if it was discovered. If a sharp-eyed constable ran the licence plates and realized it had been stolen.

An abandoned church—or "kirk" as they were called here in Scotland—set off to one side of the street as he rolled back toward the harbor area. Nearly swallowed up in the industrial sprawl spilling out of the harbor itself, awash in a ghostly sea of ancient gravestones.

Shades of a Britain that once had been, and was no more. A Britain they weren't going to bring back, no matter what they did today.

But the alternative? The man's face hardened, his eyes focusing on the signage ahead. *"You are now entering an industrial area."*

Almost there. At least no one was going to read the history books and say there hadn't been men willing to put up a fight.

"Once the perimeter has been breached," Tarik Abdul Muhammad said, looking up from the commercial satellite print-outs to meet Farid's eyes, "you and your men are to make your way quickly up the road in the second vehicle."

The Syria veteran nodded grimly, taking in the layout at a glance. "Distance?"

"Just under three-quarters of a kilometer. You will need to cover that ground before the alarm spreads, before her protective detail is able to mobilize. Do not allow yourselves—"

"*Shaikh,*" a young man's voice interrupted, "you are needed at the gate. There's a lorry outside—a British driver. He's asked for you."

Delaney felt the CZ 75 semiautomatic shift under his leather jacket as he dismounted from the cab of the artic, ignoring the guard standing just a few meters away as his eyes focused on the form of the *Shaikh* appearing around the edge of a towering stack of shipping containers. It was the first time he had seen the man since that night on Almscliffe Crag. . .when all of this had been set in motion.

Just draw his weapon and fire—end this all right here—

Delaney thought, eyeing the Pakistani as he approached, flanked by a pair of his men. *Put him down.*

Patience. That time would come soon enough. Just a few more hours. Once the man had served his purpose.

"You have delivered what was promised?" the *Shaikh* asked as he approached, his light blue eyes searching Delaney's face with their charismatic gaze. Even as an enemy, it wasn't difficult to understand why men followed this man.

"Aye," he responded, his face expressionless as he fished keys from the pocket of his jacket, tossing them underhand to the bearded young man on Tarik's left. "Everything's there. Go ahead and see for yourself."

9:08 A.M.
CIA off-site facility
City of London

"*Take her and run—far and fast. Go dark. I can trust you to do this, Harry. I know you. I know what you'll do.* Vaya con Dios.*"*

A futile prayer in the end, David Lay thought, the morning sun streaming in through the tinted floor-to-ceiling glass as he gazed down from the eighth floor of the high-rise upon the City of London far below, his eyes picking out Finsbury Circus just to the east.

Ongoing construction work for the Crossrail marring what he remembered as having once been one of London's most beautiful parks.

Futile. Because in the end, his trust had been misplaced. The oldest maxim of the spy business proving ever inviolable. *Trust no one.*

Not even Harry Nichols.

He could still remember standing in the rain on the tarmac at Dulles waiting for his daughter's body to arrive from Vegas, a cold December rain soaking him to the skin. Unheeding. Uncaring.

The plane descending out of the sky, low-hanging clouds bleak and gray as if in acknowledgment of his grief. A mute nod all he could manage when the coroner had asked him to identify her body. *It was her.* No doubt about that, a knife stabbing him to the heart.

She'd always had her mother's features. Her smile. Her azure-blue eyes, now forever closed in death.

Because of this *man*. Time to put an end to all of this. Bury the memories. Once and for all.

"All right, people, listen up," he announced curtly, turning back from the window to address the CIA personnel filtering onto the floor.

"By now, you've all been briefed on the developing situation in Leeds involving our former officer. This is now your number one priority. Harry Nichols was once one of our best. . .but he's not one of 'ours' anymore. *Find him.*"

9:47 A.M.
The safehouse
Leeds, West Yorkshire

". . .Her Majesty Queen Elizabeth has arrived at her country estate of Balmoral in the Scottish Highlands this morning, beginning a vacation reported to last a week. The Queen's visit this early in the year breaks with long-established precedent, fueling speculation that her trip north may have been prompted by the civil unrest which has wracked England in recent weeks—although Buckingham Palace has declined to comment. Here to discuss these developments with us is royal watcher Madeline Dobbs. . ."

"She's there safely," Mehreen observed, letting out a sigh of relief. The female newshost's voice continuing on the telly as she turned the volume down. "Your man was telling the truth."

"He was," she heard Harry say from behind her, his voice sounding distracted. "From a tactical perspective, it only makes sense. Given Balmoral's isolation, you want to make sure your target is already *in* the trap before you spring it. Easiest way to do that is let her get there, then keep her from leaving."

She looked back to see him looking at the screen of his phone. "What is it?"

"Flaharty," Harry replied, laying the burner back on the kitchen table after sending a brief text in reply. "He's ten minutes out."

"Are you going to tell him?" she asked, turning away from the television.

"Tell him what?"

"About Roth," she replied, her face almost impossible to read. "The part he's now playing in our operation."

"And what part *is* that, exactly?" Harry removed his Sig-Sauer from the shoulder holster, instinctively brass-checking the chamber. "Do you really think we can trust him?"

"You're serious." She just looked at him, shaking her head. "After all of this, Harry—after all you've done—do you think you have any *right* to be asking about trust?"

After all you've done. She was right, that was the worst of it. Faiths betrayed, lives shattered—pushed aside like so much rubble. But there was no stopping now, not when the end was so close at hand. The objective almost within reach.

"*Every* right," he whispered, his eyes darkening as he shoved the pistol roughly back into its holster, taking a step toward her. His hand resting on the table. "If Special Branch comes crashing through that door, it's all over. For me. For *you.* Maybe even for the Royal Family. So I need to know—is he taking this seriously?"

"He is," she replied, never flinching. "You can be sure of that."

"You're running late," Harry observed as he opened the door of the safehouse to admit Flaharty. *By a couple hours.*

"Count yourself a lucky sod that I showed up at all, boyo," the Irishman responded darkly, shoving a long, heavy bag into his hands. "Give me a hand with this."

"You were able to get what I'd requested?" Harry asked, turning to lead the way into the kitchen.

Flaharty nodded, setting his own bag down on the table with a dull *thud* and unzipping it to withdraw an AK-103 assault rifle, its polymer stock folded against the receiver. "Nearly. Four rifles, though I was only able to acquire two of these like you'd asked."

"And the other two?"

"Wooden-stocked AKMs," the former PIRA man replied, gesturing toward the bag Harry was holding.

"Good enough," he said, opening the bag and pulling out one of the rifles. The AKM was a far older design, but they'd still be able to share ammunition and magazines.

Russians were nothing if not efficient.

Flaharty shook his head. "It had better be. . .I don't suppose I'm getting paid for any of this?"

"I'll do what I can."

"Which means bugger-all," the Irishman shot back, eyeing him with a shrewd glance. "And you an' I both know it. The widow Crawford, I take it she's around here somewh—well, speak of the devil. . ."

Harry followed the direction of Flaharty's eyes back toward the doorway, turning to find Mehreen standing there. "I am."

"Sure an' I can see that." He shook his head, turning back to Harry. "So, now that we're all here together like one big happy family—is there actually a plan? I suppose I can assume you're not going after the ship, seeing as it's already left port?"

"There's a plan," Harry started to reply, the full import of the Irishman's words only then striking him. Something was wrong. *Very* wrong. "The ship's already gone?"

"You know it. Left port at Grimsby late yesterday afternoon—sailing north, last I saw of it."

11:13 A.M.
MI-5 Regional Office
Leeds, West Yorkshire

"Yes, the numbers," Darren responded, glancing around him to make sure his phone call wasn't being overhead. "What were you able to ascertain?"

"Not much as of yet," the voice of his contact at GCHQ responded, "except that all five numbers may have been used by the same party."

"Oh?"

"All of the numbers you gave me belong to pre-paid mobiles—all of them purchased at a mini-mart in the Midlands, on the same day. Just outside Long Eaton, to be precise."

Purchased all together. Whether they had all been *used* by the same person was another question, but it was shoddy tradecraft, to put it mildly.

"And the next step from here?"

"We have the time-stamp on the purchase—let me see what CCTV I can pull from the surrounding streets, if any. Maybe identify the buyer." The man paused. "Failing that, I can contact the mini-mart itself and request access to their feeds. But that's going to take longer, and if they deny the request, I'll then need a warrant, which will mean going through official channels."

"Let's avoid that if possible, shall we?"

"Right you are," his old friend laughed. "You know, some day you and I are going to sit down and have a pint together and you're going to tell me what this was all about."

"Some day," Darren acknowledged absently, finding his eyes drawn to the television mounted on the far wall, footage of an airplane coming in for a landing. If he ever got to the truth of it himself. "Get back to me when you have a name."

". . .landing at Aberdeen along with his wife, the Duchess of Cambridge, and their two children. Prince William is due to spend a rare spring holiday with the Queen at Balmoral Castle, a residence which has reportedly become a favorite of the young Prince George. The Prince has declined. . ."

My God, Roth thought, staring transfixed at the screen. If this attack was *real*—this wasn't just about the Queen. This was about the Royal Family itself.

11:39 A.M.
A farmhouse outside Harrogate
North Yorkshire

"Stay with Hale—keep close to him. And keep me in the loop." Hale picked up the field-stripped pieces of his service weapon, the words of the American playing and replaying themselves through his mind as he sat there at the kitchen table, reassembling the Walther P99.

Betrayal had always been personal to him. He could still remember the time in Iraq when his team had been sold out by their interpreter—a young Sunni foisted on them by the higher-ups.

Sold out and led straight into an ambush—one of his men losing both of his legs to a roadside IED, another man going down as automatic weapons fire filled the air.

EMBRACE THE FIRE

He'd seen the look in the 'terp's eyes—all too recognizable. A glint of exultation where there should have only been terror.

Hale picked up the loaded magazine on the table beside his hand, sliding it into the buttstock of the Walther and thumbing off the slide release. The crisp sound of metal on metal as the slide ran forward, chambering a round.

Long as he might live, he would never forget that moment. Bullets raking the air past his ear as he raised his rifle—seeing the flash of fear in the man's eyes a split-second before he pulled the trigger. *Retribution.*

He picked up the loaded weapon, screwing a long, thin suppressor into the threaded barrel as he rose from the table, walking over to the window and staring out over the English countryside.

Another twenty minutes and his men would be arriving. Paul Gordon among them. . .

11:51 A.M.
CIA off-site facility
City of London

"Nice place you've got here," Thomas Parker observed casually, gazing down upon the central atrium of the office building as the glass elevator rose toward the eighth floor.

"It's not ours." Jimenez shook his head. "We've just been renting the floor the last couple years—a stopgap that will continue to handle our overflow operations until the Embassy finally makes its move from Grosvenor Square to Battersea and we have more room to expand."

Thomas nodded his understanding. The move had been in the planning for nearly a decade—the Grosvenor Square location deemed increasingly vulnerable to the threat of terrorist attack in the wake of 9/11. Brave new world.

"Still," he said, half-smiling as the elevator came to a halt and the Agency station chief swiped his keycard to open the doors, "you have to admit. . .bankers and the CIA in the same building. It's the stuff Alex Jones' dreams are made of."

His smile faded as they passed through the portal, past the pair of uniformed Marines—his eyes catching sight of the familiar figure of David Lay standing over a nearby workstation.

Yeah, he thought, staring at the man despite himself. Finding himself transported back to that dark December night in Virginia—a figure silhouetted against vehicle lights, the crack of a revolver splitting the night. His own Beretta recoiling into his palm as he returned fire.

The form of the DCIA lying sprawled in the bloody snow.

"Good morning, gentlemen," Lay announced, looking up—glancing at Jimenez before turning his attention to Thomas. "Good to have you back with us, Parker."

"Thank you, sir," Thomas managed, unsure whether to go on. Friendly fire or no, it was hard to know what to say to someone you'd so recently shot.

"The conference room," Lay went on, solving the problem for him. "Twenty minutes. We have a lead."

12:04 P.M.
The farmhouse
Harrogate, North Yorkshire

The farmhouse had to be at least a century old, maybe two. Paul Gordon shook his head as he got out of the car, gazing up at the slate tile of the roof, the thick ivy covering the stone.

Alice could have told him, she had always been one for old buildings—architecture of a day gone by. But she wasn't going to be telling him anything ever again.

The burner phone seemed to sear a hole in the pocket of his jacket as he walked up to the door, lifting his hand to use the heavy iron knocker.

Redemption. That's all this was about, now. A chance to set things right.

A moment passed, the faint sound of footsteps on the other side of the heavy door before Hale himself appeared in the doorway.

"Paul," the former SAS man said, a shadow seeming to pass briefly across his face before he smiled, reaching out a hand. "Glad you could make it, mate. Come in."

Had he imagined it? Gordon thought, following his old comrade inside. The line between paranoia and caution. . .so hard to find.

He shook his head, closing the door behind him. This was no time to be losing his nerve.

"Lads," Hale began, turning to face the group of men surrounding the small table, "when we left Iraq, we thought that was the end. That we'd done our duty. And when they mustered us out, we believed it was over."

A low chorus of murmured *"Ayes"* rose from around Gordon, their words echoing the thoughts of his own heart. But it hadn't been that simple. It never was.

"But it wasn't over, was it?" the former sergeant asked, his eyes moving from face to face. A fierce intensity burning from their depths. "That war—those *savages* we fought, all of it—followed us home. Many of you served together with me over there. We shed our blood in those godforsaken sands. But now I'm asking more of you than I ever did back then. Everything, if it comes to that. There are no medals at the end of this, no gratitude. If we are ever remembered for what we've done, it will be as traitors. But we will know differently, and that will have to be enough. That *we* stood for England when no one else would."

He smiled suddenly, straightening. It was a smile Gordon knew well. Proud, full of defiance. "We act as though this is something new—somehow different than all that's gone before. This is the way it has *always been*. Those sodding politicians up in Whitehall—looking all high an' mighty as they preen for the cameras—they've never saved England. It's been *us*, all down through the centuries. The thin red line of British steel, all that stands between them and a world that's nowhere near as friendly as they think. And after tonight, they'll have had a glimpse of that world."

Tonight. He froze, the background noise of the room seeming to fade away, the rough murmurs of approbation nothing more than a distant roar in Gordon's ears.

"Conor," he began, struggling to mask the shock that threatened to overwhelm him, "did you mean to say 'tonight'?"

"I did," the former SAS sergeant responded, turning to look him in the eye. "Oh, I'm sorry, mate. . .you hadn't gotten here when I explained to the lads. The attack has been moved up."

No. This wasn't—this *couldn't* be happening. Hale staring at him strangely as if waiting for his response. "Is there a problem, Paul?"

"No," Gordon responded, finding his voice with an effort. Forcing a smile to his face. "Not at all."

12:13 P.M.
CIA off-site facility
City of London

"Gentlemen," David Lay began, lowering himself heavily into his seat at the head of the conference table, "before we begin, I'd like to introduce the man Thames House sent over to help coordinate this effort—Simon Norris, an analyst from G Branch."

Indeed. Thomas glanced across, meeting the man's eyes and seeing a faint smile of recognition there. "We've met."

"All right, then let's not waste any more time," the DCIA said, spreading his hands. He turned toward the British analyst. "Why don't you bring us up to speed on what you've found?"

"Right you are," Norris replied, typing a brief command into his laptop before reaching half-way across the table for the small remote lying there.

A moment later, the television screen on the wall behind Lay's head flickered to life, a grainy image flashing up on the screen as Norris tapped the remote. It was from a traffic cam, Thomas realized a moment later.

"As early as yesterday afternoon, we'd attempted to pull CCTV from the streets surrounding Seacroft after the bombing—looking at vehicles departing the area within the target window. Scanning plates. Specifically looking for any automobiles that might have been reported stolen in the last few weeks. And we got nothing. No sign of your man."

He saw Lay wince at the choice of words, "your man" sounding like a pejorative coming from the lips of the Brit. Hard to fathom—the difference a year made. A year? Scarce six months since Jerusalem. *The beginning of the fall.*

"So?"

"So this morning, after the Agency finally deigned to read us in on your suspicions regarding the attack on our surveillance van," Norris continued caustically, "we went digging again. This time cross-referencing the CCTV footage from the Seacroft area with that from the streets in the vicinity of Rahman's flat the night of the attack. And we came up with. . .this."

The image zoomed in on a single car, its plate number dimly visible in the glow of a streetlight, Thomas' eyes narrowing as he tried to read it. *Bravo-Delta-six-seven. Sierra-Hotel-Whiskey.*

"This Vauxhall Cavalier was picked up on CCTV three kilometers north of Rahman's flat only fifteen minutes after our van was hit. And here," Norris went on as he clicked to the next image, "you have the same automobile seen leaving the Seacroft area less than hour after the explosion. What are the odds?"

"That's not conclusive," Jimenez interjected, shaking his head. "You came all the way over here from Millbank to give us *this*?"

"Not quite," Norris replied, holding up a finger—the image on-screen changing once more. "Two kilometers west of that camera, there was also this."

Same vehicle. This time from the side, Thomas realized—the profile of the driver's face visible, shadowed by the interior of the car, but still recognizable. *It was him.*

"We've run the image through facial-recognition software—it came back a 63% match. It's not a coincidence. Our analysts are currently sifting through CCTV footage from around Leeds over the last four days. Trying to see if we can establish patterns—anything that can give us a fix on where Nichols might be now."

"He won't still be using the same car," Parker observed, staring at the screen.

"If it's hot, he'll have dumped it by now."

"Oh, but it's not," Norris responded with a smile. "We've run the plates. It's not been reported stolen, and the owner doesn't seem to exist. Somehow, your man got himself a vehicle 'legitimately.' Means he's going to hang onto it, long as he can, rather than risk nicking another one. And that's how we'll get him."

12:18 P.M.
The farmhouse
Harrogate, North Yorkshire

"The bird will be here in ten minutes—time enough for you lads to get your kit together. We should set down shortly after 1400 hours, giving us plenty of time to get into position."

Conor Hale's words ringing in his ears, Gordon made his way through the great room and out down the rear hall, his heart racing as he moved toward the back of the house, glimpsing the ancient stone barn set maybe fifty meters behind the house. He had to get clear unnoticed—get a message off to the American, *something.*

He pulled open the back door, closing it behind him as carefully as he could before setting off across the open ground toward the barn—fumbling as he pulled the burner out of his pocket, powering it on.

Come on, he thought, glancing toward the back of the farmhouse. As if expecting Hale or one of his men to appear there at any moment. *Come on.*

It was like his first time in combat, all over again. Worse, really. Because this time, he was alone.

The phone's screen came to life after another agonizing few moments—the signal weak, but *there.*

It would have to be enough, he realized, casting another anxious glance back toward the house.

Had to break line of sight. The longer he was gone. . .

Gordon hurried around the crumbling stone wall and into the barnyard below and behind the barn—taking a deep breath in a futile effort to calm himself as his rough, callused thumbs began moving across the touchscreen. Starting to compose a text message to the American.

Things have been moved up. They—

"Paul," a voice announced, his heart nearly stopping in that moment. His thumb reflexively pressing a key. He looked up to see the figure of Conor Hale standing not ten feet away, just inside the stone wall. Cold, hard eyes boring into his own.

12:21 P.M.
Balmoral Castle
Ballater, Scotland

Twenty-seven years, Colin Hilliard thought, buttoning his suit as he strode out from under the cover of Balmoral's carriage porch—the early afternoon sun shining down on the Commander's snow-white hair.

That was how long he'd been with the Met's Protection Command, guarding first the palace at Buck House—as it was colloquially known—then the Royal Family itself. Nearly half his life. He'd been on Her Majesty's personal detail for twelve years, its ranking officer for the last five.

The Glock 17 dug uncomfortably into his side as he moved, a reminder of the realities of his work as he glanced back toward the castle—its main keep looming large behind him, the walls thick and solid, constructed of Invergelder granite.

Relic of an England gone by.

His earpiece crackled with a momentary burst of static before a familiar voice came over the encrypted radio. "PEREGRINE has arrived—just passed the main gate. Should be with you presently."

He acknowledged the transmission with a curt reply, the shrill sound of an outrider's whistle coming from off to the east—the lead Special Escort Group Honda motorbike appearing through the trees a moment later.

And just behind it, a Black Range Rover—the familiar sight of Prince William's face behind the wheel as the vehicle neared, pulling abreast of the Met commander as it rolled to a stop.

PEREGRINE, he thought, drawing himself to attention as the the Prince emerged, extending a hand. "Colin!"

"Your Highness," Hilliard responded, gripping his hand warmly, as Catherine exited the vehicle on the other side, the young Princess Charlotte in her arms, Prince George toddling along gripping her hand. He'd first met the Prince when he'd been a boy of scarcely nine, and their paths had crossed many times over the years as William had grown to manhood. "Welcome to Balmoral Castle."

"It's good to be here again, Colin," the Prince responded, glancing around them at the grounds—the forested slopes of Craig Lurachain off to the south. "This was always one of my favorite places as a lad."

"I remember it well." Hilliard gestured toward the castle. "The Queen awaits you inside, if you please, sir."

"Of course."

12:23 P.M.
The farm
Harrogate, North Yorkshire

"Well, bugger me," Gordon responded, managing a brittle laugh. "Didn't see you standing there, Conor. Just give me a moment—I heard from Alice's doctors, and—"

"Paul. . .enough," Hale said, raising a hand to cut him off. His right hand came out of his jacket, holding a suppressed Walther. "Just stop. I *know*."

Gordon shook his head, trying to stay calm. *Go for your weapon*, his mind screamed, but Hale's gun was already raised—its muzzle aimed at his head. He was going to have to talk his way out of this one. "I have no idea what you're on about, mate. I—"

"Of all the people on this sodding earth," Hale said, cutting him off, "I never would've thought they could get to you. Turn *you* against me."

He knew. Somehow, he *knew*. And it was in that moment, Gordon realized just how this was going to end.

"They didn't," he fired back, his right hand clenching and unclenching spasmodically, "it was *you*—"

"Shut up!" The former SAS sergeant swore loudly, gesturing with the pistol as he took a step closer. His face distorted into a grimace, seeming overcome by emotion. "We were brothers-in-arms, Paul, you and I—from that first jump over Brize Norton. Always knew you'd have my back, whatever came. And they turned you—they bloody well did it."

The faint sound of helicopter rotors approaching in the distance struck Gordon's ears, distracting him. He'd seen Hale like this once before—in Iraq, the man's temper bursting through like water through a dam. But he'd been able to talk him down then. And now. . .

"But in the end, mate," Hale continued, his voice rising, "you failed them, just like you failed me. And you failed worse than even you realize—because this operation has never been about setting the *hajjis* up. It's about ensuring that they *succeed*."

12:25 P.M.
The port of Aberdeen
Scotland

"This is the day," Tarik Abdul Muhammad announced softly, looking down the line of vehicles—five blacked-out SUVs bracketed by a utility van in the fore and a white delivery van at the rear. *Carrying the faithful into battle.* "The day we illustrate once and for all the impotence of the crusader war machine—bring the war home to their soil. Show them that nowhere are they safe from the justice of God, whose precepts they have defied for so long."

He turned to Farid, extending his arms and drawing the man into a fierce embrace. Kissing him on both cheeks. "I envy you, my brother. The part you have been ordained to play in Allah's struggle."

"Is one part any greater than another?" the Syria veteran asked, his eyes meeting Tarik's in a steadfast gaze. "We must all do His will."

"You are right," the *Shaikh* relented, glancing back toward the warehouse. "From here we will monitor the emergency response—endeavor to keep them off you as long as it is possible."

He turned to Nadeem, extending his hand as the young man handed him a folded black flag.

"I give you the flag of *Rasūlullāh*, which flew above our armies in Iraq and *al-Sham*," Tarik intoned, passing it to Farid. "Tear down the Queen's lion from above the castle keep and raise this in its place."

12:26 P.M.
The farm
Harrogate, North Yorkshire

No. A wave of bile and anger rising in his throat as it hit him. His old comrade had been playing him all along. *Just like at Madina.* The sound of the helicopter again, closer now. A steady, insistent rhythm. Growing ever louder.

"You didn't know that, did you?" Conor Hale smiled, a death's head grimace, gesturing back up toward the house. "Neither do they. But this is *necessary*. The Queen's going to do more in death to help this nation than she ever did in life. Ensure people get the shock needed to wake them from their slumber—finally recognize the threat we've welcomed with open arms for far too long. That one woman die for the people—"

The helicopter swept by overhead in that moment, perhaps a hundred feet off the deck—drowning out the former SAS man's voice. Its downwash shaking the branches of the nearby trees. Stirring up a cloud of dust in the barnyard.

Now. Ignoring the pain from his wounded leg, Gordon launched himself forward, catching Hale off-guard—distracted by the passing helicopter. *Control the weapon.*

His left hand seized hold of the man's wrist, pushing the Walther's barrel out to the side. His right lashing out toward Hale's jaw in a vicious hook.

Hale ducked at the last moment, the blow failing to connect as he stumbled backward, caught off-balance as Gordon charged, grappling for his gun hand.

Delivering another pair of sharp body blows as he drove his old friend back into the wall of the barnyard, hammering him against the rough stone. Hale already recovering from his surprise—fighting back.

Get the gun. He knew now—kill Hale and this mad plan would die with him. That was all that he had to do, to make things *right*.

To atone for his sins.

He punched in hard, above the sergeant's guard—his blow catching the man high on the cheekbone, rocking him back.

Loosening his grip on the Walther.

He seized the gun from Hale's grasp with a surge of desperate strength, taking a step backward as he brought it up, the long suppressor describing a painfully slow arc. *Too slow.*

There was no time to aim, no time to even get a sight picture. He fired once, then a second time—the pistol coughing loudly—before Hale slammed into him, knocking the weapon aside.

Gordon twisted away, sidestepping a blow, his face distorted in sudden pain as he felt his bad leg give beneath him. And then they were falling together, the earth coming rushing up to meet the both of them—Hale's body absorbing the impact, Gordon on top of him.

And the Walther was. . .somewhere, lost in the confusion. But no matter. He saw his old friend's face as if through a red haze of wrath and fear—his hands clawing for the man's throat.

He could feel Hale trying to throw him off, push him away, but to no avail. *Just a few more moments.* His grip slowly constricting, cutting off oxygen.

And then he felt the hard metal of a gun barrel jab into his ribcage—time itself seeming to slow down. His mouth opening in a futile curse.

The next moment, a pair of 9mm slugs smashed into his body.

12:31 P.M.
The CIA off-site facility
City of London

"Look at this," Simon Norris demanded urgently, gesturing to get Thomas' attention. "Thames House sent over the feeds from CCTV surrounding the Leeds area, picked up a hit from traffic cameras on the A61 shortly after the bombing at Seacroft."

Thomas leaned over Norris' shoulder, looking at the screen. "It's our Vauxhall."

"Right," the analyst responded, grabbing a crisp and stuffing it into his mouth before he continued. "Thought I'd back-trace, see if it was a route he had used before—sure enough, here we have him again, caught on the same camera the night of Rahman's abduction."

That was the essence of good intelligence work, Thomas thought—monitoring your target, establishing patterns. And a good intelligence officer knew enough to avoid them in his own life. Nichols was slipping.

"But that's not all." Norris held up a finger, moving through another series of screens. "Look at these captures from the junction less than three kilometers ahead."

Thomas shook his head. "There's nothing there."

"Precisely. *Both* times, he has to have turned off before reaching that junction."

Interesting. "What are we looking at in that area?"

"Not much that I know of," Norris responded, pivoting in his swivel chair and using the Agency network to pull up satellite overlays of Yorkshire. "Looks like it's mostly residential. There's a school—and an industrial estate, about four kilometers to the northwest."

"What can you find out about the estate?" Thomas asked, an intensity creeping into his voice. It was just the kind of place Nichols would have chosen.

"The estate is pretty much abandoned. Apparently has been ever since the economic downturn of '09." He looked up. "Do you think. . .?"

"It's him," Thomas nodded. "I worked with the man for years, I know how he thinks."

"I'll have Thames House get in touch with Yorkshire. Have them dispatch a Firearms Unit."

12:29 P.M.
The farmhouse
Harrogate, North Yorkshire

Cursing loudly, Conor Hale rolled Gordon's body from off him, returning his compact Kahr PM9 to its holster inside his waistband as he stumbled to his feet—bent over, hands on his knees. Gasping for breath.

God, he thought, trying to recover himself—his shirt stained with Gordon's blood. It had been a near thing.

He wiped bloody hands against his dark pants as he reached down to pick up his Walther, wincing suddenly. Pain flaring from his side as if it had been seared with a hot brand. His fingers coming away bloody—a ragged hole in his shirt telling the truth.

Not all the blood was Gordon's—one of the man's bullets had found its mark. *Bugger.*

Hadn't even realized it in the heat of the fight.

He could still hear the rotors of the Agusta, loud and insistent. No doubt by now coming in for a landing in front of the farmhouse. Another few minutes and they'd come looking for him.

And if they found...it was at that moment that he spotted Gordon's cellphone lying in the dirt a few feet away, a sudden chill running through his body. *What if...*

It was a cheap burner, no lock on the phone as Hale ran his thumb over the screen—leaving a smear of blood. Navigating first to *Messages*, then *Outbox*.

And there it was, the only sent message to be found. Barely four minutes old. *Things have been moved up. They—*

Just a fragment, but it couldn't have been more damning. Whoever had been running Gordon, they now *knew* things weren't proceeding according to plan.

He swore beneath his breath, looking over at the man's broken body. The threat to their operation this posed, it wasn't something he could afford to ignore. It was going to have to be handled.

"Thought we were going to have to send someone after you," the man yelled, a grim smile on the former soldier's face as he raised his voice to be heard over the throbbing roar of the rotors.

Just like old times.

"Plans have changed," Hale responded, ignoring the pain coming from his side as he hoisted himself up into the door of the Agusta. A hastily thrown-on jacket covering his wound and his bloodstained shirt. "Gordon and I have some...business to take care of here yet. You'll set down at Banchory—then proceed to link up with Delaney at the rally point. Hold there for my orders."

"Aye, mate," the soldier responded, reaching out and clasping Hale's hand in his. "Solid copy."

The Shaikh *was going to have to manage this one on his own*, Hale thought—lowering himself back to the ground and hurrying away from the helicopter, its rotor wash flattening the grass of the meadow around him, the roar rising to a deafening crescendo as the Agusta rose into the sky.

He reached for the phone in his pocket, its screen coming to life as he began to compose a message. *Time to put a face to the voice.* Meet the man who had turned his old comrade against him.

Chapter 29

12:32 P.M.
The safe house
Leeds, West Yorkshire

The intelligence business was slow, painstaking work. Punctuated by moments when the truth struck home with a sudden, startling clarity.

Those moments were the ones you didn't *want* to believe. Much as you knew you had to.

"'Just met with Hale,'" Harry said, glancing around the kitchen at Mehreen and Flaharty as he read the words off the screen of the burner phone in his hand. "'Plans have changed. We need to meet, as soon as possible.' He gives a time 1400 hours. And an address, looks like it's north of the city."

Guilt. He'd once thought it would get easier with time, but it never did. "'Plans have changed,'" he heard Flaharty repeat, shaking his head from across the room. "What is that supposed to mean?"

"It means Paul Gordon is dead," Harry responded flatly, his voice stripped of emotion. *There was none left.* "And we're flying blind."

A curse exploded from Flaharty's mouth, shock filling Mehreen's eyes as she demanded, "What do you mean—how do you know that?"

Losing an asset. The knowledge that you'd sent a man to his death. A crushing load, weighing you down. "The two messages don't match up, the way the one was sent before it was finished. Now this one—the use of Hale's name. I had warned Gordon that if he needed to use text messages to maintain comms, to only refer to Hale as 'our friend from Lebanon.'"

Mehreen shook her head. "But that doesn't make any sense. I've seen his service file. He was deployed to Iraq, then Afghanistan. Lebanon?"

"He was there too," Harry replied firmly. "Along with Nick and me. Part of a CIA black op to pull out one of our assets out in the middle of the Israeli invasion in '06. Nick came home with a bullet in him."

He could see the light dawning in her eyes, as if a long-asked question had just been answered. That was the reality of this world—men coming home with wounds they could never explain to their wives, their families. Pieces of themselves, scattered in places they'd never been.

Officially.

"Less than a dozen people knew we had support from the Brits to pull that off—even fewer knew their names. I didn't explain it to Paul Gordon, just told him to be sure to use it. He might not have been experienced in this line of work," Harry said, a grim edge to his voice, "but there's no way he would screw that up."

"So you're saying what? This is. . .Hale?"

He nodded slowly. "I'm sure it is. Somehow he knows, but he doesn't know much. He's probing, trying to figure out who was running his man."

"Oh, sod this for a bloody mess," Flaharty exclaimed, shaking his head. "He's setting a trap. Tell me, old son—do you *have* a plan?"

"I do," Harry responded, meeting the Irishman's eyes. "Walk straight into it."

1:23 P.M.
The CIA off-site facility
City of London

"Bird coming on-line in ninety seconds," one of the CIA analysts announced from the other side of the floor. "Beginning thermal sweep."

Thomas Parker stood there beside the computers, hand resting on his hip as the spy satellite moved into position in low earth orbit three hundred miles above the English countryside—its live stream updating on the big monitors in the center of the room. Along with feeds being transmitted in real-time from the helmet cams of West Yorkshire firearms officers converging on the industrial estate.

Moving in tight formation from cover to cover, clearing as they went. Maintaining utter silence, only brief flashes of hand signals visible on the grainy feed.

"What's their loadout?" he asked, turning to Norris. "Less-lethal?"

The Thames House analyst shook his head, sending a chill rippling down Thomas' spine. "We're not placing our people in that kind of jeopardy. They will, of course, do their utmost to take him into custody without violence—that's what all our police are trained to do—but if he resists. . ."

And they had no leverage to do anything about it, Thomas realized, glancing over at David Lay to meet the director's impassive gaze.

My God, he thought, his mouth suddenly dry. All those years, fighting alongside Nichols—he'd never dreamed it could one day come to this. Becoming responsible for his death.

If he'd ever needed a drink, it was now.

1:26 P.M.
The offices of the UK Daily Standard
Central London

To have come this close, Arthur Colville thought, listening to Conor Hale's voice over the phone as he gazed out the window of his office five stories down into the streets of London. This close, and now risk losing it all.

Having Hale there with his sniper rifle had always been the plan. Insurance against the Queen surviving the attack.

Mirsab Abdul Rashid al-Libi. The real "Sword of the Prophet" was still in Syria, as far as they knew. His double camped out in a London hotel room, no doubt gorging himself on fast food and watching porn.

All part of the plan. . .deliberately false intel regarding the arrival of a jihadist sniper fed to the Security Services in order to cement the fiction, prepare the intelligence "battlespace" for the deployment of their own trained marksman.

And all now for naught. Hale, out of play. His men—well, this plan, like that of any successful conspiracy, had been kept close. The soldiers he had recruited were resting in the belief that the Security Services would be alerted in time. That the Queen, although placed in grave danger, would be kept *safe*.

The part they were to play had been to come after, descending in righteous fury upon the port of Aberdeen. Ensuring that the *Shaikh* would never live long enough to be brought to book before the quizmasters at Paddington Green. They couldn't be relied upon to execute the primary mission itself.

Which meant that the fate of everything they had worked for was going to be left in the hands of the *Shaikh* himself.

"Enough, Conor," Colville said finally, bringing the call to a close as he returned to his desk, lowering himself heavily into the chair. "What's done is done. Do what you must. . .make sure none of this can be traced back to us."

1:31 P.M.
Harrogate, North Yorkshire

"This is where we part ways," Harry announced, tapping the brakes of the Vauxhall as the car rolled to a stop at the side of the road.

"The man was trained as a sniper," Flaharty observed from the passenger's seat, looking out over the rolling Yorkshire hillsides. "You told me yourself. He could pick you off on the way in, easy as fallin' out of bed."

"He could," Harry conceded, tucking in a loose wire as he zipped up his leather jacket over the suicide vest he had taken from Aydin Shinwari, "but he won't. He doesn't know what he doesn't know, and getting me to talk is his only way of finding out."

The Irishman snorted, clearly unconvinced. "Sure you're willing to wager your life on that, boyo?"

There was no answer to that, Harry thought, staring out through the Vauxhall's windshield. He'd wagered his life on far less over the years, gambling on the word of Langley's analysts, a cadre whose unofficial motto was rumored to be *"We bet your life."*

"That doesn't matter," he responded quietly after a long moment. "Capturing and interrogating Conor Hale, it's the only way we get to the bottom of what's going on here. We don't *have* another option. If it means putting myself in the cross-hairs. . .then that's what it means."

He withdrew the pair of tactical headsets from the ruck Flaharty had brought with him, working the earpiece into his ear until the flesh-colored plastic was almost completely concealed. "You ever use these things before?"

The Irishman shook his head, reaching for his. "After my time, lad. I tried to get out, as you'll be remembering."

"I have both sets tuned to the frequency we'll be using," Harry said, ignoring Flaharty's retort. "We'll stay in contact through the earpieces—the radios have a range of nearly twenty miles. More than enough for our purposes."

He reached into the pocket of his jacket, withdrawing a small prepaid mobile and handing it over. "There's one number listed on this, and only one, the one that triggers this vest. If I give the word, you press *SEND*. No hesitation, no question."

Flaharty took the phone from him, turning it over in his hand idly, as if considering something. "You know," he said finally, looking up, "I could just wait until the moment you and Conor Hale are in the same room, and do just that. Blow the both of you straight to hell together—kill two birds with one stone, as it were. Save myself a lot of grief. I assume that thought's occurred to you?"

"It has," Harry replied, his eyes locking with the Irishman's in a cold, hard gaze. "But you won't do it."

A harsh laugh. "You sure of that, lad?"

"I am. If you had even the slightest thought of seriously following through on it, you wouldn't have breathed a word of it to me."

"Fair enough," Flaharty said, still chuckling. "But you have to admit, it's a risk. So I have to ask. . .why did you ask me to come along? Why not the widow Crawford?"

It was a moment before Harry replied, looking off into the distance. Over the English countryside, blanketed in the verdant green of spring. *Peace.* An illusion so soon to be shattered.

"Because when it comes down to it," he responded at last, glancing over at the former terrorist, "Mehreen doesn't have it in her to pull that trigger. I'm counting on you to have no similar misgivings."

1:39 P.M.
The farmhouse

Conor Hale wrapped the torn strips of his undershirt around his mid-section, wincing at his reflection in the mirror as he pulled them tight, forming a rude bandage.

He'd gotten lucky.

Gordon's bullet hadn't much more than grazed him, cutting a deep furrow across his side, but missing the ribs. Along with everything else vital. He'd had worse wounds in the sandbox and still picked up his rifle and ruck—headed out with his men.

He shrugged on his shirt, moving back toward the front of the house, its windows offering a clear view of anyone approaching up the drive.

The message he'd received in response from Gordon's handler had been short and to the point. Impossible to read anything into. *Solid copy. 1400 hours it is.*

Which was now less than twenty minutes off.

Hale picked up the L42A1 from where it lay beside the chair, working the bolt to bring a single long 7.62mm cartridge into the chamber as he moved toward the back door—stepping out into the afternoon sun.

Time to get into position.

1:47 P.M.
The safehouse
Leeds, West Yorkshire

Scarcely ten minutes, Mehreen thought, glancing at her watch yet again. There hadn't been so much as a whisper from either Harry or Flaharty since they had departed, leaving her alone in the old safehouse.

Waiting.

That was always the hardest part of intelligence work, the long, interminable waits. Hands tied with the certainty that there was nothing—*nothing*—you could do to alter the outcome. One way or the other.

Her mobile phone rang on the table and she grabbed it up, expecting to see the number of Nichols' burner. *Roth.*

"Mehreen," his voice came through, strained and urgent. "I just heard from my contact at GCHQ—we have an ID on the man behind Conor Hale. Put me on speaker, I need Nichols to hear this."

"He's," she began, hesitating for a moment, "not with me right now."

"What do you mean by that? Where has he gone?"

How to explain. Something she didn't fully understand yet herself.

Going to confront Hale, that much she knew. But Harry's face as he'd departed—it had been like staring into the face of Death itself.

"We received a message from his source—something's wrong. The man may have been compromised. He and Stephen Flaharty headed out to deal with it."

There was a moment of incredulous silence, then Roth swore loudly. "The two of them? *Together?* My God, Mehr. . .what were you thinking?"

"If the source has been burned, that affects *everything*," she retorted, running a hand across her forehead. "We didn't have another alternative."

"You're talking about a terrorist, and a rogue foreign intelligence officer, Mehr," Roth shot back, raising his voice. "There is no 'we' about this—or have you somehow *forgotten* that?"

She shook her head angrily. "I haven't forgotten anything. They were to meet with the asset—or with whoever reached out to make contact—at 1400 hours. I should be hearing from them soon."

"And if you don't?" her fellow officer challenged. "If they both decide to up and do a runner now that you're not minding them? What happens then?"

He went on without waiting for her answer. "I'll tell you what happens then—our careers, we're done. *Finished.* The both of us."

"I know," she said quietly. Perhaps she had known ever since the night Nichols had shown up at her flat. That this was how it could end. "Just give me the name, Darren."

"The numbers Nichols gave me belonged to a set of burner phones purchased at a mini-mart in Long Eaton. The man identified on CCTV as purchasing the phones. . .was Arthur Colville."

2:01 P.M.
The farm
Harrogate

It was a quiet place, Harry thought, shifting the Vauxhall into park. The kind of place a man could go to reflect.

Or to die.

The rough gravel crunched beneath his feet as he made his way toward the ancient farmhouse—favoring his bad leg. A sprained ankle should have healed by now, he knew that.

But then he hadn't exactly been giving it the kind of rest a doctor would have ordered.

He'd considered making a circuit of the property before he headed in, conducting the kind of reconnaissance protocol—and caution—dictated.

He shook his head, feeling the bulk of the suicide vest under his jacket as he raised his hand to knock. Protocol had no place in this. Not anymore.

2:03 P.M.
The CIA off-site facility
City of London

"Clear," came the refrain again over the comms network, the feed from the helmet cams jerky and erratic as David Lay watched the Firearms Unit officers clear their way through the industrial estate, moving carefully and methodically. Like beaters searching the bush for a wounded lion. "Clear. Clear. *All clear.*"

The gruff voice of the sergeant in at their head, "Element moving on."

"We lose coverage in another five minutes," one of the Jimenez's people announced, materializing at Lay's side. "The bird's moving out of range."

He acknowledged her words with a nod, not trusting himself to speak. Frustration threatening to overwhelm him.

Thermal had given them nothing—just a real-time image of the British officers moving in. A single unaccounted-for heat signature early on—in the northwest quadrant of the estate—but that had proven to be nothing more than a homeless man passed out drunk, still clutching the nearly-empty wine bottle.

Nichols. . .nowhere to be found.

Lay swore softly, running a hand across his mouth as the cameras shifted, showing one of the teams moving down stairs leading to a part of the facility that was below ground. This had to be brought to an end, and soon. Otherwise they were going to find themselves in the middle of the biggest international incident the Agency had seen since Gary Powers had been brought down over Russia during the Cold War.

"We've got a door—it's *jammed*," he heard one of the officers announce, cameras shifting as the team moved into position. "Preparing to breach."

A moment passed, and then the microphones crackled from the onslaught of a thunderous crash, a battering ram in the hands of five men smashing the door inward. "Clear. *Clear*. All—what is that sodding *smell*?"

There was a moment's pause, then a flurry of curses. "Hold up, hold up. We've got a body."

2:11 P.M.
The farmhouse
Harrogate, West Yorkshire

Silence reigned in the old house, the rhythmic tick of the grandfather clock in the hall without the only sound breaking the stillness.

Harry leaned back into the chair in the parlor, his eyes closed as if in sleep. Willing himself to have patience. To *wait*. Sooner or later, Hale was going to come to him.

And then—

A faint sound struck his ears in that moment, as if from a door being opened and closed softly. A footfall against the wooden timbers that made up the floor of this house.

Wait. . .

Conor Hale withdrew the Walther P99 from its holster on his hip as he entered the house. Raising it both hands as he moved, clearing each room as he went.

The man was alone, far as he'd been able to tell from his perch in the treeline, his rifle trained on the Vauxhall as it pulled up. He had never even looked his way, denying him a clear look at his face as he walked straight up to the front door.

Clearly suspecting nothing.

Hale shook his head. He'd expected more caution from a man who had been capable enough to have penetrated the group he had so carefully recruited.

And then he saw him, through the half-open door to the parlor. A man sitting there in a chair, half-facing away from him. Looking out the window.

He eased the door open with his foot, training the Walther on the target's head as he barked, "Get on the floor! Keep your hands where I can see them."

"Conor Hale," came the familiar voice of the American, the hairs on the back of Hale's neck prickling with the warning of danger as the man rose to his feet, calmly turning to face him—his hands held out from his sides.

He saw the man's face, remembering him as the man at Flaharty's side the night they had secured the weapons shipment. *But the voice.* The final pieces falling into place—a ghost from a past thought long-forgotten. His gaze falling to the man's jacket, unzipped and gaping open to reveal the all-too-recognizable wires of an armed suicide vest.

The man smiled. A grim, cold sight that chilled him to the bone. "You could start running now, Conor, and you'd never get out of the blast radius in time. So why don't you just put down that gun and we'll have a talk."

2:16 P.M.
The CIA off-site facility
City of London

"Sir." David Lay turned to see Carlos Jimenez standing there in the door of the conference room, the station chief's face unreadable.

"Yes?"

"We just received word from Yorkshire—they've positively ID'ed the body found at the estate. It's Hashim Rahman. He was shot, execution-style. A single bullet to the head."

No. Lay swore loudly, levering himself to feet. This was spinning out of control. They had created a dangerous man—sent him out into the night. Never even considered the possibility that one day he might not come back.

That they might find themselves facing off against a man *they* had trained. "Is that all?"

"I'm afraid not," Jimenez hesitated before going on. "Final results will have to await the coroner, but the initial conclusion of the ranking constable is that he was severely tortured before being executed. Perhaps over the course of days."

My God. The CIA director shook his head, remembering the last time he had seen Nichols. Standing there alone by Carol's grave as the last mourners left, a silent, haunted figure. Their eyes meeting for a moment, frozen in time—and only Death staring back.

"I'm assuming word of this has already been conveyed to Julian?"

"It has—Norris just left for Thames House and word is that Marsh will be briefing the Home Secretary later this afternoon. Once it's in her hands. . ."

There's no stopping it. A British citizen, tortured to death on UK soil by an American intelligence officer. They had lost their chance to control this.

"Enough of this," Lay said after a moment, pulling himself together. "Your mission hasn't changed. *Find* him."

2:17 P.M.
The farmhouse
Harrogate, North Yorkshire

Harry could see the fear in the man's eyes—much as he was trying to hide it. He'd met brave men over the years, fought alongside many of them. Killed more than a few. But a bomb was different than a bullet, somehow. More impersonal, more terrifying. The idea of being ripped into raw meat. Deprived of humanity, along with life.

Not even the strongest could endure that thought for long.

"You're bluffing. You wouldn't," Hale responded, swallowing hard—the pistol in his hands still aimed at Harry's head. "You don't have it in you to—"

"Trigger the vest? You're probably right," Harry responded with a shrug. "Which is why I took the precaution of leaving the detonator in the hands of a 'friend.' And unluckily for you, about the only person he hates more than you—is me. He's not going to think twice."

He reached up to adjust his earpiece, his eyes never leaving Hale's. "You there, Flaharty?"

The man took a step back at the mention of the name, the Walther's barrel wavering for the first time.

"On my mark, Stephen," Harry continued, his voice calm, almost conversational, "I'm going to count down from ten. When I reach one, you trigger the vest. If I'm cut off at any point. . .you trigger the vest. Ten. . ."

"You're sodding insane." Hale shook his head, the blood seeming to have drained from his face.

"So I've been told," Harry responded, watching the man's eyes. "Nine. . .eight. . .seven. . ."

"Enough," the former SAS man swore, lowering the Walther to his side.

"That's a start." Harry beckoned with his hand. "Drop your weapon and kick it over here."

9:21 A.M. Eastern Time
Fado Irish Pub
Washington, D.C.

"Hofstad on Appropriations," Ian Cahill said, adjusting the volume on his Bluetooth headset as the former presidential chief of staff leaned back into the booth of the darkened pub, nursing his Guinness. "You're going to need his support if you want to get it through without undue difficulty."

He listened for another moment, then, "That won't be a problem. I'll have a talk with him. There's leverage, of course—he was involved with a prostitute a few years back. Girl was sixteen. Dennis claims not to have known, but. . ."

His voice trailed off, the implication perfectly clear. He had helped the Minnesota senator out back then, and he could use that help to bury him now—if he didn't play ball.

It was the kind of thing that Cahill had become known for, ever since his early days, coming up back in Chicago as part of the Daley Machine. Just a cog in the machine, back then. And yet, it had been an education.

In power.

The kind of power he had come so dangerously close to losing, he thought, turning off his earpiece as he ended the call. With the fall of the Hancock administration. With Roy Coftey's betrayal.

Coftey. He grimaced at the very thought of the man, swearing softly to himself as he sat there, waiting for the arrival of his contact. The Oklahoma senator had once been one of their closest allies on the Hill, and so very nearly the undoing of them all. His misguided sense of "duty"—of "honor"—casting him athwart both his party and his President.

Disloyalty. It was the unforgivable sin.

He caught a glimpse of her then, her blonde hair flowing back over her shoulders—her hips swaying as she approached the booth.

"I'm sorry I'm late," she said, sliding in across from him. "We've had a full schedule."

"Of course," Cahill replied, smiling as he looked at her. "Thanks for coming to meet with me. . .Melody."

2:25 P.M.
The farmhouse
Harrogate, North Yorkshire

"It was Lebanon, wasn't it?" Harry asked, glancing back across the kitchen to where Conor Hale sat, bound with zip-ties to a sturdy wooden chair. A look of thinly-suppressed fury on the former SAS man's face.

"It was."

"July of '06, as I recall," Harry mused, coming back to stand beside the table. His jacket now off—the suicide vest removed and placed on the floor at Hale's feet. Flaharty was on his way in, but that was going to take a while. "Just the three of us—you and me and Nick Crawford, jumping off the ramp of that C-130 and into the night. I'd never seen you before that night, but I knew if Nick vouched for you—you were good. And you proved it on that hill outside Bint Jbeil."

"We all nearly bought it that night."

He nodded, a grim smile touching his lips at the memory. The fire lashing the hilltop—the supersonic *crack* of bullets whistling through the air. "We did at that. . .so tell me, Conor. What went wrong? How did we end up here in this place? On opposite sides."

"It doesn't matter, does it?" Hale asked, shaking his head. "You wouldn't understand. The war you and I fought—it didn't end. It's never going to end. Until one side *destroys* the other. And no one has the will for that. Not anymore."

"You're talking about precipitating a civil war—unleashing the kind of violence we both saw in Tikrit, in Basra, *here*—on the streets of London."

The former SAS sergeant laughed. "You just don't get it, do you—that war is coming, whether we want it or not. Whether we *believe* it or not. I only intend for it to come when we are *prepared* for it. Prepared to win, once and for all. To drive these anim—"

Harry drew back his arm without warning, his fist hammering into the man's stomach and driving every ounce of breath from his body.

Hale doubled up, cursing fluently struggling against the bonds securing him to the chair as Harry stooped down, his lips only inches from the man's ear.

"You're right, of course. How, why—none of that really matters, in the end. Because I didn't come here to reminisce about old war stories, Conor. I came here to get at the truth. And that's exactly what you're going to tell me."

"He talking yet?" Flaharty asked as Harry opened the door, letting him in.

A shake of the head served as reply. "He's not giving me anything operational."

"Oh, he will," the Irishman responded with a grim assurance. "Just let me have a go at him. I've done this once or twice, as you know, boyo."

Harry just gave him a look. No war was ever so vicious as that which pitted neighbor against neighbor, and the Troubles of Northern Ireland had been no exception, with the Provos knowing few rivals in the unspeakably brutal torture inflicted on men known—or merely suspected—of informing for the British.

And Flaharty had been right there, in the midst of it.

But to turn him loose against a man he had once gone into battle alongside. . .that was another matter entirely.

Another dark line in his soul—crossed as if it were nothing. He hesitated for only a moment before turning to lead the way into the kitchen. "Follow me."

2:34 P.M.
Thames House
Millbank, London

". . .smoke fills the sky over Birmingham this morning as young Asian men, reacting to yesterday's provocative rally on the part of the British Defence Coalition, set tires ablaze in the streets. Our local Sky News affiliate reports that the Marks & Spencer on High Street has been forced to close for business after gangs of looters taking advantage of the unrest broke into the store overnight—causing thousands of pounds in damages. Police called to the scene were unable. . ."

The discovery of Hashim Rahman's tortured body couldn't have come at a worse time, Julian Marsh thought, staring out onto the floor of the Thames House operations centre.

With the rioting overnight in Ipswich after the stabbing death of Ajmal Rafik, this was going to make for the second imam found dead in as many days. And they weren't going to be able to keep a lid on this for long.

Rahman's wife—*widow*, the DG corrected himself—had already been reaching out to prominent civil liberties groups in the wake of what her lawyer was calling her husband's "unlawful abduction by unknown government forces", clearly a veiled reference to the Security Service.

If they found out he had been tortured to death. . .Marsh swore softly. It could bring down the government.

He reached for his tailored suit jacket and threw it over one arm. Time to brief the Home Secretary—make sure everyone was at least playing from the same sheet music.

2:49 P.M.
The farmhouse
Harrogate, North Yorkshire

Demons. Harry plunged bloody hands beneath the faucet's cold stream, watching as the red-tinged water swirled in the basin beneath, draining away.

There was something he was missing in all of this, something critical, but he found it impossible to put his finger on it—memories, voices from the dark shadows of his mind, clamoring for an audience.

Hers, perhaps loudest of all. *"You swore he would come to no harm."*

What would Carol have thought of the deeds he had committed in her name? *In her memory.* It was one of the few questions he knew the answer to—knew all too well.

She had been a good person, he thought, feeling the anger well up inside him once more—far better than he could have ever deserved. And now she was dead. Like so many others. . .taken before their time.

There was no place for good people in this world.

Only for people like him, Flaharty, Conor Hale—all of them too much the same—humanity stripped away, blindly clawing in the mud for dominance. Scarce able to even remember what they were fighting for in the first place.

Justice. Redemption. Or just revenge. What you called it didn't seem to matter anymore. *All the same.*

He stalked past Flaharty, back to where Conor Hale sat—stripped to the waist now, blood oozing through his tattered bandages. He was bruised and bloodied, but his eyes glinted defiance at Harry's approach.

"You can make this all stop," Harry whispered, leaning in close to the man—his eyes only inches away from Hale's. "Can put an end to this. . .I just need you to give me the details of the attack on the Queen. A location for Tarik Abdul Muhammad. Give me that, and you walk out of here. A free man."

"Make it stop?" Hale asked derisively, laughing through the pain. He was overcome for a moment with a violent cough, recovering himself with an effort. "Like I would beg either of you for *mercy*? I'm not one of your boy-raping wogs, mate. I've seen worse than anything you could dream of dishing out."

"You've not begun to see what I'm capable of. A location for the *Shaikh*," Harry repeated, his hand resting on Hale's shoulder, bracing him against the coming impact.

"Why don't the two of you just go bugger each—"

The man's words were cut abruptly short, a raw scream of pain filling the old farmhouse as Harry's fist slammed into his ribs, blood spurting from around his knuckles as he pummeled the wound.

"We can keep this up for days," he hissed into Hale's ear, taking a step back. "And sooner or later, you *will* break."

It was only then that he realized Hale wasn't looking at him, but past him—a faint smile playing around his lips as he fought against the pain.

He followed the direction of the man's eyes over to a clock hanging on the wall. . .the realization hitting home with the impact of a rifle bullet. *This was happening soon. Now,* even."

"But I don't *have* days, do I?" he asked, glancing back to see that the smile had vanished from Hale's face as quick as it had come. "It's going down now—isn't it?"

He could feel the surge tide of anger rising within him, a murderous rage filling his body.

This was Vegas all over again. Waking up to find yourself farther behind the pace than you'd thought. Too far to catch up.

Too late to stop something that had become inevitable. "Then we're out of time. Flaharty, give me the burner."

"What?" the Irishman demanded, startled. "What are you doing, lad?"

"Just give it here," Harry responded, taking it from him and walking over to where the suicide vest was laid out on the kitchen table, his thumbs moving rapidly over the keys as he began programming one of the apps. Time to play the only card left to him. Risk everything on a gambler's throw.

He pulled his own mobile from his pocket, holding it up so the screens of both phones were facing Hale, countdown timers clearly visible on each of them.

"These are synced, Conor. One for me, one for you," he said coldly, mastering himself with an effort as he stared into Hale's eyes. "We're going to take a step just outside—close enough to hear if you call, far enough to be out of the blast radius. If I haven't heard from you by the time the countdown reaches zero, your phone places the call, triggers the vest. We were both in Iraq, I know you've seen what one these can do to a man."

"You're not going to do that," Hale murmured, shaking his head, sweat broken out in beads on his face. Defiance fading away like the mist. "If I die, what I know dies with me."

"And if you're not willing to share it with me, it might as well." He shook his head, exchanging a look with Flaharty.

"Five minutes, Conor. Tick-tock. The end of your life. . .begins now."

Chapter 30

3:02 P.M.
The farmhouse
Harrogate, North Yorkshire

Three minutes. Harry looked off into the distance across the hills of Yorkshire, the sun already beginning its declining march across the western sky. Unable to escape the feeling that, once again, he had been too late.

You could never save the ones you loved. And even avenging their deaths. . .he should have killed Tarik that day in the crowd on the train and had done with it. Anything would have been better than this. Watching him *succeed* once more.

"You really going to let this happen, lad?" Flaharty asked, glancing over at the phone in his hand, its timer rapidly ticking away. *2:17. . .2:16. . .*

He nodded almost imperceptibly, his eyes still on the horizon. "One thing you learn from spending fifteen years with the Agency: there's no margin in bluffing."

1:48. . .1:47. . .

"And if he dies?"

"Then he dies. And I contact Darren Roth again, give him what I have, let him run with it." He saw the question in the Irishman's eyes and immediately clarified, "One of Mehreen's fellow officers. Thames House."

Flaharty shook his head as if in wry disbelief, cursing softly beneath his breath. "And you were planning on telling me this *when?*"

"When you needed to know."

1:13. . .1:12. . .

Suddenly, the silence of the surrounding countryside was broken by a muffled yell from somewhere inside the farmhouse. The voice of a man calling out for help. Flaharty turned toward the door, but Harry put a hand on his shoulder, holding him back. "Give him a moment."

Hale was nearly hyper-ventilating by the time they reached him, words spilling out of him like water over a cliff as Harry reached over to cut the timer off. *0:37.*

"The attack—the attack on the Queen. It's—"

"What about it?"

"It isn't on her motorcade outside Balmoral, it's on the castle itself." He hesitated, and Harry made as if to reach once more the timer. "No, no, no. . .don't. Please *don't*. The attack was to be launched at 1800 hours."

Less than three hours, Harry thought, glancing at his watch. Scarce more than that. "Keep talking."

3:05 P.M.
The A93
Banchory, Scotland

Forty minutes, Farid thought, checking his mirrors as he turned right, navigating his way through the streets of the quiet Scottish town. Forty minutes and they would be at the staging area outside Ballater, where he would turn over control of the delivery van to the *shahid* who had volunteered to drive it up to the gates.

Keep it slow and steady, stay below the speed limit. No one was going to touch them in this land of laws. *Rules*. A country that imposed fairness and justice on its citizens while dropping bombs on the heads of innocents half a world away, he realized grimly—his dark eyes smoldering as he saw the first of the SUVs containing his men swing out into the street to follow him, hanging a couple cars back.

That was, after all, why he had left this land of his birth four years before—leaving behind his family. His job as an engineer. To fight in God's struggle, plunging himself into the maelstrom of a Syria that had descended further into chaos with each passing year.

Four years of fighting, first against Assad, then the Kurdish *Peshmergea* and the Iraqi Army. Long years of blood and terror, finding themselves fighting against overwhelming odds. Losing many recruits in their first battle—arms blown off by artillery shells, bodies riddled with machine gun bullets.

When the opportunity had finally come to leave, he had taken it—making his way first to Hungary, then across the EU before arriving in the UK with nothing more than the clothes on his back and the few remaining euros on a debit card issued to him by the *Bundesamt für Migration und Flüchtlinge* at a refugee camp outside Leipzig.

But the one thing no man could take from him was the knowledge he possessed. The skills of a man who had survived again and again in battles against the *safawi* regime of Bashar Assad, battles where his fellow *mujahideen* had fallen around him like grain before the reaper.

He shook his head. *Fate*. That was what it truly was, the hand of Allah guiding him, shielding him from harm.

Preserving him for this day.

3:09 P.M.
The safehouse
Leeds, West Yorkshire

Mehreen was on the phone almost before it could ring a second time, recognizing the number of Nichols' burner. "Yes?"

"I need you to put a call through to Roth at once," Harry's voice responded, his words terse. Clipped. "Hale talked—the attack is going down yet this afternoon, 1800 hours. An attack on Balmoral Castle itself. He has nearly forty men, according to Hale. That's more than enough to overwhelm the Queen's detail. It will be a bloodbath."

She closed her eyes. The audacity of such an attack. . .the propaganda coup should it *succeed*—was well-nigh inconceivable, equaled in impact by only 9/11 or the Christmas Eve attacks on Vegas. *Perhaps worse.*

Enough to send the UK over the brink, careening into the abyss. "They're going to tear this country apart," she whispered, finding her voice at last. "This is real, isn't it?"

"It is."

The intelligence officer's nightmare, come to life. *Not on my watch.* "And the *Shaikh*?" Mehreen asked, taking a deep breath. *Focus.* "Was Hale able to give you a location?"

"No," he replied quickly. *Almost too quickly*, she thought, the idea leaving her mind almost as soon as it had entered it. "I can only assume he'll be leading the attack. Hale knows nothing more that he hasn't told me."

"Are you sure of that?" she asked, her mind racing as she stared across the room. "We're going to need every last scrap of intel we can get."

"I'm sure," he responded simply, a chilling assurance in his voice. What he had done to obtain such certainty, she didn't know. Didn't *want* to know.

"Very well. I'll contact Darren immediately—make sure he briefs the DG."

3:11 P.M.
The farmhouse
Harrogate, North Yorkshire

"Solid copy. We'll be back on our way back, then." Harry thumbed the button to END CALL, slipping the phone into his pocket. "Let's get moving. Go get—"

He turned to find Flaharty regarding him with a keen, questioning gaze. "What are you playing at, boyo?"

"What do you mean?" he asked, knowing very well what the Irishman had meant.

"Oh, you're a cute hoor, aren't you just?" Flaharty observed, chuckling softly. "The widow Crawford. . .you lied to her—told her you'd gotten nothing from Conor Hale concerning the location of Tarik."

And so he had, yet another lie among the many. Almost easier than the truth, these days. Perhaps they always had been, for him.

"You have a problem with that?" he asked, meeting the man's eyes in a hard, unyielding gaze.

Flaharty shook his head. "Not in the least, but I'd like to know why. If I'm going to be backing your play, I need to make certain I've seen all the cards."

"Tarik Abdul Muhammad is mine," Harry responded coldly, turning away from him. "Killing him is the reason I came to this country. And there is no way I'm going to risk Five taking him into custody before I can get to the port."

The Irishman nodded, seeming to accept the response. "All right, then. So what's our next move in this grand scheme of yours?"

"We go cut down Hale—give him some of the sedative I found in his kit and put him in the trunk."

"We're bringing him with us?" Flaharty asked, the look in his eyes finishing the question for him.

"You'll have your revenge," Harry responded, pulling open the door of the Vauxhall, "soon enough. But I'm not done with him just yet. Let's get moving."

3:17 P.M.
The port of Aberdeen
Scotland

"Go with God," Tarik Abdul Muhammad said, staring into Sayyed Hassan's eyes.

When he had first met the leader of the London cell twelve days earlier in the brothel, he had been unimpressed by the bookstore owner. But now, he saw nothing but resolve written in the man's face.

Surely it was true, that Allah would give unto each man the strength required to play his part in His struggle.

He reached out, drawing the man to him in an impulsive embrace—feeling the rough bulk of the suicide vest against his chest as he did so. "*Mashallah*," he whispered, tears shining in his eyes. For what was more beautiful than the life of the martyr?

"Nadeem will drive you to the shopping centre," he said finally, pulling back. "From there, it will be left to you. Buy us time, brother."

"*Insh'allah*."

Tarik turned back to the makeshift command center they had spent the night setting up—laptop after laptop laid out on metal tables, wires running across the floor.

One man's sacrifice. . .all they needed to assure themselves of victory.

As God willed, indeed.

3:24 P.M.
The Home Office
2 Marsham Street, London

". . .and the CIA will, of course, disavow all his actions. That's not an answer the PM will find acceptable, Julian. He's going to demand that—"

You'll have to excuse me for a moment, Home Secretary," Marsh said apologetically, pulling his phone out as it vibrated insistently. *Third time now.* "I have to take this."

It was Darren Roth's number.

"Of course," she responded, dismissing him with an annoyed wave of the hand, as if shooing a fly. He had seen Napier in worse humors, but this time she had ample reason to be.

They were sitting on a bomb. Once the details of Rahman's death made the news. . .

3:25 P.M.
MI-5 Regional Office
Leeds, West Yorkshire

Pick up the sodding phone, Roth thought, staring impatiently at the screen as it continued to ring.

It was his third call to the DG since he had heard from Mehreen. All of them going unanswered. He had to be—

"Given that you've taken me out of a meeting with the Home Secretary, Darren," Julian Marsh answered finally, acid in his tone as he came on the line, "I trust I can assume this is about a matter of great importance?"

Thank God.

"I apologize, sir," Roth said, getting up from his desk and pacing across the small temporary office to the window, "but this couldn't wait. I have just received credible intel regarding a threat to the Queen's life."

"And the nature of the threat?" He could hear the skepticism in the DG's voice. They dealt with threats against the Queen on a daily basis, as a matter of course. But none of them were anything like *this*.

"There is going to be an attack on Balmoral Castle within the next two hours," he responded, still scarcely able to believe the words himself, "carried out by a jihadist cell under the command of Tarik Abdul Muhammad."

"My God," Marsh responded after a moment of stunned silence. His usual patrician reserve seeming to have deserted him. "You're bloody well serious."

"Never more so. According to the intel I've received, he has nearly forty men."

The DG swore softly. "COBRA will have to be convened at once, SO-14 alerted to handle the threat. This intelligence—who is your source on the attack?"

And there it was. The question he had hoped wouldn't be asked.

"With due respect, sir," Roth began slowly, aware that he was treading on thin ice. "Given the urgency of the situation, the identity of my source is less than material. If we are to act promptly—"

"I'm going to need full assurance that I can rely upon the information I'm passing along," Marsh responded, not giving an inch. "You're a good officer, Darren, and under any ordinary circumstance, I would rely upon your unsupported word. But this is no ordinary circumstance—I'll be taking this to the PM himself. Who gave you this, a credible asset? A walk-in?"

No way out. He took a deep breath, knowing the risk he was taking. "Mehreen Crawford."

"She's your source?" Marsh asked, pausing for a long moment—the incredulity only too audible in his voice. "I know you are close to Mehreen personally, on account of her husband—but, for God's sake, Darren—you're as aware as I am that she is suspected of having jeopardized our intelligence operations on behalf of Harold Nichols, the CIA's rogue officer. She has to be considered compromised."

"I'm aware of that."

"Then where is she getting this kind of intelligence? Do you know who her source is—or did you simply take her word for it?"

Roth shook his head, running a hand across his jaw. It didn't get any easier from here, but Marsh was a veteran intelligence officer. Lying to him wasn't a viable option—he'd see through a deception in a moment. "It's Nichols himself..."

3:27 P.M.
The Home Office
2 Marsham Street, London

Marsh glanced back down the corridor toward the closed door of Napier's office, scarce able to believe he had heard his senior field officer correctly.

"I met the man last night," Roth went on after a moment's pause. "At a decommissioned Five safehouse here in Leeds."

"And you simply decided, on your own authority, to let Nichols go. To not to *tell* anyone about him." The DG swore, lowering his voice as a Home Office functionary hurried past. The level of damage that this could do—that this already *had* done—was immeasurable. "*Why?*"

"He was still gathering intel on the attack. Based on the evidence he presented to me, I deemed it a justifiable risk. Give him rope."

No. That wasn't how this worked, Marsh thought. Every meeting with a foreign intelligence officer—even from one of the "Five Eyes"—had to be reported, logged.

Kept on record. And for good reason.

In the recruiting of a fellow intelligence professional, extraordinary care had to be exerted to make sure that *you* weren't the one actually being recruited. As had happened here. To Mehreen. *And* Roth.

"And I suppose that among the evidence he presented to you," Marsh demanded caustically, "he mentioned torturing, and subsequently executing, Hashim Rahman?"

Silence. "He didn't, did he?" he pressed, shaking his head at the folly of it all. He'd seen this sort of thing play out so many times before. Back in West Berlin, attempting to run agents across the Wall—finding your own network penetrated at the last. *Not again.* "He's playing you, Roth, and *through* you he's trying to play all of us. Buy himself time."

"With due respect, sir, I don't believe that to be the case. The attack—"

"*With due respect,*" Marsh fired back, "you are in no position to be making that decision. You've allowed your relationship with Mehreen to compromise your judgment—cause you to extend *trust* to a rogue foreign officer responsible for the torture and death of a British citizen. Do you comprehend the gravity of what I am saying?"

"I do, sir. But what about the Queen's—"

"SO-14 will be apprised that we have received intelligence of a threat against Her Majesty's life while she is in residence there at Balmoral and will receive all the details we currently have in our possession," the DG replied, his tone biting. "It will be up to them to take what action they see fit, given the unsubstantiated nature of the threat. As for you, I want you back in London. *Immediately.* We need to get this sorted—find a way to recover Nichols. And handle the repercussions. Do you understand?"

3:30 P.M.
MI-5 Regional Office
Leeds, West Yorkshire

"Yes, sir," Roth nodded, swallowing hard as he glanced at his watch. *Just over two hours until the attack was to begin.* "Perfectly. I'll be back in London within a few hours."

He just stood there for a long moment after the call ended, torn by indecision.

The threat to the Queen *was* real, he could feel it in his bones—the instincts that had kept him alive in Afghanistan rising once again to the fore.

And if that was the case. . .he couldn't stand idly by and watch it happen.

His hand moved back to the phone, hesitating only briefly before dialing a number from memory.

"Mehreen," he announced the moment the call connected, "the safehouse has been compromised—you need to get out of there at once. I'm on my way to meet you."

3:35 P.M.
North Yorkshire

So close. He could almost taste it, bitter and metallic against his tongue. The taste of blood. *Of revenge.*

Love kills, Harry thought, his knuckles whitening around the steering wheel of the Vauxhall as it sped down the trunk road.

It had killed him, that night in Vegas—Carol's blood staining his hands, his tears running down her lifeless cheek. *"Don't give up, don't you* dare *give up."*

Both their lives claimed in a single moment, only his body refusing to acknowledge the truth hers had accepted so willingly.

And now this was all that mattered. *Dig two graves.*

"The port of Aberdeen is a six-hour drive," Flaharty observed quietly from the passenger seat, his attention seemingly focused out the window. "You honestly think you stand a chance of getting there before they do?"

No, a small voice from somewhere deep within warned, reminding him of the futility of all this. The voice of reason, long since banished.

Because the idea of failure was impossible to face. *Not now*. Not after everything he had done. The lives *he* had shattered.

"We pick up Mehreen at the safehouse," he responded, his voice brittle as ice, "collect the rest of our gear. Then we start driving north. Once we've—"

The burner in his pocket began vibrating with an incoming call, cutting him off as he reached for it. *Mehreen*.

There was no reason for her to be making contact. No reason. *Unless*. . .

"Yes?" he answered cautiously, listening as she began to speak. His face growing darker the longer he listened. *No. It wasn't possible.*

He thought he had prepared for the worst case, but *this*. . .it was like looking down into an open grave, waiting to swallow you whole.

"What's going on, lad?" Flaharty asked, his voice sounding faint, far away.

How to answer?

"We've been sold down the river," he responded numbly, holding the phone against his chest. "Five isn't taking the threat against the Queen seriously. The safehouse has been compromised—Mehreen's getting ready to bug out."

The Irishman swore viciously. "*Who?* This fellow Roth?"

Harry just nodded, his mind racing. Searching for a way out. *An exit*. Finding each one closed off in turn.

They no longer had six hours to reach Scotland—they barely even had two. *And if Tarik carried out* another *successful attack*. . .

It was a thought he couldn't even bring himself to finish.

"Do you know of *any* way," he asked, turning to look at Flaharty, "of reaching Balmoral in time?"

"There might be one way," the Irishman began slowly, a shadow passing across his face. "One of the lads—name's Liam—owns a farm about thirty minutes west of here, just south of the moor near Keighley. He has a small plane, off-books. Used it for smuggling, back in the day. Hasn't been in the air in a decade, like as not."

"We'll have to try, it's our only shot," Harry responded, pulling the phone back up to his ear. "Mehreen, you still there? I'm going to need you to meet me at a farm northwest of Leeds—there's a plane we can use. I'll text you the address."

He listened for another moment before ending the call, turning to Flaharty as he tucked the phone back in his pocket, the Vauxhall slowing as it entered another small English village. "This friend of yours, is borrowing his plane going to present a problem?"

"Shouldn't be," the former terrorist replied after a moment, shaking his head. But there was *something* there in his eyes that belied the gesture.

There was no time for this. "Don't play with me, Stephen," Harry snapped, his eyes flashing a warning of danger. "Out with it."

"Liam. . .well, he's Davey's little brother."

3:42 P.M.
MI-5 Regional Office
Leeds, West Yorkshire

"He's playing you." Roth shook his head as he made his way across the office carpark toward his BMW, the Sig-Sauer holstered beneath his jacket, the DG's words running on endless loop through his head.

Marsh was right, so far as it went.

Like himself, Nichols was a career intelligence officer—had, in fact, been at it far longer—and that made anything he said suspect. He knew all that, but there was the inescapable feel of reality to this attack on the Queen. And all he had to stop it was the pistol on his hip. A couple spare mags.

And no way to get there in time.

Like it or not, the American was the only option left to them. If he *didn't* have a plan. . .

The alternative wasn't something he wanted to consider.

Roth's phone buzzed with an incoming text as he opened the driver's door of the BMW, sliding inside.

A message from Mehreen displayed on its screen. Short, to the point. *Plans have changed. Meet me.*

He tapped the address given on-screen into his car's GPS, watching as it calculated the route.

Not far.

4:01 P.M.
A farm
Keighley, West Yorkshire

"Let me handle the talking," Flaharty cautioned as Harry pushed open the door of the Vauxhall, stepping out onto the gravel of the farm lane as his gaze flickered around them.

A small stone farmhouse set just off the lane, a battered truck that looked like it dated back to the late eighties parked in front, its keys still in the ignition.

A few hundred meters farther back stood an old bank barn, a handful of more modern outbuildings clustered about it.

And beyond, to the north, the moor itself, wild and desolate. He'd always found himself struck by the majesty of desolate places. The yearning, perhaps, of a damned soul seeking its home. *Cain.*

He heard the sharp, frenzied barking of a dog from somewhere off amongst the buildings and his hand stole toward his holstered pistol, arrested only by Flaharty's voice.

"Easy there, lad," the Irishman said, shooting him a sharp look. "Liam's a sheep farmer. . .has a wolfhound, Fionchán, he calls him. Fine dog. I want to get through this without violence if there's any way we can."

As do I, Harry thought, taking his hand back out of his jacket as he gazed off toward the western sky. There was bound to be too much of it before day's end, as it was.

"Oh, it's you," the woman said as she opened the door barely a crack, catching sight of Flaharty's face. "Come in, come in. *Liam!*"

Harry followed the Irishman into the narrow hall, Flaharty's words running through his mind. *"Liam was just a wee'un when Davey and I were runnin' the streets of Belfast, trading shots with the RUC and lobbing petrol bombs at army patrols. But never ha' I seen two brothers closer. Davey always looked out for him. Even in—"*

"Stephen!" a man's voice bellowed out, and Harry looked up to see a big man in his late forties emerge from the end of the hallway. His arms outstretched. "It's been too long."

"It has," the former terrorist responded, Harry standing in the shadows of the hall behind him as the two men embraced. "Far too long."

"You heard about Davey?"

"Aye, that I did." It was impossible to read Flaharty's expression, his arm encircling his boyhood friend's back as he hugged him close. "He was a good man. Finest man I ever knew."

"And those sods killed him," Liam said, pulling back—his face stricken with grief. "He was executed, Stephen, like some kind of animal. A single bullet to the head—never stood a bloody chance."

"That's what I heard," Flaharty responded, his eyes betraying no sign that he had been the man who fired that shot. Taken his friend's life. "I would have given anything to ha' been here for his wake, but it just wasn't possible. The men that killed him, they've been after me, as well. That's why we're here this evening."

There was a perverse truth in that, Harry thought. *Somewhere.* Conor Hale had turned Davey Malone, using Flaharty's involvement with the Agency as leverage.

Lies within lies. Until they all came crashing down at the last. *Be sure your sins will find you out.*

"You *know* who killed him?" the big Irishman asked, anger shining through his tears. "They'll pay for it, or so help me—"

"We're here about the plane," Harry interrupted coldly, clearing his throat.

Liam looked up, as if seeing him for the first time. His anger seeming to have found a target.

"And who's this?" he demanded, turning to Flaharty in search of an answer.

"A friend."

Chapter 31

4:12 P.M.
The farm
Keighley, West Yorkshire

"And here she is," Liam announced, dust billowing around them as he pulled away the tarpaulins, the familiar shape of an old Cessna 206 materializing in the dim light of the barn.

"Ah, yes," Harry said, reaching a hand up to rest against the engine cowling. "The Lycoming flat-six. A good engine."

"Aye," the big man replied, favoring him with a keen, searching glance. "You've flown this plane?"

"A time or three," he nodded, all the memories flooding back. *No time.* He shoved them away with an effort, forcing himself to focus on the present. "You have fuel?"

Liam inclined his head toward a row of jerry cans lined up against the wall of the barn. "All the petrol I've got is right there. Is it going to be enough?"

It would have to be, Harry thought, eyeing the cans. Couldn't be much more than forty gallons, less than half the StationAir's fuel capacity. He met Flaharty's eyes and nodded. *Enough.*

"Let's get her rolled out into the open."

And there it was, Mehreen thought, glancing out the side window of her car as she tapped the brakes, rolling to a stop in front of the farmhouse.

The tall meadow grass waving in the warm spring wind as two men pushed a white high-wing Cessna out into the field. *Three*, she corrected herself as she exited the car, spotting Nichols' tall form on the other side of the plane's cabin.

He was coming around the tail of the plane as she came across the field, looking up at her approach.

"Did you get clear?" he asked, a weary look in his eyes as he glanced at her. Worn, haggard—the pallor of his face contrasting with the dark stubble of his unshaven beard.

The image of a bloodied prizefighter, clawing his way drunkenly back to his feet just before time was called.

"I did—Darren called to warn me right after he got off the phone with the DG."

"Kind of him," he murmured, looking at the plane, the irony only too clear in his tone.

"He said only what had to be said to get Marsh on side. Legitimize the intel he was passing along."

"And it didn't work that way, did it?" was the curt response, Harry shaking his head as if in recognition of the futility of the conversation. "Come on, let's get the gear loaded."

4:19 P.M.
The CIA off-site facility
City of London

"We've got a locked door," the Special Branch officer announced, the image from his helmet cam shaking as he nodded to another member of his team, "preparing to breach."

Final room, Thomas Parker thought, finding himself holding his breath as the officers stacked up, one of them moving forward with a breaching hammer in his hand.

The CIA hadn't been given the opportunity to independently review the intel that had led Five to this flat, but so far. . .it had turned out to be a bust.

If Harry was there or had ever been there, there was no sign of it. *Sterile,* Thomas realized, glancing over at Simon Norris, the British analyst's brow furrowed in frustration as he gazed at the screen.

Exactly the way Harry would have left it.

A year before, he would have walked through hell to pull his old friend out of the fire, Thomas thought, watching as the breacher brought the hammer back into an arcing swing. *A brotherhood washed in blood.*

And now he was powerless to do anything to stop what was about to take place. If Harry was inside—

His thought was cut short by the crash of the hammer, the door flying inward.

The second man on the team moving into the opening, the dark outline of the officer's MP-5 visible as he cleared the fatal funnel in a trice, sweeping his quadrant. *Nothing.*

"Clear," Thomas heard an officer announce, a moment passing before the Special Branch constable appeared in front of the camera.

"Sir," he began, "there's no one here."

4:24 P.M.
The farm
Keighley, West Yorkshire

"Think it will be enough to hold him?" Flaharty asked, struggling to catch his breath as he straightened, looking down at the unconscious form of Conor Hale they had just lain across the Cessna's rearmost seat. "Lord, but he's a heavy one."

Harry nodded, turning to make his way toward the door of the plane. "I only gave him a light dose, but it should be enough to keep him out until we're on the ground again."

Flaharty gave him a skeptical look. "And where do you plan on doing that, exactly?"

"The lawn of Balmoral Castle itself, if it comes to that," he replied, lowering himself from the plane and walking over to where Mehreen stood, her laptop propped up on the hood of her car. The wireless stick plugged into its USB port. "Were you able to get the maps pulled up?"

She nodded. "We don't have a good connection out here—we're having to piggyback off the mobile coverage, and that's always poor. But it's going to have to do."

Harry turned the laptop's screen toward him, brushing a callused finger over the trackpad as he zoomed in on the satellite imagery. "There's a golf course here, southeast of the castle. It's bound not to be perfectly flat, but it gives us over three hundred meters in length, in terms of a straight shot. Coming in over the trees."

Flaharty's eyes widened. "That's not enough."

"It is if we have no intention of ever taking off again," he responded, lowering his voice as Liam came into sight around the nose of the plane. "This is a one-way trip. I think we all know that."

Easy, Harry thought, holding the ignition key in place as he gently advanced the throttle, listening to the engine sputter and cough. *There.*

The Cessna's 300-horsepower engine roared suddenly to life and he released the key as the propeller began to spin, its wash whipping at the grass of the Yorkshire meadow.

And then almost as quickly as it had come alive, the engine began to choke as if it were starving for fuel. A deathly sound. *If they couldn't get this in the air. . .*

He reached down, quickly switching the auxiliary fuel pump to "HI" for a fraction of a moment, clearing vapor from the lines.

The engine continued to sputter for a moment, then came back to full power, straining against the parking brake.

Harry eased the throttle back, letting it idle as he rose from the pilot's seat, ducking his head as he exited the aircraft. He looked up to see Liam standing there a few feet away—flashed the big Irishman a tight smile. "I believe we're in business."

"Harry," Mehreen called, gesturing for him to come over to the car, "I think I've found something."

"What is it?"

"There's a gliding club in Aboyne, just twenty minutes east of the castle on the A93. They have two runways, over five hundred meters in length. It's more than enough room to land a plane like this."

He shook his head. "But then we're on the ground, without transportation. I—"

"An' what's this?" Liam exclaimed from beside him, cutting him off, his eyes focused across the meadow toward the drive. "What's this?"

He heard Flaharty swear under his breath, looked up to see a dark BMW parked in the drive. A figure striding across the field toward them.

4:28 P.M.
Balmoral Castle
Ballater, Scotland

"Of course, sir," Colin Hilliard responded gravely, holding his mobile phone close to his ear as he descended the grand staircase into the gallery just off the entrance hall. Reception was bad, as usual in the region—but the message from his superiors at Special Protection Command back in London couldn't have been more clear.

There had been a threat made against the Queen's life—credibility, indeterminate.

"You can tell the Superintendent we'll continue to exercise the utmost vigilance, as ever. Of course. Please ensure that I'm apprised of any new intelligence bearing upon these reports."

He tucked the phone inside the pocket of his suit as the call ended, his brow furrowing as he considered what he had just been told.

Threats against the Queen, nothing was more common. He'd reviewed hundreds of them in his time on Her Majesty's detail. Cranks, most of them—empowered, given a soapbox by the Internet.

Dark rantings never meant to be brought to fruition.

But this. . .this felt different, somehow. Perhaps it was nothing more than the knowledge that the Queen had come to Scotland—months ahead of her normal visit—for the express purposes of getting away from the civil unrest gripping the south of the United Kingdom. Seeking peace. *Quiet.*

But what if it had *followed* her here?

He saw the head of Prince William's detail, a Sikh inspector named Bahadar Singh, coming in off the carriage porch—his traditional turban wrapped around his head, the ceremonial *kirpan* buckled at his waist, its hilt visible just beneath his suit jacket. "The Queen, Bahadar—she's still on the terrace?"

"With Prince William and the Princess Charlotte." The man nodded, his eyes narrowing as if he sensed instinctively from Hilliard's words that something was wrong. As well he might—they'd guarded the Queen together for over five years before he'd been assigned to William and Kate. "His Royal Highness Prince Philip has retired to his chamber, he was feeling unwell. What's going on, Colin?"

"Fresh intel from London," Hilliard replied, glancing down the hall toward the gallery, "there's been a threat made against the Queen's life. I don't know that it's anything more than rumor, but we have to take it seriously."

"Of course, of course," Singh responded, a troubled look on his bearded face. "Catherine and George are down by the banks of the Dee—the young prince wanted to wade in the shallows and gather smooth stones. Should I send someone after them?"

"There's no one there with them?"

A shake of the head. "Catherine was insistent that they have some privacy."

The uneasy balance, as ever, of protecting people who wanted nothing more than a normal life and would ever be denied it.

Hilliard hesitated for a moment before replying, "No, not yet. Check in with the front gate, see if they've noticed anything out of the ordinary."

4:29 P.M.

"*Darren Roth*. . .how did he get here?" Harry breathed, wheeling suddenly on Mehreen as the answer dawned on him. "What do you know about this?"

"I gave him the address," she responded, her eyes flashing as she turned to face him. *Not giving an inch.* Moments like this, he knew exactly why Nick had married her. "He wanted to help, and he has the kind of training and skills we're going to need if we're going to make this work—your bum ankle, my lack of weapons training. . .and this sodding terrorist. It's not going to be enough."

Flaharty swore, anger bubbling just beneath the surface. "I—"

"Not now," Harry said, cutting him off just as Roth came up to the car. This had to be handled, and handled delicately. They were treading on very dangerous ground. The look in Liam's eyes betraying suspicion and bewilderment.

"I got here as quickly as I could," the British officer said, looking directly at Mehreen. "Glad to see I was in time."

"In time to sell us out again, you mean?" Flaharty spat, taking a threatening step in the man's direction. Ignoring the warning look Harry shot him.

Roth gazed at him coolly for a long moment, his gaze flickering from Flaharty to Harry and back again. "Well that's something you'd know quite a bit about, eh?"

Flaharty's face purpled with fury, his hand slipping inside his jacket. "Why, you sodding—"

Harry saw him move forward, saw the weapon come out, but too late to stop him—a hoarse cry of warning exploding from his lips.

He saw the barrel of the Kimber flash in the sun, saw Roth move in—grappling for the weapon, his elbow slamming into the older man's chest.

Flaharty went down, hard—sprawling on his back in the meadow as the former Marine took a step back, the Irishman's Kimber now in his own hand.

"This is your operation," he said, looking at Harry, "and your decision. I'm in, if you'll have me."

4:31 P.M.
Balmoral Castle
Ballater, Scotland

"Nothing that I've seen, sir," Sergeant Brian Gavron responded, hearing Inspector Singh's voice in his earpiece. "A few disappointed tourists earlier, but no one since 1400 hours. All's quiet here."

That wasn't usually the case, the SO-14 officer had been made to understand—but with Her Majesty's early trip north, bus tours had been canceled and tourists turned away. Security was paramount.

He glanced out toward the bridge spanning the Dee, perhaps fifty meters from his position, catching sight of a vehicle parked by the side of the road on the other side of the river, near the carpark. "Looks like we've got a utility van parked out on the main road out toward the kirk. Perhaps from the power company?"

"Look into it."

It *was* a power van, painted in the familiar green and blue livery of Scottish & Southern Energy—or SSE, as it was now called—Sergeant Gavron realized as he neared the western bank of the Dee, the river rushing beneath him.

Two men visible—the one near the road, the other just off the road, nearly obscured by trees.

"Everything all right, lads?" the sergeant asked as he approached, eyeing the men carefully. He'd had five years with the Met before being assigned to SO-14. . .there was something about the way the men wore their work uniforms. Something *awkward*, almost.

"Sure thing, bruv," the nearest man responded, turning toward him. He was in his early thirties, his accent unmistakably that of South London—his face marking him as Asian. Pakistani, possibly? It wasn't the first time he had seen a Londoner come north for work, though. "Just doing maintenance work on the cable—it's buried right along the road here."

It seemed plausible enough, but still. . .

"I'm going to need to see your work orders—do you have them on you?"

The man smiled, reaching in the pocket of his uniform and unfolding a piece of paper. "Here you go."

The silence seemed to drag on forever—*too long*, Farid thought, sitting in the back of the utility van, one of the Heckler & Koch G3 assault rifles clutched in his weathered hands. The safety off, fire selector advanced to single-fire.

If they were discovered. . .

"Everything seems to be in order," he heard the British policeman say finally, apparently satisfied by the forged work orders the *Shaikh* had provided them.

Another moment passed, and then Abdullah opened the back door of the van. "He's gone."

"Good," Farid responded, safing the rifle and laying it to one side in the back. "The IED, is it in place?"

"Almost."

4:34 P.M.

It was impossible to read the former Royal Marine's face—to discern what might be hidden behind his words. But there was no time for that. No time to sort out the agendas at play. They had to *move*, and move quickly.

"Don't even think it," Roth warned as Flaharty came to his feet, snarling curses.

The Irishman ignored him, starting to move forward—but Harry stepped between them, seizing Flaharty by the shoulder. "Enough, both of you. He's coming with us."

"But—"

Harry swung him around, his eyes blazing—their faces only inches apart. "I have no *choice*. In just over an hour, I'm going to need every man I can put behind a rifle."

"But he's Security Service—an' so is *she*," Flaharty spat, throwing off his hand, "you can't trust either of them. They will—"

He glanced over to see Liam Malone standing there just a few feet away, shock written across the big Irishman's face. "*Five?* You brought them *here?*"

A light seemed to suddenly dawn in his eyes. Burning with wrath. "My God. . .Davey was right about you after all, wasn't he? He told me he suspected you'd turned tout—but I never could ha' believed it, you an' him—all of us—were like brothers back in Belfast. But he was *right*."

Flaharty just stood there, looking sadly into the eyes of his old friend. "Our world changed, lad. I did what I felt was—"

But the big Irishman wasn't listening, the full implications of what he had said only then seeming to strike home, as he began to advance on Flaharty. "He was right. . .an' you *killed* him for it, didn't you? Didn't you?"

The situation had spiraled far out of control, far beyond the point of recovery. Harry glimpsed movement out of the corner of his eye, up on the hill near the barn. An Irish wolfhound sitting there—and standing beside him, the lanky figure of a teenage boy. *Liam's son.*

He stepped directly in front of the big man, halting his advance—the Sig-Sauer materializing in his hands. Aimed at the man's head.

"You have two choices," he began, his voice barely above a whisper. *Cold as ice.* "Your first is to stand down. Let us take the plane and fly out of here in peace. Do that, and you'll never see my face again."

"And my second 'choice'?" Liam asked, looking him in the eye. A gaze burning with defiance.

"I shoot you where you stand, leave you to bleed out," Harry said, inclining his head toward the boy, "right here in front of your son. It's not something I would enjoy doing. . .but I've done it before. Your decision."

4:37 P.M.
Union Square Shopping Centre
Aberdeen, Scotland

There is no God but God, Sayyed Hassan murmured, reciting the words of the *shahada* under his breath as he ascended the escalator in the middle of the shopping centre, his eyes nervously flickering around him. *And Muhammad is His Messenger.*

The bold, provocative visage of a woman drinking a cup of coffee stared down at him from an advert hanging from the ceiling—her eyes full of promise. *Seduction.*

Full…and yet empty. *Like all the promises of the West.* He reached the top of the escalator, bringing his duffel bag off his shoulder with a single, rough motion—fumbling with the zipper.

This was the moment. The moment of his destiny. *There is no God but God,* he thought once more, repeating the words as a soundless chant as he brought the Kalashnikov assault rifle out of the bag, not even thinking to unfold the stock.

Hassan pivoted, flicking off the safety with a loud *klatch*, his gaze focusing in suddenly on a middle-aged woman standing not ten feet away, staring straight at him—her eyes wide, mouth open in a perfect "o." *And Muhammad is His Messenger.*

He raised the rifle, finding her face framed in his sights for only a moment before the trigger broke beneath his finger—his creed finally finding voice in a scream as the rifle shot reverberated through the mall.

"*Allahu akbar!*"

4:39 P.M.
The farm
Keighley, West Yorkshire

"All right," Liam said finally, his eyes burning with hatred as he stared at Harry, "you win."

He raised his hands in surrender, taking a step back. "Go," Harry advised, gesturing with the muzzle of the Sig-Sauer. "Go, while you still can."

Another moment passed, and then the big Irishman turned, walking slowly back across the meadow toward his house.

"You took a chance, boyo," Flaharty said, shaking his head as he appeared at Harry's side. "All those times in Belfast, never saw Liam Malone back down from a fight before."

"Perhaps he never knew for certain he would be killed before," Harry responded coldly, his weapon still leveled. *Perhaps it was his family. It was dangerous to care. To love.* It changed a man. "You think he'll report this to the authorities?"

"And implicate himself in the possession of an unregistered aircraft? Not a chance."

If any man would know, it was Flaharty. "All right then," he said, lowering his weapon as he turned toward Darren Roth, "we'd best be on our way. Local law enforcement in Scotland. . .does your position with Five give you the authority to commandeer personnel and equipment?"

The British officer shook his head. "We can liaise with the local constabularies, but that's the extent of it. We're not your FBI—we have no jurisdiction over them."

Bureaucracy. He heard a small gasp from Mehreen and glanced over to see her looking at her phone. "What is it?"

"There's a story just breaking on the 'net, an attack is already in progress. A shopping centre in Aberdeen. The situation is chaotic, automatic weapons fire coming from the second floor of the centre. Reports of multiple gunmen."

They just looked at each other for a long moment, the question all too clear in everyone's minds. "What if Hale was lying," Mehreen finally asking it, "what if *this* is the real attack? What if this was the *Shaikh*'s plan all along?"

Then all of this. . .*everything*, had been for naught. "No," Harry heard himself say, scarce able to determine whether he believed his own words, "it can't be."

"But what if it is?" Roth pressed. "If people are dying, we can't just walk away. We—"

"Law enforcement in Aberdeen can handle the shopping centre. This is the *Shaikh*'s MO," Harry responded, more confidently this time. "It's what he did in Vegas, it's what he's doing here. Pinning down every available law enforcement asset—crippling their ability to respond—before he launches the main attack."

Roth nodded slowly, comprehension spreading across his face. "It's bloody brilliant."

"And it will work again if we don't stop him," was Harry's grim response. He returned the Sig-Sauer to its shoulder holster, looking at the intelligence officer.

"Liaise, commandeer. . .do whatever you have to do—but reach out to law enforcement in Ballater and make sure they send a pair of officers to meet us at the Aboyne gliding club. With vehicles. And do it now. We need to get in the air."

Chapter 32

5:18 P.M.
MI-5 Headquarters
Thames House, London

"The responding constables believe now they're contending with only a single gunman—in the upper level of the shopping centre, northwest quadrant," Alec MacCallum said, standing in the door of the DG's office. "Firearms units are moving in on him as we speak."

"How many casualties are we looking at?" Marsh asked wearily, running a hand across his forehead. *Had* this *been the real attack?* Roth's intelligence flawed, but not without substance in the end.

"At least eleven dead, a couple dozen more wounded. A security guard responded to the initial bursts of fire and was gunned down. He was armed with only a riot baton."

"My God," the DG whispered, distress written across his face as he rose, rounding his desk. "What was he thinking?"

"He'd been back from Iraq for five years," the analyst responded quietly. "Like my father, once a soldier. . ."

Always a soldier. "Do we have a claim of responsibility?"

"Nothing definitive as of yet. The Islamic State's Twitter accounts began broadcasting shortly after the attack began, praising the valor of 'mujahideen in the British Isles" and warning that it was only the beginning. It's unclear whether they possessed foreknowledge or were simply playing the role of opportunists."

As they had so many times in the past. Marsh shook his head. "Make sure Aberdeen has whatever resources we can provide. Apprise me when the situation has been resolved."

5:22 P.M.
The Cessna Stationair
West of Edinburgh

"Arthur Colville," Harry mused aloud, the altimeter briefly hitting twenty thousand feet as he pushed the yoke forward once more, the plane leveling out. "So he's the one behind the attacks—the man funding and supplying the *Shaikh*?"

Below them, through the patchwork of low-hanging clouds, he could see the waters of the Forth, the Scottish town of Falkirk visible farther up-river to the west. He found himself listening to the engine, feeling it vibrate at full-power, nearly red-lined. Pushed harder than it had been in a decade, perhaps longer. They had made good time, but with nearly seventy miles yet to go. . .he nosed down slightly, sacrificing altitude for airspeed. It was going to be close, if they made it at all.

No harm. Carol's words, echoing once more through his mind. Again and again. If he had given Five Tarik's location—could the shopping centre attack, could *all* of this been prevented?

Innocent lives. Sacrificed on the altar of his own vengeance. He swallowed hard, the bitter taste of bile in his mouth. Nothing for it now but to press forward. One foot in front of the other—till the bitter end.

"If the intel you provided to me is correct, yes," Darren Roth responded from his position beside him in the co-pilot's seat. "It's not going to be enough to satisfy the evidential standards for prosecution, though."

Prosecution. More red tape, more bureaucracy. . .stretching on into eternity. A man Colville's age would die of natural causes long before he ever saw the inside of a prison.

"Doesn't matter," he said, his eyes hard, "this is never going to end up in court."

"No," the intelligence officer responded, knowing only too well what he meant. "If this is going to be done, it's going to be done the right way."

Harry glimpsed Roth's expression out of the corner of his eye, something snapping deep inside him. "You were a soldier long before you became a cop, so for the love of God think like one. We both know how this ends—how *all* of this ends."

5:27 P.M.
The port of Aberdeen
Scotland

"...reports indicate that the gunman has taken a hostage and is holed up somewhere on the second floor of the shopping centre, while—as you can see behind me—police have established a cordon sealing off the area. Now we go back to London, where David Inglesworth is standing by. David?"

"Thank you, Claire. We are waiting to hear whether the Home Secretary will speak publicly on the shooting in Aberdeen, where. . ."

Buy us time, brother, Tarik Abdul Muhammad thought, gazing at the television screens mounted on the warehouse wall at one end of their makeshift command center. *Just a little more.*

The attack on Balmoral would be swift and devastating. Over long before reinforcements could be dispatched from Aberdeen, in the wake of the chaos created by Sayyed Hassan's noble sacrifice.

"A call for you, *Shaikh,*" one of his bodyguards announced, coming up to him with a phone in his hand. "It's Farid."

"*Salaam alaikum,* brother," Tarik said, his fingers trembling with nervous excitement as he raised the phone to his ear. *This was it.* The final call to establish communications before the attack.

For a moment, all he heard was bursts of static, Farid's voice fading in and out then, ". . .position. Tonight, *jannah* welcomes us."

The mobile connection was horrible, but Tarik smiled, his eyes shining with tears. "Yes—*yes.* Tonight in *Jannah.*"

5:32 P.M.
The offices of the UK Daily Standard
London

"*Earlier this evening, Queen Elizabeth was slain in a cowardly attack carried out by Muslims loyal to the Islamic*"—Arthur Colville paused for a moment before crossing out the final word with an abrupt stroke of his pen, beginning again, this time in bold capital letters. "*Loyal to the ISLAMIC State and led by a man known to our very own Security Services: Tarik Abdul Muhammad. The* Shaikh.*"*

The publisher wrote a few more sentences, the article forming in his head as he leaned back in his chair This was really happening, after all the months of preparation. The wary meetings, the moments of terrifying uncertainty.

The years of fighting against the insipid impotence of Whitehall—politicians consumed with their political correctness, their vision of a "multi-cultural" society. All of it, leading to *this*.

"*We have embraced a serpent,*" he wrote, picking up his pen once more, "*and it has bitten us in the end—leaving us once again mourning a tragedy. But how many more times must we mourn our dead before we are at last roused to action? The Queen is now dead, and the nation grieves the loss of its longest-reigning and most beloved monarch, as well we should. But how many more times will we be forced to grieve before we recognize that this cult of death calling itself 'Islam' has no place in this— or any—civilized society?*"

Colville pushed back his chair and rose, retrieving a decanter from the sideboard and pouring himself a tumbler of brandy before moving to the window—the evening sun streaming in upon his face as it descended into the western sky—bathing London in a blood-red hue.

"*Morituri te salutant,*" he murmured wistfully, raising the tumbler as if in a toast. A faint smile touching his lips as he substituted his own translation.

"To those who are about to die. . .I salute you."

5:43 P.M.
Balmoral Castle
Ballater, Scotland

"Hold up, hold up," Sergeant Gavron said, touching his earpiece as he moved out into the open, before the wrought-iron gates of Balmoral. "We have a delivery van coming across the bridge. Were we anticipating an arrival?"

He held up a hand for the van to stop, hearing the dim sound of an airplane somewhere off in the distance. Perhaps a commercial flight from Belfast to Aberdeen, although it sounded smaller, somehow.

"None that I was made aware of," came the answer over the radio. "Hold the van there at the gate, I'll apprise Hilliard."

"Aye," Gavron responded, walking toward the now-stopped van and motioning for his partner to approach from the other side, "we'll await your orders."

5:44 P.M.
The Cessna Stationair

"Everything looks quiet," Darren Roth commented as the Cessna banked right, sweeping over the estate of Balmoral from the west, barely a thousand feet above the treetops and descending, flaps extended to slow them down enough to make the pass.

He glanced over at Harry as the Cessna leveled out, gaining airspeed as it flashed over the trees, heading out toward the Dee. "I think we've made it in time."

"We're not on the ground just yet," Harry observed grimly, glancing out the cabin window at the golf course he had considered as a makeshift landing strip, glimpsing in those few fleeting moments what he hadn't been able to see on the satellite imagery—tall trees on either side of the course, rolling terrain. *No dice.* "And there's no place to set down."

"Ballater's sent out a pair of constables to meet us," Roth said, tucking his phone into the pocket of his jacket. "They'll be waiting at the strip in—"

The unmistakable sound of an explosion suddenly struck Harry's ears, his head snapping around—back and to the left, a ball of fire and black, oily smoke rising above the trees.

"What was *that*?" Mehreen asked, her voice sounding faint. Distant.

And he *knew*, a ball of ice forming in the pit of his stomach. It was a car bomb. . .just like any one of the dozens he had witnessed in the sandbox. It was beginning. *Already.*

The jihadists had launched early—for what reason, he knew not. And it didn't matter.

He retracted the flaps, shoving the throttle ahead as the Lycoming flat-six roared back to full power—the spire of Crathie Kirk disappearing off his wing as he pulled up, heading for Aboyne and the airstrip.

Getting on the ground, that was all that mattered.

5:46 P.M.
Balmoral Castle

Colin Hilliard knew what it was almost instantly as he stepped out onto the carriage porch, Bahadar Singh at his side—his head coming up as the explosion rippled through the warm evening air.

A pall of black smoke rising over the trees from the south. *The main gate.*

"We're under attack," he whispered, more to himself than as a warning—his movements feeling sluggish. As if frozen in the midst of a dream. A *nightmare.*

He glanced back, hearing Bahadar's voice behind him—low and urgent. The man's hand cupped to his ear, trying to raise the officers stationed at the gate. "Sergeant Gavron, I say again, do you copy? *Do you copy?*"

A moment, and then the Sikh shook his head, sadness written across his impassive, bearded face. "No answer. Your orders, commander?"

They were dead. He felt numb, scarce even hearing the inspector's question. All these years, and he'd never seen a serious attack on the Royal Family, let alone lost men defending them.

Before he could muster the words to form a response, something caused the senior officer to look south, his eyes widening as he saw a small group of seven, perhaps eight men emerging from the trees past the gardens and the fountain—perhaps three hundred meters away. Spread out, moving in quickly.

A skirmish line.

A faint shout, and the next moment, the supersonic *crack* of a rifle split the air—a round caroming off the granite above their heads—the sound serving to shatter the ennui gripping him.

"All teams, all teams," Hilliard spat into his radio as he dove for cover behind the engine block of the Range Rover, more rounds coming in as the staccato chatter of automatic weapons fire began to fill the air. "We are under attack, I say again, we are under *attack*. Execute SCIPIO."

Get the principals to the safe room. The bunker beneath Balmoral Castle dated back to the Second World War, and had been renovated five times in the decades since. Each time making it stronger, more secure. *Impenetrable.* They were trained for this, knew what to do.

It was just a matter of having the time to carry it out.

He reached into his suit jacket, his fingers closing around the polymer butt of his Glock 19 in its shoulder holster—glancing over at Bahadar Singh to see him kneeling a few feet away, weapon already drawn.

"Catherine and the young prince," Hilliard gasped as he brought the Glock out, leaning back against the vehicle's tire. "Where are they?"

The Sikh swore beneath his breath, his swarthy face paling at the thought. "Still down by the Dee."

Hilliard closed his eyes. *My God.*

"All right," he said, breathing heavily as another burst of fire impacted the stonework, closer now—adrenaline coursing through his veins. He was far too old for this. "We have to make contact with London, get reinforcements. Cover me when I break for the door—follow me in, then go secure Catherine and George. On my mark. *NOW!*"

5:49 P.M.
Aboyne, Scotland

"We have to be able to get a message out—alert someone about the attack."

"There's no one to alert," Harry responded to Mehreen's question, the airfield coming into view just to their southeast as he banked the plane into a long, sweeping turn over the Scottish fields below. "Just *us*. Going in with a VBIED like that, they came loaded for bear."

Loaded with munitions I once could have prevented from ever reaching their destination, he didn't say, his face darkening at the thought. An opportunity passed up, forfeited in his quest for vengeance.

His hands stained with the blood of the men who had died in that blast—and every man who was about to perish in defense of their Queen.

There was no atonement for this. Redemption, forever out of reach. Only the fight itself remained, a bloody slog to the end.

"By the time reinforcements can arrive from Aberdeen," he continued, catching sight of the pair of vans parked at one end of the strip near the hangars as he lined up the Cessna for approach, flaps extending as the airplane came in, "the battle will be decided."

5:51 P.M.
Balmoral Castle

So far, so good. *Insh'allah*, Farid thought as the SUV rolled to a stop fifty meters from the entrance of the castle.

The muzzle of his rifle led the way as the jihadist pushed his door open, stepping out into the drive, the men of his assault team spilling out of the vehicles behind him, weapons drawn. Hurrying to take up positions.

He saw a man in a dark suit sprinting across the grounds from a cluster of buildings off to the northwest and raised his rifle, a ragged burst of fire ripping from the G3's barrel.

It was like being back in Syria once more, he realized, watching the man crumple to the ground. The same feeling. The euphoria of battle, heady and intoxicating. To serve a single moment in Allah's struggle...it was worth the world and everything in it.

The lighter *crack* of pistol fire struck Farid's ears and he spotted the figure of a man taking shelter behind the hood of a Range Rover near the castle's main entrance, trading fire with the group of *mujahideen* advancing from the south.

"With me," he spat, seizing one of his men by the shoulder as he moved past, a rifle slung over the young man's back—an RPG-7 in his hands. "*There.*"

Colin Hilliard could hear bullets slamming into the thick oak of Balmoral's carriage porch as he braced himself against the door—leaning out, pressing the Glock forward in both hands.

"Come on now, lad," he bellowed, catching Singh's attention with the shout, "shift your arse!"

The Glock recoiled into the heel of his hand as he fired, again and again—laying down covering fire as the Sikh inspector rose up from behind the Range Rover, pivoting toward the door. Toward safety.

And then Hilliard saw it—a man standing out in the middle of the drive near the attackers' SUVs, perhaps forty meters off. Making out the distinctive shape of an RPG on the man's shoulder just as the Glock's slide locked back on an empty magazine.

There was no time to engage, to *respond*. The SO-14 commander dropped his now-useless weapon—reaching out, his hands seizing hold of Singh's shoulders and jerking the man the rest of the way inside.

The next moment, the RPG slammed into the Range Rover without and their world exploded around them.

5:54 P.M.
The gliding club
Aboyne, Scotland

"The name's Oyelowo," Roth said, passing over his military identification card to the tall, red-haired constable as they walked over from the plane to the parked SUVs, both of the vehicles aging Ford Transits, painted in the colors of Police Scotland. "Darren Oyelowo, military intelligence."

"Aye, sergeant said he had spoken to you on the phone," the man responded. "Not often we hear from Five. I—"

"Balmoral Castle is under attack," Harry interjected, his voice flat, emotionless. "A terrorist cell under the command of Tarik Abdul Muhammad. The *Shaikh*."

The constable's face registered shock, murmuring a curse beneath his breath as he attempted to recover himself. "And who is this?" he demanded, turning to Roth.

"An ally," Darren responded, glancing past him toward the Fords. "We're going to need your vehicles. We saw an explosion at the castle on the way in. It's already beginning."

The constable shook his head, swearing softly once more as if dumfounded by the news.

"Either of you spend any time in the army?" Harry asked, glancing from one man to the other.

"I did," the shorter, older officer responded, taking a step forward. There was an earnest look in his eyes as he gazed at Harry, almost one of. . .recognition. *Between warriors.* "In the Falklands. Scots Guards, Second Battalion. Fought my way up Mount Tumbledown that night back in '82."

Harry nodded, knowing the story well. The vicious, close-quarters fighting that had ensued as the British forces stormed Argentinian positions with bayonets fixed.

"All right then, you're coming with us," he said, heaving his duffel bag up onto the hood of the nearest SUV and extracting one of the AKM assault rifles, holding it up in one hand as he cleared the action, handing it to the man. "Time to kit up."

5:54 P.M.
Balmoral Castle
Ballater, Scotland

Chaos. Hilliard's eyes flickered open, stinging with the smoke surrounding him. His ears still ringing from the force of the explosion—drowning out all else.

He put out a hand, clawing himself forward through the debris. Struggling to rise, making it to his hands and knees before collapsing once more—the assault on his senses overwhelming, disorienting him. *Move*, his mind screamed at him, *move or you're a dead man.*

And then he realized it wasn't his mind at all—his vision clearing to see Bahadar Singh staggering to his feet just a few feet away, the inspector's suit torn and smoldering—his dark turban still firmly bound around his head. Bahadar shouted at him again, extending a hand and he took it—his body crying out in protest as the powerful Sikh dragged him to his feet, throwing the older man's arm over his shoulder as they both crashed through the inner door and into the entry hall of Balmoral.

Safe. But only for the moment, Hilliard thought, feeling another explosion rock the entryway, plaster and bits of stone raining down on them from the ceiling above.

Balmoral had been built in the middle of the 19th-Century—as a country house, not a hold-fast. Not intended to stand up against an assault from the weapons of that age, let alone this one.

And from what he had seen out there, they were outnumbered nearly two-to-one.

"Go," he said, pushing himself away from Bahadar Singh to stand erect—still unsteady on his feet. "Go. . .find Catherine and George, bring them back. *Keep them safe.*"

5:59 P.M.
Thames House
London

"Sir!" Marsh's head came up as the door came flying open, Alec MacCallum barging in without knocking. "We just received a Flash-Traffic from the ranking SO-14 officer at Balmoral, Colin Hilliard—the head of Her Majesty's bodyguard. They've come under heavy attack, small arms and RPGs."

"Good God," the DG exclaimed, his eyes wide as he rose from his desk. *It was true*. Roth's warning, come to pass. "And the Queen?"

"Being escorted to the bunker beneath the castle as per the Special Protection Command's emergency protocols. But the castle itself is under assault and Hilliard is losing men."

Marsh winced, feeling guilt wash over him. Spend nearly four decades in the intelligence business, and you knew what it was to have made wrong calls. It came with the territory. But ever since 9/11, those wrong calls seemed ever to come marked with the blood of dead British citizens. And now. . .*the Queen.*

Recriminations would have to wait for another time. Drowned in a bottle of Glenlivet.

"The PM has to be notified at once," he said, collecting himself with an effort. "What resources do we have in the area?"

"Nothing close enough, I'm afraid," MacCallum replied. "Ballater has a constabulary, but they're unarmed and untrained for this kind of situation. All available firearms units were routed to Aberdeen to respond to the shopping centre attack."

And that was its purpose, the DG realized in a sudden flash of clarity. A diversion. And it had worked. "The MoD?"

The analyst shook his head. "Closest assets would be stationed at RAF Lossiemouth. I believe they're still basing several squadrons of fast-movers out of there."

The Royal Air Force base was only about fifty miles due north of Balmoral, Marsh thought, his eyes narrowing. On the shores of the North Sea, not far from the Moray Firth.

"All right, get General Lidington on the phone," he said finally, naming the Chief of the Defence Staff. "This is going to have to go straight to the Prime Minister."

6:01 P.M.
The gliding club
Aboyne, Scotland

"I should be going with you," Mehreen said, arms folded across her chest, standing there beside the Cessna in the long shadow cast by the receding sun.

Harry looked up from adjusting the straps on his chest rig, his eyes meeting hers as he picked up his rifle. He shook his head.

"Not a chance. Five didn't give you the training you'd need to survive what we're headed into, and I gave my plate carrier to the officer. Don't have another one."

Not that it would have done him much good with the kind of opposition they were going up against, he didn't add. The plates were rated against pistol rounds, not the 7.62x51mm NATO the terrorists' rifles were chambered for.

Which meant he was just going to have to take his chances. *Come what may.*

"Nick would come back from the grave to kill me himself if I put you in that kind of risk," he said, putting a hand on her shoulder and squeezing gently. "I need you to stay here. Keep an eye on Conor Hale if he wakes up, as he's likely to. The sedative won't hold him much longer. Make sure he doesn't get away from you—we may need him later."

"Later?" she asked, looking up into his face. "What do you mean?"

He'd said too much.

"I have to go," he responded, his face darkening as he turned away from her, hearing her call out once more as he crossed the runway toward the parked Ford Transit. The older constable standing there by the open door, the plate carrier already on over his uniform. An awkward fit, but it was better than nothing.

"Ready?" Darren Roth asked, looking him in the eye. Harry nodded soberly, turning to the constable. Recognizing the look in the man's eyes as he handled the rifle. The look of a man bracing himself for a return to something he had convinced himself he'd left far behind. His mind and heart, torn between fear and. . .*lust*.

Once the taste for battle entered a man's blood, there was no getting it out. No matter how many years passed.

"I'm going to need you to do the driving," he said, "you know this area better than any of us, Constable. . .I don't believe you gave me your name?"

"McTaggart," the man responded, seeming startled from his thoughts. Shifting the AKM to his other hand as he stuck out his right. "Rory McTaggart."

Harry hesitated only a moment before grasping the older man's weathered hand in his own, forcing a grim smile. "Let's do this."

6:05 P.M.
Balmoral Castle
Ballater, Scotland

Pandemonium. Bahadar Singh could still hear the sound of automatic weapons fire from without as he made his way hurriedly down the corridor toward the great tower and the old servants' quarters beyond, bullets ricocheting off the stone walls.

He caught a brief glimpse of their attackers through the shattered glass of a window as he passed, men with assault rifles advancing on the carriage porch, laying down a hail of fire as they moved.

Singh lingered for a moment in the shadow of the window, eyeing them, his Glock drawn and carried low by his side.

But he had no shot—and couldn't afford to draw their fire on himself. Not while his charges were yet unaccounted for.

The door at the opposite end of the corridor came flying open and he turned—his weapon coming up instinctively.

It was one of the staff—a butler he recognized from earlier visits—the man's face white as a sheet, his hands raised at the sight of the gun.

"Go," Singh whispered brusquely as he lowered the Glock, pushing past the man into the tower beyond. "*Hide.*"

The door to the wine cellar—and the bunker beneath—was just down the corridor to the right as Singh entered the tower, finding a pair of SO-14 officers flanking the rear entrance, H&K G36 assault rifles at the low ready.

"What in God's name is going on, sir?" the furthermost officer asked, taking another cautious glance through the tower's windows. They would have had a better firing position from the upper floors, he realized, but that would have left the path to the bunker compromised. "Who are they?"

He had just started to respond when a third officer entered from the north, also carrying a rifle. "Winters," he said, recognizing the younger man, "you're with me."

"Hilliard's orders," the first officer countered, looking back from his position by the window, "were to take up positions here and secure the tower for Her Majesty's arrival."

"Then do so," Singh responded, his dark eyes brooking no defiance as he beckoned to Winters to follow, "but Catherine and George are out *there*. And I'm going to get them. Cover us as we go out."

The officer looked at him for another moment, then nodded, stepping aside from the door. They weren't going to be able to save everyone's life this day, but the safety of their principals was paramount. Far above their own.

"You take right, I'll take left," he instructed Winters as the more bursts of gunfire resounded from the south, pausing with his left hand on the door, his right holding his Glock. "Clear as we go. Ready?"

A nod. And then the door was open, Winters leading the way out—rifle already up and against his shoulder. His eyes searching the copse of trees not far from the tower.

Singh followed him out, the muzzle of his Glock sweeping north, back toward the eastern wing of the castle. *Clear.*

He glanced back at the younger man, gesturing for him to follow as the two of them sprinted across the pavement toward the cover of the adjacent buildings—and the banks of the Dee itself, not more than a hundred meters beyond.

And somewhere out there, a mother and her little boy. His face hardened, feeling a dark fury rise within him. He forced it away, knowing how such rage could rob a man of his judgment—his reason. *Krodh.* One of the Five Thieves.

Yet the thought of them being harmed. . .

He reached the corner of the building, his Glock coming up once more as he rounded it, Winters only a step behind.

And then he heard it, another ragged burst of gunfire—far closer this time. Felt something warm spray across the back of his neck.

Followed by a strangled cry.

6:09 P.M.
Thames House
Millbank, London

"Of course, General, I understand. Thank you," Julian Marsh responded, returning the phone to its cradle just as MacCallum entered his office.

He ran a hand across the lower half of his face, shaking his head as he glanced at his section chief. "The PM has convened COBRA to determine what measures are available to him under the Civil Contingencies Act. General Lidington," he gestured at the phone, "is on his way to No. 10 Downing Street now."

MacCallum swore, the man's eyes wide with disbelief. "So the jets aren't in the air?"

"No," the DG responded heavily, "they are not. Nor are they likely to be, not in enough time to make a difference. This is no longer the Cold War, as I was just informed by General Lidington. The RAF no longer keeps its bombers on strip alert, ready to be scrambled at a moment's notice to counter threats against the realm. Arming the aircraft alone would take forty minutes or more."

"But RAF Lossiemouth," MacCallum protested, "they're responsible for maintaining QRA North."

QRA. The Quick Reaction Alert. . .designed to maintain precisely that state of readiness, Marsh thought. A NATO burden that was, as ever, largely carried by the RAF. Based in the north at Lossiemouth, in the south at RAF Coningsby—in the heart of Lincolnshire.

"They are," he said, "but in that capacity, they're equipped for a purely air-to-air role. Re-arming them for a ground-attack mission—well the general's estimate was forty minutes."

"Then Her Majesty. . ."

"Is on her own for the time being," the DG responded, a note of morose resignation in his voice. "May God save the Queen. . ."

6:10 P.M.
Balmoral Castle
Scotland

Bahadar Singh turned just in time to see Winters go down, clutching at his throat, even as more rounds slammed into the young officer's upper chest. His rifle falling from his hands as he crumpled into the grass.

No. A life extinguished in the space of a moment—the life of a brave man. An assault on righteousness itself.

In all his years as a police officer with the Met, he'd only lost a man once. Never had one killed in front of him.

But he couldn't allow himself to dwell on that—not now. Or he too would be dead, along those he had sworn to protect. Death was ordained for every man, but not this day.

He dropped to one knee beside the officer's broken body, the Glock recoiling into his hands—allowing the fury to consume him as he fired again and again, until bullets began chewing into the wall beside him, driving him back.

Singh ejected the half-empty magazine from the butt of the Glock, tucking it into the mag pouch on his belt as he slipped another one into its place.

If only he could get the rifle. He went prone, reaching out a hand for the butt of the H&K. . .but even as he did so, more bullets split the air over his turbaned head, one burying itself into the ground only inches from his hand.

And they were closer now—flanking him, moving in on his position. He paused for only a moment before rising, whispering, "May you continue on your journey to God," as he looked down into Winters' glassy, vacant eyes.

Time to move. Time to find his principals. . .

6:11 P.M.

No help was coming, Colin Hilliard realized, hurrying down the back corridor past Balmoral's dining room toward the garden entrance—even as another explosion shook the castle. Not in time.

He knew that, somewhere deep in his bones. Could see it the face of the young officer at his side—the man's H&K G36 carried at patrol ready as they moved. Another rifle slung over his shoulder, taken from the armory while they'd had the chance.

But there was no giving up—not while they yet had breath. *And ammunition,* he thought, his grip tightening on the Glock in his hand.

The door at the end of the corridor opened from the vestibule at that moment, the figure of an SO-14 officer with pistol drawn entering the corridor—followed immediately by a footman and Prince William, cradling a weeping Princess Charlotte in his arms, the little girl's eyes wide with fear and terror.

And behind them. . .the Queen herself, her form cloaked against the spring chill in a light blue overcoat, a loose scarf covering her snow-white hair. Her old Wellington boots wet from tramping through the woods to the west of the castle with William and Charlotte—where they had been before the attack. Managing somehow to remain a regal figure in the midst of the chaos swirling around her.

Her eyes fell upon Hilliard and he drew himself up instinctively. "Your Majesty."

"Commander Hilliard," she began formally, refusing as ever to use his given name, "my husband. You've seen to his safety?"

"His Royal Highness has already been taken to the bunker, ma'am," he replied. "My men and I will escort you there at once. It's imperative—"

"What about Catherine?" William demanded, distress written across his face as he cut Hilliard off. "And George? They're safe? Tell me they're safe, Colin."

"They were down by the banks of the river when the attack began," Hilliard replied, unable to lie to him. "Inspector Singh is on his way to them now. He's a good man, your Highness—you know that. They're going to be all right."

He could see a reply forming on the Prince's lips, but it was cut off as another RPG slammed into the building from the south, the walls trembling around them—dust and chunks of plaster falling from the ceiling. "And now I must insist that we move you all to the bunker. Immediately."

"Take them," William replied, handing Charlotte over to the footman and gesturing for him to go on. "I'll wait for Catherine."

There was no time for this. He shook his head. "I'm sorry, sir but that's not possible. I—"

The Prince's face flushed with anger, his right hand clenching and unclenching spasmodically as he glared at Hilliard. "I will *not* hide here and cower like a dog while my wife and son are in danger. Give me a rifle."

Love. It drove men to madness, he thought, meeting William's eyes. "Your Highness, I am charged with protecting your life. I cannot permit you to endanger yourself in this—"

"Commander." The sound of the Queen's voice cut Hilliard short, steel glinting in her eyes as he turned to face her. "My grandson was not making a request."

6:13 P.M.
The road to Balmoral

Walking to the ramp of a C-130 high above Lebanon. Riding shotgun in a dusty old Toyota Hilux across the desert of southern Iraq. Perched knee-to-knee in the open door of a Little Bird, the stark landscape of Afghanistan flashing past at 150 knots just meters below.

It was the moments *before* a battle began that were always the hardest, Harry thought, glancing out the window of the Ford Transit—the granite bell tower of Crathie Kirk visible through the trees as they sped down the road toward the River Dee and Balmoral itself.

Those moments of soul-searching uncertainty, as a man made his peace with God.

God. Harry glanced back toward the kirk, his face hardening into a bitter mask. There was no peace to be made this time, none to be found for him—not since Carol's death. Since she had been *taken* from him.

For she walked with God. . .and she was not, for God took her.

The good, ever taken from this earth before their time. Men like himself, left behind in their stead. *Spared?*

Condemned, more like it. Damned to fight on, clawing desperately through the mud—hands drenched in the blood of their fellow man. Finding their peace only in the grave.

Curse God and die.

The anguished plea of Job's wife, resonating down through the millennia. . .to him. Never more so than in this moment.

Kill Tarik. That was the only thing left to him, the impetus that had brought him to this country. That had become the cause of so much suffering, so much death. It all ended today.

Redemption? No, there was no atonement to be found at the end of this road, but something far older. *Retribution.* As old as time itself.

He straightened in his seat as the police vehicle turned off the main road past a deserted parking lot designed for tourist traffic, hand tightening on the grip of his AK—its sling wrapped around his shoulders.

"There," he said suddenly, reaching over to put a hand on the McTaggart's shoulder, his eyes narrowing as they fell upon the sight of a utility van parked just off the road near the bridge—nearly concealed beneath the canopy of spring green that shaded the approach to the river. "Hold up, hold up."

The constable gave him a startled look as he hit the brakes, bringing the vehicle to an abrupt halt. "What's going on?"

Harry ignored him, looking back over his shoulder at Darren Roth—gesturing toward the van. "Anything look familiar?"

A moment's pause, and then a nod of recognition. "You know it."

They'd both seen it a hundred times or more over in the sandbox—an abandoned vehicle by the side of the road. A VBIED, just waiting for a Coalition convoy to come by.

Harry pushed his door open, his rifle already up against his shoulder as he stepped out, its muzzle sweeping the trees.

"Everyone dismount," he said, the distant crackle of small-arms fire borne to him on the westerly breeze. "We go the rest of the way in on foot."

Chapter 33

6:15 P.M.
Balmoral Castle

Madness. Hilliard opened his mouth to protest, but no words came out, the look on the Queen's face silencing him before he could speak. Cold resolution in her eyes—the air of one who had been born to command. "Your Majesty, I—"

"Sir!" A shout cut him off and he turned to see one of his officers stagger from a passageway farther down the corridor to the west, nearly falling against the wall as he pushed himself forward—his pistol clutched in his left hand, his right arm hanging limp and useless by his side.

"They've broken through from the kitchen court," he gasped out—the blood staining his white dress shirt only too visible as he approached. "Executed several of the staff. Collins and Morris are down."

My God. They were cut off, Hilliard realized, paling at the man's words. Two more of his men dead.

He put out his hand toward the young offer at his side, gesturing for him to hand over his rifle.

"Take the Queen back through the gallery," he ordered, his voice low and urgent even as a burst of gunfire came from the direction of the ballroom, punctuated by screams, "up the staircase to the second floor, and from there to the tower. Move quickly. Don't stop until you've reached it."

"Aye, sir."

Hilliard turned toward the Prince, rifle in hand as his officers shepherded the Queen away.

"Your Highness," he said quietly, handing the weapon over and watching as

William extended the H&K's folding stock—seizing the charging handle in his left hand and working it to chamber a round, "you're with me."

6:17 P.M.

"Your Highness!" Bahadar Singh called out, weapon in hand as he stumbled down the river bank, his dark eyes scanning for any sign of the Royals. They had to be here. . .*somewhere*, he thought, hearing more gunfire from back in the direction of the castle, a dissonant sound among those made by the rushing waters of the Dee only a few feet away.

No one had followed him, or at least he didn't think so—it was impossible to say—his eyes flickering back to the heights above as he made his way through the trees. "Your Highness!"

Movement. A flash of blue in the midst of the bright spring green and he pulled up, his breath catching in his throat. His Glock at the low ready as he scanned the undergrowth. The faint cry of a child reaching his ears. "Catherine?"

There was only silence for a painfully long moment—then a woman's voice. "Bahadar?"

Catherine. "Your Highness!" he exclaimed, pushing through the brush to find the Duchess of Cambridge kneeling there among the rocks, her young son held tightly against her body as if to shield him from harm. "Are you all right?"

"What's going on?" she demanded, eyes wide with fear and shock as he stooped down beside her. The little boy sobbing uncontrollably, despite her best efforts to calm him. "Who is it, Bahadar—who's attacking us?"

"Terrorists," he responded grimly, remembering the black flag bearing the *shahada* he had seen unfurled before the castle. *Jihadists*, to be more accurate.

His own faith had been born out of the fires of Islamic India. Two of the earliest gurus tortured and executed by the Mughals, bitter persecution from which had risen the *Sant-Sipāhīs* of Khalsa—an order of warrior saints to protect the faithful from their oppressors. *When all efforts to restore peace prove useless, when no words avail—lawful is the flash of steel. It is right to draw the sword.*

"My husband, Bahadar," Catherine began anxiously, clasping his wrist, "is he all right?"

"Hilliard is with him," he responded, doing his best to reassure her. The senior officer had been on his way to the Prince's side when they'd separated. He could only hope he had made it. "And I'm going to take both of you to him. I—"

A burst of automatic weapons fire chewed through the air over their heads, followed by the clearly audible *slap* of bullets hitting the waters of the Dee.

"Run, your Highness," Singh bellowed, giving Catherine a shove down-river as he glimpsed figures moving through the trees above them—his Glock coming up in both hands. *"Run!"*

6:21 P.M.
London

Come on, Julian Marsh thought, staring at the phone in his hand as it went straight to voicemail for the fifth time.

"Is there a problem, sir?" his driver asked, taking his eyes off the road for only a moment as they navigated their way through London traffic. With the convening of COBRA, he had been summoned to No. 10 Downing Street, along with the chair of the Joint Intelligence Committee.

"No," the DG lied, shaking his head as he tucked the mobile into the pocket of his suit. Roth wasn't answering his phone.

An ominous silence.

He *needed* to reach him, and now—the intelligence he had been given by the American of critical importance with the warned-of attack having become reality.

The mobile vibrated with an incoming call and he plucked it from his pocket, seeing the number of Thames House. *MacCallum.*

"Yes?"

"Are you with the Prime Minister?" the section chief asked, a raw urgency in his voice.

"No," Marsh responded, glancing out of the car's window at the passing street signs. "Probably four minutes out. Why?"

"MoD just red-flashed us—the RAF has been released to launch. But we're not going to be able to keep a lid on this for much longer. Photos of the attack hit Twitter five minutes ago. Pictures of Balmoral itself—the carriage porch nearly destroyed by what looks like an RPG blast, part of the building on fire, the bodies of SO-14 officers visible in the rubble."

This was bad. Very bad. "Where? How?" Marsh demanded, swearing under his breath.

"They originated from a Twitter account identifying itself as belonging to the *Jund al-Britani*. The 'Soldiers of Britain.'"

"What do we know about them?"

"Nothing—the account only went live a few hours ago. We've reached out to Twitter to get them shut down, but the images are already spreading. Jihadi accounts all over the 'net retweeting them and reposting."

A virus. Spreading out from patient zero at the speed of light. Bad enough when it was a lie, but when it was *truth*. . .

Even worse.

"Sir. . .there's something else you should know. Their second tweet—it references the *Shaikh*. Credits him with the attack."

The worst of his fears, come to bitter fruition. Marsh closed his eyes, finding no words with which to respond.

"Do what you can," he said finally, "buy us time. I'll brief the PM. And, Alec. . .have you seen anything of Darren Roth?"

"No."

Marsh grimaced. He'd had more than enough time to have reached Thames House. He—a sudden thought struck him, and he found himself unable to shake it. What if. . .*no*.

He wouldn't have—Roth was a soldier, first and always. And a soldier did not disobey orders.

"Let me know the moment he arrives, Alec," the DG said, taking a deep breath. "The *moment* he arrives."

6:23 P.M.
Balmoral, Scotland

Cold, Harry thought, his clothes still dripping from the snow-swollen waters of the Dee as they advanced through the trees, the AK-103's folding stock extended against his shoulder. Darren Roth not five paces to his left. It was a bracing thing—cleared the senses. Reminded a man he was alive. *Even if not for much longer.*

Fording the river below the bridge had been a necessity dictated by the constraints of time. Where there was one IED, there could easily be more. Snipers covering the approach, any one of a thousand things that could slow down their advance. *Unnecessary risk.*

He could hear McTaggart breathing heavily behind him, the older man clearly already fatigued by his exertion. Age taking its inevitable toll.

Harry glanced back, "You good?"

"Aye," the Scotsman replied, dogged determination glinting in his eyes. "The old woman loves to jog, always on me to join her. Thinking maybe I should have listened."

Old soldiers never die.

Press on—that's all that was left to any of them now. Committed, far past the point of no return.

The main gate of Balmoral was just ahead, their approach masked by a screen of pines. Harry took his support hand off the Kalashnikov, gesturing wordlessly for Roth and Flaharty to flank left.

Carnage. That was the only word to describe the scene as they emerged from the treeline—smoke still hanging in the air, along with unmistakable stench of burning flesh.

It was all too clear what Tarik's *mujahideen* had done—used a VBIED to overwhelm security and swarmed into the breach left behind—the charred bodies of two men who appeared to have been SO-14 officers lying not far from the burning wreckage of a delivery van. The holstered Glock still visible on the one man's hip as they advanced out into the open—his right leg sheared clean away not three inches below it, leaving only a blackened, bloody stump.

It was a sight he remembered all too vividly from Iraq. Chaos. *Blood.* But back then, that blood hadn't been on his hands.

His face darkened as he stepped over the bodies and into the nearly destroyed gate beyond, picking up the pace as another explosion reverberated through the trees, the rattle of automatic weapons fire growing more clearly audible with each step. In a just world, every man would pay the price for his own sins.

But in this world, the guilty lived on. . .and the innocent died. *Spared from the wrath to come.*

And perhaps that *was* the price.

6:26 P.M.
Balmoral Castle

No turning back. Hilliard flattened himself against the wall as rifle bullets slammed into the lintel of the door above his head, oak splinters flying through the air.

If one of the militants in the passageway beyond had an RPG like those attacking the front of the castle. . .he shuddered. *It would be over quickly.*

But if it meant saving the wife and child of a boy he had watched grow to manhood. . .

He glanced over to the other side of the door, meeting William's gaze as the Prince slid a fresh magazine into the mag well of the G36.

His eyes signaling an unspoken question: *Ready?*

This was wrong, the SO-14 commander thought—all of this was wrong. Protocol said to evacuate the Royal Family, get them to safety. Protocol said—

Sod protocol. He took a deep breath, his hands tightening around the grip of his own rifle as he nodded. *Go.*

He moved from cover, his weapon coming up through the smoke and haze as he spotted a figure standing perhaps halfway down the passage—catching a glimpse of the Prince out of the corner of his eye, mirroring his own actions.

And the halls of Balmoral reverberated with the sound of gunfire...

6:28 P.M.
The river Dee

"Keep him quiet," Bahadar Singh warned, putting out a hand behind him to hold Catherine back against the rock—the three of them sheltering beneath a rocky outcropping jutting out over the river, the waters of the Dee swirling around their ankles.

The Glock was in his right hand, its slide locked back on an empty magazine. His *last*.

Expended laying down covering fire in the effort to break contact when they had been discovered up-river.

And it had worked, but now—he heard voices not far away from them, the familiar rough accents of South London. *Searching for them*.

Now all he could do is shelter his principals and hope they weren't found. *O Lord of the Sword*, he whispered, reciting the words of the *bani* under his breath, *may we seek Thy refuge. Protect us with Thine own hands. . .protect us from the designs of our enemies.*

Footsteps sounded on the rocks only feet away and he held his breath, every nerve on a razor edge, every muscle tensed.

And then he heard young George begin to cry.

6:29 P.M.

All those years. Hilliard went wide around the corner as he entered the ballroom of Balmoral, the Prince following close at his side. Rifle pressed tight against his shoulder as he stepped over a terrorist's corpse.

Walking the beat in London. Protecting the Royal Family. He had never been forced to take a human life, until today.

Perhaps he had always known it could come to this, but knowing—wasn't the same as reality. Nothing close.

The body of the gardener lay in the middle of the room, sprawled on his back. Sightless eyes staring toward the ceiling, blood staining his faded blue shirt.

Worricker, the SO-14 commander thought, remembering the man's name. Nearly fifty years of service to the Royals. . .one of Her Majesty's favorites. Prince Charles' engraved side-by-side Purdey lay there only inches from the old man's fingers—the shotgun's breech broken open, empty shells lying on the rug.

He'd had to have taken it from the castle's gun room, been re-loading it when he was killed. A last, desperate act. *Selling his life dearly, in defense of his monarch.*

Hilliard heard William curse softly at the sight of the man's body, a bitter, regretful sound.

Loss.

"Ready, Your Highness?" he asked, hearing more bursts of gunfire from somewhere deep within the castle as they stood there in the middle of ballroom, rifles in hand. If they were going to reach Catherine, they could afford no delay.

"Aye," the Prince nodded, sorrow in his eyes as he turned. "There's nothing I can do for him here."

Let the dead bury their dead. "I remember him from when I was a lad, coming up here on holiday. He was—"

Whatever he might have been about to say was lost as another loud explosion reverberated from the south end of the castle, Hilliard's earpiece crackling with a burst of static—and then the voice of one of the men he had detailed to escort the Queen, shouting to make himself heard over the noise of rifle fire. ". . .we've been cut off from the bunker. There's no way to get the Queen down without exposing her to fire."

My God. This was spiraling out of control. "Can you fight your way through?"

"That's a negative, they have a clear field of fire on the entire hall. We don't have enough men—Nawaz and Hockings are down. Can't do anything more than try to hold our position in the tower for as long as we can."

"Hold there," Hilliard responded grimly, looking over at Prince William. "Her Majesty is under attack in the tower. I know you want to find your wife an' son more than anything else on God's good earth, Your Highness, but my men aren't going to be able to hold out much longer. And if the Queen dies, the England we have known dies with her."

He could see the agony in William's eyes, the fear and indecision. *Torn between love and duty.* Duty to his family. . .and to the realm.

A few seconds passed, and then the Prince shouldered his rifle, gesturing toward the stairs at one end of the ballroom. Stairs leading to the second floor and the tower. "Let's be going."

6:30 P.M.

It felt like a scene from another age as Harry dropped to one knee, bracing himself against the thick trunk of the oak towering over his head—the western wing of the castle on fire—angry flames leaping into the slate-gray sky above, silhouetting the figures standing in the cover of the black Suburbans.

"I have three men near the carriage porch, all of them armed. Two more by the back van, one of them with a rifle. Eighty meters," Harry heard Roth say, not taking his eyes off the AK's sights.

"Solid copy," he replied, forcing his breathing to slow, the sights wavering as he tightened his grasp of the Kalashnikov's foregrip. "Man to his left has a radio."

Command and control. Here, as in Vegas, Tarik was leaving nothing to chance. . .with Colville's nationalists facilitating him every step of the way. Blood on all their hands

"We take them both at once," he said, his finger curling around the trigger. "You have the man on the right."

". . .yes, I understand, brother," the jihadist said, hearing Farid's voice in his earpiece as he toggled the radio's microphone, turning away from the Suburban. "I haven't been able to raise them in the last five minutes. I—"

The words died in his throat, a sound like the explosion of a rotten melon assaulting his ears—something warm and wet spraying over his face.

He had just enough time to turn, mouth open in shock at the sight of his partner slumping to the ground, the back of the man's head blown away, blood and brains trickling down the side of the vehicle.

The next moment, a 7.62x39mm round smashed through his own skull, and everything went dark.

6:31 P.M.

There was a rough exclamation, followed by a splash as the searcher entered the river, coming around the edge of the rock—the muzzle of his rifle leading the way.

Protect thy disciples, Bahadar Singh breathed, dropping the empty Glock into the river as he came out of his crouch, his body slamming into that of the terrorist. *And destroy my enemies.*

He seized the barrel of the rifle in his right hand, pushing it away just as a ragged burst ripped from its muzzle—going wild in the air.

No. His kirpan coming out in his left hand, eyes locking with those of his oppponent only moments before he buried the curved blade in the young man's belly, nearly disemboweling him.

Blood spurting from the wound, a crimson flow staining Singh's hands as the terrorist tried to push him away, both of them falling backward into the river. Catherine's screams echoing over the water.

The Sikh pushed the man's hands away, his turban coming undone as he wrestled with him in the shallows, seizing hold of the dagger's hilt and plunging it between the man's ribs again and again—churning the water into a bloody froth.

A glimpse of movement out of the corner of his eye—the shape of another terrorist rushing down the bank above him—and Singh rolled over on his back in the river, his hands finding the H&K G3. Bringing it up, water and brass streaming from the rifle's ejection port as he fired.

He could see the bullets strike his target as if in slow-motion, plumes of blood rising across the man's chest as he wavered, falling backward like a broken doll.

Singh pushed himself to one knee, his long wet hair flowing unbound over his back like the mane of a lion. The rifle coming back against his shoulder as he scanned for threats. *Nothing.*

The echoes of the last shots dying away through the woods to be replaced by the more distant sound of gunfire from toward the castle itself—seeming to swell in intensity even as he listened.

He turned to see Catherine staring at him from a few feet away, her face drained of color—eyes wide with shock. He rose to his feet, rifle in one hand as he extended the other toward her and the boy. "We need to move, Your Highness. *Now.*"

6:33 P.M.
RAF Lossiemouth
Moray, Scotland

"Tyrant One Zero, this is Tower," the middle-aged man in the uniform of an RAF warrant officer announced, gazing out the control tower windows toward the slate-gray fighter jet sitting on the runway a few hundred meters away—the glow of its engines already visible in the gathering dusk. "Winds 220 at thirteen knots, runway 23 right. You are cleared for take-off, Leftenant."

A moment, and then the young flight lieutenant's voice came back over his headset. "Runway 23 right, cleared for take-off. Tyrant One Zero."

Go with God, leftenant, the older man thought, his face sober as he stared out the window. He'd been watching young pilots take off these runways for years—but there was nothing ordinary about this flight, as the cylindrical shapes of the Paveway IV laser-guided bombs hanging beneath the Typhoon's wings bore witness.

Now, the life of the Queen herself was in danger. Cut off from help. And he knew perhaps better than even the pilot out in that cockpit just what a desperate play this was.

He saw the Typhoon begin to roll down the runway, gathering speed—twin gouts of flame suddenly spurting from the tail of the plane as the afterburners fired, the roar vibrating across the airfield and rattling the windows of the control tower as it climbed into the evening sky.

He keyed his mike again, glancing back to see the second fighter taxiing down the runway. "Tyrant Two Zero, this is Tower. Winds 220. . ."

6:34 P.M.
Balmoral Castle

Open ground. Naked and bare. Over a hundred meters of it before the castle. No place to run, no place to hide.

Harry dropped to one knee on the once-manicured grass, hearing the whiplash crack of bullets crease the air above him as he ejected the AK's empty magazine, plucking another from his chest rig with a fluid, practiced motion. McTaggart only a few feet from his shoulder, the rhythmic chatter of the man's rifle adding to the cacophony surrounding him.

A man was never more alive than in the midst of battle. Death whispering about his ears.

A seductive voice. He glimpsed Roth off to his left, brass ejecting from the former Royal Marine's weapon as Harry slammed the magazine into the Kalashnikov's mag well—pulling back the charging handle to chamber a round even as another pair of jihadists emerged from the dark shadows of the treeline toward the castle's great tower, barely twenty meters away.

"Shooters on the right!" He screamed a warning to McTaggart, his voice carried away in the din of battle—his rifle's muzzle describing a painfully slow arc as he brought it to bear, iron sights centering on the lead terrorist even as the man opened fire.

Chaos. Harry threw himself sideways, hitting the ground as bullets fanned the air past his head. Rifle bucking into his shoulder as he fired.

His first shot went wild—the second and third striking his target high in the chest. The man went down, legs kicking as McTaggart dispatched his partner with a controlled burst of fire.

Two more down. But they couldn't stay here. Exposed. Out in the open.

"Flank left!" he called out, catching Roth's eye and gesturing with his support hand toward the parked Suburbans thirty meters to their west. "Move—*move!*"

6:36 P.M.

The *Shaikh* had assured him that the Queen's security would be the only opposition they would face, Farid thought, his dark eyes blazing as he made his way up the grand staircase toward the second floor, rifle in hand.

That their brother's sacrifice in Aberdeen would tie up all available units, that there would be no *time* for the British to mount a response.

None of which explained the chaos unfolding without. "*Yalla, yalla!*" he barked, stepping over the body of a dead servant as he came upon a pair of his men sheltering at the threshold of a door. *Come on, come on.*

Cowering. Like so many he had seen in Syria. Eager for the fight—to prove themselves in Allah's struggle—until the bullets began to fly, and the prospect of martyrdom became a reality.

"We can't," one of them responded, his voice cracking. Refusing to meet Farid's eyes. "They're covering the corridor—Mohammad and Amin are already dead."

"And if you stay here," the Syria veteran responded, drawing his pistol from within his jacket and aiming it at the young man's head, "I'll send you to meet them. Do you wish to meet God by my hand, or by that of the infidel?"

6:37 P.M.

Harry raised himself up on one knee as he saw Roth and Flaharty make their break for the vehicles, laying down covering fire on the treeline.

He fired until the AK's charging handle locked back, fishing another curved magazine from his chest rig as he ejected the empty. *Couldn't keep this up much longer.*

Pushing himself to his feet, Harry ran forward a few paces to where McTaggart knelt, firing as he went. "*Move!*" he screamed, placing a hand on the older man's shoulder as he reached him. "I've got your six."

A nod of acknowledgement and the constable rose, turning as Harry fired again and again, retreating backward toward the vehicles—ragged bursts of fire ripping from the Kalashnikov's muzzle. *Suppressive fire.*

And then he heard it, a familiar whine searing through the air near his head. The sickeningly soft sound of a bullet smashing into human flesh.

He turned back just in time to see McTaggart sway. A second round slamming into the man's side, going through the plate like it was paper.

His legs going out from under him as he crumpled to the ground.

No. He heard a raw scream of anger, realizing only then that it had come from his own throat. *And good men die.*

Mehreen's words echoing through his mind, hollow—filled with foreboding. Not today.

Not when victory was so close.

He reached McTaggart's side, firing as he moved. Fury clouding his vision. The chatter of Roth and Flaharty's rifle sounding distant, far away as he stooped down. He could see the pallor of the man's face in the gathering dust—his eyes slowly opening and closing as he struggled to breathe. Bloody spittle flecking his lips.

He shook his head, knowing the signs. *All too well.* "Come on now, mate—stay with me. You're going to be all right."

He reached down, his left hand entwining in the straps of the constable's plate carrier—the stock of the AK pressed tight against his shoulder, firing it in one hand as he began to drag the dying man backward toward cover.

Not today. *Not today. . .*

6:38 P.M.

"Price, what's your status?" Hilliard demanded, breathing heavily with the exertion—William at his back pulling rear security as they moved together down the upstairs hall, past one of the bedrooms used by guests of the Royal Family in years gone by. "I say again—what is your status?"

Nothing but static. The commander's lips pursed into a thin line, the sound of gunfire growing ever closer. Either his officer was engaged heavily and unable to respond, or. . .

No. He forced that thought away from him, cursing beneath his breath. *They were going to be there in time.* They had to be.

A heavy oaken door barred their entrance to the tower itself, and Hilliard threw himself against it, knocking loudly. "Price! Open up!"

A moment passed, and then the bar slid back, the door opening to reveal one of his officers—a leveled Glock in the man's hand. More of his men back toward the remains of the other door, taking cover behind a rude barricade of heavy furniture. The room filled with the acrid smell of gunpowder.

"Thank God it's you," he said, lowering the weapon and stepping back to let them in even as a ragged burst ripped from the muzzle of Price's rifle. A deafening sound in the confines of the tower. "We're running low on ammunition," the SO-14 officer continued, his face grim. "No way of telling how many men they have left, but it's too sodding many."

"And Her Majesty?" Hilliard asked, glancing around the room and finding no sign of the Queen.

"We evacuated her upstairs," the man responded, gesturing toward the winding stone steps leading to the upper levels of the tower. "Along with our wounded."

"Go join them, Your Highness," Hilliard advised, looking back at William—but the Prince responded with a shake of the head, ejecting the magazine of his rifle and hefting it in his hand.

"You know better than that, Colin. I'm not going anywhere."

Noblesse oblige, the commander thought, acquiescing with a brief nod. William's mother had understood it, and drilled it into her young son. The obligations of royalty, a prince fighting alongside his subjects. *One final time.*

"All right, then," he said, looking around the room at the handful of men—all that remained of his command. "This is where we fight, and if needs be. . .this is where we die. For England."

6:41 P.M.

"Come on, come on," Harry breathed, kneeling at McTaggart's side behind the rear wheel of the Suburban, his hand pressed tightly against the wound in the man's neck, trying to stem the flow of blood as he unbuckled his plate carrier—searching for the second wound. "Stay with me."

The older man was dying, he knew that. Knew it even before he found where the second bullet had entered—smashing through his ribcage and on into his right lung. *No exit wound.* He could see it in his eyes—a look he had seen so many times before.

Acceptance. A man resigned to his fate.

No. "Don't give up on me now," he hissed, arterial blood trickling out between his tightly-clamped fingers, dark and crimson, the deafening rattle of Roth and Flaharty's rifles sounding so very far away. Hot brass struck him in the cheek and he blinked, heedless of the pain. "Don't you dare—I'm going to get you through this, mate. Just hold on."

Lies, more of them. All that was left to him now.

McTaggart grimaced, his eyes flickering open. Coughing up blood as he tried to speak. "It—it's. . .no good, lad."

And he was right. That was the worst of it—the light fading in his eyes as he gazed up into Harry's face through the gathering darkness, muzzle flashes illuminating the gathering twilight.

"Tell. . .tell the old woman I love her. Promise me," he said, his fingers coming up grasp Harry's wrist. *"Promise. . ."*

"I promise," Harry responded, gripping McTaggart's hand fiercely, a tear streaking its way down his powder-grimed cheek. Knowing even as he said the words just how very meaningless they were. Another promise, like so many others, fated to be broken from the moment it was made. *No harm.*

Harry felt the older man's grasp loosen, his fingers falling weakly away as he slumped back against the Suburban's tire. Eyes slowly glazing over in death.

He reached down to pick up his rifle, hearing bullets impact the opposite side of the SUV as Roth took a knee only a few feet away—reloading his Kalashnikov. The question only too visible in his eyes as he glanced over.

Harry shook his head. *Good men die.*

6:43 P.M.
Thames House
London

"The cousins have a satellite coming on-line above Scotland in five minutes," Simon Norris announced, dropping his coat over the back of his office chair as he entered the operations centre, glancing over at MacCallum. "They've agreed to give us remote access to the live feeds here."

"Good work," the section chief responded, his eyes focused on the screens on the far wall. The news was already hitting the major networks, speculation and misinformation spreading across the Internet. It was only a matter of time before rumors of the Queen's death began swirling, assuming they weren't already. *And that they weren't true.* "The RAF should be able to provide eyeball shortly. What's our window on the sat?"

"Forty minutes."

With firearms units from Aberdeen still twenty minutes away, MacCallum thought. No way to tell whether any of it would be soon enough.

6:44 P.M.
Balmoral Castle
Scotland

Target down. Harry saw the jihadist crumple, framed in the sights of his AK for a brief moment before he ducked down behind the Suburban's engine block—bullets shattering the glass of the vehicle above his head.

Can't stay here. They were bleeding Tarik's men, that much was true—but every moment they were pinned down here was another moment in which the Queen's life was in jeopardy.

Had to break the deadlock. He adjusted the straps on the damaged plate carrier he had taken from McTaggart's body and raised himself up, putting a hand on Roth's shoulder, raising his voice above the insistent chatter of Flaharty's weapon. "On my signal, I want both of you to lay down covering fire. I'm going to make a break for the building—draw fire. Try to flank them."

The former Royal Marine shook his head, the look in his eyes clearly showing his opinion of the plan. "You'll be cut down before you get ten meters."

He was right. The ballistic plates in his vest, even damaged, were better than no armor at all—but they hadn't saved the Scotsman and they wouldn't save him if those rifles opened up.

So be it. The deadness inside reaching out, threatening to consume him. His hands still wet with McTaggart's blood, fury boiling just beneath the surface. "We're running short of options. I—"

And then he heard it—a low rumble growing in pitch and volume with every passing second—a sound he remembered from Afghanistan. *The sound of a fast-mover coming in for an attack run.*

There was no time to react, no time to speak as a pair of fighter jets came into view in the semi-darkness above, screaming in over the castle. Barely five hundred feet off the deck.

RAF Typhoons, Harry thought, recognizing the familiar, delta winged shape. Grasping the situation in a trice. The Queen's security team had gotten off a distress call, somehow.

But with the terrorists already inside Balmoral. . .

6:45 P.M.
The rally point
Outside Banchory

"They're saying she's dead, mate," Delaney heard the ex-infantryman say, the man's voice trembling with fear as he watched the TV broadcast on the screen of his phone. *With rage.* "They're saying they killed her—all the Royal Family. They—"

"Shut up, just sodding shut up," the former sapper exploded, turning away from the group of soldiers, the mobile pressed tight to his ear.

Something had gone horribly wrong, if even half the news reports out of Balmoral were to be believed. He had to reach Hale—had to get to the bottom of this, find out what was going on.

"The mobile number you have reached is out of service," a computer-generated voice informed him, a cold chill seeming to crawl down his spine at the words.

EMBRACE THE FIRE

He tapped Hale's number into his phone once more, his big fingers moving clumsily across the screen—raising it to his ear just in time to hear the same message repeated again.

A dark premonition sweeping over him in that moment, remembering his final conversation with Hale, days before. *"I'll be right there at your side, mate,"* he had said, standing on the deck of the *MV Percy Phillips* beside his old comrade. Looking out over the harbor of Grimsby. *"Right to the finish."*

The long, weighty pause before Hale had replied, *"I'm sorry, but you won't. I have something else I need you to do."*

Take care of the Shaikh. That's what it had amounted to, in the end. Eliminating he and his remaining men—and with them, the evidence of what they had done.

Or had that been it at all? Delaney lowered the phone, a sudden fear gripping his heart as he stared at its blank screen. Glancing out over the open farm fields toward the north.

"Tell me again," he demanded, turning back to the infantryman—one of the men who had parted with Hale at the Yorkshire farmhouse. "There at last, what did Hale say to you?"

"Said to meet you here," the soldier replied, his brow furrowing. "Await further orders."

And now Hale himself had vanished—like a ghost in the night. Leaving them twisting in the wind, facing the *success* of the attack they had been supposed to prevent.

"We need to get out of here at once," he said suddenly, tossing a set of keys for one of the spare vehicles across to another of the gathered soldiers. "Spread out, go to ground...stay there until all this is over. And remember, not a word of this to anyone. *Anyone.*"

6:45 P.M.
Balmoral Castle

"*Now!*" Harry screamed, pushing himself away from the vehicle and rising to his feet, his weapon coming up as he caught sight of the jihadists in the open. *Five targets.*

Caught off-guard by the jets, still looking up into the sky.

Controlled bursts of fire ripped from the AK-103's muzzle as he moved around the Suburban, heedless of his own safety. Advancing on the castle. *Target down. Target down.*

The rifle recoiling into his shoulder as he turned, engaging the third terrorist.

Putting three rounds into the man's chest.

He heard the rattle of gunfire behind him as Roth and Flaharty followed him out, saw another target collapse.

And then another, the three of them moving across the lawn of Balmoral toward the castle—the muzzle of Harry's rifle sweeping from side to side as he pushed forward, reaching the castle door just as the fighters came back over for another low pass.

The roar of their jet engines drowning out all else, vibrating the very ground.

A shape materialized in the semi-darkness of the front corridor, a young man in jeans and a dark hoodie. *Carrying a rifle.*

Fear visible in his eyes, his weapon coming up even as Harry reflexively squeezed the trigger—the magazine emptying as he sent a pair of 7.62mm rounds crashing through the man's skull, his head snapping back from the impact, legs going out from under him as he went down.

He kept the rifle leveled down the corridor as he plucked a fresh mag from his rig. *Last one.*

The hall stank of gunpowder and death, the sound of gunfire coming from somewhere above him—the upper floor, back toward the tower. Roth and Flaharty entering behind him.

He stepped over the young man's corpse, pulling back the AK's charging handle to chamber a round. "Clear."

6:47 P.M.
Cabinet Office Briefing Room A(COBRA)
No. 10 Downing Street

". . .this is Tyrant One Zero. We have no targets, I say again, no targets. Acquired visual on armed hostiles approx. fifty meters south of the castle on the first pass. Danger close."

"He means that the militants were too close to the castle itself to safely drop ordnance without endangering the Queen," Julian Marsh heard General Lidington inform the PM in a low voice. That should have been obvious, but upon reflection. . that never was safe to assume with a politician.

But the young RAF pilot wasn't done. "Visual was lost when they disappeared into the building."

Into the building. Marsh looked up from his briefing notes, meeting General Lidington's eyes—seeing the horror written there. The soldier shook his head. "Merciful God. . ."

They had all known that dispatching the fighter jets was a desperate gambit.

Without anyone on the ground able to serve as forward air controller—able to designate targets for the Typhoon's laser-guided bombs—perhaps it had been doomed to failure from the very start.

But to have its futility *confirmed* in such a stark manner. . .

"What does that mean?" Marsh heard the PM ask, but Lidington paid him no heed, looking instead across the briefing table at him. "The Firearms Units from Aberdeen, they're how far out?"

"Fifteen minutes."

It wasn't going to be soon enough.

6:50 P.M.
Balmoral Castle
Scotland

Hold up. Harry raised his hand in a fist, silently signaling for Roth to stop short behind him. Flaharty a few feet farther back, the three of them maintaining a loose formation as they advanced, clearing room to room.

Movement catching his eye in the darkness toward the end of the corridor toward the stairs. Picking out the barrel of a rifle, a figure of a man coming through the doorway. *Target.*

Careful. Bahadar Singh eased himself forward through the open doorway and into the corridor beyond—briefly taking his support hand off the foregrip of his rifle to keep Catherine back, hearing her gasp at the sight of a staff member's body only a few feet away. The woman lying where she had been shot, carpet stained dark with her blood. "Stay behind me," he whispered, hearing more gunfire from the upper floors. The threat was far from over.

Bringing her back here had been a risk, but she hadn't been willing to hear of anything else. Unwilling to leave as long as her husband, the rest of her family were in danger.

And in truth, there weren't that many places to go. Not without a vehicle—without some assurance that the crossings over the Dee were safe. Balmoral had always been prized by the Royals for its remoteness, but that was a double-edged sword. Aimed at their own necks this night.

Those planes above were proof that Hilliard had gotten through to London—but there was no salvation to be found there.

Movement from not far down the corridor, the figure of a armed man emerging from the shadows. His hand coming back up—steadying the rifle. Only too aware that they were caught in the open. *Exposed.*

Take the shot. Now before it was too late.

"Military intelligence!" A voice called suddenly, a black man appearing at the side of the first, his own rifle leveled. "Identify yourself."

"Inspector Bahadar Singh," he replied, his weapon still raised, motioning once more for Catherine to stay out of the line of fire. "Metropolitan Police Service, Special Protection Command. And you?"

"Darren Roth," the second man responded, lowering his rifle and taking a step toward him. "Thames House."

Another burst of gunfire sounded from upstairs after a brief cessation, bringing their danger back to the forefront. The Sikh shook his head, thinking of his dead officers—butchered at their post. *Not good enough.*

"If you're from Five, prove it. What's the SO-14 codename for Prince William?"

"PEREGRINE," came the response, a great weight seeming to roll from his shoulders at the man's words. *Help had arrived.* "I couldn't imagine London was going to be able to get here in time."

"You had that right," Harry responded, watching as Singh lowered his weapon—his dark eyes searching their faces. Still sheltering Catherine behind him, the child in her arms just visible over his shoulder. Fear written in her eyes. "We're all there is. . .and London didn't send us. We're on our own."

Surprise registered in the man's eyes, and he started to respond, but an explosion from somewhere above cut him off—plaster falling from the ceiling around them. An explosion, followed by a hail of automatic weapons fire.

Their hourglass was running out of sand.

"Get her to the safest place you can find," Harry admonished curtly, looking the Sikh officer in the eye. "And keep her there until the threat is past."

He shouldered his rifle and began to move toward the stairs, glancing back at Flaharty, who was pulling rear security—covering the corridor behind them. "Let's roll."

6:52 P.M.

Hilliard pushed himself to his feet, ears still ringing from the concussive force of the blast—smoke and dust filling the confines of the tower.

A fragmentation grenade, falling just short—their barricade of heavy furniture absorbing the impact.

Or most of it, he thought, catching sight of Price leaning against the wall—the man's face twisted in pain, hands closed around the long oaken splinter protruding from his stomach. Another of his officers slumped dead by the barricade. *Two officers down.*

The acrid taste of gunpowder on the SO-14 commander's tongue as he raised his weapon, stumbling forward through the smoke. A burst of fire rippling from the H&K's barrel as he spotted a young man charging toward the barricade.

Had to stay in the fight.

"Abdullah?" Farid asked, toggling his radio's microphone as he stared down at the broken body of the college student lying only a few feet away—bleeding out on the soft carpet of the hall. Their last grenade, and it had done nothing in terms of breaking the deadlock. "Hazim. . .Muhammad?"

No answer.

The Syria veteran cursed, fingers tightening around the pistol in his hand as he leaned back against the wall, taking cover as yet another burst of fire came from the room where the British officers had taken refuge. His men were being cut down one by one—the seven of them in the hall all that remained, or at least all that he could raise. The fate of their operation now hanging in the balance for the first time.

No, he thought, rebuking himself for his doubt. It was in the hands of Allah that their success rested. As it had ever been.

"Give me your vest," he said, beckoning with his hand to the young man closest to him. "Take it off and give it here."

The man nodded, beginning to undo the straps of his bomb vest as Farid turned toward a pair of brothers standing a few feet away, "The two of you, back—cover the stairs. Go. *Yalla, yalla!*"

6:53 P.M.
The gliding club
Aboyne, Scotland

Waiting. It seemed as if she had spent her entire lifetime waiting, Mehreen thought, glancing at her phone to check the time. The screen still displaying, *No signal.*

Waiting for information from her assets in Northern Ireland. Waiting for Nick to come home from the war. Ever the lot of the intelligence officer. . .the wife.

"Anything?" she asked, looking up as the constable came walking back toward the plane. He'd been monitoring the Police Scotland radio network, trying to learn whatever he could.

"Nothing. No one has been able to raise Balmoral Castle since the attack began."

An hour of silence.

"Perhaps they have and just aren't willing to acknowledge it over open comms."

He gave her a skeptical glance, shaking his head. "Aye. Well you're the spook, ma'am, not me. But I know fear when I hear it in men's voices."

And nothing to do for it but wait. Cut off from any ability to help. She heard a low moan from the back of the plane and grimaced. *Conor Hale.* The drugs had to be wearing off.

6:54 P.M.
Balmoral Castle

They couldn't hold much longer. That was the bitter truth of it, Hilliard realized, crouched on one knee as he laid the G36 aside, checking the magazine of his pistol. *Ten rounds.*

Another twenty in the rifle—Price and Winterson weren't much better supplied, both of them fighting on despite their wounds. The rest of them dead or dying, nearly his entire command wiped out in the scant hour since the attack began. *It felt like an eternity.*

Another rush would be the finish of them.

He glanced over to where Prince William knelt beside one of his dying men, tightening a rude tourniquet around the man's leg.

"Take him and move, your Highness," the SO-14 commander barked, even as Winterson's rifle opened up once more. There was no time for argument. Their only hope—if they were to have *any* hope—lay in a retreat up the steps, into the higher levels of the tower. "We'll be right on your heels. *Move!*"

He saw William stoop, gathering the man in his arms—saw the prince disappear into the stairs. Reached for his own rifle, the sound of a dull *thud* striking his ears, as if something had been thrown, landing in the hall without.

There was no time to react, no time to find shelter. The next moment the room erupted around them. . .

6:55 P.M.

Harry felt the entire building tremble with the force of a second, far more powerful explosion as he reached the landing ascending to the second floor—rifle snapping to his shoulder as he doubled back, covering the next flight of stairs. Roth just a couple steps behind him, Flaharty farther back.

Nightmares flashing back through his mind—memories of an operation in Beirut, years before. A suicide vest going off in the middle of a crowded apartment building.

Ball bearings turning the corridor into a charnel house, the concussive force of the TATP taking down a wall.

A blast just like this one. A mission that had ended in failure. *Innocents lost.*

He shook his head and drove forward, fighting back the fear. The loss. The despair that threatened to overwhelm him. *Not again.*

A rough exclamation was the first thing that hit his ears as he mounted the stairs, his eyes catching sight of a pair of figures not five meters away—seconds before the corridor lit up with the muzzle flash of their rifles.

"*Down!*" Harry threw himself to one side, landing hard on the steps as rounds chewed through the air he had just occupied, the rifle recoiling into his shoulder as he returned fire—Roth's Kalashnikov adding its voice to the cacophony as the British officer came to his aid.

He saw Roth stagger as if struck, one of the jihadists crumpling backward under the impact of multiple bullets, his rifle clattering to the floor. *Fire and death.*

Devastation. Hilliard opened his eyes slowly, dust and smoke filling the air around him. A numb feeling pervading his lower body as he lay there in the rubble of the tower room. *Helpless.*

He saw armed men enter the room, stepping over the destroyed barricade, a tall figure at their head—a pistol in the man's hand as he stopped, standing over Winterson's body.

Chuckling. A sound more devilish than all that had proceeded it, as the terrorist sent a single bullet through the dying officer's brain. Executing him where he lay.

No. Hilliard's face twisted in a grimace of wrath and sorrow. Struggling against the pain as he tred to roll onto his stomach—clawing for the Glock which lay only inches from his fingertips. Trying to bring it closer. If only he could reach it. . .

He wasn't going to die like this. *Not like this.*

Another harsh laugh, and a man's tennis shoe descended on the pistol just as Hilliard grasped it, pinning it to the floor.

The SO-14 commander looked up into the eyes of one of the younger jihadists—pure hatred staring back. Hatred. . .and *triumph.*

Hilliard saw the man's rifle come up, its dark muzzle only inches away from his face—all other sounds fading away, his world constricting around him.

Trembling despite himself as he struggled to summon up the last of his resolve, his honor. *Don't close your eyes, don't look away. Die like a man.*

He never heard the shots, just felt blood suddenly spray over his face—warm and wet.

The young man above him swaying slightly, looking down at the wounds in his chest as if in disbelief. Trying and failing to keep his feet.

Target down, Harry thought, seeing the terrorist fall before him—his muzzle already swinging toward the next target. Hearing Roth open up beside him as the two of them entered the nearly destroyed tower room, stone and plaster turned into rubble by the force of the explosion.

He saw the tall man turn back toward him—a pistol coming up in the man's hand just as Harry squeezed the trigger.

Nothing. Just *nothing*—the AK's bolt locked back on an empty magazine. *Useless.*

He had only a split-second to realize the truth—dropping the rifle, his hand reaching for his Sig—before the jihadist's pistol came to bear.

A pair of rounds slammed into his body, flattening themselves against the ballistic plate. It was like being hit in the chest with a maul.

The impact knocked him back against the rubble of the wall, driving the breath from his lungs—but he didn't go down, fighting through the pain. His fingers closing around the butt of the Sig-Sauer as he drew the weapon and brought it up, firing it off-hand even as another round slammed into the plaster by his head. *No time to acquire a sight picture.*

The pistol recoiling into his palm as he fired again and again, the bullets striking his target center-of-mass, mushrooming through flesh and tissue. Splintering bone.

No. This wasn't the way it was supposed to end. Farid felt his legs go out from under him, the pistol clattering to the floor of the tower as he sank to his knees. To end like this, his men dying around him as the sound of automatic weapons fire continued to reverberate through the room.

His vision fading—narrowing to focus on the single man in front of him, weapon leveled at his head. Eyes the color of blued steel boring into his.

Failure. . .so close to victory. To furthering Allah's struggle. He brought his left hand up, reaching into the pocket of his jacket for the detonator. *One final blow,* Allahu—

The muzzle of the pistol erupted in fire, a single 9mm slug smashing into Farid's forehead and into his brain. And everything went dark.

Harry stood there for a moment, breathing heavily—painfully—as he watched the body of the terrorist leader topple sideways. His shattered head striking the floor with a rotten sound.

It was only then that he realized the firing had stopped—glancing around him to see the bodies of the remaining terrorists sprawled around the room. Roth stooped beside the recumbent form of a fallen SO-14 officer, clasping the man's hand in his.

It was over. The attack averted, but at such a price. As ever, again and again through the years. . .war without end. *And good men die.*

He put a hand to his chest, still struggling to regain his breath. Looked back to see Flaharty standing there a few feet away, reloading his rifle.

Their eyes meeting for a brief moment, a barely perceptible nod of understanding. This was far from over. Indeed, it had only begun.

6:58 P.M.

"It's stopped," Catherine said quietly after a moment, her voice trembling ever so slightly.

And so it had, the echoes of gunshots dying away through the old castle. Replaced by a silence somehow more ominous than the crescendo of automatic weapons fire that had preceded it.

Take her to the safest place you can find, Bahadar Singh thought, his rifle trained on the entry of the plate room, recalling the man's words. *Keep her there until the threat is past.*

He had been an American, that much was clear by his accent. *What was he doing here?*

A question that would, like as not, never be answered. Singh glanced back to where Catherine knelt in the corner—holding onto her son as if he was the last thing left to her in this world. *And perhaps he was.*

7:00 P.M.

"*All part of the. . .job. You never lose your principal—give your life for theirs, if it comes to that.*"

Harry knelt beside Colin Hilliard, gripping his hand as the Queen's bodyguard coughed violently, spitting up blood—his strength rapidly flagging. Remembering the words of another bodyguard, from another time. *Vegas.*

Another man, so much like this one. Men who had sacrificed themselves—

but in so doing, succeeded where he had so miserably failed. In protecting all that was dear to them.

In doing their *job*.

Roth descended the stairs, moving carefully, heavily—growing pain from the wound in his side slowing him down.

It had gone straight through the flesh, in and out—missing the ribs. Had barely felt it past the impact. But now, as the adrenaline wore off. . .

He saw Nichols kneeling by Hilliard's body as he re-entered the nearly destroyed tower room—caught the American's eye, the question all too visible in his own.

A grim shake of the head serving as reply. The man wasn't going to make it.

He stooped painfully down by the bodyguard's side as Nichols rose, Hilliard's hand grasping for his and squeezing it fiercely, unable to speak for a few moments as he was seized with another fit of coughing, blood and spittle flecking his shirt. "Th-the Queen. . .is she safe?"

Faithful to the bitter end. Brass scattered everywhere through the rubble bearing testament to the valiant fight him and his men had put up.

"She is," the former Royal Marine replied, recognizing the look in Hilliard's eyes too well. The pallor of death in his cheeks. He didn't have much longer, and there was so very little any of them could do. "As are the rest of the Royals."

A duty fulfilled. Something of peace passing across the man's bloodied countenance as he heard the words, his eyes closing for the final time. "Good. . ."

Chapter 34

2:08 P.M. Eastern Time
CIA Headquarters
Langley, Virginia

". . .we need resources on that now. Get me everything we have in the area," Kranemeyer barked, moving through the op-center, his eyes fixed on the television screens, most of them now tuned to European news outlets. The BBC. Sky News. Al-Jazeera.

Russia Today—which had, up until a few minutes before, been reporting Queen Elizabeth's "death" in lurid detail—beating the nationalist war drum for all it was worth.

"Get on the horn with Alliance Base," he said, coming up alongside Danny Lasker, "find out what they're seeing there in Europe, what threats have hit their radar in the last forty-eight hours. Anything, and I mean *anything* they might have overlooked."

"Already on it, sir."

You always had to brace yourself for the potential of follow-up attacks, strikes designed to take advantage of the chaos—the intelligence resources an attack of this magnitude inevitably consumed.

Overwhelm the system.

A system he had sacrificed so much to keep in place—to *defend* against those who would have torn it down.

Turning away, he dug the burner from his pocket, reading once again the text he had received from Roy Coftey nearly four hours earlier. Before any of *this* had unfolded.

"What we discussed the other night. . .it's been taken care of. Stand down."

Stand down, Kranemeyer thought, his dark eyes expressionless, glancing over to hear the BBC breaking yet another news bulletin from Scotland.

That remained to be seen. . .

7:09 P.M. Greenwich Mean Time
Cabinet Office Briefing Room A(COBRA)
No. 10 Downing Street

". . .have located an IED in a van parked by the approach on the east side of the Dee. Inspector Connarty is concerned that the bridge may itself be mined."

Marsh shook his head as his section chief paused, glancing briefly across the conference table at General Lidington. Every moment was precious, and now *this*. "So what is being done about it, MacCallum?"

"They don't have the equipment or the technical expertise to defuse the explosives safely. 321 EOD is en route from Aldergrove."

Northern Ireland, Marsh thought, suppressing a curse. But there was no help for it. . .local Special Branch units weren't equipped to handle this kind of threat. And no one was better—or closer—than the 321 Squadron. "And in the mean time?"

"Connarty has dispatched a pair of Firearms Units to ford the Dee north and south of the bridge, close on the castle in a pincer movement. They should be there in another ten minutes. Perhaps less. Police Scotland reports they have heard no gunfire since arriving on-scene."

The silence of a tomb. The DG ran a hand across the lower half of his face, unable to shake the dark sense of foreboding overpowering him. "And the latest from the RAF?"

"Should have enough fuel to remain on-station for another twenty minutes. After that—" the section chief's voice broke off suddenly and Marsh could hear him talking in the background, as if having forgotten he was on an open line with the prime minister.

"MacCallum. . .MacCallum?"

"Sir," the section chief responded, coming back on suddenly, "we just received a transmission from Balmoral Castle. It—it's Darren Roth."

7:12 P.M.
The port of Aberdeen

My Lord, grant me victory over the corrupt people, Tarik Abdul Muhammad prayed, whispering the words of the *dua* beneath his breath as he stood by one of the computer monitors, its screen displaying a continually updating Twitter stream of the attacks, under the hashtags #Balmoralattacks and #Scotlandunderfire. The prayer of the prophet Lut, peace be upon him.

Over an hour since the attack on Balmoral was to have begun, and still nothing since the initial photographs, no confirmation from Farid that their mission had been a success. The Queen and Royal Family taken, executed on camera—their heads mounted on the tower of Balmoral. *The black flag of jihad waving above.*

Perhaps it was all to be attributed to the universally poor mobile reception in the Highlands. And though there was no word of their success, neither was there word of their failure—as much as the BBC's newshosts were urging calm.

He felt a thrill run through his body at the thought, the blow it would strike against the West. A message, written in the blood of England's royalty. *No one is safe.*

Nowhere.

7:16 P.M.
Balmoral Castle

". . .of course. I understand, sir," Darren Roth said, glancing out the windows of the tower to see a Police Scotland Firearms Unit sweeping across the lawn from the south. Advancing on the castle in a tight, disciplined formation. Weapons leveled.

If only we'd had them earlier, he thought—but didn't say, listening as the DG continued.

"And regarding Her Majesty," he began, "what are your orders?"

"Maintain your position there," came the reply from General Lidington. "A detachment of 22 SAS is in the air from RAF Shawbury. They'll be executing a combat drop over Balmoral, will aid Special Branch in securing the area and provide escort to move the Queen and the Royal Family to safety at Holyrood. They should be with you inside of ninety minutes."

"Very good, sir. We'll hold until they arrive."

"And Tarik Abdul Muhammad?" Marsh asked, interjecting himself once again.

"There's no sign of him among the dead," Roth responded, glancing back to see Catherine embracing her husband with a fierce passion, heedless of the blood staining his clothes. "I think we have to assume he survived—or perhaps was not even leading the attack in person."

How many times had they seen that, he thought, the irony too rich to be endured. The men who persuaded others to seek a martyr's death, quailing from it themselves. Lacking even the raw courage possessed by—

Roth's gaze fell on the form of Bahadar Singh standing in the doorway, a sudden thought striking him as his eyes searched the room.

"One moment, sir," he said—covering the phone with his hand as he advanced on the Sikh. "Nichols? Where is he?"

"Who? What are you talking about?"

"The American who was with me earlier—he's CIA. Where is he?"

Singh shook his head. "Saw him downstairs, about ten minutes ago. Near the kitchen court, heading out. Him and the other man."

Stephen Flaharty. Roth swore loudly, forgetting himself as he brought the phone back up. "Sir, we have a problem. . ."

7:21 P.M.
The carpark
Crathie Kirk

"You about got that, lad?" Flaharty asked, rifle in hand as he glanced back over his shoulder to where Harry crouched in the open door of a silver Vauxhall Corsa, the wires beneath its steering column pulled out.

Harry shook his head, his face twisted in pain as he removed the damaged plate carrier, casting it aside as he went back under the steering wheel, searching for the right wire. "Give me a moment."

The pain from his chest was slowing him down, purplish bruises discoloring the flesh where the rounds had made impact against the plate. Through the trees, they could see the flashing blue lights of countless police vehicles in the gathering darkness—hear the ceaseless wail of sirens.

It might be a moment they didn't have.

There, he thought, touching the stripped wires together and hearing the Vauxhall's engine falter to life. Beckoning to Flaharty. "Get in, get in."

The Irishman took a final glance back toward the bridge before sliding in on the passenger seat, removing the magazine from his AKM and checking it as he did so. *Almost out.* Harry could tell that from the way Flaharty hefted it in his hand.

Almost out—and with half their mission yet to complete. The former terrorist shook his head, looking over at him. "We're running precious low, old son. Tell me you've got a plan."

7:28 P.M.
The gliding club
Aboyne, Scotland

"You've lost, you know that," Mehreen said, the HK45 drawn in her hand as she tossed a bottle of water into Conor Hale's lap. Maintaining her distance, even in the close confines of the Cessna's darkened cabin. "This is the end for you, no matter what else comes—no matter what happens to the Queen. No one's going to remember you as a hero for the part you played today."

He shook his head, struggling for a moment to open it with his zip-tied hands. "All the heroes I ever knew are dead. Every last sodding one of them, dead in the service of a country that had turned its back on them long before. A hundred coffins, draped with the Union Jack—buried in forgotten little cemeteries all across the UK. Like your husband."

She flinched despite herself, his words striking home. Watching as he lifted the water bottle to his lips, spilling some of it down his unshaven, bloodied cheek.

"Nick was a good mate," he said finally. "An' a bloody good soldier."

It was strange to hear praise for her husband from such a man. Under such circumstances.

"As were you once," Mehreen said, trying to regain her composure. "Until you threw it all away, for *this*. And when we find the *Shaikh*, all this is going to be over."

"Threw it away?" He gave her a wry smile. "But that's where you're wrong. Everything I've done has been in the service of my country. Including this—perhaps most of all, *this*. And I didn't do any of it in hopes of being remembered as a sodding hero. I did it because it was *right*."

He paused, as if her words had only then sunk home. "What do you mean, when you 'find' the *Shaikh*. . .you mean Nichols didn't give you his location?"

The words struck her with the force of a rifle bullet. *No. He couldn't have.* But she knew all too well that he could. Nichols, ever the spy. Playing his own agenda out to the end. *No matter the cost.*

She just looked at him, struck dumb, her face clearly betraying her reaction.

"He didn't. . .did he?" Hale asked, starting to laugh. "That's good. That's too good."

It was almost impossible to believe, the realization of how skillfully she had been played. *So many lives put at risk.*

Mehreen reached out, slapping the former SAS sergeant full across the face—jamming the muzzle of the HK45 into his temple as he reeled.

"*Tell me*," she hissed, "where is Tarik Abdul Muhammad? Give me his location, or God help me, I will—"

The breath was suddenly driven from her body as Hale's bound hands came up, slamming into her stomach. *Grappling for the gun.*

She staggered back, caught off-balance as he hit her a second time—and this time she went down, hard. Crashing into one of the seats before falling, gasping for breath, to her hands and knees on the floor of the cabin.

Hale's cold eyes staring down at her as she looked up, the compact pistol looming large in his hands. His finger curled around the trigger.

For a painfully long moment—her breath still coming in shallow, rapid gasps—she thought he would fire.

End it all there and then. *All of the pain.*

"No," he said finally, seeming to think better of it. Shaking his head as he stepped over her on his way to the door of the plane—leaving her struggling to lift herself up.

And then she heard the shots.

7:34 P.M.
The CIA off-site facility
City of London

It was a strange feeling, being on an ally's soil even as they came under attack, David Lay thought—his eyes fixed on the BBC newscast across the room.

He had flown out of Madrid the day before the train bombings years before. On his way back to the States from the Middle East.

Found himself back at Langley, looking at the television in horror at the devastation which had consumed the city he had so recently left.

And yet compared to this, an assault on a royal residence, an attempt to take and behead the Queen of England. He shook his head.

Even in failure, the reverberations were going to be daunting.

"Right, I understand," Lay heard Jimenez say from a few feet away—the CIA station chief replacing the phone in its cradle as he turned to face him.

"That was Thames House," he said, gesturing up toward the screen, where the images of Balmoral were being displayed for the hundredth time—fire billowing from the castle. "They're saying Nichols was involved."

For a moment, it felt as if his heart would stop. *No.* Lay just stared at the man, searching for words. It was simply unimaginable. "In the *attack*?"

Jimenez shook his head. "In stopping the attack."

7:36 P.M.
The gliding club
Aboyne, Scotland

Gunshots. Crashing out one after another in the night, again and again and again. *A bitter death knell.*

Mehreen staggered to the door of the Cessna just in time to see the red-haired constable go down, his body sprawling broken on the runway. Dying before her eyes.

Conor Hale standing a few feet away from the plane, his figure silhouetted in the runway lights—pistol clasped in his bound hands.

A murderer. Now, if never before.

She heard a scream of fury escape her lips as she hurled herself from the plane's door, pain shuddering through her as her feet hit the tarmac.

She saw him start to turn, start to bring the pistol to bear—but then she was on him—crashing into his back, struggling to wrap her arm around his neck as he pivoted.

The HK45 fell from his hands, clattering across the macadam—the point of his elbow slamming into her ribs, delivering a bruising blow.

She cried out in pain—holding on with a strength born of desperation as the former SAS sergeant hit her again, pinning her back against the Stationair's fuselage. His face only inches away from hers in the darkness, fingers closing around her throat as she tried to fight back.

Nick. Brotherhood. None of that mattered any more, perhaps it never had to him. Words, more of them, meaningless as all the rest.

There was no mercy to be found in his eyes as he shrugged off her blows. Only a stolid, implacable determination. He wasn't trying to force her to surrender, she thought, struggling to breathe as his grip tightened—the realization striking home like a pinpoint of light through the darkness closing in all around her.

He was going to kill her.

She could feel her strength ebbing, his breath hot against her face. The runway lights themselves fading away. *Struggling to summon up whatever remained for a final blow.* A decade in the field, ferreting out terrorists, running assets in Northern Ireland. Nothing in all her training with Five had prepared her for this.

Her fist connected with his side and Mehreen heard him groan, his grip on her throat loosening—her lungs burning from lack of oxygen as she hit him again, blood spurting around her fingers, her fist pummeling into his bandaged wound.

A raw scream filling the night as his pain found its voice. She felt Hale recoil, letting go of her. His face twisted in agony as her fist found its mark once more—sending him reeling back into the tail of the plane.

Mehreen staggered, nearly going down herself—gasping for air, each breath feeling like fire passing through her raw throat. But there was no time.

Gun, she thought, stumbling away from the plane—her eyes searching through the darkness. She had to find the gun.

7:38 P.M.
The A93
East of Dinnet, Scotland

So close. Harry tapped the brakes as a police vehicle came roaring around the curve ahead—sirens wailing and lights flashing as it flew past them in the night. Disappearing down the road toward the castle, every asset Scotland had at its disposal now being deployed to protect its Queen.

So close, and yet with so much resting on the course of the next hour. *Everything.*

"You're going to get yourself killed, boyo," Flaharty said finally, as the sirens receded in the distance—the darkness closing around them once more. The first words he had spoken since Harry had finished outlining his plan minutes earlier.

He was right, Harry thought—gazing forward into the darkness, out beyond the Vauxhall's headlights. That was the truth of it.

And it didn't matter. He'd spent fifteen years of his life out there, beyond the wire. Fifteen years of fighting. Of staying *alive*, when other—better—men had been cut down. No longer.

"I know," he heard himself say, his voice curiously devoid of emotion.

The Irishman just shook his head. "And me with you, like as not."

Probably so. The odds of either of them making it out, dangerously slim. "You can still walk away, you know that, don't you? This isn't your fight, it's mine."

Walk away, Harry thought, finding himself willing the man to do it. *Now.* Before this was over, before they all went hurtling past the point of no return. Before he handed Flaharty over to Mehreen, only too aware of the bargain he had made. Handed him over to be killed.

A life for a life. The life of one *terrorist* for another, he reminded himself. There were no innocents in this.

"Maybe so, lad," the former IRA bombmaker said quietly. "Maybe so. Then again, maybe somewhere along this line, it *became* my fight. We're not so very different, you and I."

No. "We couldn't possibly be more different," he spat, doing his best to sound more convinced than he was. So many innocent lives, thrown away. *Sacrificed.*

"Sure, keep telling yourself that. A man's love of his country. . .well, it's a terrible thing, boyo. And you and I, we've spent the best years of our lives doing terrible things in the defense of all that we love."

Playing out their patriot game, he thought, the Scottish Highlands flashing past in the darkness outside the Vauxhall's window. *To the bitter end.* "But this isn't your country."

"No, it's not," Flaharty said, shaking his head as he looked away. "And I never in all my years thought I'd take any hand in saving the life of its sodding Queen. But this *Shaikh* of yours, what if he wins—what then? He an' his, you think they'll stop this side of the water? Not a chance—the six counties will be washed once more in blood, an' they'll make the Paras look like angels of light. So I'm with you, lad. Right to the finish."

Right up until the point Mehreen puts a bullet in the back of your head, Harry realized, struggling once more with the reality of the vow he had made. What he had *promised*. But what was done was done.

He took a hand off the steering wheel, pointing toward lights growing brighter in the distance. "The airfield is just ahead."

7:41 P.M.
The gliding club
Aboyne, Scotland

It had to be here, Mehreen thought, heart beating fast as she searched for the weapon in the darkness. *Somewhere.*

Run. Leave it and run, her mind screamed, hearing Hale's voice as he limped toward her.

The same dogged determination that had carried him through Selection so many years before driving his bloodied body onward this night.

"You should have stayed in the plane, Mehreen," he said regretfully, pain filling his voice as he closed in. "You had the choice. I gave you that."

"And then you killed *him*," she spat, fear in her eyes as she backed away. Those gunshots still ringing out, again and again through her mind.

"Couldn't be helped," he said, still advancing on her. Shaking his head as he glanced over at the body of the constable lying face-down just across the way. "I gave him the same choice."

She started to turn, to run—a sudden metallic clatter striking her ears as her foot caught the HK45, kicking it a few feet away.

There. She caught sight of it, its barrel glinting in the runway lights. But there was no time to reach it, no time to react before Hale's bound fists slammed into the small of her back, a hammer blow smashing into her kidneys.

She went down hard, sobbing in blinding, excruciating pain, falling to her knees on the tarmac as he moved in—his arms encircling her head, the plastic of the zip-tie scraping against her bruised throat.

Cutting off her air.

Struggling to push his wrists away, she kicked out blindly behind her—desperate to break the hold. *Nothing.*

And then her foot found the side of his ankle, catching him off-balance, unprepared. She heard a curse break from his lips as he swayed. Unable to stabilize himself—taking her back with him as he fell, sprawling across the runway.

She pushed herself away from him before he could recover, crawling across the rough asphalt. Her fingers closing around the butt of the pistol, bringing it up in one hand as she staggered to her feet—rubbing her throat with the other.

"Another move," she whispered, scarce able to speak. Glaring down the HK's sights at Hale as he attempted to rise. "Another move, and I will kill you."

She was only dimly aware of the engine sound of an approaching vehicle, headlights suddenly washing over her as she stood there on the runway—spotlighting her in their harsh glare.

Harry shoved open his door almost before the car had even stopped moving, the Sig-Sauer already out in his hand as he advanced, the Vauxhall's headlights illuminating the grim tableau laid out before him.

Mehreen. Hale. The body of the constable laying a few meters away from them.

He shook his head at the futility of it all. Two men who had put on their uniforms, left their homes—their families—in the morning. Just doing their job. And now they were dead, the both of them.

Good men die. But no matter what had happened, he needed Hale alive. For just a while longer.

"I'm here now, Mehr," he said, stopping a few feet away from her. "We've got this. You can stand down."

He saw her hesitate for but a moment, anger flashing in her dark eyes as she turned—weapon aimed straight at his chest.

"Don't you dare. . ."

7:43 P.M.
Thames House
Millbank, London

". . .an airstrip less than thirty minutes east of the castle. Here," Simon Norris said, using the stub of a pencil as a pointer as he gestured toward his screen.

"And that's where Roth believes Nichols to be headed?" Alec MacCallum asked, coming round the corner of the workstation.

"He, and possibly Flaharty as well. If they can reach there and get in the air, well, given refueling there at the strip," Norris said, drawing a large compass circle on the screen, "they could make it to Norway, Denmark. . .Iceland, even. In the space of a few hours."

"It's a gliding club," the section chief observed, his eyes narrowing as he focused in on the open windows. "I doubt they have fuel storage on-site."

"Right you are. So what are we looking at then, Northern Ireland?"

"Probably," MacCallum nodded. "Flaharty's home—he's gone to ground many times there before. Could easily do so again. What about the RAF? Can they be positioned to intercept?"

A shake of the head as Norris drew his pointer in a line toward the east. "With the kind of training this sod has, he can likely fly well-nigh nap-of-the-earth through the Grampian Mountains. Stay below our screens until he's well out over the sea. If then."

"So we're looking at needing to take them into custody before they get off the ground," MacCallum said, raising his eyes to the virtual display on the far wall, looking for all the world like an RAF operations room from the Battle of Britain, icons marking the positions of Police Scotland units sprinkled across its face—along with those moving up from the south. Most of them now concentrating on the protection of the Queen. "What do we have available to us?"

"Very little."

7:45 P.M.
The gliding club
Aboyne, Scotland

"And if Thames House had been given the location of the *Shaikh*," Harry said, advancing toward her, heedless of the weapon, "if your *mole* had found out—what then, Mehr? What then? Would Police Scotland have had the available assets to mount simultaneous operations to protect the Queen *and* take down Tarik—before he could get away? I did what had to be done."

It made sense, but of course it would. Mehreen shook her head, the anger within her boiling over. "No, this is about you, Harry. About what you needed to do to achieve *your* objectives—and it has been ever since you first arrived at my door."

He took another step closer to her, the muzzle of the HK45 nearly touching his chest. Backlit by the car's headlights, his face shrouded in shadow.

"And what if it is?" he asked, his voice low and hard. "I gave my *life* to the defense of my country—is it so very strange that I would want something for myself at the end? I had the only thing I wanted, Mehr—and *he* took her from me. And now all I want in this life is him. *Dead.*"

A desire she knew all too well, she thought, catching a glimpse of Stephen Flaharty—standing back there by the car. A rifle visible in his hands. Her own words to him, no older than the day before. *"When all this is over, when the Shaikh is dead—I want Stephen Flaharty."*

His voice, answering in reply. *"We have a deal."*

She closed her eyes, wrestling with the emotions at war within her.

"But every second we waste here," Harry hissed, not waiting for her reply as he took another step, straight into the cold metal of her pistol's muzzle, "is another in which Tarik could do a runner. So either get out of my way. . .or shoot me now."

8:09 P.M.
Thames House
London

"Welcome back, sir," MacCallum said as Julian Marsh came back through the doors of Thames House, passing his coat off to an aide as the doors closed on the sight of uniformed CO-19 officers standing in the barrel-vaulted entrance without—their Heckler & Koch MP-5s unslung. "We just received an update from the MoD—22 SAS is only thirty minutes away from making the jump. Roth has turned over operational command of the remaining forces at Balmoral to Inspector Connarty and Police Scotland is reporting that their Firearms Units have secured the castle proper."

Marsh nodded. "Good. What about the *Shaikh?*"

"Still no sign of him among the dead. Police Scotland is flooding the area with manpower, trying to get a cordon established."

If he had ever been there to begin with, as they both knew. And if he hadn't. . .he could be anywhere. "Our missing American," Marsh went on after a moment, "have you been able to garner anything from Roth's lead at the airfield?"

"Ballater sent out a couple constables," the section chief nodded grimly, handing over a photograph. "They found the place deserted. This man, lying dead on the runway—shot three times in the chest, blood not even dry. Constable Graeme Banks, one of theirs. One of two officers that had been dispatched earlier in response to Roth's call."

The director-general swore, anger visible in his eyes. This was getting out of hand. "And the plane?"

"Still on the tarmac. Wherever Nichols and Flaharty are, they're not in the air."

"Find them," Marsh spat, still staring at the photo of the dead constable. He handed it back, turning away from his section chief. "Find them and bring them in, preferably before they kill anyone else. And make sure Downing Street is apprised the moment 22 SAS is on the ground—the PM is waiting for confirmation that they have secured the Queen before he issues any public statement on the outcome of these attacks."

8:13 P.M.
The B9077
East of Banchory, Scotland

"And you think Conor Hale can get you that close to him?" Mehreen asked, glancing over at Harry as the Scottish countryside sped past in the night.

"If anyone can," he responded, eyes focused on the road before him. "Tarik is going to want to know what happened—*how* it happened. And I'm the only one who can tell him."

She shook her head, looking away from him and out the window. This went against everything she knew as an intelligence officer. Every instinct honed over the years of running assets in the field.

Mehreen glanced down at the mobile in her hand, held low and to the side, out of Harry's line of sight. A message hastily tapped out on screen giving the *Shaikh*'s location, along with her Thames House identifier code. The phone now receiving a strong signal, for nearly the first time since they had left the airstrip.

Protocol said to send it, to alert Five, ensure they could get to Tarik before Nichols could reach him. Take him into custody, interrogate him. Find out what he knew. That was her *duty*.

Duty. Honor. She looked down at her hands, the dried blood staining her fingertips. *Love*. None burned brighter than that last, no matter how important the others might have once seemed.

She could feel Flaharty's presence in the back seat of the car, his eyes on her in the darkness. Watching her, reading her.

The way he must have done in the days leading up to his attempt on her life. His *murder* of Nick.

Aydin. Ismail. Nick. Carol. They had both lost so very much. And nothing they could ever do would bring back the ones they had loved. . .but they could avenge them.

It felt as if she was standing on the edge of a precipice, the bottomless chasm yawning wide at her feet. Seeking to swallow her whole—her and Nichols both. Perhaps they were all to be damned at the last.

She closed the phone, feeling as if something had died within her even as she did so. Glancing back over at Harry, her mind once again running over what he had said. It was a mad plan.

Perhaps just mad enough to work.

"And once you're in, once you've killed him. What then—how do you get out?"

It seemed like a long time before he replied, his face masked by the darkness of the car. A touch of resignation in his voice. "Getting out, Mehr. . .has never been part of the plan."

8:37 P.M.
Balmoral Castle

"There you are, sir," the police sergeant said, rising from his knee beside Roth as the intelligence officer leaned back on a couch on the second floor of the castle, its upholstery now stained with his blood. "You should still have it looked at proper when you get back, but the bullet went straight through—no expansion from what I can see."

Which didn't prevent it from hurting like bugger-all, Roth thought, thanking the man curtly as he pushed himself to his feet, rifle in hand as he made his way back toward the tower.

The sound of sirens clearly audible through the broken windows, dozens of emergency vehicles filling the entry drive below. Blue and white lights washing over the bullet-pocked granite of the castle walls.

They were loading the body of Colin Hilliard onto a stretcher as he entered the tower itself, drawing a sheet over the bodyguard's face in a gesture of respect. Respect for a man who had died as nobly as he had lived. *Defending his Queen.*

A good man, Roth thought regretfully, running a hand over his face. Perhaps if they had only been here earlier—perhaps. . .you could torment yourself forever with thoughts like that. Condemned to a hell of your own making.

"No ID on this one either," he heard someone say, looking over to see a constable on his knees by the body of the last terrorist Nichols had shot, lying there in a pool of his own blood. Another Police Scotland officer standing over him. "But he has a mobile."

The man pulled the phone out with a gloved hand, his voice changing suddenly even as he did so. "And—it's ringing."

It was the *Shaikh*. It had to be.

"Give it here," Roth barked, extending a hand as he advanced toward the men. "Get Thames House on the call."

Number withheld. He stared at the phone's screen for a long moment as it rang for a second, then a third time—the signal weak, but the call still coming through. Trying to delay for as long as he could.

It was as the phone rang for a fourth time that he swept a dark, bloodied thumb over the screen, lifting the mobile to his ear. His lips suddenly dry as dust.

"*Salaam alaikum. . .Shaikh.*"

There was a perceptible pause, and then the voice of Tarik Abdul Muhammad responded, "Where is Farid?"

"He fell in the assault, *Shaikh*," Roth replied, the suspicion only too audible in the terrorist's voice. *Stall for time.* "A martyr in Allah's Struggle."

"And the Queen?"

"She is herself dead, along with her family, praise be to God. I—"

The line went dead suddenly, and Roth swore—glancing over at the Police Scotland technician standing a few feet away. Knowing even as he did so that they hadn't had enough time.

8:40 P.M.
The warehouse
Port of Aberdeen

They were compromised, Tarik thought, a wave of premonition washing over him as he stared at the mobile in his hand.

Knowing *somehow* that his men were dead. That the British had managed to foil the attack.

He threw the phone away with an angry curse, taking in the sight of Nadeem standing there a few feet away. Surprise filling the young black man's face.

"Don't just stand there," Tarik spat, pushing past him as he strode out into the center of the warehouse, getting the attention of his remaining fighters. "We need to pack everything up. Destroy everything that can't be moved quickly. Rig the building. Now move, quickly—*yalla, yalla!*"

8:42 P.M.
The quay
Port of Aberdeen

"And that's the warehouse?" Harry asked, glancing across the harbor toward a fence-enclosed row of buildings, the cold waters of the North Sea lapping at the quay a few meters away.

A silent nod from Conor Hale served as his answer, the former SAS man sitting there on the boot of the Vauxhall at Harry's side. Rubbing his wrists to restore circulation to them—the marks of the zip-ties which had bound them still visible in the harbor lights. "It's where my men delivered the weapons."

Weapons he had permitted to arrive at their destination, Harry realized, regret gnawing at him from within. Weapons that had *killed* brave men in the halls of Balmoral.

But regret had never brought anyone back from the dead. Or avenged their deaths.

"What do we have, three guards on the perimeter?" he asked, glancing over at Stephen Flaharty.

"Aye," the Irishman responded. "Maybe more. There are so many sodding containers—he could be hiding men anywhere."

"And that's precisely why we're not going to waste time looking for them," Harry said, feeling Mehreen's eyes on him as he turned back to Hale, pulling his Sig-Sauer from its shoulder holster.

He'd been a good man. . .once, Harry thought as he stared into the sergeant's bloodied, defiant countenance. A brother in arms. A *guardian*.

But somewhere along the line, the protector had become a predator. *Time to put the dog down.*

"You understand how this is going to work, right?" he asked, brass-checking the weapon before handing it over to Hale, butt-first.

Another quick nod, sweat beading on the man's forehead, even in the chill of salt night breeze. "I take you to meet the *Shaikh*, get you past his guards as my 'prisoner.' Tell him that the attack was a failure, offer you up."

"Right. You get me in close. Put me in the same room with Tarik." With Flaharty providing overwatch with the rifle and what remained of their ammunition, Harry thought but didn't say, glancing at the Irishman. And Mehreen.

Hale just stared down at the pistol in his hand, his fingers trembling ever so slightly. "What if he doesn't buy it?"

"Well that's a problem you're just going to have to overcome, mate," Harry said, shaking his head. The exposed wires of the suicide vest visible beneath the sergeant's unzipped jacket. "Because your life depends on it."

Hale started to speak, but Harry cut him off—nodding to Mehreen. "We're both going in wired for sound. Everything that happens around us, every single word that is spoken, she'll hear it. If you fail to take me to Tarik. . .she triggers the vest. If you try to kill me, she triggers the vest. If you try to signal him, she triggers the vest. If you try to do a runner or go off the reservation in any way, she triggers the vest. In short, the only way you walk out alive is to make sure everything—and I mean *everything*—goes according to plan. Is that clear?"

The man swore in anger and fear, his face pale as he met Harry's eyes. "But you've seen as well as I what one of these bloody things does. If she detonates the vest, you—"

"Will be dead right along with you," Harry replied, ice in his voice. "That's a gamble I'm prepared to take."

Hale held his gaze for a long moment, cursing once more under his breath. "You're insane."

Harry just looked at him.

"It's time we got into position. Flaharty, take him with you. I'll be along in a moment."

"Wait!" Hale exclaimed, raising his empty hand as he pushed himself to his feet—glancing back and forth between Harry and the Irishman. "Once I get you to him—what then? You have a plan for killing the sod? You're not going to get that close to him with a loaded weapon."

Harry gestured to the Sig. "That's why I gave one to you."

8:46 P.M.
Thames House
Millbank, London

". . .flights departing from Scotland's Aberdeen Airport have been grounded on the runways as the Prime Minister implements emergency measures under the Civil Contingencies Act. Inbound flights have been diverted to Edinburgh as officials with the Home Office suggest that the measures may expand to all flights in and out of Scotland. Here to discuss the still-developing situation with us is former Home Secretary, the Right Honourable Lloyd. . ."

Marsh closed the door of the conference room, shutting off the sound of the BBC newscast without. "Where are we at on the intercepted call?" he asked, glancing at Norris as he walked past them, taking his seat at the head of the table.

"Tarik Abdul Muhammad is in Scotland, likely Aberdeen based on the mobile towers," the analyst responded, looking up from his tablet. "That much we can establish with a reasonable certainty, provided he wasn't routing the call through a relay."

"How probable is that?"

"Based on the sophistication of these attacks. . ." Norris' voice trailed off for a moment. "I don't think we have any way of ruling it out completely until GCHQ completes their final analysis."

"And how soon can we expect them to do so?"

"Several hours."

Several hours they didn't have, Marsh thought, drumming his fingers against the table. Nor the manpower to go searching blindly, not with so much of it now concentrated on Balmoral.

"Downing Street will need to be apprised. The PM has already indicated that flight closures may be extended south to Dundee and Edinburgh and the RAF is mobilizing to escort flights in if it proves necessary."

Emergency measures, measures he had thought he would never see implemented. "What is our status on the security of Her Majesty. . .MacCallum?"

"22 SAS just jumped, MoD estimates a half hour will be time enough for them to regroup on the ground and reinforce the police perimeter. SO-14 is coordinating with Police Scotland on transit to Holyrood."

8:47 P.M.
The port of Aberdeen
Scotland

Just a few more steps, Harry thought, his eyes alert—scanning the quay as he walked forward, his face bruised and bloodied from the impact of Flaharty's fists. His hands bound before him.

Above them, the ghostly shape of a massive shipping crane loomed in the darkness, the cold muzzle of the Sig-Sauer pressing into the back of his neck. Tension clearly palpable in Hale's grip on his arm.

Just a few more steps and they would be visible to the *Shaikh*'s sentries. And then everything was going to depend on Hale's ability to keep them both alive long enough to get to Tarik.

To get him inside the blast radius.

It was a strange feeling, walking to one's death. Mehreen's words from moments before, still ringing in his ears. *"Even if you succeed, even if you kill him, what have you gained by sacrificing yourself? There'll just be another to replace him. And someone else after them."*

And another and another and another. . .war without end. Harry's face tightened. It was like fighting a Hydra, cutting off one head just to watch another grow in its place.

"And that's all the more reason this has to be the end," he had told her, his hand touching her arm. *"For me."*

Only the dead have seen the end of war. The end of all sorrow, drowned, itself, in the grave.

The gate came into view as he rounded the stack of shipping containers. Shouts of surprise and alarm breaking the silence of the night as a pair of Tarik's foot soldiers—young men in jeans and light jackets—reacted to the sudden appearance of the two men.

He saw them moving forward, rifles leveled at the two of them. Felt Hale's voice ring out, the former sergeant's hand on his shoulder, giving him a rough shove—sending him to his knees on the asphalt.

The pistol aimed at his head, only inches away from his temple.

The end of the road.

Chapter 35

8:49 P.M.

"...don't know me," Mehreen heard Hale say—rougher shouts in the background as she listened over her headphones in the cold, forbidding silence of the car, "but your *Shaikh* does—and I need you to take me to him at once. You've been betrayed, and *this* man knows who is responsible."

It was hard to believe this was happening, she thought, staring down at the phone in her hand—a single number displayed on screen. *The number that would trigger the vest.* That they were actually doing this, that any of it was real.

The look of haunted resignation in Nichols' eyes as he turned to leave still burned into her memory.

"Even assuming you can get the gun from Hale in time," she had said finally, speaking only once they were alone, the figures of Flaharty and the SAS man disappearing into the darkness between massive shipping containers, *"you're going to be dead the moment you pull the trigger. But you know that, don't you? That's what you meant by saying you never planned to get out."*

A faint, weary smile crossing Harry's face as he shook his head slowly, reaching forward to place his hand on her arm. The cold chill seeming to reach her very bones as he whispered, *"No."*

"But then—you said..." Her voice had trailed off, trembling despite herself. *Knowing*, in that moment, exactly what he expected from her.

8:51 P.M.
The warehouse

"*Here?*" Tarik demanded, shoving the laptop computer into a carrying case—his brow furrowing as he looked up into Nadeem's dark face.

"Yes, just without and demanding to be allowed to speak with you, *Shaikh*. And he's brought a prisoner—an American. Says we've been betrayed."

That much seemed certain. But it was impossible to know if Colville himself might have been behind the betrayal. The *Shaikh* gritted his teeth in barely-repressed fury. Used and thrown away at the last, despite all his precautions. "Did they come alone?"

"As far as the lookouts know, yes." A belief that counted for nothing, Tarik knew. The young men didn't have the training or the experience to have been able to discern that. But Nadeem wasn't done. "And the man—Hale—he's been wounded."

Tarik slung the case over his shoulder, picking up his Browning from off the table. "Take me to them."

8:52 P.M.

Fear. Harry could see it, raw and naked, in the eyes of the young man standing not ten feet away—the assault rifle grasped awkwardly in his hands.

Feel it, in the tension of Hale's grip of his shoulder—the pistol barrel's muzzle scant inches away. Trembling, but never leaving his head. *Ready to blow his brains out.*

"Put your gun down, bruv. Drop it—*now!*"

He had known they wouldn't get inside armed, no matter what he had told Hale. *Never a part of the plan.*

"No," Conor Hale responded, shaking his head. Desperation, defiance in his eyes. "Not until I've handed this man over to the *Shaikh*."

"If you don't put the gun down, I'm going to end you right here. Take him to the *Shaikh* myself."

"And he'll kill both of you fools with his bare hands."

The young man swore, glancing over at the guard backing him up and then back at Hale, his grip on the rifle tightening. Too proud to back down in front of his partner. A perverse, twisted sense of honor.

"I'm not telling you again, bruv," he repeated, his finger curling around the trigger. "Put it down before I kill you."

Another minute and they'd be dead—the both of them, like as not. Harry raised his head, catching the sergeant's eye for a brief moment. Feeling him waver.

He inclined his head toward Hale, a nearly imperceptible nod. *Do it.*

"All right, all right," Mehreen heard Hale exclaim, punctuating his words with a curse. Her heart sinking as she heard the scrape of gunmetal, a weapon being kicked across the asphalt.

A last, faint hope extinguished in that moment. A futile prayer that this might end in some other way. *Fate.*

She heard the dull sound of a blow, Nichols grunting as if in pain. *A rough laugh*. The clearly recognizable accents of South London, a young man barking orders.

Fire. Pain flooding through Harry's body as he reeled from the blow of the young man's rifle butt to his bruised ribs, nearly going down in the mud and broken asphalt of the loading yard—the metallic taste of blood filling his mouth as he bit deeply into his lip in an effort to keep from crying out.

He glanced over to see Hale standing there a few feet away, his face ghostly pale in the glow of the harbor lights. Defeat etched in his countenance.

And then he felt the young men step back from around them, giving way as if parted by some invisible force.

Raising his bloodied face to see a young, muscled black man maybe five feet in front of him—carrying a rifle. Another figure emerging from the semi-darkness to his right.

Ice-blue eyes sweeping over him.

Eyes he had seen many times before—in the club in Vegas, seemingly an eternity ago. *Another lifetime.* On the train out of London. In a hundred vengeful dreams.

Tarik Abdul Muhammad.

To be this close to him—it was all he could do not to lunge for the man. Wrap his bare hands around the *Shaikh*'s throat and strangle the life from him. Tarik seemed to glance from Harry over to Conor Hale, then around at his men. "What's going on here?"

"You've been betrayed," Hale responded desperately. "The attack was a failure. This man—this American, he got to one of my soldiers—*turned* him. Used him to penetrate our operation."

Truth. It always made for the best of lies.

"Did he?" Tarik demanded, a Browning materializing in his right hand as he raised the pistol. Aiming it straight at the former SAS man's head. "Or was this Colville's plan all along? To use us and betray us in the end? Sell us out to the Security Services."

EMBRACE THE FIRE

Harry could see the tension—the anger—written in the *Shaikh*'s face, his finger tightening around the Browning's trigger. A man on the brink, made desperate by failure. Another moment, and—

"He's telling you the truth," he interjected, raising his voice above Tarik's.

One of the young men moved to hit him again, but the *Shaikh* waved him to one side—stepping closer to Harry, pistol in hand. "And who are *you*, really? CIA. . .Special Forces? Who sent you?"

The CIA. Harry closed his eyes, remembering that day—standing in Kranemeyer's office there at Langley. *"Just let me take the team to Britain. Let me be there. For God's sake. . .you owe me this, Barney."*

The sadness in Kranemeyer's eyes as he'd responded, *"Parker will go to Britain to liaise with Five. As for you. . .I need your resignation by the end of the week. Clean out your desk—turn over your access cards. And then leave. Put all of this behind you."*

A weapon was owed nothing. Particularly not a broken weapon. He lifted his face to meet Tarik's gaze, shaking his head. "No one sent me."

"Then why. . ."

"That night, back in Vegas—you were responsible for the death of a woman."

The *Shaikh* looked around at his men, laughing in disbelief. "I was responsible for the deaths of many *kuffar* that night. What makes this woman so special?"

"She was the woman I loved," Harry responded, his voice flat, emotionless. Betraying nothing of the rage surging within him.

"Ah. . .I see." Tarik smiled, taking a step closer to him. "I begin to understand it now. And you came here—intending to do what, exactly?"

The moment of truth. This wasn't the way he had foreseen it over the months of planning, but perhaps it was better this way. An end to all things. Harry raised his face to the dark heavens above, nerving himself for all that was to come. The fire. The pain. *Into Thy hands, I commend my spirit.*

"I came here," he began, his eyes locking with those of the *Shaikh*, "to kill you. Embrace the fire. . ."

8:55 P.M.

No. Mehreen heard Harry's words, heard him give the signal—her whole body shuddering as she stared at the phone in her hand. A voice somewhere deep inside her screaming at her to *do it*—to just enter the number and press SEND. Trigger the vest.

It was *his* plan. And yet, all she could see before her when she closed her eyes was that morning back in the country. Nick's face as he'd kissed her good-bye for the last time. Walked out the door to the car.

And moments later a ball of fire expanding outward, the windows of the house shattering, covering the kitchen in shards of glass. Cutting deep into her bare feet as she made it to the door.

Knowing that it was already too late, hoping against hope that everything her mind told her was wrong.

That he could have survived.

Her free hand balled into a tight fist, struggling to master herself as she entered the first three digits of the number—the screen blurring as something akin to panic seemed to overwhelm her.

Hating Nichols in that moment for asking this of her, yet finding herself unable to do it. To hit SEND, to detonate Hale's vest. To do to Harry what had been done to Nick. . .to *reenact* that morning through her own actions.

"I'm sorry," she whispered, hot tears streaking their way down her face as she stared out the window of the Vauxhall into the darkness of the port. Knowing that he was going to die one way or the other, and there was nothing she could do to prevent it. *Nothing*. . .

8:57 P.M.

"I'm sorry." The words hit Harry with the force of a hammer as he stared unblinking into Tarik's eyes, the sound of Mehreen's voice seeming to paralyze him for a moment. A sick, *empty* feeling in the pit of his stomach—bile rising in his throat.

Something dying deep within him. His own words from hours before, a haunting echo in his brain. *"Mehreen doesn't have it in her to pull that trigger."*

True enough at the last. . .and yet that there had been no one else. No one he could *trust*.

He screamed, a scream full of bitterness. *Defeat.* A raw, feral sound, anger and pain echoing across the loading yard as he pushed himself to his feet. Heedless of the guards. Of the rifles leveled at him.

Launching himself at Tarik, his bound hands outstretched, reaching out for the man's throat.

He'd made it four steps when a rifle butt slammed into his side—catching him off-balance and sending him sprawling into the dirt and broken asphalt. A booted foot catching him in the ribs as he tried to rise.

Pain. Blows raining down on him as he lay helpless, unable to rise. To *fight*.

Darkness closing in around him. Death had come for him so many times over the years, with so many faces. A welcome visitor, at the last.

But not *yet*.

He heard voices in the darkness, distant and far-away. Voices calling out, one finally stronger than the rest. The *Shaikh*'s.

"Enough!" Harry felt the men recede from around him as he lay there on his back on the broken asphalt, his eyes flickering open to see Tarik standing a few feet away. *Out of reach.* "There's no time for this. We have to be leaving. *Now*—before the Security Services can arrive."

"Then what do you want done with these two?" another voice asked and Harry raised his head painfully—seeing the young black man enter his field of vision. "Just go ahead and kill them now?"

Tarik seemed to consider the idea for a long moment, his gaze sweeping over Harry. "No," he said finally. "This one—I need to find out who he's been working for, and how much *they* know."

"But he said—"

"He's lying," the *Shaikh* responded, shaking his head as his eyes locked with Harry's. "There's no way one man, acting alone, has accomplished so much. As for the other. . .it may be that Allah has willed he serve as our means of escape. We take them both with us. Go, get the rest loaded. *Yalla, yalla!*"

9:00 P.M.

Ten minutes, Flaharty thought, shifting his position to check his wristwatch—shielding its luminous dial in the darkness. His Kalashnikov aimed over the heaping pile of rusting anchor chain he was lying upon, maintaining overwatch two hundred meters down the docks toward the warehouse entrance where Nichols and Hale had disappeared.

Ten minutes, and nothing. No gunfire. No *explosions*, he winced, knowing all too well what Harry had planned.

But nothing. The shrill blast of a tug's horn out to sea the only sound reaching his ears. He shifted restlessly, his eyes searching the darkness—the cold fog beginning to roll in off the North Sea. *Impatient.* Cursing his inability to communicate, to hear what was going on.

There just hadn't been enough headsets to go around, and without comms—he was flying blind.

Like he had so many times before. The streets of Belfast, seeming so very far away in this moment. Ducking the RUC, throwing petrol bombs at the British soldiers. Him. . .and Davey Malone.

Flaharty swore, his face darkening at the memories. Of how they had all been betrayed at the end.

Perhaps by himself, most of all.

He shook his head, pushing himself off the chains and picking up his rifle as he rose to a crouch, his eyes sweeping the quay. There would be time for that later, time to get royally drunk and think about the past. On another day, if he lived that long.

For now, he had to get in closer, find out what he could.

9:02 P.M.

Fate is what a man makes of it, Harry thought—feeling the cold muzzle of the black man's rifle in his back, prodding him forward toward the open door of the Land Rover, its engine already running—headlights piercing the night.

That's what he had told Hamid Zakiri, standing over the broken body of his former friend in darkness of the *masjid* beneath the Temple Mount. Perhaps he had even believed it—then.

His bloodied face twisted into a grimace, blood trickling into the stubble of his beard, dirty with grime. Was it true—or was choice itself little more than an illusion? A tantalizing mirage produced by hindsight. . .when you looked back on the past and saw everything else you *could* have done.

"*We walk on the edge of a knife out there.*" Kranemeyer's words, playing themselves again and again through his mind. "*A razor-thin line between light and darkness. And you've crossed that line. You've been out in the field too long.*"

It was always the choices you didn't even know you had made that killed you in the end. That killed the ones you loved.

He stumbled, and the young man swore at him, jabbing him again in the back with the muzzle of the rifle.

There was no question that he could have taken it from him, disarmed the jihadist before he knew what was happening—even with his hands bound—but he would never have made it ten steps before being cut down. Let alone found Tarik.

There had to be another way. But he was passing the exits one by one—and running out of highway.

He reached the vehicle, lifting himself slowly, painfully into the seat. Catching sight of Hale through the open door—standing there on the other side of the Land Rover—hands shoved into the pockets of his jacket. Under guard, but not restrained, one of Tarik's men standing a few feet away.

Their eyes met for a brief moment, and then Hale looked away quickly. The *Shaikh* materializing out of the mist at his side. "It's time we were leaving," he said, putting a hand on the sergeant's shoulder. "Everyone, load up."

The former SAS man started to move toward the Land Rover, toward Harry, but Tarik's voice arrested him. Calm—in control once more, a smile crossing the *Shaikh*'s face. "No, Mr. Hale. . .you're riding with me."

His eyes locked with Hale's for just a brief moment in time, sensing the fear, the uncertainty there. *Foreboding.*

9:05 P.M.

There had to be a way to get to him in time, she thought, hurrying along the docks. To pull him out. To *save* him yet. Even if she didn't know how.

". . .*riding with me.*" Mehreen heard the words, stopping in her tracks as she glanced over the waters of the harbor toward the neighboring quay. The harbor lights haloed by mist as they shone down upon her, the HK45 held beneath her coat. Only then realizing their import.

She froze for a half-second, glancing back down along the docks toward where she had left the Vauxhall, swallowed up in the night and fog.

And then she began to run. . .

9:08 P.M.

"Let's move, bruv," Harry heard the black man say from beside him—reaching up to clap their driver on the shoulder. He saw Tarik's Land Rover pull out in front of them, headlights sweeping across the loading yard—their own vehicle lurching into motion as it swung into a following position.

Maybe twenty meters behind, if that, he thought—measuring the distance at a glance. Danger close.

It would have to be enough.

He shifted his position carefully, every movement sending sharp pain through his bruised ribcage. Looking over into the eyes of the man on his left—*man?* More of a boy, really. Barely out of college, if that. A rifle in his hand, a Glock just visible beneath his jacket—jammed carelessly into his waistband.

Eyes burning with hatred as they stared back into his. Like those of so many young men he had seen through the years. Minds corrupted by indoctrination. *By hate.*

But there was no time to think of any of that. Not now. Harry looked away, forcing himself to focus. *So close.* Eyeing the lead Land Rover as it drove between the warehouse gates, rolling out onto the road leading inland off the quay.

Now or never.

"Mehreen," he began, his voice low and urgent, "for the love of God, do it—*do it now!*"

He saw the young man's eyes open wide at his words, saw the rifle shift in his hands. . .time itself seeming to slow down as its muzzle came up.

And then the night exploded in fire—the lead Land Rover suddenly engulfed in flames, a shockwave expanding outward from the center of the explosion. A pillar of fire rising into the darkness of the sky.

Lives extinguished in the blink of an eye. *A funeral pyre.*

Their own vehicle swerving to avoid the burning wreck—spider veins spreading across the glass of the windshield as it was struck by flying debris.

Ignoring the pain wracking his body, Harry threw his weight into the guard—slamming him against the door and knocking the rifle away as he reached forward, grabbing the Glock 19 from the young man's waistband and bringing it out in his bound hands.

Out and all the way around. He caught a brief glimpse of panic on the black man's face as he saw the pistol now suddenly aimed at his head, as he started to react—the trigger breaking beneath Harry's finger in that moment.

Lights out. Blood and brains spraying across the window of the Land Rover as the bullet smashed through the jihadist's skull and out through the glass beyond—the roar of the gunshot reverberating through the enclosed vehicle.

Harry swung the barrel of the Glock to the left, putting a pair of 9mm rounds through their driver's shoulder—the vehicle fishtailing as he lost control. His scream of agony nearly swallowed up by the report of the weapon.

The raw, sulphurous smell of gunpowder filling the Land Rover. Two of the jihadists guarding him dead—only seconds having passed since the explosion, since the first gunshot.

He turned back toward the young man on his left even as the Land Rover slammed into a stack of shipping containers and came to a stop, throwing him into the seat in front of him—steam hissing angrily from beneath the vehicle's destroyed hood, the airbags deploying to fill the front seat.

He nearly dropped the Glock in the force of the impact, struggling to bring the weapon to bear. Seeing the look in the young man's eyes as he clawed for his rifle—hatred replaced by naked fear at the sight of Harry's face. Bloodied, pitiless.

A boy once more in that moment, young—scared out of his mind. But going for his gun.

The choices we make. Life and death. . .no *or* about it.

The Glock spat twice—point-blank range, the bullets tearing through the young man's jacket and into his belly.

A look of shock and surprise spreading across his face as he stared down at the blood soaking his shirt—his empty hand groping blindly for the handle of the door. Finding it and pushing it open even as Harry shot him again in the forehead, his head snapping back.

No mercy. No time for anything of the sort, not now—hearing the squeal of tires as he pushed himself up, catching a glimpse of the third SUV through the Land Rover's back window. Pulling in behind them.

He unzipped the young man's jacket and began rifling through his pockets, finding a small knife clipped to his belt—dropping the pistol to the seat. His hands working awkwardly to open the knife, pressing the blade against the hard plastic of the ties binding him. Sawing back and forth, knowing he had only seconds left. *Time to move.*

There. He pressed his hands outward, the ties digging into his flesh until they snapped with an audible *pop*, his hands free at last even as shouts began to fill the night. *Out of time.* There was a spare mag for the Glock in the front pocket of the kid's jeans and he took it, pushing past the corpse as he heard a door slam shut—throwing himself from the vehicle. The impact nearly taking him to his knees as he hit the concrete, pain shooting like fire through every muscle.

He glanced just up the road toward the burning hulk of the lead Land Rover, thinking for a moment he could hear screams of anguish and pain coming from the wreckage. Realizing only then that he was silhouetted against its hellish glare. *A perfect target.*

There was nowhere to run—easily fifty meters of open ground between him and the water. The nearest cover easily twenty meters off as the doors of the rear vehicle came open. *Nowhere to hide.*

Last stand. He brought the Glock up in his hands, thrusting it forward—getting off a shot as the first of the jihadists exited the vehicle. The bullet going wild, burying itself in the frame of the door.

He could see the rifle in the man's hand, its muzzle sweeping toward him as he fired twice more, the bullets catching his target high in the chest. *Double-tap.*

The man went down against the concrete, legs kicking in the spasms of death—the muzzle of Harry's Glock already traversing to the next target as another man came around the front of the vehicle, rifle already up.

And then another. Muzzle flashes lighting up the night, flickering like strobes in the fog. The supersonic *crack* of rifle bullets snapping through the air past his head as he moved back toward the shipping containers. Firing as he went, again and again and again.

Knowing he was running low on ammunition, knowing that he could only last so long.

John Patrick Flynn's words echoing through his mind, as true now as when he'd first heard him utter them in early October of 2001, the two of them sitting astride horses atop a ridge in northern Afghanistan. Gazing through binoculars at Taliban positions in the valley below as Northern Alliance fighters unslung their weapons all around them, preparing for a charge. *"Some days, son—doesn't make any difference how good you are. . .there are just too many Indians."*

Too many Indians. That about summed it up. Death coming for him once more. The face of a friend.

He fired again, seeing a man go down in the mist. Hearing the death rattle of a rifle on full-automatic as bullets tore through the metal of the container, inches away from his head.

And then the Glock's slide locked back on an empty magazine.

9:09 P.M.
Thames House
Millbank, London

"Sir," a voice called out as MacCallum passed through the Centre, "you need to see this."

The section chief glanced down at the phone in his hand, closing it before moving over to join his analyst at his workstation. "What are we looking at?"

"Reports are coming in of an explosion in the port of Aberdeen—an explosion followed by sustained gunfire."

Tarik Abdul Muhammad, MacCallum thought, knowing what he had to do. "Where are the nearest response units?"

"Fifteen minutes away, but they're nothing more than constabulary. Aberdeen's scattered—still dealing with the scene at the shopping centre, assisting 22 SAS as they escort the Queen to Holyrood. Nearest Firearms Unit is nearly forty minutes out."

It was a bad situation all the way around. No good solution to it, no way to avoid sending good men to their deaths.

"Liaise with Police Scotland," the section chief said finally, "have them dispatch all available units to the harbor, but they are not, I repeat are not, to move in until the Firearms Unit arrives on scene. Establish a cordon a mile out and hold fast. I'll notify the DG."

9:11 P.M.
The port of Aberdeen
Scotland

Sooner or later, your hourglass ran out of sand. It was as simple as that. Death, the end of every man. *Long overdue.*

EMBRACE THE FIRE

Didn't mean you couldn't go down fighting. Harry thumbed the Glock's mag release, hearing the magazine clatter to the concrete even as bullets whined through the air past his ear, tugging at his jacket.

Fishing the spare out of his pants pocket, knowing even as he did so that it was too late—that he would be dead before he could release the slide. Dead as he had lived.

By the sword.

And then he heard the distinctive crackle of a Kalashnikov off to his right, shots ringing out over the water as bursts of fire tore through the night.

He saw one of the jihadists go down, the weapon dropping from his dying hands—saw another crumple in a bloodied heap as the third man turned to confront the new threat.

His thumb hit the release, the Glock's slide running forward as he raised it once again—acquiring a sight picture for only a brief second before he fired, the pistol recoiling into his hand.

The bullet smashing into the base of the jihadist's neck, severing the brain stem. He dropped like a puppet whose strings had been cut, sprawling across the concrete.

Silence falling across the port once more. Harry rose slowly from his crouch, weapon still leveled—searching for threats. He glimpsed movement off to his right toward the water, pivoting to meet the threat as Flaharty came walking in out of the fog—his AKM raised in one hand.

"Easy there, boyo," the Irishman cautioned, taking in the sight of Harry's pistol. "Is that all of them?"

A silent nod as he lowered the weapon, glancing around at the corpses strewn around them, the scene lit in the glare of the burning wreckage.

Running a hand across his bloodied face. Scarce able to believe he was still alive. . .scarce *wanting* to.

Knowing that he owed his life to the Irishman, but finding himself unable to thank him. Knowing all that was to come—the *deal* he had made.

A devil's bargain.

He turned away without a word, the Glock still in his hand as he limped across the road toward the burning Land Rover.

The vehicle well-nigh gutted by fire, flames licking at the windows. Seeing the driver's side door pushed open as he rounded the rear of the SUV—the driver's body slumped half-way out of the vehicle, flames licking at his charred legs. As if he'd tried to drag himself to safety. *Tried and failed.*

He stepped closer, the heat of the flames searing his face as he peered into the wreckage—his foot catching on something. He looked down to see a severed human hand and part of a forearm lying there in the road, bloodied but curiously intact.

A dark shadow passing over Harry's face as he recognized the watch encircling the wrist. *Conor Hale.* Or all that was left of him. Perhaps it was better this way—that he be remembered for all that he had done before. *Not for this.*

He turned away, seeing another body lying farther away from the vehicle, mangled and torn—its right leg missing, the left skewed away from the torso at an obscene angle.

Tarik Abdul Muhammad, Harry thought, his fingers tightening around the butt of the Glock as he stood over him—gazing down into what remained of the terrorist's face, near half-blown away. Marred almost beyond recognition.

But it was him. Lying dead at his feet, at long last. *Retribution.* For all those who had lost their lives this night. For the hundreds who had died in Vegas. For *Carol,* most of all.

Justice. Too long delayed.

It was strange, but he felt no triumph—no satisfaction—in this moment. There was just. . .*nothing.* Nothing but a gnawing emptiness, somewhere deep within. Like a black hole, threatening to swallow him up.

"Those who seek to take that which belongs to the Lord of worlds. . .do so at their peril."

Ismail Bessimi's warning, ringing again and again in his ears. *Truth.* But the wolf was dead.

And perhaps that would have to be enough.

Flaharty was kneeling by the bodies of two of the fallen terrorists when Harry returned to the vehicles—searching them for ID, for weapons. His back turned at Harry's approach.

"Well?" he asked, still not looking back. "Are they both dead?"

"They are," Harry replied flatly. Emotions warring within him as he brought the Glock up in one hand, aiming it at the back of Flaharty's head. *He couldn't do this.* But he *had* to do it. For Mehreen. *For Nick.* There was no other way. "Turn around, Stephen."

He saw the Irishman stiffen, leaving his rifle where it lay as he rose slowly to his feet. Turning to face him, his face pale in the dying light of the flames.

It was a long moment before either of them spoke, the haunting wail of distant sirens overshadowing the scene. Then, "What are you playing at, old son?"

"I think you know," Harry responded, an overwhelming sadness in his voice. Knowing that Mehreen could hear him over his earpiece. Was already on her way, like as not. "I think we *both* knew it would end this way."

"Aye," came the simple reply. Flaharty's face drawn and tight, his jaw set. "That we did."

"And yet you came anyway. Why?"

"Why did I walk right in, you mean—like a sodding lamb to the slaughter?" The Irishman shook his head, staring into the muzzle of the Glock. "Don't know as I could explain it—perhaps not even to myself. Was it a chance at redemption? Maybe so. We've both done things we regret. Horrible things—blood staining our hands the like of which no sacrament will ever be able to wash away. 'Bless me, Father for I have sinned. . .'"

Flaharty turned his head aside and spat at the words of the confession, bitterness written in the lines of his face. *Faith lost.*

He straightened, seeming to draw himself up. Looking Harry in the eye. "Do what you're going to do, lad. I've never begged a man for mercy in my life, and I'll be buggered if I start with you."

Enough. Harry's face twisted into a grimace, his fingers clutching the Glock in a death grip.

Struggling with what he *must* do. . .and finding himself unable to do it. Looking into the eyes of the older man and seeing decades of sorrow, decades of war looking back. A damned soul, seeking rest and finding none.

He reached up suddenly, removing his earpiece and dropping it to the pavement. His booted foot closing over it with a sickening *crunch.*

"Go," Harry said simply, his body shuddering with emotion as he lowered the pistol. Inclining his head back toward the city behind him. *Enough blood had been shed this day.*

"*Go now.*"

9:17 P.M.
Thames House
Millbank, London

". . .still fifteen minutes out. 22 SAS is diverting a team to Aberdeen to assist."

"Whose idea was that?" Julian Marsh asked sharply, glancing up from his notes.

MacCallum and Norris traded glances, and then the section chief spoke. "It was the MoD's, sir. Straight from General Lidington."

The DG shook his head. "And Police Scotland?"

"Have expressed a desire for the SAS to lead the assault on the quay once we begin to move in."

Marsh swore under his breath. It wasn't what he had wanted, but he understood the reasoning behind it. They were short on trained men. "Do we have any way currently of establishing what we're up against?"

A shake of the head from Norris. "Police Scotland is hoping to have a drone in the air within forty minutes, but we're going to need to launch before then."

"Satellite coverage?"

"I've spoken with the cousins. Nothing on-station for over an hour."

So be it, Marsh thought, placing both hands on the conference table as he rose to his feet. They were going in blind, come what may.

He buttoned his suit jacket, pausing as he glanced over at his section chief. "Make sure the SAS is properly briefed before they go in—if at all possible, we need Tarik Abdul Muhammad taken alive."

9:21 P.M.
The port of Aberdeen
Scotland

He never knew what hit him, Harry thought, looking into the dead, vacant eyes of the young black man lying slumped there in the back seat of the Land Rover—the dying light of the flames reflected in their lifeless depths.

Taken off-guard, unprepared. He'd never had a chance.

He shook his head, pulling open the dead man's jacket and retrieving his confiscated Sig-Sauer from within. One of these days, it was going to be him. *Sooner or later.*

A man couldn't cheat Death forever and he'd been on borrowed time for far too long already.

He replaced the pistol in the empty shoulder holster beneath his jacket, wincing in pain from his damaged ribs as he did so.

Headlights washing over the vehicle in that moment, a car pulling to a stop not far away.

Harry left the Glock where it was on the seat, recognizing the familiar shape of the Vauxhall as he walked out into the glare of the headlights.

Bracing himself for what was to come.

The sound of a car door opening and closing serving as harbinger, the figure of a woman emerging into the light. A pistol visible in her right hand.

"Mehreen," he said, his voice stopping her in her tracks. She looked at him and he could see the uncertainty in her eyes. Searching for words, the both of them.

"The *Shaikh*?" she asked at long last.

"Dead," he replied flatly, nodding toward the smoldering wreckage of the Land Rover. "Along with the rest of his men. It was a close-run thing."

Closer than it had needed to be, he thought, but didn't say. All it would have taken was the press of a button. . .and she could have ended it all. *In a blinding flash of light.*

The end of all sorrow. *An escape.*

She opened her mouth to speak again, hesitant—her dark eyes searching his face. "Harry. . .where is he?"

He didn't need to ask who she was talking about. He *knew*, far too well—the look in her eyes stabbing him deep to the heart. The decision he had made resting heavy on his shoulders. Crushing him beneath its weight.

"He's gone, Mehr," he said finally, knowing there was no good way to answer her. No way to *explain* what he had done. The faith he had betrayed. He wasn't fully capable of understanding it himself.

"What do you mean?" She shook her head, taking a step toward him. Her voice brittle as ice. "He was here. You were with him—I *heard* both of you, over your earpiece. I heard you speaking to him, I—"

"He was," he admitted, struggling within himself. How to explain what had happened—how it felt to look into the eyes of a man and see yourself looking back. Unable to pull the trigger in that moment. "And I. . .let him go."

Such a simple statement, yet so devastating. *No.* Mehreen felt herself recoil as if he had struck her, her right hand clenching and unclenching around the HK's grip as she struggled to regain control of herself, the textured polymer digging into her fingers. Desperation washing over her like a flood tide. *It wasn't possible.* He was lying. He *had* to be lying.

And yet when she looked into Harry's eyes, all she could see in their weary, gun-metal blue depths was truth. *For once.*

"But. . .why?" she heard herself demand, her voice trembling with anger. Raw sorrow mixing with an all-consuming rage. The pistol coming up in her outstretched hand—a rough, instinctive motion, devoid of conscious thought. Its barrel wavering as she looked down the sights into his eyes. *Hammer back on a loaded chamber.* "We had a *deal*."

An eye for an eye, and a tooth for a tooth. The oldest law known to man—both of them seeking vengeance in this night. *And he'd found it.*

She shook her head, tears of pain and fury shining in her eyes—something snapping within her in that moment. Her finger curling around the HK's trigger. *Taking up slack.*

Enough. Enough with the lies, the deception.

The sound of the shot shattered the night, reverberating out over the harbor—startling her as the compact pistol recoiled hard into her unsupported hand, its muzzle blossoming with fire. . .

Pain. Sudden and unexpected, searing heat—like being stabbed in the side with a hot iron.

Harry staggered back from the impact of the round, his mind struggling to process what had just happened—looking into Mehreen's eyes as she fired again, a second .45-caliber slug tearing its way through his body. He stood there for a long moment suspended in time, swaying slightly—and then his legs went out from under him.

Seeing the look on her face change from fury to shock, then horror as he went down, falling to his knees on the pavement.

The impact shuddering painfully through him as he tried and failed to stay aright, toppling sideways—his body sprawling in the road.

So this is how it all ends, he thought, lying there staring up into the night sky above. The harbor lights haloed by fog, shining down upon him.

Struggling to rise, to push himself up—his body refusing to accept what his mind already had. That Death was coming for him once again. No longer to be denied.

All of the sorrow, all of the pain. *The years of war.* Ended now. . .at the hand of a friend.

Irony of ironies.

He heard footsteps approaching and looked up into Mehreen's face, finding nothing but sorrow written there.

Tears running down her cheeks as she stooped beside him, the weapon long since discarded. Cradling his head against her arm as she pulled him backward, propping him up against the wheel of the wrecked Land Rover. Her free hand pushing his jacket to the side to examine his wounds.

Her fingers came away sticky with blood, the look on her face telling him what he already knew. It was bad. *Very bad.*

"I'm sorry," she whispered, her body seeming to convulse in a silent sob. A tear falling from her eyes to splash against his face. "I never meant—"

"Don't be," he said, reaching up to touch her wet cheek with the tips of his rough, callused fingers. "You were right, and I was. . .so very wrong. But it's too late for any of that, now."

"No, it's not." She reached up angrily, brushing away the tears and leaving her cheek smeared with his blood. "There has to be a way, *something*—I can get you to a hospital. I can—"

The shrill, discordant wail of police sirens sounded once more in the distance, seeming closer now. "You need to go, Mehr," he responded, his voice little more than a whisper. "Go now. *While you still can.*"

Before the Security Services arrived. Before everything came crashing down, for the both of them. "Don't sacrifice yourself for me."

"*No.*" He could see the angry denial in her eyes, hear the desperation in her voice. "I can't just leave you here to die, all alone."

Harry shook his head, a sad smile crossing his lips. Feeling weak in that moment, painfully weak.

"Everyone dies alone, Mehr," he said, a cough seizing hold of him—pain wracking his body. "Every last one of us, in the end. *Now go.*"

She nodded finally, seeming to choke back a sob as she rose wordlessly to her feet—making her way toward the car. Pausing with her hand on the door, looking back to where he lay.

"*Go*," he mouthed, well aware his voice couldn't reach her. Willing her to leave. *To save herself.*

The car door closing finally, the Vauxhall's headlights sweeping out over the road as it swung toward the far side of the quay, turning back toward the city.

He sat there for a long moment, leaning back into the wheel of the Land Rover, his chest rising and falling with deep, labored breaths. Summoning up whatever remained of his strength.

He put a hand back against the vehicle, rolling over onto his hands and knees as he struggling to push himself aright—fighting against the pain and nausea threatening to overwhelm him.

Biting deep into his lip to keep from crying out as he staggered to his feet, feeling unsteady, light-headed. Looking down at the wounds in his side and abdomen, the lower half of his shirt soaked with blood.

Knowing from hard-earned experience just how gravely he was wounded, knowing he only had so long before he would go into shock. *Make the most of it.*

He cast one final look back toward the city before pushing himself away from the vehicle, pressing a bloodied hand against his side in an effort to staunch the bleeding as he began to make his way down the quay, making out the ghostly outlines of ships in the fog, riding at anchor.

And beyond them, the waves of the North Sea—the lonely, haunting blast of a tug's horn piercing through the mists.

He stumbled, nearly going down—gritting his teeth as he caught himself, the pain all but overwhelming him. Forcing himself to push on, to keep moving. *One foot in front of the other.*

Another ten steps, and the night swallowed him up. . .

Epilogue

7:29 A.M., April 8th (Four days later)
United Airlines Flight 831
Heathrow Airport

"We're just finishing up some last-minute paperwork, ladies and gentlemen—should be underway shortly."

Shortly. Thomas Parker adjusted his seat, glancing out the window over the wing of the Boeing 767, toward Heathrow's looming Terminal 2.

It couldn't come any too soon. For any of them, he thought, looking back as if to assure himself that the rest of his team had taken their seats.

Director Lay had departed for the States the day following the attacks, leaving them to attempt to sort through what pieces remained before the British government had stepped back in, requesting the CIA team's immediate departure from UK soil.

The ruins of Balmoral's western wing were still smoldering, the Queen herself reportedly being brought back to Buckingham Palace under heavy guard. The Security Service struggling to identify the remains of the corpse they believed to be that of Tarik Abdul Muhammad.

And Nichols was nowhere to be found, at least if the Brits were telling them the truth. Vanished, as if the earth itself had swallowed him up.

Harry. He passed a weary hand across his face, still wrestling against the memories. The sight of Harry standing there in the stairwell of the council block only a few days before—raw desperation in his eyes, his weapon aimed at Thomas' head.

A different man than the one he had followed all through the years of war, and yet somehow. . .so very much the same.

And now he was, what—*dead*? It seemed impossible to believe. Wrong, that it should have ended this way. And yet. . .

There was nothing he could do about any of that. Powerless, at the end of it all. *Impotent*. He leaned back his seat, opening his phone's browser—a scrolling headline catching his eye as he went to CNN.

"*Capitol Hill In Turmoil: Prominent Senate Democrat Changes Parties, Throwing Control Of The Senate to the GOP.*"

Washington. He shook his head. Ever torn apart by people vying for power.

Someone paused by his seat and Thomas looked up to see a flight attendant standing there over him, a smile on her face. "Would you like something to drink while we're waiting, sir? We have scotch, bourbon. . .gin?"

Temptation. He just stared at her, torn by indecision. *Weakness*. Three days dry, knowing all too well what it would mean to go back down that road once more.

"No," he said slowly, forcing the words out with painful, tortured deliberation. "No thanks."

9:47 A.M.
An interrogation room
Paddington Green, London

Silence. Mehreen took a sip from the bottle of spring water she had been given, replacing it on the table before her as she glanced around the bare, featureless room. Waiting, just waiting.

She'd been doing a lot of that, ever since she'd been stopped by a Police Scotland roadblock on her way out of the port of Aberdeen on that dark night four days earlier, part of the cordon thrown out in the attempt to capture the *Shaikh*.

Four days, and no word of Nichols. Nothing since her last glimpse of him in the darkness, lying there propped against the tire of the Land Rover. If Five had found his body, they weren't talking about it—not that anyone had done much talking to her.

The door opened suddenly and one of the constables looked in, seeming to assure himself that her right hand was still shackled to the table before turning to address someone without. "Right this way, sir."

A moment, and Julian Marsh appeared in the doorway. As commanding a figure as ever—although he looked worn, more worn than she could ever recall seeing him. His suit appearing as if it had been slept in.

"Director!" she exclaimed, rising to her feet. Although they had spoken, briefly, on the phone days before, she hadn't expected him to come in person. *Could it be. . .*

"Uncuff her," he ordered, gesturing to the constable as he crossed the room, setting a thick folder on the table. Watching in mute silence as the officer used his key to unlock the cuff, the metal falling away from her wrist.

Then, "Leave us."

"Are you sure, sir?"

"I am," Marsh responded icily, his tone brooking no disagreement. Looking at her finally as he pulled back the chair on his side of the table—gesturing for her to take her seat.

He waited until the door had closed behind the constable before he took his own seat, sinking heavily—wearily—into the chair as he opened the folder, spreading it out before him.

"You were right, Mehreen," he said finally, the words seeming to cause him pain. "It checks out. It all checks out."

A grimace crossing her face. *No joy in this moment.* "So then MacCallum. . ."

"Has been playing us all false," the DG confirmed, a grim edge to his voice. He shook his head, swearing under his breath. "Alec's been my most valued advisor in his years with Five, one of the finest section chiefs Thames House has ever seen. None of which changes the simple fact of his betrayal. We have the swipe card logs, his terminal log-ins, everything he's accessed from the Registry over the last six months and the counter-intel lads over at D Branch are digging back further. This has been in the planning for a very long time."

Betrayal. She winced, looking down at her hands, struggling against the emotion. It was like a cancer, eating at them from within. Turning them against each other. "What's to be done with him?"

Marsh glanced at his watch. "The Met should be arriving at Thames House even as we speak. They'll place him under arrest on charges of espionage, conspiracy, and treason."

She took a deep breath, struggling to think that someone she had considered a close friend could come to such an end. *Perhaps you never really knew anyone in this business.* "He was a good man."

"*Was.*"

10:03 A.M.
Thames House
Millbank, London

". . .matching his description broke into the house of a doctor in Stonehaven, twenty kilometers south of Aberdeen, three days ago. The details are still coming in, but it seems he took the doctor—one of the heads of the Royal Infirmary's new trauma centre—hostage, forcing him to patch him up at gunpoint."

"So that confirms Crawford's report, then," Alec MacCallum nodded. "Our man's wounded."

He shook his head, his brow furrowing. "Three days. Good God, in that time, he could be anywhere. Why didn't Police Scotland inform us of this before now? They should be aware of the national security implications entailed."

Simon Norris shrugged. The formation of Scotland's police service might have streamlined things on an organizational level, but it hadn't necessarily guaranteed the expeditious transfer of information. "Hard to say," he said, glancing over at the section chief. "I've asked Glasgow to dispatch one of our own people to interview the doctor, will let you know as soon as more details are available. I—"

His voice broke off suddenly as a pair of men in the uniforms of the Metropolitan Police came through the doors of the Centre, a cold chill running through his body. *Premonition.* "What are they doing here?"

"I don't know," MacCallum said after a moment's pause, the both of them watching as a middle-aged man wearing thick glasses crossed the room from one of the conference rooms to meet the officers, "but that's Philip Greer from D Branch with them."

A counter-intelligence spook, Norris thought, knowing all too well what that could mean. Doing his best to focus his attention back on his workstation as he saw Greer begin to head their way, followed by the officers.

The game was either up, or it wasn't. Not much he could do about it either way.

"MacCallum," he heard the D Branch officer begin. *The moment of truth.* "I'm going to have to ask you to come with us."

A load lifted from his shoulders in that moment. MacCallum's face showing bewilderment and concern. "But of course. What's this all about, Philip?"

"I think you know, Alec," the counter-intelligence man replied, his eyes cold and emotionless. "All too well. You're being taken into custody under the Official Secrets Act, on charges of espionage, conspiracy, and treason. I need you to turn over all your access cards, surrender any and all files you may be working on at the present."

"What are you talking about?" Norris looked up to see the section chief's face drain of color. Shaking his head slowly in disbelief. "There—there has to be a mistake of some kind."

"There's been no mistake," Greer said, a grim certitude in his voice. Stepping aside to let the officers advance. "Except the one you made in betraying the Service."

"I have done nothing but serve my country and my Queen faithfully,"

MacCallum protested, glancing in Norris' direction. "What do you know of this, Simon? What in God's name is going on?"

"I don't know," he responded, feeling a knife twist in him as he spoke the words. He had known this moment could come, but still, to have to watch it happen, before his very eyes—that was something different. "I'm sure it's something that can be sorted. . .some kind of misunderstanding."

I'm sorry. Norris stood there, watching as the older man was escorted out, a constable on either side of him—the rest of the operations centre looking on. His face tightening into a grimace as they disappeared through the doors.

Spurred by a sudden impulse, he reached over to his workstation, retrieving his jacket and hat. He needed to get out, take a walk. *Get hold of himself.*

Or this would all be for nothing.

The sun beat down warm upon his face as Norris walked out onto London Bridge, the spring breeze whipping at his jacket. He had done only what was *necessary*—to defend his country against those who would have destroyed it. To protect himself. But it was hard to feel any joy in it.

He stood there by the balustrade, allowing the crowd to pass him by, looking out over the sparkling waters of the Thames as he had on that night less than a week before.

"England confides that every man will do his duty."

And do it he had. He pulled the burner phone from his pocket, punching in a number quickly before lifting the phone to his ear—waiting a few seconds until the call was picked up, hearing the familiar voice of Arthur Colville on the other end.

He hesitated for a moment before speaking, glancing back toward the southern end of the bridge—where once had been mounted the heads of traitors.

"I'm in the clear."

10:15 A.M.
The interrogation room
Paddington Green

"There's no way for you to come back to Thames House. Not after all of this."

Mehreen sat there for a long moment, looking away at the bare wall as she struggled to digest the DG's words. To come to terms with the reality of what they meant.

A lifetime of work, to be ended like *this*. In disgrace. She had known the risks she was running in helping Harry—in attempting to save her nephew, and yet. . .

To hear the words from Marsh's lips was like listening to a death knell.

"I'm sorry, Mehreen," he said finally, something of regret in his eyes. An unaccustomed humanity. "But you know this is how it has to be."

And she did. . .the Security Service wasn't a line of work that lent itself to second chances, to clemency. Nichols' words echoing back through her mind. *"Go now. While you still can. Don't sacrifice yourself for me."*

But sacrifice herself she had, long before, she thought, her face twisting into a grimace at the memory. It was a strange feeling, looking back on the path that had led you to this place—trying to sort where the point of no return had even been.

Had it been when she procured the dead-ground map at Harry's request? Or had it been the very moment when she'd looked out the door to see him standing there on her stoop? Like an angel of death, of destruction. *Malak al-maut.*

Questions like that could drive you mad.

"But you won't be charged in connection with your actions of the last week," the DG went on after a long pause, "nor will a cloud be attached to your departure from Thames House. That's the most I could do, Mehreen."

And it was, perhaps, more than she had any right to expect. "Thank you, sir," she responded numbly, still not looking at him.

"And just because it's out of the question for you to continue further in the employ of the Service doesn't preclude you from seeking employment elsewhere. You're a good analyst, Mehreen, and private intelligence is on the rise, whether we like it or not. I was briefed just the other day on a company expanding its reach in the Middle East. . .the Svalinn Security Group, I believe it was. Run by one of the cousins' former officers. You'll find a place to make use of your talents, of that I'm quite sure."

"More likely I'll retire to the country," she retorted, her voice dripping with bitter sarcasm. "Raise chickens and knit myself a throw."

Live the life she had always seen for herself and Nick in their declining years. *Growing old together.*

"And Arthur Colville," she began quietly, resignation in her voice, "what's to become of him?"

Marsh seemed taken off-guard for a moment by her question, but then he let out a long, heavy sigh, taking a paper from within his folder and sliding it across the table toward her. "Colville is another problem entirely. . .with tensions running higher than ever before in the wake of the attempt on the Queen's life—several Muslim-owned businesses in Liverpool were torched by rioters last night—he's only continuing to stoke the flames. And more."

It was the front page of the *UK Daily Standard*—this morning's paper, she realized, glancing at the date—the headline blaring in bold print:

"DERELICTION OF DUTY: How A Politically Correct 'Security' Service Placed Her Majesty In Mortal Peril."

Her eyes scanning down the broadsheet, opening wider as they went.

"My God," she whispered, finally looking up to meet Marsh's eyes. "This—this is PERSEPHONE. This is the operation we ran against the *Shaikh*—the operational details, the decisions made by the Home Office, all of it. How did he—"

"MacCallum," the DG replied simply, shaking his head. "It has to be him. He sold us all down the river."

"But this," she said, continuing to scan the article, "this is all highly sensitive, classified information. Its publication. . .it should be enough to put Colville away for the rest of his life, even without being able to prove his complicity in the attack on the Queen."

"It should," he said, reaching out a hand to take the article from her. "And *would*, were it ever to be pursued. But it won't be."

"But *why?*" She demanded incredulously, scarce able to believe her ears.

"It's politics, Mehreen, pure and simple. These articles of his—this is the second in a series he began publishing two days after the attacks—are igniting a firestorm in Parliament. There have already been calls from the Shadow Cabinet for an inquiry into the government's handling of this affair, and the Home Secretary was on Sky News this morning, broadly hinting that blame for the near catastrophe lies entirely on the doorstep of Thames House and promising viewers a 'full and thorough' investigation."

Keep your friends close, your enemies closer. And never were enemies closer than in the politicians of Whitehall.

"With the Security Services under this kind of scrutiny from the press, no one is going to risk furthering the perception of a cover-up by going after Colville. There's no one at Downing Street who would sanction it."

And he wins, she thought, shaking her head at the folly of it all. *The sod wins, after all of this.* "So you're telling me he's untouchable, then?"

"Yes."

10:23 A.M.
Colville's estate
The Midlands

"Good," Arthur Colville responded, rising from behind his desk. "What we've set in motion—it's now far beyond their power to stop."

Even with Her Majesty's unfortunate survival, he thought but didn't say. His informant at Thames House had never been made privy to the true nature of their objectives and even now. . .

No. Keep the circle close. That was the secret of any conspiracy that stood a prayer of succeeding, he thought, a shadow passing across his face. Remembering with a very real sense of disquiet his words to Conor Hale, only hours before the attacks. *"Do what you must. . .make sure none of this can be traced back to us."*

It was the last he had heard from Hale, the former SAS sergeant vanishing as completely as if he had dropped off the face of the earth. The one man who could be the undoing of them all. *Simply vanished.*

It had yet to be seen just how "successful" they were to be, he thought, glancing over toward the window of his study—the morning sun streaming in through the curtains. What price they would yet be asked to pay.

But it was a new day. *For England.* For her people. A future purchased—as ever, down through the centuries—in blood.

Norris' voice in his ear, sounding haunted. *Uncertain.* "Are you *sure*?"

"Of course I am. You can see what's happening in the streets for yourself," the publisher responded, putting the phone on speaker as he moved over to the window. Gazing out over the the pastures to the west, the grass moving gently in the breeze. "People are desperate, they're angry—more importantly they're waking up, and they're not going to go back to sleep just because some boffin in Whitehall tells them that everything's going to be all right. They *know* differently now."

"But the Security Services—"

"Are going to have all they can do to handle the revelations of these last few days," Colville interjected, cutting him off. "And those yet to come. It may well bring them down."

Nothing but silence on the other end of the phone. *Was it remorse? Regret?* "We both knew going in that this could be the result," the publisher said, a stern edge to his voice as he looked down into the courtyard below, the rose bushes already blooming between the close-trimmed hedges. "But in the end, to what does your loyalty truly belong? An institution, corrupted and crippled by bureaucracy? Or to the *ideals* that institution was intended from the first to rest upon? *Regnum defende.* The defence of the realm. We are on the cusp of bringing to birth a new world, Norris, and the actions we have taken will ensure that it not only comes into being, but that those who are entrusted with its defence are able to do so. Unhampered by the restrictions of a government which has proven. . ."

His voice trailing off suddenly as he caught sight of something out of the corner of his eye, in the garden below. The body of one of his bodyguards—one of the men *Hale* had secured to protect him—lying prostrate on the cobblestones of the walk, only his head and shoulders visible from behind the hedge.

Something dark pooling around the man's head. *Blood.*

A cold chill ran down his spine, his mouth dry—a faint sound from somewhere in the house striking his ears in that moment, even as he struggled to grasp what was happening. The sound of something—*someone*—falling.

The phone slipped from his grasp to fall unheeded to the floor, the sound of Norris' voice suddenly muffled as he hurried back across the room to the desk—hands trembling as he jerked open the top drawer.

Fingers closing around the butt of his grandfather's old Webley, a service revolver Second Leftenant Rupert Colville had carried into the trenches of Passchendaele. *Heritage.*

"Don't even think it," a voice warned sharply, Colville's head snapping up to see a tall, dark-haired man in the open doorway of the study, leaning heavily against the doorframe as if it were the only thing holding him aright—his jacket gaping open to reveal a shirt torn and sodden red with blood, his face pale and drawn beneath the dark stubble of his beard. Eyes the color of blued steel staring into his own. The eyes of a man half-dead already.

The suppressed pistol in the man's outstretched hand aimed straight at his head.

"The Security Services are getting desperate," Colville said, managing a false, nervous laugh, raising his empty hand from the drawer, "if they think they can send someone here—to my *home*—to try to frighten me."

"No one sent me," the man replied grimly, shaking his head. "And I didn't come here to frighten you. I came here to kill you."

10:26 A.M.
London Bridge
Central London

"*. . .came here to kill you.*" The muffled words struck Norris like a thunderbolt, his face draining of color. His hand suddenly trembling as if he had been taken with a fever.

"Then who are you?" he heard Colville ask. Desperation, *fear*—filling the publisher's voice.

A part of him wanting to do nothing more than throw the burner into the Thames. To *run.*

But it felt as if he was rooted to the spot, the phone held tightly against his ear. Straining to hear every word.

10:27 A.M.
Colville's estate
The Midlands

"My name really isn't that important," Harry said, taking a limping step forward—his bloodstained hand finding the back of an antique armchair, steadying himself with an effort. *Still so desperately* weak.

His eyes never leaving Arthur Colville's face, framed in the sights of the Sig-Sauer. "What's important is that I know who you are. *And* what you've done."

"What I've done," the publisher responded, seeming to master himself with an effort, "has been done for England. For all that she once was, for all that she may yet be. Her *future*—if she is to have a future."

"For the greater good, then?" Harry shook his head. "That's an old refrain, and one that rings down through the pages of human history, ever accompanied by the weeping of widows and orphans, mourning their dead."

"For the only good there is in this world," Colville spat, his eyes flashing. "Islam is a cancer, and if the patient that is this country is to survive, it must be *excised* by force. Wholesale. Every last vestige of that pestilent cult driven from our shores, lest it return to grow again once more. If you think that can be done without the necessary—if tragic—sacrifice of a few innocent lives. . .you're a fool. If you don't think it needs to be done, you haven't begun to understand the threat."

"Oh, I understand the threat," he said, his grip on the chair tightening as he stared into the publisher's eyes. Fighting through the pain, struggling to keep himself aright. "Far better than you could even begin to imagine. I've spent the last fifteen years of my life fighting it, all across the Middle East—more than a fair bit of the rest of the world. I've buried friends I loved more than brothers, stood by their graves as their wives wept in my arms. Comforted their children as a color guard came to 'present arms', rifle shots crashing out through the hush."

"Then for God's sake, *why*—"

"You'd be surprised," Harry went on, continuing as if the man had never spoken, "how much you remind me of them, the tactics they're willing to employ. They've never hesitated to kill their own, by the thousands, to advance their agenda—to achieve their ends. Religion, nationalism. . .the excuses change, but the reality doesn't. That all of these excuses are little more than a mask for something far older—the desire to *rule*."

His face hardened, biting back the pain—the weapon trembling in his outstretched hand, his finger curling around the trigger. "And if I've learned anything over the years, it's that if there's any cancer in this world, it's to be found in the hearts of men who seek to control—to exert power over—their fellow man.

To *sit* in the seat of God. Men like *you*."

The trigger broke beneath his finger in that moment, the Sig-Sauer recoiling into his hand—the sound of a suppressed shot echoing through the study. Followed by another.

The rounds tearing their way through the publisher's lungs, mushrooming and expanding as they went. *Fire and death.*

10:30 A.M.
London Bridge
Central London

Norris ripped the phone away from his ear, his entire body shuddering—the deathly handclap of suppressed gunfire still ringing in his ears, harsh and discordant. *Applause at a funeral.*

Knowing with everything in him that he should report the murder he had just borne witness to, but daring not. Glancing around wildly, his eyes searching the crowd of passers-by.

As if suspecting that even now, Death was coming for *him*.

Seized by a desperate impulse, he took the phone in both hands—snapping it in half and dropping both pieces into the turgid waters of the Thames below as he turned, beginning to shoulder his way through the press, his panic rising with every moment.

Get away.

10:31 A.M.
Colville's estate
Central London

Colville staggered back at the impact of the bullets, his eyes wide and staring—his mouth opened as if in one last, desperate protest. *Too late.*

So always to tyrants. Harry shook his head remorselessly, raising the Sig-Sauer one final time. "Good-bye."

The pistol bucking against his palm, a single red hole appearing between the publisher's eyes—blood and brains spraying over the painting on the wall behind him. *Nelson at Trafalgar.*

He went down hard, his body striking the chair and taking it over with him—crumpling to the floor in a heap.

And it was over. The last echoes of gunfire fading away through the old house as Harry safed the pistol, returning it to its shoulder holster beneath his jacket.

He pushed himself away from the chair, starting over to check Colville's body. The adrenaline draining from his body, leaving him suddenly faint, light-headed—still weak from the wounds, the loss of blood.

Staggering forward. . .Carol's face seeming to rise suddenly before his eyes. So real he could have touched it, felt the softness of her skin. Her eyes beckoning to him. *Come, and be at rest.*

Another step, and then his legs gave way—the floor coming rushing up to meet him as he fell to the carpet of the study. Everything else fading away, his hand reaching out as he tried and failed to pull himself up. *So very weak.*

And then the darkness closed around him. . .

The End

Coming Soon...
A New Novel From Stephen England

He's a man without a country...fighting a war without end.

Gravely wounded and at the point of death following the terrorist attacks on Balmoral, Scotland, former CIA officer Harry Nichols finds himself a fugitive.

On the run from the British security services, and his own former employers, the combined might of the Western intelligence community closing in upon him on the continent of Europe.

He's never been farther out in the cold. He's never been more dangerous.

There's nowhere to run.

And the only place left to hide...
is among the very people he's spent a career hunting.

Look for *Presence of Mine Enemies*, the fourth full-length volume of the Shadow Warriors series from bestselling author Stephen England, coming soon.

For news and release information, visit www.stephenwrites.com and sign up for the mailing list.

An author lives by word-of-mouth recommendations. If you enjoyed this story, please consider leaving a customer review(even if only a few lines) on Amazon. It would be greatly helpful and much appreciated.

Author's Note

As I work here today, finishing up final edits, I can't help but be amazed at how much our world has changed since the late fall of 2013, when I first sat down to write the opening scenes of *Embrace the Fire*. The rise of the Islamic State, massive terrorist attacks in France and Belgium. . .real-life events have begun to mirror those laid out in these pages to a disturbing degree.

But that has, after all, been the goal of this series from the very beginning—to bring readers into the realities of the War on Terror as seen through the eyes of those who fight it.

It's been nearly five years now since the Shadow Warriors saga first broke onto the thriller scene with the debut release of *Pandora's Grave* in the summer of 2011, and not only has this series come much farther than I could have imagined. . .the vision for what is yet to come has only grown. There is so much more of Nichols' story remaining to be told.

Any undertaking of this scale is impossible to accomplish on one's own, and I owe heartfelt thanks to all those who have aided me along the way. I regret that there is not place to thank everyone, but I will make an attempt at a partial list.

To my parents, without whose support through the earliest years of my writing I would likely not be where I am today. I thank God for their influence and encouragement.

To the artistic geniuses behind the *Shadow Warriors* series' visuals. Louis Vaney, my cover artist—and Jānis Zunda Kalnins, the creator of *Embrace the Fire* video trailer.

To the ever-diligent members of the *Embrace the Fire* beta-reading team: Tyler Donoghue, Joseph Walsh, Mary Thompson, Dan Keller, Jessica Keppler, Chris Herron, Paula Tyler, and Jeannie Clarke. The hours they put in reviewing the unproofed manuscript were indispensable to the process.

To the tight circle of highly-talented independent thriller authors who have become dear friends through the course of this journey. Steven Hildreth, Jr., Robert Bidinotto, Nate Granzow, Ian Graham, and R.E. McDermott. I strongly encourage any fan of the *Shadow Warriors* series to check out these men's work and it is my hope that they will know success equal to their skills.

To the many members of both the American and the British military and intelligence communities who have offered advice and guidance along the way. What mistakes which remain are mine, but they would be vastly more numerous without the technical expertise and tradecraft these men and women have provided.

And perhaps most of all, I owe thanks to my readers, whose outpouring of enthusiasm for Nichols' story has been a font of inspiration through the years. I look forward to continuing this journey together.

May God bless America, and watch over those who defend her.

Printed in Great Britain
by Amazon